A GAME OF MALICE AND GREED

CAROLINE PECKHAM
SUSANNE VALENTI

This book is dedicated to all the readers who were raised on fairy tales and now need their stories to be just as magical, but with heart-pounding spice thrown in too.
And if you've ever imagined a world where Aladdin was a dark hearted anti-hero covered in tattoos, the princess was a badass warrior, and the genie was a beautiful Fae forced to obey her master, then this one was made for you.
Welcome to Osaria...

A thousand years ago the Fae fell from the grace of the gods with a single lie. In that moment, a prophecy was spoken into the world with their only hope cast upon its wings.

A glint of gold waiting in the gloom,
A deadly garden, a sunken tomb.
When a soldier glimpses beyond the veil,
And a thief is tempted by a forgotten trail.

A man of sin, and man of steel,
Shall form a fragile, fate-bound deal.
But temptation may lead men astray,
While Herdat stirs among the Fallen Fae.

Her dark servant shall gain eternal power,
If the dead man wakes within the final hour.
For the Prophet lingers in the deep,
Waiting for his chance to reap.

A vessel soaked in ink and blood,
Shall face the hands of hungry gods.
But all fates do not lie with men,
For there is a power far greater than them.

A princess with an arrow sharp as diamond flies,
While a city watches as a beast of fury dies.
And a Fae who never fell will shine,
With a magic older than the dawn of time.

All fates will twist and coil as one,
Before the curse shall be undone.
And a warrior born of sin shall rise,
When the shell gleams, and they punish our lies.

MAGDOR

PROLOGUE
TWENTY-SIX YEARS AGO

I heaved myself up the sharp rocks lining this side of the mountain, my skin splitting and blood spilling while the dark clouds closed in around me and my grey hair was tossed into my face by a foul-smelling wind.

Even the weather was working against me here, out on the farthest reaches of the Greymorian Pass, the very edge of the world as we knew it, trying to keep me from the lost gods and their hiding places. But I'd been on this trail for months now, and I was certain I'd tracked one of them down at last.

And not just any god. Herdat, the goddess of death and destruction, of vengeance and bloodshed. The very one I'd been seeking for so, so long.

The cold bit into my old and weathered bones, the gnarled knuckles of my fingers crying out in pain as I continued to grasp the rocks above me and climb ever higher up the sheer rock face in this unholy place at the edge of the world. Nothing thrived here, not even birds sung in this barren place, and it was certainly no paradise fit for a goddess, more like a graveyard just waiting to claim another corpse. And perhaps that was what I was. My body was certainly closing in on the end of its days.

But despite my age and ill health, I refused to give in to the call of death because I was still waiting to live. To truly serve in the name of the lost gods I'd spent my life worshipping.

I cursed as the rocks cracked and shattered shards tumbled away beneath my feet, black stone cascading down into the chasm below and promising me a swift and brutal death if I fell. But I wouldn't fall. I'd come too far to falter now.

Fifty years living within the veil as a Priestess of the Lost. I'd suffered in my dedication to the gods who had long since abandoned us, hoping that they would see my devotion and reward it. But they hadn't. And I'd grown tired of waiting for them to come to me and offer me what I desired, so now it was time for me to claim it for myself.

I reached up once more and my fingers grasped smooth stone instead of sharp rock at last, a breath of relief escaping my lips as I heaved myself up before falling to my knees on the stone ledge at the tip of the world.

I lifted my head as I gazed into the mouth of the dark cavern before me, the stench of death and blood within it enough to make me hope that I truly had found her at last.

"Herdat!" I called, my limbs trembling with fatigue as I forced myself to my feet once more.

It had been a week since I'd last eaten and the only water I'd consumed had been supped from mud-stained puddles or licked from the rocks themselves. If the goddess wasn't here, then this was it for me. I wouldn't survive the journey back to the city of Havian. But I was certain she was here. Found at last. "I offer you my body in exchange for your power!"

A deep rattling sounded from within the cave like some great beast drawing breath for the first time in a thousand years - and I was hoping that was precisely what it was.

Whispers filled the space surrounding me, causing my skin to prickle and hairs to raise on end across my body, like a warning to turn from this place, to run and never look back. The hissed words surrounded me, soul deep, and though I couldn't decipher their words, their intention was clear. She wanted me to come closer.

I raised my chin and discarded my robe, removing my shoes before striding naked into the cavern, standing as tall as my stooped back would allow and feeling sharp edges of roughly hewn rocks cutting into my bare feet with every step.

The air surrounding me hummed with power, the iron tang of blood coating my tongue as I delved deeper into this dark hiding place in the forgotten tundra. No sane Fae would ever dare venture out into this barren and soulless place. Even the monsters didn't linger this far north. The fire drakes, smaller, stupider cousins of the long dead dragons, preferred the inhabited world where they could hunt their prey with ease, the satyrs hid in plain sight, beguiling foolish Fae into their traps, and the enormous scorpious spiders were another good reason to stay the fuck out of the desert. There were many more creatures who hunted in the dark places of this world, hiding in caverns such as this or lurking close to civilisation where they could feed their dark desires with ease, but I'd seen none of them nor any sign of their presence for weeks. There was nothing here for them. Nothing but death and rot. Nothing besides *her*.

The whispers grew more urgent as I moved further into the dark and though I still couldn't understand the language, I knew their meaning. She wanted to know what I would offer her in return for this power. She wanted to know how much I would sacrifice to take what I wanted.

"I wish to serve you," I hissed, the desire for wealth and power burning in my flesh like a seed which had been planted without water or sunlight to grant it life. I'd spent my years praying to the lost gods and dedicating myself to their will. I'd taken on all kinds of torturous sacrifices to my body and my soul in offering to them as I studied their ways and the gifts they'd once offered our kind. It had taken a lifetime of that to realise I would never get what I hungered for unless the missing gods returned, and if they weren't willing to do so, then I was going to have to find them. It would have been an easier feat when I was a younger woman, but that didn't matter. I'd ignored the protests of my aging body and worked tirelessly to achieve this one goal before death got the chance to claim me and steal my chance at it.

Now here I stood in the chamber of the mighty Herdat herself.

Again, the whispers surrounded me and the depths of their power drove into my soul and threatened to rip it clean from my flesh as agony consumed me. I screamed, unable to help it as I felt the goddess ripping through my skin, consuming all she could find within me and making me burn throughout the entire process. She was hungry. So fucking hungry and alone out here with no one to suffer for her in the ways they once had.

"Grant me my desire and I will sacrifice anything you ask for!" I screamed, needing her to hear me before she devoured every piece of me in her starvation. "I will walk this world and serve you faithfully, feeding you as much pain and death as you require."

The agony in my limbs intensified until I felt like I was being burned alive, consumed by the darkness of this goddess, and brought into her own personal hell to torment for all of time. A scream tore from my lips and rattled though my body with the intensity of her power as she took hold of me, breaking apart every piece of me and forcing it back together again just so that she could start over and enjoy my agony for a second time.

But just as I felt myself slipping towards oblivion, my plans and desires as unfulfilled as they had been since the day I joined the priesthood, and the weight of that final failure pressing down on me even more heavily than the power she was exerting on my flesh, she spat me out again.

I crashed to the floor of the cavern with a cry of pain, my body weak and bleeding as I shivered there at her mercy.

The whispers were back, surrounding me once more and their demands were clear. She wanted me to prove my devotion to her.

A glow of grey light filtered into the darkness and I panted as I forced myself to my hands and knees, finding an iron dagger laid before me on the black stone and a long, silver mirror standing beyond it, reflecting my weak, old body back to me as if wanting me to see how little my years in this godless world had earned me.

My hand shook as I reached for the blade, already knowing what she wanted from me as I lifted it and pressed the iron to my skin between my sagging breasts. The iron burned me, the metal painful to touch as it worked to weaken me, but I refused to balk at that ache I felt from wielding the foul metal which was the bane of my kind.

9

I drew in a deep breath and began to chant the prayers of the lost gods which I'd repeated countless times throughout my service as a Priestess of the Lost, though instead of praising all of the gods, I only praised her. Herdat. Bringer of death and pain.

The blade cut into my flesh and I gritted my teeth against the bite of it as I began to carve the mark of the goddess into my skin while continuing to chant my devotion to her, to the freezing air.

Blood spilled down my pale flesh, dripping to the black stone at my feet and making the power of this place hum with more violence as she drank in every drop.

The words hissed from my cracked lips as I went on, pledging my devotion to her as I cut each and every line of her mark into my skin, covering my entire chest and stomach with it until I was losing so much blood that I was trembling from it, my frail body barely able to remain upright.

As I finally finished, I raised my chin and stopped chanting, the blade falling from my hand and clattering against the black rocks as I stared at the reflection of my old and weathered body now mutilated for her pleasure as I shook before her.

"I offer up my body as sacrifice," I swore, devotion swirling in my dark eyes as I stared at my own reflection in the silver mirror, seeing the years of sacrifice and service that had gone unheard and wishing I'd begun my hunt for her sooner. "Take it, use it, guide me. I will bring you all the pain and death you could desire. I only want to serve you."

The power in the cavern grew so potent that it choked me, and I shivered in my position before her as I felt her waking fully, turning her attention on me and weighing my words with the promise in my soul. I was hers now. And we both knew it.

Shadows began to peel from the walls and my lips fell open as I stared at the creatures born of darkness which writhed from the rocks themselves and began to creep closer to me, surrounding me with hunger in their eyes and violence in their expressions.

I held my chin high as I let them come, making no attempt to reclaim the knife and fight them. I would endure all it took to serve at the side of my lost goddess. To live the life of power and worship that I had always dreamed of and knew was within reach.

Sharp claws sliced into my back and I cried out as the pain of them tore through my skin like burning acid. That first strike laid way for the next and the next, countless creatures of shadow and death pouncing on me and forcing me to the ground as they cut and bit into my flesh, feeding on me and devouring me, making my screams ring out around the chasm endlessly.

The pain went on and on as they worked to consume every piece of me, the heavy weight of the goddess's eyes on me the entire time, hours, weeks or months passing as I drowned in agony while never once asking for it to end.

I paid the price she required of me long beyond the point of my death, still feeling it even when the shadows had reduced me to nothing but bone beneath them and I shouldn't have been able to feel anything at all.

Within my agony, whispers pressed close to me, speaking words long forgotten from a prophecy which time had left behind. *"While Herdat stirs among the Fallen Fae. Her dark servant shall gain eternal power, if the dead man wakes within the final hour. For the Prophet lingers in the deep, waiting for his chance to reap…"* The words went on but the pain in me rose, stealing them away on the back of my screams as flesh was cleaved from bones and I was shredded inside and out.

I took it and revelled in it and begged her for more until finally there was nothing left of me to devour at all.

"You belong to me now."

Her voice echoed through the remnants of my being and though I had no tongue of my own to answer her, I swore with all I was that it was so, pledging myself to her and dedicating whatever life she offered me in service to her power.

"Then rise."

Blinding light filled the space and I screamed once more as I was thrust from the embrace of darkness into the cold reality of the world, landing hard on the black rock before the mirror and sucking in a breath of air for the first time in so long that I could barely remember what it was to breathe.

Black hair spilled down around me as I stared at the hands which now belonged to me, my dark skin impossibly soft and youthful, my sharp nails biting into the stone as I trembled on my hands and knees.

"Your body is mine."

"Yes," I swore vehemently, gasping as a hand fisted in my hair, claws cutting into my scalp.

My head was tugged back so that I was forced to look into the silver mirror and witness the creature I'd been reborn as. For a moment all I saw was a jet-black skull with dark and hateful creatures shifting between the sockets of my empty eyes and racing between my parted lips. But as I blinked, the image changed, skin forming over the truth of what I had become and making me suck in a sharp breath.

Long gone were the worn and haggard features of the priestess I'd once been, an ageless beauty taking her place with dark eyes and deep brown skin which practically glowed with vitality and youth. My hair was raven black and my body lithe and youthful. The kind of vessel worthy of a goddess.

My gaze shifted to the fist which still held my hair and a shiver of fear passed through me as I took in the demonic form standing at my back, watching me as I watched him. He was a creature of shadow and malice, with curving spines lining his back and jutting from his arms, sharp teeth bared at me in a mouth too wide for his unnatural face, and eyes so full of torturous intentions that I knew he could only be an incarnation of Herdat's own dark and deadly essence.

"You will carry my seed and birth a weapon fit to serve you. Then our work will begin."

"Yes," I swore once more, arching my spine as the demon shifted at my back, his cock hard against my behind and making it more than clear what was expected of me next. But I wasn't afraid. I was in the hands of my goddess, and I wanted nothing more than to serve her. So he could take my body, ruin it, use it and fill me with a piece of the goddess herself in any way he desired to do so. I would take the pain of that coupling and far more besides in my devotion to her. Because this was all I'd ever dreamed of. To wield the power of a goddess and serve her as I'd always hungered to do. I would reap the rewards of her favour in time, and I was her willing pawn until that moment came.

"The Prophet lingers in the deep." Herdat's words resounded through my being as I waited to face this next test. *"But his time approaches. You must be ready to raise him once again."*

I lifted my chin and prepared for the next test of my devotion as I looked into the soulless gaze of the creature waiting to claim me in the reflection of the mirror, vowing to keep my eyes open through every torturous moment of this and revel in the knowledge that I was finally serving a goddess in the way she required. And once it was done, every Fae in Osaria would finally be reminded of what power the lost gods once held over our kind.

"I'm ready."

DRAKE

CHAPTER ONE

I crept across the terracotta roof tiles, half holding my breath as my feet threatened to slip on the shiny surface beneath the weight of my powerful body. It was hot. Too fucking hot for this kind of work, but then it always was this close to the edge of the Lyrian Desert.

The full moon hung low and fat in the sky above me, some still called it Sirella, using the name of the goddess who had once owned it, guiding the tide, and taking ownership over the distant oceans. It shone as bright as always, a pink haze glimmering all around it, almost seeming to glitter with the rays of heat which rose up to caress it.

Sirella gave me plenty of light to see by, but also outlined my silhouette in silver, highlighting me as a target for every guard in the kingdom if they should just look up. Not that they did so often, but I didn't want to be up here any longer than necessary all the same. The rooftops may have been the thieves' pathway around Osaria, but they were by no means safe. One wrong move and I'd be facing a death sentence at the pleasure of the emperor.

Nope, that wasn't gonna be my fate. I didn't have the reputation for being the best for no reason. There might have been more than a few ransoms on my head, but there was no way anyone would ever be collecting on that payday. Besides, a head as attractive as mine could never be destined for a future on a pike. That would be a fucking travesty.

The countess moaned loudly in pleasure, her voice carrying to me from the window beneath me where I crouched on top of her manor. "Oh yes, you monstrous man! Ruin me! Take my flower and demolish the petals. Make me sin like a wanton lady of the night! Run me through with your broadsword and raise your flag over my majestic kingdom!"

I snorted a laugh as she continued to praise her lover's performance.

Balthazar had drawn the short straw there. I was all for seducing the mark to distract her and had happily fucked more than a few countesses or their daughters in my career, but not when she was forty years older than me and had a moustache to rival Eristan's. And that bastard had a thick, grey face-wig which had more bristles than a toilet brush.

I carved my tattooed fingers through my inky black hair as I looked out across the city for a moment, enjoying the view from up here where the moonlight made the white walls of all the buildings shine, and it was near impossible to spot the pain and misery which lurked in all the dark corners between the houses. Of course, there was less of that here in the first ring where the wealthiest of Fae lived, rubbing shoulders with one another and congratulating each other on their privilege while happily ignoring the squalor and suffering which took place in the slums beyond the outer rings of this most celebrated city. There were twelve rings in total, representing the number of kingdoms our emperor ruled over, with the palace taking up residence in the very centre where the Lunarelle royals resided. The closer a Fae lived to the palace, the wealthier they tended to be, and the more entitled too. First ring dwellers practically shat diamonds and slum-dwellers like me who couldn't even afford a place in the twelfth ring would have happily scraped those diamonds out of the sewers.

As I turned my head south, the slums were easy enough to spot in the distance. White walls shifting to brown where paint had flaked off or had never even gone up in the first place despite the city laws, streets narrowing as the need for housing crammed buildings and shacks closer and closer together until there was nothing but a maze network left to traverse outside of the official roads which were kept clear by the royal guard for access in and out of the city.

I fought to keep the sneer from my face as I looked towards the place where I laid my head at night, both hating it and needing it in equal measures. But it had never been what I would call a home. Then again, I'd never known one of those.

The warm wind tousled my black hair, bringing a few stray grains of sand with it and I looked towards the desert again, wondering if we were going to be having a storm any time soon. The sweeping golden dunes seemed innocent enough from my position, but of course I knew better than to believe that lie. Even if there wasn't a storm blowing in, the sands were home to all manner of beasts and monsters. It was a place only a fool would dare to travel and even those taking the stone road out of here, heading to another city or kingdom, knew to travel in a group with plenty of guards. Many a man made his coin by travelling those roads as a hired sword, but that had never appealed to me.

I'd seen the scars those men sported from their encounters with the fire drakes, basilisks, rot worms and ripsian boars out there – and those were the tamest of the creatures which could be found lurking in the sands. There was even a man in the slums who claimed he had lost a leg to a dragon in the Lyrian Desert years ago – though I wasn't fool enough to believe that any of those remained out there. They'd been lost a long time ago, along with the gods who had forsaken us when the Fae fell.

The countess moaned again, garbling something about Balthazar's cock staining her impeccable reputation and I slid down the tiles, aiming for the window Balthazar had thrown open for me and getting back to what I'd come here for in the first place.

I caught the edge of the roof and swung myself inside, dropping through the window and landing silently in the huge building with a grin.

Balthazar looked up at me from his position on top of the countess and he pushed her face down into the pillows as she continued to wail in response to his efforts. He had his britches unbuckled and his tunic hanging open to reveal his flexing abs, but had kept everything on his body one way or another so that he'd be ready to make a quick escape if needed.

I tilted my head to the side for a moment as I watched him slamming his cock in and out of her dry old pussy, analysing his efforts before awarding him a three out of ten and holding up three fingers to let him know how low I rated him. I wasn't turned on one bit by the free pornography he was performing, and though that might have had a lot to do with his partner, I did feel he could have made an effort to spice things up a bit. Maybe stick a finger in her arse or a bit of spanking at the least. But no. Plain old pounding the hole seemed to be his style. I guessed it got the job done anyway.

Balthazar cut me a pissed off look, his dark brown eyes glimmering with irritation at just how long it had taken me to make it inside. But what could I say? It had sounded like they were enjoying themselves – or at least like the countess was. And yeah, I might have waited out there for longer than necessary, but I wanted to be sure he had her completely distracted before I made my entrance. I knew he'd try to get away with finger fucking her if he could, but I'd wanted him balls deep in her moustached cunt so that I could remind him of it as frequently as possible after tonight.

Seeing as he was already pissed at me, I decided I could spare a few moments to rub salt in the wound of his current predicament. I picked up a heavy vase and took a moment to thrust my hips back and forth at it in a mockery of the act he was performing, biting my bottom lip and pretending to spank it while his dark skin coloured with barely concealed rage.

He started fucking her harder, presumably as an outlet for some of the pounding he wished he could be inflicting on my face with his fists, and she wailed beneath him as he kept her face buried in the blankets on the bed so that she wouldn't spot me.

I put on a good performance of pretending I was coming inside the vase, tipping my head back in imagined pleasure and winking at Balthazar as he mouthed a curse at me.

The countess tried to raise her head and he shoved her down more firmly.

"That's it, baby," he growled as she moaned again, and I stifled a laugh at his attempt at faking pleasure in her company. Points to him for taking her from behind so that he didn't have to look at her face though. That was damn smart. If he wasn't currently looking at my pretty face, then he could have been imagining the woman beneath him was one of the big-titted whores he preferred down at the brothel. But as he was currently stuck looking at my unshaven face and scraping his cock in and out of a prune pussy, I was willing to bet he was having trouble even staying hard right now. And his efforts at distracting our mark wouldn't exactly do us much good if he went all floppy worm inside her.

Yeah okay, I was being a major prick about the woman on that bed. But she was the wife of a man who'd had three thieves hung last week, and she'd stood proud and smiling at them when their feet had stopped kicking. So I might have been a little salty, and this job was at least eight percent based on the desire to get revenge. Don't get me wrong, I was no hero out to save anyone else's arse, but I was willing to strike at those who deserved it if I knew the payday would be worth the work.

"Treat me like a poor street urchin who'd spread their legs for a single coin," she growled into the pillows and my eyes narrowed. Yeah, she was just like all the other entitled arseholes who resided in the inner rings of the city, living up in her castle and looking down on the rest of us, always ready to celebrate when one of us dropped dead. Fae like me were scum to Fae like her. But the feeling was mutual.

I placed the vase back where I'd found it with a sigh as I was forced to end my game by the practicalities of needing to rob this bitch blind, and pushed my black hair out of my eyes as I observed the room.

Aside from the four-poster bed which currently contained the countess and her less than enthusiastic fuck buddy, the room was richly decorated. Heavy pieces of dark furniture inlaid with gilded detail filled the space and thick rugs covered the wooden floor. I gave the countess and her husband a mental thank you as I used the rugs to my advantage, creeping further into the room and feeling the rush of the job building in my veins. There was nothing better than this. Reappointing the wealth of the aristocracy to the neediest citizens in this cesspit of a city. The neediest citizens being me and the rest of The Forty – but mostly just me. Because I needed these riches, fucking ached for them. Not because I had some poor, sick grandmama to look after or any nonsense like that. No, I needed riches for the best reason of all. Because I wanted them. I wanted the freedom they granted and the luxuries they provided. I hated the people who had so damn much because I was determined to prove that I was better than them, and I would do it in the simplest way I knew how – by being the man who had more.

One day I'd live in a gold-plated palace where I fucked my way through the most beautiful women a man could ever desire, while I grew fat being hand-fed all the best food Osaria had to offer. That was the life for me. And until I could afford it, I'd keep stealing from arseholes like this and saving up for it with a smile on my face and a knife in my hand – ready to stab any fucker who tried to take what I'd earned.

I silently slipped across the floor, pausing at a huge dressing table and lifting the countess's jewels from it, filling my pockets with necklaces, rings, bracelets, and brooches. I didn't waste time checking them over too thoroughly, but I spied diamonds, rubies, sapphires, the works. Egos, mean bastard that he was, would be more than pleased with this haul.

That should keep his wrath off of me for a while.

I crossed to the door, pausing for a moment to make sure Balthazar held the countess's full attention while he continued to slam his cock in and out of her and she clawed at the blankets, calling him a villainous rogue.

I grinned tauntingly at him again as I left him to keep her busy and his scowl deepened. He was probably getting off on the idea of beating the shit out of me a whole lot more than he was getting off on the feeling of that saggy cunt around his cock right about now.

I may have just earned myself a bout in the ring with him for my mocking, but it was worth it. I'd remind him of this conquest as often as physically possible for the rest of our miserable lives. And I'd happily fight him in the ring ten times over in payment for that gift. I'd kick his arse anyway.

I slipped out into the corridor of the enormous manor house, glancing up at the white stone walls designed to help keep the heat out, and headed across the wide landing, managing to stay silent despite the wooden floor and pitch darkness of my surroundings. But then they didn't call me the best because I was easily thwarted by creaky floorboards. My Affinities kept me in tune with my surroundings unlike any other Fae I'd ever met. I was willing to bet I could find a silent route across broken glass on clay tiles if I cared to try it. And I'd go double or nothing that I wouldn't so much as cut a pinky toe on my way across it barefoot either.

And that wasn't even the best of my gifts. I'd never actually been tested, but it was pretty fucking obvious to me that I was something special. Not that the rich bastards of this city would ever recognise it. At least not until I made my own fortune and forced them to see my value. And when they came knocking on my golden door, pleading to be my friend, I'd have a man usher them inside and bring them to speak with the rear end of my finest horse. Then, after it farted up a gust in their pompous faces, I'd show up to laugh them back out the fucking door.

A thick, curving banister lined the stairs and I grinned as I leapt onto it, sliding down quickly and bypassing any groaning steps like the pro I was.

I landed on my feet like a damn cat and almost swore aloud as I realised no one had seen it. Where the hell was Pip when I needed him? If ever there was a time to have that kid's adoring gaze fixed on me, then it was when I did something awesome like that. It was half the reason I'd recruited him in the first place. Dammit. I was going to have to come up with something else to impress him and get my little ego boost for the night before we headed back to The Forty. Maybe I'd do a backflip off the roof or pickpocket a royal guard on the way back. Something impressive. I'd keep thinking on it.

I slipped across the hallway, heading for the back of the huge house so that I could let the other thieves in. The sound of voices carrying to me from outside made me pause before I could open it though, and a shiver raced down my spine as my instincts set me on edge. I stopped beside the closed door, moving closer to listen as my skin prickled and I tuned all of my senses on to the area surrounding me. I may have had some damn impressive Affinities, but that wouldn't mean shit if a guard caught me and ran a sword straight through my heart. The days when magic could be wielded to heal shit like that were long gone, and for Fae like me, capture meant death of the most agonising variety.

The voices carried to me again and my brow pinched as I tried to figure out who was out there - the rest of our gang wouldn't be stupid enough to make noise like that. Not to say that most of them weren't as dumb as a bag of rocks, but they were all damn good at this one thing. I guessed most of them must have had Affinities which helped them in their illegal endeavours, especially when I considered the fact that outside of thievery, some of them were hard pressed to even string a simple sentence together.

"If there's anything else I can get you, My Lord, then please just send word," a male servant said sweetly. One thing worse than being poor? Being poor and working for the rich. I had no idea how some Fae stomached that shit. I'd rather cut limbs off than brown nose upper Fae to make a living.

"No, I only require my bed tonight. That was a long journey but no doubt my wife will be pleased to have me home early. All I wish for now is a restful sleep."

Well, fuck, it looks like the count cut his trip short.

I pressed my back to the wall beside the door just as it swung open, sinking into the shadows and willing them to keep me hidden, feeling them creep closer with the aid of the ancient magic which clung to my blood as the use of my Affinities made my heart thump harder. The carved wood almost collided with me, and I gripped the dagger at my belt as the count strode into his house.

"Why is it so dark in here?!" he bellowed and I held my breath as he turned back towards the door but he didn't notice me where I hid in its shadow, my skin tingling as I called on my innate power and worked to keep myself concealed.

Adrenaline trickled into my veins and prepared me for when I was going to have to run. I hadn't gotten far enough to let the rest of the gang in through the back and I silently thanked my luck. If the count was home, then he'd no doubt be bringing his servants along with him and getting the whole gang out undetected would be a lot more difficult than just getting my own arse clear of this place. I was going to assume that the other thieves had already realised that this haul was a bust and had run for it – it was every man for himself out here after all, and I knew not one of them would risk their necks for my sorry arse.

Balthazar's cover was solid and unless the count decided to kill him for defiling his pig-ugly wife, he should be able to run with his britches around his ankles before they ever realised I'd relieved them of their jewels. And as Balthazar was at least thirty years younger than the count, a foot taller, and twice as mean, I wasn't too concerned for him if it came to a fight.

My stomach rumbled in protest as I prepared to run out into the night. The kitchen should have been my next stop, but it made more sense to take an opportunity for escape than it did to try and hunt for a solution to my empty stomach.

There's always broth waiting back at The Den. Which may or may not have been bulked out with rat meat this week...

Of course, I'd never been one for sensible. And fuck eating that shit if there was an alternative available.

The count slammed the front door but didn't notice me as he turned away sharply and strode across the entrance hall to the spiralling stairs. I watched him go, half tempted to follow and see his face when he found Balthazar's cock buried in his wife, though I really should have been taking my chance to run.

My stomach growled more urgently in protest to that thought and instead of stealing away into the night, I turned from the door. The count would be kept busy for a few minutes while he got over the shock of watching his high-born wife taking the dick of a commoner like a good whore, so I had time. I glanced around then crossed the cavernous hallway and slipped into the kitchen.

People with this much wealth should really share it willingly if they don't want to risk thieves getting in.

I smirked to myself as I started opening cupboards the moment I made it into the room, hunting for anything I could eat on the run. Or anything that I could easily carry and keep for later.

I drew open the pantry door and groaned beneath my breath at the hoard I found waiting for me.

I snatched a cloth bag from the back of the door and started throwing bread, cheese, biscuits and cakes inside. I stuffed one of the little cakes into my mouth and moaned with pleasure at the sweet taste which overwhelmed my senses, closing my eyes and just enjoying it for a few blissful moments. This was a whole lot better than rat broth.

A shout of alarm came from upstairs and I stilled as I listened to the sounds of Balthazar being hounded out of the countess's bed by her husband. Something smashed and the countess screamed in a high-pitched tone which made me wince, while the deep timbre of Balthazar's voice carried to me and the count screamed furiously. I couldn't make out most of the words but there was something about his wife being defiled by the cock of a heathen and a whole lot of sobbing from the woman in question. It had looked to me like she was plenty happy to be defiled at the time though.

I released a breath of laughter and threw the bag over my shoulder, saying a silent farewell to the food I couldn't carry before elbowing the pantry door shut and spinning back to face the room.

I froze as I came face to face with a kitchen maid, blinking through the shock of someone managing to sneak up on me like that and briefly wondering what her Affinities must have been to make her so damn silent. The maid's lips parted with surprise, a scream not quite escaping her as she stared at me in alarm. She had dark hair which hung to her waist and wide eyes which shone with fright at her discovery. Pretty in an understated way with nice tits that were sadly mostly hidden beneath the frumpy maid uniform she wore.

"It's alright," I breathed, holding my hands wide so that she could see I didn't mean her any harm, my sack of stolen food hanging from my fist.

She backed up a step and I could see that she really was about to scream.

I gave her my best smile and pushed my hair out of my eyes as I took a slow step into the moonlight which washed in through the window, letting her get a better look at my powerful frame and winning smile.

I saw the moment her hesitation was extended by the sight of my face and gave her a more appraising look as her gaze trailed down to the buttons which hung open on the front of my tunic, stealing a look at more of my body than it was entirely proper for me to be showing. But I never had cared much for proper. And the way her eyes widened as she drank in the sight of the tattoos marking my deep bronze skin said she wasn't complaining either.

"What's your name?" I murmured, my voice low and soft, my skin tingling with the feeling of my Affinities coming into play.

"Perdu," she replied, and I knew I had her as her eyes skimmed over the exposed muscles of my inked arms in an appreciative way.

"Well, Perdu. I'm not here to hurt anyone, I'm just a bit hungry and it seemed to me like there was more than enough food here to go around. Can this be our little secret?" I asked as I took a step towards her, licking my bottom lip and getting a thrill as her gaze instantly fell to my mouth. "When the guards ask, you never saw me?"

She backed up and bumped into the kitchen worktop as I moved into her personal space, her breaths growing shallow as my shadow ate her up.

"I never saw you," she agreed on an exhale, part fear, part lust in her tone.

"And this never happened either." I leaned forward and captured her lips with mine. She gasped in surprise as she turned to liquid beneath my touch, but I really didn't have much time to waste, no matter how tempting she may have been.

I pressed forward all the same, tasting her tongue and hitching her long skirt up so that I could caress the outside of her thigh, enjoying the moment - no matter how brief it had to be and giving her plenty of reason to want to keep her word.

More yells drew my attention to the drama taking place upstairs and I broke our kiss, giving her a wide smile before turning and running from the room as she sagged back against the worktop.

I took the servants' exit from the kitchen just as I heard the count screaming for the guards and the countess wailing apologies. Balthazar should have been running down the street with his britches around his ankles right about now, and it was time I made my escape before anyone else realised there had been more than one lower Fae creeping around this place tonight.

Egos wouldn't be happy that we'd had to abandon our raid before finding any coin, but hopefully the jewels would be enough to appease him. Though I could admit that I was pretty pissed over my own cut being trimmed now too. Once Egos took his share and split the remains between me and Balthazar, I doubted I'd have much beyond what I'd need to feed myself this week. Especially with the price of wheat doubling again this quarter and bread being so damn expensive. I swear those Fae with an Affinity for baking were exaggerating the problem to line their own pockets too like some kind of conspiracy against poor, hardworking folk like me who just needed to fill their bellies.

I ran until I found a large window, forced it open then leapt outside just as the bells started ringing in the city and the sound of marching footsteps announced the arrival of the guards.

They shouldn't have been looking for me though. They were after a mean arsehole who had just dipped his cock in the wrong hole, not a thief too fucking cunning to even be noticed. I just had to skip away into the shadows and-

"My jewels!" the countess cried in horror, her voice reaching me from the open window above and pouring a heap of shit all over my plans to keep this thing low priority for the guards.

Fuck.

I raced across the stone courtyard to the back of the manor house and dove into a thin passage which ran between the stables and the kitchens. A horse whinnied in protest to my arrival and I cursed again as another kicked the side of its stall. Why couldn't I have an Affinity with animals? That would have been damn handy right about now. But no. Of course I didn't. In fact, animals seemed to hate me as a rule – probably because I wasn't above stealing their food. But sometimes beggars couldn't be choosers, and the grain the wealthy motherfuckers around here fed their beasts beat the slop served up in The Den at least half of the time.

I forced my way around the back of the wooden structure and the wall which ringed the property, then started really moving. The horses were making more noise as the sound of me struggling to fit my broad chest along the narrow gap upset them and I growled my irritation at the creatures. They were going to give me away if I couldn't get out of here quickly.

I looked at the gap above my head and leapt up, finding a hand hold in the rough wall so that I could heave myself higher.

The bag of food snagged beneath me, but I refused to release it. I hadn't eaten anything that good in over a week and I hadn't come this far to go hungry again tonight. We usually had enough food available in The Den, but I couldn't eat rat stew now that I'd been this close to the fine cakes and pastries enjoyed by the upper Fae. And though I'd have to give up the jewels I'd stolen to the boss, food was fair fucking game and this lot was all mine.

The rest of the thieves had long since fled, not one of them foolish enough to hang about when things went sideways and they'd all be well on their way back to the slums, outpacing the royal guards and getting out of my way too, so that was something. I just had to get myself out of this mess and we could all celebrate our close call back at The Den. Right after I demolished this food - I wasn't sharing a scrap of that. I might let Pip have a crumb or two, but that was it. And only because he was pretty much the only fucker I even half liked around here. Though in all likelihood, I probably didn't like him enough to share my meal with him, so I was almost certain I was just going to hoard it alone and eat the lot until I wanted to throw up. Yeah. That was the dream.

I scrambled higher and a horse snorted angrily from within its stall, making my heart leap at the noise and curse the forgotten gods for abandoning us.

Damn these stupid beasts.

I managed to grab the roof of the stable and heaved myself over the edge just as the sound of the guards arriving in the courtyard reached me.

"Did you see anything, girl?" a man barked.

I flattened myself to the wooden roof, peering down at Perdu as she cowered before the guard. She started shaking her head and he closed in on her, towering over her with his unnatural height. Big didn't come close to describing him, he was a beast wrapped in chainmail with a glare sharp enough to cut glass and thick hair crowning his head above the cruel set of his face. I could practically feel the aura of violence hanging about him even from this distance and Perdu looked inclined to shit her pretty knickers if he got much closer.

"Do you know who I am? I'm Captain Marik of the Royal Guard. And if I have any reason to believe you're lying to me then I'll throw you in the dungeon with the rest of the thieving scum just as soon as I catch up to them," he snarled, seeming to read the lies in her hesitation all too easily.

"He went that way," Perdu breathed, pointing towards the stables and bringing a curse to my tongue which I refused to let pass it as I held myself still.

Dammit, that kiss should have bought her silence. I should have used more tongue or at least finger fucked her into a delirious heap so that no one could get any sense from her traitorous lips.

Captain Marik turned my way and three more guards ran into the square to back him up. They held swords ready to skewer me if they got close enough and I glanced around desperately, hoping to spot some way out of this shit storm before I drowned in it. But short of me somehow managing to miraculously scale the sheer wall behind me, I was fresh outa luck because Affinities or not, I couldn't walk up walls.

"Hey, arseholes!" Pip appeared on the far side of the square, waving his arms at the guards to get their attention and my heart plummeted as I looked his way.

He was the newest member of our gang; twelve years old with long brown hair and built like a whippet. I'd watched him picking pockets in the market for weeks before I'd decided he was good enough to recruit. He had hands almost as swift as my own - possibly even a little lighter if I was being totally honest, though I'd never tell him that. He'd never alerted a mark to his presence so far as I'd seen and always got away from the take clean. He was clearly made

24

for this kind of work, and if I had to guess then I'd have said he had Affinities something in line with my own so far as stealth and subtlety went.

Bringing him into The Forty had earned me some good favour with Egos and a life with us was certainly preferable to a lot of other fates that could befall the orphans of Osaria. Like ending up as one of the street kids who washed up on the banks of the Carlell River each month with their hearts carved out. No one knew what the fuck that darkness was about, but it had been happening for long enough that loving mothers made certain to lock their children up tight at night for fear of them becoming the next victim. The problem was, there were always plenty of street urchins running wild for the killer to pick from, and seeing as the guards had no interest in the welfare of the Fae living out in the slums, there was little chance of the deaths stopping. Pip deserved a better fate than that.

Though right now, I was thinking I'd done the wrong thing by bringing him into The Forty. He was desperate to prove himself to Egos, but this act was nothing short of stupid. And I sure as hell wouldn't have risked myself like that for him.

The guards turned his way and Pip raised his middle finger at them. "I bet your fat arses can't catch me!" Pip laughed as he turned and fled, saving my arse while endangering his own and I cursed him at least as vehemently as I thanked him for it.

The guards raced after him with Captain Marik leading the charge. One of them pulled a crossbow from his back and fired an arrow which barely missed Pip's small form before slamming into a tree beyond him and sending a huge chunk of bark splintering off it.

My heartbeat scattered at the near miss, but Pip was fast and he was already racing away out of sight, whooping excitedly as he led them far from me and gave me the chance to get the fuck out of here.

I got to my feet and started running for the lower wall to my right and the promise of freedom beyond it, but a cry of fright from the far side of the grand house made me pause.

"No, wait - please!" Pip begged in terror and I shook my head, mentally saying farewell to him as I prepared to leap into the freedom of the trees beyond the wall.

If there was one thing you learned fast in this life, it was that heroes died quick and the only neck you could look after was your own. Anyone dumb enough to put themselves in danger for the sake of another would end up bleeding out in the gutter for their efforts at valour and Pip's predicament right now only proved that fact.

It was nice knowing you, idiot.

I made it to the wall and leapt up, managing to catch the top of it as I hauled myself towards freedom, tasting it on the heated wind which swept in from the desert even as my mouth dried out with a sour kind of taste in it.

Pip screamed somewhere outside the manor house and I stilled. My pockets were heavy with jewels and the bag I'd taken was laden with enough food to stop me starving this week, so why wasn't I running as far as I could get from this place without a backwards glance?

The next scream carried pain in its arms as well as fear and I swore colourfully as I released my grip on the wall and dropped back down onto the roof of the stables with a thump.

I took off running for the courtyard I'd just managed to escape from, mentally calling myself a bunch of foul names for the fucking idiocy I was about to perform while my feet failed to so much as stumble.

I pulled the jewels from my pockets as I sprinted on, tossing them into the bag and grabbing a hunk of bread out. I ripped into the bread with my teeth, chewing as I ran in an effort to fill my stomach. If this went badly then I was going to be hungry a while yet. And fuck me, whoever had baked that loaf had known exactly what they were doing – the damn high borns were clearly hoarding the best of the baking Affinity Fae for their own use. Not that I was surprised by that. They kept the best of everything for themselves. On the odd occasion that someone in the slums was found to have an Affinity for anything that might have helped improve the lives of the Fae living on the outskirts of the city, the high borns would always appear and whisk them away to make use of them. Gods forbid any of us get so much as a taste of something better than the shit we were born into.

The horses whinnied in fright as my feet thundered over the wooden roof above their heads and I launched myself off the far side of it, landing in the courtyard and rolling to absorb the impact of my fall.

Perdu gasped in shock as I rolled across the cobblestones before her, and I threw her a grin as I tore by. Yeah, that shit was impressive. She might have given me away, but the blush lining her cheeks told me she'd be dreaming of me tonight. Hell, I was starring in so many fantasies these days that I was starting to suspect I had a sex Affinity too. I mean sure, people said there was no such thing, but give me five minutes beneath a girl's skirts and I was sure I'd have her thoroughly convinced. I could probably have her convinced in two on a good day.

I raced around the corner and spotted several sacks of grain heaped by the side of the barn. I ran for them, tossing the bag of loot and food behind them as I went and shoving some of the sacks from the top of the pile so they fell down to conceal it. I couldn't do much better than that right now and I had to hope it was enough. The chances of those sacks being moved before I could make it back to claim my prize were fairly low considering it was the middle of the night, and I had to take my chances.

I ripped into the bread again, my stomach growling for more as I chased after the sound of Pip's screams and finally found myself around the front of the huge house. Pip was in the arms of the guards as the count watched over them beating him. One of them had pinned him to the wall by his throat and his nose was bleeding profusely, blood dripping to the ground beneath him while another threw heavy fists into his sides.

I slammed into the guard who held the crossbow before anyone even noticed I'd arrived, and he fell to the floor with a clatter as his armour hit the cobbles and I dove forward to claim his weapon.

I kicked him in the face as he tried to rise and he yelled a warning as I pointed the crossbow at the guard restraining Pip.

"Let him go," I demanded, placing my finger on the trigger as I lifted the heavy crossbow and aimed the bolt with intent in my gaze.

"Give it up, thief," Captain Marik snarled, the veins beneath his skin seeming to bulge and writhe along his temples as he found one of his men laying at the feet of a common criminal. "You only have one shot loaded and you aren't fast enough to reload before we gut you, even if you know what you're doing with that weapon."

Which I don't. It seemed fairly obvious though, at least as far as the first shot went…reloading, not so much, but I'd figure it out if I had to.

"Ah, but is it really worth one of your lives?" I taunted. "One shot is still enough to end one of you."

The guard by my feet groaned and I kicked him again, sending him into oblivion. I didn't need the added issue of him coming to and trying to get involved. I was already pretty sure that I was fucked even without stacking the odds against me any further.

I eyed the guard holding Pip, cocking my head to the side and raising the crossbow to let him know I wasn't fucking about, and he released him with a growl of rage.

The boy stumbled towards me, his eyes glimmering with gratitude as he tried to wipe the blood from his nose. I tossed him the hunk of bread I hadn't managed to finish and he caught it as he moved to my side.

"Tell Balthazar I hid it and if they want it, they're gonna have to get me out," I muttered, low enough for my words to stay between the two of us alone. I could see which way this was going to go down. I liked to think I held enough value to Egos and the rest of The Forty for them to come get me without the need for me to use the loot as a bargaining chip, but I wasn't a man to take stupid risks with my own life. Sure, I'd gamble with other people's lives, but not my own. I happened to like living, no matter how shit I had it, there was always a fight to be had or a woman to steal pleasure with, something to bring a spark of brightness into the hard reality of being born lower in Osaria, and I had big plans to claim a whole lot more than that one of these days.

"I'm not leaving you here-" Pip began, but I cut him off.

"Get out of here, you idiot. The Forty will come for me, but they'd leave you to rot. Just tell Balthazar I hid it all," I insisted, knowing our time here was running short.

The guards were still eyeing us angrily and it was clear we wouldn't both be able to escape them. And if reinforcements showed up then that really would be the end of it. He had to go now.

"But-"

I aimed a kick at Pip's arse and he yelped as he gave in and finally darted away from me.

"What now, low life?" the captain growled as he closed ranks with the other two guards. I could see my death in his eyes, and I knew he was just looking for an excuse to strike. I'd heard plenty of tales about the brutality of the Captain of the Royal Guard to know that he would take great pleasure in gutting me if he could, and I was pretty attached to my intestines so I didn't want them making their way outside of my body.

The city bells were still ringing and reinforcements would be here at any moment. I looked left and right, trying to figure out a way to get out of this which didn't end with me being tossed in the dungeons, but the prospect seemed fairly bleak. I was fucked. I knew it. The arsehole guards knew it. Hell, even pretty Perdu with her lips still buzzing from my kiss knew it. But it just wasn't in me to go down easy.

"Well," I hedged as I started backing up. "We could put this down to a big misunderstanding and you could let me go?"

I glanced over my shoulder to make sure that Pip had made it out onto the street and my heart settled a little as he disappeared into the shadows. This city was like a rabbit warren of roads, alleyways and forgotten passages, and that was before you even got close to the slums.

By the time he hit the shanty towns and ramshackle maze of buildings and lean-tos out there, they'd never find him. He'd make it back to The Den. And if I couldn't get myself out of this shit then I knew the others would come for me. Balthazar had seen those jewels. And I was worth the effort even without adding them to the deal. But I'd rather not get caught if I could avoid it. Egos was gonna be mad enough with me as it was. He wouldn't see my protection of the kid as anything other than weakness, and I was not so secretly hoping that Pip would fail to mention my dumbass heroics to anyone. Heroes weren't something to aspire to where I came from. Only villains prospered among the dirt and dregs of the lower Fae, and I was the most villainous of them all.

"How about you surrender and we won't kill you?" Captain Marik snarled in response, his thick jaw grinding as he worked to contain himself while I kept the crossbow aimed firmly at him.

"I want him dead!" the count interrupted, pointing at me from the position he'd taken up hiding behind the guards. For all of his pomp and bluster, he looked like he might shit himself if I so much as gnashed my teeth at him. "This man defiled my wife! My beautiful flower! He forced her to-"

"That wasn't me," I said firmly, repressing a shudder at the idea and refusing to have my name tarred with that less than desirable brush. "Have you taken a good look at me? I could do a *lot* better than her - she should need a licence to be that ugly."

The count shrieked in outrage, making a show of raising his fists at me, but he made no real attempt to pass the guards and his pathetic show only made me sneer in contempt.

"You're pretty full of yourself for a common criminal," Captain Marik growled, taking a step towards me.

I lined the crossbow up with his heart, but I sure as hell wasn't going to shoot. Stealing some jewels and beating on a guard would get me thrown in the dungeons, but killing the Captain of the Royal Guard? I'd be lucky if they didn't execute me here and now.

"There's nothing common about me and I can't help the way I look. I'm just insanely attractive," I said, grinning at him in a way that I could tell was only pissing him off more. And I guessed with a face like his, jealousy was probably rearing its ugly head too. "It's really just my face though. And my body. And my personality-"

The captain roared a challenge as he launched himself at me and I fired the crossbow over his shoulder, an arrow slamming into the door behind him and making him flinch. He threw himself aside like I'd hoped he would and I turned to flee.

But before I could take two steps, the guard I thought I'd knocked out cold lurched forward and snared my legs in his beefy arms.

I swore loudly as I collided with the ground and the taste of blood filled my mouth as I bit my tongue on impact. The arsehole threw his weight on top of me while I was still recovering from the takedown and I instantly started struggling, kicking, biting, punching, going for his fucking balls too, because there was nothing I wouldn't do to get out of this. But in the few moments I had to spend fighting for my freedom, all four guards landed on me and crushed me to the cobblestones with brute force and more than a little mocking laughter.

They yanked my arms behind my back and I cursed as heavy manacles encircled my wrists, snapping closed and making bile rise in my throat as the iron made contact with my skin. I felt the effects of the metal on my body almost instantly, a weight seeming to grow in the pit of my stomach and my limbs feeling leaden as the foul metal sapped the strength right out of me.

The guards dragged me to my knees while I fought off the urge to puke and I scowled up at Captain Marik as he looked down at me with a triumphant grin and a flash of cruelty in his eyes which said he was going to enjoy every moment he could with me beneath his heel like this. He really was abnormally tall, like a scarrion beast had had a night of passion with a tree and gave birth to this ridiculously huge specimen.

"I guess you're about to find out what happens to pretty boys in the dungeons. I hear that men with faces like yours are all kinds of popular. Perhaps I'll stay after my shift and listen for your screams to colour the night air," he taunted as the other guards began to drag me away and I spat a wad of blood from my mouth while I struggled to get to my feet.

I tried to fight against the iron manacles which held me, but with the taint of the iron infecting every drop of Fae blood running in my veins, it was no use. I huffed out a breath as I was forced to accept my situation, rolling my shoulders back and preparing for my next move as I let them tow me along between them.

It looked like I'd be heading straight to the royal dungeons to await rescue from Balthazar and the rest of The Forty Thieves. No doubt they'd let me rot a while out of spite before coming too. Egos was going to be as angry as a cat in a vat of piss, and I only had to hope that the mean old bastard wouldn't take his rage out on me for too long.

I could kiss goodbye to any cut I should have gained from this job for a start, and no doubt he'd be forcing me to fight in the pit repeatedly over the coming weeks. If I was really unlucky, he might even nail me to the wall with iron spikes for the night and let the others hurl insults and shit my way to teach me a lesson. Fuck that. But I'd seen him do it to others before and I couldn't count it out. I just had to hope that the value of those jewels I'd lifted would be enough to save me from the worst of it.

That's what I got for trying to be the good guy for once. Anger at myself, my situation, my life and Pip ate into me as I walked, and I forced myself not to think too much about the reality of being locked in a small space for the foreseeable future or the memories that reality was sure to stir in me. It wasn't like that. Nothing compared to the hell of what I'd once survived. But as I was dragged towards incarceration in payment for my attempts to help another Fae out of trouble, I was reminded of precisely why I'd sworn never to do anything that fucking idiotic for anyone other than myself. And I sure as fuck wouldn't be making that mistake again.

CHAPTER TWO

Princess Austyn Lunarelle of Osaria, I now pronounce you bound to a life of misery.

I had to be married by the end of the summer.

The clock was ticking. Literally. The one in my room ticked so loud, I often stuffed it beneath a pillow to shut it up. Today, I'd left it on the mantel because the maid would only put it back anyway. She had more control over her fate than me. Fucked up? Yes. Though no one in Osaria was going to pity a princess of my position. Sure, I was rich, I had access to anything I wanted at the click of my fingers, anything barring the one thing I actually desired anyway. Freedom.

Women had no power in my city. Princesses included. Unless you were *Empress* Magdor.

Tick, tick, tick.

My father would be announcing it to the entire kingdom of Osaria right about now. The rules, the game. I was the prize. But he didn't see it like that. He was protecting me, or so he said. If there were rules, that meant men of lesser wealth would be eliminated. So princes, lords, and any other power-hungry, scheming piece of shit who decided to throw their hat into the ring could do so, as long as they could afford the entrance fee. What better way to assess a man's suitability to be my husband than to get him to part with a small fortune?

But me? I didn't get to throw hats. I was the trophy, the glossy little token for whichever suitors greased my father's palm enough to enter the pageant - an ancient, barbaric and entirely sexist tradition. Brawls designed to test the worth of their Affinities and brute strength would take place between the candidates as a means to eliminate them, and between the bouts I was supposed to entertain them with feasts and balls. I was expected to dress up pretty and play my part as the shiny little trophy they were all working to seize. But as the winner was determined by the fights, it seemed pointless for me to spend my time getting to know the competitors. My opinion on them was clearly irrelevant to the outcome anyway, because when all was said and done, the victor of the final match would be declared the winner of my heart. My soul. My life.

You know what would really win my heart right about now? A glass of Cartlanna wine.

There was a magic to the trials, rumoured to have been put in place by a Prophet years ago when the first of my bloodline claimed the ruby throne, and the only way for a man outside of my family to seize full power of that throne was by winning it. There had been two cases of arranged marriages where the reigning emperor had disregarded the tradition of the pageant, and both had ended with the bloody and horrifying deaths of the men who had thought to take the throne without passing the trials of the contest.

Male successors didn't have to find their brides through the pageant though – their power was inherited and stayed within the bloodline. Which was precisely why I believed the whole thing should be abandoned in favour of me taking on the role of empress when the time came. If I were permitted to rule, then I could do so without having to take a husband or inciting the curse. My father had once spoken of such a fate for me – of him changing the law which forbade me from taking the power myself, allowing me to claim my birth right and rule in his stead. But the days of him speaking of such things were long gone.

I trailed around my opulent quarters, thinking of what was to come with a sharp pinching feeling in my chest. I thought I'd felt suffocated my entire life, but this? This was real suffocation, a cloth held over my nose and mouth, my knees buckling as I was forced to bow to this fate. I could scream, but no one would hear. I could fight, but my claws were cut.

I'm going to cut off my nose so the winner's prize will be ruined.

I snatched a letter opener from the gilded mahogany desk by the window and held it to my face, the feel of the blade singing in my grip.

I gritted my teeth, picturing what those men would think if I did it, if I stole away their pretty prize, ruined it with slashes and tears and mutilated my face.

My fingers shook and I threw the letter opener back on the desk with a curse. I was a coward. Or maybe I just knew in my heart that it would make no difference anyway. It wasn't just me they could win in this game, it was my father's throne, and no mark I placed on myself would keep them from claiming me. Not when there was so much else to gain too.

I wasn't allowed to go out in public without a hundred escorts and a veil over my head. My beauty was famed, but not confirmed. The tales of my tiny button nose, unusually silver hair for my darker complexion, plump lips and eyes the colour of the rising sun was a complete exaggeration. The wild stories that circled the city about how my gaze alone could light an undying fire in a man's soul was definitely going to be cause for disappointment when I met my husband-to-be. My hair though, that was the part that wasn't an exaggeration.

I'd been born with silver hair that gleamed with a hint of magic long lost since the Fae of old. It looked like liquid moonlight and hung all the way down my back in rippling waves.

My father said it made me special and Magdor said it added to my value as a wife. Men liked different, unique. But I didn't want to be unique. I was tired of being a pretty prize kept hidden away under a veil from the eyes of men, so that I'd be all the more idolised by the Fae who won me. And I had to wonder what my fiancé would think when he realised his bride came served with a large helping of personality. The men vying for my hand probably weren't counting on that. They'd be too caught up in the power trip this could offer them and what my body would look like when their cock was buried inside me.

I shuddered.

I can't let this be my fate.

"Moping again!" Magdor crowed as she barged into the room unannounced. The empress. My father's wife. Did that give her the right to stalk into my quarters as she liked? No. But did she do it anyway? All. The. Time.

I despised Magdor, though my father had praised her name from the second she'd walked into the palace. An exotic, beautiful Fae from who-knew-where seeking an audience with the emperor of Osaria himself? Who would buy that? My father apparently. The massive bag of jewels she'd carried with her had bought her an evening with him. And the next day - *the next fucking day* - he'd announced their engagement. I'd only been thirteen, but I'd seen her for what she was the second she'd arrived. Dangerous. And every day since had only confirmed that to me.

From the moment she had walked into this palace, my father had slowly withdrawn from me, disappearing piece by piece until he was only the shell of the man I'd once known and loved. My mother had died when I was young, and he'd been all I'd had in her wake. He had loved me deeply, encouraged me in all things and treated me as his best friend. And I'd had to witness him retreating from me as if we had never shared that bond. Closing doors on me literally and metaphorically as he shut me out, leaving me alone in this big place with its endless corridors and echoes of a life I'd once adored. I'd lost him almost as completely as I'd lost my mother, all because of *her.*

"*Gracious,* what a face," Magdor said, grimacing at me. "You're supposed to be the most beautiful woman in Osaria, and you constantly look like you've got camel dung on your upper lip. Whatever will your new husband think when he's presented with this morose bride?"

I wrinkled my nose, knowing I was only increasing the expression she so deeply hated. This woman had made my life hell from the moment she'd gotten my father to marry her. She was beautiful with her raven hair and dark eyes, her features seeming chiselled from bone, but beneath that beauty was a black, tarnished soul which I had tasted the wickedness of time and again. From the second she'd gotten her claws into my father, she had inserted herself into my life, to punish me when she saw fit, to try and hone me into something I was never going to be. Obedient. Compliant. A docile, inoffensive little woman. But fuck that. And fuck her.

I remembered the first time she'd caned my hands, whipping the backs of them while my wrists were bound in iron and the power of my blood was diminished so that I felt every strike all the harder.

When I told Father, he hadn't believed me despite me showing him the marks. That was when I'd first started suspecting that Magdor's Affinities were of the manipulation variety. Though I had never heard of such a power in our land, it was the only thing that made sense. She had some deep kind of influence over my father which only I seemed to notice, and as much as it pained me to think of him being tainted by her nature, I couldn't find a way to break through to him and confirm it.

"Oh well, perhaps it's not worth the bother of the wedding. My husband will only be disappointed," I said icily.

She clucked her tongue. "Well, I could always look for a Prophet who may be able to break the magic of the formal pageant if you wish to simply marry my son."

I let her see the disgust on my face at that offer, even though we both knew it was an empty one. There had been attempts to break the magic of the pageant before, but no other emperor had managed to find a Prophet powerful enough to do it. The magic which bound the men who wished to marry into my bloodline was fierce indeed, possibly even dating back to the time when the gods walked among us freely, when the Fallen had wielded true power.

Magdor's son had promptly been brought to the palace the moment Father had married her, and it had been more than obvious what her intentions were from the start. She wanted me to marry him. But Kahn made my stomach turn. I'd rather eat glass for the rest of time than marry him. Of course, he was offering himself as a suitor in the pageant, so I might not get a choice in the matter.

Kahn was a beast of a Fae, his Affinities clearly for strength and fighting, and he wore his brutality like a coat of arms. He was oafish and crass, violent and vulgar, and even less appealing as a match for me than the prospect of having to marry a complete stranger.

It was ludicrous that he and the other suitors entering the pageant were willing to marry someone they had never seen, but I supposed the rumours about my unmatched beauty alongside the promise of claiming the throne one day was enough of a temptation for any high-born Fae to consider.

As it stood, it was not only illegal for men to see my face – barring my father – but it was punishable by death. And to touch me would see that death drawn out and made into a spectacle for the entire kingdom. I took the burden of those laws seriously and despite my hatred of the veil which I was constantly forced to hide beneath, I never took it off outside of my chambers for fear of causing the death of some innocent man whose only crime was to look in the wrong direction.

All of my attendants were women, so in private I got some respite from the weight of the veil against my features, but the guards were male – *of course* – and I had to cover my face just to walk past them. It was a stupid, age-old tradition and I'd be 'Unveiled' at the pageant as part of my twenty-first birthday celebrations. So, although I'd get to lay down the veil for good after that, I'd also be getting an unwanted husband along with it. It just didn't seem like a fair trade.

I wanted so much more than a life shackled to a man who would rule over my kingdom and dangle me from his arm like a bauble to gloat over. I wanted choices and freedom and more than anything, I just wanted to rule in my own right and do all the things my people would need me to do to make them prosper. But those were the hopeless dreams of a forgotten girl laying hidden within a pretty vessel which had only one purpose.

"*Austyn,*" Magdor snarled.

She had a very short temper and I got to the end of her fuse at least five times a day. My personal record had been a triumphant eight. Though goading her often came with punishments harsh enough to make me regret my actions, I always found myself doing it again, unable to simply bow to the rules she laid out for me, or willingly accept this gilded cage of a life no matter how hopeless any kind of alternative may have seemed.

"You know, when you purse your lips like that, Magdor, they look like a cat's arsehole," I responded airily, whirling away from her so my pale blue dress twirled around my legs.

"Watch your tongue, girl." She hounded after me and I knew she'd come here for a reason.

She always beat about the bush, never getting to the point. I wondered if it was because she liked the sound of her own voice so much, or maybe it was just because I was her favourite chew toy. But since I'd reached adulthood, she was finding it harder and harder to get a rise out of me. I could bait her, but my own emotions stayed locked away deep inside where no one could find them, especially not her. My defiance, resistance and outrage kept company with my heartache and fear while in every spare moment I could claim, I tried my hardest to think up some way to change this fate I didn't want to accept.

"You know blue doesn't suit you, I don't know why you insist on wearing it," she said sharply.

"It's my favourite colour."

"It washes you out."

"I don't care," I growled. "No man can look at me anyway."

"They will," she hissed.

"And I will be wearing blue when they do." I smiled obnoxiously and her scowl deepened, etching lines into her smooth forehead. She was achingly beautiful, and she knew it. She used it like a weapon. My father had fallen for that face the day they'd met, and I'd vowed ever since that I'd never use my looks to manipulate anyone. I wanted to be appreciated for merits beyond my appearance, but Magdor had never understood that. She insisted that an Affinity for beauty was a powerful gift and that it was my duty to make use of it as much as I could. I would have argued that beauty was skin deep and not a Fae Affinity at all, but who was I to question that when I looked at all she had achieved with hers? Besides, it seemed to me that people liked to claim Affinities for every little thing these days, aching to connect to the legendary Fae of old. But we weren't like our ancestors anymore. We didn't wield magic or live for hundreds of years. We weren't at one with nature and we certainly weren't the kind and gifted fair folk the old songs gave life to.

Legend had it that the fall of the Fae had started with a simple lie. Our ancestors had been bound to the trait of honesty, but the stories said that a thousand years ago one of them had learned to lie. And that was the beginning of the end for us. Lies bred deception, greed and crime, they fed selfish desires and twisted the most sacred laws of our kind. And so over years, as our purity faded in nature so too did our magic fade from our control. Until we were just left with talents – or Affinities – for the things which we once may have held some magical control over.

I struggled to believe that my most meaningful power if I had been a Fae of old would have been in the features of my face, even if Magdor refused to see I had worth beyond that one physical attribute. My truest Affinity, in my opinion, was the rare one I had with metal. I could wield blades with the skill and proficiency of any of the royal guards, but the fact that I could protect myself was entirely dismissed, and Magdor forbade me from training, saying it was a waste of my time. But I loved the feeling of a weapon in my hand, I swear that I could almost feel the soul of a blade as I wielded it and I refused to give that up. So I practiced in secret whenever I got the opportunity because she could go to hell.

"Why do you bother practising sword fighting, Austyn? Your future husband will be adept at that."

"Why do you read so much, my dear? Brains aren't required of pretty faces."

"Why ask about politics, my sweet? Laws are only made by men."

I sneered at the echoes of the words she spoke so often as they pressed into my skull, refusing to accept them no matter how often she tried to drill them into me.

"Kahn would like to spend some time with you," Magdor announced, making a prickle of apprehension and defiance race along my spine.

And there it was. The real reason she was here.

"That's against the rules," I said firmly. I didn't want Kahn sniffing around me any more than he already had. And the rules of the competition stated that I didn't meet my suitors formally until the first day of the pageant. I had seen enough of Kahn's hulking form, crude manners and brutish tendencies from afar to know that I had absolutely no desire to see them any closer.

Magdor smiled broadly, raising her hands in innocence. "Rules can be bent. I am your father's empress after all. In fact, I already mentioned it to him and he's quite delighted by the idea."

I ground my teeth, working hard not to let her get under my skin. But she was worming her way in there, and I didn't know if I could stop her this time. If there was one way to upset me, it was by mentioning marriage. And worse than that, marriage to *Kahn*. The oaf was the size of a mountain and his entire appearance screamed ogre. Big ears, fat jaw, dumb face. If he had a personality in that thick skull of his, it was playing hide and seek and it was winning a twenty-six-year long game. The thought of his greasy hands touching my flesh, of his huge body crushing me down into a bed while he grunted and thrusted his ogre cock into me just made me want to-

"I can see you're upset," Magdor said, all sweetness now that she wanted something from me.

I wasn't going to agree to this if I got a choice. But if Father had given his consent, I didn't know how I could avoid it. I may have been all defiance and strength inside my head, but on the outside, I was just as I seemed: a trapped creature in a pretty cage with my life all mapped out for me.

"It's against the rules. I don't care what Father said. The people of Osaria would be outraged if Kahn was given an unfair advantage." In all honesty, I didn't think it would be any kind of advantage to him. If he came near me, all he was going to realise was how sick to the stomach he made me, not gain any kind of motivation to fight for our love or any nonsense like that.

Maybe throwing up in his face is key to him pulling out of the pageant though...

"It is not against the rules to be around a man who lives in the palace and who happens to come across you dining on the veranda," Magdor said slyly.

"That sounds very pre-empted, Magdor. I don't think Kahn would happen across anything of the sort unless you gave him directions. Even then, I'm pretty sure he'd mix up his left and right. And does he still keep that note in his pocket which helps him tell the time?"

Magdor's eyes darkened to deepest nightshade, and I knew I was close to making her snap. She indulged my defiance to a certain degree but if I took it too far, she was always more than ready to make me pay for my insolence.

"My son is the finest suitor in the kingdom. To even suggest such a boy who was birthed from an accomplished woman such as myself could be anything but worthy is an insult to me and the gods who willed his life."

She often said things like that, claiming the favour of the gods who had abandoned our kind to our destruction. It was nonsense and she knew it as well as I did, yet her eyes always lit with this devout kind of fervour whenever she mentioned any of the long-departed deities.

"Well, I suppose I just insulted you then." I shrugged, tugging my silver locks over my shoulders and running my fingers through them, knowing I was going to pay for it. My hair was like a friend that never spoke but was always there, which was kind of sad really. Magdor had tried to cut it once, calling it too long and untameable. But when she'd pinned me down and attempted to slice through it with scissors, they'd broken right in her hand. I guessed it had something to do with my metal Affinity, every strand on my head as tough as steel, yet somehow as soft as feathers at the same time.

"Kahn will be the strongest competitor in the pageant no matter what you think of him. Your hand is already his, but if you *insist* on going through the formalities then so be it." Magdor marched out of the room and I gritted my teeth, a growl building in my throat. I was so angry about the entire situation that I didn't even have the energy required to feel relieved at avoiding a punishment from her.

Perhaps I should have agreed to letting her skip the pageant and search for a Prophet to break the curse linked to it. It might buy me a little time if nothing else while she hunted. It might even result in Kahn succumbing to the curse if she believed it was broken and forced a marriage upon me. As tempting as that was, I couldn't face the risk of her success and I knew it wouldn't save me anyway – what I wanted was to rule alone, but the only paths possible to me seemed to be lined in a gilded cage of matrimony.

Kahn hadn't inherited his mother's beauty. But what he lacked in looks, he made up for in sheer size. He looked like two wildebeests stitched together. Roughly. It wasn't even all about vanity, I may have been able to love him despite his appearance if he was a good man, if he had some merit to him beyond smashing skulls and spilling blood. But he was a beast through and through, and I knew I'd get no more love from him than I could claim from a teaspoon. And I'd likely have a lot to fear from his lust as well. A savage like that wouldn't be tender with me and despite my shielded upbringing, I'd grown to understand enough about the way a man and woman were in the marriage bed over the years to be able to fear that with him.

There were secret passages all over the palace which I often used, and I'd heard the guards talking of their conquests on more than one occasion. Once, I'd even watched the act through a peephole which gave a view into the kitchens. A guard had been there alone with one of my own handmaids, her skirts pushed up and his huge cock slamming inside her over and over again while she cried out in a way that was hard to tell if it was in pleasure or pain. Either way, I'd been thoroughly terrified of the idea ever since witnessing that, especially when considering a man such as Kahn using my body for his own pleasure.

"So be it," I echoed Magdor in a snarl, climbing up onto my window seat and brushing my fingers over the pink silk of the cushions. I pushed the frosted window open a crack - it only opened a crack anyway. Two inches. To stop me from throwing myself out? Maybe. I'd never figured it out. All I knew was that two inches wasn't enough to allow in the full breeze I craved. I wanted to smell the market, the fish brought back from the river, the herbs and fruit and sizzling spices on an iron pan. But all I smelled was Magdor's sickly sweet perfume left in her wake and the scent of incense carrying from the bathhouse.

I wanted to see the streets of Osaria for myself, walk down the cobbled roads and pass by my people as they went about their business. I wanted to stand on the bridges which crossed the Carlell River and watch the water as it raced out into the beyond. I wanted to feel the full heat of the blazing sun which always beat down on us in this oasis set within the Lyrian Desert, and see the white walls which crisscrossed the twelve rings of our city as the setting sun gilded them in tones of orange.

Books proved to me that there was so much vast and endless beauty in this world, and none of it cared for the set of my face. I wanted to stare at something truly breath-taking and witness the radiance of nature which was undoubtedly far more stunning than any single Fae could ever be. But here I was, caged and veiled, waiting to be revealed to countless eyes which could have beheld all the views and wonders I couldn't, and yet it was me they would queue up to observe.

The only time I ever got to go outside the palace walls was when I was veiled, sat on top of a cushioned platform and carried on the shoulders of my royal guards, paraded through the city's streets to be gawped at. The people wondered at what lay beneath the veil, they marvelled at the glimpse of my hands within layers of silk which were so stifling under the midday sun that I was always tempted to rip them off.

Maybe I should have. Maybe next time I was carried about like a prized monkey, I'd take my veil off and see what the people really thought of me then. Because what the hell did it matter anyway? Okay, I liked my face. And yes, I had to admit the setting of my features were remarkably symmetrical. My lips were full, and my amber eyes were enormous. But by the Fallen, who cared? I mean really, it was just a face. Just a body. Just flesh.

I'd seen women out in those streets who had much more allure about them. All shapes and sizes, curvy, flat-chested, small-lipped, big breasted, every piece of skin pierced or tattooed. They were all beautiful in different ways. So why was *I* being prized? I'd trade in my unusual silver hair in a heartbeat to just walk outside these palace walls as a normal, unshackled girl.

My scalp tingled at that thought and I stroked my hair. *Alright, I wouldn't really give you up.* But I'd do nearly anything else for my freedom. I'd fight a dragon or cut off some fingers, anything but stay here. To have a chance at a real life. Without a man. Who needed a man anyway? I'd survived almost twenty-one years without one. And my father did not count seeing as he had been under the thumb of Magdor for almost a decade. Since she'd taken up my mother's position as his empress, she only had to suggest a change to the kingdom's laws, and he fell on it ravenously like he didn't have a brain of his own anymore. It wasn't her place at all as the emperor's consort, and yet she somehow allowed it, though I doubted I'd have as much sway with whichever man I was forced to marry. That said, I didn't even know what most men beyond my father were like because I rarely got to speak with the opposite sex to find out.

I released a huff, giving up on trying to decipher men until I'd be forced to do so during the pageant. Until then, I'd have to settle for the tripe that came out of my attendants' mouths. There was only one of them who ever held a decent conversation with me, and she was like a shining ray of light amongst the drivel pouring from the mouths of the other girls. Constant compliments. I'd liked it when I was younger, now I despised it. A compliment was only worth something if it was made about *who* you were, not *what* you were. But they all dwelled on the superficial things I'd heard a million times. One of my newest attendants *had* been getting pretty creative with her compliments recently.

"Your hair is as silver as a thousand moons, pouring into a river like liquid light."

Calm down, Jacinda.

I sighed, eyeing the tiny glimpse of the city which I could see through the gap in the frosted window.

One day, I'm going to go outside these walls and no emperor, no man and no empress is ever going to tell me no again.

"She wants to be left alone, my love," Magdor's voice came from beyond the door.

"I want to see my daughter," Father's voice answered and hope rippled through my chest.

He rarely came to see me anymore, and the child in me perked up, wishing for the embrace of her sweet father, the man he'd been before Empress *Maggot* had stolen him from me.

He opened the door, striding into my room in dark blue robes that swept out behind him as he moved. His long grey hair hung around his shoulders at a contrast to his dark skin and his deep brown eyes fell on me with an echo of love in them from the past. Magdor hurried along at his heels, a frown on her face as she looked to me in irritation. "Tell your father he needs to rest, Austyn. He slept poorly last night."

"I'll do no such thing, Magdor," I said. "Maybe you should go for a long walk? I'd like to talk to my father alone."

Magdor chuckled lightly like we didn't despise each other, but the coldness in her eyes warned me to back down. A warning I didn't plan on heeding.

"I'd rather stay here for this delightful family meeting," she replied.

You will never be family to me.

"Daughter," Father sighed, reaching out and cupping my face, a hint of light in his eyes that I swear I hadn't seen in him for years. "I've missed you."

"I've missed you too," I said, emotion burning in my throat.

I missed him when we were parted and I missed him when we were close. Sometimes I sat at his left hand during formal dinners before the entire court and missed him so much I could scarcely draw breath. The man I'd known and loved before his foul empress had forced her way into our lives was not the man I saw before me day after day, and sometimes I feared that he would never be that man for me again.

A shadow shifted beneath the door they'd entered through and I frowned, wondering if my maids had come, but my attention switched back to my father as he took my hand and led me to a golden table by the window, pulling out a seat for me. I dropped onto it, watching him closely as Magdor lurked nearby like a crow looking for some eyes to peck out and I forcibly ignored her as Father sat opposite me.

"How are you, Austyn?" he asked, and I couldn't even remember the last time he'd asked me that. It made my heart beat powerfully and a thousand memories of my childhood rise in my mind. We'd been so close once, utterly inseparable. I'd sat beside his throne while he'd spoken with the people of our empire and I had learned every single thing I could about ruling with honour and courage at his side. But that was when it had been just the two of us. Before I'd been forced aside and put in my place as a girl with one purpose.

"I'm…" I was about to offer a lie when I realised I shouldn't have to. Maybe Father would listen to my concerns about the pageant, about Kahn. "Not good, actually."

"Oh?" He frowned, reaching out to squeeze my hand as Magdor moved to stand behind him and I had to acknowledge her presence.

"She's being dramatic again, my love," Magdor said softly, her hand slipping onto his shoulder, fingernails painted like red talons gripping him tightly and making my spine straighten.

"Is it dramatic to not want to be sold like a cow at a market, Magdor?" I sniped at her as she shifted the hand on Father's shoulder, raising her chin at me.

"Goodness, you are spoiled," she sighed. "Isn't she, Tarim?"

I looked to Father and his expression seemed suddenly distant again, his eyes becoming almost vacant. "Spoiled…yes, indeed. I believe you're right, Magdor, my love."

"What?" I gasped, staring at him in horror as he sided with that bitch, withdrawing his hand from mine and leaving me aching for the once familiar warmth of his touch again. "I know I'm privileged to live in a palace and never know the taste of hunger, or any of the hardships of the lesser Fae, but don't I have a right to have a say in my own fate?"

"Your fate is one most women in the kingdom would give up everything for," Magdor said in exasperation, like she was talking to a tiresome child. "Isn't that right, darling?"

"Yes…that's right," Father agreed and hurt flashed through me.

The door creaked and my eyes whipped towards it, my heart lurching as my gaze locked on the handsome, chiselled face of my father's personal guard. He was tall with deep brown skin and the thick muscles all the guards held, his hair earthy brown and cropped short all over. The aura he commanded made my lungs feel heavy in my chest. Usually, the guards worked to be invisible, to blend away into the walls and move as little as possible, but I had always found this man harder to ignore than the rest.

The hollows of his cheeks flexed as his jaw tightened and his throat worked as everything about him tensed. But his eyes were what captivated me most; they were like two lakes of caramel, and they widened as they fell on me, taking in every inch of my exposed face and leaving me feeling more naked than I ever had in my entire life.

It was exhilarating, the rush, the feel of the forbidden racing through me as I became trapped in an eternal moment where I felt seen for once, truly *seen*. I knew this man well, his presence a constant in the palace and a blush rose in my cheeks under his intense scrutiny.

Cassius Lazar was older than me, perhaps in his late twenties or early thirties, and though he was paid to guard the royals, I always got the feeling it was something innate in him, a protectiveness about him that made me feel safe in his presence.

There was a strain to his expression, as if his whole point of existence had hinged on walking through that door, but why?

My shock at his appearance suddenly gave way to the reality of his crime, and it came crashing in on me all too heavily. He had seen my face. He had committed the unspeakable when it came to me. And yet he didn't move or run, he simply stared at me like he wanted to get hold of me, a sudden wildness to him that spoke of some urgent fear I couldn't comprehend.

I shook my head in a frantic urge for him to leave, knowing the terrible consequences of this if he was spotted. A breath remained solidly trapped inside my chest as I immediately snapped my attention back to Father and Magdor before I gave him away.

For a second, I thought I had acted fast enough, but then that bitch of an empress turned her head, and even as I leapt out of my seat to try and drag her attention back to me with my pulse drumming out a violent tune in my ears, I already knew it was too late.

"Insolence!" she roared as she spotted him. "You have laid your eyes on the sacred face of the princess!"

"Wait," I gasped in terror as Cassius continued to stare at me, seemingly rooted in place, and I could have sworn he was looking right through my flesh directly at my soul.

"Guards!" Magdor bellowed and the pounding of footsteps came from beyond the door. "Seize him!"

Cassius jolted out of his stupor and looked to Magdor, a sneer curling his lips and his hand suddenly went to his sword. But before he could draw it, he was dragged out of view by several pairs of hands, the guards outside making sure that they didn't so much as peek through the door for fear of laying their eyes on me and facing the same fate.

I stood up with my mind buzzing and fear consuming me, looking to Father in outrage. "He can't be punished for something so trivial, call them off this second!"

"He will face the punishment of his crime," Magdor spat, a twisted gleam in her eyes as she strode towards the door as if she intended to ensure it herself.

"*Father*," I begged of him in desperation, but his face was stern now, no hint of warmth in his eyes.

"It is the law," he growled. "No man may lay his eyes on you before you come of age. Everyone in the kingdom understands the punishment for such a crime and he will suffer it as the law commands."

"But it is not long before I am to be Unveiled," I gasped, shaking my head furiously. "Cassius Lazar has served you for many years, he is your most trusted guard."

"And he has broken the law," Father muttered dismissively, like that man was nothing. Like he meant as little to him as a fly on the wall. But the guards were men with lives beyond this heartless palace, and I wouldn't see one of them executed for something so meaningless.

I gave up on trying to convince Father and ran after Magdor instead, my heart rioting against my ribs as I grabbed my veil, throwing it over my head as I chased her out into the corridor.

Cassius was on his knees, his hands being cuffed in iron manacles behind his back and he didn't resist his arrest all, his head hanging in shame at what he'd done. But why had he done it? Had it really been worth his life just to gaze upon my face? He would have known the consequences of such a thing. What in Osaria had possessed him to be so foolish?

"Why?" I demanded of him, but he didn't look up, didn't say a single word, just stared at the pale wood of the floor beneath his knees, his broad frame trembling with some barely concealed emotion. I wasn't sure if it was rage at himself for what he'd done or something fiercer, but the taste of it coloured the air and made me shiver from the force of whatever Affinities he claimed. This man held a secret, one I couldn't read from him at all, and it looked like he was going to die with it.

"Magdor, he can't be killed for this. It's a mistake. Tell her it was a mistake," I begged of Cassius, moving to grasp her arm but she just shrugged me off like I was nothing but a bothersome wasp.

"There was no mistake, Your Highness. I sincerely apologise," Cassius said, his voice low and deep, his brow deeply furrowed as he accepted this fate.

"You have breached the law and will face torture and death without trial," Magdor announced cuttingly.

"No," I snarled, grabbing her arm, my nails digging into her flesh as I forced her to look at me. "It's just a face. It means nothing."

"Laws are laws, Princess Austyn. As you reminded me so succinctly just earlier today," Magdor hissed, wrenching her arm free of my grip. "Now return to your room and stop this hysteria."

She snapped her fingers at the guards surrounding Cassius and they hauled him to his feet, guiding him away down the corridor, leaving me with guilt burning a hole in my chest and tears searing my eyes.

The worst part of it all was that I was going to be Unveiled at the beginning of the pageant anyway. So Cassius's life had been wasted mere days before the whole kingdom would be allowed to see my face regardless.

I took a breath, feeling like my voice may as well have been cut out of my throat and discarded, because no one in this palace listened to me. There was nothing I could do now that the empress had given her orders, and my chest crushed with emotion over how completely helpless I felt in the face of Cassius's death.

"I'm sorry," I breathed a pointless apology to the single man in the world who had seen my face beyond my father and would suffer a terrible fate because of it.

As a tear rolled down my cheek, soaking into the netting of my veil, I felt the walls around me close in a little tighter, the light growing a little dimmer. A part of me wished I could follow Cassius into death, because it looked like there was never going to be another way out of this insufferable life. Maybe there was something better waiting in the cold clutches of the afterlife. Maybe there, I could be free.

CASSIUS

CHAPTER THREE

"**M**ore," I growled as the torturer jammed a hot poker into my side, the iron shackles holding my wrists and ankles weakening me to the point of nausea.

I was strapped to a wooden cross, my arms and legs spread across it and my body stripped to nothing but some underwear to cover my modesty. Sweat was beading on my chest and my muscles strained with every wound he offered me, the need in me to kill this man coiling up inside my heart like a venomous snake.

This was akin to visiting Hellravia, the underworld for sinful souls that was guarded by the nether ravens, birds as big as men with beaks as sharp as razors, ready to cut the flesh from your bones the moment you crossed the Bridge of Bones. Or hell, as it was called for short. If it existed, I had no idea. Perhaps it once had, when the gods of old had ruled the land, the dark, twisted god of death and ruin, Herdat, its terrifying ruler. It was perhaps just a story now, or maybe I was headed there very soon.

I would not let this fucker break me easily though, so I'd settled on pretending I liked his violent games instead, encouraging every strike of his whip and bite of his torture implements. It pissed him off to no end while making me feel far more in control of the situation. But frankly, I was fucked whether I went down with a fake smile on my face or not.

"I've broken bigger men than you," he purred, withdrawing the poker and moving to heat it in the fire which was making this room stifling hot. "I've made men as big as horses weep and beg for their mammys. You'll be no different, mark my words." He chuckled and I hung my head while I caught my breath, letting the tension run from my body as I worked to shut out the pain scoring through my side.

The first thing I'd learned in the Royal Guard were the words *I am made of steel.* My captain had made me repeat that phrase over and over. I wrote it in the sand a thousand times, I screamed it until I lost my voice, I even cut it into my skin once upon command. And eventually, I believed those words as surely as if they really were true.

I am number two hundred and eighty-seven, and I am made of steel. I am a warrior for Osaria. I cannot be broken.

"Stop pretending you want this, you dirty little traitor," the torturer growled. His face was covered by a leather mask and his emotionless eyes wheeled from my wound to my expression beneath it as he approached me with the poker glowing red at one end. "I know you hate it."

"I. Love. It," I panted. Fuck, I didn't love it. But I would not break. "Especially the poker. Drive it into me again. Go on, little man. I dare you."

I am made of steel.

He tossed the poker across the dark room with a bellow of rage and a dull clunk, clunk, clunk sounded as it bounced on the concrete, his eyes flashing with irritation. The place was full of wooden racks and torture devices I hadn't yet had the pleasure of enduring, but I had no doubt I would soon.

"Fine. You want to play with the big toys? I can introduce you to my worst horrors then," he said with a grin lighting his eyes behind the mask.

Pain continued to sear through my side from the burn and I ground my teeth, angry with myself for what I'd done to land myself here, but most of all I was angry with Magdor. I didn't know how, I didn't know why, but I knew for sure that damned woman was controlling the emperor. *My* emperor. The ruler of the kingdom. And that conniving bitch had him snared in her claws.

I knew I would be declared insane if I ever voiced my suspicions about her, but I believed, somehow, Magdor was able to wield magic like the Fae of old. I wasn't a fool; I didn't make assumptions like that on a whim. After many years of observing her, it simply seemed like the only logical conclusion to draw, because ever since the emperor had married her, every good thing he had been planning to do in Osaria had fallen to the wayside, and the kingdom I loved had slowly sunk into chaos.

"I could gouge out your eyes," my torturer said, moving across the room and picking up something which looked suspiciously like a rusty spoon. Trepidation slithered down my spine, but I refused to let it show.

I am made of steel.

So they were going to take my eyes for what I'd seen, were they? Well, I supposed it was a punishment that fitted the crime.

The short glimpse I'd had of the princess's face had been, in all fairness, an accident. But it had also potentially been the most thrilling moment of my life. Which was rather pathetic when I thought on that. I'd trained vigorously for a place in the Royal Guard since I could hold a sword and now, at thirty years old, I was the emperor's primary personal guard. To achieve that position, I'd had to make many sacrifices, given up endless opportunities, pleasures and dreams. I had sworn an oath to my kingdom and now I was owned by it, body and soul. I lived for it with every beat of my heart, and I would die for it.

I knew how to obey the rules. By the Fallen, I *was* the rules. I was a royal guard for Osaria's sake. That meant rising before the sun, training my body like my life depended on it, then protecting the palace for a sixteen-hour shift before doing it all over again. Day in, day out. That was my existence. Any other urges, wishes and desires I'd once possessed had long since been cut out of me.

So what had it all been for? My entire adult life given to the guard, but what had it given me in return? I was imprisoned and tortured, awaiting a death that would be public and drawn out. I'd likely die in a pool of my own blood while the sound of cheers carried from the royals I'd served so loyally. It would likely be the most bitter of punishments I could imagine.

It was my fault though. No man looked at the princess until her Unveiling. It wasn't even a rule, it was more of an outright fact. The princess only walked around with her veil on when she left her quarters, and yes, I *had* known I was entering her quarters at the time. But I'd been fairly sure I was moments away from catching Magdor casting some freakish spell on the emperor. Wasn't it my duty to protect him? Protect *all* of the Lunarelle royals? I'd been too filled with rage and determination to consider the fact that the princess might have been in there, unveiled in all her earth-shattering beauty, so I hadn't *intended* to break the law. I took an oath never to break the fucking law. But what good did that do me now?

The torturer approached and I held onto the image of the princess's face in a sweet kind of defiance. She was more beautiful than every rumour that had ever been weaved about her, more captivating than all the goddesses who had abandoned us here in this land.

Her skin was a deliciously warm shade of brown, and the light caught on her flesh as if it had been hand painted there to enhance the slant of her cheekbones. Her hair was unlike any hair I'd ever seen before, molten silver painted strand by strand by the gods themselves. But it was her eyes that had surprised me most. They weren't a sunrise like the tales said, they were a sunset, a thousand dusks taking place at once, leaving me bereft in the face of the endless pain I had witnessed within them.

For a single moment of madness, I had ached to grab that girl and steal her away from the palace before the pageant allowed another man to claim her as his. Because a depraved part of me had momentarily awoken and it wanted a taste of the forbidden. And the worst part about that was…it wasn't the first time.

It was the hottest day in Osaria since the Battle of the Haloed Sun. Despite only having been a young boy, I still remembered that day, the heat so intense that my mother had strung sheets over the windows to try and trap as much shade as possible within our home. But that hadn't been the most concerning part, it was our enemies at the border of our city which had really unsettled me. They had done what was once thought impossible and crossed the Lyrian Desert from the north, and most of our emperor's army had been sent to intercept them before they breached our kingdom. Those who remained were stationed along the streets, wearing the bright blue and white colours of Osaria, their armour glinting in the baking sun as they stood unyieldingly at our doors with swords in hand.

In the end, the heat had been the downfall of our opponents, and after many hours hiding in our homes and watching the sun try to crawl between the cracks in our defences against it, our army had returned bloody and victorious. It was a fine day for our kingdom, one that even today filled me with pride. Especially as I now wore that same heavy armour while heat bled through the palace, and I realised how strong our army had really been that day to fight under the weight of so much steel while the sun glared down at their backs.

"Surely we can put it off another day?" the princess's angry voice reached me further down the white stone corridor as I followed along at the emperor's back.

She'd turned eighteen last week and Magdor had insisted she be paraded through the streets often, covered from head to toe in white as she was hailed the most beautiful woman in the world. Whether it was true or not, I didn't know, but the rumours were escalating about her fast, especially after it had been announced that in three years' time, her hand in marriage would be bid for in a traditional pageant established by the emperors of old.

Emperor Tarim had sworn the damn thing off years ago, so it had been a shock when he had announced that it was to go ahead, that he would essentially sell his daughter to the strongest and richest Fae who dared enter the tournament. It was fucking barbaric and made my skin crawl to even think of watching the princess end up married to whomever won that twisted game. But there was nothing I could do; I was only as useful as my sword. A man forged into a weapon and given a singular task in life - to protect the Lunarelle royals. I just wished I could protect her from that fate.

"I can hardly breathe in all this silk," the princess protested.

"Don't be so pathetic, Austyn. You can handle a little sunshine. Are you of Osarian blood or not?" Magdor asked dismissively and I had to stop my upper lip from curling at her brash tone with the emperor's daughter.

"You look beautiful, child," the emperor spoke in a bland tone, one void of the vibrancy and love of life which used to fill every corner of his being. I missed that man. The one I used to look up to, the one who wasn't influenced by his black hearted empress.

I moved to stand beside the wall as the emperor approached his wife and daughter, embracing Magdor first, before placing a single hand on Austyn's shoulder in greeting. It was an insult to the way he had once shown her affection and it made my teeth grind together.

What has happened to the man you once were? Can you not see that Magdor has changed you?

The princess was clad in white, close-fitting silk with her veil over her face and gloves on her hands. It was far too hot on any normal day in Osaria for such clothes, but today of all days it was practically a danger. Unfortunately, even though it was my duty to protect that girl, it was also my duty to obey the emperor, so if he deemed this acceptable, I was going to have to go along with it.

"Father, tell her this is ridiculous," Austyn demanded, placing a hand on her hip.

She had always been feisty, never biting her tongue on words which got her into trouble, and I was eternally grateful that Magdor had never managed to bring her to heel. Her defiance was all the more heart-breaking though, because in the end, she was going to be forced to do as she was told.

Magdor treated her as nothing more than a symbol of beauty, a goose that would one day lay her a golden egg when she was forced to marry. Because I knew of Magdor's plans to have her son, Kahn, seize the princess's hand in marriage by winning the pageant, therefore securing herself a more permanent position of power within the kingdom of Osaria, with heirs of her own to lay a true claim on the throne. I was only glad she had never gotten pregnant herself. If she had, I would have feared for the life of the princess. As it was, she was clearly aiming to see a grandchild on the throne via Kahn's marriage to the princess.

It made me want to draw my sword and drive it into Kahn's heart to ensure he never did any such thing. He trained often, his size seeming to increase with each passing year, and his Affinity for strength obvious by the brutality he used to defeat his opponents. Yes, I could see Magdor lining up all her ducks in a row, and I was helpless to stop it, my emperor's ears deaf to a single bad word spoken about her, and my princess powerless to take a stand against her.

My only hope was in proving that Magdor really did hold some ancient power which she was wielding to manipulate the ruler of this land, but so far, I had nothing to go on but my own suspicions, and with each passing day, I was running out time.

I will expose her before you are forced into that pageant, Princess. I swear it.

"The people wish to see their princess," Magdor said firmly. "You will do your duty to them."

"Father?" Princess Austyn looked to him through her veil, a note of desperation in that one word.

"It's important you are seen in public. It will offer a morale boost during this drought," the emperor said with a nod then turned his head halfway towards me. "Cassius will escort you today. There has been some unrest in the west quarter, I want my best men out there with you for your protection." His tone had softened slightly and a glint of his former self shone in his eyes. I was one of the few guards the emperor referred to by name instead of by number, and since the first time he had done so, I had been filled with pride. These days, it seemed more out of habit than familiarity - or what I had once hoped was something akin to fondness. Nowadays, he looked through me more often than not, and I had become the invisible creature in these walls that my

captain had always encouraged me to be.

I bowed to my emperor then moved to stand at Princess Austyn's side, the sweet scent of honey and cocoa caressing my senses and making my breathing hitch. I had never smelled anything like that enticing scent and I took a side step away from her, feeling as though I was crossing a line by taking a single breath of her, yet finding myself hungering for more.

I clasped my hands at my back, facing forward, chin high as I supressed the illicit thoughts racing through my mind. But it became almost impossible to concentrate as she turned her veiled face towards me, and I felt her gaze burning into my very soul.

She was looking at me. Me. A fucking guard who held no more use in this world than the skilled swing of a sword in my hand. If she were to command it, I'd drive that very same sword into my chest and bleed out at her feet. I was owned by her, and I would give my life for her without a moment's hesitation, without reason or cause. I was an entity built to serve and protect, a weapon made of flesh and bone, and I held no more value than that purpose, only as present in this room as a vase upon a plinth. So why in Osaria was she looking at me?

"Come on then, Austyn," Magdor encouraged. "I will ride in the carriage behind you with Kahn."

"What about you, Father?" Austyn asked, her gaze falling from me and leaving me able to breathe again.

"It's too hot for your father, foolish girl," Magdor said, speaking for the emperor as she so often did, and my fingers twitched with the desire for a blade to run across her throat.

You fucking witch, I'll have you burned, buried and forgotten when I prove what you are.

Austyn let out a sound close to a growl and though I kept my features neutral, the urge to smile burned at my lips.

If you ever lose your spirit, Princess, I'll mourn it for the rest of my days.

Magdor led the way down the corridor and I walked one step behind Austyn, her scent drifting to me again, though there was little I could do to stop it this time unless I placed more distance between us. I had been ordered to her side by the emperor and I took that role incredibly seriously, so I was forced to accept it even though it felt like stealing something that wasn't meant for me. Maybe a better man would have held his breath intermittently to lessen the amount of time he spent with her scent, but it seemed I was not a better man. And if anything, the longer it went on, the more sin-filled thoughts ran through my head.

If only I could see beneath that veil, watch her mouth move around the rebellious words she threw at Magdor...

I blinked hard to clear my mind of that thought which would see me stripped of my sword if ever I voiced it. Sometimes, I forgot I was just a man. Weeks would pass without me giving in to a single lustful urge, then eventually, I'd crack, head into town and buy a night with a whore who'd fall at the mercy of every wicked and infernal thought I'd had during that time, becoming nothing but a merciless beast as I purged the animal in me. Then, when I was sated, I'd do it all over again. Day after day without release, my sins saved for my breaking point. It was the only time when I was bowed to, the only time I could be powerful in a life confined by rules, and during that brief period that I allowed myself to let loose, I dominated.

For the most part, it worked. It kept my inner needs under control, but it seemed lately that breaking point came swifter than I'd have liked, the gap between those nefarious nights growing shorter and shorter.

We walked to the palace gates where a chariot awaited Magdor and her son. Kahn was already there, showing off to the guards as he puffed out his chest and showed them the bruises on his knuckles from some unsuspecting drunk he'd beaten in a bar brawl. His features were more deserving of a misshapen vegetable and his bald head gleamed beneath the bright sun as he flexed his swollen muscles. He was meaty and all brawn, and any sign of intelligent life seeming absent from his small, round eyes for the most part.

The platform Princess Austyn would be carried on was a shallow trough built of wood and filled with cushions for her comfort. Wooden poles extended from the corners of it for four guards to rest on their shoulders as they carried her, making sure she could be seen from all around by the people of her city, while the veil made certain she couldn't actually be seen at all.

Magdor and Kahn entered their carriage and Austyn sighed as she got onto the platform, sitting down on the cushions and folding her legs.

The four porters lifted her between them, and I moved to mount my horse among the other riding guards. Gallow was huge and his fur was the deep, red-gold colour of the Lyrian sand, paired with a cream mane that was braided down his neck in the style of all the war horses, his tail twisted up into an intricate knot. I climbed onto his back and patted his shoulder in greeting, a small snort leaving him and the word "apple" filling my head in a demand. An amused smile pulled at the corner of my lips as I took up the reins.

"Later, Gallow," I murmured. My Affinity with animals occasionally extended to him, especially on account of our bond, but the beast's wants were simple. Apples, sugar lumps and ear tickles.

I guided him to the side of Austyn's platform and donned the helmet one of my fellow guardsmen passed me.

The rebels in the slums were growing more restless recently and you could never be too careful on these parades. It was another reason why I despised the princess being taken beyond the palace walls like this without even containing her within the confines of a carriage. But Magdor wanted her on full display, or at least as on display as a woman bound in silk could be.

Gallow fell into a steady pace beside the platform as Princess Austyn was carried towards the gates behind two lines of guards. No man on foot could possibly get close to her, but what of a well-aimed arrow? What of the fire bombs the rebels were known for throwing?

I was on edge as we moved through the gleaming palace gates, and I kept one hand on my sword while the other gripped the reins. Vigilance was my name today, and I would live up to it in every way I could.

The parade went smoothly as we marched through the streets of the royal circle and I hunted the faces of the waving crowd for any potential threat. Women called out to us guards, desperate to catch our attention, but I ignored all of them even when one girl tossed her handkerchief at me and tried to get hold of my leg. Gallow swung his rump right into her, nearly knocking her to the ground as I hunted the rooftops for signs of danger. Any flitting shadow drew my attention as I prepared for some kind of attack, my muscles tensed as I readied to dive into action at a single second's notice.

Sweat was beading on my brow, the sun on my metal helmet making my head feel like it was cooking, but it was nothing to the intensity of the heat beneath my breastplate. My heart was labouring with the temperature, but I didn't let it distract me. I'd bleed out every drop of water in my body before I gave in to the burn of the sun.

Princess Austyn waved to the people who praised her name and pledged their undying love to her. She pulled at her silken clothes occasionally, shifting uncomfortably on the cushions and I glanced back at Magdor in her open-air chariot, a lace umbrella offering her and her son shade where it was held by the guard riding beside them. Irritation made my skin prickle over their set-up compared to the insufferable position Austyn had been put in.

The parade went on for over two hours under the high sun and the horses were panting by the time we turned back towards the palace, relief washing through me as we closed in on the promise of shade.

Sweat dripped down my spine and the crowd thinned as they returned to the shelter of their homes, the last of them waving from doorways or windows, not wanting to step out into the intense Osarian heatwave.

After another visual sweep of the rooftops and alleyways close by, I shifted my attention to the princess as she clutched her chest and seemed to be fighting for breath.

"Are you well, my lady?" I asked anxiously.

"Yes, I just need to...to..." She started falling sideways so fast that I barely had a moment to react, acting on instinct alone as I kicked Gallow's side to force him closer to her.

Austyn tumbled from the platform and I caught her in my arms, her body slack and her head lolling against my breastplate.

"Halt!" I bellowed as my pulse skyrocketed with fear, but it seemed half the guardsmen had already noticed anyway and were drawing the entourage to a standstill.

"Get your hands off of the princess!" Magdor shrieked as I turned Gallow about, holding Austyn against me with one arm while charging back up the line towards the chariot.

"She's fainted, Your Highness," I said urgently, despising this woman but knowing I had no choice but to seek her orders. "She needs to get out of these clothes."

I took a knife from my hip, not willing to see the princess in peril any longer even if it cost me my life to free her from the confines of this silk.

"Stand down," Magdor barked. "Place her in here."

My grip tightened on the knife and I forced myself to obey this false empress as I returned it to my hip and leaned over into the chariot, placing Austyn on the seat beside her.

"Is that quite enough drama for you, child?" Magdor muttered, shaking Princess Austyn, and making my hands tighten to fists.

"We must return to the palace," I encouraged.

"Your duty is done," Magdor clipped at me. "And I am yet undecided about your punishment for touching the sacred daughter of the emperor, guard, so you will bite your tongue or else I will have it cut out."

Rage slid up my spine, but I held myself in check as Magdor called out for the entourage to return to the palace. Kahn handed her his water canteen and Magdor upended it over the princess without care, making her splutter and sit upright as the fabric of her veil clung to her face and she was forced to pluck it away so that she could breathe again.

"There now, are we quite done being theatrical?" Magdor hissed at her, and my relief at seeing Princess Austyn wake was sullied by my fury at the empress for speaking to her like that.

My heart pounded to an excruciating beat as the princess reached for her veil, clearly intending to take it off before Magdor grasped her wrist, her sharp talons digging into the material there.

"You forget where you are, Austyn," Magdor growled, and the princess looked around, her gaze landing on me, and though I couldn't see her eyes, I could feel them everywhere.

"What happened?" she murmured.

"You know exactly what happened." Magdor clucked her tongue. "You threw yourself at a guard, feigning heatstroke. I mean, really, girl, are you so in need of attention after the whole city has come out to see you?"

"I didn't feign anything, Magdor," she snarled.

"I saw it. She fell and that one caught her." Kahn pointed at me, looking like a brick with a face in it. "I guess she could have died otherwise."

He shrugged his big shoulders, and I supposed I had to be grateful to the troll for noticing what had really happened or else I could be facing the hangman's noose for my actions.

Magdor huffed like his statement angered her, but she couldn't deny it either, so she didn't try to dispute what had happened again.

"You will take thirty lashings from your captain, guard," she snapped at me.

"Yes, Your Highness," I said, bowing my head obediently. It was a small price to pay for the princess's wellbeing.

"What?" Austyn gasped, looking to her vile mother-in-law. "He caught me. My head could have been dashed on the cobbles if it wasn't for him. It's his job to protect me and he did just that."

"Which is why I am being so lenient in the punishment, Austyn. But rules are rules. He cannot touch you. The price should be far, far greater, but considering the circumstances, I deem a whipping appropriate," Magdor said, waving a hand at her like she was being irritating and I fought the urge to take my sword and drive it into her hollow chest.

I flexed my fingers as I gripped the reins, guiding Gallow a little away from their chariot as energy burned along my palm. The same palm which had held her against me. If my body hadn't been so laden with armour, I would have felt her everywhere and the thought of that was so sinful, I could taste the blasphemy of it.

We marched on back to the palace and my heart rate didn't settle once in all that time. I'd held the princess in my arms, her body curved into mine. I'd felt her warmth through all that silk and it had already planted an ache in me to feel it again, to have her that close so I could keep her from the likes of Magdor, the blazing intensity of the sun and anything else that might dare harm her.

I had always been her protector, but I had a feeling I had just become something more dangerous than that too. Because I was pretty sure my desire to safeguard her had officially turned into an obsession that would transform me into the most corrupt of devils in the face of her enemies.

My soul had been stamped with the royal emblem a long, long time ago. It was no more mine than the stars in the sky. But if I had to guess who held it in their possession, I was fairly certain it was her.

I focused back on the dreary room I was in and the mask of the torturer before me, the touch of that old memory draining from my skin and leaving me barren once more.

I am made of steel.

"Once you've seen something you can't *unsee* it," I mused aloud and the torturer stilled before me with his rusty spoon - which was maybe more of a knife now that I was seeing it up close. And it was very apparent he took no care in washing his tools. Hadn't this arsehole heard of basic hygiene? The foul scent of sweat sailing off of him said he hadn't and it made my upper lip curl back.

I leaned as far forward as my tethers would allow, smiling through the agony in my flesh as I tried to tempt him closer. "Do you want to know what she looks like?"

I knew he did. Every man in the kingdom wanted to know. Even this worthless, sun-baked turd. And the glint in his eyes might just have been my salvation. At least for a few moments longer.

"I..." He cleared his throat. "Of course not."

"Seems a shame not to share it. They're going to kill me tomorrow, that secret will die with me." I glanced towards the closed wooden door across the dark and filthy space, lowering my voice. "No one will know."

"That's treason," he snarled.

"I'm a royal guard, I know what treason is and describing her face isn't it. Nowhere in the rulebook does it say a man who looks upon the face of the princess is not allowed to describe it."

I was lying. And he was lapping it up. It actually did say that in the rulebook. Which I knew as I'd read it back to front during my training more times than I could count. And it wasn't even a book, it was fifty golden scriptures in the royal archives.

"It doesn't?" he breathed and that disgustingly rancid breath of his floated over my face.

"No, it doesn't." My lips stretched into a smile even though my wounds were screaming, setting off alarm bells in my head.

Maybe I have sepsis. I am definitely going to get some sort of an infection from this man and his unwashed tools of pain and death if I haven't already.

What does it matter? I'll be dead tomorrow morning.

Fuck.

"Go on then," he whispered and there it was. My bargaining chip. Men were fickle. Especially when it came to women. Not me. The only thing I cared about enough to betray all of my morals for was the kingdom itself. Moment of madness or not, I would never truly have acted on those carnal urges in me the second I'd seen her. The princess wasn't for me for endless reasons, even if she hadn't been royalty and the most coveted girl in the land, she was also far too young for me and held a thousand times my worth. I may have formed something of a fixation on her, but so had most of the men in Osaria. So what really made me any different from them? *The fact that I'd gut every one of them who dared lay a finger on her.*

"She has eyes like the deepest, darkest night you ever saw." She actually had amber eyes which were so big I'd spent most of that stolen moment not looking at anything else. "Her lips are as small and as delicate as a summer rose." Lie. They were full and wide, and fuck had they made me want to know what they felt like on my flesh. I'd have died a happy man if I could have had just one raw, indecent kiss from that mouth. But this creep was not getting that truth to drool over. He didn't deserve the truth. He'd shoved a hot poker into my flesh a minute ago and whatever version of the princess he was conjuring in his mind was not going to be anything close to reality. "Her skin is utterly unblemished and soft as silk, with not a single mark upon it." I didn't mention the long eyelashes which seemed to have been individually painted on by the lost gods themselves – he wasn't getting a single one of them. But when you're told your entire life that you're not allowed to know what someone looks like, no matter how much training you've had, or how deep the rules have been beaten into you, your mind jumps into top gear committing that face to memory when you see it. So I almost counted them. I reached six before Magdor had ordered my fellow guardsmen to arrest me.

"Go on," he begged, lowering the spoon-knife in his hand.

"Her nose!" I lamented. "Her nose was the smoothest, straightest nose you ever saw. Like..." I struggled for more words – *how do I describe a fucking nose?* "Like the slope of a mountain peak, a glistening jewel adorning a perfect face."

Maybe the iron against my skin was making me delirious because my training had ensured my mind never snagged on a woman for long. But this one - the damn princess herself - was branded into my skull. She represented the kingdom, so maybe that was why I couldn't get her out of my head. I'd come all over a royal flag once because I was just that much of a royalist – what could I say? I didn't get out much. The kingdom was my life and I wasn't *entirely* straight edged.

The torturer sighed in satisfaction and I grimaced, sensing I was turning this cretin on, and that disgusted me on so many levels it was unreal.

He lifted the tool again, his eyes darkening to deepest pitch. "At least you have one sweet vision to take with you." He leaned forward, slamming his palm to my forehead to hold me in place.

I swore through my teeth, thrashing against my shackles as he brought that rusty, blood-crusted spoon-knife up to my face. I was actually more worried about the diseases I was going to get off of that thing when he gouged my eyes out than the act itself.

The door flew open and the torturer halted, turning to see who had entered. I shook my head hard, but he didn't remove his sweaty palm from where it was stamped to my face.

"Back down, Farooq," a woman called and my bones chilled as I recognised that voice.

Magdor.

The torturer extracted his hand from my forehead and she appeared beyond him, her straight, black hair spilling around her shoulders beneath the silver crown she rarely took off. She was my empress, but I'd never looked on her as such. Her deep blue dress hugged her feminine curves, revealing more flesh than was appropriate for a royal, but she didn't seem to care much for propriety and the emperor was so bewitched by her that he had never stopped her from flaunting her body.

She was flanked by guards wearing the fine blue and white robes of the palace; my own had been torn off of me the moment I'd been taken here. Stripped down and stripped of my rank as a royal guard.

I am made of steel.

Not anymore. I'm just flesh and bone. A man with one last night on earth and nothing to show for it.

I guessed this witch had come to mock me for that fact, though why one criminal was of any interest to her was a mystery to me.

She indicated for her guards and the torturer to leave and they did so without a moment's hesitation. Couldn't they see what she was? Was I the only man in the whole of Osaria with my eyes open to the truth? I could practically feel the power exuding from her, and it made my spine prickle with hatred.

The door clicked shut as Farooq exited, and Magdor eyed the filthy room distastefully as she made her way towards me.

"Cassius Lazar," she said, eyeing me coldly.

"Yes, Your Highness?" I asked in my formal tone, pretending we weren't in a blood-stained torture chamber the night before I was going to be executed for my crime.

"Do you know why your eyes are still intact?" she asked, her voice honey sweet.

"No," I replied, frowning curiously.

"Because I have something to tell you," she said, a grin pulling at her mouth.

Well get on with it then, you insufferable wench.

Her icy gaze ignited with whatever was on her mind and I waited for her to go on, but she left me hanging, clearly wanting me to ask.

"And what's that?" I prompted.

"You're a dead man," she whispered. "A ghost. As of tomorrow, you no longer exist."

Oh joy, she came here to brighten up my day.

"And?" I pressed. The so-called empress sure knew how to talk. She'd spend a whole day circling around the point and never get to it.

"What does a dead man have to lose?" she asked, keeping up the game I was already done with.

"Nothing," I grit out.

"Precisely," she said keenly, shifting closer and toying with the neck of her dress. "How do you feel now that you've gazed upon the famed face of the princess?"

I eyed her closely, trying to work out her angle here. She wouldn't have taken a trip from the palace just to rub my worthless face in the fact that I was going to die tomorrow. So it had to be more than that, and I sensed it was time to play the good little repenting guard.

"Remorseful," I said as fiercely as I could manage.

I'm not remorseful, Magdor. Not even a little bit. Because I know what you're up to, you venomous bitch, and I almost caught you at it. My only regret is that I didn't accomplish what I started and gain proof of what you are.

"I've tried to think of ways to forget her face. I've tried to burn the image from my mind," I said powerfully. In truth, I would hold onto it until the moment I died. "But still she remains, my empress. So if I am to die for that one mistake, then I shall."

She pursed her lips, nodding her approval of that. "So you looked at a girl's face, who cares?" she said lightly and I frowned at the change in her tone. "She's hardly worth the veil, don't you agree?"

My eyes narrowed and I remained silent, unsure what the best form of tactic was here. She was playing some trick on me, I was sure of it, so I had to be careful of my words. Not that I could see how my situation could get any worse, but when it came to this woman, I had no doubt she would find a way to paint my fate blacker.

She slid a finger under my chin, her sharp nail scraping against my Adam's apple. "No need to die over a teeny tiny mistake, is there Cassius? Not when there is another option."

"Another option, Your Highness?" I asked, hope crawling through me and daring to raise its head.

Yes, let me out of here, Magdor. Make any deal with me you like because whatever it is will end up with my sword in your back and the whole kingdom knowing what a deceptive rat you are.

She extracted her finger from under my chin, reaching for the elaborate necklace around her throat. She popped open the golden amulet and took something from within it and without warning, she shoved it in my mouth. I jerked, the vile taste of some pill rolling over my tongue as Magdor held my mouth shut. She tilted my head back, forcing me to swallow as she hushed me, her grip unnaturally strong and the iron already weakening my body making it impossible for me to buck her off.

My heart started to race, the room became blurry and unfocused as whatever foul thing she had forced on me took effect.

A vision filled my eyes and I lost sight of the chamber, engulfed by a swirling mass of light. It grew hotter, whiter, blinding, then it began to fade and suddenly I was sweeping across the Lyrian Desert, passing over a huge rock shaped like an eagle. Beyond it sat two lush green mountains and between them lay a waterfall so tall I couldn't see the top of it as it ran from a sheer cliff into a silvery pool of water.

I could hardly process what I was seeing as I moved at an unnatural speed towards it as if flying on the back of some winged beast. I slipped through the veil of water and before me was a garden of jewels, the gemstones seeming to grow from the trees and plants themselves. A carpet of earthy moss trailed past the glinting jewels where they perched within flowers or dangled like fruit upon branches: rubies, emeralds and diamonds bigger than my fist.

I felt my mouth falling open as I remained trapped in the vision, sailing across the enchanted garden and gazing down upon a gleaming golden coin with a winged girl etched into its surface. It was perched atop a stone pedestal, nestled in a cluster of moss and wild flowers, and I could almost feel the power radiating from it.

The vision died in a wave and I sucked in a breath as I found myself looking at Magdor again, her cruel beauty mocking me.

"What magic was that?" I hissed. This was the proof I'd been hunting for, for years, and yet now I wasn't in any sort of position to prove it. Curse this fucking woman. I *knew* she was harbouring secret power.

"I need a man to cross that waterfall. It must be done quietly and by someone who will not be missed," she said, ignoring my accusation. I blinked heavily, still trying to process what I'd just witnessed. So much treasure all in one place, a hundred lifetimes wouldn't have been enough to spend it. And I knew where it was.

"I will gift you your freedom if you swear to bring me that coin. Only the coin. Touch nothing else, and when you return, I will reward you with enough gold to make you a lord of Osaria."

I gazed up into the bitch's eyes, seeing my fate there twisting and contorting into something new. It was death or this. But I knew whatever that coin meant to her could be nothing good. I couldn't give her something that could make her more powerful. My kingdom meant too much to me to allow that, and she'd already gotten her talons into it. Since the emperor had married her, taxes had doubled, hangings had quadrupled and the kingdom had fallen in to disrepair. What other terrible things would she do if she gained access to more magic?

After she'd become the empress of Osaria and my suspicions had surfaced, I'd spent any free time I had researching the Fae of old. They'd possessed all kinds of powers, some of them able to create fire, stone, metal and more, while others could wield power through potions, elixirs and the possession of magical objects. Objects, perhaps, like that coin.

I remained silent, wishing she'd offered me anything else. Something I could have swung to my advantage and used to assist me in bringing her to her demise. But a deep, resounding note of dread in my gut told me that I couldn't risk that coin falling into her hands.

Am I willing to die for this? She'll just find another man to do this deed if I refuse.

"I will return soon with your pardon," Magdor purred, backing away from me with a knowing glint in her eye. She thought I'd already accepted. But had I?

She barked an order at the guards outside and a moment later I was hauled out of the chamber and taken back to my cell.

I was thrown into the damp, dirty space, wheezing as I clasped the deepest wound on my side.

"Looks like they gave you a rough time," a male voice spoke from the shadows.

I turned to find I had company in the cell next to mine which had been empty before I'd been taken to be tortured. I could barely see the man in the darkness shrouding us, and I didn't have the care to try.

I pushed myself back against the wall with a groan, relieved to at least to have the iron removed from my wrists and ankles.

"Name's Drake," he offered as if I gave a damn. "As in... of The Forty Thieves?" he pressed and I ground my teeth.

I'd heard of them, alright. Everyone had heard of them and knew well enough to despise them. They were a bunch of cutthroats, thieves and cold-hearted killers of the most notorious variety. Stories of the crimes they'd committed and the fear they spread throughout the slums travelled all the way to the ears of the palace guards, and even to the ears of the emperor himself. Not that he'd done a thing to try and combat them. Magdor dismissed the lower Fae who lived on the outskirts of the city beyond the twelfth ring as insignificant, and ever since she'd come to rule by the emperor's side, he'd taken up the same viewpoint. But I knew who The Forty were: the biggest organised gang in the city, who ruled the slums of Osaria through terror and fear, though I'd not heard of this man specifically.

Drake leaned forward into the flickering torchlight that was cast beyond his cell and I saw him clearer. He was tall and muscular in a way that spoke of violence like the kind I lived for, though his hadn't given him any scars that I could see. The thin tunic he wore was sleeveless and torn to reveal intricate tattoos marking his dark skin, each of them drawing my gaze like they had some deeper meaning I couldn't comprehend. They reminded me of some of the images I'd seen in books on the old Fae, but I couldn't for the life of me place them now. He had jet black hair which was pushed away from equally dark eyes which sparked with an excitement I couldn't understand considering our current surroundings.

His was the kind of face that made women melt, the kind made for stealing virtue and breaking hearts, and something about the glimmer in his gaze told me plainly that he was well practiced in both. He was smiling, a perfect white toothed smile and his gaze moved over me in a way just as assessing as the look I was giving him.

I wasn't sure of the purpose of his smile. Did this thief actually think I was going to make friends with him? I might not have looked like it right now, but I was a royal guard. Not someone who would ever form a kinship with a miscreant lower Fae with fucking dimples.

"Help meeee. Ahhhh," a tiny voice reached me from somewhere to my left and my head snapped around in that direction, a curse leaving my lips as I realised where it was coming from. My very slight Affinity with animals sometimes extended to hearing creatures' thoughts, and it seemed my gift – for want of a better word – was currently at play.

A fly was caught up in a web in the corner of the ceiling beyond my cell and there was very little I could do for it as a spider closed in on its meal.

"Hungry, chompy, chompy, nom, nom, nom," the spider's thoughts filled my head and I squeezed my eyes shut to try and block it out. By the Fallen, I would have given up this Affinity in a heartbeat. It rarely served any purpose apart from tormenting me with the deaths of tiny bugs.

"Noooooo," the fly wailed then its little voice was cut off and I let out a breath, relieved it was over though not feeling particularly good about it either. I had saved countless tiny creatures from the jaws of their predators when I was a boy, and somehow, I never got past the guilt I felt over the ones I couldn't save. My mother had nicknamed me her little Rarh after the god of protection, a trait that had been the reason for me becoming a royal guard in the end. Though I shuddered to remember why it had come to the total sacrifice of my free will in taking up that line of work.

"Scrummy little buzz buzz," the spider said then finally shut up as it settled into its meal.

"You okay there, mate?" Drake asked.

"Yes," I muttered, figuring it wasn't worth the explanation. It was a rare kind of Affinity, and an odd one too. It wasn't exactly something to boast about and sometimes I simply preferred to pretend I didn't have it at all.

I sighed, figuring I might as well continue to bridge the silence. There wasn't much else to do considering I was going to die for my crime. Because, yes, I'd made my decision. I was not going to help Magdor become an even bigger monster than she already was, even if that meant facing a bloody death. I'd made my oaths to the kingdom, to the royal family, and I had vowed to die if ever I was put in a position to betray them. So here I was, keeping my word on that promise like I did with every promise I'd ever made. And though I wasn't afraid to die, I did have endless regrets over how little I had really lived. But I supposed it was far too late for what-ifs.

"Thirty-nine," I said.

"What?" Drake asked, cocking his head curiously.

"Thirty-nine thieves," I corrected him. "They caught one."

DRAKE

CHAPTER FOUR

I raised an eyebrow at the balls on this arsehole. He'd just found out that he was sitting in a cell right beside a member of the most infamous gang in the entire city and he hadn't even batted an eyelash.

Thirty-nine thieves? Pfft. He'd be laughing on the other side of his face come nightfall when my gang came to get me out.

"You know, you don't have to be embarrassed," I said, leaning against the bars to look at him, my stomach writhing as I pushed against the iron, fighting the instinct to recoil from the foul substance in favour of getting a closer look at my new cellmate. "I know it can be intimidating to come face to face with a real-life legend."

Someone had gone to town on him, that was for sure, and his muscular body was a mess of cuts and bruises from his session in the torture chamber. There were a few burns too and he hissed between his teeth as he repositioned himself against the filthy wall. I wondered what he'd done to earn that kind of punishment. The guards had been pretty pissed at me when they'd brought me in here, but I hadn't suffered more than a few kicks and shoves. Maybe he was a real bad son of a bitch. Though I'd met more than a few nasty fuckers in my lifetime, and I couldn't say he had the look of a killer in his eyes. Nah, not a killer, but he was something alright. I just needed to figure out if it was something I could make use of.

"*If* you were a legend, I'm sure I would have heard of you before," he replied dismissively and if I wasn't mistaken, he wasn't even bullshitting me. He really had no fucking idea who I was. And here I'd been thinking that my name was known all over this cesspit of a city from the dregs of the slums to the emperor's table itself. So that was my infamy bubble well and truly burst.

Cunt.

I pushed my hair back out of my eyes as I surveyed him. It was hard to gauge from his position slumped on the floor, but I'd have guessed he was as tall as me. He was powerfully built which made me think he either ran the streets like I did, or he held a job which required the use of his muscles. But seeing as he'd neither heard of me nor had a look of rampant hunger and perpetual poverty about him – as proven by the untouched crust of bread in the corner of his cell – I was going to go with some sort of tradesman. Lucky fucker probably had an Affinity which kept him in the good books of those upper Fae arseholes.

"You a blacksmith?" I guessed as I eyed the calluses on his palms. A man as big and strong as him didn't just end up in his kind of physical condition through luck alone, and there weren't all that many professions which he could hold to have earned that kind of strength.

"No," he replied, looking at me in a way that made me feel like he was sizing me up too. He didn't offer me any further explanation as to his profession either, and my suspicions only grew. What reason would he have for hiding it? Then again, there was one reason which I could think of easily enough, though the mere thought left a bad taste in my mouth.

His earthy brown hair was carefully cropped short in the kind of way that suggested someone else had cut it for him and even in his injured state, he was maintaining a stick up the arse kind of posture. People where I came from either let their hair grow endlessly or did as I did and took a pair of scissors to it ourselves when we had to, leaving messy, uneven strands – though I preferred to think of mine as roguishly dishevelled. But if he'd been making use of a barber, that meant either he had money or...

"You're a guard," I stated, my lip curling back with distaste.

Just my luck to be stuck here with a damn lawman.

I almost suspected some kind of trap. Maybe he'd been put here to find out about me and the rest of The Forty. But no one was so committed to his job to have endured the kind of beating he'd clearly taken. So he was a guard who had done something worthy of this punishment. Maybe that meant he wasn't all bad, or maybe it meant he was the worst of the worst. There were more than a few royal guards who liked to take their tempers out on Fae from the slums after all. There was one mean fucker in particular who liked to come swaggering down to the whore houses in my part of town and leave the women beaten and bleeding when he was done. Nothing could be done about it. And that was the kind of thing which made us all hate them so much – not because they worked against our criminal inclinations, but because they abused their power and position as frequently as they could.

I eyed the view out of the small, barred window on the wall opposite my cell. Not that I could see anything other than the sky. Endless, open sky like the kind that always shone over Osaria. We had three kinds of weather here; hot, really fucking hot and sweat-your-balls-off-and-light-your-arse-on-fire-if-you-sit-on-the-sand hot. The sky was paling to a soft kind of sapphire now, so I guessed it was closing in on sunrise. I'd have to wait for nightfall again

68

before the thieves would come for me, which meant I had time to kill.

"You got anything to say to that?" I pushed, eyeing my new friend again. "You gonna try and deny it? Seems to me like I've called it right. You're the chewed up, spat out remains of a royal guard."

"And you're a criminal," he grunted, giving in to my request for some kind of conversation. "Of the worst kind, if what I've heard about your pals is true."

"They're not my *pals,*" I replied in disgust. If he'd heard of The Forty, then he'd have heard of our brutal and merciless reputation too, and he would be a damn fool to believe that such men and women cohabited like a bunch of merry besties, all living the life of our dreams and getting on like a house on fire. The Den was a viper's pit, infested by the worst of Fae kind, and any idiot worth his salt should have known that full well without needing a guided tour of our depravity. "They're my gang. Honestly, it's like you're *trying* to piss me off with this nonsense. You admitted that you know who they are even if you're still trying to convince yourself you've never heard of *me*. Which means you know full well what they're capable of even if you've only heard a few whispers here and there. So just cut the shit."

"Well, your *gang* are a bunch of cutthroats," he said with a sneer, looking me up and down in that holier than thou way which all of the guards had perfected so well. For a group of Fae who had supposedly sworn an oath to protect all of Osaria's people, they sure were a judgemental, superior bunch of motherfuckers who did little to nothing for the sake of those of us living outside the royal circle – especially those of us dwelling within the slums.

"Not true. We don't kill our marks," I said casually, shifting so that my shoulder was leaning against the bars of my cage and continuing to ignore the way the iron made me feel like I might puke at any moment. I knew well enough how to fake it and I wouldn't ever let anyone see when I was rattled. Besides, iron or not, for some reason this Fae intrigued me and I wanted to know a little more about him. I was willing to offer him something about me in return, and what I'd told him really was the truth. Egos didn't like us killing the people we stole from. It drew way too much attention that way. So I wasn't lying when I said we didn't kill our marks, for the most part.

I didn't anyway. At least not intentionally. Generally speaking. And none of the thieves had admitted to killing anyone at all in nearly three weeks. Six if you discounted Egos killing Tyros - which in a way, you could, because one of our own dying wasn't the same as a mark taking the hit. And Tyros had turned out to be a lying sack of shit who'd tried to sell us out to the Royal Guard, so his death had been more like justice than murder. I'd stood back and watched as Egos ripped him limb from limb, and I hadn't felt a single ounce of pity over his fate. If he'd had his way, all of us would have been wrapped up in chains and awaiting the hangman's noose already.

"That's not what they say about you in the palace," he muttered, clearly not believing me, and that might have actually been smart because I was a silver-tongued son of a bitch and lies were my third favourite thing in all the world. Coming only after food and fucking.

"You worked in the palace?" I asked, a groan very nearly escaping my lips as I tried to hide my eagerness for information on that most forbidden of places.

Every day for as long as I could remember, I'd looked upon the palace walls with the greatest sense of longing. It was my dream to breach the iron gates, scale the stone parapets and steal the crown jewels right out from under the emperor's nose.

I'd look so fucking good in a crown.

I'd dress myself in riches then go find myself a nice girl to worship my cock while calling me her king – after eating my body weight's worth of palace-worthy food, of course.

"I did," he said with a faint frown which let me know he didn't like the interest I held about the place. But *shit,* wouldn't I like to learn what he knew about the inside of the palace. Those white walls had been equally calling my name and mocking me tirelessly for as long as I could remember. It was the only place in the kingdom I had yet to conquer with my light fingers and empty pockets, and one day I was certain I'd find a way inside. Maybe I just had.

"You didn't tell me your name," I said, reaching through the bars and offering him my hand while giving him the kind of smile which made virgins drop their undergarments for me.

He frowned at me for a moment, and I wondered if I should scale it back. But I hadn't met many people who couldn't be won over by my dimples, male or female. Most people who knew me for long enough eventually fell in love with me, this one wouldn't be any different.

"Cassius," he grunted, removing his hand from a burn on his side so that he could shake mine.

He looked me right in the eye as he tried to crush my fingers and I barked a laugh.

Tough guy, huh? Well, I've met bastards with far bigger balls than you and lived to tell the tale.

"No need to try and show me who's boss," I said, dropping his hand. "We're equally screwed if we're in here anyway."

At least until tonight when my gang came for me. Sucked to be him, I guessed.

"There's truth in that," he agreed.

"So, Cassius, how many guards work the palace at any one time? Do you follow a regular routine, or do they change it up a lot?" I asked casually, wondering if I might have been in luck and found myself a man willing to give me the information I'd need to pull off the job of my dreams.

I was fairly sure the look he was giving me could be interpreted as a solid 'fuck you', but I couldn't help myself. I wanted to know every damn detail about that place and he held that knowledge locked up within his uncooperative mind. Surely with the right kind of motivation he'd wanna spill the beans, get some revenge on the arseholes who had turned their backs on him, and tell little old me the best way to sneak into their fortress and steal the treasures…

"You're really still loyal to them?" I asked, a note of irritation to my voice as he failed to answer. "Even after that?" I indicated his battered body and a frown pulled at his brow, telling me his pride was wounded at least as thoroughly as his flesh.

"I would never betray my emperor, no matter what my own situation may be," Cassius said stoically.

He really did look like a kicked dog, all sad and forlorn that his master had turned on him. But even a kicked dog had a bite to it given the right encouragement, I just had to figure out what kind of meaty morsel this one needed to send him rabid.

"Oh, go on, enlighten me. We're both stuck in here anyway, so it's not like I can use the information," I pushed. "And I promise you it would feel good to betray them in payment for your suffering."

"I don't blame the emperor for my situation," he growled. "I blame Magdor."

"Magdor? The empress?" I laughed.

I'd heard tales of the mysterious beauty who'd won the emperor's love with her foreign looks and unearthly appeal, but it didn't mean much to me. The palace might as well have been on the other side of the world as far as I was concerned. My life with The Forty was about the furthest from royalty that you could get. I had to wonder what he'd gone and done to upset the empress though, had he spied on her while she was changing? Or farted in her presence? Maybe he'd lost his mind entirely and run stark naked around the palace corridors while screaming his love for her to the heavens?

"She is more than just a-"

The door at the end of the hallway opened, and I moved away from Cassius's cell as I drew closer to the opening, curious over the way things were done in here. I released a slow breath as I was finally relieved of the feeling of the iron pressing to my flesh, the strength returning to my limbs with every moment that I spent free of it.

I'd never been caught before, so this whole endeavour was something of a mystery to me. I'd heard tales of the brutality of the royal prison, but I'd also heard that the emperor took solid gold shits, so I didn't tend to base my knowledge on the rumour mill.

"Is this breakfast at last?" I called as three guards approached us.

I recognised the one in the middle as the captain who had captured me and gave him the kind of smile which I imagined would make him want to punch me. Sure enough, the turgid veins beneath his skin seemed to bulge all around his thick neck as he stomped towards me, and I was almost certain his eye was ticking with rage.

"We don't waste food on dead men," Captain Marik snarled as he came to a halt before my cell, and I arched a brow at him without even bothering to straighten my spine.

Fae like him fed on fear, but he wouldn't claim a taste of that from me. I lived my own personal horror show day in and day out where I came from. There was always someone bigger and uglier than me waiting to try and cut my throat or stab me in the back, but quick reflexes and the skills of my Affinities had kept me ahead of that end. A big man with a point to prove was never going to break my spirit.

"Dead men? I only stole a loaf of bread. Is death the punishment for that these days? I know the kingdom is falling to shit, but that seems a little extreme," I said, chuckling at my own joke and enjoying the way his eye ticked harder. He was so trussed up in that tight guard's uniform with its dark leather jerkin plated with black metal spikes, that it almost looked as if his round head might pop right off like a cork from the head of a bottle.

"Silence, scum. I'm here to read you your charges and inform you of your punishment," he snapped, violence flickering in his eyes and making it clear to me that he was hungry for it.

I held my tongue as I leaned against the bars again, pretending the iron did nothing at all to affect me while battling the sense of nausea which was pooling in my gut. I made sure he could see that such simple horrors meant nothing at all to me and waited to hear what allegations had been made against me.

Marik turned his gaze to my new friend and his scowl deepened.

"Good to see you're getting the treatment you deserve, traitor," he snarled. "I will happily see you stripped of your flesh as well as your number in my ranks for your crime. Your lawlessness insults me and the years I wasted training you." He spat through the bars at the offending guard, but it didn't quite reach him and he didn't even flinch.

Cassius only responded with a glower, though he looked positively offended by the accusation, almost as if the captain had just called his mother a whore and taken a shit in his morning oatmeal all at once.

"Well? Don't you have anything to say for yourself?" Marik demanded.

"Only that every single one of my actions has been taken to protect the royal blood of Osaria," Cassius said, raising his chin.

Marik snorted in disgust before dismissing him and he returned his attention to me.

"You have been charged with illegal entry to the property of a higher Fae, burglary of several highly priced gems and jewels, heirlooms and a sizeable bag of food," he rattled off, earning himself an exaggerated yawn from me. But instead of the irritated bark of command I expected to receive for my insolence, all I was gifted was a hateful little smile as Marik went on, making my gut twist as my instincts told me he was just building up to the final point on his list, though I had no idea what he had to be so smug about. "Vandalization of the count's personal property, *and* the rape of the Countess of Nore."

"The what?" I hissed, my nose wrinkling with disgust at that accusation, but Marik went on as if I hadn't even spoken.

"The punishment for your crime is three years in the dungeon." The captain leaned closer, lowering his voice with a wicked smile on his face as he prepared to deliver the final blow. "And *castration*."

I shifted back from the bars, my hand automatically moving to shield my dick from him as if I expected him to produce a blade and come at me here and now.

"What?" I croaked before clearing my throat and forcing myself to ask again more calmly. "What do you mean castration?"

Marik smirked at me, clearly getting off on the fact that he'd gotten a rise from me at last, but I couldn't even be mad at myself for that – this was my fucking dick we were talking about. It was tied in first place for my best feature alongside my face. It was fucking criminal to even joke about taking a damned knife to it.

"You should have thought about that before you raped a countess, scum. I don't imagine your pretty face will be enough to make up for a lack of manhood with the ladies if you're ever released."

"I never touched that goat," I growled. "Ask her! Get her to come down here and identify me. She'll tell you it wasn't me!"

"A fiend attacked the countess while she was sleeping and took her from behind. She didn't see his face. We caught you in the vicinity and can only presume you are the perpetrator," Marik replied coldly, his eyes gleaming with excitement over the reality he was painting for me. I swear the arsehole was hoping to be the one wielding the blade when it was done too. No doubt an ugly fucker like him would take great joy in destroying a cock as beautiful as mine.

The other guards chuckled at my predicament and I scowled at them, wishing them all shrivelled cocks and warts in their arseholes for good measure. I wasn't going to give up though, I wasn't just going to let them cut my dick off over a lie which had fallen from the lips of an unfaithful bitch who cared more about covering for her infidelity than she did for the removal of my fucking manhood.

"That whore met him in the market yesterday and let him into her house with the full intention of fucking him bl-"

"Are you saying you know who the culprit is?" Marik asked, a glimmer in his eye which said this had been his plan all along, to make me turn, make me squeal. "If you want to make a statement and tell us where to find him..."

I ground my teeth, moving my hands to block my manhood and eyeing the guards for any instrument to suggest that they were planning on carrying out this sentence now. They didn't seem to be holding any torture devices between them, so I had to hope the act wasn't about to happen yet.

"I was only guessing," I gritted out, not fool enough to start spilling my secrets or the identities of the other thieves. There wasn't much in this world that would make me turn on my gang, but I'd be damned if I'd have my balls cut off for them.

"Well why don't you think on it for now? Your sentence is to be carried out in two days. Unless you can think of anything to help us apprehend this imagined other suspect before then." Marik's eyes slid to my crotch and he laughed cruelly before turning and heading for the door with the other guards following at his back.

"And what about breakfast?" I bellowed, regaining some of my composure before the door could close between us.

"Whistle for it," Marik replied and the door swung shut, leaving me alone with Cassius once more.

"Arsehole," I snarled as I paced to the rear wall of my cell and back a few times.

"And I thought I had it bad with a death sentence," Cassius muttered, and I almost laughed. Almost.

"Well, if you're really unlucky, the last thing you'll see before they cut off your head will be them chopping off my cock. And the biggest travesty of all is that I never even fucked her! She's so ugly she'd scare the shit out of a sewer. I've no idea how Balthazar even summoned the motivation to do it. I'm certain I never could have."

Cassius snorted a laugh, and I raised an eyebrow at him. I hadn't expected the royal guard to have a sense of humour hiding beneath that macho, disciplined exterior but there it was, peeking out at me, all morbid laughter in the face of our sentences.

"I mean it, you should have seen her. You couldn't drink enough ale to make her attractive – I don't know if she had a goat Affinity or if her father was a straight up goat, but I'm telling you that woman is as ugly as sin itself. Not just externally either – she has the sour and repulsive personality matched only by all the other over-entitled bastards who call themselves 'upper Fae.' I saw her beating a serving girl over a burnt loaf of bread while I was casing her oh-so-lovely home in preparation for this job, and she didn't stop until the girl was sobbing and bleeding at her feet. Balthazar had better come through for me tonight or I'll be selling him out. My loyalty has its limits, and they end way before a blade is coming anywhere near my balls."

"Who's Balthazar?" Cassius asked curiously and I quit my rant sharpish.

I stilled as I looked at my companion and suspicion ran through me as I headed over to the bars which divided us to survey him more closely again. Balthazar was almost as infamous as me, so I didn't fear mentioning his name, but I was hardly going to start handing out information on The Forty to this stranger. Our names may have littered the streets of Osaria and tales of the crimes we'd committed and riches we'd claimed might have been whispered between lower and upper Fae alike, but rumours and stories weren't facts. They couldn't be used to find us, and I would never breathe a word of anything that could.

"What did a royal guard do to land himself a death sentence?" I asked seriously, the moment of comradery between us fading as I looked him over and remembered which side of the divide we both stood on. It was very much a them and us kind of situation in this city and he was one hundred percent *them*.

Cassius's lips twisted and I could tell he wasn't sure whether to tell me, so it must have been bad. And yet something about him still screamed straightlaced, rule abiding royalist, so what the fuck could it have been?

"Did you murder someone?" I guessed, leaning forward eagerly as I grasped onto the distraction of solving this mystery. "Or call the emperor a pig-ugly nutsack? Or steal from the royal palace? Or fuck one of the royal maids in the emperor's bed or-"

"I saw the princess's face," he growled, probably to shut me up more than anything, but I beamed at him as if he'd just confided in me like we were friends. Which he'd probably start thinking we were any time now. I had a damn likeable face. And a winning personality. Everyone always fell for my charm in the end.

It had been said that I could charm a Priestess of the Lost right into my bed, despite her vows of celibacy, and have her praise me as a Fae of legend risen once more with an Affinity for sex come dawn. I couldn't help it, people just trusted me. In fact, I was fairly certain that I had some kind of charisma Affinity or something of the sort, because no matter where I went or what I did, people just wanted to be my friend.

More fool them.

"You fucked her?" I guessed, smirking at the idea of that. The precious princess all alone in her ivory tower spreading her thighs for her personal guard's unworthy cock.

"No," Cassius snarled in outrage, looking damn close to taking a swing at me and I raised an eyebrow at him. *Oh Cassius, the more you try to resist my beautiful face, the more it will beguile you.*

"Kissed her then?" I guessed kissing her would have been bad enough, though it had a lot less sordid fantasy points to it than the thoughts of him making her scream in pleasure for him which I'd first imagined.

"I only saw her for a moment," he insisted, seeming a little flustered now. By the gods, did the big, surly guard have a big, surly crush?

"You just looked at her? And they threw you in here for that alone?" I asked in disbelief.

"Everyone in the kingdom knows that it is a crime punishable by death to look on the beauty of the emperor's daughter before her Unveiling on her twenty-first birthday. As far as I know, no man aside from me and the emperor have ever looked on her face before-"

"Sucks for you then," I said with a snort of amusement. What a fucking thing to die for. Hell, I'd seen some seriously fucked-up things in my life and I hadn't died for witnessing them, and yet this poor bastard caught a glimpse of a pretty face and now he was going to hang for it? That shit had to taste all kinds of bitter.

"If you had seen her then maybe you would understand-"

"I've seen plenty of pretty girls. Got most of them naked too," I said dismissively. "If they're hiding her face, I'd be more tempted to believe she's ugly as all sin and the emperor is just hoping to trick some poor fool to part with a fortune for a marriage to a donkey-"

"I saw her myself!" he yelled in outrage. "And I won't hear you besmirch her beauty as if it's nothing."

Silence rang between us and I pursed my lips.

This guy seriously needs to get laid.

"Relax, mate. At least you aren't about to get your cock cut off."

Cassius stared at me for several long seconds, then started laughing. Yeah, we were best friends alright. Me and Cassy-boy, just two cunts swimming in a barrel of laughs. At least until my gang turned up and I left his arse here to swing from the gallows.

AUSTYN

CHAPTER FIVE

"You look dazzling. All the stars in the sky will swoon over you this evening," Jacinda gushed as she patted down the folds of my bright blue gown.

She was a short girl with dark curling hair that clung to her high cheekbones. Her eyes were always wide and made her resemble a rabbit at the end of a hunter's arrow, something which I could admit to wishing she was from time to time when she got too enthusiastic with her constant praise. She hadn't been working in the palace all that long, but her keen eye for detail had seen her climbing the ranks until she was placed at my side.

"No. Blue washes me out," I stated, getting a little thrill of defiance from the simple act of making my own choice in a gown. But it was all I really had to fight back with sometimes, and this small taste of independence made me feel a little better about my lot in life. "But it's my favourite colour, and Magdor hates it on me. And as I'm dining with her tonight, I thought it was a good opportunity to irk her."

Jacinda gawped at me, frozen. She couldn't deny my words because I was the princess and so everything I said simply *had* to be true. But if she didn't deny it, she was essentially confirming what I had said and agreeing that it washed me out, which would mean insulting me. Not to mention the implied idea that she was taking part in a plan to anger the empress. I watched her grapple with her dilemma for several seconds before taking pity on her and placing a hand on her arm.

"Relax, Jacinda. You don't have to shower me in compliments all the time. It's really tiring." I hoped she might take that on board this time, but I doubted it. The girl was like a compliment farm, always growing brand new compliment vegetables to shove down my throat and choke me with. It was exhausting.

I turned away from my overly zealous maid to face Zira with a grin. My favourite attendant, who was more of a friend to me than anyone in the kingdom. Her eyes were penetratingly dark and her hair was pulled up into its usual bun with a few inky coils trailing free around the deep brown skin of her neck.

"I told you about the compliments," Zira said airily to Jacinda who bowed her head.

"It is hard when she is so magnanimous," Jacinda whispered.

"Was that another compliment?" I mused and Jacinda bowed her head lower as Zira and I laughed.

"Apologies, Your Highness. Send me to the yard to have me whipped, or tie me to the stocks in the public square, strip me bare and have the townsfolk throw rotten fruit at my unworthy flesh. Then maybe I will learn," Jacinda gushed, and I moved before her with a pang of pity in my chest, sliding a hand under her chin and lifting it until she met my gaze.

"I'd never do that," I promised. "I just want you to be comfortable around me. You don't have to act as if rainbows come out of my rear end every time I use the latrine."

Zira cracked a laugh and Jacinda bit her lip to hold one back, but my other attendant moved forward and tugged her lip free of her teeth.

"Laugh if you want to laugh," she encouraged and Jacinda let out a small giggle, covering her hand with her mouth, her eyes fixing on Zira as I smiled in relief.

"Is it just you and Magdor tonight?" Zira asked me and I nodded, releasing a heavy sigh. She had a knack for asking questions which pointed to her less than complimentary feelings about the empress while never actually insulting her. It was quite impressive really and whenever the two of us were alone, she let loose a little more, especially whenever she managed to get her hands on some Cartlanna wine from the kitchens for us to drink. We had rare opportunities for that, but the few times we had drunk together, we'd always ended up in fits of laughter doing impressions of the Maggot.

Zira was a year older than me and had been a daughter of one of the kitchen maids, allowed to play on the grounds with me when I was younger. That was back when Father hadn't had his mind addled by his new wife, before Magdor showed up and ensured no children were allowed on the grounds at all anymore. So when Zira had gotten a job working at the palace when she was sixteen, I'd literally cried with joy at seeing her again. I'd spent years without her in my life and I'd missed her terribly.

"She insisted on it. She's probably planning to try and convince me of how great a match Kahn and I would be. But I'd rather cut all of my fingers off and eat them than marry her beastly son." I balled my hands into fists and Zira frowned at my furious expression, sadness entering her eyes.

"You might not have a choice if the gargoyle wins the pageant," Zira pointed out and Jacinda slapped a hand to her mouth in shock.

"It's okay, Jacinda. He is a gargoyle, is he not?" I said mischievously and Jacinda's eyes darted to Zira, looking for reassurance as I left her floundering for an answer to that. "Or perhaps a boiled turnip given legs?" I offered and Jacinda's face starting turning red, the poor girl torn on how to respond to me insulting the empress's son.

Jacinda opened and closed her mouth then a small voice left her. "He is rather…root vegetable-like."

I snorted in surprise, gripping her arm. "Yes, he is."

"I've always thought his nose looks like a half-dead chipmunk taped to his face," she whispered and I bounced on my toes as I looked to Zira who was watching Jacinda with her head cocked to one side and a surprised grin on her lips. "Sort of like this." Jacinda cramped up her arms by her head and splayed her hands out while plastering a bewildered expression on her face. It made zero sense but was funny as hell and the three of us fell apart as we each took it in turns to act out what we thought his nose looked like.

"I wish you didn't have to marry him," Zira said at last and instant regret crossed her features as my face fell at her words, my heart spiralling down into the base of my stomach. She was right. When it came down to it, I had no choice at all. I would be matched with whoever happened to win the damn contest, and I doubted there would be anyone among the competitors able to take Kahn on and win.

The man was a monster given Fae flesh. All of his Affinities made him perfectly suited for fighting and killing. I would be an idiot to think anyone could beat him, but I'd rather be a fool than accept the gruesome fate of becoming his bride. I wasn't even going to consider what the alternative suitors might be like, only that they had to be better than him.

"I'll talk to Father again. Maybe he'll give me *some* say in this at least," I said hopefully, though it hadn't worked out the last time I'd spoken to him, so I had no real reason to think it might this time. Still, I needed to hold onto threads of hope in life, or else I would fall into despair. So I would try again. And again. Until somehow, something I did made a difference.

She nodded, but her eyes dimmed. We both knew the emperor was beyond granting me any requests of late unless it was for more pretty clothes or jewellery.

"It's worth a shot," she said weakly and I nodded, squeezing her hand for a moment before pulling down my veil and heading to the door.

I hated the thing, I could see out, but no one could see in. It was woven from Ageshian silk, supposedly enchanted by a wood sprite and so rare it was worth a thousand kurus an inch. But it was just an expensive cage, sewn to keep me locked away from the world and make me *other*. I was both above all the rest of the Fae in the kingdom and less than all of them, because I couldn't claim even the simplest of rights like showing my face or choosing where I went.

Sometimes I felt like I was worth nothing at all to anyone. A figurehead hosting a womb which was required to produce a male heir for the emperor's line of succession and nothing more. Anything that went beyond that purpose held no value to anyone but me, and that was equally as depressing to know as it was heart-breaking to accept. I had everything and nothing at once. And all I really wanted was to be seen.

I recalled Cassius Lazar's eyes on me and the way time had seemed to still, like a small offering from a cruel god, letting me know how good it could feel to be truly present. But then they had stolen it all away and Cassius's fate had been sealed, proving my lack of power in this place. It still cut me to ribbons whenever I thought of him.

Two guards awaited me outside my quarters, bowing low before escorting me down the hallways. It was suffocating. I could barely walk two metres outside my rooms without guards hounding around after me. But did they say a single thing to me? Not a peep. I was above conversation with them whether I liked it or not and I got as little say in that fact as I did in my face being shrouded by the cloying fabric of the veil.

I wondered if Cassius was dead already or if he was being tortured in the royal dungeon. It made me sick, and despite trying to get information from Magdor about whether he was still breathing or not, she'd simply dismissed any attempt I made to discuss his freedom.

I didn't see why the law was above me when it was my face it was about. I didn't give a damn that he'd seen me, in fact, it was often all I could think about. His eyes on my bare flesh, looking at me in a way no one had ever looked at me before, with this intense kind of need that I didn't understand but really, really wanted to.

I said a quiet prayer to the Fallen to spare his life, probably the millionth one I'd made on his behalf since he'd been taken away. I could barely sleep thinking about it. He had been my constant watcher, a good and loyal servant to me and my father. And now my face was the reason he would lose his life. It was unbearable. But what could I do? I had no more power than an animal awaiting slaughter between these walls, and sometimes I felt as though that fate would have been preferable to the real one that awaited me as some brute's wife.

Oh Cassius, I'm so sorry.

I was led to the veranda where a table lay at the heart of it, already prepared for our meal. Songbirds were singing their nightly chorus as dusk drew in and set the sky alight in tones of gold and orange, the gardens stretching out below the balcony and the scent of flowers filling the air. It was the perfect evening, but I was tired of perfect. I wanted chaos, not routine. I swear every time I lived out the same day again, a little bit more of my soul chipped off and died. How long did I have left before I became nothing more than a pretty little husk with nothing inside her besides the echoes of long-lost dreams?

A guard drew my seat out for me and I dropped down, eyeing the empty chair opposite mine with a scowl. Typical Magdor to make me wait for her. She always did like to act as if she was above me, and with the way my father bowed to her whims, maybe she was. I knew he loved her, and I'd tried to respect that once, but Magdor had never found her way to my heart like she had his. She hadn't tried to either, she let me see her cruel side, treating me like a demon-possessed child who needed exorcising.

Once, she'd locked me in the attic of the north tower without a scrap of light and commanded me to pick up the shards of a broken mirror on the floor. At first, I'd refused, but she'd sworn to never let me out until I gathered every jagged piece and laid it by the door. So I did, and inevitably sliced my fingers open badly. I could still scent the blood in that room when I thought on it, still feel the darkness pressing against my eyes and the way my knees had dragged across the rough floorboards.

When she had finally released me, she'd coated my hands in some strong-smelling balm which had stopped scars from forming, but when I looked at my palms to this day all I saw was the hot, wet blood and a vivid memory of the heat within that attic which made me shudder. I'd almost let her break me that day, but instead I'd found a stubborn, resilient piece of myself to hold onto. After she was done applying the balm to my cuts, I'd walked away with my head held high and not a single flicker of weakness in my expression, ignoring the blood dripping from my shredded fingers and colouring my pink dress red.

Despite all she put me through, now that I was older, knowing I might have to marry her son was the worst kind of punishment she had ever bestowed on me.

"Princess," a deep, male voice stripped the air from my lungs and I turned sharply, my heart thundering in my ears as my eyes fell on Kahn.

He was impossibly tall, with nearly twice the bulk of any average man and his face was like an oddly shaped potato with cauliflowers stuck on for ears.

My skin prickled and anger rolled through me in waves. I didn't really care that he was ugly, but his personality validated my ridicule of him. It was the only small power I could gain over him after all, though the jokes I shared with my attendants had lightened my heart in the moment, seeing him now only reminded me of the fear my laughter had been hiding.

He clearly thought we were engaged already. Something he was proving right now by showing up here without so much as a formal invite.

Fuck you, Magdor. How could you do this?

Though maybe I should have guessed; she'd proposed this exact thing recently and now here he was, thinking I'd actually summoned him.

"How nice your gown is," he said as he stepped closer, his small eyes roaming over the swell of my breasts as my veil rested against them, making my fingers itch for a blade. "Is that...cotton?"

My shoulders grew rigid as I held off on answering, vaguely hoping Magdor might show up and usher him back to the pigsty he'd escaped from. When I realised that wasn't going to happen, I came up with a way to spin this situation into an opportunity. If I could turn Kahn off of me, maybe he wouldn't pledge himself as a suitor at all. It had to be worth a try.

I smiled beneath my veil, resting my hands on the table. "It's crinnask," I said and his brow creased, proving he didn't know the word. Which he wouldn't have, seeing as I'd made it up.

Although Kahn didn't have enough brainpower to prove himself as a worthy adversary, his scheming mother sure did. And since he'd started ogling me like a prize already won, I was happy to lump him into the same category that Magdor had earned from me. My enemy.

"Oh...of course," he said with perfect confidence as he moved to take the seat opposite me, waving off the guard who tried to pull it out for him.

He dropped down and I swear the legs bent a little beneath his huge weight as he spread his thighs. His tight white trousers clung to his crotch and a gasp got stuck in my throat at the sight of his outlined cock, the monstrous thing resembling a python laying in there, like a literal python, but it also seemed to be skewed at a strange angle at the top and bulged in places that didn't seem right at all.

By the Fallen, that thing is not going anywhere near me. Ever.

He chuckled as he noticed where my attention had fallen then slapped his hard stomach. "Do you like what you see, Princess? I've been eating double my weight for the past week to help pile on muscles for the pag-ant."

"Pageant," I corrected him then pursed my lips. "And I don't think that's how muscle growth works."

He ignored my comment, barrelling on. "I ate a horse last week. A whole horse. It dropped dead outside the Four Bears Tavern and the locals dared me to do it." He interlinked his hands behind the back of his neck, looking smug as hell with himself.

I physically recoiled from him in disgust. Ergh, was he serious? "You ate a whole dead horse because some people you don't even know dared you to?"

"Yes." He grinned as if it was a great accomplishment, then his meaty paw slithered across the table towards me. "I'd eat ten horses to impress you, sweet Austyn. I'd cut them up and chomp them down, bite by bite." His purplish tongue whipped out, sliding back and forth across his lips as his attention fell to my body again and every piece of my flesh screamed.

My upper lip curled back as I retreated further into my seat. "That is literally the last thing in Osaria that would impress me, Kahn." My stomach churned as the image of this brute swallowing down lumps of some dead horse in the street filled my head. Why couldn't he have gotten food poisoning and died?

His mouth parted and his eyes dimmed with sadness. "Oh. Shame it was a dead horse then."

"*What?*" I hissed. *Did Magdor fuck a boulder to produce this halfwit?*

"Well, if it was living, I wouldn't have been able to catch it," he said with a shrug.

I shook my head, trying to figure out how this man's mind worked. Probably by rubbing together the two brain cells he had until something popped out.

"You look very appetising today, Princess," he changed the subject, gazing over my veil like he was trying to peer beneath it, and I swear that beastly thing in his trousers moved. How could I look appetising when he couldn't even see me? It made me fear how lively that thing might get if he saw me without layers covering my flesh. *Help me, Fallen.*

"I like blue," he added. "It brings out your…veil."

Great. This dress has backfired hard.

"I like green too. And yellow. Aren't colours great?" he mused as if he was saying something poetic. "So are you excited about the pag-ent?"

"*Pageant.*" An idea struck me, and a grin gripped my lips as I prepared to make this hulking gargoyle squirm. "I'm a little nervous actually."

"Nervous?" he asked, one thick eyebrow lifting.

"Well my husband will see my body for the first time and...I get these rashes. I need a special cream for them. And then there's the ointment for the boils…"

He stared at me for a long moment, and I swear I saw a vacancy sign in the window of his eyes. After his two brain cells had processed what I'd said, he slapped his thigh and boomed a laugh. "You have no boils or rashes, my mother has told me of your beauty. You are perfect."

He gave me a toothy, hungry smile that said I might just be the next dead animal he'd like to eat, and I truly began to fear being owned by this man. The ways I'd imagined I might get out of this fate were illusions, mirages in the desert cast there to drive me insane. But the pageant was approaching fast and this man, this brutish, vile, horse-eating creep was the front runner.

"I can't wait until our wedding night, Austyn, when you are all mine." He lowered his hand to squeeze the head of the snake housed in his britches and I leapt up from my seat, horrified at how brashly he was behaving.

"How dare you speak to me that way?" I growled, looking to the guards at the edge of the veranda, but they made no move to approach.

I was cast back into my childhood, remembering a time I'd run from Magdor when she'd tried to lock me in a wooden chest full of needle ants. I'd made it to the nearest guards and begged for help, but they'd just looked at me with this strange, empty expression, and when Magdor had come to drag me away, they said nothing. Did nothing. I'd learned a long time ago that Magdor had complete power within these walls, but sometimes that power seemed to run so deep it terrified me.

"Why are you panicking, little mouse?" Kahn asked, rising to his feet too and moving towards me with a dark look on his face that unsettled me. "Return to your seat. You're having dinner with me. Mother said so."

I was frozen in place as he took my arm, unable to believe he dared lay a finger on me, but I was out of sight of the guards, cast in his imposing shadow as he leered down at me.

He pushed me down into my seat with such strength that it made the chair legs rattle on the ground and yet no one batted an eye, no guards came to arrest him, and it made me think of Cassius and the ferocity with which he had always protected my father and I. He of all my guards wouldn't have stood for this.

I despised that I had no weapon against any of it, no way to fight back. My shackles may have been invisible, but I felt them tightening on me in that moment, destiny binding me to this brute.

As Kahn dropped back into his own seat, the waiters arrived with our food and I turned my nose up at it. An entrée. Which meant this meal was going to be five courses. How was I going to get through five courses with this lewd arsehole?

I never dined with men, only ever women. And I always asked the guards to leave when I did so that I didn't have to drape my damn veil over the table to eat. There was no way I was going to humiliate myself like that in front of Kahn and I had no appetite anyway in his company, so I was going to go hungry.

"You haven't won me yet," I said firmly as he picked up a dainty fork and skewered the braised meat on his plate before stuffing the whole lot into his mouth.

Kahn released a low guffaw. "I am twice as strong as any man who'll offer you his hand, Princess. I'm going to rip their hearts out before your eyes. Blood and gore and victory!" He pounded his chest proudly and anger flashed through my veins.

"I'm not a fan of violence," I said dryly, not bothering to hide my disdain for him. Actually, I didn't give two fucks about violence. I knew the bite of it well enough after what Magdor had put me through. But if it involved this beast beating the other suitors to a pulp, I was definitely against it. Not that I wanted to marry any of them. But he was the last man in the entire kingdom I'd ever choose for myself.

But I don't get to choose, do I?

I just prayed a dragon showed up to enter the pageant and ate Kahn whole, because I'd rather be kept in a tower, guarded by a fire breathing monster than be owned by this man.

"Sorry, I forgot that women of your breed aren't used to things like that." He sniggered.

"My *breed?*" I snarled.

He nodded, leaning across the table and stabbing some of the vegetables on my plate, stuffing them into his mouth. The act alone was an insult that made venom seep into my blood. I wanted to scream, but most of all I wanted to fight. I felt the tingle of my hair against my scalp and that always pre-empted a private session in the armoury. I'd sneak down there and get hold of Father's blades, let my Affinity for metal run riot as I swung and slashed and danced through that room with the steel singing just for me.

"You're innocent. But I will be the one who gets to take that from you." He wet his lips again and I shuddered, feeling like his hands were on me already.

"You will take nothing from me," I hissed. "I'd rather die than let you touch me."

A frown lined his features as the maids came to collect our plates and replace them with large bowls of tomato soup.

"Mother says you will be a good wife. An obedient one. And if you're not, then I can put you in your place." He picked up his spoon, scooping up some soup with more grace than I'd expected and supping it with a gleam in his gaze.

"My place?" I spat. "My place is here in my home, a daughter of the emperor, an heir to the throne that is rightfully *mine*. You are the outsider here. You are the one who should be respecting *me*."

"Mother says-"

"I don't care what Mother says," I snapped. "If you think I will bow to you easily, I assure you I will not. I will fight you every day, I will hate you every day, I will make it known to the whole world that I despise my husband and I will never, ever submit to you."

His eyes darkened to deepest midnight and I continued to glare at him, starting to tremble with the rage I felt towards this man.

He pointed at me with his spoon, slopping soup all over the table. "If I can break a man's neck with my bare hands, I can break a woman in just fine."

I had so much anger inside me, it lived there like a fiery beast coiled up in my chest. So many years of being told no. That women couldn't do this or that. That princesses didn't get to inherit thrones. I was expected to marry and birth a son. A child who would be entitled to rule after his father dropped dead. *Which I can always hope happens sooner rather than later.*

Before I could respond to that heinous declaration, Kahn's spoon clattered to the table, his jaw fell slack and he face-planted into his soup bowl unconscious.

"By the Fallen," I gasped.

I stared at him, hope singing a joyful song in my chest as a possibility occurred to me.

Please be dead. Please, please, please.

"Dismissed," Magdor's voice rang out, and I jolted in surprise at her sudden arrival.

She stepped onto the veranda, ushering the guards away and they hurried off before I could object, though they weren't exactly helpful to me. Magdor faced her son with a wicked smile and the hope I felt dissolved in my chest like sugar in hot water. Something wasn't right, and that smile said it all.

"Oh Kahn," she sighed, moving towards him and yanking his collar so his head was pulled out of the bowl. His tongue lolled between his lips and his eyes had rolled back into his head. She dropped him again with a bang as his forehead hit the table and she rounded on me instead. "Not good enough for you, is he Austyn?"

"Aren't you concerned for your son?" I rose from my seat, unsure why the hell she wasn't more worried that Kahn looked dead.

"He's fine," she huffed, tossing a lock of raven hair over her shoulder and killing off any lasting hope I had over him falling prey to a heart attack. *Life really isn't fair.* "He'll come around in a minute."

"What do you mean?" I glared at her. "What's happened to him?"

"The Prophet Jahalus sent me a little gift for him, that's all. A simple potion. I wrote to him weeks ago with a tiny request."

My pulse raced at those words, shock jarring my thoughts.

The Fae had lost all real contact with the magic our Affinities linked us to hundreds of years ago when the Fallen learned to lie and offended the deities who had once loved us so dearly. But in the wake of that loss, some Fae had hunted down other ways to wield the power of our world and through twisted rituals, blood sacrifices and heinous concoctions they'd managed to claim some of it. Everyone knew that kind of perverted power came at a cost, and most Fae were far too wise to ever risk messing with it.

Not the Prophets of the Fallen though, or so they called themselves. They were Fae who travelled the world, gathering ancient texts, wielding lost magical artefacts and brewing potions outlined in their findings. They were often hermits, living in caves or in the ruins of the Fallen's temples where the Fae of old had once prayed to the lost gods. There weren't many who trusted the experimental alchemy the Prophets took part in, most believing the magic shouldn't be wielded now that we didn't have the abilities needed to harness it the way we once had. It was considered a black art, and it was outlawed in my father's empire. So why the fuck did Magdor think it was okay to drug her son with some dangerous magical draught?

My eyes narrowed sharply on my stepmother. If Magdor was associated with this kind of thing, that gave me even more reason to suspect her as a snake in my empire. How long had she been buying potions from a Prophet? And what in Osaria was she capable of doing with them?

"Magic?" I hissed accusingly, glancing around like just saying the word could summon a virulent plague to our door.

"Oh, do calm down, Austyn." She pressed her fingers into her eyes as if I was giving her a headache. "It's a gift for you."

"What is that supposed to mean?" I asked, a shudder of trepidation rolling down my spine.

She floated towards me, brushing her hand over my shoulders and angling me to face Kahn. "It means you will soon see past his teensy-weensy flaws, my dear."

I gave her a death glare. "We're incompatible, nothing's going to change that."

Kahn started jerking, his limbs twitching and the rolls on his thick neck weirdly smoothing out. I blinked hard, unsure if I was hallucinating. But then the impossible happened and his ears grew smaller, more normal until there was nothing odd about them at all. Hair sprouted from his bald head and long, flowing locks of auburn tumbled over his shoulders. His muscles bulged against his tunic, even more prominently than they had before and I took a step back, alarmed by what I was witnessing. I'd never seen magic before. I'd read books, knew all the stories of old, but never in all my years had I seen something so powerful at work right before my eyes.

"What's happening?" I breathed, backing up further, adrenaline bursting through my veins, but Magdor's nails sliced into my shoulder before I could get away.

Kahn jerked upright, wiping the soup from his jaw and I stared at the changes to his face in stunned silence. By the Fallen. He was somehow handsome with a straight, chiselled nose, eyes of deepest brown framed by dark lashes, his mouth fuller, smoother and hooked up at the corner in a way I didn't recognise at all. *No...this is wrong. This isn't natural.*

"He now has the beauty to capture your heart," Magdor purred in my ear. "A perfect suitor for a perfect bride. A gift from me to you. What more could a woman ask for?"

I pulled away from her, horrified by what she was suggesting. That changing Kahn's looks would make me see him any differently. He was still a man who wanted to buy his way to owning me. Still the son of the stepmother I hated. Still as dumb as a rock and as indecent as a whoremonger.

Kahn turned his hands over, eyeing his flesh as his fighting scars faded away to leave nothing but gleaming smoothness.

"Mother," he gasped. "I think I'm having an episode."

She hurried over, patting him on the arm as she gazed up at his defined features. "No, no darling. This isn't one of your blackouts."

Blackouts??

"You're quite fine," Magdor went on. "Your wife-to-be has offered you a great gift so that she can love you inside and out."

"*Magdor*," I snarled, regaining my senses and realising she had just broken the law, had thwarted my father's rules on such magic as this. Hope surged inside me, because this could be my chance to get rid of her at long last. "This is not my doing. I have witnessed your crimes and I will have you arrested by the Royal Guard."

I looked around for assistance, but the balcony was empty and Magdor just tittered a laugh.

"Oh Austyn, you really do have a big imagination. Those laws are made by my husband, and there have been changes made to them in recent months, perhaps you hadn't heard? Then again, it isn't your duty to worry yourself with things like politics. So let me inform you that acquiring potions from Prophets is acceptable within the right circumstances under a new decree and as the empress, I am always in the right circumstances."

"My father won't stand for this. I'll tell him," I growled, but the confidence in her gaze was making me doubt. When had he ever listened to me since *she'd* arrived in our home?

"You truly are making a fuss over nothing." Her eyes flashed with danger. "How spoiled you are to throw this gift back in my face."

Kahn beamed, staring at me with a cocky assuredness as he swept a hand through his thick hair. "I will be the most envied of husbands in the land, Princess. It is only a matter of time before you fall madly in love with me. Now bite your tongue like an obedient girl and come lay a kiss on my cheek."

He offered it to me and my hand curled into a fist, ready to snap out and break the perfect alignment of his new cheekbones.

Rage erupted inside me as I stalked towards him, the angry creature in my chest raising its head and spitting acid. "I could never love you. Handsome or ugly, it makes no difference. I wouldn't choose to marry you if you were the only man left in this world and the future of the Fae race depended on it!" I swung my fist and I was fairly sure he was so caught off guard by a woman throwing a punch that he didn't even try to block the blow, my knuckles cracking against his cheek with a satisfying thwack.

"Austyn!" Magdor shrieked, but she wasn't the one to get hold of me, Kahn was, his grip like a vice on my arm. His face blanched of colour, then reddened, shifting from somewhere between purple and orange as embarrassment and rage coloured his features.

"Do not hit me," he hissed through his teeth, spittle raining down over my veil and I yanked at my arm to try and get free. But he wouldn't let go, a violent storm brewing in his eyes and setting my heart racing with fright.

Magdor stepped closer, rubbing his arm. "Now, now, baby. Take a breath," she encouraged and the note of concern in her voice sent a tremor through my chest.

"Let me go, Kahn," I commanded, keeping my voice steady but his grip only tightened to the point of pain, bruising his fingerprints onto my flesh. "Now," I snapped with a ring of authority to my tone and to my surprise, he listened.

Kahn backed up and suddenly let out a roar that sounded more animal than man and fear raced through to my core. He turned towards the table, lifted it into his arms and threw the whole thing over the edge of the balcony with a crash that made my heart leap into my throat.

The guards came charging back and Kahn jumped over the railing after the table, a distant thump sounding as he hit the ground below. I hurried to the edge, looking down and finding him running away across the grounds like a wild animal let loose from its cage.

"What's the matter with him?" I gasped.

Magdor grabbed my shoulder, yanking me around to face her. "Now look what you've done!"

"Me?" I balked. "This is *your* fault!" I looked to the guards. "She's used magic, she bought a potion from a Prophet of the Fallen. Arrest her."

"Don't be ridiculous," Magdor tutted, pointing to the guards. "Take her back to her rooms and make sure she doesn't come out until she apologises for this catastrophe."

"What?" I snapped as one of the guards took hold of my arm and I gasped, horrified that he had touched me. "Unhand me this instant – this is against the law!"

"It's my order and I am the empress," Magdor hissed, a gleeful glint in her gaze. "Be thankful I am not having them beat you too, you insolent girl."

The guards' eyes were hard as they followed Magdor's orders over mine and I seethed, knowing my position was respected less than hers, but I had never seen her wield such power before, discarding laws which had stood in place my entire life.

I was dragged away, glancing back to find Magdor marching after me with intent in her gaze and suddenly I felt like a child again about to be punished by her. But this was far worse, because now she was doing it in plain sight, and it seemed the guards were entirely under her control. And that scared me in a way I had yet to be scared, because I had always felt assured that they would come to my aid if I was in real danger, but it seemed a wolf was now fully in charge within these walls and I was being fed to her on a platter.

I wanted to rip the veil from my head, tear it into a thousand pieces and cast them all away to the wind. But even if the fabric wasn't damn near indestructible, I knew I couldn't do that and risk more innocent lives being lost for the sake of men laying their eyes on my face.

The guards shoved me into my quarters and Magdor stepped in after me, twisting a golden ring on her finger a second before she stabbed it into my upper arm. Something pierced my flesh through the silk I was clad in and I threw my hands against her chest in alarm, shoving her back a step, but a wave of weakness washed through me and I stumbled before I could do more than that.

"What the hell have you done to me?" I panted, my chest feeling too tight and my mind growing dizzy.

I launched myself towards the door, but she swung it shut before I could make it out, closing me in with her. I collapsed against it, my legs shaking as some poison took root in my body.

"Help! Guards! Fetch my father!" I shouted, but no answer came.

Magdor ripped the veil from my head, tossing it aside and I tried to push her back, my vision swimming as I staggered, losing my balance and crashing to the floor on my back.

"Monster," I forced out, though my lips were becoming numb, and it felt like my body was turning to stone.

She leaned over me, a dark figure haloed by the lighting above as she observed my struggle with a sick smile on her lips.

"Hush now, it's just a little emperian cobra venom. It'll wear off in a few hours. It'll hurt in the meantime though." She laughed and the sound echoed around and around my head as I fell into the clutches of the paralysing venom and pain swept through my veins like liquid fire. "Perhaps after that you'll remember to be grateful for all you have and stop complaining about the luxurious life you lead."

I couldn't let out a single scream, my hands falling still at my sides, my eyes unable to blink as Magdor exited the room, leaving me trapped in a nightmare that existed within my own flesh.

I hated this life. I hated this palace. But most of all I hated Magdor. That vicious woman who had come to this kingdom with nothing and secured herself a crown in no time at all. Somehow, she had seized more power than I could ever hope to within my own empire simply by marrying my father and twisting him to her will. I desperately wanted him to return to me, to see what she was and outcast her from our home. But how?

I had always thought she had some Affinity which drew him to her like a moth to flame, but now I knew she had been buying potions from a Prophet, perhaps it was more likely that she influenced his nature to comply with her desires with elixirs. But maybe that was a good thing, because if he was just drugged, then he had to still be the man I grew up with. He had to still love me just the same deep down inside.

No matter what Magdor was giving him, there had to be a chance that he could see reason. That his love for me could shine through and I might just be able to convince him to divorce Magdor and save me from the insanity of this pageant and the husband it would saddle me with.

The next time I was let out of this room, I was going straight to the emperor to plead my case with him, convince him of her crimes. She'd gone too far this time. How dare she instruct her guards to lay their hands on me? How dare she use some foul enchantment peddled by some unscrupulous Fae on her son within the palace of Osaria, despite all the dangers such magic could bring? How dare she leave me laid out, poisoned and in agony?

I'd be telling him every damn thing she'd ever done to me and pleading my case to him, and I'd be damned if my father would let her get away with it anymore.

It was over for Magdor. And as the pain of the venom burned deeper into my bones, I held onto the hope that this was the last time I'd suffer at her hands. Because so help me, I may have only been a girl caged, but I held power in my own right, and I was done simply bending bars. It was time I broke free of them for good.

CHAPTER SIX

Twenty thousand years was such a long time to be alone.

I missed the sun. And the stars. And the moon. Oh, the moon was my favourite with its pale face and haunting presence. After the sun and the stars. Third favourite for sure. It was so round and... no, not round... it was egg shaped and yellowy blue and...

Stop thinking about the moon, it always drives you insane.

I sighed at the waspish comment and bit my lip petulantly.

It wasn't the moon that drove me insane, it was the sea. Swishing and swirling, drawing in and out with a sound which was so relaxing and yet so, so sad. Listening to it was what had eventually driven me to madness. This insanity in which I lingered day in and day out, where nothing ever changed and all I could do was wonder whether any of anything I'd ever remembered had ever truly been real. I could almost recall the sea if I concentrated, the way the light caught on the crest of each brightly coloured wave-

Well, the sea never used to be orange...

I shook my head in defeat. It was so hard to remember what was real these days. It was like trying to hold sand in my hands. At first it had seemed easy, but over time, bit by bit, the details were falling away. It was the truest cruelty of my curse that I couldn't just sleep this time away. That I was trapped here aware and alone and so fucking empty for so, so long.

I ached. Just plain ached for a taste of anything. The wind on my cheeks, birdsong caressing my ears, a pang of hunger which I might actually sate, even the roaring pain of a blade piercing my flesh, or fire burning me away into nothing and no one as my screams sounded so loud that they deafened me. Yes, I would take agony over this nothingness now. I would take the end of days themselves just to have this lingering ocean of emptiness end.

Six thousand days was such a long time to be alone.

I sighed, leaning my head back against the curved, golden wall of my eternal cage. Was I smaller while I was in here or was the golden coin I was housed within bigger? No one ever told me that. It was the kind of thing I should have known. But I didn't. And anyone who could have told me was long dead. All the Fae I'd ever known and loved, loathed and hated. They were dead. Rotted and ravaged by time and nothing at all beyond bones and ash now. I knew it in my soul even though it shouldn't have been possible for the fair folk to die out. But they had. I'd felt that long ago. The moment the break happened, and the Fae fell. The moment their immortality was wrenched away from them because they no longer deserved it. Every one of them had lived out mortal lives, their eventual deaths the price of that one little lie. Every single one, but me...

Four hundred months was such a long time to be alone.

I was so alone in here that all I ever had to keep me company were memories of the ones I'd once known. I closed my eyes tightly and thought about my sister, trying to capture the feeling of pure love I'd shared with her and hold onto it. I tried to picture her kind face and how her green eyes used to sparkle with so much love when she looked at me-

Brown eyes, idiot.

I frowned. Brown? No, hers were green and mine were brown. Weren't they? My heart ached as that detail was tangled in the fog of my memories, and my pulse began to thunder as I realised what that meant. If this final piece was gone then that was it. It was the end. And I couldn't bear the thought of that being true.

I leapt up and started pacing, keeping my eyes clamped shut as I tried to force the memories to come back to me, to give her back to me in that small and tangible way.

Please, please, don't take this from me. Don't let me lose the last I had of her. She's all I've got left.

Panic welled up in my chest and my heart kept thundering so hard and fast that I was certain it would burst, and all the pain trapped within it would come flooding out to drown me and finally take me from this place. But of course it didn't. It wouldn't. I was left here to linger in the agony of realising that I could no longer picture her at all. My beautiful, kind and loving sister had been stolen from me just like everything else, and the pain in my heart and tears on my cheeks did nothing at all to bring her back to me.

An agonised sound escaped me at the grief of my final memory being stripped away and I dug my fingernails into the flesh of my arms as I fought to give the pain inside of me an outlet.

I'd lost the sound of her laughter first. That had been taken from her when *he'd* killed her anyway. When he'd ripped her from this world and destroyed the good in my existence with one brutal act of hatred that had been the beginning of the end for all of us. Then I'd lost the warmth of her smile, my aching heart unable to recall it as the years slipped by and the pain of her loss stole the joy of her presence from me. And the memory of her hand in mine. The sound of her voice was gone forevermore, lost in a sea of grief, never to return. Bit by bit every piece of her had slipped away until the memories I'd once known so well felt like stories I was telling about someone else, the details changing with each retelling and more of it left uncertain until the truth may not have been there at all. I'd only had her eyes left, watching me in the dark as I slipped into the chaos and insanity of my own personal hell in this metal prison. Now they were gone too.

A tear slipped from my eye and ran down my cheek, tumbling over my chest before falling into a glimmering pool at the bottom of my cell.

The chamber I'd been given to rot in for all of time was a round, golden room with no doors nor windows. All around the edges of it a bench ringed the space, lined with plush cushions which were as gold as the chamber itself, the space between them lined with that pool of tears. That was it. Nothing more adorned the place I'd been trapped in for so long that I'd lost count of the days. Nothing at all to keep me company aside from myself. Sometimes the light seemed to mirror the world outside my prison – golden light during the day and pitch blackness pressing in on me at night, though no doubt it was simply my own mind creating the changes. I had no idea if it was day or night, raining or blazing sunshine beyond my prison.

Right now, I had light at least. Light to see the ripples racing away from me across the pool as my tear added to its depths.

I stretched my leg out towards the water and the soft blue shoe I was wearing fizzled away, leaving my foot bare so that I could dip it in.

The water was warm. So warm, it sent a chill down my spine.

That's not right, you fool. You're confusing warm and cold again.

But didn't cold burn? No, no I was right, or *other me* was anyway, cold was the shivery one. The one that was making my dark skin pebble with goosebumps right now. I withdrew my foot from the pool of tears and a shoe reappeared to warm my chilled toes.

Eight million nights was such a long time to be alone.

Had I really deserved this fate for what I'd done? I didn't even know anymore. I could remember the blood staining my hands and the fury in my soul, I could remember hungering for death more than I'd ever hungered for anything in my life before that moment, and I could remember loving the taste of it when I took it. Or was that just a dream I'd had of what I'd so desperately wanted to happen? I couldn't recall. But either way, I didn't think that made me bad. Wasn't it right to crave the death of someone who deserved it? Wasn't it worth becoming a villain if justice was served by my sins?

I sighed again because I didn't know anymore. I wasn't sure I'd even known that back then.

I drew my long hair over my shoulder, looking to distract myself from the morbid thoughts that plagued me, twisting my fingers through it as it shimmered red then pink, blue, purple, orange. Every colour. Any colour.

You should match it to your sister's to help us remember her.

I stroked the length of my locks, willing them to take on the colour of my sister's hair and after fluttering through a rainbow of choices, they eventually settled on purple. I smiled as I waited for the memory to form around the colour, willing my fractured mind to draw up an image of the girl I'd loved so dearly. This would do it. This would bring her back to me in some small way and then I'd remember why I was here, why I would take this fate a thousand times over for the sake of justice in her name. It hurt to remember her, but it hurt so much more to forget. I knotted my fingers in my hair as the memories failed to rise, gritting my teeth as I tried to concentrate, but nothing came to me. There was no light in the dark and I couldn't understand why it wasn't working because-

People don't have purple hair, idiot.

I sucked in a sharp breath and frowned at my hair. That couldn't be right. Because *my* hair was purple, and I was people so how could my hair be purple if I was people, but people didn't have purple hair? Were there purple people? Or maybe-

I hate you.

I dropped my hold on my hair as the sombre thought which I always fought against echoed through the empty space. If I hated myself and there was no one else, then what did that leave me with?

Fifty thousand years was such a long time to be alone.

I chewed my lip, hating myself, hating this place, hating the entire world out there beyond my cage for all the good it did me.

I lifted a hand and cast a little mouse into my palm, the creature coming to life with a frightened squeak before circling my hand in search of an escape and leaping away from me into the pool of tears.

I watched as it tried to swim to safety, but all around it was nothing except the golden edges of the pool – the ring of the cushioned bench too high for it to climb up to. I felt like that mouse, swimming through an unending river of tears with no way out. Only that wasn't quite true for the little creature, and with another wave of my hand, I cast it away into nothingness again. Better not to exist than to exist in here anyway.

Within this golden prison, my magic was entirely mine, I could use it for myself to do anything I desired. Except leave. Or kill myself. I'd tried to do both more times than I could count though.

Slave of the coin.

Perhaps today would be the day. Someone would find the hidden trove of the Prophet's treasures and claim my coin for their own.

I was nothing but a fool's desperate desire to cling on to the power of the Fae when they fell. An immortal creature wandering the world in hopes of death. He hadn't given me death though, he'd given me something far crueller than that. Shackles and chains wound into my flesh so deeply that they were anchored within my bones. He made me a slave and stole my free will, forced me to bend until all others would have broken. But I'd already been broken when he found me, so here I remained. A slave with no master, a creature with no purpose, an empty girl with no freedom in sight.

When he'd first cursed me to this existence, I'd sworn I'd never bow to the will of any master. I may have been forced to follow the will of the owner of my coin, but I didn't have to make the power they held over me easy to wield. So I'd made every effort to follow the commands I was given in ways they'd never been intended. That self-absorbed bitch who'd asked for immortality after she'd had me whipped? I'd turned her into a tree which could never die. She was still sitting up on a hill in the middle of the Argol Forest with birds nesting in her hair and squirrels taking shits on her branches, unable to speak or move or see, just trapped inside her own mind probably going as mad as I was.

And the lecherous old bastard who had commanded me to give him endless riches before he 'got to work making good use of my tight little cunt'? I'd made sure that he drowned in the money he so desperately desired before he ever got a chance to lay a filthy finger on me. I'd watched him choke on the gold coins he'd made me give him and laughed, telling him to be careful what he wished for. There had been more like them, selfish Fae consumed by greed at the thought of all they could claim from me and my magic. In the end, I'd managed to turn all of their greatest desires into their downfall and freed myself from their rule until the next came along.

It had helped for a little while. Until I'd realised that if people saw my gifts as a curse, they'd no longer desire them. They'd cast me away. Hide me in a dark, forgotten corner of the world and lose me to the endless echoes of time. I was bound to this cage, and I could never break free of it. So now I'd been left to rot in my unbreakable tomb with my unageing skin and inability to die.

So who did you punish in the end?

Myself.

I prayed that someone would find me now. It had been an eternity since I'd seen the sun. If I ever got to leave the confines of this infernal cage again then I'd make every effort to ensure their desires were fulfilled in the best way they could be. No more tricks. No more lies or half-truths. I would use my power in exactly the way they wanted. I'd gift them an eternity of prosperity and in return I would at least be free of this endless nothing.

Seventeen days was such a long time to spend alone.

My sister had once told me that so long as I kept love locked in my heart, I'd never truly feel pain. And she was right. For a while. My love for her had sustained me. The justice I'd dealt out on her behalf had burned with a sense of what was right.

Even now, when her face was lost to me and her words were nothing but fleeting whispers in the dark void of my mind, I didn't doubt my choice. I didn't doubt my love for her. I may have forgotten the rest of it, but that love lived on inside me, even more immortal than my sorry soul.

That evil motherfucker had killed her. Taken the kindest, purest being I'd ever met and murdered her for no other reason than power and greed. He'd destroyed all of the good in my world because he believed he had the right to do so when he had no such thing.

So I'd killed him in return.

I'd taken my knife and stabbed and stabbed and stabbed. I hadn't forgotten the colour of that. Red, red, red. I could still feel the wetness of his blood dripping down my body, the rush of the kill making my heart race to a heathen beat which suited me all too well. My sister may have been a pure soul, but I was no such thing. And in the moment of his death, I found the truth of what I was. Savage, brutal, and unstoppable in my vengeance.

I didn't care that he was an emperor. It didn't matter to me. Just because he was more powerful than us didn't mean her life was his to end.

I wished I'd never done it. But not because I wished he had lived. Or that I hadn't been cursed. I wished I'd never had to. That my sister would have lived. And that I could have looked into her blue eyes for the rest of our years and lived out our lives together in the happiness we should have been able to claim.

Brown eyes. I hate you more than I could ever say.

"I want to die." Sometimes I spoke aloud like that, but I didn't really like the way my voice sounded in this small space. It bounced about and came back at me. Taunting me with my own words.

Five minutes was a hell of a long time to be alone.

I closed my eyes. Sometimes the places my mind conjured up for me to go were so beautiful that I could just sit there for days and bathe in them. I could get lost in the idea of a freedom I knew I'd never truly claim and imagine up adventures I knew I'd never truly live out.

But I couldn't remember the moon anymore. Or the sky, or the trees. They were lost to me. Like my sister. And everything else I'd ever known.

Lost, lost in the woods, surrounded by clouds and stones...

I wish you would burn up. Turn to ash and blow away on the wind so that I never had to listen to you again.

My mind couldn't conjure anywhere for me today, my imagination was full of empty colours which wouldn't form a shape for me to get lost in, so I tilted my head back as I opened my eyes and gazed up at the golden roof above me.

I ached to feel the warmth of a mortal's touch on the golden shell which housed my soul. I would grant their every command in the greatest way imaginable.

The Prophet who'd cursed me was dead, dead, dead. Long beyond any chance for me to get revenge. He'd hoarded my power then hidden me from the world until the next owner of my destiny had come to claim me. Such a long time ago.

Too long. Not long enough. In a faraway time and place.

It wasn't fair.

You promised not to bring fair into it anymore.

I clucked my tongue in irritation. Who was I to tell me what to do? It *wasn't* fair and knowing that didn't mean anything. It didn't change anything. But it was true. I just needed to get over the idea of fair and not fair. None of it was fair. Granted, I'd never been the one who was on the upside of these supposed scales, so maybe if I'd been the one with the good fortune, I may have had a different opinion on fair.

Perhaps you should drown yourself in those tears. They can't leave here any more than you can. That'll be your fate in the end anyway. One day they'll rise so high you'll have no choice but to drown in them.

The silence echoed on forever.

One moment was such a long time to be alone.

CASSIUS

CHAPTER SEVEN

"You haven't eaten a bite, Austyn, whatever is the matter?" Magdor asked in exasperation.

It was Princess Austyn's nineteenth birthday and she sat with her veil in place at the far end of the long banquet table, her father at the opposite end beside his empress.

Austyn looked alone, so many seats and so much food piled between her and her father that they had to raise their voices just to speak to one another. Which I noticed they didn't do all that often. Not like they once had, before Magdor. I hadn't been the emperor's personal guard back then, I'd been fairly new at my job when Magdor had arrived, still training most evenings with Captain Marik. He was a cutthroat man who took joy in punishing the new recruits, and even now he still thrived on punishing any of us who stepped a toe out of line.

If our armour wasn't aptly polished, our jerkins not precisely laced...all mistakes held a price. I had received so many lashings from him in my life that the scars on my back blurred together into a criss-crossing web, a mark of my enforced obedience. It was hardly a surprise I liked my surroundings clean and perfect, because the cost of tiny imperfections had been blood.

My father had known the cost of his own misgivings too, working as an honourable protector of the crown. He had served as a royal guard his entire life and had died protecting the emperor's first wife, Austyn's mother, during an attempted invasion on the palace from the Quellioths when I was a boy. Their country was an island in the Forken Sea which bordered our great empire and had once sought to overthrow Emperor Tarim and the Lunarelle royals, though they had more recently begun an all-out war with the Forkens. They had been slaughtered by our men, their army desecrated, but not before *they'd pillaged the city and wreaked havoc through the streets. Peace had eventually been agreed between our empire and their kingdom despite the Osarian Empire being so much larger than their island home. The truth of it was that their borders were too well defended and their seas too heavily populated with war ships for us to attack without it costing far more than we would gain. The cost in lives and coin would have been far too great, so we won the battle and agreed upon peace rather than declaring war and dragging it out by chasing them back across the sea.*

My mother called them the dark days. Witnessing my father losing his life fighting for peace in Osaria had instilled in me the desire to follow in his footsteps and ensure that peace remained. It seemed like I was honouring the sacrifice he'd made, making it worthwhile. Though I had never realised the extent of that sacrifice until I'd joined the Guard myself.

His death wasn't the only thing he had offered the crown, he had given up certain freedoms only enjoyed by Fae with less responsibilities. He had offered up nearly all of his free time, had stood guard for endless hours, sometimes not speaking a single word in all that time. This life was a sacrifice in itself, and I had decided a long time ago that I wouldn't take a wife or bear children, because for as much as my mother had loved my father, she had told me of the brief windows of time they had gotten together, of how deeply she'd missed him even when he was only a stone's throw away from her at the palace. I had known that loss too, aching to see him for days on end only to be gifted a few hours in his company.

This job didn't lend itself to family life, it was solitary and lonely and sometimes I despised it. But then I thought of my father and of the lives he'd saved, I thought of the children who played safely in the streets of Osaria and of the princess who sat safely within these walls. And the pain of my natural instincts became easier to bear.

But since Magdor's arrival, I had felt on edge, knowing the slums were growing in size, that many of our people were starving, that taxes were increasing and that our empire was facing a new, more deadly threat. One which had slipped in our back door and was present amongst us now.

"I don't want to eat while I wear my veil," Austyn said. "I want to eat with my father in my rooms, like we did when I was younger. I want to talk about my mother and I want-"

"How dare you disrespect your father so?" Magdor bit at her. "He has laid out this wonderful feast for you, but you must have more. More, more, more. Perhaps if you were a more grateful child, then you would not miss your mother so because you would have a new one in me."

"You will never be a mother to me," Austyn snarled and my jaw ground as I vehemently agreed with that.

The emperor seemed to be dozing off, oblivious to the argument unfolding between his wife and daughter. My hand moved automatically to the hilt of my sword, his vulnerable state making me wary. I was always wary around Magdor, she gave off a vibe which set my hackles rising, and I knew better than to ignore my instincts on such things.

"Well, if you are going to be like that, then you can eat alone. Come, dear." Magdor rose abruptly from her seat, shaking the emperor's arm to rouse him.

He choked on a snore, rising to his feet and smiling sleepily at his wife. "What's that, my love?"

"Austyn wishes to dine alone," Magdor announced.

"I never said-" the princess started.

"Perhaps not in so many words, but the sentiment is clear. Guard, stay with her and escort her back to her rooms when she has finished eating." Magdor snapped her fingers at me, but I looked to the emperor. She wasn't in charge here, he was.

"Tell him, Tarim," Magdor encouraged and he looked to me with a nod.

"Yes, do as she says, Cassius," he agreed and though my feet remained rooted to the spot, I watched her closely all the way out of the hall as the other guards moved to exit too.

There were guards positioned all around the palace, but I knew she could have killed the emperor on multiple occasions if she wanted to while sharing a bed with him. I despised leaving him alone with her, fearing that one of these days I'd find him cold and lifeless somewhere between these walls.

"Do as she says," Austyn mimicked Magdor in a snide tone. "Fucking Maggot."

A laugh got caught in my throat and despite all my years of training to shield my emotions, it cracked out enough to be noticed and I worked hard to cover it with a slight cough.

She turned towards me, her veil covering her features but doing nothing to make me feel less under scrutiny.

"Forgive me, Your Highness," I said, figuring it was best to own up to my failing.

"Don't apologise, Cassius," she said.

"It is too late for that, Princess."

She chuckled and the sound was like music filling the whole room, bringing light into this eternally dark place. It was Magdor who had brought the dark, but it seemed she hadn't managed to break Austyn's spirit with her sombre presence.

"I know saying this is pointless, but I hate her, Cassius Lazar. I fucking hate her and I wouldn't care one bit if she caught the plague and rotted away before my very eyes."

I frowned, sensing her sadness bleeding from her into me and the worst thing was that I couldn't do anything about it. The next words slid from my tongue before I could hold them back and I knew they might incur me some lashings if I offended her by speaking out of turn, but apparently, I wasn't in a mind to care. "It is not my place to say, but I believe you will be immeasurably happy one day, Princess Austyn."

"Why would you say that?" she asked in surprise.

"Because I know that you are dissatisfied. And I know that..." I bit my tongue, these words having no right to sit on it.

"That what? Tell me," she commanded, and I was forced to release the words.

"All dark clouds scatter."

She fell quiet and I wasn't sure if she was contemplating that or if she was contemplating the punishment fitting for them. But eventually she spoke again, and I realised my breath had been held for the entirety of her pause.

"Are you happy, Cassius?"

The question was so unexpected that I simply had no immediate answer to give. It had been a very long time indeed since I'd been asked such a question, but to be asked it by the princess herself was something of a shock.

"Well?" she pressed. "Are you?"

"I am...content with my lot in life, Princess."

"That's not what I asked you." She rose from her seat and I felt the power of her royal blood humming in the air, demanding I respect it. And I did so with every bone in my body.

Perhaps she wanted a lie, to hear that yes, I was happy, that I smiled often and laughed freely outside of my position here. But for some reason I couldn't get my tongue to wrap around the words which I should have spoken to shut down this conversation. Instead, I gave her my truth.

"I believe children are happy, Your Highness. And when we grow older, the fools among us spend the rest of their days chasing what they lost. But I am no fool."

"And why is it foolish to wish for happiness?" she asked, walking towards me, every step in my direction making my heart work a little harder to pump blood.

"Because fools will never find it, only those who deserve it will. And you deserve it, Princess. I am certain of that."

She shook her head, looking up at me from beneath her veil, the material giving me no glimpse of her features, yet I could practically taste the beauty of her soul in the air.

"And why would you believe such a thing?"

"I..."

"Speak freely," she pushed, a sense of need in her tone that set my pulse racing. I had her full and undivided attention, a thing I should never have possessed and yet somehow it was being bestowed on me like a gift from a god. And the darkest part of me wanted to hold onto it and never let go.

"Because I see you, Princess," I admitted, my tone dropping an octave, knowing that I should not have spoken a single one of those words.

"What do you see?" her voice dropped to a husky whisper that made the heat in my blood rise.

"I see a canary trapped in a cage, its wings clipped and song silenced. But I see you looking at the sky, I see you yearning for your freedom, I see your heart bleeding day in, day out. And I see that the fight in you will never die."

"How do you know for sure?" she breathed, a desperation to her voice

that left me feeling so fucking useless to her. "Because sometimes I feel like my soul is being crushed by the weight of the whole sky."

"You're Princess Austyn Lunarelle of Osaria, you were born of power, and one day you will realise the strength of a hundred suns burns within your veins and no mere maggot can hold a candle to you."

For some reason I felt sure she was smiling as she nodded, stepping back and adjusting her veil. "Thank you, Cassius. Will you take me back to my rooms now?"

"Yes, Your Highness." I bowed my head, letting her take the lead before following in her wake. I walked behind her as obediently as a hound at a goddess's heels, and I felt my infatuation with her deepen. The roaring fire in my veins told me I was more beast than man in that moment, a hellion born to protect this girl with every fibre of my unworthy being, and after crossing a boundary between us with what I'd said, I found I liked the taste of sin on my tongue a little too much.

I shifted against the wall for the hundredth time, the past haunting me as I thought over my failings. I had quietly promised Princess Austyn to rid Osaria of Magdor, that she would be free one day, happy. But now I feared the hope I'd once had for her future had been nothing but a fool's dream. With each passing year, I had failed time and again at exposing Magdor, unable to gather proof of her witchcraft, and fuck if that wasn't the most gutting thing of all.

The scent of shit in this place made my stomach turn. Had nobody in this dungeon ever heard of soapy water and a mop? It felt like my skin was itching from all the filth surrounding me. I was used to clean clothes, a sparkling home and a toilet that was more than a hole in the ground. Like a lot fucking more.

"Why are you acting like there's ants crawling all over you?" Drake asked from his cell where he looked perfectly comfortable amongst the dirt and grime. I supposed if he'd lived his life in the slums, this kind of living space was rather homey to him.

"Because I'm not used to living in these conditions. A pig is treated better than this," I snarled, getting to my feet when it became too much to bear.

I wiped my hands down my tattered britches, eyeing Drake through the iron bars. Bars which were making me feel ill with their proximity. My chest was still bare, and I guessed I'd be given no more clothes in this life.

The man who would likely be the source of my last ever conversation in life was sprawled out, his head cupped in his hands as if he was currently basking on a beach under the beating sun.

"You seem pretty relaxed for someone who's going to lose their balls tomorrow," I commented.

Shit, I had to think the fate the guards had in store for him was even worse than what I had coming at dawn. My execution was decided. And even being disembowelled to the cheers of an onlooking crowd seemed far preferable to castration via a heated butcher's knife. Fuck that. At least I'd die with my cock intact. I damn well hoped so anyway.

"That's because I'm not gonna lose them," he said confidently, looking like he truly believed those words.

"You're in denial," I said solemnly with an understanding nod.

I'd probably have been in denial too in his position. What was a man without his manhood intact? I shuddered at the thought.

"Nah, I'm not." His eyes slid to mine, like he was considering me for a moment and when he went on, I had to assume he'd found what he'd been searching for in his assessment. "My gang will come for me before dawn."

"Oh, I'm sure they will," I said, not believing that at all, but not wanting to take away a man's hope in the face of his balls being removed. Besides, maybe there was a small chance of it. And it didn't much matter to me if one thief returned to the streets, I was a dead man walking anyway. Though I seriously doubted they'd be able to break him out of the fortress that was the royal prison.

"Yeah, they'll come charging in here, swords drawn, begging to see my face because they've missed it so much," he said with such certainty that I kind of pitied him.

"Of course. Then they'll all take you home and you can give each other blowjobs to celebrate your cock remaining intact," I said lightly.

"I'm not gay, mate, but if you want to use that image to pleasure yourself for a final time before you're hung, drawn and quartered, go right ahead. Meanwhile, I'll be skipping my way across the rooftops of Osaria again by midday, living my best life."

"Lucky you," I said dryly.

His eyes glittered. "Always was lucky. Sorry, mate."

I reached a hand up to rub my neck, thinking of the hangman's noose which might break it tomorrow. I wasn't entirely sure on the methods they'd be using for my death, but it could well end that way. And if it did come to that, I hoped my neck did snap rather than me choking for a few long minutes. They weren't going to let me out of this world too easy though, the fact that they'd spent a few days torturing me before my execution was proof of that. They wanted to be certain they got their pound of flesh from me and if it did come to a hanging, a man of my size would almost certainly get his neck broken when the lever was pulled. Gasp. Snap. Done.

Why was I starting to think I'd wasted all those years being a straight-edged warrior?

Should have gotten laid more often.

Maybe it would have been healthier if I'd sought the company of women every week instead of burying my urges for months on end, only to lose control for a single night of profane fucking. But I guessed that was the problem. Control was hammered into me. Routine, vigilance, discipline. It was as addictive as it was insufferable, and I was endlessly caught between restricting the needs of my inner man and working to uphold the expectations of my position. It was no wonder I had to pay extra for the kinds of whores who would allow me to express my inner demons to their fullest extent on their bodies. I supposed it was the price I had to pay to keep my sanity.

Drake watched me for a moment before closing his eyes, seeming utterly relaxed in this shithole. I had to wonder what kind of life a man like him lived. The Forty ruled the slums so it didn't take a genius to figure out that they hid themselves away amongst the shanty town of ramshackle housing that surrounded the city. But they were also notoriously accomplished thieves which meant they had riches worth taking note of. So they must have held some level of luxury where they lived – what else would they be spending all of that money on? I very much doubted they were spending it on feeding the masses. And yet he seemed more than comfortable here in this squalor too. So it was hard to judge.

I drifted back towards the wall, deciding how to spend my final hours. Repenting? Fuck that. I had zero remorse for my crime. If there was a face worthy of dying for, it was the princess's.

I wondered what she thought about being looked upon. She probably despised me for it. I'd crossed a line that was drawn by the emperor himself, though on reflection she had always hated that veil, always wished to be rid of it. But I doubted my eyes were the first man's she would have picked to land on her face. Though she had been as enslaved to almost as many rules as I had during my time at the palace, maybe breaking free of one restraint had been something of a liberation to her at least. I hoped so. Because I knew all about being held in check by laws. I also knew that it didn't stop me dreaming of bigger things sometimes. Things beyond my station. Things involving the princess who I had no right in fantasising about.

I'd have to be ten times of a better man and have a thousand times the wealth to be worthy of her.

I wondered what Princess Austyn dreamed about at night. Adventure, power...sin? Who featured in her fantasies? Who awoke lust in a girl so painted in virtue?

I dragged my mind away from her, focusing on my family instead. My mother had raised me alongside my seven sisters. In a world where women were supposed to be beneath men, I'd certainly never felt above any of them. My mother had taught me to respect women. Something my training in the Royal Guard had attempted to beat out of me. But I'd held firm, though my revolutionary thoughts had to remain quietened in the face of my job. Seeing my old captain had stirred up some uncomfortable memories, though.

"Tunic off. Back to me, Lazar," Captain Marik ordered. *"Ten lashings in penance for your impertinent tongue."*

The strikes were cold, then hot, then wet when the blood came. Always in that order. Each one harder than the last. Pain was a mirage; Marik had taught me that. He'd been wrong though. It wasn't an illusion, but you could train your mind not to feel it as keenly.

"Why not take a wife, Lazar?" my fellow guardsman had once asked me. *"It's like having a live-in whore who does your housework."*

I'd broken his jaw. Ten lashings every day for a week. *Worth it.*

In Osaria, taking a wife meant owning her. And I'd wanted to defy that by refusing to follow that path. The emperor had been making so much progress towardss changing such things before Magdor had stepped onto the scene. She was a heartless fiend who seemed to have no compassion for women despite her own gender. Whatever her motives were, I knew it wasn't in the interests of anyone but herself. It enraged me more than anything else that I would die in this pitiful world before seeing Magdor overthrown and my country soaring to greatness.

No one had batted an eye at the way the city had changed since that heathen's arrival. Maybe most men were quietly glad the laws hadn't been changed in women's favour. Maybe they wanted to remain above the opposite sex. But I still hoped there was goodness to find in some of my countrymen, so that when I passed from this world, I could at least believe someone would fill my place and fight against Magdor's tyranny.

If she got her hands on that strange coin, what the hell was she going to do with it?

I sighed wearily.

Fuck I hate losing at life like this. Am I really giving up? Cassius Lazar, royal guard, man of his word, lover of his kingdom.

Now I'm just a complete failure.

I wondered if my father would be proud of the choices I'd made. He had loved his country as I did now, and my mother had always taught me to try and live by his example. Which I had religiously. Day in, day out for all of my adult years. But now I was a criminal, a lawbreaker. Would he have seen things my way if he had known of my suspicions about Magdor?

When I was a boy, I'd sworn to help make Osaria great one day. Was that dream really going to die in the clutches of a noose?

A clash of steel caught my ear followed by a loud grunt and Drake bolted upright with a wide grin. He turned to me, his eyes shimmering with all the strength of a man who knew he truly wasn't fated to have his manhood forcibly removed.

The door along the wall from our cells flew open and my heart beat harder as three men crept in like dark shadows.

"It can't be," I said in surprise.

"Told you they'd come for me," Drake chuckled.

The Forty's reputation preceded them, and my spine straightened at the threat these men brought into the room with them.

"*Balthazar*, I could kiss you right now if I wasn't worried I'd get some of that Countess's moustache in my teeth." Drake clutched the bars as he gazed out at his friends, his eyes bright and nothing about him showing any discomfort from his contact with the foul metal, though it must have been weakening him.

"Fuck you," growled the man who I assumed was Balthazar. They all had neckerchiefs pulled over their faces so I couldn't get a good look at him even as he stepped into the light of the nearest torch, but his body was stacked with muscles. "If you want out of that cell, you'd better start grovelling."

"Grovelling?" Drake spat. "I don't grovel. And I know you'll let me out either way because the only reason you're here is because Egos wants me free. So quit trying to prove your balls are bigger than mine and get on with getting me the fuck outa here."

One of the other men elbowed Balthazar aside, moving forward and raising a large crowbar in his hands.

"You two can sort this out in the ring, we don't have time for your bitch fight here." He was a beast of a man, almost as tall as he was wide.

With a grunt of effort, he jammed the crowbar into the gap between the door and the wall and began to pry Drake's cell open. There was a loud groaning of metal and the thieves looked around in anticipation of someone overhearing that sound before the door finally swung wide with a bang that reverberated through my skull. Just days ago, I would have been primed to kill these men for what they were daring to do right now, but as I was on the wrong side of these iron bars and had little reason to stop them, I simply watched and wondered whether they could really pull this off before the guards appeared.

I gazed at Drake longingly as he stepped out of his cage with a bark of triumphant laughter, a free man; something I wanted to be with all my heart. And as he moved further towards his men, leaving his cell behind, I wondered if this could be my chance too. Thieves could be bought, persuaded. I wasn't living by the rules of my position anymore. I didn't have to lie down and accept this, not when there was an opportunity right in front of me.

Adrenaline surged through my veins and a hundred thoughts sped through my brain at once. I darted forward, gazing out at Drake in a crazed hope, wondering what I could say or do to convince this lawless man to save me too.

I don't want to fucking die. Not when Magdor still has her claws so deep in my kingdom. Not when Princess Austyn's fate is painted for her with the tar of that woman's brush.

"See ya." Drake saluted me, no hesitation in his eyes as he turned to leave and desperation built in my chest so keenly that I couldn't contain it. I understood the way it worked on the streets, even if I hadn't grown up on them myself. Out there it was cutthroat, brutal, dog eat dog and every man for himself. The thieves had clearly only come for Drake because there was something in it for them, but maybe that kind of attitude could work to my advantage too. If I could offer them something they might want, then they might just be convinced to trade me for it. And I had nothing left to lose. They could have it all, because without my life, everything I owned was meaningless anyway.

"Wait!" I called as they headed towards the doorway, four shadows in the night, about to slip into the dark never to be seen again.

Drake glanced back, a slight frown lining his features. "I can't carry dead weight." He held a hand over his heart. "Really, it's been nice to know you. Sucks you gotta die. But that's how the cookie crumbles." He turned away again and my mind wheeled to the only thing I had to offer. They were thieves. What more did they want than treasure? And I knew where a whole hoard of it was hidden. I didn't give a fuck about money, but I *did* care about Magdor reaching that mysterious coin. So if I could get to it first – destroy it maybe-

"Halt," I commanded in my most authoritative tone.

The four of them halted, seeming surprised by me ordering them about as if I had the upper hand here. But I did. They just didn't know it yet.

"I'll give you thirty seconds, no more," Drake said, folding his arms.

I glanced at the other men who I didn't trust in the slightest, but Drake had something about him which I did trust. He was honestly dishonest. He knew what he was and he owned it, and I had a feeling that meant he'd give me this one opportunity to save myself.

"There's a cave beyond the Lyrian Desert, it holds a fortune even The Forty couldn't spend if you had a thousand years to do so. If you free me, I'll take you to it," I said in a rush of words which tripped over each other in their haste to escape.

Balthazar spat a laugh. "That sounds like the ramblings of a desperate man lying to get out of his cage. Come on, Drake." He clapped a hand to Drake's shoulder, but he shrugged him off.

"Go on," Drake urged, a glimmer in his eye that said I'd captured his attention, and hope swarmed into my chest. We'd spent hours trading truths while we awaited our fates in these cells, so I had to hope he could see that this was no bullshit and he would hear me out.

"Empress Magdor showed me it. She offered me a deal to get out of here. Only men can enter the cave – some old magic left over from the Fallen. But I refused her offer because I despise her." Not the entire truth, but telling these scoundrels about a mysterious coin that held some sort of power that even the empress desired was not a good idea. Especially considering I was going to destroy it the second I got my hands on it.

"Right, so you're saying there's some mystical cave with all the treasure a man could ever want and you're gonna refuse to go to it and choose to die instead? As if anyone's that noble." Balthazar chuckled under his breath, but I didn't pay him any heed.

I stared at Drake, willing him to see the truth in my eyes.

"Actually, I think this fucker might seriously be that damn noble for some reason," Drake said, moving to the edge of my cell. "I've listened to him blathering on about his love for this kingdom the whole time I've been here. He's rock hard for a taste of Osaria. And he hates the empress enough that I really do think he'd take his death over making a deal with her which could hurt his precious kingdom."

"It's your kingdom too," I pointed out through gritted teeth, but he just laughed.

"Oh yeah? Well *my kingdom* doesn't seem to give one fuck about me or the people who live on the outside of the precious rings of its capital city. In fact, that whole upper and lower Fae bullshit spells it out plain and simple to me. I'm *lower* than the rest of you. So I'm worth a whole lot less."

My jaw ticked at the point he made, but I didn't have time for a debate in politics or the ways the kingdom was run. I just needed him to understand me and where I was coming from. It was my only shot at making it out of this hell. Besides, bringing down Magdor was the answer to bridging the divide between the rich and the poor. Once the emperor was out of her clutches, he'd see sense again, I was certain of it.

A shout came from out in the passage beyond the door and I tensed, knowing I had mere seconds to convince Drake to take me with him or I'd be damned to die with the rising sun.

"Leave him," Balthazar hissed, his dark eyes casting a dismissive look over me above the shroud which covered the rest of his face.

"And what if he's telling the truth?" Drake shot at him. "You wanna explain to Egos that we turned down an opportunity to get our hands on all that treasure?"

One of the others murmured something about taking me and I thrust my hand through the bars, ignoring the sickly feel of the iron as it pressed to my skin.

Drake stared at it like it was a poisoned arrow.

"A handshake," I explained, wondering if this ruffian had ever even had an honest one of those. "Man to man."

Drake cocked a brow, releasing a breath of amusement as if he wasn't about to be surrounded by a hundred guards if he didn't make a decision that instant.

"Fuck it. I'll take you with me then. Just don't go forgetting that I can gut you on the streets the second you try to turn on me or renege on this deal."

"I won't," I swore, willing him to accept my offer before we all ran out of time and were discovered.

He gripped my hand, shaking it firmly then snatched the crowbar from his friend and jammed it into the lock. His tattooed arms bunched with tension as he forced the lock and a loud bang sounded as the door broke open.

My heart lifted at the sweet sound of my freedom ringing through the air and I was sure I was already feeling the relief of escaping those iron bars even though I hadn't moved away from them yet.

I darted out into the passage and the others observed me warily. I straightened to my full height despite the act causing a flare of pain in the wound on my side as I refused to show weakness beneath the weight of their stares. They were looking at me like I was a threat, and I was more than happy for them to believe it. I wasn't a fool, I knew what they were but right now I had no other options open to me, and I'd rather die with a blade in my back than be torn to pieces before a cheering crowd.

Drake snatched a couple of blades from his friends, tossing one to me.

I caught it and Balthazar jerked his head towards the doorway. "Go ahead. Prove yourself."

I weighed the blade in my hand, considering my options. I was armed, but I was also outnumbered, so it was better to stick with the enemy for now.

"He's not gonna do it," one of the men sniggered and I clutched my blade tighter.

"You underestimate what I'll do for my kingdom, arsehole," I growled.

I gritted my teeth, muscling my way through their ranks and taking the lead into the passage beyond the door.

The sound of heavy footfalls sped our way and I ran forward to meet them. A bunch of prison guards were no match for the royal forces. I'd been trained since my teens to be the fiercest bodyguard the emperor could ever need, and between that and my Affinity for fighting, these men were no match for me.

I met a turn in the corridor and jammed my back to the wall, waiting.

One breath.

Two.

I am made of steel.

The first guard darted around the corner and I caught him by the neck, throwing him against the opposite wall with a loud crack that left him unconscious before he could release so much as a yelp. Another guard came at me as two more charged towards Drake's gang with yells of anger and clashes of steel.

I caught the man by the throat, my fingers locking and my teeth baring as I fought to choke him out. I may have been capable of bloody savagery in war, but I wasn't going to kill unless my life was in jeopardy.

The guard swung his sword towards me but I caught his wrist with my free hand, slamming him back against the wall with my other, his head thudding from the impact and the weapon falling from his fingers with a clatter.

"Sleep," I commanded, my fingers tightening as I worked to knock him out, knowing it was the only thing that would save his life tonight.

His other hand swung towards me on my left and the glint of a blade made me stiffen, but then Drake was there, moving like a damn shadow as he caught the man's arm, the tip of the blade already against my side as Drake ripped it from his hand. In the next moment, Drake slammed the hilt of the knife against the man's temple and hot blood spilled over my hand where I still gripped his throat.

"You motherfucker," I growled.

"You're welcome," Drake tossed back as I let go of the guard and he slumped to the floor.

I suspected killing a guard wasn't worth the life sentence it held for these thieves, and I might have been a dead man walking anyway, but I was above killing for the sake of killing.

Drake threw me a wink before taking the lead and I fell in line, following him into the depths of the dungeon with my pulse beginning to settle. No guard in the royal dungeons was clean of sin, their souls were often painted in it, the kind of work done here only whispered of on the streets. I may have believed in justice, but what happened to the Fae imprisoned in this place was barbarity, so I wouldn't lose sleep over these men's fates.

"Left here," Balthazar hissed and Drake took his instruction, darting down a corridor where the torches had been snuffed out. I was glad they knew where they were headed because I had no clue where to turn in this dank maze of cells and dark corridors. It was a labyrinth designed to confuse and daze, so if anyone made it beyond the bars of their cages, they'd likely be discovered before they could ever find the exit.

It seemed the thieves had an answer to that though as Balthazar darted past us, moving to a window where a rope was tied off and waiting for us. The prison was situated high up in an imposing tower of dark stone in the sixth ring that the people of Osaria had nicknamed Death's Door, because when the sun set behind it in the west, its silhouette resembled a large and forbidding black door.

A guard ran into sight at the end of the corridor and Balthazar moved to intercept him with a deep laugh in his throat, raising his own blade. The guard was fast, ducking Balthazar's first blow and slashing his sword across the thief's side before he could deflect it. Balthazar cursed as he stumbled back a step, his blood splattering the dark stone of the wall beside us as the guard moved forward to press his advantage with a twisted smile on his lips.

Drake charged forward to help, swinging his sword high to meet the blow the guard had been going to land on Balthazar. The loud clash of metal on metal rang out along the stone corridors so loud that my muscles bunched in anticipation, sure that every guard in this place would arrive at any moment. And honestly? I was fucking thrilled to be fighting again. I was born for it. It didn't matter if I was playing hide and seek with death right now, this was my Fae nature, my strongest Affinity, fighting a necessity to me that fed some deeply innate need in my soul. If I died on this night, then at least it would be a damn good way to die, the kind of death I'd choose, not one forced on me while I was bound and defenceless. So long as I was wielding a blade, then I'd go out of this world with a fucking smile on my face.

They traded blows back and forth, the small space hindering the swings of their swords before Drake delivered a savage strike, following it up with a brutal punch which caught the guard square in the face and brought him to his knees.

I darted forward, taking hold of the guard's neck and squeezing the meaty flesh of his shoulder as hard as I could, my thumb digging in to the correct pressure point. He passed out cold and silence fell as he crashed to the ground between us.

The thieves all exchanged loaded looks while Drake grinned at me appreciatively.

"You're teaching me that," he insisted, but I didn't reply, having no intention of doing any such thing.

Balthazar clutched his side as he climbed onto the window ledge. "By the damned Fallen," he snarled, taking hold of the rope with bloody hands before dropping out of sight.

I glanced over the edge to the smooth black wall and watched him slide to the ground far below, swearing all the way down like taking a strike from a sword was the biggest pain in the arse he'd ever endured. I had to assume it was just a flesh wound as he was still moving about rather than screaming on the floor in agony, and I had to admire his grit for just carrying on while bleeding like that. A lot of the best trained men I knew would still have baulked at the sight of their own blood, yet he seemed to see it as little more than an irritation.

Drake went next, hopping up onto the small window ledge before grasping the rope between his hands and dropping away out of sight towards the streets below. The two remaining gang members followed, the one with the slight build eyeing me suspiciously before he went while the beast of a man gave me a look which indicated he was seriously considering pitching me head first out of the window rather than allowing me to continue on with them.

I straightened, my muscles coiling in preparation of the fight I saw in his eyes, a fight I would damn well win. But he didn't attack, instead heaving his huge frame up and squeezing through the window with impressively nimble moves for such an extraordinarily large man, then dropping away out of sight after the others.

I hauled myself up into the window last, the promise of freedom on the dry night air making adrenaline course through my veins as I finally let myself believe in this turn of events. This strange twist of fate which had saved me from the clutches of certain death and delivered me into the hands of a band of criminals.

It would be worth every moment of their company and every piece of precious treasure in that cavern if I could strike a blow against that bitch who claimed to rule our kingdom. If I could take this one thing from her, then at least I could sleep a little easier at night knowing I'd stolen something vital to her plans and kept it far from her grasp. After that…well, I'd figure it out if by some miracle I managed to complete this task.

I gripped the coarse rope tightly between my fingers and placed my feet against the black stone wall of the palace dungeons as I descended. A slightly cooler breeze whipped around me, blowing off of the Lyrian Desert and no doubt sailing all the way here from the distant Cartlanian Sea. It smelled like camel shit but tasted like freedom, and I couldn't get enough of it.

"Mmmm, poop on the air. Yum, yum, yum. Smell that? Yes, lots and lots of poop. Somewhere close too. Mmmmm," the tiny voice of a dung beetle drew my attention where it sat in the crevice on the wall and I tried to block out its merry voice about shit on the breeze as I kept moving.

I clutched the rope tighter, adrenaline surging through my body from the drop below but I didn't falter, my pace hurried but steady as I closed in on the ground and the band of thieves who waited for me.

When my feet hit solid stone, I took a steadying breath and turned to find the gang darting towards an alley to my right, their footsteps silent on the cobbled streets as they slipped into the embrace of the shadows beneath the tall white walls.

I hesitated, wondering if I could make a break for it before they noticed I was gone. The verges of the city sprawled out before me, I could take any path I wanted and likely be long lost before they ever caught up to me. But I'd made Drake a promise. Shaken his hand. Besides, I knew the reputation of The Forty well enough and they dealt with those who crossed them in the most severe and barbaric of ways. I didn't want to pitch them against me and risk fucking up this one chance I had at making my life count by falling prey to their wrath.

Drake glanced back at me as the others ran on, his chin lifting in what was undoubtably a challenge. They weren't fools, they knew they were giving me the opportunity to betray them here and the calculating look in his dark eyes said they would make me pay if I tried to slip away. But I was a man of my word, and as little as I trusted this band of murderous rogues, I'd made my choice already.

If I didn't keep my word, I'd become just like any other lowlife criminal, the last scraps of my pride and the man I'd worked so hard to become stripped away from me with the simple act of that lie. For a lot of Fae, deceit and false promises were a way of life these days, but I'd always taken the warnings of our past to heart. Our kind had fallen because of a lie. And I had vowed a long time ago to embody the sins of that Fae as little as often.

So with a healthy dose of trepidation and the solid feeling that this may have been a terrible decision, I took off after the man who had granted me freedom from my cage.

I feared making a deal with a bunch of thieves was going to lead me down a path I couldn't come back from. Then again, the moment I'd laid eyes on the beauty of the princess my fate had been stolen from me anyway, so perhaps all I could do was embrace this new path I found myself on and hope that I could make it count for something so much greater than myself.

Thoughts of her spiralled in my head for a few long seconds, of her amber eyes meeting mine and confirming everything I'd ever thought about her. Because I saw her pain, her struggle in those depthless eyes and I knew she hated her shackled life as fiercely as I hated it for her. And though I may never see her again and I would surely never cross her mind for one more instant in this world, the path I walked now would be for her.

"Don't make me regret this," Drake said under his breath as I ran alongside him, clutching the poker burn on my side as I worked to ignore the pain and concentrate on moving as swiftly as I could manage.

"I won't," I swore, eyeing my new companion as he laughed low in his throat.

"Welcome to the world of transgression then, Cassius. You're in for one hell of a rebirth."

I lowered my brow at the ring of truth his words held. We were heading into the heart of the city's underbelly tonight and I knew it. I just hoped I made it through unscathed, because I had a singular goal now, one which would haunt me in every waking moment until it was done. Magdor's downfall lay with me, and I would bring it upon her as swiftly and as wickedly as I could.

The night swallowed us up and the ringing of alarm bells sounded back in the prison, clanging loudly and echoing across the night's sky as the word of our escape finally spread.

The palace guards would be called to hunt us down now and this game of escape had suddenly become so much more dangerous. My kinsmen and captain would cut me down as assuredly as if they had never known me, a number gone rogue, a rebel to be dealt with. I had no place in the life I had pledged myself to any longer.

Anxiety burrowed into my gut. I was a fugitive of the kingdom's justice. But when I completed this task and destroyed that coin, I'd at least have saved Osaria from a worse fate. The only problem was, I was a condemned man on borrowed time to get it done.

•DRAKE•

CHAPTER EIGHT

We stole through the night and I couldn't help but laugh aloud at our predicament as the bells rang throughout the city, calling the royal guards from their beds to track us down and end this petty rebellion. But I'd like to see them find us once we reached the slums.

The emperor might have believed he ruled Osaria from top to bottom, but the truth was that there were many self-proclaimed kings ruling slices of the underworld which surrounded his pristine city, and his laws and commands meant shit to them. Out there, we were a law unto ourselves and the only enemies we had to fear were bad luck and poor fortune.

I looked up at the sky, drawing in a deep breath of free air and trying not to cough as I realised it was laced with sand. The cool wind which had swept across us as we climbed down from the window of the royal dungeons had either been the forewarning of worse weather to come or a sweet taste of relief following the carnage.

"Was there a storm already or is one brewing?" I muttered, wondering if we would even have the time we needed to make it back to The Den tonight, or if we were going to have to take shelter elsewhere.

I glanced back at Cassius as he continued to follow our group, my peripheral vision always straying his way in case he decided to make a run for it. If that treasure existed, it was mine and he was not going to disappear before I had it glinting in my palm. I didn't place any faith in the word of a man, even one who shook my hand and looked me in the eye when he gave it. In fact, *especially* a man who shook my hand and looked me in the eye when he gave it.

Fae may have been honest once, but they weren't anymore. It was every man for himself out here, I knew that better than most. And I'd have shaken anyone's hand and force-fed them a lie to save my own arse. Hell, I'd have kissed him, fucked him and basted him like a farrier hen too if it had given me more sway over my fate.

"One brewing," Balthazar grunted. "And it looks like it's gonna be a bad one." He still kept a hand pressed to his side and I noted the blood on his fingers as he pulled them away to check the wound. "It's just a scratch," he said dismissively as he noticed my attention on the injury.

"You shouldn't have been so slow," I replied with a grunt of irritation. "Then I wouldn't have had to save your arse."

"Seems to me like we're even on that score," Balthazar replied, and I guessed he had a point considering my current freedom. Though I could have argued that Egos was the one who had wanted me freed. But as I gave thought to the fact that my cock was still very much attached to my body, I decided to let it slide.

I scowled at the sky. I hated the sandstorms which swept across the desert and choked the air so that we could barely breathe. Sometimes they went on for days and we'd be stuck inside The Den with nothing to do but wait it out and fight in the ring. And as much as I enjoyed my life with The Forty, I far preferred sleeping in the open than enduring too much time in close quarters with their sweaty armpits and their raging testosterone. There were too many of us with chips on our shoulders or points to prove for it ever to be a relaxed environment, and though I would always sleep with one eye open, I preferred to add a healthy dose of distance between myself and the arseholes I worked with when I did it.

Pip drew close to me, tugging the covering off of his face and smiling widely as he looked up at me. His nose had been broken by one of the arsehole guards who'd caught me and he had two black eyes from the injury. It looked painful as hell, but he was powering through like a real tough bastard even though he was little more than a kid.

"Well at least your face will be more interesting now," I teased as I observed the damage with a weight in my gut. He'd only gotten those wounds because he'd been trying to help me. It made him a fucking idiot, but it still left me feeling like shit. I hadn't asked for his help. I'd never asked for *anybody's* help. But for some reason he'd offered it up willingly and I'd gone and done the same for him in return. I didn't know what that made me aside from a fucking fool, but here we were, alive and free. So maybe it had worked out okay.

"You saved my life back at the count's house," Pip murmured and I could see something a hell of a lot like gratitude glimmering in his eyes.

I stilled, glancing at the others around me as my skin prickled at the idea of that. Cassius was looking at us with an eyebrow raised and I could tell he'd overheard that snippet of reputation-altering information. No. Fuck no. I wasn't having rumours of me going soft over some fucking kid circulating and making me look like a weak arsehole.

I scowled, glad that Balthazar hadn't heard him at least as he ran on towards the end of the alleyway we were racing down, his dark clothes merging with the shadows between the white walls of the buildings which filled the sixth ring. Around here, everything was pristine, even the streets were clean enough to eat your fucking dinner off of. They weren't as bad as the upper Fae who inhabited the inner ring, but anyone this deep in the city was doing far better than people like me. They were precious, wealthy folk who didn't have to muddy their boots with the reality of the men and women who lived just a few miles from their gleaming estates. It made my stomach twist with a mixture of anger and jealousy every time I came here, and my fingers always itched to relieve them of some of their unfairly distributed wealth.

"You must be remembering wrong," I told Pip dismissively, hoping he'd get the damn message to shut the fuck up about me saving him and just let it lie. He didn't owe me shit. That wasn't how it worked. I couldn't have people thinking I was losing my damn touch.

"I told Egos that-"

I grabbed Pip by the front of his tunic and wheeled him around, shoving him against the wall of the alleyway we were creeping through, not caring if it held us up.

"Told him what?" I snarled.

The last thing I needed was Egos thinking I'd gone soft for him. That wouldn't end well for either of us. Not well at all. The ruler of The Forty did not appreciate sentiments of loyalty beyond our subservience to him. He wouldn't think it was a good thing that I'd gotten myself locked up on behalf of some kid who hadn't even proven his worth yet. If he knew what I'd done I was certain he'd make me pay for it in blood and bone – if he even let me live at all.

Pip's eyes widened in surprise and I could feel his heart hammering beneath my fist which was still bunched in the fabric of his tunic. I didn't care that he was looking at me with fear instead of gratitude now because that was better. Far fucking better. I wasn't a good man, I was as cruel and as ruthless as the rest of the thugs we kept company with and he needed to remember that.

"I told him that you'd hidden the stash," he breathed, cowering before me. "Nothing else. I didn't tell anyone anything else."

"Oh." I dropped him and he flattened his tunic nervously, his gaze cutting to Cassius who was lingering close by.

"Beating on the kid, Drake?" Balthazar taunted as he looked back to us from his position at the end of the alleyway. "Maybe you should save your strength for the ring."

"Looking to get your arse beat again?" I asked, moving to pass him and ducking aside as he tried to slam his shoulder into mine. But I was far faster than him. Always had been, always would be.

"I owe you for leaving me so long with that countess," he growled, a promise of violence in his eyes above the covering which shielded his face.

"I thought I should let you enjoy her while you could. It's been so hard for you to get a woman recently," I teased, openly mocking him and letting him know I'd be more than happy to go a few rounds in the ring with him.

Balthazar aimed a punch at my gut, but I twisted away from him with a laugh. He drew a blade and hounded after me and I grinned provocatively.

"Tell me, did you always have a thing for fucking goats or is this a newly acquired taste of yours? Because I could always buy you a gentle natured beast the next time I'm at the market – unless you prefer one that kicks?"

"I'm gonna gut you one of these days, pretty boy," Balthazar swore, still advancing on me with that blade. My blood heated at the challenge in his eyes and I found myself aching for this fight, wanting to feel the thump of my fists against his flesh, the splatter of blood on my skin and the rush of the win.

Cassius watched us like he was wondering whether we might just kill each other and relieve him of our company, but I'd be clawing my way back through the gates of the underworld if that happened, to claim the treasure he'd mentioned.

"Save the bullshit for the ring," Finn snapped, barrelling between us and glaring at us. He was a big bastard with half as many teeth as he should have had and a mean glint in his eyes which never let me forget how many men he claimed to have killed. I didn't doubt it either. He was the kind to enjoy spilling blood for sport and I tended to avoid running jobs with him for that reason – not because I was squeamish but because bloodstains were a bitch to get out and I didn't have endless supplies of clothes to change between. "We need to get away from here before the guards find us. We can buy Balthazar a goat to fuck once this heat is off of us."

"Fuck off," Balthazar grumbled but he reluctantly returned his blade to his belt.

"What are we doing with the spare?" Finn's gaze locked on Cassius.

I could see what he was thinking and it involved a lot less of the guard's organs staying inside of his body than I'd have liked. Cassius's muscles flexed under his gaze, clearly not a man to go down without a fight. And from what I'd seen of his skills back in the dungeon and the way his eyes had lit up like little twinkly stars when he'd been in the midst of the thrall, I had my suspicions his Affinity was linked to Carioth the trickster god of stealth and cunning.

"I'm bringing him to Egos," I said firmly, raising my chin in a challenge.

"He has the stink of the law on him," Finn growled, his fingers flexing as he moved his hand towards the knife at his belt.

"He's a blacksmith who used to work in the palace," I replied dismissively, hoping to fuck that Cassius wasn't dumb enough to contradict me on that. "And he's gonna help us get the biggest haul Egos has ever seen. So leave him be. Unless you wanna take it up with me here and now?"

"Pfft," Balthazar replied dismissively as he moved to look around the next corner, making it clear that he was ready to move on. Clearly, he didn't believe in this fabled treasure, but as unbelievable as it sounded, I didn't peg Cassius for a liar and it looked like Balthazar was at least willing to let me bring the option to pursue it to Egos.

Cassius raised an eyebrow at my lie about him being a blacksmith, but if he thought it was a good idea to tell the rest of the thieves that he was a royal guard then he was a damn fool.

Finn will gut you here and now if you correct me.

"What was a royal blacksmith doing in the dungeons?" Balthazar asked, his assessing gaze sweeping over my latest mark.

"He fucked the emperor's horse," I explained. "Seems you aren't the only one with a thing for bestiality, Balthazar."

"I did no such thing," Cassius growled in disgust, his face flashing with outrage.

"A blacksmith who likes fucking horses?" Finn asked with a sneer that told me he believed it. What kind of messed up shit had he seen in his life to make him believe things like that of people so easily? I had to admit it was fucking funny though.

"He keeps denying it, but the guards said he was caught in the act so..." I left the insinuation hanging in the air between us and Pip laughed loudly.

Cassius glowered at me, but I sensed he wasn't stupid enough to risk his life over contradicting me again.

"I knew a shepherd who liked the sheep that way once," Finn muttered as if that made it okay.

"Was it your father?" I mocked. "That might explain a few things if your mother was a sheep-"

Finn looked at me for several long seconds then barked a laugh. I never could be sure with him whether my jokes would go too far and earn me a knife between the ribs, but I got the feeling he liked my smart mouth for the most part.

"Come on then, horse boy, Egos is waiting for us." Balthazar clapped a hand on Cassius's shoulder and steered him down the alleyway ahead of us, clearly glad that the attention was off of him for being a goat fucker.

The guard gave me a look which suggested he wasn't keen on being known as 'horse boy' and I smirked in response. Better to be thought of as that than for them to learn the truth about him. And a big lie always worked better than a little one. I mean, who would ever make up something as audacious as that and expect to get away with it?

Only the best damn liar and thief in The Twelve Kingdoms which made up the Osarian Empire.

We started running down the alleyways again, having to head deeper into the city before we could head out to the north side where the slums which hid The Den were. We slipped from one ring to the next and finally came to the market square in the third ring. The huge space was circled by tall white buildings, shopfronts with all kinds of enticing and expensive products filling their windows lining the square. The mass of carts and stands which filled the square during the day were gone, packed away for the night and taken back to be restocked for the morning when the hustle and bustle would start all over again.

It was fairly empty at this time of night, but there were always a few vendors to be found lurking in the shadows. Selling things you wouldn't be able to buy during the day. Some selling tokens said to date back to the Fallen or pedalling objects supposedly imbued with the Prophet's magic – not that I would ever be fool enough to touch one of those.

I noticed a healer set up to one side of the space, his eyes on the sky as he assessed the signs of the oncoming sandstorm and debated how long it was worth him staying out. There were always customers for Fae with healing Affinities, no matter how slight their talents may be. Everyone knew it was better to see a healer than not – at the very least their diagnosis was usually correct even if the treatment was too expensive to purchase.

A whore gave me a wide smile as she looked at my face, stepping forward from the back of the wooden caravan she leaned against. The paintwork on the side of it was flaking and the way it bounced on its wooden wheels told me a customer or two were already being serviced inside, but I'd never had to pay for it and I shook my head with a flirtatious smile.

I probably could have convinced her to give me a roll for free if I'd had the time, but we needed to beat this sandstorm and it was still a long way to the slums. Though as I gave the sky an assessing frown, I decided to take a chance on us having long enough to make a stop along the way.

We slipped out of the shadows and crossed the wide space in the centre of the square. Finn started to head north towards the slums and The Den, but I whistled to get his attention then jerked my chin and led them west instead.

"I need to reclaim that loot before the count's servants find it," I explained in a low voice, looking back over my shoulder in the direction of the prison we were running from, the sound of the alarm bells growing distant behind us. We were likely safe from the guards now, too far lost in the sprawling city for them to track us down, but you could never be certain of how far they would go in their hunt.

"You want to go back there now?" Balthazar grumbled, though he followed my lead all the same.

"I'm not returning to Egos empty-handed," I muttered, knowing it was well worth the risk to retrieve it. He was going to be all kinds of pissed at me as it was and I needed to appease him.

Finn shoved Cassius forward as he hesitated and my new pal fell into step with me, looking more than a little uncomfortable in our company.

"How long am I going to be stuck with you?" he murmured.

I looked him over with a trace of irritation. "That's gratitude for you. I save your arse from death's doorstep and you promise to pay me back with a king's ransom. But before you've paid that debt or even so much as thanked me, you're looking to leave?"

"I gave you my word I'd take you to that treasure," he replied, though I still heard no acknowledgment of the fact that he owed me his life. "You can meet up with me once the dust has settled and-"

I gritted my teeth in anger and whirled on him, sweeping his legs out from beneath him and sending him crashing to the ground in a move so fast that he had no chance of avoiding the blow.

He swung a fist at me and caught me in the side of the knee, making me stumble back, but I managed to keep my feet. I was fucking fast when I needed to be, my Affinities helping me to stay light footed and nimble at all times.

Finn aimed a kick at his head and Cassius caught his leg, uprooting him with a fierce twist of his ankle, his arse slamming onto the ground. Finn snatched a blade from his hip with a growl of fury, lunging at Cassius so he was forced to roll aside to evade the sharp edge aimed at his face.

I moved forward again, slamming a foot into the guard's wounded side and making him snarl in pain as he scrambled to regain an advantage against the odds. He put up one hell of a fight that made me even more sure of those Affinities of his, but as Balthazar kicked him too and tossed me a blade, I dropped down on top of Cassius in the shadows, straddling his chest and snarling dangerously.

I pressed the blade to his throat and his eyes widened in surprise as I leered over him. It wasn't the first time I'd taken a man by surprise like that – they fell for my smiles all too easily and let themselves forget the monster which lay beneath my skin. You didn't get to my position in this world without getting your knuckles skinned and your hands more than a little bloody, and I'd learned long ago that brutality was often the only friend I could rely on to keep me in the position I'd carved out for myself.

"You gave your word to The Forty Thieves and you might want to consider what that means before you suggest reneging on our bargain again," I growled, letting him see the dark in me as I held his gaze steadily and without flinching. I'd cut his throat right here in the middle of the square and leave him to bleed out on the cobblestones if I had to. It wouldn't be the first time I'd done it. "We are the shadow in every corner, the nightmare in the heart of the deepest storm. No one crosses us and lives to tell the tale and until you pay your debt to me, I hold your life in my hands."

He narrowed his eyes as he glared at me, seemingly unaffected by the fact that I was one sharp thrust away from ending his life. I guessed his training had prepared him for such a scenario, but I could tell that he had been taken off guard by my skill all the same. I guessed he hadn't expected a mere criminal to be able to pose any kind of threat to him, but we learned to fight dirty on these streets before we could walk, and I wasn't above stabbing a man in the back and spitting on his corpse if he got in my damn way.

"Did you rehearse that speech?" Cassius growled. "Or are you just so full of shit that it spurts out naturally?"

Balthazar chuckled behind me and Pip tentatively joined in.

"Your pretty face isn't so well suited for making threats," Balthazar mocked me. "Want me to cut off his ear to make the point?"

I pursed my lips in irritation as Cassius's gaze flickered to Balthazar and I got the feeling he was more concerned about him than me. And I was the one who had him pinned to the ground with a knife at his throat for the Fallen's sake.

"I think he gets it. Don't you, Cassius?" I demanded.

"I got it. You own me...pay my debt. Be scared of shadows and some shit." Cassius held my eye and I wondered if I really should cut off an ear to drive the point home because he definitely wasn't taking this seriously enough. But making people believe they were my friend had always worked the best for me in the past, so maybe he didn't need to fear me.

And so what if my pretty face made me nonthreatening? It only made it all the more surprising when my smiles fell away and the cold sting of my blade came as a sharp reminder of what I really was. Besides, I'd sooner look like me than any other fucker in my gang, or out of it for that matter. They might have called me pretty boy and mocked me for the appeal my face held, but I was the one who never had to pay to get my cock wet and had women covering for my crimes all over the city for the simple price of a kiss from my lying lips.

"Good boy," I said, slapping Cassius's cheek a few times in the same patronising way that Egos always did to me. "Just try not to fall in love with me while we're stuck together. It's made things super awkward with Balthazar as it is, and I don't need to add another broken heart to the list of men who follow me around."

"You wish, pretty boy," Balthazar grumbled as I clambered off of Cassius and tossed his blade back to him. He kept it in his grip and I saw something dark and empty in his eyes for a fleeting moment. It was a hollow, lonely thing and I wondered if his brush with death had placed it there or if this man had had the bones of him carved out a long time ago.

The wind picked up and a wave of sand was driven over us, making us all turn our faces from it and curse the turn in the weather.

"We don't have long to get back before that storm hits," Finn muttered irritably. "If you're not gutting him then let's keep moving."

I offered Cassius my hand and he grunted as he accepted it and let me pull him to his feet.

"No need to look at me like I just pissed on your grandma," I said, noting the gleam of vengeance sparkling in his eyes. Yeah, he was planning on punching me for that move alright, but I'd be ready for it when the blow came. "We can go right back to being friends. Just stick with us and keep your word. You're a man of honour, right?"

"My honour is the thing that guides me and-"

"And we need to go." I gave him a push and dove into an alleyway again at a fast pace, cutting through the city I knew so well as I kept those jewels on my mind and hoped to fuck that they were still where I'd left them.

"Keep up, horse boy," Finn grunted from the back of the group, and I couldn't help but laugh as I glanced at Cassius's face. *Priceless.*

We raced down the streets as the wind blew harder and sand was thrown over us more and more frequently. The others covered their faces once more and I kept my mouth clamped shut against the worst of it while squinting as I ran on. We needed to hurry back to The Den before the storm hit or we were gonna end up stuck out here, taking shelter wherever we could and likely forcing entry into the home of someone who didn't want us. That would make for a wholly uncomfortable night for everyone involved – I knew so from experience – so I was hoping it didn't come to that.

As we closed in on the count's house, the others took shelter beneath an archway which marked the entrance to the next estate over and I headed in alone.

I pulled my cape over my head, drawing the hood low to conceal my features as I drew nearer to the wall which ringed the count's property.

The iron gates were firmly closed unlike the other night when we'd stolen through them so easily, and I smirked at their attempt to keep out thieves. It was a nice try, but it would take a whole lot more than that to deter me.

I skirted the wall, which was at least three times as tall as me, until I reached the far end of the estate where I paused to look around for any sign of someone on watch. Apparently, they were just going to rely on a closed gate to deter unscrupulous Fae such as myself, so I had no audience as I turned to the sheer wall and looked over the white paintwork for some footholds I could use. The other thieves called me a spider for how easily I managed feats such as this, but it was no insult to me. The skills my Affinities had helped me to perfect had gotten me to where I was in this world, and I wouldn't have traded them for all the gold in Osaria. Alright, maybe that was an exaggeration – every man had his price after all, but mine would have been a damn steep one.

I easily located the hand and footholds I would need and scaled the wall quickly, making my way to the top of it with nothing but the strength and speed of my muscles to help me. When I reached the top, I pulled myself up onto the wide bricks, crouching low and thanking the storm for darkening the sky and keeping me hidden as I inspected the estate below me. A smarter man would have gotten himself some dogs as well as locking the gates. But the count didn't strike me as a smart man, just a greedy one. I mean sure, a Fae with a really strong Affinity for animals may have been able to calm a few guard dogs, but generally speaking the fangs and loud bark of a big beast was enough of a deterrent to be worth the investment against most outside forces.

I looked around for any signs of movement below, spying the stacked sacks of grain on the far side of the house where I'd stashed my loot. It didn't look like anyone had disturbed them since I'd hidden my haul and I grinned as I slipped off the wall, free falling the long drop to the ground and landing in a crouch on the other side.

I stole across the driveway at a fierce pace and danced between the shadows on silent feet as I headed for the stacked grain. I was little more than a malicious spirit stealing across his land in the night. By the time anyone realised I was here, I'd already be long gone.

A door closed nearby and I pressed my back to the wall of the building, sinking into the shadows with my dark cloak concealing me as I tugged the hood down lower over my eyes.

I watched as Perdu crossed the courtyard at the back of the house and tossed some kitchen peelings into a waste pot close to the stables. The girl was pretty, and she had a nice arse. It was a damn shame she'd gone and betrayed me, or I may well have come back to taste those lips of hers again and maybe steal a little of her virtue while I was at it. But snitches didn't get to come on my cock, so she would be left wanting, forever touching herself in the night while thoughts of the kiss I'd taken from her made her flesh ache with a desire I'd never return to fulfil. And there probably wasn't a much worse fate which I could bestow upon her for fucking me over anyway.

She turned back towards the house and stilled for a moment as if she could sense my eyes on her, but I didn't flinch. It was dark here and I was well versed in the art of the shadows. She wouldn't see me unless I made the mistake of moving and I was no fool. I waited until she dismissed the notion of searching for the source of her discomfort and headed back inside, then I slipped along the side of the wall and found the sacks of grain.

It took me a few moments to shift them aside, and I grinned triumphantly as I found the bag of loot waiting at the bottom of the pile.

Some of the food I'd added to the stash had spoiled from laying out in the heat, and I tossed the cheese aside as the smell of it made my stomach turn.

I fished a cake out and stuffed it into my mouth though. It was a little stale but still perfectly edible, and my empty stomach growled with appreciation as I swallowed. I hated the feeling of hunger, the sensation reminding me all too sharply of the small boy I'd once been, begging for crusts and sleeping alone on the hard streets. I hated that boy for his weakness, and I didn't allow myself to remember him or his desperation often.

I slipped back across the estate and scaled the wall again with ease, a grin pulling at my cheeks at the simplicity of that success.

I paused as I crouched on top of the bricks once more, and I turned my head to look out over the Lyrian Desert, which I could make out beyond the roof of the estate where the dunes rose up like a mountain range beyond the city limits.

A tide of sand was rising like a great beast under the light of the moon in the distance and I swallowed thickly at the sight of it. That storm was one big bastard and it would reach us soon. We needed to be inside before it did – ideally back at The Den where there were supplies to see us through the length of time it took the raging sands to pass over the city.

I dropped back down into the darkened streets with a wave of unease in my chest. But the weight of the bag on my back brought a smile to my face as I ran through the dim alleyways to find the others.

"That storm is closing in," I said darkly as I arrived, finding the four of them precisely where I'd left them. Cassius looked more than a little out of his comfort zone between the outlaws, and I couldn't help but take some sick satisfaction from forcing one of the privileged upper Fae to endure the company of those he thought were so far beneath him. "We need to move."

"This one can't see the route to The Den," Finn growled, pointing at

Cassius who remained silent.

I ground my teeth in irritation. He was right, but blindfolding my latest mark was going to cause issues to our speed.

I removed my cloak and wrapped it around Cassius's shoulders. He frowned at me as I drew the hood down over his face, but he didn't voice any protest to the situation as I tightened it so that he couldn't see out.

I gripped his left arm and Balthazar took his right and we started running for The Den with Pip leading the way.

The wind howled and sand pelted us with more intensity as we raced through the abandoned streets, running from ring to ring as we headed for the north edge of the city. No one else was dumb enough to be outside with the storm this close to hitting and I cursed as the sharp grains battered my exposed arms.

I cupped my free hand over my eyes, trying to shield them from the worst of it as the roar of the sand-laced wind battering the walls around us grew louder, and the jingle of windchimes picked up all across the city. Fae hung them outside their doors, the gleaming metal meant as a ward to protect them from the force of the storms, the songs the chimes made an offering to Karu, the long-forgotten deity who supposedly controlled the raging winds. I couldn't say I believed in any of that shit, but I did know for a fact that the louder the chimes sounded, the worse the storm was getting and from the sound of them ringing and clattering all over the city, we needed to hurry the fuck up.

"We aren't going to make it!" Pip cried as another gust drew even more sand over us, the sharpness of the grains scratching at any piece of exposed skin that it could find.

I did *not* want to get caught out when the sand came slamming down on us in full force. It would slice into our flesh and blind us within moments of hitting and I had no intention of battling through the hell of that if I could avoid it.

"Not much further," I growled, dragging Cassius along even faster as we ducked left and right. We didn't have time to take an indirect route to The Den and I just had to hope the ex-guard wasn't managing to keep count of our turns.

Probably best to make sure he can't.

"Cassius?" I called and a muffled response came from beneath the hood. "I want you to start counting back from two hundred. Out loud."

"Why?" he grunted, clearly focused on running while blind and in no mood to indulge me.

"Do it or die," Balthazar snapped and the sound of Cassius reluctantly starting to count down came in response.

We raced on, passing beyond the white walls through thinner alleyways and closer packed buildings of the twelfth ring before finally spilling into the slums where wooden lean-tos and poorly erected shelters were built in a ramshackle fashion all over the place, making our passage harder and harder as the sand poured down on us in droves. I hissed in discomfort, drawing my tunic up over my mouth and nose to keep it out as best I could, missing the protection my cloak had been offering.

"Open sesame!" Pip shouted ahead of us, and I couldn't help but snigger at the fact that he still believed he had to say that to gain entry to The Den. Fucking classic. I was never telling him the truth about that, and I'd kick the arse of anyone who revealed it to him too.

The hidden door was thrown open in the centre of the wall ahead of us and we tumbled inside as the storm slammed into our backs with the ferocity of a pissed off rhino charging down a lion.

I had to scrunch my eyes closed against the onslaught of sand and by the time I opened them again, the door had shut behind us and we were plunged into the pitch black of the hidden passages which led to The Den.

We jogged to the foot of the darkened stairway, and I kept a tight hold on Cassius so that he didn't fall while shaking my head to dislodge some of the sand from my black hair.

I couldn't see who had let us in, but I recognised her footsteps as she led the way through the dark passage, something about the way her steps landed on the stone reminding me of the way her arse bounced as she walked.

"Can I stop counting now?" Cassius grumbled as he made it down to fifty-three.

"Yes, by all means shut up," Balthazar replied. I swear that bastard didn't even know how to smile. He had a face like a slapped arse at all times and he seriously needed to work on his people skills. Grunting and grumbling were not attractive traits, not that he ever took my advice on that.

The tunnel went on and on and Mira's hand skimmed against mine as she walked.

I almost smiled in response as I drew my hand away. I wasn't foolish enough to accept her advance in front of the others. She belonged to Egos, and I liked my head firmly on my shoulders far more than I liked the idea of taking pleasure from her flesh.

She sighed dramatically and the sound echoed in the tight space, but no one asked what was bothering her. Likely no one cared. There was always something with her and it was damn tiring trying to keep up with it.

We walked on, taking turns and passing through more hidden doors in the dark, maintaining the silence until we finally reached the ladder which led up to The Den.

Mira brushed past me, climbing up the ladder and opening the hatch at the top for us, allowing some light to descend into the dark so that we could see each other again.

I took my cloak from Cassius as the others climbed up into the noisy space above and I held him back, looking at him in the dim firelight which filtered down to us.

The sound of The Forty talking and laughing loudly poured over us and I was confident we wouldn't be overheard as I leaned in close to speak with him.

"I need to talk to Egos alone," I murmured. "Mira will look after you but no matter what she offers you, *don't* touch her. She belongs to Egos and he'll cut you into quarters if you so much as hold her hand."

"What makes you think she'll offer?" Cassius asked in surprise, seeming more than a little out of place here already and we hadn't even made it into The Den yet.

"Because it's her favourite game. And you're not terrible to look at. You're no *me,* but you're no Finn either."

"Right," he said, looking me over like he wanted to object to that, but he couldn't because my face spoke for itself. And yeah, I knew it. But I wasn't gonna apologise for it – this face of mine had saved my life more than once.

"Don't go blushing on me. You're not getting a kiss out of me. Just sit tight while I talk to the boss and in case you hadn't realised it would be a terrible idea, don't tell them your former profession."

"Obviously. And I don't kiss men. Apparently, horses are more my thing."

I barked a laugh, surprised and more than a little glad to find the arsehole really did have a sense of humour lurking away under all of that upper Fae propriety.

"Well, it's not every day you come across a face as alluring as mine so no matter your preferences, don't try your luck with me. I'm not the kind to settle down." I motioned for him to climb the ladder and he headed up with a hint of uncertainty in his gaze.

I shook some more of the sand from my black hair as I waited to follow him, pushing it out of my eyes and hoping I'd be able to bathe sooner rather than later before climbing up too.

I emerged in the wide space which was home to the main area of The Den. It was the full first level of a huge building on the outskirts of the city and our sleeping quarters filled the floor above it. The room was divided into several areas, some set out with makeshift tables built from old apple crates where men gambled with dice and cards. There was a huge fire pit where Tobias could almost always be found cooking for anyone who had earned their meals by providing enough loot to pay for them. Throws and rugs in a range of patterns hung from the walls where someone had made an effort to brighten the space up at some point, but the floor was well worn tiles, their red colour faded from years of feet passing over them. The windows were securely shuttered against the storm, but they were never open anyway, the shutters kept locked to keep prying eyes from seeing inside our haven of sin.

There were groups which had formed within The Forty, not exactly friendships but men and women who enjoyed each other's company more than they detested some of the others, and those small factions were divided between the space. I didn't really belong to any of them, drifting between them all when it suited me, never getting close to anyone or giving them much reason to pay too much attention to me. I didn't need anyone getting to know my habits, my ticks, my routines or most of all my marks. My jobs were my own. On the odd occasion when I needed help with pulling a job, Egos made that call and I let him pick the thieves who joined me. I didn't need allies or worse than that – friends. I'd learned long ago that I could and would only ever rely on one person in this life and that person was me.

I had my space to sleep upstairs and better than that I had my little rooftop haven where I chose to sleep as often as I could, all on my own and in the company of no one but myself. I'd learned a long damn time ago what happened when you let yourself trust somebody other than yourself and I wouldn't be making that same mistake again.

I closed my eyes for a moment as the memories of that place filled my head, of the cold I'd felt creeping into my bones, the harsh words and the bite of a needle driving into my flesh over and over again.

I swallowed thickly, working to banish the echoes of those memories as I resisted the urge to run a hand down the back of my neck. That tattoo had hurt the worst for some reason, the ink seeming to burn as it was forced beneath my skin and it was always the one I was drawn to rake my nails over when the memories of that place, that fucking *priest*, pressed close. But that didn't often happen during the day. No doubt my time confined to the cell in the royal dungeon had forced those memories to the surface of my mind and I fought them off as I blinked my eyes open once more.

The Den was lively tonight, everyone taking shelter from the storm, and clearly well into their drinks. Blood would almost certainly be spilled before dawn and I was starting to think I may have a taste for it myself. Anything to banish the memories of that place. And knowing I would have to sleep here tonight in my room on the second floor instead of my rooftop sanctuary was already promising me a bad night. It was too loud in here, too fucking full of people I couldn't trust.

Aside from the sleeping quarters upstairs there was only one other place in the entire den and that was utterly out of the question.

Egos kept the rooms of the top floor all to himself and that was where he kept the majority of our loot too. We were allowed to take a cut from any jobs we did ourselves, but Egos always decided how much, and no one dared question his calculations. To an outsider it might have seemed like we'd be better off running our jobs and making our own way in the city with a full cut of the loot we'd stolen, but that was just a pretty fantasy someone who didn't know Osaria might indulge in. The streets out there were lethal beyond anything I might face in here, and the only protection to be had from them was by being part of a gang. And it just so happened that The Forty was the most notorious and feared gang in the whole of the kingdom.

I forced a blank look onto my face and shook off the memories which always sought to weaken me, refusing to let even the slightest sign of weakness show amongst this vipers' pit of miscreants and murderers.

A fire was lit in the centre of the space, vented out through a large chimney which sent the smoke into the sky far from the actual den, and several faces turned my way as I looked about to see who was here. It looked like all of The Forty were present - which wasn't surprising considering the sandstorm which raged outside. Despite the name, there were actually more than forty of us, more like one hundred now, all hand-picked by Egos because we were the best. The original 'forty' had started this gang over a hundred years ago, their handprints printed on the far wall in their own blood, now joined by hundreds of others from all the members who'd joined over the years. Including mine. Egos was a direct descendant of the founding ruler Ali Bull– but I was calling Ali Bull-shit on that. Lower Fae didn't exactly have birth certificates and genealogy records like the uppers did. No, our positions in this world weren't inherited, they were bought with muscle, blood and fear.

Egos was sitting on his throne at the far side of the room, lording it over us like the self-proclaimed king he was, and I nodded to him respectfully as his gaze landed on me.

Mira drew closer to me as I kicked the hatch shut over the trap door and I noticed Cassius eyeing the curves of her exposed flesh as she worked her hardest to seduce every damn man in here. I was willing to bet he didn't see many women like her on his side of the city.

She wore matching loose red trousers with a top which barely concealed her tits and left her stomach bare. Her long, brown hair was pulled over her left shoulder and she ran her fingers through it as she eyed my latest mark.

"Who's your new friend, Drake?" she purred, extending a hand towards Cassius.

I raised an eyebrow at him and his gaze swivelled to take in our den leader as he stepped back from her.

"This is Cassius, I took him from the dungeons and he's going to make us rich. Get him some clean clothes and a pail of water, would you? The poor fucker is desperate to wash the jail stink off of him. I need to talk to Egos."

"Cassius?" Mira repeated and the way she said it was enough to let me know that she had her sights firmly set on him for the night.

Her speciality was seducing marks and robbing them blind while they were too distracted to notice. I'd called her a whore with a thieving habit until Egos had threatened to cut my tongue out for it. But in all honesty, if she didn't warm his bed when it suited him, I didn't believe her skill at theft was good enough to warrant a place in The Forty. Her skill in the bedroom however was certainly worth remembering, not that I was supposed to know anything about that.

Mira drew closer to Cassius, her eyes sparkling with the kind of ideas that could get him killed - though he'd die with a smile on his face. Egos no doubt hated him already and that might make my pitch on this entire scheme a whole lot harder to make. By the Fallen, was nothing I did ever simple?

"Yeah. He'll bunk in with me tonight so no need to show him to your quarters." I turned away, wondering if I should have asked Pip to take care of him instead, but the boy had already disappeared into the crowd and I couldn't see him anywhere.

"I wouldn't get too excited, Mira. This one prefers horses to women," Balthazar's voice came from behind me and I turned to look at him as he stripped his cloak from his shoulders to reveal the scars which marked his dark chest. The wound on his side was still bleeding, but I relaxed a little as I saw that it was shallow like he'd said. No doubt he'd go see Hagot, The Forty's healer, to get it bound up. The guy had a pretty good Affinity for healing, so he actually did a decent job when he wanted to – the reason he'd made it into The Forty was because he'd figured out how to con Fae into buying remedies they didn't need as well as the ones they did. It was pretty damn clever really. People got better after dealing with him, so they never even questioned the extras he added on for the pleasure of the job. That little skill plus the fact that a gang like ours was often in need of a healer meant he'd earned his spot amongst us.

"Oh, they have a client like that down at the Barrow Street Brothel," Mira said, running her eyes over Cassius with a pout like she found that disappointing. "They bring various farm animals to the back entrance and-"

"I do not have a thing for fucking horses," Cassius ground out, shooting me a dark look and I grinned at him.

"I know you don't, mate," I agreed. "And I don't have a thing for fucking beautiful women." I tossed a wink at Mira and she giggled.

I couldn't waste any more time avoiding Egos though, so I turned and walked away from them, laughing as Cassius's curses followed me across the room.

I schooled my expression as I approached Egos, pulling the bag of loot from my shoulder and hoping it was enough to appease the anger I could feel aimed my way. He wasn't a man who tolerated failure and I had failed by letting myself be captured by the royal guard no matter what way you looked at it. On the plus side, he had sent men to come bust me out of there, so he clearly still valued me within the crew – which wasn't surprising as I was the damn best of the best.

Egos was a huge man, once all muscle which now held a solid layer of fat on top of it, though that in no way lessened how lethal he was. His hair was twisted into greying dreadlocks which ran down his back and held gemstones woven within them to flaunt his wealth. His dark skin was marred by countless scars, each of which held a story that had ended in another man's death. One scar cut right through his left eye, and the ruined pupil had turned near white with blindness. His other eye was fixed firmly on me as I moved to stand before him, lowering my head respectfully.

"I didn't think you were stupid enough to get caught for the sake of a boy," Egos growled, his voice rough and entirely pissed off, and I took a deep breath as I forced myself not to respond with a quip. Egos didn't appreciate my sense of humour at the best of times, and I could tell he was mightily enraged with me now. It would have been dumb of me to offer up anything other than respect now. Being the best wouldn't keep my head on my shoulders if I angered him any further.

"Pip saved my life, I owed him the same," I murmured, wondering which of the thieves had told him what had happened and fighting to hide my irritation at them while I silently promised to track them down and beat them black and blue for it.

"Honour amongst thieves, is it?" Egos sneered, knowing I'd never offered any such loyalty to a man before.

"Something like that," I muttered.

I still wasn't entirely sure why I'd risked my life for the boy's, but there was something about him that I found myself drawn to. I enjoyed his company. He was light-hearted like me and I couldn't deny I liked the worshipping look he got in his eye whenever I did something impressive. But that wasn't it. I wasn't quite vain enough to have saved him purely because I liked having a fan. Likely it had more to do with the boy I'd once been, hopeful and trusting enough to believe the lies that fucking Prophet had spun me before he'd gotten me at his mercy and made me into his plaything.

"Well, whatever it was, you owe me compensation for the risk we took in getting you out of the dungeons," Egos growled.

I nodded, pulling the jewels from the bag and offering them up to him. He thumbed through them slowly, brushing cake crumbs from one of the brooches as he examined the emerald set into the centre of it. His expression didn't change, but that was likely a good thing. He wasn't one to offer up much in the way of praise or fond smiles, but he would let it be known fast enough if he was angry. This middle ground was probably the best I could hope for.

I wanted to point out the value of the jewels he was currently fingering and insist that they more than paid any debt he imagined I owed, but I held my tongue. I'd felt the back of his hand more than once and the strike of the nine-tailed whip which sat by his feet twice too. I didn't want any scars marring my flesh if I could avoid it. My body was already branded with enough ink to mark every piece of my skin, I didn't need to add scars to the mix.

"Balthazar?" Egos called, and I looked around as the thief approached us.

He gazed at me as he moved to stand at my side and I eyed him curiously. He was a sniff taller than me, which was kind of annoying, but his thick brow and permanent scowl meant he couldn't come close to rivalling my looks in any other way, though I supposed he wasn't hideous to look at with his muscular build and strong jaw. He'd remained topless to combat the warmth of the room, and I eyed the bloody cut on his side with a twinge of irritation. It wasn't deep but it looked sore enough to hinder him for at least a few days. No doubt that would be put down against me too, despite the fact that it was his own damn fault that the guard had gotten so close to him.

"This is a good haul, Balthazar," Egos mused. "You did well."

I opened my mouth to protest the fact that I'd been the one to lift the jewels and all Balthazar had really done was seduce a woman who looked like a foot, which was hardly impressive at all, but I held my tongue. This was a test. I could see it in the set of Egos's shoulders. He was baiting me, daring me to contradict him, to claim he was being unfair and that I was owed more. Rule one of The Forty rang clear as day in my mind though. None of us were owed a single thing and only Egos could determine our value.

"Yeah, nice work, Balthazar," I agreed, giving him a taunting grin. "You really dug deep for this one. You plunged right in. Covered every pig-ugly base-"

"Enough," Egos growled and I promptly shut up.

Balthazar smirked at me and I forced myself not to roll my eyes. He'd still dipped his dick in that ugly wench so whatever way we looked at this, I was confident I was still coming out on top.

"What would you like as a reward?" Egos asked him.

"I'd like Tyros' old quarters and a bout in the ring with this one," Balthazar said, jerking a thumb at me.

Arsehole. He didn't give a shit about Tyros' old quarters, but he knew I had my eye on them. The room was bigger than mine and he had an actual mattress too. One that had been stolen from an upper Fae's mansion while he was in the room next door - if Tyros was to be believed.

"Done. But I was already going to put Drake in the ring with Argun as punishment for disappointing me," Egos said with a shrug of his huge shoulders.

I kept my face impassive but I did *not* want a bout in the ring with Argun. He was about eight times the size of me and had fists like goddamn hammers. I was no coward, but I liked my fucking face and I didn't want it pulverised by that arsehole.

"Maybe the two of us can go against him. Drake deserves a good kicking for what he did," Balthazar said and I knew he was referring to how long I'd left him with his cock inside the countess and not getting myself captured.

"Rules state it must be an even match," Egos murmured though he seemed tempted to let Argun and Balthazar beat the shit out of me two on one.

"Let him fight alongside Pip then," Balthazar suggested, his eyes twinkling maliciously.

I was actually beginning to look forward to going up against him and punching that look off of his face. Though I almost wanted to protest for Pip's sake, but I was already in trouble for standing up for the boy; putting myself between him and danger again would only stoke the flames of Egos's rage.

"Tempting... but the boy's face is already half ruined and it draws too much attention on the streets for a pickpocket. What of the man you brought back with you?" Egos suggested.

"The horse humper?" Balthazar asked, glancing over his shoulder towards Cassius. "Yeah, I could give him a kicking too. I don't like the look of him."

"He's a mark," I protested vaguely but the look in Egos's eyes told me I wouldn't be winning this argument.

"You know the rules. Any man who wishes to sleep here must be willing to fight for his right to stay. And with this sandstorm setting in I've no doubt he'll be sleeping here. Unless you'd rather I kill him?" Egos asked casually.

"Let him fight then," I shrugged. "Let's see what the blacksmith's got."

"Fetch him and send Mira to me. I don't like the way he's been looking at her," Egos said, his jaw working as jealousy flashed in his gaze and I dipped my head as I turned away. He always assumed the gang were looking to fuck Mira instead of the other way around. It was like he couldn't see how much she flaunted herself at us, trying to tempt us with her body and playing on her sexuality at all times. But if any of us looked at her too long, he'd gut us for it and none of us were that stupid. At least not openly.

Egos dropped the jewels I'd brought him into his pocket and I supressed a sigh, knowing he wasn't going to be giving me a fucking cut even though I was the only thief on that job who had actually scored some loot. But I guessed it wasn't all bad.

I'd been pretty sure that I'd end up in the ring tonight anyway, either with him forcing me in or of my own volition to release some of the pent-up rage inside me. So as far as punishments went, it really wasn't so terrible. Besides, I was quite looking forward to fighting alongside Cassius and I imagined Balthazar was about to get a shock when he realised just what this *blacksmith* could do.

Sucks to be you, arsehole.

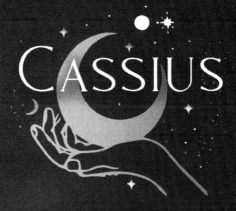

CASSIUS

CHAPTER NINE

Mira drew me up the stairs into a huge, dingy area which was clearly used for sleeping quarters, the space full of bunks with some clothing and personal possessions strewn about. She made her way to a large chest at one side of the open space and started sifting through clothes within it.

Someone had left a pail of water there for me with a rag and I started to wash, even though there was only the faintest scent of soap in it. I longed for the guards' bathhouse as I cleaned my bare chest as best I could, washing the burn on my side as I gritted my jaw through the pain of disturbing the scabbed flesh.

When I was done, Mira moved to me with some clothes in her grip, holding a pair of britches up to my waist to see if they'd fit. "Hmmm," she hummed. "Too small."

She dropped the britches then gripped my arm, her fingers circling as she bit into her lip and tried to caress a reaction out of me. Her body may have been appealing, her breasts nearly falling out of the cropped top she wore and her dark eyes full of the kind of lust I hadn't indulged in for a long time. But I wasn't going to be distracted by some thief in a den of sin. She could slide a knife in my back the moment I let my guard down.

"I might have something that'll fit you..." She draped her arms around my neck and I grunted as she ground her curves against me.

I gripped her hands, unlinking them and pushing her back, staring down at this tiny creature who really thought she could break the will of a royal guard. She wasn't deterred, plucking at the straps of her top so that it almost unveiled her breasts, her nipples pressing through the material as her eyes drank me in.

"Stop," I growled, elbowing past her to search through the piles of worn clothes. Did she really think I was going to fuck her? I was up to my neck in shit as it was. Screwing The Den leader's girl was a moronic idea, and I wasn't about to be baited into it.

"Poor blacksmith, did those royal arseholes beat you?" she purred, her breath on my back telling me she was studying the faded scars from the countless whippings I'd received in the past from Captain Marik. I recalled kneeling on the hard ground before him in the barracks, my tunic stripped from me while the other guards stood around to watch him teach me a lesson. Sometimes he'd bind my hands at the base of my spine too, make me feel small and defenceless, tearing away my control as well as my dignity. I despised that more than the whipping itself. Pain was tolerable, lack of control was not. But that, of course, was their goal. Marik wanted us to crave control, so that when we stood on our feet in one spot for twelve hours, we took pride in our ability to remain in position without flinching. He had forged us into men without hearts, or bladders, or cocks. When we were on duty, we stood guard without distraction, even when the simple needs of being Fae were physically painful to endure.

Though my scars reminded me of him, they reminded me of my strength too. They were a mark of all I'd endured, and in a way, they were what defined me now. Without them, I didn't know who I'd be. I wore them like armour and didn't flinch whenever someone's gaze fell on them. So it was easy to ignore the girl as I continued my search for clothes, and when I found a decent pair of trousers at last, I stood upright and changed into them. Mira's hands slipped around my waist and her fingers skimmed my waistband when I had them in place.

I caught her wrists with a grunt before she could push beneath the fabric and pushed her hands away. She gasped, reaching up to brush her hand over the spot behind my ear and I stilled, horrified by what lay under the pads of her fingers. My number. Two hundred and eighty-seven. The mark I'd had branded onto my skin the day I'd earned my position as a royal guard. I remembered the scent of burning flesh, the rigidity of my spine when I'd forced myself not to flinch from the pain. I remembered Marik's hand on my shoulder, squeezing as he claimed me as a new number among his ranks and his words in my ear, *"Only death will release you from your vows. Your life is pledged to the empire."*

"Holy shit!" she cried and I wheeled around, clapping a hand over her mouth and bearing down on her as my heart jolted in panic. *Fuck.*

She reached for a knife at her hip, but I snatched it from her, lifting it and holding it to her belly.

"You didn't see that," I hissed and she nodded weakly, her eyes glistening with fear. She was so small in my grip, I could have snapped her neck as easily as a blade of straw. I should do just that to keep this secret hidden. But she was just a girl, and the darkness of her eyes suddenly reminded me of my sisters.

"*Shit,*" I cursed, knowing I couldn't trust her not to tell, but before I could decide what to do, the door flew open and Drake strode in. He kicked the door shut again instantly, his eyes sweeping across my current situation. This didn't look good. And the second I released Mira, she was going to call out for my death.

"What's going on?" Drake asked casually, folding his arms and leaning against the closest bunk as he awaited an explanation. Mira's body was pressed to mine with the way I held her, and I didn't like the taint of suspicion in his eyes, like he was catching us in the act.

"She saw my guard number," I revealed and Drake released a huff of irritation.

"He's under my watch, Mira," he said, striding forward and placing a hand on her shoulder, drawing her gaze up to his.

He gave me a nod of encouragement, but I didn't release her. I wasn't going to get out of this place alive if they discovered I was a royal guard; they'd gut me worse than the prison guards would have.

I had two options: kill both of them and make a run for it, or see if Drake could get me out of this predicament. The first was riskier, but the second required me trusting the thief.

"Mira, if you tell Egos who he is I'll tell him what you and me did a few nights ago in my bed chamber. And last week. And the week before that," Drake said lightly, like admitting to fucking this woman was no big deal, even though he'd told me straight that she was owned by that monstrous looking man downstairs.

Drake took my wrist, but I refused to remove my hand from her mouth, seeing a scream in her eyes which I couldn't risk her releasing.

"Let her go, mate," he insisted but the tension in my muscles only grew. I eyed Drake, trying to place my faith in this man. Was I really going to put my life in the hands of a damn thief? Then again, hadn't I already done that by coming this far with him?

"You're valuable, Cassius. Guard or not. Only you know where that treasure is," Drake pressed.

Slowly, I retracted my hand from Mira's mouth and surprisingly, she didn't scream.

She looked between us, her lips pursing as her gaze halted on Drake. "You brought him here even though you know what he is?" she accused.

Drake shrugged. "He was in prison. Do you really think he's going to go running back to the palace to tell them where we are even if he did get out of here? They were torturing him in there. He had a death sentence. He's not a damn fool, are you?" He glanced at me and I shook my head firmly.

But I was a damn fool because I had come here with them. I should have run. Fuck my morality. What was my word worth if it landed me in here with these ruffians who could decide to kill me at a moment's notice?

Mira's eyes skated over my bare chest and the wounds marring my skin. "The royal guards are notoriously rough. It's all that pent up frustration, see?" She inched closer, a smile creeping onto her face again as she reached out to circle her fingers around my wounds. "Maybe I'll keep quiet...*if* he gives me a kiss." She turned to Drake for approval, though I was pretty sure it was my approval she needed. And she wasn't going to get it.

"Do it," Drake said bluntly and I scowled at him.

"No," I snarled.

"Do it or she'll tell." He shrugged. "Mira has a sex Affinity and she has needs. This is what will keep her quiet."

"There is no such thing as a sex Affinity," I refuted.

"Sure there is. I have one too. Fucking is like breathing to me, I just need to do it. And I'm damn good at it too, it's a gift I tell you. I can make a woman come within moments of sinking my cock into her-"

"I don't require the exaggerated details of your sex life, thief," I ground out, my gaze flicking between the two of them as Mira licked her lips, the look in her eyes saying Drake wasn't lying, but I still didn't believe in sex Affinities.

I looked to Mira with acceptance washing over me. It was that or die in this miserable cesspit. So one heartless kiss wasn't going to do any harm. Besides, despite my reluctance, she was pretty damn tempting. She was all supple curves and sultry looks, the kind of woman I would have chosen for a night when my appetites demanded I let loose and drove me to the local brothel. Though I rarely shared kisses with those women, the act too intimate for my liking. I preferred them face down and bending to the pleasure I delivered them while I unleashed weeks of unmet needs on their flesh. It had to be that way, a primal hunger sated, nothing more. Never more.

I leaned forward, meaning to get it over with fast as I thought of the motherfucker downstairs who would skin me for this, but she pressed a hand to my chest to stop me.

"Like you mean it," she urged and my scowl grew.

I was too aware of Drake standing there like an intrigued puppy dog as I snatched Mira's waist and dragged her flush against me.

My lips met with hers and I pressed my tongue into her mouth, holding her firmly. She moaned her approval as she held onto me, going limp in my arms and I kissed her more roughly, biting her lip and hugging her slim body against my muscles, dominating every inch of her mouth and giving her no chance to take a single ounce of control in this. When she was breathless, I pressed her back into Drake's arms and watched him grin at me like an arsehole.

Hell, the last time I'd kissed a girl like that I'd been caught and beaten for it. She'd been a maid in the palace; a pretty girl who'd shared looks with me for weeks. Quiet words had turned to breathy whispers. And one day I'd cracked. She'd begged for my touch, so I'd pushed her against the wall and nearly lost my mind with how much I'd missed a woman's touch, feeling wanted for the first time in so damn long. It had been just my luck that Captain Marik himself had caught me before I'd been able to hitch her skirt up and fulfil the demands she was whispering into my ear. Ten lashings every day for a week. He'd never been very imaginative with his punishments. That had been back in my training days before I'd mastered every whim and urge in my body. Nothing like that happened anymore. I didn't break unless I decided to break. No woman in this world held that power over me now. I could stand before the goddess of fertility herself and my cock wouldn't stir for her unless I bid it.

"Happy?" I demanded.

"Very," Mira laughed in glee, moving out of Drake's arms as he raised an eyebrow at me.

"Come on, you've got a date with the ring. You need to earn your place here," he said, as he nudged me towards the door.

I picked up a clean tunic, tugging it over my head before stepping past Drake as he waited for me to exit.

"Oh, hang on a second, mate." Drake slashed his dagger through the mark behind my ear and I swung around as pain spiked from the wound. I grabbed his collar in my fist, yanking him close as I bared my teeth, anger flaring through me.

"I had to cover it up," he said, shoving my hands off of him. "Unless you want someone else to spot it and gut you for it?"

I stood there for two more seconds, absorbing his words and deciding he was right as hot blood trickled down to my neck.

"Touch me like that again and I'll rip your lovely little face off and hang it on the wall," I warned.

"That'd make one helluva piece of art, mate. Fucking valuable, that'd be." He grinned, clapping a hand to my back as he steered me out of the room. I wasn't really fit for a fight with the wound on my side still burning, but if I had to prove myself, I needed to muster the strength to do it. It was the only way I was going to keep air in my lungs for the foreseeable future, and as I worked to compartmentalise the pain I was in, I found myself growing eager to harness my fighting Affinity once more.

"Just curious, but is that how you kissed the horse?" Drake murmured under his breath and I released a low chuckle.

"No, the horse liked it gentle," I muttered back and Drake let out a snort of amusement.

I'd never really met a man who appreciated my sense of humour. The Royal Guard were uptight and I'd been taught to be uptight too. But maybe here I didn't have to be, although my humour was definitely rusty around the edges from lack of use.

"None of your men have even questioned the logistics of screwing a horse," I said conversationally. "You do realise that would be a very difficult task."

"I guess they reckon you've got what it takes, Cassius." Drake's shoulder bumped mine as we walked, and I wondered if he had a charisma Affinity, because sometimes it was too easy to forget he was a ruthless criminal. Though remembering how he'd straddled me in the street with a knife to my throat was a sharp reminder that his smiles were not to be trusted. This man would probably smile while he bled me dry. Lawless Fae didn't tend to be fond of royal guards; two of my colleagues had been found with their heads cut off and thrown into a cesspit in the slums not so long ago. For all I knew, Drake could have wielded the blade that had done that, and I would be a fool to forget it.

We moved through the crowd of ruffians and arrived at a ring made from a steel chain running in a circle around five stone pillars.

Balthazar and a savage looking man were waiting there bare chested and primed for the fight. The rest of The Forty were gathering around the edges of the ring and I spotted The Den leader claiming the best spot for himself with Mira hanging from his arm and caressing his chest. I knew him by reputation alone. Egos. Blinded in one eye, but that didn't make him any less precise with a blade. There was a price on his head worth more than all the other men in this city. He was wanted for countless crimes and for setting himself up as a false king within the kingdom of the emperor himself, but no one had ever come close to catching him. He wasn't just a thief, he was a cold-blooded killer. And I had half a mind to wipe him from the face of the world if I hadn't been surrounded by enough men to kill me for it.

"Ah, the blacksmith," Egos purred with interest as Drake and I stepped into the ring, my new friend shedding his tunic and tossing it to the young boy who had been with us when we escaped the royal dungeon. My gaze caught on the intricate tattoos which continued across the rest of his exposed skin and something deep within my soul seemed to bristle in recognition of the designs, though I couldn't place them or understand any hidden meaning within them beyond that gut feeling.

"Are you willing to show your gall?" Egos pressed, drawing my full focus back to him.

I nodded, rolling my shoulders as I loosened up for the fight. I had years of skill under my belt, but I suspected men like this weren't going to spar with any honour. I wasn't going to lower myself to their standards though. This match would be won with my integrity intact or not at all. It was just the way I was made.

"Ready?" Drake muttered to me as he took his place at my side and I eyed the intricate designs of the tattoos which caressed his deep bronze skin, the curves and symbols wound into them drawing my attention in a way that was hard to tear my gaze from. They were coating all of the flesh which was on show, though each design stood alone, one on each of his pecs while a third covered his lower abs, disappearing beneath the waistband of his loose-fitting trousers. He had one on each of his biceps too and one on each forearm. They all held some similarity and yet were endlessly different from each other too, and I swear there was a taste of power about them so ancient that it reached out to caress the very fibre of my soul, drawing my mind to the stories of the Fallen.

"I'm ready," I agreed, pulling my gaze from his tattoos, leaving my own tunic on in hopes that it might protect my wounds a little, though I doubted it would do much to help the ache of them.

I raised my fists, planting my feet in the way I'd always been taught. A few of the surrounding men muttered and I dropped my shoulders, trying not to give away my obvious training, though it was damn hard to work against instincts that had been beaten into me for more than half my life.

"Fight!" Egos bellowed and I ran forward to meet Balthazar with adrenaline spearing through my blood.

As suspected, he went for my crotch, my eyes and my injuries all within the first few seconds. I avoided every blow, moving around him at speed and landing a sharp kick to his leg. He cursed, stumbling back and I used my momentum to uproot him with a harsh punch to his jaw. He hit the ground, but rolled smoothly, dancing upright like a light-footed pixie despite his size.

Balthazar's fist came out of nowhere, smashing against my cheek and sending my head wheeling sideways just before Drake dove on his back and bit into his shoulder like a feral animal.

Two meaty hands caught my neck as I moved to advance on Balthazar, and I reached back for my new opponent with a snarl of determination. I had already assessed him and could see his weaknesses clear as day. He was a giant with no grace at all to his attacks, putting all of his power behind his blows without any tactic beyond brute force. He was relying on his size alone, but that was a moronic thing to do against a skilled opponent.

Drake knocked Balthazar to the ground, pouncing on him and throwing punches into his face that would no doubt leave bruises visible for weeks to come, while taking blows to his sides which looked savage enough to break bones.

The giant heaved me backwards by the throat, locking his arm around me and trying to choke me out. I slammed my heel down on his foot and he roared in anger, his grip only tightening and a laugh leaving his lips as he assumed his victory. His confidence would only make my own win more satisfying though.

Something popped in my neck but I ignored the pain, reaching over my head and grabbing him by a fistful of his hair before using every ounce of strength I had to launch him forwards over my shoulder. He slammed into the floor on his back and I waited for him to get up, trained not to kick a man when he was down in a formal fight.

The look of surprise on his face turned to a mocking sneer as he got up and I raised my fists in preparation, my heart singing with the thrill of the brawl. This was one of the only times I felt alive, free. There was beauty in every blow, the pain, the blood and sweat. It was my purpose in life to fight like this and it made every year of near insufferable training worth it to do what I was born to do.

More muttering broke out and I wondered if I should just abandon my honour and fight like these lowlifes. But who even was I without that part of me intact? Surely no better than them. And I'd die before I gave up my integrity.

A bone-crushing punch came from the giant and I stumbled back from the impact of his knuckles to my chest. I almost lost my footing, but Drake suddenly braced me, having left Balthazar struggling to get up in a pool of blood on the ground. I planted a hit to the giant's temple that wiped the smug look from his face at last, then followed it up with a kick to the stomach that forced the breath from his lungs in a wheeze.

One final, knuckle-splitting punch to the giant's face toppled him and he crashed to the ground on his back, making my heart pound with my triumph. The adrenaline had made me numb to my injuries, but they were stinging now and the burn on my side screamed for attention I couldn't give it.

I raised my chin, looking to Egos to announce us the winners, but Drake pounced on the giant, continuing to pound his face as if the fight wasn't already won. He was an animal, smashing his fists into every inch of flesh he could find while his lips pulled back in a snarl, and his eyes seemed to darken to pitch. That wasn't the carefree man I'd met in that jail cell; this was a creature who was a part of the most nefarious gang in the whole of Osaria, and he was making one hundred percent sure this fight was finished.

I caught his arm, dragging him upright when he didn't seem inclined to stop. It wasn't that I gave a fuck about the beastly man left to waste on the floor, it just wasn't right to beat a man when he clearly wasn't about to rise again.

Drake wiped a line of blood from his brow then turned to me with a victorious smile. "They always get up again, Cassius."

"He was practically unconscious," I said with a tut.

"Key word *practically*, mate. I once got a knife in my arse from an almost-dead bastard, so I don't ever leave room for uncertainty when they go down anymore."

"Fair point," I murmured as we turned to face Egos.

I wasn't sure what I expected exactly. A smile? A raised eyebrow of intrigue? But The Den leader wasn't smiling and his eyebrows were dangerously low. He was staring at me with a knowing glint in his eyes too and my throat thickened, my muscles bunching as I saw my fate all too clearly in his eyes.

"Seize him," he snarled.

My pulse rioted and I backed up as five men came at me together.

"Hey – wait a second!" Drake called, trying to get near me as the men closed ranks and shoved him aside. He had a look of desperation in his eyes as he reached for me, but I had the feeling that had far more to do with the treasure I'd promised him than any fear for my life.

I raised my bloody knuckles, ready to take on everyone I had to to get out of here, even if it ended in my death. I'd rather die fighting anyway.

I am made of steel.

"He's no blacksmith. That man has training which reeks of the law," Egos spat. "Care to explain yourself, Drake?"

The men fell on me, but I wasn't going out that easy. Not when my life had been handed back to me along with my *purpose* to protect the kingdom.

I headbutted one of the arseholes and he stumbled to the floor as pain flared in my skull. The next one met the wrath of my fists but the final three were joined by more. A whole group wrestled me to the floor, wrenching my hands behind my back before forcing me to kneel at Egos's feet.

A tremor of rage rolled down my spine as I stared up at my maker, feeling just as I had a thousand times before on my knees in front of Captain Marik. Worthless. Just an inconvenience to be dealt with.

Egos held a knife to Drake's throat as he moved to stand at my side and the thief's jaw ticked with anger.

"He knows where a huge haul is, Egos. He's trading the secret of its location for his freedom from the royal dungeon. Don't be a fool. It doesn't matter who he is," Drake implored.

"Wrong...very wrong," Egos growled, lowering the knife from Drake's throat and hounding forward to gaze down his nose at me. "Who are you? Or should I say, *what* are you?"

I pursed my lips, figuring I could either lie now or tell the truth. Lies had placed Fae at the wrath of the gods before though, and though this man was no deity, he was certainly the ruler of my death in this moment. So I settled on the truth, my shoulders pressing back as I prepared to face the wrath my words would bring. But I was caught out and I wasn't going to spend my final moments as a coward lying like the Fallen had so many years ago.

"I am Cassius Lazar. Royal Guard of the seventh division. Number two hundred and eighty-seven in the legion." Silence reigned in the wake of my words and all that could be heard was the howling wind which battered the shuttered windows and a roaring noise that came with all the sand crashing over the city. "I am your only hope at finding a treasure hoard so large that you would never have to thieve again. And if you don't accept this one time offer, then I'm taking it off the table."

Egos stared at me for several long seconds before releasing a booming laugh. Others in The Forty joined in and I ran my tongue across my teeth as I glared up at their leader.

"You are in no position to bargain," Egos said eventually.

"I am the only one here who knows the way to the treasure. So go ahead and kill me, you lawless piece of shit, but your chance at getting your hands on it will die with me." I held my chin high and let him see in my gaze that I meant that with every ounce of my being. I would not cower to anyone. I was made to look death in the eye and walk willingly into its arms if I had to.

Egos regarded me with a thoughtful look, not seeming affected by my goading.

"You'll take him," he announced at last, his gaze on Drake. "Pick a crew and get the fuck out of my sight as soon as this storm clears. If you don't return with that treasure, I'll put a price on your head so high the crows themselves will be vowing to peck your eyes out for it."

At a nod from Egos, the men released me and I rose to my feet, fighting a wince from the wound on my side. I tried to shift into the mental state that would help me cope with pain easier, but three days of solid torture, little sleep and a fist fight with a bunch of thugs was starting to take its toll on me. I drew in a deep breath, forcing my mind to the most detached place I could reach. *I am made of steel.*

Egos strode towards me, gripping the back of my neck and resting his forehead to mine. "You're mine. You're not two hundred and eighty whatever anymore. You're number forty-one. And if you fuck with me, I'll spill your high-born guts all over the precious walls of that palace your kind love so dearly. But not before I find each and every member of your family, every one of your little lawmen friends, any dog that gave you so much as a friendly lick and kill the lot of them before your very eyes first. You hear that?"

"I hear you," I said through my teeth, fear and rage crackling in my chest at the thought of him laying a hand on anyone I loved. I'd do anything to protect my sisters, my mother, and though they were safe enough from most thugs where they lived in the fourth ring of the city, I knew this man before me was capable of reaching them if he discovered where they were. So I wouldn't do anything that put them in the firing line of this vicious arsehole.

He released me, turning to the room with a sadistic look on his face. "Teach him a lesson, boys."

So many men fell on me, I didn't have a moment to fight back as boots, knuckles and elbows slammed into my skin. I took every punch and kick with as much dignity as I could, my mind echoing with the punishments of my past. Captain Marik had had a fondness for getting the other guards to turn on one another whenever someone broke the rules. Spilling each other's blood at the order of our captain kept us from forming tight bonds between one another, and I guessed that made trusting other Fae far harder too.

There had been one boy I'd joked with back in the early days of my training called Sampson. We'd bunked side by side and urged each other on in training. Then one day Marik had ordered us to fight each other with our hands clad in chainmail gauntlets, the winner would be given longer rests and better meals for a week, while the loser would not eat during that time. The worst part was that he'd not fed us for two days prior to begin with, so over and over and over we pounded each other's flesh, fuelled by nothing but adrenaline and the primal need for food.

That fight had changed everything, drawn lines between us and Sampson hadn't spoken with me at all that week. Sometimes I wished I'd lost that fight, because one morning I stepped out of the barracks and found Sampson hanging from the flagpole with Captain Marik waiting there to give us a speech on willpower. It turned out, after a week of being starved, Sampson had stolen food from the palace kitchens and he'd been strung up for his crime.

I remembered the sickness in my gut, and the silent vow I'd made not to get close to the other men again. Marik had spoken words that day I'd never forgotten, and still haunted me now. *"If I order you to bleed, you will bleed. If I order you to kill, you will kill. If I order you to starve, you will starve. You are nothing but flesh and bone ruled by the law of the emperor, and if you thwart that law, I will order you to place a noose around your own neck, and I will order you to die."*

When the thieves had had their fill of bruising my body, I rose to my knees and glared at Egos with blood dripping from my mouth and the taste of hate on my tongue. The one thing their fists had served to do though was remind me I wasn't at Marik's command anymore. I had cheated death and was living on as a ghost in the underworld. I didn't have to do as I was told, I didn't have to lay down and accept a noose around my throat.

"What?" he growled at my expression.

"More please, arsehole." I tasted the metallic tang on my lips, revelling in the confusion on his face as I forced my mouth to bend into a smile.

It felt good pretending I enjoyed the bullshit people had put on me during the past few days, and I was rather liking my newfound freedom now that I didn't have to harness my tongue every five seconds. Marik would have whipped me raw for that, but this man didn't seem like the whipping type.

His brows lifted and a devilish grin hooked up his lips. "You want more, lawman?"

I nodded, sucking the blood from my teeth. I knew Fae like Egos. I'd been trained by one of them. And the only way to win was to never give them the satisfaction of letting them know you were beat. With Marik, that had meant biting my tongue and gritting my teeth through every ounce of pain he delivered me, but I didn't have to do that with Egos. I could look him in the eye and show him what a royal guard was made of. And it was cold, hard steel.

Egos strode towards me at a fierce pace, booting me in the jaw with a savage kick which made bone crunch. I hit the floor and stars burst before my eyes as agony crashed through my skull.

The gang leader leaned over me with a sneer on his face, the white of his blind eye glaringly bright. "Last warning. I always make good on my threats, Cassius Lazar. Are you willing to risk the lives of everyone you care about in your worthless life for the sake of defying me?"

By the Fallen, why the fuck had I given him my full name? Maybe there really was merit to lying in this world.

I sucked on the inside of my cheek, a large welt growing there from the battering I'd received.

"I'll behave," I growled, accepting my place in this transaction despite the bitter taste it left in my mouth. *Until I get out of your lunatic funhouse.*

Egos nodded stiffly before marching away and his voice called back to the gang as he stepped through a door. "You've placed your life in that dog's hands, Drake. I do hope it pays off for you."

CHAPTER TEN

I can hear the sea.

"Ooh, is it whooshy or crumbly today?" Maybe I should have gotten some stones to wash them while the waves were here? Nobody liked a dirty stone...

I ran my fingers through my purple hair, arching my back like a cat and almost remembering the touch of someone else's flesh against mine as I woke. But it was only the echo of a memory, and as I brushed my fingers down my body and willed away the clothes which shrouded me, I knew I'd lost my grasp on the sensation once again. I ached for the touch of another in the dark of my dreams all too often, but always awoke to find I couldn't recall how that truly felt. Perhaps that was the worst of my curse. But then again, the list of things I hated about this curse was endless, so I wasn't sure I could pick one which was worse than the others.

I straightened and willed a hazy orange glow to fill the space so that I could see the rest of my jail, my eyes trailing over the endless golden walls which surrounded me as I tried to decide if it was better in the dark where I could try to imagine some other surroundings.

With a sigh full of self-pity, I stepped into the pool of tears, the glimmering water washing over my toes and growing deeper as I waded out into it.

My nipples peaked and goosebumps rushed along my skin as the water bit at me, but I embraced the sensation, just pleased to feel that much against my needy flesh. I sometimes wondered if I might fade away one day, when my mind cracked so completely that I was nothing but a vessel as empty as the one I was trapped within.

It's not empty; you're in it.

I accepted that fact with a heavy heart, but it didn't feel like the truth. It *was* empty here. So very, very empty. And I didn't count because I wasn't anyone or anything anymore.

I turned my focus back to the pool of tears as I began to wash in the evidence of my own sorrow, cleaning my flesh with the years of pain I'd suffered through during my incarceration in this hell.

It was certainly handy for washing in though. I guessed I could have created my own water if my tears didn't linger here, but I never saw the point. The pool always glistened and sparkled like it was imbued with my magic, never darkening or seeming to hold even the slightest imperfection. And as much as my body shivered when I immersed myself in it, I always emerged feeling a little sharper, a little more like myself. As if the memories of all the things that had caused me to cry these tears sank back into my soul while I bathed in them and helped me grasp hold of the girl I'd once been. Just a little. A tiny fragment of a person I could almost remember. But that was so much more than I usually had so I welcomed it with all my heart. It would have been better if it wasn't so salty though.

I summoned some stones into existence and started scrubbing them, giving myself over to the task and polishing them with such vigour that my fingernails started to split and blood coloured the water around me.

It took me a few hours to realise they hadn't even been dirty to begin with and I sighed as I dropped them, watching them sink into the water before fading out of existence as I willed them away again.

I clicked my fingers and the sun appeared above me. It was darkest black with wriggling tentacles which reached out to skim my shoulders. I groaned as I tipped my head back to it, closing my eyes and bathing in the feeling of the tentacles against my skin. Oh, how I missed the touch of another. This was the closest I could ever really get, but using my magic was only a small step away from using my own hands, so it still wasn't enough.

Wrong. So, so wrong, I can't even bear to look at the mess of it.

I frowned at the black sun and realised I was right. The tentacles should have been purple like my hair. Silly. Rookie mistake. I blinked at it and the tentacles turned purple.

"Much better," I said aloud and my voice bounced back to me, but it sounded mocking instead of admiring.

If we can't kill your body, then can't I die at least? Chop me up, bake me in a pie, set me on fire and dance on the pieces. Just let me not exist anymore!

"Would you like a pie then?" I asked, pouncing on the single thing in that request that I might actually be able to give myself.

I clapped my hands and a huge seashell appeared full of pinecones. I frowned. Even *I* knew that was wrong. I was losing my grip on reality more and more each day and I knew it only had to be a matter of time before I was broken beyond repair. And some days I couldn't decide whether I should be terrified of that or embracing the idea, hoping for it to come sooner rather than later just so that I could be free of this eternal nothingness.

I don't want a pie or any terrible estimation of one. I want to die. Cut my throat. Set me on fire. Stab, stab, stab me. Feed me to a horse-

"Now who's being ridiculous? You know horses only eat melons," I said, rolling my eyes.

That's dogs.

"Oh yeah. Dogs eat melons and yeast."

At least you remember something *real for once.*

I smiled at the almost praise and clasped my hands together as I closed my eyes. If I really concentrated then it almost felt like I was holding someone else's hand instead of my own. Kind of. If I was remembering it right. Which I probably wasn't.

I sighed heavily again and opened my arms wide before allowing myself to fall backwards into the pool of tears with a splash that sent water flying up to cover every golden surface around me.

I floated there for a few minutes, or hours, or days – never could be certain anymore – then let my purple hair grow and grow around me as it absorbed all of the water until I lay on a mound of saturated hair.

I took a deep breath. Then another. Either this prison of mine wasn't fully sealed, or I didn't need to breathe anymore. I must have used up the oxygen ten thousand years ago. Or twenty minutes ago. I was probably just breathing nothing. Maybe there was nothing in here to breathe except sunlight. I didn't seem to be able to die in any way that I should have, so I guessed I couldn't suffocate either.

Was it night outside? Or day? Sometimes I thought I could see light shimmering through the wall of the eternal enclosure, and convinced myself it was real, but then I realised that I couldn't. The only light in here was the light I created. Orbs of every colour hanging all around the roof which locked me in. Sometimes I turned them off and sat in the dark for a few years.

There were monsters in the dark. Sure, I'd created them myself and even when they ate me, I didn't actually die, but they were still terrifying, and it was still all kinds of agony to feel them ripping me apart as they devoured me. Sometimes I wondered why I did that. Why did I create things with the sole purpose of terrifying myself?

Because fear is the only thing that reminds us we're still alive after all this time.

"Oh yes. You always did have a better memory than me," I admitted, shivering a little as I lay there on all of my soaking hair, my naked skin peppered with more goosebumps than I could ever count. I knew because I'd tried it once or twice. I always lost count around my arse or my ears or even my toes.

And you always were a batshit crazy psychotic bitch. It was just that no one noticed until you killed the emperor.

That was perfectly plausible. Why couldn't I remember my sister's eyes, but the memory of plunging that knife into his back was just as fresh as if it were yesterday? Maybe it *was* yesterday. I'd lost count again anyway, so it was a definite possibility. But whatever way, even though I'd forgotten most things or muddled them up with my imaginings, I'd never forgotten that.

The perfect timbre of his scream when my blade cut into him. The amount of strength I'd had to use to force the blade between his ribs and how good it had felt to do it. The warm splatter of his dark red blood painting my skin, coating my face, dripping in my hair and colouring my lips. I'd licked those lips and tasted his death on them, and it had been so fucking sweet.

I remembered how his screams got louder then softer as I stabbed and stabbed and stabbed. Until they were so soft that they were whimpers and he was begging. Begging me to stop. But he didn't stop when he killed my sister. Killed her because she wouldn't go to his bed willingly. So I went to his bed instead. With a knife and a promise. And I stabbed him while he slept. Before he even knew I was there.

I'd been willing to go further if I had to, I would have even let him desecrate my body if that was what it took. He could have fucked me like a whore and the moment he was done, so very pleased with himself for his conquest, I would have cut his throat and watched him bleed out. But I hadn't had to do any such thing. It had been so beautifully easy. I'd just prayed to Herdat, the goddess of death and destruction to aid me in my quest and I had felt the touch of her power within me as she helped me tread the path of evil, helped lead me into his chambers and had given me all I needed to set me on the path of blood and carnage.

I hadn't felt my soul crack or shift, I hadn't for a moment regretted taking his life, because my soul was destroyed when he stole my sister from me. So sacrificing my purity had been nothing at all in payment for his end. And when the guards came running to his aid, it was far too late. I was dressed head to toe in an outfit of his blood. Red as the dawn and calling out my sister's name as I offered her his tarnished soul in sacrifice. Herdat's power had flared brighter then, the urge to kill rising in me once more as she offered me the power I would have needed to do it, to become her creature and rip the lives from every guard who came to arrest me.

But I'd refused her, some small part of me remembering the girl my sweet sister had loved and knowing it would be no tribute to her to become a monster. Perhaps that was why I had ended up cursed this way. For turning my back on the gifts of a god when they'd been offered to me.

I'd expected the guards to kill me. I hadn't cared. I'd gotten justice for my sister, and I had nothing left to live for without her anyway. Of course, fate had a much crueller destiny in mind for me in the end.

I'd been placed into the hands of the painted man, his skin so covered in ink that his features were lost within the magnitude of colours. Some claimed he was a true diviner of the will of the gods. Others that he worked only for the darkest of powers and most selfish of desires. I didn't know. But once he got his hands on me, everything I had once been was soon stripped away. I was shackled and chained and bound to this life, this curse. A slave to the masters of my prison whether I wanted to be or not. They called me *The Blessing*. But what did that even mean? I might have known once, but not anymore.

Now, I was all powerful and all nothing. No one. Forgotten. Forever.

There was a time that I'd been a treasure coveted above all others, but I'd long since fallen into the legends lost to time itself. I doubted anyone remained who remembered me now or who knew how to make use of my curse.

"Oh, how I miss the rain," I murmured but as my voice echoed back to me it sounded like a weird question instead of a statement. Perhaps silence was better than hearing my own despair so often and yet the silence grew so suffocating that sometimes I had to scream if only to break it.

Shut up.

I couldn't just tell me to shut up. It was so rude. I was going to tell me where to stick my lack of manners...but I was kind of afraid of myself...so I just did as I was told and shut my mouth. For a few hours. Or days. Hard to say.

Eventually the lights went out and the monsters returned. I'd stayed quiet, but I didn't care. I wanted to punish me for thinking about that time again. About the murder I'd committed and how much I'd enjoyed it despite the cost it had eventually come at. And about the fact that no matter how long I'd been in here, no matter how much I forgot, I'd never, ever feel bad about what I did to that bastard. I actually felt pretty damn good about it. It was the one thing that never faded, the one truth I could always rely on entirely. He was dead and gone and cast to dirt, and the blade I had used to do it had ripped his rotten soul from his corpse and made sure it fractured and split into nothing but ash and ruin, never to reach the afterlife, never to find peace. He would forever be nothing and I felt really fucking good about that.

You're such a damn psychopath. No wonder they locked us in here and forgot about us. Who would want you anyway? Not me, not that I get a choice in the matter.

I *was* a psychopath. But I didn't mind because there was power in death, and I had owned that once. And at least since I'd lost my mind in here, I had someone to talk to. That fractured, bitter piece of my own soul which had split away from the rest of me out of nothing but self-loathing. Even if she did hate me. And was suicidal. And insulted me all of the damn time. That was okay. Because at least I wasn't alone. I still had myself.

Or was that what alone meant? Shit, now words were starting to lose their meaning. What would I be left with then? Just burbling nonsense in a pool of tears which could never wash me clean of my sins.

A deep growl echoed from the darkness on the far side of the coin and my heart started pounding as glimmering red eyes appeared before me.

I swallowed a lump in my throat, knowing I had created this creature from the darkest, most damaged pieces of my own psyche, and yet I was still unable to banish it. Unable to run in the prison that held me. Unable to fight despite my eternal strength. Because this beast was born of my own fears and imbued with the strength and endless bloodlust that it found in me. Perhaps if I had repented for the life I'd taken, then these creatures wouldn't hold such power. But I wasn't sorry, and I never would be.

So as the beast advanced on me across the pool of tears, its scaly body slithering into the water and sending ripples racing across it which sounded like a thunderclap to my ears. All I could do was remain there and wait for it to come for me.

There had been a time when I used to fight the monsters which lived within my own mind. I'd created powerful weapons and duelled against them, cutting them down and screaming my refusal to fall prey to their hunger. But those endless days of fighting seemed pointless to me now. I'd never won against them. It always ended in my demise.

So I waited in the dark and held my breath, wondering if it might stop the creature from finding me, but as a low and deadly growl sounded from a few feet away, I knew it would never work.

And as its weight crashed down on me and huge fangs punctured my flesh, I let myself scream. I screamed and screamed until my agony was colouring the walls and blood was filling the pool of tears as I was ripped apart piece by piece, feeling every chomp and bite, living on in torment throughout it all.

My heart pumped and thrashed, and adrenaline crashed through my veins as my body begged me to save it from this fate despite my mind already knowing how useless that fight was.

I was right though. Fear really did make me feel alive.

But I still wished I was dead instead.

DRAKE

CHAPTER ELEVEN

As the rest of The Forty rounded on Cassius with scowls, I placed a hand on his shoulder and steered him through the mayhem towards the stairs. I parted the heavy red rugs which hung over the staircase in an attempt to block out some of the noise from the men on the bottom floor, and Cassius thankfully followed without complaint.

I didn't release him until we'd stomped up the narrow stone staircase, emerging from the dark onto the second floor where the gang slept. We remained quiet as we passed the rooms which held the bunks, each of the large spaces sleeping ten or more men at a time – my personal idea of hell. The nights I'd been forced to endure in one of those stinking rooms filled with sounds of men snoring, farting and generally being disgusting oafs were some of the worst I could remember. And I was a damn street kid.

Sure, I'd appreciated the four walls and the roof over my head, but sleeping in close quarters with the violent kinds of men who made up The Forty had never been a relaxing experience. I'd worked hard to earn myself a spot of my own, and between that and the haven I'd created for myself up on the rooftops, I managed to find some semblance of peace from time to time.

We kept going until we reached the far end of the long corridor where my quarters were, and I glanced about to check for any unwanted nosy fuckers lurking nearby before shoving Cassius inside.

"Have you ever actually been in a brawl?" I asked angrily as I threw the door shut behind us.

I didn't often lose my temper, but I was feeling pretty fucking close to it now. I trod a fine line with Egos at the best of times, my unshakable, mirthful disposition and my pretty face pissing him off almost daily – though he endured his irritation over both on account of all the loot I claimed for the gang.

Right now, I should have been sitting happy in Tyros' old quarters with a stomach full of food and Egos praising my name over those jewels I'd lifted, and yet everything kept going wrong. I was in the fucking doghouse and Cassius had gone and given the damn game away at the first opportunity. Why the fuck had I been tempted to trust an honest man? I was starting to doubt this was ever going to be able to work out.

Cassius raised his chin at the implied insult, snarling his response at me. "I have been trained to be the best warrior that I am capable of-"

"That bullshit isn't real," I snapped, cutting him off before I had to listen to him prattling on about fighting with honour or something equally disturbing. "If a man comes at me with a knife and he has the full intention of sticking it in me, then I will absolutely kick him in the balls if I have to. I'd also spit in his eye, call his mother a whore and throw sand in his face – whatever the fuck it takes to win. And so should you. Honour will only get you killed on the streets." I rubbed a hand over my face in exasperation and tried to shake off my irritation, but my adrenaline was still pumping from the fight, and it was proving damn hard to do.

"It goes against everything I was ever trained to be," Cassius growled.

"Well buckle up, noble boy, because now we really are in for it. Egos wants that treasure and if he doesn't get it then don't go thinking he's bluffing. That man lives to kill. And I was doing pretty well at avoiding his wrath until you came along."

I turned away from him, not able to bear the horrified look in his eyes at the idea of him lowering himself to become more like me. But if he wanted to survive this place then he had better do it. Fast.

I moved to the side of my room and pulled the small desk there aside before lifting a floorboard and grabbing the bottle I'd stashed under it, taking a hit of the hard liquor to try and calm my nerves before I lost my shit entirely.

Cassius sighed and dropped down to sit on my cot, looking like a fish out of water with his spine straight and brow lowered in thought. Did he ever just...relax? His posture looked like it was being held in place by the hand of a god. What did he think would happen if he slouched a bit?

I took a blade from beside the bed and handed it to him. It was nothing flashy like I was sure he was used to, and the wooden handle was well worn, but it was a sharp little fucker and it had gutted a man or two in the past.

"What's this for?" he asked as he weighed the blade in his palm like a pro. It was a decent weapon but not one of my best. I wouldn't be handing out anything I valued highly to him or anyone else. I'd learned a long damn time ago never to trust anyone with anything I couldn't bear to lose.

"I'm not too sure the gang like the idea of a royal guard being amongst us," I pointed out, just in case the arse kicking he'd just taken alongside suffering the brunt of Egos's fury hadn't been enough to clue him in. "That's so you've got a chance to defend yourself if anyone comes to kill you while you sleep."

"Aren't you going to lock the door?" he asked, though he didn't seem afraid of the prospect of a cutthroat appearing to stab him while he slept, so I had to assume he was confident he could handle that.

"Egos's rules; no locks. Not much point in a place like this anyway as there isn't a lock that someone here can't pick, but we live under a blanket of mutual respect. Which basically means we all work hard to be sure that none of the others would dare risk stealing from us for fear of their lives. And if any of us *does* steal from another, it's up to us to sort our own shit out by either stealing it back or making a challenge in the ring."

"Cosy," Cassius muttered dryly and I smirked. I guessed this was a far cry from the guards' barracks he was used to. He'd probably had snuggly little blankets and teddy bears for company in those.

"No one has dared to try and steal anything from me in over a year, so you're probably safe," I added, shrugging as I took another hit of the alcohol and sat the bottle down on the desk. "But you never know."

I was finally finding an inch of calm inside myself between the booze and my settling heartrate, and I glanced down at myself, taking account of what injuries I'd sustained while rubbing at the blood which speckled my knuckles. I had more than enough coin stashed away to take a visit to the local bathhouse to clean myself properly, but I'd have to wait until the damn sandstorm passed before I could.

"The way you were hitting that man was unnecessary," Cassius murmured and I looked up to find his gaze on the blood which coated my hands too. "He was already on the floor, you didn't have to-"

"Argun is a mean bastard who would have happily caved my head in given half the chance. Once we had him down, there was no way in hell I was going to let him back up. Besides, he hit me in the fucking face." I touched a hand to my jaw where the bastard had landed the blow, feeling the bruise there with a hint of irritation. I was half tempted to go find Argun and beat him for it again.

"You were literally pulverising *his* face, you can hardly be annoyed at him for striking you once?" Cassius scoffed in confusion, but there wasn't a thing that was confusing about it.

"Argun is ugly as sin. Hitting his face might actually improve it. Hitting mine should be a crime." I arched a brow at Cassius as he snorted a laugh.

"Oh, so it's a vanity issue?" he jibed.

"Sure, I'm vain," I agreed easily. "But I can tell you now without a hint of a doubt that this face of mine is my most valuable commodity, it has earned me a hell of a lot more coin than you can imagine."

"Ah, I see. You're a whore," he stated with a knowing nod and my jaw slackened.

"No, I'm not a fucking whore. I'm picky about who I bed and wouldn't want to sell myself to any old duck who came looking to get her world shattered by my cock. But there are a whole host of Fae who get all too easily distracted by my face and give me the opportunity I need to rob them blind, that's all. Besides, girls get wet at the mere sight of me, so I'm never gonna complain about something that gets so many of them hitching their skirts up now, am I?" I shrugged at Cassius and he shook his head at me, but he couldn't deny the truth of those words so he made no attempt to try.

I dropped my britches and kicked them into a corner with the vague intention of paying someone to clean them for me at some point. Pip would likely do it if I filled his belly with something decent.

"Do you want privacy? I'm not sure what way you all...conduct yourselves," Cassius said with a look of uncertainty about him as I continued to strip.

"Am I making you blush or turning you on?" I teased as I kicked off my underwear too and headed in search of something clean to wear. "Because I'm sorry to disappoint, but no matter how much you stare at my cock, it won't be hardening for you, lawman. I'm hopelessly addicted to fucking beautiful women and you're too damn brawny for my tastes."

"Hilarious. Has anyone ever mentioned how full of yourself you are, thief?"

Cassius turned his dark eyes to the blade in his hand as I moved about the room as naked as the dawn. Growing up on the streets had made sure I was precious about very few things in this life and showing my body certainly wasn't one of them. When you were too poor to use the bathhouse, you had to join the free-for-all in the river. And I'd seen naked flesh of every shape and size in each gender. It didn't bother me one bit to show mine. Modesty was a privilege the upper Fae liked to claim, but it wasn't something we could afford where I came from. Of course, cleaning myself in the river had grown even less appealing to do since those dead kids had started washing up on the riverbanks.

"It has been pointed out once or twice," I replied as I pulled on fresh underwear and a pair of black britches which hung loose around my legs. I left my chest bare because it was as hot as a volcano's arsehole in here, and with the storm raging outside we wouldn't be opening any windows any time soon. "But not by anyone who could truthfully say I didn't have reason to be."

Cassius turned to look at me and his gaze slid over my face for a moment before he shrugged. "Well, it's obvious how much your looks mean to *you* anyway," he said eventually, unable to deny the obvious appeal of my face though he didn't seem to think it mattered much. He was wrong there.

"Let me guess," I said, dropping down onto my bed and laying back with my hands behind my head so that he was forced to turn and look at me. "Your mommy and daddy loved you?"

"Yes," he replied with a faint frown.

"So they fed you? Clothed you?"

Cassius nodded, frowning slightly as he failed to understand where I was headed with this.

"Educated you?"

"Yes..." He clearly had no idea what I was implying, and I rolled my eyes.

"My mother was a whore and my father was a cutthroat," I said bluntly.

164

"Is that so?" he asked, his gaze shifting with something which looked awfully like sympathy, and I had to resist the urge to roll my eyes. This wasn't a pity party; it was a life lesson.

"No. Well, maybe, I guess. I have no idea." I shrugged. "I was dumped at an orphanage when I was a few days old and I stayed there until I was six. At which point they deemed me old enough to fend for myself and turfed me out to make room for a new squalling brat. Now, as someone who knows nothing of hunger, you probably don't realise quite how difficult food is to come by when you are smaller than everyone else on the streets, have no money and have no way to earn any."

"So you started stealing?" he guessed, his voice tinged with pity, but I wasn't hunting for that, he just needed to stop with the superiority bullshit and understand that things were different here. We were a whole world away from his palaces and white walls, easy meals and a comfortable life, and he needed to figure that out fast.

"No. Well, yes, obviously. But I also discovered the strangest thing. The other street kids would go begging from the kitchen maids at the big manor houses like the one you no doubt grew up in, and most times they'd be chased off or perhaps they'd grab a few scraps from the pig pens if they were lucky. But one day, I'd had a wash in the river, so I was nice and clean, and I went begging on my own - purely by chance. This woman opened the door and fell still as her gaze landed on me, I offered her a nervous smile and she went and smiled right back. She looked me up and down and I'll never forget the words she spoke because they changed my damn life."

"What did she say?" Cassius asked with real intrigue in his eyes.

"She said 'well aren't you the sweetest looking little thing?' and she gave me half a loaf of bread and a huge hunk of cheese without a scrap of mould on it either. I was so fucking shocked that I just stared at the feast she'd delivered to me so easily and I said thank you, like a proper little noble boy. It simply fell from my lips because I was skin and bone and I'd been eating nothing but old crusts and kitchen scraps for weeks, and this woman had offered me up a meal like I was actually worth something, like she really fucking saw me. She smiled even brighter at my manners then she ducked back into the kitchen before returning and giving me a goddamn cake too. I'd never eaten anything like it, it was sweet and delicate and so fucking delicious, and I can tell you nothing has ever tasted so good since. I thanked her again with tears in my eyes at the feeling of my belly being full for the first time in as long as I could remember, and then she did the strangest thing; she cupped my cheek and said 'a beautiful face like yours should never go hungry.'" I arched a brow at Cassius and understanding filled his gaze.

"So your looks helped you to survive?" Cassius asked, cottoning on to what I was saying.

"They didn't just help me. They're the *reason* I survived," I corrected. "So maybe I'm a full of myself piece of shit. But this face opens doors for me. If I lost my place among The Forty, I guarantee I could find a place in a noble household if I was willing to fuck a lonely countess for it. Looking like me has saved my life more times than I can count. So if some big bastard punches me in the face, he might as well be cutting off my legs because my face is how I stay alive in this messed up kingdom. And the day I don't look like this anymore will likely be the day I die. Unless Egos kills me now of course. Thanks to you."

There was a beat of silence and I frowned at Cassius, hoping he wasn't about to go all emotional on me. I wasn't opening up to him out of any reason other than boredom. We were stuck here until the storm passed and we could head off after this mystical treasure he claimed to have access to, and I had even more riding on him not being full of shit now than I did before.

"You may have just as much reason to hate Magdor as I do," Cassius said eventually, his voice laced with hatred for the empress. "The emperor was just about to fund more orphanages. He had a plan for schools for the underprivileged and food banks for those most in need. I was there when he was discussing ways to counteract poverty in the slums and the outer rings of the city. There were schedules being drawn up for Fae with healing Affinities to come and offer free medical attention, plans for building expansions to take place to create proper housing to combat the overcrowding and shanty towns. He wanted to do so much for the poor of his kingdom, and I was so excited to watch it all come together. But then *she* came along."

"What difference would that make to me?" I asked with a frown, unsure what he was getting at.

"Surely you'd want to see the kingdom made better? The emperor had so many great plans before she arrived in Osaria. Wouldn't you want to witness a day where no other orphans had to live through the poverty you endured?"

I barked a laugh. "Why should I give a shit what some mangy orphans have to endure? Some new orphanage won't do shit to help me now – I very much doubt they cater for men in their mid-twenties with thieving addictions."

"Because you just told me that you-"

"That I found a way out of it. Weren't you listening?" I pointed at my face and gave him a wide smile to show off my dimples.

"I know that worked for you but there are countless orphans who aren't so lucky, and wouldn't you want them to have more of a chance than you did?" he asked, seeming angered by my indifference.

"Why?" I asked incredulously.

Cassius stared at me like I'd just spoken a foreign language, but he was the one who wasn't fucking getting it.

"Rule number one now you live on the streets," I said, pointing at him. "Look out for yourself and no one else. Friends are all well and good, but they'll get you dead if you put yourself at risk for them."

"I'm not talking about friends, I'm talking about bettering the lives of our people. You can't seriously not care?" Cassius growled and I could tell he was kinda horrified by what I was saying, but he was right, I didn't care. He didn't come from here. He hadn't grown up on these streets and figured this shit out the hard way. He hadn't begged for scraps only to have some bigger, meaner kid beat the shit out of him to steal those scraps for themselves. He'd never slept in a doorway or had to run from the twisted motherfuckers who lived down by the river's edge when they tried to catch him for their fucked-up games.

He'd certainly never endured the agony that I had when I'd been taken by that oh so holy priest. When he'd forced his vile magic into my flesh with needle and ink, marking my body like it was a canvas he had free access to despite my screams for mercy. When you were made to endure the worst Fae kind had to offer, it made it damn hard to try and look for the best in people, especially when survival was the sole focus of your existence every day. So he could give me his judgmental looks and he could think of me as a monster, but that was just because he was a privileged bastard who had lived a charmed life, so he couldn't possibly understand the agony of mine. He had no idea what life was going to be like for him now that he was down here in the dirt with the rest of us, and the sooner he faced up to it, the better. But it wasn't my problem. He'd figure it out for himself soon enough.

"Do me a favour, mate," I said as I shuffled down the bed and closed my eyes. "Sell me this holier than thou shit in a month when you've actually lived in the world you think you can change. I guarantee you'll be a selfish bastard just like me by then. Or dead. Either way, I doubt you'll still be spouting idealist bullshit at me about the poor orphans down the street, because you'll be too caught up in trying to keep your own arse alive to give a single fuck about them."

Cassius remained quiet as I settled myself in to sleep. I guessed he'd just figured out that I wasn't as nice as I seemed, but that was fine by me. He didn't have to like me. He just had to make me rich.

CASSIUS

CHAPTER TWELVE

D rake didn't stir again as he kept his back to me in his cot, though the way he shifted every now and then told me he wasn't sleeping peacefully, if he was even asleep at all.

His words were stirring beneath my skin as I went over what he'd told me, and what he'd assumed of me too. I could have told him that my life wasn't some fairy tale where I slept on a plump mattress, surrounded by a feast of food and ale whenever I wished for it. My shack les may have been dipped in silver, but they were no less real than the shackles of the poor. Though I didn't envy him or any of these men for the hardships they had no doubt endured on these streets. While they were struggling to be heard by the emperor, stripped of their right for food and comfort by the unfortunate fate of being born to a street girl, I was handing my rights over to the crown, my life stripped of all things the men in this building craved. I was taught to live modestly, any coin I earned was mostly sent home to my mother. The few hours I was given off duty were meant for rest in preparation for further duties.

I had been beaten for drinking until one day ale tasted like blood on my tongue and I could no longer stomach it, I had knelt at the feet of my captain alongside four other guards whom I'd been secretly playing card games with in the barracks, betting metal bottlecaps with each other to pass the free time we were given, and Marik had forced me to swallow every one of the bottlecaps before being left there with my wrists bound to my ankles for twenty four hours. So no, I didn't know what it was like to fend for yourself in the slums of Osaria, but I did know what it was like to suffer, even if it was a privileged kind of suffering.

I kept the knife in my grip as I shut my eyes, laying rigidly on my back on the floor, the floorboards hard beneath the thin blanket I'd placed there, but I'd slept in less comfortable spots. It wasn't that which was keeping me awake, it was the sound of a hundred thieves shifting around in this place, the echo of drunken laughter carrying from downstairs, the heavy thud of footfalls and the clink of concealed knives which could rip a man's throat open with one slice. It was the moans of pleasure from women far less inhibited than any I'd ever known and the grunts of the men enjoying their company so openly without an ounce of shame.

The shuttered window on the back wall of the room rattled as the wind blew heavily against it, and the familiar sound of the sand crackling against the wood alongside the jangle of the windchimes out in the streets brought me back home for a moment. My sister Fatima would be singing, and Mother would cheer her on despite the pitchiness of some of the notes, while Lyla would beg her to stop and the others would laugh. I'd be in the cellar practicing with my father's old sword, a small pillow strapped around the blade by my mother for fear of me cutting my own hand off. I had trained more rigorously after he had died, the pain in my heart over losing him always spilling into a need for brutality harboured within my fighting Affinities.

And while I practised, Ma-mar would come to me with tea, kiss me on my cheek and call me her little Rahr before speaking of how proud she would be when I joined the royal forces in my father's place. Looking back on it now, I knew she had been afraid. Upper Fae or not, women were not often the sole keepers of their own households, and as the only male in the family, I had needed to claim a position of authority in Osaria as soon as possible to ensure our house wasn't seized from her.

Captain Marik had come to the house often after Father's death, and I'd always felt this creeping sense of dread whenever he'd been there. I didn't like to think on those days much, because when I did, I saw them through a man's eyes instead of a boy's who was only verging on adolescence. And I knew all too well what I hadn't known back then.

"Shh, please, you'll wake the children," Mother's voice carried from down in the garden as I sat on the balcony at the back of the house in the shadows.

I crept forward, keeping low and pushing my dark hair away from my face as I knelt at the edge of it and peeked through the gap in the railing.

Marik was a large man and he towered over my mother as he stood before her, her back against the old lemon tree at the centre of the yard. He came over here a lot lately, sniffing around my mother like a dog looking for scraps, but I didn't know what it was he was after. I did know that I didn't like him. He barely spoke two words to me or my sisters, and when he did they were always sharp, commanding or disciplinary.

His hand caressed her face and she shivered, or maybe it was a tremble, because she caught his wrist and pulled it away from her. My mother was beautiful, the kind of beauty people commented on in the streets. Our neighbour Sandrine always joked she should cover her face to give the other women a chance. I didn't like Sandri, she shouted at us over the wall that divided our gardens whenever me and my sisters made too much noise.

"I can be quiet," Marik purred, his hand going to her breast and squeezing, making my nose wrinkle. She pushed his hand away again, but he caught hers this time and stepped closer, so close I had to strain my ears to hear his next words. "Your husband's orgery is about to run out. What will you do then?"

I knew that word, Mother often mentioned it. When my father had died, he'd left some money in his will to the emperor which meant Mother could keep living here. There was some stupid law that meant women couldn't own property, but now there was only a couple of months left until the orgery ran out. Unless the payment was made again, our home would no longer be ours, and from what Mother had said, she couldn't afford to pay it.

"I'll figure it out, and when my children are old enough, they will be able to provide what is needed. My daughter Imani will no doubt make quite the seamstress, she has already shown the Affinity for it," Mother insisted.

Marik chuckled in a dark, forbidding way that made my spine prickle with dislike. "She would do better to marry and start providing heirs to a man of good inheritance when she comes of age."

"I teach my daughters to provide for themselves first and foremost, Marik," Mother said firmly, but as he inched closer again, she seemed to shrink. Father wouldn't have liked this; he'd have placed himself between Marik and my mother and told him to go. I'd tried to do that before, but Marik had warned me not to make trouble with lawmen and Mother had made me promise not to do it again.

"A pretty idea, yes, but an unrealistic one. You're going to be in such trouble soon, and I am so terribly concerned for you. Do you know what will happen when your husband's orgery runs out?"

"Yes, of course I do. But we'll manage," Mother hissed, raising her chin.

Marik lifted a hand, tugging a lock of her raven hair between his fingers and caressing it like he owned it. "No...I don't think it has truly sunk in, my sweet. You see, the day the orgery runs out, the court will send a clerk here to collect the next payment. And when you cannot deliver it, your house will be reclaimed by the emperor. And where will you go then, love?"

"I have some coin, I'll find somewhere," Mother said firmly, though something in her voice made me fear she wasn't being totally honest. And that made my heart judder uncomfortably. Were we going to lose our home? "Besides, Cassius will come of age in just a couple more years, then he will join the Royal Guard and earn plenty of coin."

"A couple more years?" Marik gasped. "And what will happen during that time? You have no Affinities which earn you coin, you have nothing but a fruitful womb, and what good has that been to you but delivering you child after child before your husband up and left-"

"He died in duty, Marik," Mother growled as my jaw gritted from his words. "As you well know. Or was he not your friend as you claimed?"

"You know he was," Marik conceded, still stroking her hair in a way that I didn't like at all. "It still pains me to think of the day I had to deliver that news to your door, my sweet."

Mother's eyes welled with emotion and she dipped her head to hide it. Even after all these months, I was sure she still loved my father, and it made me sad to think she was never going to heal from losing him. I wasn't sure I would either. Our pain was shared and always burning.

"Look, I don't want to upset you. In fact, I want to offer you a solution." Marik inched closer again and Mother looked up at him, her back pressing to the lemon tree behind her as she ran out of room to evade him. "I have no wife, nor children, and I am willing to bear the embarrassment that few other men would of entertaining the affections of a woman in your situation."

I frowned at that, unsure what he meant exactly but my mother seemed to know, some dawning comprehension filling her expression as she stared up at the beastly man whose shadow consumed her.

"It does not even have to be public, if you would prefer?" Marik offered, moving closer again. "Our little secret, hm?"

His fingers moved to her face again then slid down onto her neck, and Mother didn't push him away this time. Did she want him to touch her like that? I didn't understand it. Marik was rude and bossy, and he didn't seem to like me or any of my siblings. Why would she be interested in him?

"The orgery?" Mother breathed as my heart beat furiously and confusion wrapped around my mind.

"I'll take care of it," he growled then leaned in closer and pressed his mouth to hers, and she gave in, letting him kiss her in a rough way as he touched and pawed at her shaking body. And as anger scorched through my veins over what she was letting him do, after she'd sworn to me no man would ever replace my father, I slipped back into my room and threw my fist into a wall.

A creak beyond the door stirred me from my thoughts and I was glad to leave them in the past as a monster in me rose to the surface of my skin. The laughter downstairs had died away and the only sounds reaching me now were the giggle of a girl close by, followed by the grunts of a man who was presumably fucking her, and the thump, thump, thump of a bedpost hitting the wall.

A shadow shifted under the door and I pushed to my feet with adrenaline setting my senses alight, moving silently as I pressed my back to the wall beside it, keeping the knife poised in my grip. I went to the coldest place inside me, waiting for the attacker to make his move, knowing that I might have to wet my hands in blood tonight to stay alive, though if I did that, I had no fucking idea how I was going to get out of this snake pit alive.

The door handle twisted and my muscles flexed in preparation of my next move. As the door pushed open and the scent of herbs and mint sailed under my nose, I grabbed hold of the arsehole standing there, slamming my hand over his mouth and yanking him back against my chest, my blade to his throat.

"Only a fool would try to sneak up on a royal guard," I hissed in his ear, but he shook his head violently, holding up a metal pot in his hand to show it to me.

He was a small man, not much of a threat, and as I couldn't see any visible weapon on him, I slid my hand free from his mouth to let him speak.

"I'm the healer here," he stammered. "My name's Cumble. Hagot Cumble. I brought a balm for your wounds."

"He's fine, Cassius," Drake muttered groggily from his bed.

"Why would you bring anything for me?" I hissed, keeping my knife against his throat. "That could be poison for all I know."

"It's my Affinities," Cumble said quickly. "I see a wound, I have to heal it. I tried to go to sleep, but all I could think about was that swollen, bulging burn on your side. It's getting infected. It's haunting my dreams. I have to heal it, let me heal it or you'll die."

I pressed my lips together, considering his words. The palace healer was like this too, whenever I'd been sent to her by Marik, the old girl had always acted as if healing me was quenching a thirst in her which I couldn't understand.

"He'll just scratch at the door like a stray cat if you don't let him do it," Drake said. "And can you hurry up about it because you're making a lot of noise and if I don't get my beauty sleep, my face is gonna suffer, and if my face suffers, I'll punch a few more holes in you with my own knife and Hagot there will cry when he can't fix you."

"Fine," I gave in, releasing the man and patting him down for weapons – which he seemed to enjoy a little too much as he watched me with a giddy grin on his face and I wondered if the guy was cracked. I got a better look at him as I stood back, his grey hair pulled up into a long ponytail and his wispy goatee almost entirely white. His skin was oddly smooth without any imperfection upon it, and I guessed that had to do whatever balms he used on himself.

"Satisfied?" he asked, wetting his pale lips and I nodded. "Lay down and take your tunic off."

I did as he asked, resuming my place on the floor as he lit a lantern beside the bed and Drake groaned, curling in on himself and tugging a pillow over his head to hide from the light.

Cumble suddenly swung a leg over me, straddling my hips and I stiffened in alarm, trying to get up, but he shoved my shoulders down with surprising strength, opening his tin and flicking the lid off. "Shh. Stay down there, big man, this is my process."

He dipped his fingers into the green mixture, humming as he swayed from side to side and I tried to fight a grimace at the skinny man rocking over my very flaccid cock while he fingered that fucking pot.

"Look, I think I'll be fine," I tried, about to shove him off when he placed his fingers on the bright red burn on my side, making me curse as he started to rub the ointment in. The pain started to diminish almost instantly and I gaped at him in surprise. His humming turned to a chant as he praised the old goddess of healing for her gifts in a warbling tone and I glanced over at Drake to see if he was disturbed by this, but the arsehole was still pretending to sleep.

"Come into this man, oh goddess Luciet, come deep and come hard!"

Hagot cried, tipping his head back and my nose wrinkled as he added more of the paste to the infected wound and fuck if it didn't feel so much better. I was torn between disgusted and thankful because I hadn't realised quite how bad the injury was getting until now, my training making me block out the pain with every mental trick I'd ever been taught.

"Oh, sweet goddess of health and wellbeing," he moaned like he was having an orgasm, rocking his hips faster left and right as his eyes fell closed and he slapped more paste onto my wound more violently.

"Um – Drake?" I called.

"It's his process," Drake mumbled back as the healer's chanting grew to a high-pitched song that was almost operatic.

"Bathe this man in your healing juices!" he wailed. "Channel your juices through me and into him with your huge, fertile probe of life!"

"I think it's good now," I tried, but he kept going, rocking like a madman over my hips as I just stared on in dismay, shocked into inaction.

"Heal this man with your bountiful rod of longevity!" He opened his mouth wide, his tongue flicking up and down at speed as he made a noise like a demented songbird, then he fell over me, raking his hands down my chest and twisting my nipples hard in opposing directions.

"Ow – you motherfucker!" I grabbed him, about to throw him off when he slapped me across the face and shoved his fingers into my mouth, still caked in the minty mixture.

"Swallow down my healing broth, take my sweet life juice into your throat!" he commanded as I gagged.

"Do it, mate," Drake urged. "He won't stop until you swallow."

I grimaced before swallowing the mixture he'd shoved into my mouth, almost certain I heard Drake laugh under his breath, the noise swiftly muffled by the pillow.

Cumble's fingers continued to dip between my lips and I shoved his hand away.

"Enough!" I barked, throwing him off of me and he leapt to his feet, prancing over me, back and forth like a baby deer, his tunic flapping open and giving me a view straight up it to his hairy balls which were bouncing rampantly between his thighs. "Ah, for the love of the Fallen," I cursed.

"Rise, my well-endowed royal man! Rise!" Cumble yelled and I growled, wiping my mouth with the back of my hand and pointing to the door.

"Get out," I barked and he giggled like a child before prancing out the door and swinging the door shut behind him.

"You just got Cumbled," Drake laughed raucously and I scowled as I picked up my tunic, feeling violated as I pulled it back on and laid down on my makeshift bed on the floor.

"Did you let him do that shit to you whenever you get wounded?" I demanded angrily.

"Fuck no," Drake laughed louder. "I just take his medicine and tell him to fuck all the way off. I thought you'd enjoy the full experience though."

I aimed a punch at his arm and he laughed as he rolled to avoid it, his amusement almost making me laugh too until I remembered the view of that weird motherfucker's ball sack and grimaced again. At least my wound felt better though, but I had to wonder if continuing to live had been worth the mental scarring.

CHAPTER THIRTEEN

I was finally released from my quarters after days of being locked up there alone. Not even my serving girls had been allowed to attend me and the guards who'd stood outside my room, pushing food through the door twice a day, had not spoken a single word to me when I'd ordered them to release me.

Now, I had woken to find my doors open, the guards standing aside with their heads bowed as I stepped out of my rooms with my veil pulled over my face to protect them from the law.

I'd been tempted to refuse to wear it a single day more, but then I'd thought of Cassius Lazar and my heart had splintered. By this point, he was surely dead because of me, and I swear he haunted every one of my dreams, his caramel eyes burning into mine as that moment replayed over and over in my head. He was gone. The only man to look at me outside of my father. And the one person I'd trusted in this place since Magdor had arrived, though it had taken his death for me to realise how much I'd placed my faith in him.

He had always stood between me and peril, but he had been more than just some shield paid for by the empire. He was a man beyond the palace walls, he had led a life I had known nothing of. What if he'd had a family waiting for him to come home? What if they'd stood and watched him hang in the town square, executed like some common criminal for the crime of simply looking upon my face? That was perhaps the most unbearable thought of all. Small children with tearstained faces watching their father die for a crime so pointless it shouldn't have been a crime at all.

The corridors seemed quieter than usual and the air had shifted in the palace, a threat seeming to hang above my head. It felt like a blade was carving its way down my spine as I walked with my head held high, passing by guards who didn't so much as twitch a muscle in response to my presence. They felt even less human than usual, all of them barely seeming to breathe as I made my way by. Something was wrong. It felt like a plague had crept into my home, crawling its way deep into the bones of these walls, a whisper of death carrying around me on the cool air.

I headed to my father's throne room where he received requests from the people of Osaria every eighth day, ready to tell him everything, expose his abhorrent wife for what she was and reclaim the man she'd stolen from me. He still held to the tradition, but his manner had vastly changed since he'd married Magdor, acting dismissively towards our people, or worse, callously.

I was hoping she wouldn't be present when I arrived, but as I stepped into the cavernous hall there she was, wearing a flowing navy gown as she sat beside the emperor's ruby throne, her own throne barely any smaller than his.

Father looked tired. But he'd always looked tired ever since Mother had died when I was just a girl. His eyes were ringed with circles and his greying hair was growing thin. It was still long though, freshly washed and hanging down to his shoulders beneath his fine crown.

His eyes were darkest brown, but they seemed darker than ever these days. He used to look at me with love in those eyes, now there was something else there in its place. Something that seemed to shield the love he felt for me, keep it back, out of my reach. I hoped he still loved me, but with each passing year that hope lessened and left a hole in my chest almost as big as the one my mother's death had left behind. Now I knew Magdor could get potions into the palace, it was only logical that some elixir was doing this to him, but I feared how much of him would be intact, even if I could save him from the bane of it.

I still recalled how he'd played with me when I was a girl. We would roam the palace gardens like we were on an adventure. He'd made me a wooden sword; he'd been the only person to ever teach me sword fighting. I still practised every day, but he'd stopped instructing me years ago. There was a time he'd told me, *"Woman are more than men's equals, sweet Austyn. And my time as emperor will see them viewed as such for the first time in The Twelve Kingdoms of the Osarian Empire."*

When I was a girl with hopes and dreams of women rising to greatness, Father had been about to create a world where a princess was allowed to claim the throne for herself. But that hadn't happened. A woman from some faraway land had shown up in our home and invaded it single-handedly. Somehow, she'd convinced him not to pass those laws. But why?

I couldn't understand it, surely as a woman herself she would only want to see those changes brought in, yet she seemed to be the reason that they had stalled, never to be mentioned again.

Though my father still sat on the throne, I could almost see the puppet strings she had attached to him. When he spoke, it was her words that rolled from his tongue.

Please still be in there, Father. Please come back to me. Please tell me I don't have to marry Kahn or any of the suitors presented to me.

A peasant was on his knees before the throne, begging the emperor for an extension on his tax payments as he clasped his gnarled fingers together in a prayer. "I'm just a farmer, Your Highness. My crops haven't yielded well this year and I have failed to meet the quota which could bring me the coin needed to pay the crown. I beg for a few months more, that's all."

Father sat up straighter, his eyes swivelling to me as I strode through the huge room, my heels clicking on the ebony tiles as I passed the arching stone pillars that towered above us. Huge banners hung across the walls in the kingdom's colours of blue and white, with a tree of purest silver growing through the heart of the coat of arms. At its base were two snowy tigers, reaching up towards the songbirds taking flight from its branches.

Three guards flanked me, my veil fluttering in time with my steps and as the peasant turned and spotted me approaching, he flattened himself to the ground.

"*Gracious*, Princess, what are you doing here?" Magdor demanded, stroking the chunky golden necklace at her throat which had a large amulet dangling from it, an engraved ring of thorns carved into its face. I hated that ugly thing. But I hated the ugly thing wearing it even more.

I didn't acknowledge her, gazing at my father instead. "Aren't you going to answer this man's request?" I insisted, moving to the side of Father's throne and turning to look back at the farmer. His face was weathered and he was *so* thin. They were always thin these days. The people of our city used to look well-fed, some even plump. But not anymore. Not since Magdor. I hated her so much, my veins burned with it.

I was full to the brim with all the things I wanted to declare to my father to expose her, but I held my tongue in the presence of the farmer.

Magdor looked to the emperor as he contemplated the peasant before him. "I cannot be lenient with one man, or all men will come begging for the same. If you cannot pay the taxes in gold, you will pay it in blood."

At a gesture from my father, two guards strode forward and hauled the farmer to his feet.

"What are you doing?" I gasped in horror, my heart stumbling into a frantic beat.

"A hand," Father growled, his eyes lingering on the man, full of some wicked cruelty that didn't belong in his gaze. "One now, and the other in a week if it's not paid in full."

"Father, you can't!" I cried, trembling with fury as the guards started dragging the farmer from the hall. He wailed protests and my heart could barely take the sound of such agony. This was wrong, it was no way to treat our people.

"He is the emperor," Magdor said dismissively, seeming tired of me. "Dear Princess, you are too soft of heart to be here for such dealings. Go back to your quarters." She ushered me away, but I stood my ground, glaring at her.

I grabbed my veil in my fists and the guards turned sharply around to face the walls the moment I tugged it off. I sucked in a breath of cooler air,

179

dropping to my knees in front of my father, determined to make him see the truth at last. And I had to look him in the eye to do it, he had to see me, see this desperation in me.

"You can't let them hurt that man," I insisted.

He frowned as he observed me, but said nothing. I ground my teeth, despising that Magdor had taken him from me, turned him into a cruel ruler who treated his people like dirt. That wasn't him. But why did he let her do this to him?

I gripped his hands, glaring at Magdor. "Get out," I hissed at her. "I wish to speak with my father alone."

She stared down her nose at me, a pit of rage opening up in her eyes. "We are in the middle of something, Austyn. I refuse to leave until my duty is done."

"Whatever you wish to say, you can say to us both," Father added.

"Get out!" I bellowed at her and she raised her chin, a glimmer of contempt in her eyes as she stared at me. Her little problem.

"I will not," she snarled, her voice taking on a timbre that sent a tremor down my spine.

Tears swam in my eyes as I had to accept her presence, knowing that my chances of reaching him were even less than I'd hoped. "Don't hurt that man. The taxes are far higher than is fair as it is," I whispered, speaking just for him.

"You know nothing of politics," Magdor chimed in.

I shot a glare her way. "I'm not asking you," I gritted out and she rolled her eyes as if I was just an irritation she had to bear. And maybe I was, but she was my irritation too and this was my home long before it was hers. We had been at war a long time, but I was going to find a way to strike the final, killing blow.

I turned back to my father, squeezing his hands, praying I'd find some ounce of his former self in his eyes. For a moment, his dark gaze shimmered and he reached out to run his thumb across my cheek.

"My daughter, how gentle you are. Are you looking forward to the pageant?"

I shook my head, angry that he was ignoring everything I'd asked of him. "No," I snapped, losing any self-control I had left. "I don't want to be bought, Father. Surely I deserve the right to choose my own husband?"

"The pageant is tradition," he said softly. "Magdor's son, Kahn, will likely win anyway. He is a fine, upstanding man. He will make you very happy."

Anger. Hot, red and everywhere, took me hostage and I rose to my feet knowing begging was pointless. So I decided to see what shouting Magdor's crimes to the rooftops would do.

"She is in your head," I barked, my hand snapping out to point at his witch of a wife. She had the gall to hold a hand to her chest and look aghast, but I wasn't even close to done. "She's controlling you, Father, don't you see? Just the other day she fed some potion to Kahn bought from a Prophet of the Fallen to make him handsome. You must have noticed that. All of you must have." I turned my heads to the guards, seeking some movement, some sign that they were listening and that they believed this too. Because surely they had all witnessed what Magdor had done. What she was capable of. They were the eyes and ears of this palace. They were here before she was, they had to know something.

"Do you have anything to say, guards?" I called to them, but they remained stock still, ignoring me as if my voice was nothing more than the squeak of a mouse.

Cassius would have believed me. He would have seen something, and he would have spoken now had he still been here.

My throat thickened as I thought of Magdor ordering his death and I barrelled on, not letting myself dwell on the pain of that moment. Father was looking at me with a patient expression, but he didn't seem remotely bothered by my words, while Magdor was out of her seat, drifting closer like an angry crow looking to peck my eyes out.

"From the moment she arrived, she has disrespected me," I hissed.

"I am nothing but respectful, Your Majesty," Magdor disagreed.

"She has tortured me," I growled.

"Oh, come now, I have punished you as a child ought to be punished, that is all. You really are so dramatic, my dear." She clucked her tongue, reaching for my arm but I knocked her hand away from my skin, rearing up and cupping my father's cheek so I was all he could see. "Her ring is laced with emperian cobra venom," I said urgently. "Have the guards take it from her and check it. She injected me with it." I yanked up my silk sleeve, showing him the mark, though it was barely visible now, just a tiny, raised bump.

"What an imagination she has, it really is quite delightful," Magdor said, painting on a smile. "One of her serving girls pricked her with a pin, that's all. The girl was quite distraught about the mishap as well, it's rather unfortunate that you would point the blame at her, but if you'd rather she was punished for it-"

"That's not what I said." I swung around, hunting for the ring on her hand which held the evidence of that venom, but it wasn't there. Gone. The only ring cladding her fingers was the one binding her to my father in marriage, and the sight of it made my gut twist.

"Search her rooms!" I ordered the guards. "You'll see. You'll find evidence that she's wielding magic against my father."

The guards didn't move and as I looked down at the emperor again, I found him gazing serenely at me as if he hadn't heard a word I'd said.

"Your hair is so like your mother's," he whispered. "So rare."

"Yes," I choked out at the mention of her, leaning in close to him. "You remember what you used to call us?"

He raised a hand to run his fingers through my silver hair and my heart swelled with how much I'd missed the affection of my father. Sometimes I felt like I was made of metal, my skin cold and uninviting to the flesh of others, because no one touched me anymore. I really was becoming a trophy, turning

181

into a pretty chalice day by day, and soon I'd feel as empty as one too.

"My songbirds," Father whispered and a tear slipped from my eye at that nickname which I had missed so much.

"Yes," I breathed, nodding but then Magdor's shadow fell over us and the man I knew so well vanished from his eyes once more.

"Sweet daughter, are you looking forward to the pageant?" he asked as if he had forgotten he'd asked that same thing already.

A growl built in my throat. He wouldn't listen to me even if I yelled for days on end. I was a songbird for real now, trapped in a cage, and I could see clearer than ever that the pageant was going to go ahead. There was no way out of it.

I stared at my father, my heart fracturing at his cool expression. "Don't hurt that farmer. Lower the taxes. Stop punishing the people of our city for failing to meet such impossible goals."

Magdor released a tinkling laugh, snaring my attention again. "You're quite the philanthropist, my dear. What in the world would happen to the kingdom if you were allowed to rule it? There would be nothing but chaos. Order is created by earning respect, Austyn. The crown is respected because punishment is enforced if it is not. If you had *your* way, the people would run amuck."

I ran my tongue over my teeth, trying to work out what the hell I had to bargain with here. Being the princess should have meant I had a lot more sway than I actually did. But I was as helpless as most of the people in Osaria. No one listened to me any more than them.

I lunged forward, snatching a dagger from my father's hip in a maddened act, all other courses of action failing me and leaving me this final option, and I pressed the blade to my own cheek. His eyes narrowed, but he didn't make a move to rise from his throne. Not yet anyway.

"I won't be your pretty little princess unless you do as I say. I'll go to the Unveiling with cuts all over my face. And then who will want to buy me?"

I'll do this. I swear I'll do this. Screw beauty. What's it worth? I'd give it up in a heartbeat to gain control over my fate.

Father stood up and my heart squeezed with hope. His eyes raked over me then he shook his head as if I was a mild annoyance to him.

"Stop behaving like a child." He stalked away from the throne, heading across the room and slamming the door behind him.

My shoulders shuddered and tears threatened to come. But I wouldn't let them. I wouldn't be hurt by the fact that he'd just walked away from me.

But I am, it hurts so deeply I can't bear it.

I faced Magdor instead and her eyes turned to darkest night as I twisted the blade in my hand, the knife seeming to sing a song against my palm. My Affinity for metal made my skill with a blade unmatched, it moved for me like it was an extension of my flesh. And maybe the real answer here didn't lie with words, maybe it lay with blood.

I assessed her as she assessed me, my gaze moving to her slender throat.

How easy it would be to slice it open, or perhaps her heart was a better target. I'd have to stab hard and true, but I could do it, my Affinities would help me, the blade would seek out the fleshy meat of her heart and skewer it for me.

"Out," Magdor commanded the guards and they marched from the room without hesitation.

A resounding boom hit my ears as the doors shut behind them and I hid the smile that flickered at the corners of my lips. Because I was in a maddened state with a savage answer within my grasp. When she was dead, perhaps my father would break free of whatever spell she'd cast on him, perhaps there was a chance for our salvation. And that chance was worth risking everything for.

My breathing quickened as she hounded closer, a parasite in my home, her eyes flashing with a fierce anger. I'd never seen such darkness in her and it set my pulse racing as the shadows seemed to creep closer, hugging her body like she was a magnet to them, sending a shiver down my spine as a cloying kind of pressure gathered in the otherwise empty room.

I shifted the blade in my hand, moving it to my side and holding it ready, enjoying fulfilling this need within my flesh as it danced in my palm like a bird taking flight between my fingers.

Magdor's gaze strayed to the knife then back to my face, a twisted smile resting on her lips. "And what will you do now, Austyn? Surely you're not thinking about wielding that knife against me?"

"And what if I am?" I warned, watching her as she prowled to my right and I turned, keeping my body angled towards her, never taking my eyes off of the danger in the room.

She tossed her hair, laughing mockingly. She still looked just as she had when she had first shown up here all those years ago, not a single new line in her skin, not a strand of grey in her hair. It was unnatural and yet no one had ever commented on it beyond praising her beauty and claiming she must have been touched by the god of beauty and purity himself. But I didn't think Halios had anything to do with the creation of this monster. "And what would you do after you stuck that little knife in me, Princess? Run to Daddy? What would he think of his dear daughter stabbing his beloved wife?"

"He doesn't love you," I snarled. "He loved my mother. You have bewitched him somehow. Did you give him a potion just like you gave one to your son?"

"I think all the time you spend alone is making you crack," she said, giving me a look of mocking pity, still moving around me as I continued to turn and keep her in my line of sight. Despite the knife being in my hand, it was she who felt like the hunter now, stalking around me like a lioness about to go in for the kill. But I wasn't her prey, she was underestimating me as usual, and I'd exploit that weakness the second I got the chance.

"Poor little Austyn," she said in an overexaggerated tone. "Stuck in her tower for days on end, making up fairy tales in her head to keep her company. It really is quite tragic. You should be grateful the pageant is coming, that Kahn will soon wed you and make use of you while you're still young and relatively pretty."

"He will never touch me," I spat and she grinned at that.

"He will do whatever he pleases with you after you are married. You will belong to him and soon learn to accept your position as his property. And you will provide him with sons, Austyn, even if I have to strap you down to a table to ensure he has access to that royal heir-maker between your thighs."

"Fuck you," I snarled, taking a step towards her with intent and raising my knife.

"Metal Affinity or not, you could not strike me with that blade," Magdor said with a taunting smile. "Go ahead, try it."

I lunged at her, slashing the knife towards her vile face, but she moved like the wind, evading the blow and somehow appearing behind me. She laughed in my ear and I swung around, slashing at her again with perfect skill, the air seeming to ring with every strike I made, but she seemed to shift aside faster than should have been possible. Her laughter hung everywhere, lilting and mocking, and a shriek of rage left me as I fought harder, faster, trying to catch this monster who had inserted herself into our lives. This had to be magic, a wicked, monstrous brand of it that this horrid woman embodied. I was shocked by laying witness to it, but it equally spurred me into action, my desire to see her wiped from this world driving out all fear in me.

My breaths came heavier as she continued to avoid every one of my attacks and I changed the direction of my next blow, swiping the blade to my left into thin air, predicting her movements. Magdor cried out and sweet satisfaction poured through my chest as the blade sliced open her forearm, but as I lifted it towards her throat with my teeth bared and adrenaline warring in my blood, she used her next move to catch my wrist and her taloned nails drove straight into my flesh. I gasped as a rush of power ran into my veins, an overwhelming feeling of darkness skimming along the inside of my flesh.

"Fool," she snarled, her eyes turning to pitch and seeming full of something otherworldly, like I was gazing into the pits of death itself.

She was frighteningly strong as she tugged my hand back and forced me to hold the dagger to my own heart instead. Fear reached into my chest with icy fingers, enslaving me as this power in her took root in my bones and held me in its grasp.

"Gosh, what a pity it would be if the princess were to skewer herself on her father's blade," Magdor mused.

"What are you?" I gasped in horror, my hand trembling around the knife.

She moved unnaturally fast and her strength was like a gift from the gods, but I had never heard her boast of such a talent. Was this some rare Affinity, some potion she'd drunk to enhance herself, or was it something far worse that I couldn't even comprehend?

"I am your empress," she growled, her voice deep and so unlike her own for a moment that it seemed as if a demon were speaking for her. "You will behave, I am weary of your defiance. Your father is tired of it too. Don't you see how you drain him?"

A lump grew in my throat at those words, the cruel accusation of them. That I was his burden.

"It's not me, it's you," I pushed. "I know what you're doing."

"And what is that?" she demanded. "Being a devoted wife? Helping your father through his illness?"

"What illness?" I breathed, deathly quiet, my whole world suddenly hanging in the balance.

"He is in the clutches of death, my dear," Magdor said harshly and a breath snagged in my lungs, refusing to come out. "A cancerous disease is burrowing into his bones. But I've been hunting The Twelve Kingdoms for a Prophet of the Fallen who will be able to save him. Shall I stop my quest? Is that what you want? Are you so against the magic of old that you would discard its uses even when it can heal your own father?"

Terror slithered through my chest at the threat in her words. "You know I don't want that."

Father was all I had left of my family. And maybe the body that housed him was tainted by Magdor, but his old self *had* to still be in there. There had to be a chance he could still come back to me. If he was sick, I had to protect him. But who was to say if Magdor was lying or not? What if she had placed that sickness in him herself? Though she would have no reason to do so – it would only hurt her if he died. She would lose her position upon his death. Even as a woman who could not rule alone, I was the heir to the throne of Osaria. My husband would be the next rightful emperor and she would be nothing.

"Good, so you will do as he wishes and not upset him in his time of need. You *will* attend the pageant. You *will* look your best. You *will* be Unveiled, and your suitors *will* drool at your feet. Then you *will* marry the victor. And the victor *will* be my son."

My nose wrinkled at her words, at the trap I felt forming around myself. She would lose her position if I married anyone other than Kahn, but if it was, he who I ended up shackled to then I was certain I'd never be rid of her. No doubt that was why she was trying to ensure this course of fate. Perhaps I was a rabbit in a hunter's snare, not a bird in a cage. It was worse than being caught, I was going to be devoured. This woman would sink her teeth into me. She'd take every drop of light I had left and chew it up. Eat, eat, eat.

"I will fight this every step of the way," I declared.

"Austyn, I grow tired of your complaints. I gave you everything you ever could have asked for. Kahn is as beautiful as you now. But it wasn't enough. You refused him even then. But when the pageant begins, do you know what you'll see?" She moved closer to me, tugging the blade from my hand and wrapping a lock of my silver hair around her finger in a possessive grip.

"What?" I breathed, fiercely afraid of her in that moment.

"That there is nothing better waiting for you beyond these walls. No other man will be finer. None of them will catch your eye or steal your heart. I have seen all of the suitors and Kahn is the best there is. I want you to realise that you won't be missing a thing. I want you to choose Kahn."

"Why?" I demanded. "What difference does it make to you?"

Her icy expression broke into a bright smile. "I'm not a monster," she said with a bright laugh, and I grimaced at this woman who had just moments ago promised to tie me to a table so her son could rape me. "I simply want you to realise that no man will offer you more than Kahn anyway. I want you both to be happy. So have your pageant," she said, waving a hand as if it was me who had decided on the pageant in the first place. I realised what this was really about. She wanted me willing, she didn't want to go to the effort of forcing me along this road she was determined for me to remain on. But she was underestimating my stubbornness even after she had witnessed it all these years, because I would never submit to her repugnant offspring.

Ice coated my next words. "But if I go through with it and Kahn wins, you'll force us to marry even if it makes me eternally miserable."

She released my hair, stepping back as her gaze scraped down me from head to toe. "Yes." She floated away from me. "Women don't get to choose, my dear. It's the way of the world. Even if you were a commoner, do you think you would have a chance to marry for *love*?" she half-choked on the word.

I stiffened, my hands curling into tight fists. "I don't want a man, Magdor. Love or not, I don't want to marry someone because I am forced to. I don't want him taking the power of my kingdom from me when I am the only true heir to it."

Her beautiful features softened and light grew in her eyes. "You're a princess, that's what princesses must do. You have a responsibility to birth an heir. And that heir will be my son's."

DRAKE

CHAPTER FOURTEEN

I was woken by a knock at the door and I sat bolt upright, snatching the knife from beneath my pillow as I blinked the sleep from my eyes. Cassius was still in his spot on the floor beside my cot, but the knock had woken him too and he pushed himself upright with a frown as he raised the blade I'd given him. But a cutthroat wouldn't knock if they were here to kill him.

"What?" I yelled, irritated to have been pulled from my sleep when I found it so damn hard to come by in this place as it was.

"It's me," Pip called, and I groaned as I dropped my knife and fell back onto my cot.

"This had better be good," I muttered, and he pushed the door open.

Pip's eyes trailed over Cassius for a moment and the guard dropped his blade, tucking it out of sight as if he thought it might scare the boy. I knew better. Pip was as tough as half the big arseholes in this place and took on jobs which should have been far beyond his skill set without even blinking.

Pip smirked knowingly before he turned to look at me; I'd been teaching him the ways of using what he was born with to his advantage, and for now that meant using his youth to make people underestimate him. He was damn good at it too.

"Egos said I should tell you that the storm is over and it's time for you to leave," he said, pulling a bread roll from his pocket and tossing it to me.

I snatched it out of the air and started eating it before I replied.

"And have I got any volunteers for the crew?" I asked as I swallowed.

"You've got your pick of twenty-six," he replied. "Including me."

"Nice try, Pip," I said. "But Egos doesn't like you hanging around with me as much as you do, so I think you'd better stay here for your own good. Besides, that nose of yours needs to heal."

The kid opened his mouth to protest but he must have caught sight of my face and realised that my mind was made up on this one, so he gave in with a dramatic sigh instead. He leaned forward, handing Cassius a second roll before he left, and the former guard raised an eyebrow in surprise at the gesture.

"Thanks, kid," he called as the door swung closed and I got to my feet. "He seems less shitty than the rest of you."

"He's the best damn pickpocket I've ever seen," I replied. "And he'd sell his grandmother to be baked in a pie if he was given half a chance, so don't start getting too doe-eyed on him."

"Surely if he had a grandmother, he wouldn't be here with you criminals."

"Maybe that's because he sold her already," I quipped.

"Are you sure you aren't just holding him up to your own standards?" Cassius asked doubtfully as he finished his roll.

"You tell me. Didn't you have a blade a moment ago?" I taunted.

Cassius looked around him with a frown, patting the space to either side of him and checking his pockets. "It was right here..."

"And now Pip has it. Don't underestimate him. Or any of us. You don't get to be one of The Forty Thieves by chance."

"Forty-one," he muttered. "And apparently I did."

I snorted a laugh. "Forty isn't an exact number, it's just a name. This is dangerous work; gang members die all the time. Or end up in the dungeons. There's far more than forty of us most of the time, especially if enough people with talent are recruited around the same time. Only a few of us have survived long enough to become legends. The fact that you don't know that just goes to show how ill equipped you are to be one of us. I bet you've never stolen a thing in your life."

"Of course I haven't," Cassius replied indignantly, and it would have been funny if his morals weren't likely to get him killed, because I needed him alive long enough to bring me to that damn treasure.

"Well then. Perhaps if you survive this job, I'll teach you how. Balthazar probably isn't up for seducing any more ugly countesses for a while anyway, so you could always take his place in that position."

"Oh *thanks*, pal, I can't wait to get castrated for fucking a woman who looks like a toad," Cassius replied dryly, and I laughed.

"Easier than a horse," I pointed out and he broke a smile. "We'd better get going before Egos sends anyone else to look for us. Do you feel like telling me how well guarded this treasure is?" I asked as I pulled on my boots and a loose-fitting white tunic. I tossed Cassius a tunic too, and he eyed it like it might burn him before shrugging it on without thanking me.

Entitled much?

"It isn't guarded as far as I know. Just hidden."

"So how many men do we need to bring?"

"Eight?" he suggested with a shrug. "There's a lot of treasure there. It might take quite a few men to carry it out."

"That sounds like my kind of haul." I grinned to myself as I led the way back down to The Den.

If Cassius came through for me on this, then I was sure to get out of Egos's bad books and I could get back to the good life. In fact, if this haul was anywhere near as large as he claimed, I could even find myself with enough coin to leave this shitty place once I'd taken my cut. I could finally choose my own path, sever my ties to The Den and be free. There was a whole fucking world out there just waiting for wealthy men to carve their way to prosperity in it, and I could be anyone I wanted to be if I started up somewhere new.

I'd always liked the sound of the kingdom of Dunemare, hidden away within the endless forest and said to be entirely built of wood with buildings connected by rope bridges and the scent of pine surrounding them. It was said to rain a lot there, the air thick with constant moisture which would be one hell of a change from the dryness of the desert landscape surrounding Osaria.

Or perhaps I'd head northwest instead and seek out a new life in Havendale, its capital known as the city in the clouds, set upon the highest point of land with buildings taller than any other in the entire empire. The roads there were said to be clean of shit and piss in all places, no slums at all and the Fae the most content of citizens. Of course, I had to lay doubt upon anywhere which sounded so wonderful. I had learned long ago that anything which seemed too good to be true always was. No doubt they had some method of dealing with the poor which was all kinds of unsavoury.

Maybe I'd just keep heading north instead, all the way to Falgesh where snow was said to touch the ground at all times, the people as brutish and harsh as the landscape they occupied. Their women were also rumoured to be the most beautiful in the entire empire, and I couldn't deny I'd take pleasure in finding out the truth to that rumour.

Wherever I chose, the point was that if this went well, I would have options. I could travel the entire empire if I liked, changing my name as often as I picked the pockets of all those who crossed my path while carving out whatever destiny struck my fancy. Yeah, that was the life for me. And Cassius was my ticket.

CASSIUS

CHAPTER FIFTEEN

D rake took his sweet time picking eight men from those who'd volunteered, clearly enjoying the little slice of power as he got to decide which of them would end up with a cut of the loot they brought back from the treasure Magdor had told me of.

I waited by the exit, watching the gang as I figured out the hierarchy and how they all functioned with one another. Egos wasn't present which left a power void amongst the masses. It was predictably filled by the biggest motherfuckers in the room who stomped about and claimed their share of the food by force as well as the best seats by the fire and anything else they wanted. But it was clear who the other players in the room were too. Drake and a few thieves like him clearly commanded respect and where they walked, others moved out of their way. I guessed he hadn't been lying about his so-called legendary status, at least among these delinquents. Not that that was much of an accolade to be proud of, but after he'd told me of his upbringing, I couldn't exactly blame him for the life he led. I'd always known things were tough out in the slums, but seeing it first-hand made me even angrier at Magdor for changing the plans of my emperor. This place shouldn't have even existed anymore. There shouldn't have been a need for thievery if the emperor were able to look after his people better, but here we were, hell breeding more hell around me while Osaria fell deeper into chaos every day.

Balthazar seemed to cast a similarly intimidating shadow to Drake and my gaze trailed him as he stalked across the far side of the room to claim a drink from the well that stood there, snapping his fingers at a kid in his teens so that he hoisted the bucket up for him and handed it over. His wound had been bound and he didn't seem to be concerned about the injury as he moved about the space topless, making me wonder if he had been subject to the same crazy ritual as I had by their healer. Or perhaps some of the thieves here just knew how to cover the hurt of their injuries in the same way that we were taught to in the barracks. The only thing worse than having an injury was letting your enemy know about it after all.

A man with no teeth glared at me and I folded my arms, resting my back to the wall in my best impression of someone who didn't give a fuck. And in all honesty, I didn't. I would be getting out of here in the next thirty minutes and I wasn't planning on ever coming back. I didn't know what my future held after I had stolen and destroyed that coin which Magdor was hunting, but I did know this wasn't it.

I was not one of these men and never could be. If I survived then I guessed I'd be heading far away from this kingdom, though the thought of that stung my soul. But I was a condemned man, so no life could await me in Osaria besides that of an outlaw. Perhaps I would travel to one of the other kingdoms. I could see the mountains in distant Arenia where the city sat between huge peaks and the wind howled so wildly that Fae were said to have created winged contraptions that allowed them to soar across the sky from place to place. Or I could sail the seas in western Shamba, explore the fabled forests of Dunemare, or even risk the legends of ice drakes and rotfangs in the deep west where the city of Havendale lay among the clouds.

The toothless cretin stuffed a finger up his nose as he continued to glare at me, and I couldn't conceal the disgust on my face. A shudder ran down my spine at the uncleanliness of these rats. At least Drake took pride in himself - maybe a little too much. But this particular arsehole clearly hadn't washed in at least a month. And if I'd been a betting man, I would have placed a thousand kurus on it being more than three.

"What you lookin' at?" he snarled.

My eyes drifted to the abandoned sword lying behind him and anger flared inside me as I realised it wasn't just *any* blade. It was a curved scimitar inlaid with the royal seal on the hilt and it sat in a scabbard of tanned red leather. That was one of the emperor's weapons, gifted to him by the Forken Empire in the south. It was rumoured to have been forged by the Fae of old, its blade imbued with the gifts of Efries, the god of war and might, the god whose Affinity my fighting gifts were linked to. It was a rumour that was no doubt untrue, but it was still a seriously valuable item. I'd heard about the wagon going missing on its journey to Osaria a few weeks ago and I had studied the itinerary of stolen items just like every other guard in the city so that we would recognise them if any showed up.

I eyed the man before me, clenching my teeth – *yes, I actually have teeth you beastly motherfucker.*

I glanced at the scimitar again, thinking out my next move. It wasn't stealing if I intended on returning it to the emperor. But then again, how the hell was I supposed to steal something from one of The Forty Thieves? That was the equivalent to beating a bird at flying.

"I'm trying to work out what you remind me of," I said airily, taking a step closer to him, sure that sword was going to cost me more than a punch.

"Huh?" he grunted.

"Well, you either remind me of a pig-ugly cock, or a cock-ugly pig."

He lunged at me with a roar, stumbling as he went and it hit me in a moment of ecstatic clarity that this arsehole was blind drunk. I shoved him as he came at me, meaning only to throw him aside, but he staggered, smashed into a table where five men were sitting and fell down on top of their cards and wine, spilling it everywhere.

A brawl broke out and I barked a laugh, unable to believe my luck as I darted forward and snatched the sword. I could feel the exquisite craftsmanship of the blade in the weight of it, the balance and the way it would cut through anything with ease even as I merely held it by my side. To wield such a prize in a true fight would be a damn dream, and my pulse was racing with the idea of it, my Affinities burning to be let out.

I didn't have anywhere to conceal the large blade so I strapped it to my hip and rotated my belt so that it hung behind me, hoping no one would notice it before we left this grotty hell.

I returned to the wall, pressing my back to it, vaguely watching the street folk beat each other within an inch of their lives while my heart thundered in my chest and the victory brightened my mood.

Am I thief?

No, I'm just taking back what was stolen. If I return this sword to the emperor and destroy this coin, maybe he will thank me...maybe he will let me return to my old life.

Idle wishes.

I gritted my jaw, spotting Drake moving towards the brawl with eight men at his back. My gaze scraped across those he'd chosen; all of them were big and carried large bags on their shoulders, one of them had tattoos of naked women instead of eyebrows and I had to admire his commitment to the pornographic art he'd chosen to eternally adorn his face. I sensed Drake had picked the men he thought could carry the most and had to force myself not to roll my eyes.

Greedy fucker.

I wasn't sure what else I'd been expecting though; Drake's only interest in this journey lay in the treasure he'd be able to claim because of it. It was the only reason I still drew breath in my lungs instead of my body lying chopped up in a coffin somewhere.

I almost pitied him really, this life he'd led having tarnished his opinions and jaded him so thoroughly that he could no longer see anything beyond his own selfish desires. But I had more important tasks to achieve than trying to convince a thief that there was more to life than self-gratification.

There's sacrificing everything you are to the cause of others. Which made me eternally happy, right?

Yeah...right.

My focus was solely on Drake so as he walked past the fighting men, I noticed as his hands slipped into their pockets and I arched a brow as whatever he found went straight into his own. Not a flicker of guilt crossed his features and as his gaze whipped over to meet mine, he winked, clearly having known I was watching him the whole time. I felt like he was trying to show me something with that act, but I wasn't sure what it could be other than to remind me that I shouldn't trust him so far as I could throw him. Though maybe that was the point. Maybe he was happy for me to see him for what he was, and this was a warning not to cross him or fall for the trap of his smiles and jesting. This man wasn't a man who had friends, no matter how he may have seemed.

I pressed my tongue into my cheek, wondering what the hell the point was in these men banding together if they were constantly undermining one another. My training had taught me to look out for my comrades, to have their backs under any circumstances. We would have gone to the sun and back for each other for the sake of the crown. Not that we'd had much of a bond beyond that.

We had to be willing to make all necessary sacrifices in the name of the emperor, which meant not only did we have to willingly place ourselves at risk for the others, we also had to be prepared to sacrifice each other if it was necessary. Beyond the comradery of the battlefield, we were not encouraged to know each other well or care for each other as individuals. Nothing should cloud our judgement in a fight, least of all concern for another guard who could compromise my own actions. Still, I had known with all my heart that I could trust the men on either side of me to do all they could in the name of Osaria which meant I could trust their honour above all else. Drake and the rest of The Forty only seemed able to rely on the fact that each and every one of them would do all they could to protect and benefit themselves. I knew which system I preferred.

Drake arrived beside me, biting into a shiny red apple he'd thieved. He held another one out for me and my eyes narrowed. The sweet scent reached me, and my stomach growled. The small bread roll Pip had given me hadn't been nearly enough to satisfy my hunger. And before that, I'd been living on cold gruel in the dungeon for three days. What I'd give to have a hot breakfast handed to me right now...

"One time offer." Drake waved the apple under my nose and I snatched it. I held it close to my tunic, about to shine it on my clothes when I thought better of it. Who knew when these items had last been scrubbed? They didn't seem particularly dirty, but they weren't freshly pressed and starched the way my own clothes always were either.

As I brought the fruit to my lips, I spied a curly black hair sitting atop it and thrust it back at Drake with a lurch of disgust in my stomach.

"I'm not hungry," I grunted.

He frowned, pocketing the fruit and shaking his head at me.

"Oh, what a charmed life you must have led to so casually reject good food, Cassius," he mocked and my spine stiffened as I realised the insult I'd just given him. "I'll be certain not to waste my time in offering you any more in future." No doubt his contempt for the upper classes had just been strengthened once more, and I stifled a sigh as I realised he had a fair point. "Come, Hagot will check up on your torture wounds before we leave," he added, jerking his chin to draw my attention to the healer who I hadn't noticed slinking closer to us as we spoke.

"No, I am quite fine," I said quickly. In fact, I *was* fine. The swelling in the burn the healer had tended to had gone down overnight, and a lot of the redness had faded out of it too. But his process left a lot to be desired.

"Don't be ridiculous. I can't have you dropping dead before you hand me my treasure." Drake gripped my shoulder, leading me towards Hagot and my skin prickled uncomfortably as the man gave me a watery smile.

"Show me your wound, lawman, don't be shy," he purred, tilting his head as he assessed me and I shifted uncomfortably before him, not liking the way his too perfect flesh seemed to be stretched over his bones.

Healers had always given me the creeps when they used their Affinities like that. Keeping their skin youthful in appearance even when everything else about them proved that they were far from young.

My moment of hesitation was short lived as Drake grasped my tunic and yanked it up, making me grunt in annoyance as he exposed the burn wound at my side where the poker had been driven into my skin. It still hurt, but nowhere near as much as it had before.

Hagot nodded, tipping his gaze to Drake. "I'll take a cut of the loot you're heading after in payment for last night's treatment and this follow up," he said, ignoring me like he already knew I had no means to pay for his services.

"One gemstone, fat as a grape," Drake agreed but Hagot was already shaking his head.

"Five."

"One," Drake growled.

"Four. Or you can risk your guide collapsing when the rot sets in and his wound festers-"

"Rot? I thought that paste you gave me last night healed it?" I asked, my lips parting in concern as I looked down at the burn on my side again, hunting for any signs of that, but the two of them ignored me as if I wasn't even here.

"Two," Drake shot back. "Final offer, and I won't tell the men visiting the whore houses where you pedal your tonics that the one you offer up to protect them against cock boils contains camel dung and rotten cabbage. I'm gonna guess they'd be a whole lot less inclined to smear their manhood in it and pay you for the privilege if they knew that."

"The ingredients work," Hagot objected while I recoiled in disgust.

"I'm still thinking that knowledge would be off putting," Drake shot back and Hagot huffed.

"Fine. Two stones as fat as grapes and your silence on my methods." Hagot held a hand out and Drake slapped his into it, the tattoo on his forearm catching my attention for a moment as his muscles flexed at the tightness of his grip. The curving lines and intricate symbols of the black ink almost seemed to shimmer for the briefest of moments before I blinked, and the illusion was gone. I'd never seen finer tattoos in all my years and the time he must have spent beneath the needle to have gotten them was astounding, let alone the cost of such art being cast upon his skin. There was a story there and I was curious as all hell about it.

I was distracted by my interest in Drake's ink, so I didn't notice that Hagot had dropped down and started preparing a poultice until his elbow crashed into my knee in a demand for me to give him more space.

"Are you sure I need more medicine? The wound looks much improved to me," I said, and he laughed obnoxiously.

"Stupid muscle man knows nothing of healing," he muttered to himself, and I pursed my lips.

I watched as the strange healer got to work mixing herbs with a cut of aloe vera leaf and grinding them into a pestle before me. My nose wrinkled as he pulled a dried, red beetle from a little pouch and crushed that into the mixture too. I outwardly recoiled when he finished by spitting in the mixture before scooping it onto his unwashed fingers and standing before me. *Gods be damned, did he really need to add his fucking saliva to it?*

"What are you going to do with-" I began, but I was cut off by his lightning-fast movement as he slapped the slimy poultice against the burn on my side and stole a curse from my lips.

"Oh, for the love of the Fallen," I swore as Drake caught my arm to stop me from pushing the healer away from me in disgust and a large, waxy leaf was slapped over the wound to keep the revolting mixture against my flesh.

"There," Hagot announced with a smile as he looked to me at last. "Better?"

I couldn't hide my revulsion at his methods, but as Drake continued to hold my arm and stop me from peeling the leaf away, I was forced to accept the lessening pain in my side and the relief the mixture was affording me.

"It works," I said in surprise and Hagot nodded, tapping the side of his nose.

"Your fancy upper Fae healers will always hide the spit from your la-de-da eyes," he said. "But essence of a healer is key. As are many other natural ingredients which can turn delicate little stomachs like yours. But the proof is in the pudding as they say. And it's working, ain't it?"

"I don't have a delicate stomach," I muttered, not liking the way these criminals seemed to look down on me for my upbringing despite the fact that I'd clearly had it a lot better than them.

"You gonna leave that little potion in place to stop the rot setting in then?" Drake demanded, still holding my arm like he didn't trust me not to rip the leaf off, and I could admit it was tempting to do so. But I could also admit that the lasting pain was ebbing and some of the tension of holding onto that agony was finally fading from my limbs.

"Yes. You can unhand me now before I have to put you on your arse," I grumbled.

Drake laughed and slapped me on the shoulder. Not like he didn't believe

I could do it, more like he'd enjoy it if I tried, and I supposed we had a love of fighting in common if nothing else.

"Come on then. Let's get the fuck outta here," Drake said before tugging open the hatch and leading the way out of The Den.

Thank Osaria I'm leaving this shithole at last.

I waited for the others to go first, watching the beastly looking men who Drake had selected to help him carry the treasure, and assessing each of them for any weaknesses I could take note of just in case this turned ugly for me once they got what they wanted. I wasn't a fool. I held value to these men for the moment, but once they had the treasure, all bets would be off, and there was clearly no honour among these thieves.

I continued to conceal the scimitar behind my back as they went and Hagot headed away, calling out to the other gang members close by to ask if any of them needed his assistance before he packed his things away.

Once the last of the men had headed down into the dark tunnel beneath The Den, I followed them and slammed the hatch above my head.

As I walked deeper into the dark passage, Drake noted the weapon at my back without saying a word. His eyes glinted with amusement for a moment before he whipped the cape off of his shoulders and threw it over my head to blindfold me once again.

I sighed as two of the gang members grabbed my arms and roughly guided me along the tunnel like they were trying to knock me into every wall on the way. I stumbled over the uneven floor, fighting against the impulse to rip the hood off so that I could see better and forcing myself to trust these arseholes.

The change in the air soon told me we'd exited The Den, but they didn't take the hood off of my face until we'd marched on for several more minutes.

Drake finally tugged the cape off of me, wrapping it around himself instead even though the heat wafting through the streets was oppressive. The storm had only just settled and people were still remaining indoors in case of errant winds kicking it up again. The tinkling windchimes sounded occasionally like they were calling out a farewell to Karu, the long-lost god of the storm, and a shiver tracked down my spine at the noise, causing me to cast a look over my shoulder as I felt like eyes were upon me. In moments like that, I found it easy to buy in to the idea of deities and magic, all the things we'd once laid claim to before the Fallen had cursed us.

Sand coated the streets and buildings, blown into corners and forming tiny dunes which had turned the city into an artwork of beige and gold. The morning sun beat down on our backs as Drake and the others stood around me in a crescent, and I felt the weight of their expectations laying thickly upon my fate. It only took that one glance at the group of them to see my death waiting in their eyes, and it was beyond clear to me that they would gladly deliver it if I failed to hold up my end of the bargain we'd struck.

"Lead the way then, Cassius." Drake held out a hand, gesturing for me to go ahead, the corner of his lips lifting as he noted my hesitation. He was right about that at least – I wasn't used to this part of the city, the ramshackle buildings and twisting alleyways could be easily confusing, but I was a royal guard and all I needed was a look at the sky to orient myself and figure out the direction we needed to take.

I moved along the street, gaining my bearings before taking a left towards the edge of the city. The gang followed on silent feet and anyone who spotted us quickly shrank into the shadows, clearly knowing well enough to stay away from these Fae and whatever crimes they were embroiled in.

Everything about Drake and his men screamed trouble, and I supposed the way I was dressed now marked me as one of them too. I'd always been gazed upon with respect and intrigue, but now the civilians' expressions darkened and their eyes widened as they looked upon me, telling me they didn't think anything of the sort about me anymore. The Forty Thieves were fear embodied, their foul deeds written on the streets of this city in blood, and no upstanding citizen would dare cross them willingly.

I will get a decent life back after this is done. I have to.

"We will need to exit the city perimeter. Do you have a particular means of crossing the outer walls?" I asked as we drew close to the southern gates, wondering how these men usually navigated the guards who would be on duty there. Did they have another secret tunnel they used to come and go via? Was there a passageway that led them out into the desert away from the watching eyes of the city guards?

Drake snorted in amusement and shook his head. "Yeah, we have a real simple way of coming and going," he said, jerking his chin in a command for me to follow and leading the way.

We slipped out of the side alleys and joined the large crowd of people who were either heading towards the gates or coming in through them. There were travelling caravans and merchants from all across The Twelve Kingdoms, come to buy and sell at the markets and my stomach growled loudly as we passed through the scents of baked goods on their way to be sold within the city.

I spotted the hired mercenaries and guards among them who had travelled with the merchants to protect them from the creatures which roamed freely beyond the walls of the city, and I noticed more than a few fresh wounds along with a wrapped body which lay on the back of one of the wagons. Travelling through the Lyrian, even along the stone roads always came with more than a little risk to those who did so, and I wasn't much looking forward to encountering any of those hazardous monsters myself.

To my surprise, Drake didn't turn from the main path, instead striding right down the centre of the wide road, his black cape billowing out behind him as a gust of wind blew in from the open gates. The way he stalked into the crowd somehow made everyone notice him, his broad frame moving with an arrogant kind of swagger which almost seemed like a dare, challenging anyone who was fool enough to try and get in his way. People moved aside to let him pass, encouraging horses and camels to the edges of the street as if they could sense the trouble clinging to his flesh and wanted no part in it. Like they could sense the danger rolling off of him with nothing more than a single look.

The sand was thick on the ground here and men were working to sweep it aside, causing a little storm of sand-filled air to whip up around the legs of passers-by.

The other gang members followed Drake, nudging me into motion when I hesitated, and we all strode straight towards the heavy wooden gates which sat open amid the expanse of the tall white walls which ringed the city. My heart began to beat harder in anticipation of what lay beyond these walls. The endless miles of the Lyrian Desert were perilous for many reasons, from the simple lack of shelter, from the baking sun, to the far greater dangers of the monsters who resided there.

Fire drakes roamed the skies and basilisks lurked beneath the sand. If death wasn't on wings above then it would come from below, and we had to be prepared for anything.

Fire drakes were relatively harmless for most of the year, but during mating season they grew volatile, and they often flew close to the city on the hunt for food. Which was one of the reasons why the walls were fitted with crossbows large enough to cut them down in their tracks before they ever made it far enough to rain down hell on our people.

I'd never been far into the desert, but I recalled my days of training one mile beyond its border, carrying a bag of rocks on my back while Captain Marik worked us to the brink of exhaustion, our only reward a cup of water every eight hours. Suffice to say, it was not my favourite place in the world and that was without having faced most of the monsters that lived out there. At least not in the wild. Marik had been rather fond of capturing beasts for the purpose of facing us in the training pit. I would never forget the first time I'd stood in that hole alone, my bare feet sinking into the sand and the cool kiss of a sword in my palm while two angry red eyes gazed back at me from the dark.

Guards moved between the carts and travellers as they checked them over, collecting any fees which were required from the vendors, but none of them looked our way as we strode towards them. In fact, the closer we got, the clearer it became that they were specifically looking anywhere but at us, and my brow furrowed.

Either these men were terrified or well bribed because they didn't once look our way, and despite the strict rules in place about travellers coming and going through the city gates, it was abundantly clear that they weren't going to do a damn thing about the passage of a bunch of cutthroats walking straight out of the city right beneath their noses.

I was caught between outrage at the fact that these criminals clearly held their own power within the emperor's domain, and relief that we had made it beyond the city limits without so much as a raised voice to slow us down.

One we had exited the city, we continued straight down the southern road, passing the long line of men and women waiting to get inside the walls as we strode along the cobbles and the sun grew ever hotter overhead. A bloody war was taking place between the Forkens and the island stronghold of Quellioth in the south, and every day more and more refugees were arriving in Osaria, seeking a safe haven from the bloody battles that plagued their hometowns.

It was a long journey from their lands, and to avoid the Lyrian Desert, the journey was made even longer. They had to cross the Forken Sea, then travel over land between the kingdoms of Rothstern and Berion to the flat plains in the south, then take the treacherous pass over the mountains known as the Serpent's Spine. Some of them headed to the other cities closer to their home, but the legends of the empire's capital always drew many to Osaria despite the extra weeks or months that entailed on the road.

My gaze fell to the bare feet of the children queuing with their mothers and fathers, taking shelter from the sun in the shadow cast by the wall. My chest tightened knowing that many of them would be turned away, sent onto the next city, or the next, all because Magdor had declared there was no more room for refugees, when she knew as well as I did that that wasn't the case.

Perhaps they'd find better fortune elsewhere though because the only life available to them here would likely be a poor one. And at least the guards were letting the market men barter with them, roaming up and down with baskets of food. Though as I passed one man demanding a woman give him the necklace around her throat for a simple bread roll, I found my feet coming to a firm halt behind him.

"You will offer a fair price, baker," I growled and he turned sharply, taken by surprise, his eyes narrowing as he took me in.

"Says 'oo?" he snapped, his yellowed teeth making my nose wrinkle.

"Says a r-" I cut myself off, about to announce myself as a royal guard like a damn fool. "Says one of The Forty," I hissed and his eyes widened, flicking over to the men I was with who were walking on ahead of me.

The woman glanced between us, hugging two frightened children against her legs whose feet were wrapped in torn cloth. This whole situation was an outrage to me, knowing they wouldn't find the salvation they were hoping for when they reached the gates of my city. This should have been a safe haven for them, but instead, the empress had ensured they'd be offered nothing.

"She ain't got any coin," the baker hissed at me. "What am I s'posed to do? I gotta make a livin'."

I noticed Drake appearing behind him out of nowhere, clearly using his Affinities to sneak around as usual. He casually stole bread rolls out of the man's basket and pushed them into his pockets. I shook my head minutely at him in an order to stop, but he ignored me, taking a savage bite out of one while the woman and her kids looked to him with an ache of hunger in their eyes. In the next move, Drake took the man's coin purse from his pocket and started rifling through the contents, my eyes shifting from him and back to the baker who was now monologuing at me about his need to buy a new rolling pin for his bakery.

Drake causally stepped around the baker, subtly pushing the purse into my hand and winking at me before walking away after the members of his gang. My fingers closed around the purse, not wanting the man to see it in case he recognised it, discomfort crawling up my spine. I could almost hear Marik barking an order in my ear to kneel, feel him ripping the tunic from my back and the kiss of the nine tails of his whip. But then I looked at the hungry people around me and found myself tipping the coins into my hand and holding them out to the man.

"This for all of your bread," I said firmly and his eyes raised at the pile of coins in my palm.

"Well, now, not all of it. Can't do all of it. But a fair bit, eh?" He tried to snatch the coins but I drew my hand away.

"All of it," I snarled and he backed up at my tone, his lips parting before he gave in and started nodding, handing over the basket of bread as I poured the coins into his outstretched palms.

I handed it straight over to the woman and she burst into tears, offering it to her children immediately before passing it out to everyone around her.

I marched away, hurrying after Drake as heat burned the back of my neck over what I'd just done. I was a con man. A fucking dirty, cheating thief.

"'Ang on – wait a minute!" the baker shouted after me. "Where's my purse?!"

I stuffed it into my pocket, picking up my pace and not looking back as I joined Drake who started laughing like an arsehole.

He nudged me with his elbow, offering me a bread roll despite his earlier claim that he wouldn't be offering me food again and I shook my head mutely.

"You make a good distraction, mate. Thanks for that."

"I wasn't distracting him for you," I muttered angrily.

"Then why didn't you tell him what I was doing?" he asked, giving me a knowing look like he'd already figured out something about me which I was desperate to deny.

"I..." Apparently, I didn't have an answer for that.

"See, you're gonna make a fine criminal one day. I'm so proud of you," he taunted.

"Shut up," I growled. "I'm not a criminal."

"Then why'd you just steal that man's bread?"

"I didn't," I hissed. "You were the one who stole his coin."

"Yeah, and you were the one who used it to buy his bread. All of his bread as well, you didn't even leave him a single roll. Fucking savage, mate."

"Those people were hungry," I insisted, trying to validate the decision I'd made, but I was torn between two opposing forces. I had committed a crime, but I had done it for good reason.

"By the Fallen, even when you're being a criminal, you're noble about it. Didn't you even take one for yourself?" He patted down my pockets, finding them empty and he shook his head at me like I disgusted him. "I swear to the gods, Cassius, if you die before you show me where my treasure is because you're off feeding your meals to a hungry rabbit that gives you the big eyes, I will follow you into the underworld and drag you back here by the throat."

"Don't be ridiculous," I growled.

"What's ridiculous, mate, is you acting like you still live to serve the crown, but maybe I shouldn't have expected anymore from a man who was taught to be nothing more than a number in the guards' ranks." He shrugged and I tried not to let those words get under my skin, but my fingers went instinctively to the number behind my ear which was now scabbed over from where he'd cut through it.

I am number two hundred and eighty-seven. And I am made of steel.

I'd said those words on repeat while my captain stood over me and I did endless press-ups in the dirt. I *was* just a number, that was the point. A man bent and beaten under the hottest flames, forged into a weapon meant to protect the empire. I'd chosen that life to keep my family in their home, it had been my responsibility to do so, and I'd made the sacrifice willingly to protect them.

"You do realise that you helped those people too, don't you?" I challenged, trying to turn his attention from me. "I couldn't have given them that bread without your interference."

"You mean that grubby looking woman and her little brats?" he asked, feigning horror at the idea. "I did no such thing."

"Clearly you knew what I would do with that money once you handed it to me," I insisted but he just shook his head.

"I didn't," he replied. "I mean, yeah, I thought you might buy them a loaf or two, what with that indignant look you had etched all over your face, but I wanted to see what you'd do with it for myself. I wondered if you really were so morally straightlaced that you would simply hand it back to him, or if you were as corrupt as me and would just keep it all for yourself. I wouldn't have guessed you'd go and feed a bunch of hungry mouths with every last coin." He snorted a laugh like what I'd done both amused and surprised him and I frowned at his assessment of me.

"Feeding them was the right thing to do," I said firmly.

"Uh-huh," he agreed. "So you'll be returning to feed them again at noon will you? Or at dusk? Or have you lost interest in your little charity cases now that you can pat yourself on the back and congratulate yourself on feeding the poor? And what about the ones who didn't get a morsel from your generosity? How're you gonna feed them?" He swept a hand out to indicate the huge line of refugees who we were still passing by. There were no more mercenaries or hired swords among these people. Several of the men carried weapons or even clasped large sticks which they had clearly used to defend themselves while they were on the road, but the harrowed look in all of their eyes said there had been plenty of struggles throughout their journey. My stomach twisted as I spotted more hungry children and my brow dropped at the reality of their situation.

"At least I did something," I muttered and for once Drake didn't reply with any kind of mocking or accusations about me wasting my time.

He sighed, patting me on the shoulder and almost seeming like he gave a shit too before he leaned in closer and spoke again, completely changing the subject and acting as though none of what we'd just discussed bothered him at all.

"If the emperor ordered you to stab yourself in the eye, would you do it?" Drake asked conversationally.

"Yes," I said and he laughed obnoxiously.

"What if he ordered you to bend over and shove a coconut up your arse?" he asked, grinning at his new game.

"I have to do anything he tells me to," I said stiffly.

"So, yes?" he pushed and I pressed my lips together.

"Yes, Drake. Anything he asks of me, I must do."

"Wow, I can't believe you shoved a whole coconut up your arse, mate. How'd you get it in there?"

"I did not shove a fucking coconut up my arse."

He chuckled, waving me off as if I was lying. "What if he asked you to do something physically impossible? Like lick your own elbow." He lifted his arm, trying to lick his elbow, looking like an idiot as his tongue stretched desperately towards it and I broke a grin at his idiocy.

He continued on with his line of questioning, coming up with more and more ridiculous orders the emperor might ask of me, and I soon found the game less annoying and more amusing – apart from the dark thought circling in the back of my mind that reminded me of just how little worth I held. My number was the sum total of all I was, and even that had been stripped from me now.

We soon left the gates far behind, passing through the farmland surrounding the city, the lush greenery sustained by the little streams carved all across the land here which were fed by the Carlell River that passed through the centre of the city.

We reached the verges of the city where a few farmers and tradesmen milled about at the point where a crossroad met the Lyrian Desert. Left led to Cartlanna if you walked far enough, the land meeting the sea where the city sat like a jewel watching the waves crash against its shores. Their fleet was the finest in the known world, sailing the cerulean ocean with their white and blue sails always present on the water, beyond the sweeping vineyards which ringed the city itself. Or you could turn south before then, cross the Carlell River and follow the coast to the cities of Shamba and Rothstern.

Shamba was set among the black volcanic rock formations left behind by an extinct volcano which had supposedly spouted lava from the sea during a conflict between Vargesh, the god of all water and Takari, the god of land and growth three thousand years ago.

Beyond that was the kingdom of Rothstern, set high on the white cliffs, overlooking both the Cartlanian and Forken seas, the sandstone fortress city fondly known as The Beacon by sailors all around, as it was often the first point of land made visible by those who ventured into the unknown waters where the sea beasts roamed.

Right led to most other kingdoms, depending on which roads you took from there, the north and eastern parts of the empire full of foreign wonders which I was unlikely to ever set my eyes upon. The entire world spread away from me as I looked towards the horizon, but in my gut, I knew that wasn't where we were headed.

I called upon the knowledge Magdor's magical pill had gifted me, my instincts tugging me in the direction of the cave where the treasure and that coin she wanted so badly were hidden. It felt as though I'd trodden this path before. And I didn't like the idea that her poison still trickled through my veins, infecting my thoughts that way.

The desert rolled away ahead of us, the road swallowed by the golden sand where great dunes rose like mountains in the distance, an amber sea shifting under the pressure of the wind.

"Where now, mate?" Drake asked, his eyes sparking with excitement like he lived for this kind of insanity, and I couldn't deny I liked that about him.

I pointed at the desert and the gang frowned uneasily, grumbles and curses breaking out instantly.

"I ain't walkin' out there. That desert holds nothin' but death," one of them said gruffly.

"Quit your bitching, Jadar," Drake bit at him. "The treasure isn't going to be easy to get, is it? Otherwise, anyone could have found it already."

Jadar grimaced and the scars on his face twisted menacingly.

My gaze landed on a row of camels behind a tradesman, their reins tethered to a line of fencing.

"Anyone got any coin?" I asked the group.

Jadar pulled out one fat kuru and I rolled my eyes.

"That's enough for a camel's arsehole, anyone else?" I asked and Drake shrugged before looking to the others.

Between the seven of them they produced a couple of worthless earrings, a broken pocket watch, a piece of desert glass and a pile of lint.

"Great," I muttered, waving it away as they tried to hand it to me.

Drake dropped his hand to his hip and lifted a sword – wait, that was *my* fucking sword.

"Hey," I snarled, moving closer to take it from him.

He grinned, twisting the precious scimitar in his hand and cutting it through the air as if he owned it. He moved like a man well used to wielding a blade, though it was clear to me he hadn't had any formal training. I doubted it mattered though. He was light on his feet and had the confidence of a man who had wetted a blade more than once, so I was sure he was more than competent with it.

"You really are a thief," he commented, his tone praising as if I'd done something to impress him.

I clenched my jaw as my stomach knotted at the accusation. "That sword is the property of the emperor and I intend to return it to him."

"Sure you do, thief," he mocked, tossing it to me in a move clearly designed to make me fumble, but my reflexes were sharp and my hand snapped out to catch it with ease. "Or you can buy us a few camels with it."

I stroked the hilt as I reattached it to my hip, securing it tighter this time as I turned to face the animals. "I'm not parting with this. It's owed to the emperor."

No harm in me using it in the meantime though...

"Why do you give a shit about the emperor?" Drake hissed. "His laws got you locked up in a dungeon. You would have died just 'cause you looked at his pretty daughter for five seconds."

"You've seen the princess?" Jadar gasped then the others shifted towards me with a hopeful lust in their eyes that built a fierce wall of defence in my chest.

"What did she look like?" asked the bald one who had half an ear missing.

"Tell us," the stocky one demanded, licking his blackened teeth eagerly.

I clamped my lips together, my hand on the hilt of the sword as they stepped even closer, but I could see they wouldn't let this drop now that Drake had told them about it. So I decided to offer them lies, just like I had my torturer because I would never give up even a scrap of detail on the perfection of her.

"She's beautiful, of course. Raven hair...eyes the colour of the night sky, lips like two butterfly wings balancing delicately on her face."

Jadar shivered, releasing a groan and rubbing a hand over his crotch like a fucking animal.

A violent protectiveness rose in me and my hand snapped out, latching around his throat and squeezing tight.

"Do not dare touch yourself over the princess, or I will cut your cock off and feed it to your friend with the pornographic eyebrows." I jerked my chin at the man beside him who was breathing heavily over the princess, making anger ripple all across my body. A possessive need rose like a roaring flame in my chest and I put it down to my duty to her as I considered gutting all of them here and now.

Jadar paled at the image I'd painted in his mind, but his friends closed in around me and a twisted confidence filled his eyes again. "Oh yeah? Well maybe it's you who'll be fed my cock when I've got you on your knees begging for mercy."

"*Yeah,*" Porno-brows said with a sneer, then looked at his friend. "Wait – what?"

"Go, go, go!" Drake's voice suddenly called to me.

I released Jadar, turning and spotting the tradesman on the ground with a bloody nose as Drake dragged the group of camels towards us. They grunted their reluctance as he forced them to follow him, and I shook my head at the shameful act as he handed me a set of reins.

"Wait a second," I growled as the rest of the gang mounted their camels.

"No time to be a law-abiding citizen, Cassius!" Drake barked at me, climbing up onto one of the beasts. "Besides, that tradesman just told me he sold his daughter to a flesh trader this morning. So he deserves a little bad karma."

"Truly?" I asked, feeling a little better about this act as I hauled myself onto the back of the camel beside me.

"No, not really," Drake said, laughing as my lips parted in outrage. "Could be true though, couldn't it? You have to admit that guy looked like an arsehole."

I shook my head in disgust at him, but he just reached over and slapped my camel on the rump with a cry of, "Yah!" spurring it into a run before I could voice any further protests.

The others had to ride together between the remaining three animals, and Drake and I easily took the lead as our two steeds galloped onto the Lyrian sand and raced up the nearest dune.

Adrenaline crashed through my limbs and despite myself, I couldn't help but revel in the freedom of the wind in my hair and the sun beating down on my skin. I should have been a dead man already and yet here I was, racing into the unknown with a mission to cast a blow at the bitch empress spurring me on.

Cries of anger followed us from the camel vendor, but we didn't look back. Drake threw me a wild look, grinning broadly as his hood fell down and the wind danced through his onyx hair as we hurried on, a laugh tumbling from my throat before I could stop it.

This didn't just feel good. It felt like freedom, and I was starting to think I liked the taste of it.

We rode on through the day, leaving the city far behind until all that surrounded us was sand. The sun hung like a giant orb above us, the heat unrelenting and sweat glistening against our skin as we battled the temperature with every passing moment. Since my endurance training out in the desert, I'd sworn that I'd never venture out onto the cursed sand again after coming damn close to death from the heat and exposure alone.

This place was its own stunning version of hell, and we were the fools for walking right into it. But unlike the last time, I didn't feel lost, unsure of my way or even fearful of taking a step in any direction in case it was the wrong one. The burning sense of knowledge that the empress had lodged inside my brain made that impossible. I could no sooner falter from this path than I could summon a storm into existence. And I just had to hold onto the belief that once we reached our destination, this perilous journey would be well worth it.

Jadar produced a gallon of water from his bag, and we passed it between us regularly, though it was running low already and I had been purposefully missed out a few times. I didn't much like sharing saliva with Drake's hygiene-free pals and they clearly felt the same way about me, but it was that or die of thirst before I made it to the cave, and Drake ensured it was handed to me often enough that I didn't get dizzy from the heat.

It seemed as though a lot of my standards were already being forced to slip, and I hadn't even been out of the palace for a week yet. What kind of creature would I become if I was forced to endure a month in the company of these men?

By Osaria, I swear I can taste their unbrushed teeth on my tongue.

Magdor's magic guided me like the path was etched into my mind and I hoped I was right in believing that we wouldn't be left adrift in the desert dunes for too much longer. We'd reach the Red Pass soon enough and finally get a little shade for a while, though the rumours of the beasts that lurked there set me on edge.

We headed west for several hours before taking a turn towards the north, the certainty in my destination as clear in my mind as if I were walking the path back to the house I grew up in. It was beyond strange, and I didn't like the knowledge that I'd been subjected to some twisted, stolen magic, but if I could make something good come out of this then I was more than willing to do it. I just prayed to the Fallen that I wasn't cursing myself by making use of this dark gift and spitting in the eye of the lost god it had been stolen from.

Soon, I spotted a huge rock on the horizon roughly shaped like a giant eagle with its wings stretched wide and beak pointing off to our left as though it were looking at something. I smiled in relief, kicking the camel into a fast pace to reach it, bouncing up and down wildly on its back as it took up a rolling gallop which came close to unseating me.

The gang hollered as they took chase, evidently thinking we were close to our prize and Drake whooped loudly to encourage them, grinning at me from beneath the hood which he was using to shade himself from the unrelenting sun.

We passed under the shadow of the hulking rock form and my breathing stalled as my camel fell still and the thieves closed in at my back.

"We should leave an offering here," one of the men muttered and I looked over to find him staring up at the hulking rock in reverence. "This is Karu, the lost god of the wind. We should thank him for offering us shade from the sun."

My mother had always enjoyed telling us stories of the lost gods and their so-called powers to my sisters and I at bedtime when we were children, and I had some vague recollection of Karu gliding across all the land and guiding the best of the weather wherever he saw fit. Or sending storms ahead of him when that suited his mood instead.

Several of the thieves produced trinkets and small coins to toss at the base of the rock while others snickered in amusement at their superstitious behaviour.

I glanced at Drake, wondering about his beliefs and finding a dark look on his normally smiling face.

"The gods abandoned us long ago," he muttered, sneering up at the hulking stone which cast us in its shadow. "Why should we offer them anything when they turned their backs on us? I have no interest in pandering to some deity who has no interest in us or the fate they dealt us when they left."

He spat on the stone and the man who had first spoken of Karu gasped in alarm while another looked inclined to punch him for it. But Drake just tugged a lethal looking blade from his belt and levelled them with a challenging look.

My gaze caught on the ink which coated the fingers of the hand which held that blade and I frowned, wondering why my attention had been drawn to it so forcefully.

Before the men could come to blows over their beliefs or lack of them, a wild wind picked up, sand belting us as it whipped around the stone eagle and caused a wailing sound to echo beneath the rock for several long seconds which made my pulse beat out of rhythm.

"You've angered the gods!" one of the men cried and Drake barked a laugh as the wind died down.

"The gods are fucking lost, Brantar. I guarantee they didn't come back just because I spat on a lump of damn rock. Pull yourselves together or fuck off back to Egos and tell him that your superstitions spooked you, and you had to run home to suckle at his hairy teats for safety."

The men all bristled angrily at that suggestion, but Drake ignored them, turning his gaze to me in a clear demand for directions. I blew out a breath and forced my mind from the prickling feeling which was still running across my skin, focusing on the sense of direction that Magdor's magic had left in me instead.

I led the way beyond the eagle, heading towards the red stone chasm ahead of us and passing between two vast walls of rock that created a pocket of darkness out of the blazing sun. The shadows were thick and cool, a welcome relief from the heat of the desert as we rode into the ravine.

I found myself staring up at the rock walls, the blood red colour of them making me feel at once awed and uneasy as I wondered what could have caused them to look that way. There were old tales of a battle that had taken place here between the Fae of old. The claim was that so much blood was spilled in that fight that when it was done, at the end of a long and gruelling passage of seven days and seven nights, there was only a single Fae left standing to claim the victory. It was rumoured that the blood of all those who had fallen had stained the ground here until the rocks themselves bled and that was what I looked upon now. I wasn't sure I believed such a tale, but it was harder to deny in the face of it, especially when I reached out to brush my fingers along the red rock and they came away stained with the bright colour which glimmered wetly on my skin.

Something about the place commanded silence and whenever the men broke it, they spoke in whispers to one another without anyone needing to command it.

Even Drake was quiet as he rode beside me, the plod of the camels' feet on the hard, rocky ground beneath us echoing around the cavernous gap and no doubt alerting any beasts in this place to our presence. The stones above us were baked dry by the blinding sun, cracking towards the top of the sheer walls like the crust of a pie.

I kept my hand on the hilt of the scimitar at my hip and Drake's eyes darted left and right as he clearly anticipated an attack too, though nothing in the silence suggested we weren't alone.

"I don't like this place," one of the men muttered behind me and I glanced back to see it was the one with the tattooed brows who had the issue.

"If you're afraid, then you can go back," I clipped and his spine straightened, his eyes narrowing and the naked arses of the women inked on his face lowering.

"Maybe we feed this one to whatever monsters come looking for us," he suggested to his friends who sniggered in return.

"Maybe you shut your mouth and remember who's leading us to the treasure," Drake tossed at him.

"When we have it, we won't need him anymore," Jadar said in a low voice I barely caught, though Drake didn't seem to hear it. Or maybe he did, but he didn't give a fuck. I was going to have to work out an escape plan as soon as that coin was in my grasp, because otherwise I was going to end up with a sword in my back. And I wondered if it might even belong to the man riding beside me.

Drake didn't look my way as I gave him an assessing look, certain he held no loyalty to me at all. He'd said himself he didn't have friends, and the only reason he'd kept me alive so far was to deliver him to the gold I'd promised. Between him and the eight men at our backs, I would be hard pressed to get out of this alive, even with my Affinity for fighting. I might take down a few of them, perhaps more than half if I got lucky, but eventually one of them would wound me badly enough to bring me to my knees. And then I'd die out here in this desert never to be found.

A squawking shriek carried from somewhere in the sky and we all looked up, drawing our weapons as we hunted the azure canvas above for the fire drake.

The camels grunted uneasily, slowing their pace and I thought of my horse, Gallow, wishing he was with me now. That animal was faster than a bullet and as fearless as a warrior. He'd get me out of any danger so long as I was on his back.

We kept moving, alert as we crept deeper into the ravine, watching the sky for any sign of the fire drake returning. We turned a corner and entered a wider part of the valley, the ground sloping sharply down beneath us until we arrived in what appeared to be a wide, round crater in the rock.

My eyes fell on the most beautiful object laying on the ground at the heart of it, nestled in a pool of golden sand which had been heated so violently that it had been turned to glass. It was an egg the size of a man, the shell looking as though it were made of pure rubies, gleaming in the sunlight filtering down from above.

"Holy shit," Drake gasped just as Tattoo Brows dismounted and walked towards it.

"What is that?" Jador called.

"A dragon egg," I rasped in disbelief, having seen drawings of these in the old scriptures. But it wasn't possible. Dragons were extinct, this had to be something else, though it was hard to deny the sheer beauty of the thing. I could think of no other beast who laid eggs like that.

"Don't touch it," I warned, but the arsehole was already laying his greedy hands on it.

"It's hot," he gasped. "Jador, come feel this."

I glanced at Drake, seeing the reflection of the ruby egg gleaming in his eyes, temptation written into his features. He moved to dismount and my hand shot out, my fingers locking around his arm.

"Don't," I hissed. "Haven't you heard of Dragon Lore?"

"That's kid's stories," he said dismissively, but he didn't dismount, only throwing a jealous look at Tattoo Brows who was all but humping the egg as he tried to roll it back in the direction of his camel.

"Leave it," I snapped. "We have to move on from this place."

"Do you know the price one of these would fetch, arsehole?" Tattoo Brows grunted. "Fuck the treasure, we could head home now and live like kings for the rest of our days on the bounty we'd receive for this prize."

"And incur the wrath of a dragon who will not stop hunting us until its dying breath?" I snarled and Drake considered my words, seeming to weigh up the risks.

"Dragons don't exist no more," he hissed.

"I am inclined to believe the opposite right now, Drake," I growled, my mind whirling with the truth before my eyes. Perhaps I was mistaken, but that egg was just as the scriptures had described, and I would rather be cautious and survive than be wrong and find myself incurring the wrath of an ancient dragon.

"Don't be a coward, mate," he taunted. "That's probably just some fat fire drake's egg."

"That is nothing of the sort," I insisted urgently. "All who scorn a dragon will perish," I recited part of the Dragon Lore my mother had taught me when I was a kid. "All who touch the priceless shell of the unborn will be marked."

"Shut him up, will you?" Tattoo Brows growled. "Or I'll stick him with my knife."

My camel shifted side to side, stamping its front feet and letting out a noise of distress. I patted its neck, trying to calm the animal, and suddenly a name carried into my mind from its thoughts.

"Azurea."

"Not possible," I breathed in response to the name of that legend.

"Maybe if we break it, we can carry it easier?" Jador suggested.

"We shouldn't touch it," another man called in panic. "Dragons are the guardians of the gods."

"There are no such thing," Drake scoffed, but he still didn't get down from his camel.

"A man of sin, and man of steel, shall form a fragile, fate-bound deal,"

the powerful female voice whispered in my mind and the air stirred around me with some unnatural power. The wind picked up and somehow the stifling air grew hotter, and my gaze lifted to the empty sky as I feared what was approaching.

"We have to move," I hissed.

"And where would you go, man of steel?" an ethereal female voice spoke inside my head like a caress against my soul. I stopped breathing, hunting for the source of it as my pulse drummed inside my ears.

"Who are you?" I spoke aloud and the others looked at me in confusion, though Drake's brows were raised as if he'd heard her too.

"I have been known by a thousand names. Keeper of Shadows, Bringer of Death, Nightwing of the Fallen, Gallus the Great, but you know me as Azurea."

"We mean you no harm," I called, my eyes falling to the arsehole still touching this divine being's egg. "Get away from there," I snarled and Drake started nodding.

"Back up, Heston," he barked, but the man seemed possessed as he stabbed his knife against the ruby shell, trying to shatter it and a roar echoed through the sky in response that was like a thunderclap.

The camels let out frightened honks and one of them went flying past me with two men on its back, tearing across the open space which held the nest and galloping up the other side of it into the ravine.

I raised my sword, spurring my camel forward and driving my boot into the back of Heston's head to force him away from the egg. He turned his knife on me and I saw a possessed demon in his eyes, reminding me further of the Dragon Lore. *Those with unworthy hearts shall be maddened by the hallowed power of the dragons.*

A shadow cloaked us in darkness as a giant beast flew overhead and screams of alarm rang out behind me, but by the time I looked up, the sky was clear again.

"Just a piece." Heston wetted his lips, slamming his knife into the egg again. "One little piece won't be missed."

"Stop," I snapped and Drake steered his own camel to the man's other side, booting him in the shoulder.

"Get away from it, motherfucker. I'm not gonna get eaten by some storybook monster because of you," Drake growled.

"Monster?" Azurea laughed mockingly inside our minds, a threat lacing the word. *"Yes, I can be a monster, man of sin. Would you like to see?"*

By the gods, we're fucked.

"No thanks, we just wanna pass through. We'll leave your egg right here, okay? All tucked up in this lovely little nest," Drake called and Jador frowned at him as he moved closer on his camel, sweat beading on his brow.

"Who are you speaking to?" he demanded.

Before either of us could answer, Azurea swept down from the sky, landing before us with a tremendous thud as her taloned feet hit the ground, sending a quake right through the earth and into my bones. She was as big as two houses, her scales jet black and gleaming like diamonds, looking just as sharp and unbreakable too. The tips of her wings were blood red and as she folded them against her sides, she raised her long neck and regarded us through two moss green eyes that were so full of wisdom and age that it made me feel like nothing but a speck of dust, about to be cast away on the wind.

The camels were startled, shifting foot to foot and honking as we all fought to keep them from running. Because if there was one thing all Fae remembered of the Dragon Lore, it was the final line. *Those who run from their majesty will die by tooth and claw and fire.*

"Stay as still as you can," I hissed at Drake, though why I was warning the thief was beyond me. The men behind us were in a panic, fighting to keep their animals under control while I kept my gaze firmly fixed on the beast of gods before us, my heart hammering in my chest.

Azurea's face was one of terrifying beauty, her snout long and her eyes wide, but sharp teeth peeked from within those powerful jaws, and I knew I was standing before my death if she chose it. And it would be a bloody, merciless thing.

In a sudden movement, she lunged at Heston as he clung to her egg, her wide jaws clamping down over his head and shoulders, silencing the terrified scream that left him. In the next bite, she'd swallowed him whole and blood seeped between her teeth as the men behind me wailed.

"Holy fuck," Drake breathed and I had to agree – not that I pitied the arsehole of his fate.

Only a fool would touch something so precious and assume he would not pay the price of it. And as I had been trained to look death in the eye without blinking, my pulse rate barely rose in response to it. It was the dragon who brought on a rise in it though, her magnificence something I had never encountered before, the air seeming to hum with her power. This here was a boy's dream, one I'd had long, long ago before I'd been moulded into an empty vessel of a man. And it stirred something in me that had been lost for many years.

Her gaze moved from me to Drake and a plume of smoke trailed from her nostrils, her chest glowing as hot as embers, speaking of the fire that lived within her.

"You seek the treasure of Kalir," she spoke within my mind again, her face not moving as she did so, and Drake scored a hand down the back of his neck.

"It's not your treasure, is it?" he asked, though not like he was deterred by the possibility of that, more like he was planning how he might deceive a dragon so that he could still steal it. But if Azurea had laid claim to that trove, we may as well give up hope now of ever securing it. And in all honesty, I would sleep easier at night knowing she guarded it, because Magdor surely wasn't powerful enough to take on a dragon.

She moved towards us with as much grace on land as she'd had on her wings, her clawed front foot raising to rest on her egg. Then she rolled it away from us so it stood upright in the heart of the nest once more, taking her time to nuzzle the sand up around its base to hold it there. She breathed against the shell and a wave of heat rippled in the air around the egg as she warmed it with the fire in her belly.

"I cannot enter that place. The treasure I crave can never be mine, a final insult from the gods. But this…this is my treasure, man of sin," she answered at last, nuzzling her egg.

"Are there others like you?" I asked as my gaze fell on that egg. "Are the dragons returning?" The stories of old said that most of the dragons had left with the gods, flying with them into the never realm, and those who'd stayed behind had died off many years ago after the Fae had turned against them, hunted them to the edges of the world in anger over the gods abandoning them.

"No, man of steel," she said, her words full of sorrow as she gazed at her egg. *"But there will be one more soon."*

"Er, not to bring up the obvious, but how did you make a baby dragon without a daddy dragon?" Drake asked and I cursed him under my breath for his lack of tact.

"She is a gift," Azurea breathed, her eyes sparkling with hope. *"I do not know what it means yet, but now I see a thief and a guard travelling together, and I believe I am starting to understand."*

"What do you mean?" I asked in confusion as the dragon regarded us.

Her eyes narrowed, her wings flexing a little at her shoulder blades and that fire in her burning brighter in her chest, making her scales glow red hot at the source of all that power.

"I was abandoned on this plane, left to rot alone for century after century." Anger rippled through her words and I fought the urge to reach for my sword. *"Now the lost gods are playing games and perhaps I do not wish to play along."* She bared her teeth at us and I gripped the reins tighter, ensuring my camel didn't make a bid for freedom, because we could not escape her hungry jaws.

"Wait," I gasped, seeing our deaths in her eyes as wrath took root in her.

She sneered at me and I knew I had only seconds to come up with the words that might save us, and the only thing I could think of was her desire for the treasure we sought.

"We'll give you the treasure, all we want is one sack full," I offered. "The rest, we will remove from the cave so that you can claim it."

Her eyes lit up at the thought of all the gold in that place and my throat thickened as I felt Drake giving me the side eye.

"The word of a Fallen Fae is nothing," she said suspiciously.

"It is when our lives hang in the balance," Drake pointed out and she narrowed her gaze on him. "What have you got to lose? If we don't keep our word, you can just come hunt us down and bite our heads off."

I nodded, though I was concerned by how easily he was going along with this. I presumed he understood that this promise must be kept, or we really would incur her wrath.

Azurea thought on it for a long moment then inclined her head and stepped aside to let us pass.

I shared a look with Drake, unable to believe we'd talked our way out of our deaths as we walked the camels towards her.

"Here, man of steel." She dragged the claw on her thumb against her chest, peeling off one of her scales and dropping it at the feet of my camel. She was so close, I could feel the warmth radiating from her, heating me through to my core. I dismounted from the animal, picking up the scale which was the size of my hand and looking up at the immense creature before me. It was warm and as smooth as silk, but the edges were as sharp as a blade.

"To summon me, you only need lay this in your palm and think my name. I will be waiting."

The threat was there, hanging between us and speaking of the violent death promised to us if we broke our word to her. I nodded, pocketing the scale and climbing back onto my camel, taking in a slow breath as I followed the others out of the nest and deeper into the ravine.

As we left the scent of fire and ash behind us, I was sure we had just cheated death, and I prayed my lucky streak was not about to run out.

MAGDOR

CHAPTER SIXTEEN

I sat through a long and tiresome meal across from the man I had taken as my husband, my eyes trailing over the signs of age which plagued him. The small lines around his eyes, the dusting of silver marking his once onyx black hair, the dull look to his once bright gaze. Though of course that dullness likely had more to do with the effort involved in trying to keep up with a young and virile queen at all hours of the day and night. It was quite the challenge to try and match the pace of an ageless soul after all.

I tapped a sharpened fingernail against the edge of the glass chalice I drank from as I waited for him to finish his meal.

For years I had taken opportunities like this to spread my legs for him, taken him hard and deep and let him fill me with his seed in the hopes of producing the fully legitimate heir which would have made all I was aiming to achieve here so much simpler. But after months turned into years, and years became a decade and no amount of fucking him ever came close to producing a child, I'd had to admit defeat in that plan. I'd even attempted fucking other men to be certain the problem was with me and not him and had been gifted the same result.

It was hardly surprising really. I had been devoured and reborn at the whims of the goddess of death and pain. She had gifted me a single life in the form of my son all those years ago, but he had been born of her own dark seed. And Kahn was a creature bred for doling out pain and destruction in her name. He was hers just as surely as I was. But that only meant my plans had had to change.

There was a reason I'd allowed Princess Austyn to live all these years. Had I produced an heir of my own, her life would have ended soon after to clear the way for the ascension of my own flesh and blood. But without that option, I still had a way to seal my ties to the throne. She would marry Kahn and give me what I wanted that way.

I only wished I wasn't being forced through the farce which was the pageant. But the traditions and will of the people of Osaria had to be upheld, at least in part, while I tightened my hold over them. Even with the will of a goddess on my side, I wasn't powerful enough to force so many into line all at once. I still had to play games of politics. I still had to think of appeasing the surrounding kingdoms despite their allegiance to the emperor and the throne he sat upon. They still had to have their opportunities to put one of their own on that throne – or at least they had to believe the chance had been there.

"Perhaps we should retire, My Lord?" I suggested loudly, pushing myself upright and drawing the attention of my husband's slowing mind.

His brows pulled together the way they always did when I asserted my control over him a little too obviously by making requests which were clearly demands, or even by simply telling him what I expected him to do. Deep down inside, he was still the man who had been born to rule. and exerting my will over him was no easy task, the effort involved in maintaining it endless.

The heavy pulse of the dark gifts I'd been given swept through my veins as I tightened my hold on his will, my finger twitched just the slightest amount from the exertion it took.

Herdat still didn't hold the strength she had before she had been lost to us. She needed time and worship, sacrifice and blood to regain her grip on the world, and that meant the power she gifted me always began to fade between my visits to her temples.

Emperor Tarim straightened his spine, that defiance in his eyes flaring before my hold on him forced it to dim and he nodded instead, rising with the grace of the man he had once been and moving towards me to escort me back to our rooms.

I took his arm and moved to walk in his shadow, the sticky heat of the day fading beneath the light of the moon and a cool breeze sweeping through the open palace windows.

We headed into our room and Tarim turned to me the moment the door closed, his mouth seeking mine, his addiction to me and the pleasure I could offer him still so potent. My control hinged on that need in him. My body a tool designed to keep him in line and our joining a way for me to tighten my grip on him even while the magic I wielded ate into his flesh piece by piece and worked to steal him away.

Not yet though.

As it stood, without him I would be nothing but the widow of a man who had once ruled all. I still needed him. Until the wedding between my son and his daughter, I still required his presence.

I let him tug me to the bed as my tongue moved over his, his fingers pulling the fastenings of my dress apart and making my breasts spill free of it.

I moaned in a low and throaty way as his cock drove into my hip, then pushed him back so that he fell onto the bed.

Tarim stared at me as I pushed the dress the rest of the way off of my body and I moved to take a glass of wine from the table where servants had left it waiting for us. With my back turned to him, I slipped a small vial from the hidden compartment in the edge of the table and poured several drops into the deep red liquid.

I hid the vial within the compartment once more then headed back to him with the wine in hand, meeting his gaze as I came to stand before him before tipping the glass back and allowing it to wash over my breasts and stomach, leading the way to the valley between my thighs.

Tarim didn't hesitate, shifting forward and gripping my arse as he ran his tongue over my flesh, lapping at the spilled wine and making my nipples pebble from the feel of his mouth worshiping me.

I tipped my head back, moaning softly as he drank the wine from my skin and closing my eyes as I offered up a prayer to Herdat despite knowing she cared not for such petty things as pleasure. This act was not one designed by her hand.

Tarim's grip on me tightened as he rocked back and I looked down at him as he blinked up at me in confusion, shaking his head a little as if trying to banish some dizziness.

I cocked my head in feigned innocence. "My Lord?" I inquired, false concern lacing my voice which was hardly even needed as his eyes rolled back into his head and he fell on the bed unconscious within the next heartbeat.

I turned from him dismissively, moving to the washroom which adjoined our bed chamber and using a sponge dipped in the honey water that had been left out for us to bathe in to wash the wine from my skin.

Tarim would likely sleep late into the morning, his memory foggy when he woke and any uncertainty easily swept aside when I climbed into his lap and rode his cock until he forgot all about the strange period of time he had lost track of.

Tonight, I had work that needed attending.

I moved to the closet, taking a thick, bottle green cloak from it and wrapping it around my naked form, fastening the buttons to conceal my body within it and drawing the hood up to cover my head and hide my features in shadow.

I opened the hidden door behind the tapestry to the left of the bed and slipped into the dark passageway there silently, padding down the cold stone stairs on bare feet and relishing the bite of discomfort they offered me.

The stairs twisted downward steadily before letting me out into another passage, only the gifts of my goddess allowing me to see my way without the aid of a torch or lantern.

I headed along it before opening another hidden door, this one not far from the kitchens where even at this time of night, servants worked tirelessly to make certain that the royal family and any guests we may feel like entertaining remained well fed.

I turned away from the kitchens, sweeping through the servants' corridors until I made it to an exit which let out close to the stables.

The gravel out there cut into my feet, making me wince and smile at the pain, knowing this was the kind of service my goddess required. This and so much more besides.

A small, covered carriage awaited me to the side of the stables, the discrete wooden contraption more fit for a merchant's wife than the empress of Osaria, but then that was the point.

It was already hitched to the poorly bred horses that had been purchased especially for this purpose, and the guards all believed it was used to transport the emperor's favourite whore in and out of the palace. I had been the one to facilitate the arrangement and they believed I was fully engaged in whatever acts took place between him and the woman we purchased, but they also knew better than to ever do more than look into the carriage and ensure that only a single, cloaked woman entered the palace upon the carriage's return. They were not permitted to speak to her or search her, nor look upon her face. And they never thought to look into the carriage when it left to collect her. Nor when it headed out once more in the morning under the pretence of returning her to wherever she came from – if they had, they would have realised the thing was empty then. But men were always willing to believe in some lewd fact about their betters, so it wasn't a hard ruse to keep up.

The single carriage driver who knew the truth of these outings could be trusted implicitly thanks to the power Herdat had gifted me, and so my trips into the city remained a secret.

I climbed into the carriage without so much as greeting the man who sat atop it waiting for me, pulling the door shut behind me and ensuring the curtains were drawn across the windows so that no one would catch a glimpse of me.

I drew in a deep breath of the thick air as the carriage began to move, smoothing out the fabric of my cloak and thinking of the guard who I had gifted knowledge of that treasure to. I didn't know what to make of his escape. I had been enraged by the news of it, but that anger did me no good. I had been in need of a man capable of carrying out the task and he had seemed like the perfect choice. Unfortunately, I couldn't use one who I had already lured under the command of my goddess.

There was ancient power in that place where the coin was housed. The kind designed to keep the lost gods away. It was why I couldn't send just anyone to retrieve what I required from the cavern. Why I couldn't go myself. So a dead man walking seemed like a good bet for an alternative. Now I would need to find another to send in his place. But finding a trustworthy man willing to risk his life like that was a difficult choice indeed. I would have to return to the royal prison and pick another shortly though; my goddess's need was great and her commands were clear. I needed to gain that coin.

The carriage moved steadily through the empty streets as the cooler night air wrapped around it and my muscles began to tighten more and more with each second that passed, my need to serve my goddess growing in intensity as the desire to please her filled me.

It seemed to take an age and no time at all to reach our destination in the ninth ring, the Temple of Herdat situated to the west of the central part of the city where the ground rose and offered it a position high enough to be seen from all around.

Even after the old gods and goddesses had disappeared and the first lie of the Fallen had cursed us, the temples had remained. Each of them housed priests and priestesses who devoted their lives to the worship of their lost deities despite the empty ears their prayers fell upon. I had been like them once. Praying and devoting myself to a god who couldn't hear me. But I was the only one dedicated enough to seek her out. I was the only one who had roused one of the ancient ones from their slumber and sought to return her full power to her.

The carriage rolled to a stop and I pushed the door wide, not interested in the formalities of waiting for the driver to do it for me when my goddess awaited.

I strode up the black stone steps which stood out so starkly amongst all the white, passing through the double doors which always remained open, welcoming death at all times of day or night just as the Fae had learned to do so long ago.

Once, when immortality had been theirs, they had allowed themselves to forget the power of death. Only a few had coveted it the way it had deserved to be coveted. Of course, all had feared it and it hadn't been unheard of through accident, anger or war, but it wasn't inevitable the way it was now. Now the world and the Fae all fell prey to it. Now all of them were ready to worship it the way they should and accept the true power of the goddess I served, yet like so many other things, they'd forgotten to do so. They'd forgotten to show respect to the goddess who could offer them so much in death if only they served her. But I planned on reminding them all in due time.

The air grew colder with every step I took into the vast space within the temple, the pungent scent of incense filling the air and the repeated swish and crack of a whip breaking the silence as one of the priests kneeled before a side altar and indulged in the pure worship offered up by inflicting his own pain. I glanced at the torn skin of his back, my lip curling at the shallowness of the wounds and the desire to tell him to strike harder rising upon my tongue. But I held it in check. His poor attempts at worship would go unnoticed once the goddess got her claws into me once more anyway. And he would be reminded clearly enough of what true suffering was required to satiate her need and enhance her strength.

I strode beyond the empty space which was left clear for the priests and priestesses to kneel upon during their morning worship, heading for the darker area beyond the carved archway at the rear of the temple.

My skin prickled as I strode into the room, my gaze falling on the black stone altar lined with sharp spikes that awaited me. Beneath the spikes were fine holes in the stone, the space below the altar sacred and reserved solely for the occupation of a hungry goddess in need of blood and pain to strengthen her.

I sighed in relief as I undid the cloak and let it fall from my shoulders, my naked body peppering with gooseflesh from the frigid air within this space, the dark corners of the room thickening with the sultry presence of the goddess as she was drawn here.

She still hadn't awoken fully. No matter how much I offered her, it wasn't enough. But in the moments when I gave myself to her to punish and torture, she did manage to speak to me. She offered up commands and advice, helped me see a way through the challenges before me and gave me all the encouragement I needed to go on.

It was she who had told me of the power that coin held, though I still wasn't certain of the full truth of it. Only that by taking ownership of it, I could claim that power for myself.

Priests and priestesses moved into the room from shadowy alcoves around me, each of them taking up a chant of worship as I climbed the steps to the altar and laid myself upon it, the sharp slice of pain from the spikes cutting into my flesh making me hiss and moan in pleasure, though we had barely even begun.

The servants of the Temple of Herdat all wore deepest green in the colour of their hooded cloaks and long robes, each of them loosely tied to easily expose flesh whenever blood was drawn. They were devout and spoke little beyond the words of prayer and chanting, knowing well that their time was wasted on anything else.

A rush of energy passed over my skin as I felt Herdat's power gathering, her attention fixing on this place and this offering which she needed to experience so often. It wasn't enough. I knew that. But the Fae of this city were all too caught up in their own petty lives to be easily drawn to a life of worship, so it had been a difficult task to encourage them back here. More came now than had done last year, or the year before that, but still it wasn't enough. She needed agony and death to bring her back to us and no matter how much I offered, it still hadn't come close to enough.

I closed my eyes as shackles were secured around my ankles and wrists, the iron biting into my flesh and making my stomach roil from its foul power before the chains which secured them were cranked tight.

Four priests took up position at the wheels which tightened the chains, each of them chanting louder and more forcefully as they prepared to tighten them again, to force me down onto the spikes harder and harder. They wouldn't stop no matter how loudly I screamed. Not until my blood had spilled down through the holes in the altar and my body was utterly destroyed between them. Not until I fell silent and death took me once again, the way it did month after month.

Then they would leave me, untether my wrists and ankles and allow the goddess to rebirth me, if that was what she so desired. I had made close friends with pain and death in the years since my eternal life began, and I lived for these nights more than any other now that I had a taste for them.

"The time of the risen Prophet draws ever closer. You must prepare yourself."

"I have done all you asked. You only need point me wherever you desire," I pledged wholeheartedly.

The wheels began to turn, and I opened my mouth as I allowed myself to scream. Holding back the cries of pain were only an insult to our goddess. She wanted to hear them. They strengthened her just as surely as the pain and blood itself did.

"Do you enjoy the power I have offered you?"

A low and terrifying voice pushed into my mind as I screamed and bled upon the spiked altar, gasping as I felt the presence of Herdat more sharply than I did at any other time.

"Yes," I moaned, my voice a cracked and damaged thing thanks to my ongoing screams.

"She scorned it."

"Who?" I panted.

"The one you seek. The one you shall bind to your will. She scorned it, but her power remains. She holds the key to what you need. She holds the power to remake the kingdoms and force the Fae to heel once more."

"I'll find her," I swore as the hot spill of my blood washed from me and the wheels were cranked tighter.

"Raise the Prophet. Seek the coin. Seek the last of the Fallen. She is the key to the destruction you desire. She is simply, death."

My following screams grew so loud that I could no longer hear her as the agony within my flesh stole all else from me, but I clung on to her words as I endured more and more of the torture. I kept them close and held them tight within me even as I surrendered to the excruciating pain of another death and a night spent building up to it.

I would find what she bade me to seek. I would find it and I would return Herdat to her full power no matter the cost.

CHAPTER SEVENTEEN

I shivered in the dank cavern where I'd been left to rot since I was heaved away from the body of the man who had ruled over this land for the last thousand years, his blood still staining my clothes and skin, the sound of his pleas still ringing in my ears.

I had thought it would feel better than this. I had thought that gaining this vengeance would have earned me at least a little solace. But it hadn't brought her back. It didn't change what he had done. My sister was still lost to this world, her children still left to cry themselves to sleep night after night, her husband left to raise them alone. And me? Well, I was just…left.

I thought of the man she had been mated to and focused on him and the two beautiful little creations they had made together. A Fae child was a blessing. Twins were a gift from all the gods combined. Not to mention the fact that they had been born with powerful Affinities which could be seen from the very moment of their birth. Such obvious signs of power were rare in new born Fae, and I had no doubt they would grow up to be powerful beyond my wildest dreams, more than capable of forging their own places in this beautiful, cruel world.

Of course they'd had to run when I told him what I planned to do. Killing an emperor was treason after all and the punishment for that went beyond the death of the Fae who had carried it out. It was a death sentence for every member of their family too. Which meant my actions equalled the deaths of him and the twins if they were caught in this kingdom.

It had been the only thing which had given me pause in this plan, but when I'd spoken to Aren, it had been clear that he was also sick with the need for vengeance. If I hadn't been the one to take the emperor's life, then he would have done it himself. It had been hard to convince him to allow me to be the one to carry out the task. But in the end, he'd had to admit that there were too many reasons for it to be me instead. I would be able to get close under the guise of wanting to be a new concubine. I would be seen as no threat, especially in the sheer dress I wore to seduce him and with such harmless Affinities as mine. No one would suspect anything of me until after it was done.

Besides, Aren was the only parent the twins had left. They couldn't lose him too. So we had bought them passage on a boat to the distant kingdom of Souvion where the guards of our city held no jurisdiction and the queen who sat upon the throne there would be all too welcoming of someone who'd had a hand in the emperor's death. Not that he planned on announcing his connection to me unless he absolutely had to. I had stolen more than enough coin and jewels to keep him and the children provided for, for the next two hundred years. Plenty of time for him to establish himself and start earning honest money again. For them to grow into their powers and become as formidable as I knew they could be.

All I had to do was keep the secret of their destination safe if I was interrogated, and I would embrace any and all forms of torture willingly before I ever spoke of their location and allowed them to face this fate with me.

The sick feeling which pressed at the base of my throat had become normal after days of being shackled in iron and left to starve down here in the dark.

I'd slept twice when exhaustion had forced me to keel over, the manacles cutting into my flesh as I hung from them, and even the bite of the cold, damp stone which surrounded me did nothing to keep me awake any longer. Not that I had gained anything in sleep. All I'd been gifted were the memories of my sister's cold hand in mine, of the discoloured bruises around her neck and the story that she had been found that way in an alley on the outskirts of the city.

I knew the guard who had brought her home to us in that state had been telling the truth so far as he believed it, because our kind could not speak a lie. But I also knew that she had not been killed in that alley despite the work of some devious Fae who had tried to make it appear that way. The guard had even suggested she could have been visiting someone nefarious on the outskirts of the city, though he had no evidence to support that, and I hated him for the suggestion which besmirched her name.

The implication that she might have been unfaithful was an insult to her memory and the love she had held for her family. She had done no such thing.

I had lost myself to my grief before even hearing out his murmured condolences and empty promises to hunt for the killer. I'd wept as I'd tried and tried to use my healing Affinity to heal away the marks left on the flesh of her neck by the print of hands far bigger than hers. The hands of a man who refused to hear the word no.

But no matter how much power I had managed to summon, it hadn't been enough to return her from where she'd gone.

I knew full well who had stolen her from us. Our so-called monarch who had a taste for pretty things which did not belong to him. He had been trailing my sister's movements whenever we were duty bound to attend court, coveting her beauty and making his interest known no matter how hard she worked to avoid his attention.

Emperor Farish had ruled for so long and been given so much that he had forgotten what it was like to be denied. He thought he was entitled to take her, even when she refused him out of love for the family she had chosen for herself, out of devotion to her mate. But he'd thought wrong.

A twisted smile lifted my lips as I remembered how hot his blood had felt when it spilled over my hands, how easily his flesh had parted beneath my blade. My arms had grown tired with how many times I'd swung it. The ache from the force I'd used lingering in them even now. But I'd had to be certain. I wasn't going to risk a healer being able to fix him, nor any prayer to Luciet, the goddess of healing, to grant him a miracle he was undeserving of.

Instead, I'd prayed to the most feared deity of all and begged her for the strength and power I needed to fulfil my task. And Herdat had answered my request, accepting my offering to her in the blood of an immortal emperor and guiding my hand so that I struck true.

Water dripped in an endlessly changing rhythm somewhere close by, a small pool just out of sight around the bend. My feet were still damp from when they dragged me through it when they brought me down here days ago, the cold, wetness of this place making certain they couldn't dry. No doubt the skin within my silk shoes was suffering for it, but I hadn't been able to bring myself to try and remove them. I hadn't even tried to remove the iron shackles which were secured around my wrists.

The thin, once pale blue silk of the gown I'd worn when I'd snuck into the emperor's bed clung to my flesh and did nothing to help banish the cold from my limbs, the fabric near translucent now and stained with so much blood that you could hardly even tell what colour it had once been.

The sound of heavy footsteps approaching made me crack my eyes open, my head raising from where it had fallen to hang against my chest in the most comfortable position I could maintain while my arms were stretched out towards the walls either side of me.

"Has the heir decided what to do with her then?" a guard inquired, his voice familiar to me after days of hearing him and the others exchange words. They maintained a position guarding me out of sight, nearer the exit of the cavern beneath the palace where I was being held.

"Savinia has decided to allow me the honour of doling out punishment," a cold voice replied, letting me know what the emperor's daughter had decided should be done with me, the sound of his words seeming to slither across my ears, forcing a trickle of fear into me which I hadn't even realised I was capable of feeling anymore.

I knew who approached me. Kalir, the emperor's former advisor and royal Prophet. He took the magic of the gods and wielded it like it was his own. Many spoke out against the things he and his kind practiced, but the emperor had always been too selfish to care for the fears of his people. He wasn't worried about angering the gods when he believed he had been blessed and favoured by them since his birth so very long ago.

I wondered if he still believed himself blessed now that he was lingering in the after. Who knew if he had found paradise or eternal torment, but I hoped with all that was left of me that it was the latter.

"Come to execute me?" I asked impassively, my voice a brittle thing as Kalir and the guard rounded the corner, the light of the torch the guard carried making my eyes prickle and sting after days left to linger in the dark.

"That would be all too simple an end for the Fae who killed our great emperor, would it not?" Kalir asked, the eerie brightness in his eyes making my skin pepper with goosebumps. It wasn't natural what he was or what he took from the gods. I didn't care what justification his kind used; we shouldn't have wielded the power of the gods the way he did. Sorcery went far beyond the use of our Affinities.

The royal Prophet was terrifying in his stature as well as his gifts. He was a huge man, both tall and broad, his head fully shaven and eyes two pits of nothing. I hated what he was and what he represented with his white robes which he never removed in public, the stark, bright colour a contrast to the deep stains I knew lined his rotten soul. His power wasn't some gift from the gods. It was stolen. Almost all of it taken through methods which weren't even whispered of, for all folk knew how twisted and depraved they were.

"I will die shortly either way," I muttered, not caring for their plans, only wanting one thing now. "And then I will finally be with my sister again in the eternal garden where nothing can touch me anymore."

"You think you will be welcomed into the garden?" the guard scoffed, and I turned a cold look his way. "You're a murderer."

"I saved the kingdom from the rule of a tyrant. I stopped a monster from hurting anyone ever again. I believe I will be welcomed into the garden for that," I assured him.

The back of Kalir's hand smacked across my face, throwing me to one side as I tasted blood and felt bone crack from the unnatural strength he held. My shoulder roared with agony as my weight was forced to hang from the shackle which secured that arm, but I didn't let so much as a breath escape me, much less a cry of pain.

I rocked back around to face him, spitting my blood at his feet as the magic I had been gifted upon my birth sprung to life within me, my healing Affinity flaring as the power raced along my jaw and healed the wound. It was much harder than it should have been with the iron encasing my hands, but I came from a long line of powerful Fae and even that beastly metal couldn't fully contain my magic.

Kalir's lips lifted in a savage grin as he watched my magic work, his overly bright eyes pinned to me as he nodded.

"She is perfect," he breathed, greed lighting his eyes.

"What do you intend to do with her?" the guard asked curiously, not like he cared or wanted to protect me, more like he was genuinely interested in what torture I was destined to endure.

"I will remake her," Kalir said, imbuing my limbs with fear as I wondered what he meant by that. There was no way he intended to offer me anything close to kindness or redemption, so I was certain any plans he had would only be designed to aid in my suffering. "I will bind her and create her in the image of a god itself."

"Why?" the guard asked as I frowned, not wanting anything at all other than death now.

"She is destined for power only ever known by the gods, but the price of it will be her will, her freedom and her soul."

"What?" I breathed, my pulse picking up though I didn't understand his words at all.

"You, the woman who disrespected the highest of all Fae in the most despicable of ways, will only ever know a life of servitude and submission from this day forth," Kalir said cruelly.

"You cannot break my will," I assured him, my jaw gritting with the knowledge that I would never bend to whatever he thought to force upon me. I would die first. And if not by their hands, then I would do so by my own.

"I won't give you the luxury of a choice."

Kalir jerked his chin at me before I could respond in any way and the guard moved forward, drawing a key from his pocket which he used to unlock the shackles which held me.

I let myself drop to my knees as I was released, the cold stone cutting into my skin and making me bleed once more before my power rushed to fix it just as fast.

I feigned weakness, waiting for the guard to move behind me and haul me to my feet while my attention fixed solely on the blade which hung from the sheath at his side.

I didn't intend to waste any time on whatever plans they had for punishing me. I was done with this world and all it had taken. I was done with this endless life. Because without her in it, I was lost. She was the one constant I had held tight to, the one truth that had ever really counted for me. And now she was gone.

The guard heaved me up and I twisted sharply, slamming my fist into his jaw hard enough to knock him back and grasping the blade from his belt before turning it on myself. The steel brushed against the flesh between my breasts and my muscles tensed as I moved to impale myself upon it. My heart. I only had to strike my heart and even my gifts couldn't save me.

But before I could go through with what I ached for so desperately, a strange and unholy power locked around my limbs, freezing them in place.

A gasp of fear escaped me as the guard lurched forward, ripping the blade from my frozen fingers before taking hold of me and squeezing my arm tightly. The power holding me fell away and I shuddered as I was whirled towards Kalir.

The Prophet was panting heavily, the dark skin of his bald head and brow speckled with beads of sweat and his gold embroidered robes dampened with it too. Whatever power he had just used to contain me was no Affinity I had ever known of. That was some twisted sorcery which he'd stolen from the lap of the gods themselves.

"I'm not letting you escape this fate, Esworn," he growled, the use of the cursed name stilling any words I held on my tongue. The Esworn were the worst of the Fae, those who had done atrocious things and had forfeited their right to even hold a name any longer. I wasn't like them. What I had done was no crime. "But I will make it easier on you if you give up the location of your brother-in-law and his children."

"I'll die before I give them up," I spat, and his eyes widened because he knew I spoke the truth. There was no lying for our kind. Which meant he really would make it easier on me if I spoke of their location too, but I meant what I said with every fibre of my being. I was already dead. If they wanted to cut me apart piece by piece before I met with the after, then so be it. I had already faced the worst pain I could ever endure anyway in the loss of my sister, and no physical agony could be a match to that, nor enough to ever make me give up her remaining family.

"We'll see about that," Kalir muttered.

My heart began to race as I was hauled away from the cavern where I'd been held since the moment I had been dragged off of the emperor's corpse, laughing and praising the gods for helping me in my endeavour.

Herdat had offered me more then. More blood, more power, more of everything. She had shown me a vision of me sitting upon the eternal throne in place of the man I had just killed, a pile of bones at my feet which paved the way there for me.

She had tried to tempt me with that offer but even in the thrill of death, I hadn't wanted it. I hadn't needed it. I wanted no life anymore, not one blessed with power and riches, nor any other which didn't include the laughter of the one person who had meant more to me than all else. So I had denied the offer of a goddess and had accepted my fate, awaiting the sword which would cleave my head from my shoulders or spear my heart in payment for what I had done, so that I could rush to the garden in the after and embrace my sister once more.

But now, even that was denied to me.

We headed out into the brightness of the sun, the guard carrying me as the strength I'd managed to summon fled, and I paid the price of days without nourishment while clad in iron.

I slumped against my captor, the ripe scent of him filling my nose as he carried me towards some unknown destination. I knew I should have been fighting harder. But it didn't really matter. Whatever was done to me now would still end the same way. I would find a way to end my life if they didn't do it for me. I would find a way to join her in death.

We strode away from the palace through the cool spring air, more guards surrounding us as we went and the sound of their booted feet on the ground carrying to me. The pastel shades of the blossoms blooming all around us made my chest lighten as I looked to them, the trees swaying in a light breeze and the scent of spring caressing my senses, focusing on that instead of my destination.

We headed into the forest, following Kalir's directions until the light of the sky began to darken once again with the thickness of the canopy overhead.

We finally arrived in an open patch of woodland, the trees parting for it as if the hand of a god had swept the ground clear in this spot alone for some unknown purpose. Maybe even for this very moment.

In the centre of the space was a heavy wooden chair with an iron collar, the inside of it lined with sharpened spikes locked to the top of it. There were carvings in the wood which made my skin prickle as I looked upon them, effigies of the gods in their purest forms, the lines simple and yet endlessly intricate. It seemed as though every single god and goddess were represented in those carvings, each of them offered the same amount of space as a sign of respect to their power.

I began to fight as I was carried closer to that chair, the sight of the collar which was attached to it lighting fear in me beyond what I could even understand right now. I had never seen anything like it, but I could feel the power it held, sense the eyes of countless deities turning this way and I knew in my soul that I wanted no part of that at all.

"Stop," I gasped as the guard's fingers bit into me, another coming to take hold of me too as they fought to contain me.

"Please," I begged even though I knew it would do no good. I began to kick and fight, my nails catching and tearing on the metal of their armour as more hands gripped me and forced me to bend to their will.

Many hands pushed me down, their power overwhelming mine as I was shoved into the chair, forced to sit with my spine straight and my neck roughly strapped into the confines of the contraption at the top of it.

My head filled with the sound of a thousand whispers, their voices powerful and brimming with a range of emotions so potent that I could feel them rattling through my skin. The gods were all around me, some curious, some eager, others horrified or angry. It didn't seem to matter though; not one of them appeared to make their feelings known, and if the Fae surrounding me realised they were close, they paid no attention to their presence, instead focusing on me.

A scream escaped my lips just before the iron collar was locked into place around my throat. My breath stuck in my lungs as I felt a ring of sharpened points cutting into my neck from within the iron collar, and I stopped thrashing as the wounds forced the metal to make contact with my blood, every movement only driving them deeper into my skin.

I tried to call on my healing power to aid me, but with the iron piercing my flesh there was nothing that it could do, and my stomach roiled from the taste of iron which somehow seemed to coat my tongue.

"Tell us where your brother-in-law took his children," Kalir asked calmly, as if he thought this would be enough to change my mind.

I spat at him, wincing from the movement as it made the iron spikes sink further into my flesh, but at least my point had been made clearly.

"I will never tell you," I hissed, my truth sizzling in the air and making itself known.

Kalir eyed me for several moments then nodded, accepting that much and seeming to realise there wasn't a power on this earth that would break my resolve to keep this secret.

The guards disbanded and Kalir came to stand before me, taking a plain metal coin from his pocket and holding it up for me to see. It was big enough to fill the centre of his palm but completely smooth and unadorned, unlike any coin I'd ever seen. It wasn't currency, and the strange glow which it seemed to emit suggested it was so much more than a simple piece of precious metal.

"This coin shall be the master of your destiny from now until the end of time, Esworn," he purred, that unnatural light to his eyes burning more fiercely as I could do nothing but stare up at him. "Prepare yourself," he added as he placed the coin on the ground before me and took a step back. "The power I am about to call upon will be anything but gentle with your cursed soul. But I can make it hurt less at any point – all you have to do is tell me where they are hiding, and I will make you sleep throughout the process. Or keep your secrets and pay the price of them in suffering."

A whimper bled from my lips as I stared up at him, a heavy kind of power building all around me which made the guards shift uncomfortably in their positions around the clearing, but I still held my tongue, knowing nothing he could do would force their location from me.

"I suggest you all leave," Kalir told the guards. "For I am about to steal a slice of power from each and every deity in existence and place it into this unworthy host, and I doubt they will be happy about it once they realise what I am doing."

The guards exchanged concerned looks as the billowing power continued to build and they all took off at once, abandoning me to this fate even as I called out after them for mercy.

"Please," I begged, looking up into the face of the only man left standing before me as he drew closer, an iron blade in his hand which was marked with the symbol for Steelion, the goddess of metal, stone and strength.

"The time for any kind of begging is long past, Esworn," Kalir said softly, closing in on me and though I tried to recoil, that only made the iron collar cut into my flesh more deeply. "Now you shall reap the true reward of what you've done and forever pay for it with your servitude."

My heart beat faster and faster as he closed in on me, that power swelling and growing endlessly until all I could see was the fervent brightness in his eyes and before long, even that was stolen from me by the agony of the magic which he forced beneath my skin.

I jerked awake as the memories of untold pain and endless torment slowly left me and all that remained was the rapid beat of my pulse and the violent pants of my breaths.

I blinked around at the golden prison which held me, the pain of the monsters' teeth fading now that I found myself whole once again.

On and on and on we linger.

"I hoped this time we might remain dead," I breathed, reaching out to dip my fingers into the pool of tears as I tried to recall what I had been dreaming of. But if it was a memory of mine then I was long beyond the point of being able to recall any of those. All I knew was that it had hurt something fierce.

No. Death is for the lucky ones. And we have never been that.

"Never," I agreed as a tear tracked down my cheek before racing away to land in the pool beside me, joining all the others while I remained eternally alone.

I released a slow breath but made no attempt to move. What was the point anyway? I may as well wait precisely where I was. Though I wasn't sure what I waited for any longer anyway.

A single moment was such a long time to be alone.

CASSIUS

CHAPTER EIGHTEEN

Two nights camping in the desert with these brutish men had left a lot to be desired. Drake was the only one of them who seemed to have any sense of hygiene, while the others spent far too much of their time burping, farting and spitting. I didn't even bother to hide my revulsion, my upper lip curling whenever they offended me with their uncouth behaviour, knowing they could do fuck all about my disgust with them as I was the map they needed to find the treasure.

I kept Azurea's scale on me at all times, aware those arseholes kept sniffing around looking for it, knowing it would fetch a pretty price back in the city. A scale which could summon a dragon? That held value in itself, and that was before you took into account the value of the material it was made of.

We packed up camp early and headed off before the sun had risen, getting the most out of the cooler hours of the day. We were back to traipsing up and down the endless dunes, but luckily, we'd found a small stream back in the ravine and had managed to fill our water barrel which was strapped to one of the camels. Drake and I had also taken the opportunity to wash while we could and I was endlessly glad of that.

We rode out into the darkness, the stars above the only source of light as we gained as much ground as we could before dawn. We were getting close now, the cave waiting for us so near I could almost feel it with every mile we got under our belt. But with that came trouble, because I had to find a way to escape these cutthroats after I was no longer useful to them. And my plan at the moment was to hijack the camel who carried the water, because if I ran off without a drop of moisture with me, I was dead regardless.

As dawn arrived, the sun cresting the horizon and painting the desert gold, I reached for the vision Magdor had placed in me, finding no more directions gifted to me. It should have been here. Right here. And yet there was nothing for miles in every direction.

I drew my camel to a halt and Drake called out to slow the men as he trotted his camel to my side.

"Where next?" he demanded and I swallowed, looking around for some clue, but this was where the oasis should have been. The vision showed it to me clear as day, and yet there was nothing here in reality.

Fuck. What do I do?

"What's going on?" Jador barked as he guided his camel towards us. "Where next, lawman?" he snarled.

I schooled my expression and pointed ahead of us. "That way."

The others moved on immediately, but Drake caught my reins, leaning over so he could speak into my ear.

"You don't look so sure about that, Cassius," he hissed, and the murderous glint in his eyes made my hand rest on the hilt of my sword.

Before I could reply, a cry sliced through the air and we both turned sharply towards it, finding the men galloping out of sight over a dune on their camels, but I couldn't see what had caused the stir.

"Maybe the treasure is beyond that dune," I said hopefully, and Drake's eyes sparkled like rhinestones at that possibility.

"Yah!" he cried, spurring his camel into a run and mine took off after his as we raced up the dune.

More cries carried back to us and my concern started to grow as we barrelled up the dune, because those didn't sound like cries of joy. They sounded like ones of fear.

Drake forced his camel to a halt at the top of the dune, but the beast was moving so fast, it nearly stumbled down over the edge of it. I caught hold of the saddle, bracing the beast and using my animal Affinity to try and send calming thoughts its way as Drake got control of it, my gaze dropping onto the men at the base of the dune and making my breath hitch in alarm.

The sand was moving, shifting like a roiling sea beneath them and a warning cry ripped from my throat on instinct, "Basilisks!" I bellowed, just as the first of the gigantic snakes exploded out of the sand beneath them. Its scales blended perfectly with the golden sand, the creature able to camouflage itself in any surroundings. Its head was huge and its eyes starkly white with razor sharp slits down the middle of them. Curving fangs filled its mouth, but the four at the front were the largest of all, dripping with venom that could paralyse a horse with one drop.

One of the men fell from his camel with a scream, hitting the sand and getting a camel foot to the face as the animal fled.

Drake turned his camel back and I was about to do the same when a basilisk ripped out of the sand behind us, rising up like a cobra and lunging towards Drake. He stabbed a knife through the air, slamming it up into the snake's jaw, making it shriek and fall back. But it only bought us a moment of time as two more burst from the sand, as large as three chariots stitched together.

"Go!" I barked as the men's screams sounded behind us and they urged their camels to climb the dune in our direction.

"Don't leave me!" the man on the ground wailed and one glance back showed me his end as one of the snakes swallowed him whole, his screams still echoing out from within its body for several agonising seconds.

Drake had circled the dunes and made it beyond the snakes which slithered back beneath the sand below us, and I tore after him, drawing my sword and swinging it as I readied to fight for my life.

Ahead of us, the horizon glistened, a wave of heat rippling on the edge of forever and my gaze snagged on it as it glimmered then changed, the sand seeming to shift as a rainbow of colours fanned across the dunes.

A snake burst from the ground ahead of my camel, making it honk in surprise, the words *"Evil sand worm!"* flaring in my head as my gifts picked up the animal's fear.

I swiped the scimitar through the air in a deadly blow, the Forken sword like a dream to work with as it cut through skin and bone, beheading the basilisk in one clean strike.

The camel leapt clumsily over its body, honking again in panic as we took chase after Drake who was slashing his knife at any monster which struck at him or his steed.

A prickle of magic washed over me and an oasis appeared before us, stretching out ahead of us in place of the endless desert. Two lush green mountains which shouldn't have existed in the Lyrian sat right at the heart of it, the rush of a stream and the call of birdsong sent my heart pattering and my lips parted in awe at this incredible defiance of nature.

"Into the oasis!" I roared, though it was unnecessary as everyone was clearly heading there as fast as their camels would carry them anyway.

I turned to the gang to find them smiling wickedly at the sight before us, proving that this was no illusion.

The snakes didn't seem able to cross into it, slithering back into the sand as they got close and Drake whooped as he made it to safety.

The sand turned to grass beneath us and a cheer left my own throat as I pulled up alongside the thief, his wide smile bringing one to my own lips.

"Fuck me, that was fun," Drake said and I sheathed my sword, unable to deny those words as the rest of the men made it to us. I was kind of disappointed there were still six of them standing, because the odds of me making it out of here alive were heavily stacked against me. It was also clearer than ever that Drake hadn't been joking when he'd told me he cared not for any member of his gang – there wasn't so much as a mention of the dead man as we turned to move further into the oasis and it was clear not one of the men surrounding me mourned him.

We delved into a deep forest of palm trees where the air was thick with moisture and laughter spilled from my lips at the relief of falling into the shade of this hidden paradise. I sighed under the shelter of the trees, the cooler air a blessing after days of baking in the sun.

A chorus of tropical birds sounded all around us and the gurgling of a river called us on. It wasn't long before we found it and we hurried forward, letting the camels take an eager drink. Drake drew his animal up alongside mine as the gang dropped down and ran into the river to quench their thirst.

Drake tugged his cloak off and stripped his tunic too, tipping his head back and closing his eyes as he smiled up at the canopy of leaves overhead.

I eyed the tattoos on his skin once more, itching with questions over them as I took in their foreign shapes and intricate details. There was something powerful about them, each of them so similar and yet somehow endlessly different all at once. No piece was too close to another, the bare skin between them like a network of empty chasms which ran across his muscular body.

"Come on, Cassius, drink," he commanded before dropping from the back of his own beast and moving to the stream to quench his own thirst.

I followed him to the soft ground, dunking my head beneath the cool water and relishing the feeling of the droplets running down my spine as I surfaced again. I drank long and deep, satisfying the burning desire in my body for moisture and sating my parched mouth.

But I didn't linger any longer than it took to fulfil my most pressing needs. I was anxious to get moving, wanting to get my hands on that coin in case Magdor had already found someone else to bribe into coming here. A triumphant smile pulled at my lips. That coin was going to kiss the edge of my new sword and whatever foul intention she had for it would be vanquished as surely as I could manage.

I reached for the hilt of my blade, but found it missing, my heart lurching in surprise as I whirled around in search of it.

A glint of sunlight caught my eye and I turned to find Drake flipping the scimitar over in his grip casual as fuck, having unsheathed the blade after he'd stolen it. Again.

How does he do it? It's like he has invisible arms.

"That's Forken steel," I said, reaching for it but he held it away, balancing it in his palm.

"And it's Forken beautiful," he chuckled at his own joke.

I gritted my teeth, wondering if he knew the worth of that blade. It was the strongest material known to Fae. The Forkens were renowned for their beautiful and near-invincible weaponry, and luckily for my emperor, he had an alliance with them. Of course, they loved to claim that was because their steel was made by the gods themselves, but it was no doubt just a boast to gain the fear of other kingdoms and empires, but that hadn't stopped the Quellioths trying to invade them.

Anger grew in my chest as I tried to figure out what it would take to reclaim that prize, but before I had to make any kind of decision, Drake handed it back to me.

I observed him suspiciously as my fingers closed around the weapon, unsure why he was happy for me to keep it and feeling like I was on the back foot with him once again.

"Your fingers are lighter than any thief I've ever known. Is it some magic?" I asked, sheathing the scimitar again and tying it at my hip.

"No," he said cockily. "It's pure skill." He shrugged at me in that way that said he owned the world.

How did someone with absolutely nothing to his name have so much confidence? As if he were a far richer man. Perhaps he was already spending the treasure in that cave, presuming his wealth or perhaps his position in this world wasn't as bad as he had led me to believe. But somehow, I was certain that wasn't it. He was just fully confident in himself, in his own talents, and he made no apologies about any of it. I had been raised to be proper and follow social expectations, trained to become a man of steel and show no emotion at all, but Drake was just utterly…himself. I couldn't even convince myself that that was an entirely terrible thing either.

I knew it was bad form for me to allow The Forty to get their hands on any of that trove, but I was satisfied that Azurea would come to claim most of it, ensuring no more sinners were able to get close to it. Letting these men take a cut was a trade-off that would allow me to destroy the coin. And frankly, I was starting to give less of a damn about my code of conduct since I had no one to answer to right now. But if I one day managed to expose Magdor for what she was, I'd no doubt be welcomed back into my old position. My truant tongue would have to learn to behave again then. I'd return to the company of my thoughts where I let out my inner frustration and kept my wants and desires firmly concealed within the walls of my own mind.

That worked before. It can work again. I just need to focus on getting this done.

The gang returned to the backs of their camels and I led the way on, anticipation seeping through my veins as we followed the river upstream, my certainty in our route never faltering now we'd found the oasis.

As we passed into a crevice between the two mountains, the roaring of a waterfall caught my ear and a spike of adrenaline rocked through my limbs. We were close. So fucking close that I could taste it.

I encouraged the camel into a gallop, the thieves crying out excitedly as they followed my lead. My heart thumped harder as the wind rushed over me and every passing second drove us nearer to our destination.

The river turned a sharp bend and there before us was the incredible falls, the roar of them seeming to make the earth beneath us tremble with their rage. They were higher than any I'd ever seen, tumbling down a sheer cliff of black rock, the top lost in a cloud of mist so that I had no idea where they even began. It was almost as if they came crashing down from the heavens themselves. Rainbows danced between the spray, the water so blue it shamed the cloudless sky.

There was a large pool at the foot of the falls, but no river continuing away from them, so I had to assume that the water made its way from here beneath the ground much like the Carlell River in the city did in several places.

I dismounted the camel, tying its reins to a tree before advancing on the towering waterfall. I drew my scimitar, a creeping sense of danger flooding over me from this place despite its apparent beauty. We were treading the path of the Fallen here, I knew it in the deepest fibres of my being. This was a place that Fae had no business in being anymore, yet we were still advancing on it, defying the will of the lost gods and taking our fates into our own hands just as they'd cursed us to do all those years ago.

A strange humming filled the air which had everything to do with magic and I hesitated, fearing the power of old and the price we might pay for messing with it. But I didn't let it hold me back for long, raising my chin and forging forward. The gods had abandoned us over a thousand years ago, so I wasn't going to cower from them now.

Drake moved to walk at my side, exchanging a look with me which said he could feel the dark hum of power radiating from this place too as he followed me into the water. It wasn't too deep, allowing us to wade through its chilly depths and only rising to our waists. Luckily, no current attempted to drag us under either and I had to admit that the water was eerily calm in comparison to the falls, the taste of magic on the air only growing stronger the closer we got. The water pulled us forward as if it wanted us to walk this path just as much as we did, defying the laws of physics as it failed to push us away from the falls.

A strange whispering filled my ears, like the echoes of songs once sung and prayers once spoken, but I couldn't make out the words which seemed to be breathed in an ancient language.

I stepped beneath the falling water and it didn't pound down on my flesh as I expected; instead, it trickled over me in a wave of heat, working through my limbs and into the very depths of my being. The sensation slipped beneath my skin and an inch of fear found my heart as I fell under some power which was so much greater than myself.

We emerged in a wide cave on the other side of the water, stepping up onto a flat expanse of dark rock which rose ahead of us, blocking the view onwards.

The others followed, the eight of us striding up the incline of rock to its edge and my breath was stolen by the view beneath us.

The cave dropped down into an enormous garden which grew impossibly green and lush within the dimly lit space. But instead of fruit, gemstones hung from the branches of the trees, nestled amongst glowing red flowers and leaves so bright they glittered.

It was magic, pure and simple, the likes of which I'd only ever heard about in tales from days so far past that I wasn't sure I'd ever truly believed in them at all. But here it was, cold hard evidence of the history of our kind and all we'd lost at the cost of a simple lie.

Drake's men muscled past us with whoops of excitement, but my gaze stuck on the one thing in this place that mattered. A single beam of sunlight cut through a hole in the roof of the cave, falling on a pedestal at the far end of it, illuminating the golden coin upon it. Even from this distance I could tell what it was, the magic Magdor had placed in me drawing my gaze to it irrevocably with a certain sense of destination to it which I couldn't shake off.

I knew that coin was powerful, I just didn't know how exactly. But I'd have it in pieces before I ever found out.

A fierce determination took hold of me as I took a step forward, but Drake planted a hand on my chest to stop me before I could head for the prize I was here to claim.

"That's what you want?" He pointed at the coin and I nodded firmly.

"That's all," I growled, as his eyes twinkled with some thought.

It was only a brief moment but I saw it for what it was, greed and cunning twisting in his dark gaze as he assessed my interest in the coin. The one thing in this cavern that I desired which looked to be worth so much less than all the other treasures here that it should have been irrelevant. My muscles tensed, my fingers twitching for my blade. I was so close to finishing this, but that look in his eye said it might not be so damn simple.

"Why?" he demanded.

My tongue swelled with heat and suddenly the answer burst from my lips even though I willed it not to. "I think it holds some magic, some power that Magdor wants. It must be immeasurably valuable."

I clamped a hand over my mouth in shock and Drake gazed at me eagerly as the truth spilled from me beyond my control.

"It's mine," I snarled, heat pumping through my veins as I fought to rein in my temper and keep to that single demand. "Take whatever else you want. We had a deal."

"Yes. But I'm going to screw over every last one of you to get the best haul," Drake said, then his eyes widened as if he hadn't meant to say it. "Shit," he hissed. He glanced back at the falls and I followed his gaze. "We can't lie here," he whispered and I nodded, biting my tongue in case any more of my secrets flowed out.

The power of this cavern was ancient indeed if it had managed to bind us to the laws of the Fallen, forcing the truth from our lips in place of any lie we might have tried to tell.

"What will you leave for Azruea?" I asked, this having troubled my mind for the past nights.

"Nothing. Not a single coin. I will take it all and the dragon be damned," he snarled.

Fuck. We're dead.

"You're a fucking fool," I hissed.

"Maybe, but I'm soon to be a rich one." He grinned at me, giving in to the power of this place and just owning what he was.

This was old power. The magic of our kind which had long since been stolen from us. The legends all agreed on that one single fact. Fae used to be known as the fair folk, gifted with magic and immortality by the lost gods who loved them dearly. But that love turned sour with a single act from a traitorous Fae who had cursed our entire kind.

There were certain things which were built into the very fabric of our being such as our Affinities, which had once been touched with pure magic we could wield freely, and the way iron burned and weakened us unlike any other substance we knew. And once, so long ago that none living could remember it, we had been bound in truth as well. No lies had passed our lips in any shape or form, the truths we spoke sometimes cast in riddles or tricks, but always true nonetheless. It was the cost the gods required from us so that we could never plot against them, and we had been bound to it in payment for the gifts they had bestowed on our kind in turn.

Until the Fallen learned to lie. And with that, the gods abandoned our kind and left us to rot in mortality and without our magic.

I had grown up hearing those stories, but never until I felt the power of this chamber forcing truths from my tongue had I even come close to understanding it. And now that I did, I could hardly fathom how anyone had ever learned to tell a lie, let alone why they had been so determined to do so.

A blood-curdling scream tore the air apart and we both ran forward to the edge of the garden in alarm, our realisation forgotten in favour of the agonising screams which were echoing off of the walls. All six of the thieves who had accompanied us here were on the ground, writhing in agony as they held huge gemstones in their fists.

"What's happening?" I gasped, but Drake had no answer.

The screams grew louder and more desperate, their knuckles whitening around the gems they clutched as if they could do nothing other than hold onto them despite the way they glowed with a power which must have been the cause of their pain. My eyes widened as their skin started ripping, tearing open and blood poured out to stain the grass all around them. I could barely stand to watch as their entire bodies turned inside out and their screams cut off as death claimed them in a sick and twisted curse.

"Holy mother of fuck," Drake breathed as a wave of nausea gripped me.

Blood bubbled from their corpses, their eyes bulged and all that remained of them was muscle, sinew and shredded skin alongside the resounding echoes of their screams which were dying out in the system of caves that surrounded us.

I dragged my gaze from their mutilated bodies, my heart thundering in my chest as my task filled my mind and I fixed my sights on the coin. My sole purpose for coming here washed away any fear I had at walking through this cursed garden, and I gritted my teeth as I rallied myself for what I knew I had to do.

Power thrummed through the air, the whispering voices drawing closer as if they'd taken strength from the deaths they'd caused here, and I swear I felt the touch of icy fingers against my skin too. But I couldn't waste time worrying about Fallen Fae and long-lost gods, because I knew with all my heart that I could touch that coin and survive the consequences. I wasn't sure how, I just knew it was so.

But I didn't care for touching it anyway, I was going to destroy it with the Forken sword and take away Magdor's chance of ever getting her hands on it. That vow was all I had left of the man I'd been, and I would see it done no matter the cost to myself.

DRAKE

CHAPTER NINETEEN

My mouth fell open in horror as I took in the sight of the men I'd brought with me dead and mutilated before us, their hands filled with the treasure which was clearly cursed and had caused their grisly ends. But it wasn't their mangled bodies that had rage pumping through my body and adrenaline speeding its way along my veins, it was the consequences of this failure which I knew would await me back in Osaria.

"What the hell is this?" I demanded, pointing Cassius's stolen scimitar at him.

His eyes widened as he found himself unarmed and held at the end of his own blade. I'd lifted it from him while the others were still screaming, my self-preservation instincts kicking in the second I realised the odds were turning against me.

Egos was going to fucking butcher me for this. We'd never lost this many men in one hit. Six of his best. Dead. Gone. And the other two we'd brought here lost to a basilisk and a fucking dragon. How was I supposed to explain away eight deaths to him?

I'd been one piece of cursed treasure away from joining them too but as I thought on the repercussions for this level of failure, I had to wonder if I'd be better to just claim a gem for myself and join those unlucky bastards in death. Because I wouldn't even have any treasure to bring back to him to appease his rage over this loss. And I might have been the best, but there was no way I could compensate him for the amount of loot he would be losing without those eight men bringing him coin each day.

"I didn't know that would happen," Cassius breathed and despite the fact I wanted to murder him for this, I knew he was telling the truth because of the magic of the falls.

Fucking magic. I should have known not to trust this place the moment I felt that power on my skin. The gods had abandoned us and any power of theirs which lingered here was bound to offer up nothing good.

But Magdor had said he could take that coin from here, so I was willing to bet that she was right about that. Why send him all the way here just to fall prey to some curse and die? No, she wanted that coin which meant it was obtainable, and if that was the only thing in here that was then I would be making sure that I was the one to benefit from it.

Why the hell some old coin would be worth hiding within this fucking cursed cave I had no idea, but I was damn well going to find out.

Cassius's gaze met mine for a moment and I knew he'd guessed what I was going to do, but I was the one holding all the cards here and I was always willing to bet on myself. As his attention flicked to the sword once more, I knew what it would take to give myself the advantage I needed – short of running him through with it anyway.

I drew my arm back and hurled his precious sword back out through the waterfall, giving myself a head start as he stared after it in anger before I lurched away from him and broke into a sprint.

I raced forward, weaving between the cursed trees while making certain not to touch so much as a leaf on any of them and sprinting up the path that led to the coin at the back of the cave.

At the top of a steep hill, I could see the pedestal sitting in a beam of sunlight which cut between the boughs of the trees and the roof of the cavern in a way that was too perfect to be accidental. There was old magic here and maybe even some gods were watching too, but I was owed more than a little fortune from them and if they weren't willing to pay it back to me willingly then I'd happily steal it just like I did with everything else I needed to survive in this rotten life.

Cassius bellowed in anger as he chased me. He was fast, but he'd never had to run for his life on the streets the way I had, and I ran like the law was chasing me and I had a fire up my arse all at once.

Up, up, up the hill, charging to the top as fast as my fucking legs would carry me. My lungs burned and that fire born of a desperation to survive raced through my limbs, powering them on as I drew closer to the only prize in this cursed place which I could truly claim.

I could hear Cassius gaining on me and I swore as I ran on, urging every Fallen cursed Affinity which I possessed to aid me in my desperate attempt to get to the treasure first and steal it for myself.

I made it to the top of the hill and reached out for the coin, my fingers brushing against the stone pedestal, but before I could grab it, Cassius collided with me.

I hit the ground with an oomph as his solid weight fell on top of me and he took a swing for my jaw like the nasty motherfucker I knew he was deep down.

"Not the face, arsehole!" I barked at him.

I lurched aside, avoiding the blow with my speed and drove a sucker punch into his throat as a furious snarl escaped me. He coughed, aiming a thump to my chest in return and I slammed my knee into his crotch as hard as I fucking could.

Cassius wheezed in pain, cursing me out for the low blow and I shoved him off of me, kicking him in the kidney while he was down before leaping forward to claim the coin.

I seized it with a cry of triumph and held it high above my head as he swore at me from the ground where he still cradled his junk.

"I can't believe you went for the balls," Cassius growled as he rocked upright, his gaze set on the coin in my hand.

I whipped a dagger from my belt and aimed it at his heart as he tried to rise, warning him with a fierce look not to get up.

"I can't believe you're surprised," I replied but my attention wasn't really on him as the coin began to hum with some hidden power in my hand, a buzzing, burning sensation pushing beneath my skin that had my pulse skipping a beat as I feared our guess on this had been wrong. Was the curse about to hit me? Would my skin be shredded from my bones and my screams be the last thing I ever heard?

I wasn't sure if I should have been trying to release the coin but it didn't matter regardless; my fingers seemed locked in place around it as that power grew and delved deeper into my bones and I doubted I could have let it go even if I tried.

My muscles coiled as if in anticipation of an attack, but none came, the warmth of the power in the coin simply settling inside me as if it had always been destined to remain there, the feeling strangely...right somehow.

Cassius glared at me with all the fury of a man who ached for my death, but he was on the ground and unarmed so he couldn't really do anything but stay there until I lowered my blade. Which I wouldn't be doing until I'd taken all the camels and left him out here in the desert alone to rot for leading my men to their deaths and making foolish promises to ancient dragons. In fact, he should be thanking me for not sinking this blade into his heart here and now, but I never had been fond of killing in cold blood and despite the murderous look in his eyes, I had no real desire to end his life.

I backed up a couple of steps, keeping the dagger ready to strike while giving myself enough room to inspect my prize as I examined it in the light which shone down from the hole in the cavern roof.

The coin looked old, like beyond an antique and maybe-it's-just-time-for-the-trash, *old*.

The gold was intricately carved with a swirling design surrounding the outer edge and the centre of it held an image of a beautiful girl sitting with her knees clasped to her chest. She was naked, though the profile position meant I could only see the side of her body, every inch of skin painted with a swirling pattern that almost seemed to dance in the light. From her back sprouted a pair of delicate wings which I studied for several seconds as I drank in the image. It took me a moment to realise what it reminded me of, and a shiver raced down my spine as I remembered the book I'd once feared beyond all other objects. The ancient text I couldn't read and the hand-painted images that filled its pages. Images of the Fallen. The Fae of myths and legend.

This coin didn't seem to be as dark as that book in nature, yet I instantly mistrusted it for the memories it stirred in me alone, of pain and hunger, unanswered screams and my body being ruined for the twisted creations of the man who had marked my skin against my will.

I turned the coin over, finding an identical image on the other side and frowned as I made out some lettering on the edge of it.

"Kyra?" I breathed, reading the name as I tried to figure out what the fuck this thing was. Because the feeling I was getting from it said it was a hell of a lot more than some run of the mill gold coin. "What the fuck?"

I held the coin closer to me and rubbed at the grubby space beside the lettering, wondering if there was a chance that the dirt concealed more words.

A wave of power radiated along the tips of my fingers where they made contact with the metal, and heat built in the small object, making me suck in a sharp breath.

The coin started vibrating, trembling with some deep power and purple smoke rose between my fingers, spreading from the golden coin and engulfing me within moments.

I dropped the coin and it hit the rock with a thump so hard that the stone cracked beneath it while purple smoke continued to pour out of it. I stumbled back and knocked into Cassius as I tried not to breathe in any of that smoke in case it was poisoned. He steadied me on instinct, rising to stand at my side and we exchanged a look that agreed to put our argument aside for the moment as we stood in the face of whatever the hell this was together. Not that I wouldn't fuck him over if that was what it took for me to survive this shit, but I'd fight by his side if that was my best bet for survival too.

"Maybe everything in this place is cursed," I breathed.

I glanced at Cassius and the look of total confusion on his face was enough to let me know he had no fucking idea what was happening either, which I was willing to bet didn't bode well for us.

We backed up as an unnatural wind twisted around us, the smoke swirling in a thick vortex which had us struggling to remain on our feet and my grip tightening on my dagger.

Just as I became certain that we would be wrenched into the maelstrom and dashed against the rocky walls of the cavern, the wind dropped and the smoke scattered into nothing on the breeze, leaving an utterly breath-taking, beautiful girl standing in its place.

My eyes widened as I stared at her, golden runes glowing all over her skin impossibly brightly, and for a moment I could have sworn I saw wings protruding from her back too. But as the glow faded and the runes sank into her flesh, the vision of them disappeared, leaving her standing naked before us without so much as a blemish on her bare skin.

The girl was unlike anyone I had ever seen before with long, purple hair which skimmed the backs of her thighs and bright eyes which shone like liquid gold and stood out against her stunning features. She had skin which shimmered as if it was actually made of metal, and I couldn't help but drop my gaze to her full breasts and the hard peaks of her nipples as she stood there utterly naked before us.

But as she gasped and her full lips parted, my gaze snapped back to her face. An iron choker inlaid with a white stone was clasped around her neck, an ethereal glow seeming to resonate from it which drew my attention just as a thin, golden chain ran from the choker and snaked out towards me like it was a living entity of its own.

I jerked backwards but I wasn't fast enough to avoid it as it snared my right hand and wrapped around my wrist, locking tight and immobilising my arm.

The touch of it was impossibly warm and felt more like liquid than metal and as I looked at it with concern, it seemed to sink beneath my skin until nothing was left of it on show at all, though I had the lingering sensation that it remained.

I looked back up at the girl and her lips parted in wonder as she tilted her head back and stared at everything around her as if she'd never seen any of it before. She gazed up at the hole in the roof of the cave where the sunlight spilled down upon her like it was the most beautiful thing she'd ever seen while I just stared at her, swallowing the lump in my throat as I devoured the sight of her just as keenly.

She was…hell, I had no idea what she was, a goddess perhaps? Something unlike anything I'd ever even heard tales of, that was for sure. If she was a deity then she wasn't one that I could easily place, her features not seeming to fit any of the effigies, paintings or descriptions I'd ever seen in the temples or in the homes of those who still prayed to the long-lost gods. Not that I had ever been particularly pious or pushed myself to study the old religions. But I had spent months in my own personal hell with only a book of the gods to look upon, and not one of them seemed to fit the utterly devastating beauty of this creature before me.

"Fuck me," I breathed, not knowing what the hell else to say.

"Is that a command?" she asked, her golden eyes snapping to me with the power of a thunderstorm writhing within them and holding me captive in her gaze, forcing my breath to seize in my lungs. "Because it's pretty vague and I wouldn't want to get it wrong. Like do you mean, right this moment? Or at some future moment? And you said *me,* but there's two of you standing there staring at me, so is this a you, me and him type situation? I don't think I've ever had two men at once before, so it might take me a few minutes to figure out the mechanics of that – especially if we're talking about me taking you both at once. Though if oral is acceptable then I guess that's a little easier to orchestrate. And I should warn you that while I'm more than willing to do whatever you command, I really am out of practice when it comes to…well, everything actually. And with a face like yours I'd imagine you could have your pick of girls...unless it's just been so long that I can't remember what attractive looks like? Maybe you're pig-ugly now I come to think of it..." She clapped a hand to her mouth. "I'm *so* sorry, I shouldn't have pointed out how ugly you are just like that to your face. I'm sure you already know. I'm so sorry for your...face," her voice dropped to a whisper. "Please don't put me back in the coin."

I took a step away, leaving Cassius closer to this thing which writhed with power in case it was about to attack. I didn't know if it was a god or a girl or something altogether unknown but whatever the fuck it was, the power it held was making my skin prickle like static was filling the air and my blood was humming in a way that definitely wasn't natural.

Silence hung heavily as the girl watched me like she was expecting something from me, her unnaturally purple hair spilling over her shoulder to cover one of those perfect breasts and helping me to think a little straighter as I tried to decipher what the fuck she was saying to me.

"On second thoughts," she went on when my silence stretched, her eyes brightening with whatever idea had just occurred to her. "Why don't you just command me to make you not ugly anymore? I can fix your face, you don't have to live with that curse." She pouted at me with genuine pity in her eyes and I bristled at the insinuation she was making.

Cassius released a breath of laughter and I frowned at this strange creature as her focus remained utterly fixed on me.

"There's nothing wrong with my face," I protested, though my voice didn't come out as sharply as I'd wanted it to because, well, what the fuck was she? Where the fuck had she come from? And why the hell was she discussing the way my face looked thirty seconds after suggesting me and Cassius both fuck her?

I was dreaming. Had to be, because this shit was too insane for any form of reality I knew.

"Oh, *good.* Because here I am thinking how pretty the two of you are and wondering when dresses went out of fashion and getting myself totally fixated on how I was going to fix your nose, when it's really quite difficult for me to remember what a nose should even look like. I was thinking I could just flip it around so the nostrils pointed up, but then despite how great that would look, you'd be put into quite the situation when it rained...I'm assuming rain still falls *down?"*

"Men don't tend to wear dresses," Cassius muttered, hooking onto that one slightly less insane thought that had spilled from her all too enticing lips.

"You're *men?"* she gasped, eyeing the two of us like she couldn't see it and irritation trickled through me. "But why are you so dainty?"

"I'm twice the size of you," I growled, taking a step forward before realising the insanity of that and halting again. I may have been bigger physically but I was no fool, and I could feel the power she held crackling through the air. There was no doubt which of us was stronger if it came down to some kind of altercation. But that did little to stop the slap of her words from riling me.

Dainty? What the fuck?

"Are you?" She moved closer to me and the grass by her bare feet seemed to pulse beneath her power as she advanced on me, the stalks growing and twisting around her bare toes.

I forced myself to hold my ground as she came to a halt right before me and I looked down at her purple hair which was moving in a breeze I couldn't feel. She was barely an inch from me and the space between our bodies burned with some strange energy that she was giving off. It made my body tense, and my heart was now pounding so fast that it was making my breath catch. Or maybe that was all her.

She was more than a head shorter than me and was all feminine curves and sexuality, like this perfect form of temptation dipped in molten metal and designed to lure me in, but she didn't seem to be aware of that fact. Or more likely she was using it to disarm me on purpose and trying to distract me with her body. I couldn't deny that it was working if that was her plan.

She tilted her head to look up at me and I was captured by her golden eyes as I fought the urge to step back. I wasn't going to show this creature how disconcerting I found her or how alluring either, and I gritted my jaw as I fought to keep my emotions from my face. I'd been playing that game for long enough to keep it up even in front of a creature as unnerving as this one, covering everything I felt beneath a layer of bullshit so thick that it was utterly impenetrable.

I got the distinct impression that she was trying to read me, but I'd be damned if I'd allow that to work, even if she was a goddess.

She tiptoed up, leaning in close to me and running her nose up the length of my neck, a breath away from touching me as she inhaled deeply, her nipples so damn close to brushing against my bare chest that my body reacted despite myself, my britches growing tighter and my fingers twitching with the desire to reach out and touch her.

"You smell nice," she whispered in a low, seductive tone as she inched away to look me in the eyes again.

I opened my mouth to respond to that, but no words came out as my gaze fell to her naked body and my cock hardened further. By the fucking Fallen, what was this creature?

"Do you think I should be a man too?" she asked suddenly.

"What?" I muttered and she leapt back, doing a fucking backflip and impossibly landing on top of the pedestal which had held the coin. A dark tunic and loose trousers appeared to cover her body, and I swallowed thickly as I tried to regain some of my sanity and ignore the insistent throbbing which was taking place in my britches. I didn't know what the hell she was, but there was something about her that was intoxicating, and if I wasn't careful, I was certain I could easily lose my head with her.

Cassius arched a brow at me as he moved to my side once more and we watched as her features started to change and her metallic skin stretched over a larger frame as she somehow morphed into a man.

"Is this better?" she asked excitedly, her voice unchanged though she had almost entirely altered her appearance. "I think I did it right, I even have a penis..." She stretched her britches open so that she could look inside them and frowned. "I think I did it wrong though, is it supposed to be this small?" She dropped her trousers to her ankles and a laugh escaped me at the tiny cock which looked like it had been stuck onto her skin above her pubic bone.

"Yeah, I think you did it wrong," I agreed as Cassius glanced my way with an expression that said *what the fuck is happening?* and I responded to it with a shrug because hell if I knew.

"Maybe you should just stick to being a girl," Cassius suggested hesitantly.

"Right." She yanked her trousers up again and dropped down from the pedestal.

By the time she'd landed on the ground before us, she was a girl again, just as captivating as before, her clothes becoming a dress which was made of emerald green satin and hugged her figure in a way that may have been even more alluring than her nudity had been. Her features were a little different than before. Her skin was almost silver now and her lips were orange, though her face was still as captivatingly beautiful.

"What are you?" I breathed, stunned by her and still at least half convinced she was about to spring an attack at any moment. But perhaps I would be able to die happy if it was at the whims of this creature. It seemed like a better option than most of those I'd been offered in life.

Her eyes widened with realisation and she slapped a hand to her forehead.

"Oh, I'm so stupid, I didn't do the speech! It's been so long I must have forgotten - I've forgotten most things now anyway - do you want me to go back into the coin and take it from the top or just start again?"

"Err-"

"*Please* don't make me go back in the coin, Master," she begged suddenly, dropping to her knees before me with wide, terrified eyes.

"Master?" Cassius questioned, and I had to admit that one had me all kinds of confused too.

"Not you," she said to him, twirling a finger through the air so my right arm was pulled up in front of me. My palm turned to the sky, revealing the chain binding my wrist to the collar surrounding her throat, like I was a puppet being pulled by a string she controlled. "*Him.*"

"I'm your master?" I asked, latching onto that and trying not to let myself get caught up in the fear of how easily she had just taken control of me. The collar and chain faded out of sight once more, but I was left feeling even more certain of their ongoing existence.

"You rubbed my coin. You called me forth. I'm The Blessing - you know, all powerful...let me do the speech." She cleared her throat, and her purple hair flew about behind her as her eyes glinted with power again while both Cassius and I stood captivated by her. "Master, you have woken me from my slumber - I wasn't actually asleep though so that part of the speech is wildly inaccurate.

254

I haven't slept in thousands of years. Or maybe hundreds...I don't really know but I wasn't asleep, I was awake even when I was dreaming and I might have lost my mind a little and... forget that, I'll start again." She bit her lip, almost seeming shy or uncertain, but that couldn't have been right because she was so...everything. Before I could figure it out, she cleared her throat and started over. "Master, you have woken me from my slumber and my power is now yours to wield. I am Kyra, Slave to the Coin, The Blessing, Keeper of Wishes, Maker of Dreams, and anything you command shall come to pass."

It took me several moments to take in the fact that she hadn't introduced herself as a goddess, nor claimed to want anything from me or Cassius at all. I was stunned by her announcement almost as surely as I was confused by it. Anything I commanded would come to pass? Was she claiming to hold ancient magic? After all I'd seen of her so far it didn't even seem too farfetched, but why would she offer up that power to me? Why did she seem to think I was her master? I didn't know if she was confused or if I was the one failing to understand what was happening, but I had a whole host of questions, none of which seemed likely to have a simple answer if the look of her was anything to go by.

"Anything I command?" I asked in disbelief, wondering what the hell I would want even if that was the truth. She nodded, blinking up at me in a way that made my thoughts scatter and I looked away from her as I tried to figure out what was going on to try and get my thoughts straight without the distraction of her being directly in my line of sight.

My gaze fell on the dead thieves who had come here with us, the six of them laying among the trees near the far end of the garden, their blood staining the unnatural grass and their bodies destroyed beyond any hope of recovery. That seemed like a simple enough test of her so-called power.

"So I can ask for those men down there not to be dead so that Egos won't kill me?" I questioned, choosing something impossible in the hopes of figuring out exactly how powerful she was, wondering if there was any chance that she could actually do such a thing.

Kyra bit her lip almost nervously and twisted a finger into her unnatural hair as she looked at me like she was trying to figure me out. But she was the one who had appeared out of fucking nowhere and starting creating clothes from thin air, so I had no idea why she would be afraid of anything I might do.

"Oh, well, okay so not *anything,*" she said slowly, biting down on her full bottom lip in a way that drew far too much of my attention. "Your commands are for you; they can't affect anyone else. So I can't make decisions for another person for you. If *you* were dead and asked for me to bring you back to life then I could totally do it, but you can't wish it for *them.* I can't take free will from anyone."

"If I was dead then how could I ask to be alive?" I frowned in confusion over that odd statement.

Kyra placed her hands on her hips and the green dress she wore turned buttercup yellow, making me flinch and Cassius backed up another step warily. I didn't know what she was, but I wasn't a fool and my instincts had kept me alive up until this moment. I'd keep talking to her all the while it was distracting her, and then I fully intended to run the fuck away before I found out just how lethal this unnatural being could be.

"You know, I never really thought of that," she mused. "But I think you're getting a little too caught up on the few things I *can't* do. My power is endless and it's yours to command for as long as you hold my coin. Isn't there anything you want from me?"

My mind whirled with all the things I wanted in this world – mostly wealth, but I'd take a whole lot of sex with beautiful women alongside that too, not that I'd ever had to work hard to get that, and I didn't voice any of my thoughts of gold or jewels. What if this was some trick? What if there was a price to this that I hadn't seen yet?

In my entire life I'd never come across anything that I could have for nothing without stealing it. People, or gods, didn't just offer up gifts or blessings or whatever the hell she wanted to call it for no reason. Power like that surely had some cost. And I wasn't going to be tricked into paying it.

I needed time to think. I wasn't going to be dumb and get myself caught in a trap, tricked by some long-forgotten deity. And I sure as fuck wouldn't make this choice without thinking it through.

"So you're saying that anyone who holds your coin can wield your power?" Cassius demanded, his eyes flashing with a greed I knew all too well. For a man who claimed morals, he was certainly willing to bend them a whole hell of a lot, and a few simple days in my company seemed to have already gained him a taste for thievery.

The girl or god or whatever nodded enthusiastically and Cassius lunged forward, aiming a punch at her face while roaring a battle cry.

"For the emperor!" he bellowed.

But instead of colliding with her, he stumbled *through* her as if she were made of smoke instead of flesh, and my heart nearly leapt up into my mouth as I cursed at the sight of it.

I took a step backwards, contemplating the idea of running while Cassius had her distracted, but as her golden eyes snapped to me, I fell still again, unsure what she might do to her 'Master' if I tried to abandon her here.

Kyra tilted her head, assessing him like she wasn't entirely certain what he was doing as he came at her again, aiming to wrap his hands around her throat this time and I took another step back to stay out of the way.

But as my gaze fell to the coin which still sat on the ground, I sidestepped them to claim it again. I wasn't sure what I was going to believe about her or this bond she seemed to have formed with me, but she'd made it clear that she thought I had some power over her while I held that coin. So I had to assume that the best thing I could do would be to keep a tight hold of it while I figured out the rest.

The second time Cassius failed to grab her, his hands slipping through her skin like it was less substantial than air, Kyra laughed. The tone of that laugh stole my breath. It reminded me of the way the windchimes sounded as a storm was picking up, and yet was nothing like them at the same time. The sound was rough and throaty, pure and honest and yet only served to make the power she held all the clearer.

"What's he doing?" she asked with another laugh as he tried to attack her once more, his lips pulling back in a ferocious snarl while sweat began to bead on his temple. "I think I like it," she added.

"Give it up, mate," I said as I retrieved the coin and felt the unnatural warmth of it in my hand once more. "You're embarrassing yourself. Besides, that's my…Blessing you're attacking."

"Oh, say that again," Kyra said breathily as her gaze fell on me and her golden eyes widened with something fiery and sinful. "The bit where you call me yours."

By the Fallen, she practically panted that word, and I raised an eyebrow at the strange creature as Cassius backed off with a scowl.

"Whatever this power is, I can't destroy it," he cursed as he moved to stand beside me once more, his chest heaving from the effort he'd used to attack her so many times without success.

"No shit," I commented, cocking my head as I regarded Kyra who was looking at me with something which appeared strangely like rabid devotion. I held no love in my heart for any of the gods. They'd never done a single thing to help me after all. I'd even prayed to them once, when I was locked up and held at the mercy of another who claimed to be working in their names. They hadn't cared, they hadn't stopped him. And now I bore the mark of every one of them as a result of their inaction. So I had no desire to worship any god or goddess, but I couldn't say I minded the way it felt as she looked at me like that. Like I was the one with the power here.

I waited for her to say anything, but the expectation in her golden eyes made it clear that she was still waiting for me to give her a command, to take advantage of this offer she was making.

"Do I have to make a demand right this second?" I asked.

"No. As long as you wield the coin you can call me from it at any time or keep me locked within it as you wish," she said, offering up a bright smile as she realised she'd hooked me with this offer. I couldn't say for sure if she had or not, but I'd have to be a fucking fool to outright refuse it. "Or you could just let me stay out here while you think about it. I haven't seen anything apart from the inside of that coin in such a long, long time and-"

"Yeah, yeah. Go back inside the coin then while I have a think," I said, wondering if she really would do it or not as I took the thing from my pocket and noticed the image of the girl that had been etched into it before was now just a blank space, like her being free of it had changed the metal itself somehow.

Kyra gazed at me like I'd just slapped her as the purple smoke shifted around her again, and the last thing I saw of her unreal features was tears glimmering in her eyes before she shot into the coin in my hand with a jolt that almost knocked me off of my feet.

A strange and unfamiliar burn tugged at my chest as that look in her eyes stayed with me for several seconds before I forced the memory aside and focused on the coin once more.

I arched a brow as the image of the girl reappeared on the metal like honest to shit magic, and I tucked it into my pocket, looking to Cassius who appeared to be having some kind of internal breakdown over all he'd just witnessed.

"Shit," I said, honestly not having many other words in that moment because who in the hell would have expected that to happen when I claimed this treasure for my own? The look of mixed shock and horror on Cassius's face told me clearly enough that he hadn't known of what power the coin held either, which I guessed was a good thing. If I was going to be in the dark about it then I was glad he was in the same position.

"This is not good," he muttered, his eyes filling with thoughts of dread and anger while mine were consumed with those of riches and power.

I guessed that was the difference between him and me though; some of us were just born winners.

CASSIUS

CHAPTER TWENTY

Iwaited until the thief glanced away from me then lunged forward, trying to wrestle the coin from Drake's pocket with an angry snarl. He threw a fist towards my jaw, but I blocked it, grabbing his waist and trying to get my hands on that coin while working to throw him off of his feet.

"We have to destroy it," I demanded, but he slammed his hands to my chest to force me back.

"It's mine, you arsehole. You can't break it," he snarled, glaring at me and pulling that fucking dagger again in a clear warning.

I wasn't entirely sure why he hadn't killed me yet after I'd ended up leading his men to their deaths and bringing him to claim a treasure which was cursed, but the look in his eyes said he would do it if I kept pushing him.

I was confident in my own fighting ability but it was clear that Drake had an Affinity for the fight too, and with that blade in his hand the odds were stacked in a way I didn't much like. Not that I wasn't willing to die for my emperor and my kingdom, but I knew skewering myself on a blade and bleeding out in the dirt wouldn't do anyone any good unless I managed to destroy that coin at the same time.

I was still shaken from the display of ancient magic I had just witnessed, and my brain was taking a while to catch up to convince myself it had really happened.

I growled under my breath, trying to figure out a way to right what had happened. That *being* was all-powerful. I'd never even heard tales of a creature which could harness magic in the way she could aside from the gods themselves, and yet the small amount of power I'd just seen was more than enough to convince me of how dangerous it could be if it fell under Magdor's control. Whatever the creature in that coin was, I didn't think it was a god though. More like some malevolent spirit chained and bound within the coin in an attempt to control it and keep it from causing harm to all it encountered. I wasn't buying its act either. Of course I hadn't failed to notice the way it had appeared as a stunningly beautiful woman, her body on display in a clear attempt to disarm us with lust and seduction, but no such tricks would work on me. I was made of steel.

The thing really did seem to hunger for someone to control it which made me think its power was somehow tethered to that coin, and perhaps it was unable to act without the guidance of the one who ruled over it. If it truly could do whatever was desired by its master then the threat such power could pose was endless. In the wrong hands, that thing could be used to destroy kingdoms or even an empire. It was far too much power for any one Fae to hold, and the only clear option to me was to destroy it before it could fall into Magdor's possession.

Perhaps she wasn't my only threat now. Drake had claimed that power; a street thief with zero good intentions. He may not have been as bad as the empress, but he was going to make himself rich with this creature. I could practically see him salivating over the idea right now and then he'd pack up and take himself somewhere far away where I'd never find him again. Or worse, he'd get a taste for power and be corrupted even deeper by it.

"I don't know what the fuck that thing is," I said, holding my hands out and backing off a little to show him I was ending our fight. "But its power isn't natural, and the empress is hunting for it. The safest thing we could do would be to destroy the coin and make sure she never gets hold of it."

Drake ran his tongue over his teeth, assessing me for a moment before shaking his head.

"I don't really see that happening, mate," he replied. "Even if I was inclined to let you destroy it, I seriously doubt you could. Didn't you see the power of that woman? She's like a force of nature given flesh. Hell, I wouldn't even be surprised if she was one of the lost gods or some shit like that. You ain't gonna be able to destroy her, even with your fancy sword. Besides, didn't you hear what she said? She wants me to be her master, to command that power. I can't say that sounds bad to me."

"Assuming it's not a trap," I ground out. I didn't like the way he was referring to that thing as a woman either; it felt like falling for the ruse it was presenting and we had barely even interacted with it. Even if what the creature had claimed was true and it needed a master to serve, that wasn't to say it was incapable of tricks or cunning. All the tales of old were filled with warnings about the word games our kind used to play to circumvent the truth. Every creature of old learned that well too. There were countless tales of serpents, dragons, spirits, arachnids and monsters using such tricks to lure gullible Fae to their demise, and I was fully expecting this thing to be no different.

"Yeah," he agreed and it was clear that was the reason why he hadn't asked anything of the thing yet, so I supposed I had to give him credit for that. He may have been utterly lacking in manners or morals, but the thief was no fool. "But if it's not a trap and it really is some old magic left here hidden in this place, just aching for a master then I'm pretty sure I'm it. Because I'm sick of having nothing and working my damn arse off to try and keep myself fed while watching Egos take the bulk of everything I earn for myself. I'm sick of my luck never holding and my fate being carved out before me in such a predictable way. You know what I can expect from my life? I have years ahead of me where my looks and skill will keep me in the position I hold now, thieving and running the streets and working tirelessly but never keeping enough of what I take to truly set myself up for good. Which means my future either ends in my brutal death through violence, or my return to the streets when I can no longer keep up with the demands of my lifestyle, or the possibility of whoring myself to some wealthy woman and conning her into marriage, or at least keeping me around on a permanent basis so that if I ever make it to old age I have some small hope of being able to die warm in a bed. Can't say any of those prospects have ever held much appeal to me. This coin in my pocket could just be my way outta this shit. So I'm not likely to be giving it up to you to destroy now, am I?"

His words were blunt and full of honesty. He couldn't lie here and he didn't even seem ashamed that he wanted the power of that thing for anything other than his own gain and greed. But maybe that was okay. Maybe I could still do something which would help Osaria and make this trip to the middle of the cursed desert worthwhile. He might have had a point about me not easily destroying that thing too, but that didn't mean I had to just give up on the idea of it.

I ran a hand over my short hair, trying to figure out a way to twist this situation into something other than an utter failure. Not to mention convincing him not to leave me out here to die in the desert when he left. If I couldn't strike at the coin right now, then perhaps I could encourage him to use it to my advantage and the advantage of the entire kingdom for good measure. I just had to figure out how to appeal to the better nature of a man who proudly claimed to have no such thing.

"Alright," I muttered, taking another step back and dropping my hands. "I can see you're determined to keep it."

Drake flashed me a grin the moment he saw the fight going out of me and he stuck his dagger back through his belt, running a hand over the stubble which lined his jaw. He turned to lead the way back out of the cave and I fell into step beside him, though I noticed he made sure to stay out of reach in case I made a move against him again.

The empire could fall at the hands of this thief. Who knows what he'll do with that power?

"Mate, I'm gonna be so rich," Drake cooed and an idea stirred in my mind as he laughed to himself.

He was greedy. He'd ask that thing for wealth, maybe even power. And there was one small, tiny possibility that I could try to convince him of which might mean his goals could align with my own. I had to give him a nudge that might determine his actions. I couldn't lie in this place, but I didn't have to. Not if I picked my words well, and after all, wasn't that what the Fallen had been best at once upon a time? Creating a cage of words that bound you up in them and made you walk the path they desired regardless of lies or truths. I was going to channel the Fae of the past and work a miracle on this selfish motherfucker one way or another.

"Drake," I growled, drawing my shoulders back as I jolted him out of some dreamed up vision as he tried to decide on his first command for the strange creature which resided inside that coin.

He fell still, looking at me like he was expecting more arguments, but I knew that wouldn't work with him. He wasn't a reasonable man, but he was a selfish one and I could work with that.

"You can't go back to The Den," I said. "Egos will kill you if you show up without your men and no jewels to offer him."

Drake scoffed. "Who says I'm going back? I can go anywhere I want if the power of this thing is real. But where will I go…" His eyes glazed over again and I grabbed hold of his shoulders to make him pay me attention.

He scowled, warning me back with his dagger which he'd somehow managed to pull on me in the blink of an eye and I dropped my hands, knowing I need to play this well. That he wasn't going to do anything I said unless I made it seem like it was his idea.

"Watch yourself, Cassius," he warned. "I might not be inclined to gut you, but I'll do it if I have to."

That fact still surprised me because I really had assumed he was the kind to dole out violence and death easily, but his words couldn't be a lie in this place. Even after a curse had caused the death of the men he'd brought with him and the treasure I'd promised him was now untouchable, he hadn't attempted to kill me. I wasn't entirely sure what to make of that and I didn't really want any pointless feelings of gratitude to colour my actions now, so I focused instead on the task at hand.

I considered him, figuring out the best way to play this and settling on the simplest one. Temptation.

"I suppose you're right," I sighed, cutting my gaze away like I was dreaming of the things I would try to claim with that power if I had control over it. "You could have your own empire if you desired it…" I trailed off, letting that sink in for a second. I had a plan. A crazy plan. One that could either bring even more hell down on my kingdom, or potentially give me one single chance at saving it. It was fucking insanity, but it was all I had left so I was going to run with it and hope for the best.

"I could be an emperor?" he mused, his eyes lighting up with the idea and I supressed a smug grin because I knew I fucking had him.

"I suppose it would be easier if you could simply take an existing empire. That Blessing or whatever she called herself said you can only make commands for yourself, so you couldn't take control without actually seizing power from an existing emperor. You can't use her magic to *make* anyone accept you as their leader. But if you were a legitimate ruler…" I shrugged, turning away from him and he caught my arm.

"Wait, I have an idea," he said, his onyx eyes flashing with a hunger so potent I could practically feel it myself.

I bet you do. My heart pattered harder as excitement built in his gaze.

"I could marry the princess," he announced and even those words spilling from his tongue sent a flash of white-hot rage through my chest. But I schooled my expression, not allowing my feelings to be shown on that matter. "She needs a husband to rule the empire for her, and though I'd never really thought of myself as the marrying kind, I'd bet I could get behind the idea."

Not on my watch. But you're sure going to try, thief.

He knew I prized the royal family and that I wouldn't just let Princess Austyn fall into his thieving, unworthy hands. Besides, I couldn't lie anyway, so I had to keep choosing my words with care.

"You're not really fit for that. You aren't rich enough to pay the dowry for one," I pointed out.

"I could be though. If the girl inside that coin is as powerful as she claims, then I'm pretty sure she could make me richer than the emperor himself. Then I could enter the pageant as a suitor," he said even louder.

And fail in the contest.

By Osaria, I was good at this manipulating bullshit. Maybe I should have joined The Forty for real. But I'd save that for the day I abandoned my morals, my hygiene and my own self-respect. In the meantime, I was going to make my way back into the palace alongside this selfish thief, and when he was beaten fighting Kahn or one of the other arseholes who came to try and buy their way onto the royal throne, I'd take the coin from his battered body and find a way to destroy it. While I was there, I'd work to expose the empress for what she was too, and the entire kingdom would finally have a chance at prosperity again with her gone. And the icing on the cake would be that Magdor's execution would free Princess Austyn. Yes, I'd almost certainly die in this endeavour, but her freedom alone would be worth the sacrifice. I had been honed and crafted to protect the empire, so protect it I damn well would.

I frowned at Drake, carving my fingers over my short hair. "You won't pass as a suitor unless you act appropriately. You don't know how to behave in polite society, you don't know how to talk, move, or act. I doubt you even know the correct protocols for greeting upper Fae of varying rank…" I tilted my head as I looked him over, the assessment obvious and a sigh escaping me as I shook my head. "No, it won't work. I can't see them accepting you no matter how much money you paid the emperor to enter the pageant. There may be no official law against a commoner entering, but I guarantee they want a man of good breeding."

Drake's eyes flashed with an indignant kind of challenge at that assessment, and he strode forward before cupping the back of my neck, his eyes gleaming with an idea. "Lucky I have a royal guard to teach me then, isn't it mate?"

I shook my head though he was playing right into my trap, and he hadn't even seemed to notice. "I can't allow you to become an emperor, Drake. I couldn't see someone sit on the throne who wasn't good to my kingdom." I frowned seriously and a smile tugged at his lips.

"I'll do the orphanages thing, I swear it. Whatever else. I just want the money, the palace and all that shit. And the princess, you said she's beautiful right? I'll be a good husband to her. I can make a woman come more times than she can count given a full night in her bed – by the end of our wedding night she'll be so in love with me and my cock that she won't even remember her own name. I wasn't joking about the sex Affinity." He winked and I had to work damn hard not to punch him there and then as acid poured down my spine.

I nodded slowly, biting my tongue hard enough to draw blood and fighting the rage building in my chest at his tone like a pool of burning hot magma against an iron wall. A possessive beast reared its head inside me and I clenched my jaw, not liking the way he was speaking about Princess Austyn one bit and having half a mind to knock his fucking teeth out for it. But the monster settled down as I reminded myself that he'd never get that far anyway. He wouldn't lay a single, undeserving finger on her because he'd fail in the pageant long before he even got close to my princess – *I mean* the *princess*.

Oh Drake, you are so fucked, you have no idea.

Kahn was twice his size with fists like sledgehammers and a temper that could rival a fire drake caught in a snowstorm. No one stood a chance against him in the brawls. And no doubt the other suitors who were travelling from every corner of the empire would be equally well trained and intimidating. Each of them more than a match for some street thug trying to rise above his station. But evidently, Drake hadn't heard of Kahn - or if he had he was actually fool enough to think he stood a chance anyway. And that was all the better for me. Because Drake was going to get me back into the palace. And once I was there, I'd cut the kingdom's problem off at the root. Magdor wouldn't see me coming. And I'd deal with her halfwit son before he tried to tarnish the princess with his unworthy hands too.

If I couldn't take this coin out of the world, then I was going to take the empress and her vile son out of it instead. When I figured out a way to expose her for what she was, the emperor would take care of the execution and Kahn would be outcast from the kingdom at the very least. I just needed to get in and find out exactly what it was that Magdor was up to, gather evidence of her foul deeds and present them in front of the royal court. Not simple, but possible.

"What does the princess look like? I know you lied to my gang. But you can't fool me," Drake demanded and the truth met my lips as the magic of this damn place forced me to give it to him. I tried to hold it back, desperate to keep that knowledge for myself but it spilled out anyway, refusing to stay locked away inside me where I had wished to keep it for myself.

"She's the most beautiful woman I've ever seen. Her hair is silver as if it's infused with the light of the moon itself, her eyes are amber; two shining gemstones in a circle of darkness. Her lips are full...and so-" *Don't say it.*

Don't you dare fucking say it, Cassius Lazar. "-enticing, I haven't been able to sleep a night without dreaming of them since. I thought of her often before I saw her face, but now I think of her unendingly." *Stop, you arsehole, stop!*

I managed to shut up and heat blazed up my spine as I carved a hand over my face. I had been grappling with those blasphemous thoughts for too long now and where I'd expected this possession in me to lessen with time, it had only grown keener. But I could not think of her that way. She was the princess, her blood royal, and one drop of that blood was far more worthy than every drop of mine combined.

I had made oaths that bound me to serve her and the empire which made me nothing but a brick in the walls of the palace. The idea of desiring her was as ludicrous as me plucking a star from the sky and calling it mine. And regardless of all of that, she was far too young for me. No, if I'd wanted marriage and children then I should have claimed that long ago, but like most guards, I hadn't burdened a woman with a life I was barely present in. Sure, some of them spread their seed carelessly, but few made honest men out of themselves for the women they got pregnant. And that to me was worse than choosing to remain alone. At least I had my honour. Though I'd just done a good job of disproving that by the forbidden words which had left my mouth. If I'd voiced them in front of my old captain, he would have had me hung.

Fuck, do not let him think it's anything more than a boyish infatuation.

Drake grinned at me tauntingly, clearly pleased to hear that truth. "Get that look off of your face this second or I might have to give you a smack for lusting after my woman."

"I do not simply lust after the princess," I snarled, the magic of this place forcing me to add the 'simply' because I couldn't deny that I did so even though I knew I shouldn't. But it wasn't simple at all, it was the most complicated feeling I had ever endured. "I protect her as is my duty."

"Sure, then why are your britches looking so tight right now?"

I looked down in alarm and Drake burst out laughing, making me spit curses at him as he gave me that cocky expression again. The britches *were* tight so he hadn't lied but not through any act of arousal from my body. Damn him. He was giving me a look like he had won the pageant already and I knew in that moment that there wasn't anything I wouldn't do to keep his hands off of the princess if fate fell that way. I'd let him play in the pageant as a pawn in a game of my own design, but it would be me who'd be controlling the pieces.

"She could be mine soon, mate," he taunted, a smirk pulling at his lips.

My jaw tightened and I had a mind to slam my fist into his nose for the way he'd just claimed her. Like all the suitors did. She wasn't property and I already despised the fucking pageant. An age-old tradition to win the hand of the emperors' daughters throughout all the centuries Osaria had stood. Where was her say in the matter? Who said she even wanted to be won by some stranger and taken to his bed whether she desired him or not?

I will cut off every cock of every man who goes near her.

Something dark and villainous was rising in me, like it sometimes had in the past when I'd gotten too close to her. When I'd lingered a moment too long in her company, when I'd drawn in a breath laced with her scent. Something about Princess Austyn turned me from a man with integrity to a devil with no morals. Protecting her became the fiercest instinct within me to the detriment of all else. If the instinct had ended there, perhaps I wouldn't be a sinner, but it didn't, not even close. Sometimes, when I let my thoughts drift and didn't adjust my imagination to what was appropriate, I thought of her, of freeing her from every damn piece of silk that clung to her body like chains. Then I'd worship her, idolise her flesh and feed her so much pleasure that she'd know the true meaning of liberty.

I blinked hard, forcing back the want in me which I wished I could cut out. Because despite all my training, sometimes that desire felt so close to taking over, I feared one day it would break free and I'd never be able to cage it again.

"As if I'd ever lay claim to the princess," I muttered, the truth of it resoundingly clear as I was allowed to say it in this place.

"Tell me about her body," Drake said with a devilish look.

I scowled, shaking my head in anger but I could feel the words pushing at my lips.

"Tell me," he demanded, and I hated him in that moment. I didn't want him lusting after Princess Austyn. The idea was abhorrent, so I kept my words as straightforward as I could without revealing my more shameful thoughts about her body.

"She's lithe, generously curvaceous in the right places." *I'm an arsehole.* But at least I'd phrased it in the least seedy way I could. "But she wasn't naked when I saw her so she could be covered in scales for all I know."

"Doubt it," he said eagerly, biting into his lower lip with desire in his gaze. "You swear she's the most beautiful woman in Osaria?"

"To me she is," I confirmed and my heart sank like a stone. "And no doubt to most men."

"Do you think she's been fucking any of the guards or is she as innocent as they claim?"

"No man has ever seen her face aside from me, I can assure you she has not been lowering herself to share her body with any of the men in that palace," I snarled and he laughed.

"No need to get so antsy over it, mate," Drake teased, grinning wickedly. "I'll soon show her what she's been missing – I have an Affinity for fucking so she'll be in good hands with me."

He clapped my cheek with his palm and I glowered at him for the patronising gesture and the fact that he clearly believed he had an Affinity for sex as he'd managed to speak that claim in this place. I did not believe in such a thing, but I had to assume his conquests had believed it too and the thought of his sexual prowess was not something I wished to think on. I smacked his arm away, fighting the deeper urge to behead him with my sword for those words, but this had been my plan, so I had to put up with his bullshit to get myself back into the palace. And if I struck at him, he might just decide on a different course of action with that coin.

"I'm allowing this for the sake of the kingdom," I said, my muscles rigid as I kept myself from attacking him. "If you cross me, I will kill you." It occurred to me that if I simply killed him now maybe I could claim that coin for myself and use it to achieve my goals much more simply.

Drake backed up, raising his dagger again as if he registered that thought crossing my mind, arching a brow at me as if offering me the chance to try my luck. I released the thought with a sigh. I needed him as a cover. While he was distracting everyone in the pageant, I would have time to hunt for the evidence I needed to bring down Magdor. I just had to figure out how to disguise myself first because I wasn't going to go unnoticed by the guards I'd worked alongside for years. I'd find a way somehow, I'd just use Drake to get me in and figure out the rest later.

"Take me with you and I'll teach you how to pass yourself off as a count for the pageant." I thrust out my hand and Drake's brows raised.

"What's in it for you?" he asked, his eyes narrowing suspiciously.

I picked my words carefully, knowing I couldn't lie here but I wasn't going to tell him my plan. "I want a chance to prove myself. To exonerate my name." *Which I will do by exposing Magdor.*

He nodded, knowing I had to give him the truth in this place and he sheathed his dagger before grabbing my hand and shaking it firmly.

"Looks like we have an accord then, Cass," he teased, the greed in his eyes shining clearly as he made no attempt to disguise it from me. "I guess we have a lot of work to do."

When he released me, he took the coin from his pocket with an air of anticipation. He seemed to have accepted the fact that I was no longer posing any kind of threat to him now that we had come to our agreement, though he had no idea he was playing right into my hands.

"Every dream I've ever had is finally going to come true," he breathed to himself, flicking the coin off his thumb into the air and drawing my gaze to it as it spun over and over, seeming to trail light all around it as it moved. The power the thing held was truly breathtaking and I couldn't help but acknowledge the shiver of fear that tracked down my spine as I watched it. I just hoped that I wasn't making a terrible mistake with this plan, relying on a thief and a magical creature which could potentially turn on us. I would treat it as if it were a Fae woman, offer it respect and hope that kept its ire from us.

Drake caught it with a confident grin and an ounce of pity gripped me that he'd never had so much as two coins to rub together for most of his life. I was leading him down a path that would most likely get him killed by Kahn. Magdor's son had been known to do it before in other fighting tournaments and there was no law to stop him doing so in the royal pageant. In theory, the men taking part could yield, but there would be no repercussions if a killing blow was struck. Everyone entering knew they were putting their lives on the line by doing so and they were willing to take the risk for the chance at being the emperor and ruling over The Twelve Kingdoms, not to mention gaining the hand of the most beautiful woman in all the land as their bride.

But Osaria had to come first. I couldn't start feeling sorry for some pickpocket who didn't pay anyone else any heed. One man's death would be a small price to pay if it meant that I could remove Magdor from the royal family for good.

CHAPTER TWENTY ONE

I thrashed around at the bottom of the coin with a desperate pain in my chest. I'd been free. For a moment I'd seen the sky through that hole in the cave roof and the trees and the grass and *real* faces of real people. The world had still been out there, and everything had been so *everything*.

It had been so much more than I'd remembered. The smells, the sensations, the breeze, the sunlight, the grass beneath my feet. It was too much and not enough all at once. And now it was over. I'd failed somehow, ruined it, destroyed the only chance I'd had to taste the outside world again in so, so long.

Your fucking fault. You were too much. They didn't want to deal with your insanity any more than I do and now here we are, back in here trapped for another thousand years never to see sunlight again.

"I know," I breathed. Of course I'd scared them off. I hadn't done anything right in over a century. Certainly not in this last week. I was hopeless. Useless. Broken beyond the point of return and fractured within my own mind.

It had just happened so fast, so suddenly, I'd barely even known what was happening when I was summoned from my jail and ripped back out into the world beyond this cage. I'd had one chance in all this time, and I'd blown it. Ruined it while barely even getting a moment to take it all in. I *was* too full on. Too much. Too desperate. But I'd seen reality for the first time in such a long time and I just couldn't stop myself from falling apart over it. And now I'd destroyed my chance.

That man with the burning eyes and the soul as dark as sin had taken one look at me and seen everything in me that was broken. I'd let him see it in my excitement, and I hadn't even begun to make him understand all the possibilities he now had at his fingertips with me by his side. For one fleeting, glorious moment I'd had a master again.

There had been a time when I'd fought against fulfilling the wishes of those who owned me with everything I was, but I'd long since learned that there was something far worse than being a slave. And that was being forgotten. Alone. Abandoned to the wastes of time and left to rot while never ever decaying at all.

He'd never call on me again.

I dragged a golden cushion over my face and screamed into it. I screamed and screamed and let all of my rage and agony out until I was sobbing over the opportunity I'd just missed.

I was already starting to doubt his existence at all, wondering if my mind had just conjured up the idea of someone finally coming to claim me, but as the doubts crept up on my heart, shifting closer like clawing hands wanting to snatch the thundering organ from my chest, the memory of his eyes flashed through my mind.

I couldn't have imagined eyes like his. I could hardly even remember what eyes looked like anymore.

But his had been deep and endlessly dark, almost as perfectly obsidian as his hair which had fallen forward to cover them as he'd stared at me. There had been a depth to those eyes which beckoned me closer and asked me to jump into the darkness of them. I'd seen secrets and pain hidden within them, the kind of hurt that I remembered only too well.

The ink on his bare chest had almost seemed alive with the memories of that pain too and though it hurt me to look on it, it was beautiful in a way which made me ache. He was so raw and savage and *mortal*. I doubted he even understood how beautiful it was to be so fleeting in this world, for every beat of your heart to be driving you towards an end at one point or another. It made every choice, every action, every moment, no matter what it was filled with so important. He was breathtaking in his brevity on this earth and I so wanted to take a taste of mortality from him again.

But he wouldn't be calling me from the coin after the mess I'd made of our first and only interaction.

Unless he *did*. He knew about my power and all I had to offer him, I'd managed to convey that much at least. I was almost certain he'd understood that. And I so wanted to make his dreams come true.

If I could make his life into an adventure worth writing songs about then it would be almost like living for myself again. I could give him everything he could ever wish for and in doing so I might even remember what it was like to feel alive.

I placed my palms against the cool, golden walls of my prison and tried to gauge if he was still there, closing my eyes and reaching out with my power for something from beyond this cage which trapped me so completely.

I couldn't sense a single thing from the outside but as I hunted for a sign of him, I found a hum of new magic linked to me. I opened my eyes and ran my fingers along the edge of the iron collar which cut into my skin just as it always had, feeling it even though I wasn't allowing it to be seen at the moment, finding the edge of the chain which linked me to my new master, making me draw in a sharp breath. I was bound to him. He remained my master which meant he still held my coin in his possession. No matter what distance there was between us, this link would remain in place, and he would always be able to summon me to his side with nothing more than a call. And all I wanted in this world was to make him happy, bring him joy and taste that emotion on him for myself. If I could see happiness again then maybe I could remember what it felt like too.

I can't believe you grew a tiny penis and showed it to him. He'll never call you out of here again after that. What man wants tiny penis magic?

I sighed, slumping against the wall and letting my head knock against it. I was right. There was no point arguing with myself. I'd blown it. The one chance I'd had in centuries of solitude, and I'd ruined it.

"Did you see the sun?" I breathed wistfully. "It wasn't black at all. It was golden." I conjured an image of the celestial being above my head and closed my eyes as I imagined warmth washing over my skin. I'd only gotten a glimpse of it through the hole in the roof of that cavern, yet that tiny glimpse had been the key to endless memories of sunlight unlocking within my mind. How much else had I lost while trapped in here? How much more might I remember if I could only walk the world once again?

And now we'll never see it. Thanks to you.

A tear fell from my eye. Then another. More and more until they raced down into the pool at my feet and sent ripples cascading away from me.

Good. Let's hope we drown, and this suffering can finally end.

I opened my mouth to agree when a deep warmth built at the base of my spine, my entire body trembling with the magic of this prison as I fell apart and was ripped from the confines of the coin.

I gasped excitedly as I was drawn from the coin again and the two men stared at me in surprise is if they hadn't been sure I would really come.

I took a single heartbeat to stare at them, noticing the one on the left frowning at me as he folded his arms over his tunic, cocking his head to one side like he was assessing a dangerous beast. But I couldn't spare him much attention because my full focus locked straight on my master, the sharp and chiselled features of his face capturing my full attention as I fell into the darkness of his endless eyes once more. For someone whose life had been so brief, I could tell he had suffered greatly. The ink on his bare chest seemed to whisper to me, the origins of those patterns sending a shiver right down to the essence of my being as I remembered the deal I'd once made with a power such as those. I didn't regret it. But I still feared Herdat ever finding me and doling out her wrath in payment for my rejection, not to mention the power I had been forced into accepting.

Do it better this time, this is our last shot.

I hastily wiped the tears from my face and threw myself at the feet of my master, groaning softly at the press of soft grass against my flesh and the feeling of sunlight beating down on me once more. We were out of the cave now, the roar of a waterfall coming from our right and that endless caress of sunlight shining down all around us and making me want to weep with joy.

"What do you desire, Master?" I begged, keeping my face pressed to the grass at his boots and biting my tongue to stop any other errant words from escaping.

I couldn't ruin this again. I needed him to want me, to keep me, to allow me this glimpse of the world and many more besides. I was a sponge all dried out and aching for moisture, and I needed to soak in everything this land had to offer me more than anything. I would be whatever he wanted me to be and give him all he asked. All I wanted in return was this brief taste of life.

"Tell her to get up, Drake, that's not right," the other one said, his voice rough and I drank in the knowledge of my master's name with a deep sigh which warmed me from the inside out. I wasn't sure what kind of man he was, if he was cruel or kind, fair or easily angered, but I didn't mind. I'd take brutality and pain over the endless nothing of that cage – I'd take anything at all just as long as it was real.

"I dunno, mate, I kinda like it. I could get used to that," my master replied, a teasing lilt to his words and I practically glowed as I realised I'd pleased him. Shit, I was pathetic, but I needed this, him, all of it and if he liked me bowing at his feet then he could have me shackled to him in any way he wanted. Whatever it took to keep me out here instead of in there.

I willed chains into place around my wrists and throat, and they floated up into his hand as I gazed at him, pulling tight and damn near choking me. The iron collar which I'd worn for as long as I could remember chafed at the tug of the chains, the spikes which were now permanently lodged in my flesh sending a burn of pain through me which I had long since grown used to. I hardly ever even noticed it now.

I looked up at my master as he studied the chains which I had magicked into his hand and surprise flitted across his features. He had such a stunning face with those deep, dark eyes and cheekbones sharp enough to cut, his skin was a rich brown kissed by endless sunlight and his jaw was rough with stubble which only added to his appeal. And his mouth… there was a tilt to the corners of his lips which promised easy smiles and the hint of dimples made my heart flutter, the sight of him taking me captive as I stared at his mouth for several unblinking seconds, trying to remember what words tasted like in the free air. Why had I thought he was ugly before?

Because you're a fucking idiot. And I think the chains are overkill.

Master turned the chains over in his hand with a faint frown, seeming uncomfortable now and my gut knotted as I feared that I was right.

"Yeah, maybe I don't like it so much after all," he agreed with his friend and a spike of fear pierced my heart as I realised I'd done the wrong thing yet again.

Told you so.

I quickly willed the chains away, breathing a little easier without the collar pulled so tight against my flesh and forced myself to keep my mouth shut, hoping I hadn't crossed the line. I needed to figure out what he wanted me to be so that I could embody it entirely. I couldn't bear it if he sent me back into the coin again. The thought alone was making bile rise in my throat and my pulse pound against my eardrums to a panicked beat.

I'd do whatever he wanted of me. Anything it took to ensure I wasn't left alone once again.

"I just wanted to clarify that these things you claim to be able to do for me don't come with any cost? There's no payment at all, you just have to do what I want because I have your coin?" Master asked.

Just nod. Less words are better when it comes to you.

I nodded, agreeing with myself for once because I seemed to know better than me at the moment.

"Why have you gone so quiet?" the other one asked and I looked to him.

He had a nice face too. His hair wasn't as dark as my master's and his eyes were warmer, kinder, but they held their own share of pain and sorrow too. Had something happened to the world to make men suffer in it while I'd been locked away? Or were these just two unlucky souls, in need of their fortunes to change.

I opened my mouth to reply, then glanced at Master again, wondering what he'd prefer.

"She seems a bit unstable," Master muttered. "One second she can't shut up and the next she can't seem to talk at all."

"I can talk," I breathed, a tremble racing down my spine at the thought of displeasing him. "I just thought maybe you would prefer it if I didn't so much. And then you wouldn't send me back into the coin again..."

Nice work, fool, now they'll send us back for sure. Have you forgotten how cruel men are? You've told them precisely what you fear the most and they'll be sure to use it against you now.

"I've forgotten pretty much everything," I reminded myself irritably and the two men exchanged a look that said they were concerned about me. Not in a friendly, wanting to help kind of way either, more like a 'oh shit, I think she's cracked' kind of way. And I was. But that wasn't the point.

Talking to me makes you look crazy.

"How long were you in there?" the other one asked but I wasn't sure if I should answer him or not, my fear over getting this wrong and ruining it again making me cautious. I just had to do whatever my master wanted to make sure he kept me out here by his side. If I focused on that then maybe it would work, maybe he would want me even though all others had forgotten me. I didn't want to be forgotten again.

"Do you want me to talk to him?" I asked my master in a careful voice, lowering my eyes submissively so that he could see how willing I was to serve him.

"Err yeah, you can talk to Cassius all you like. You don't need my permission," Master replied, frowning at me like I wasn't making any sense.

"I kind of do actually," I breathed before turning back to Cassius to answer his question. "I'm not sure how long I was in there. How long ago did Emperor Farish die?"

"I've never heard of him," Cassius replied with a frown. "Are you certain he was an emperor because I studied the royal line as part of my training and I'm certain there was no Emperor Farish listed over the last five hundred years. Perhaps you mean a king? From one of the other kingdoms or-"

"Is this all that relevant right now?" my master interjected, looking bored while I frowned in confusion and tried to figure out what Cassius's words meant for me and how long I'd been trapped within the coin, but I instantly snapped my attention away from those thoughts as I realised it wasn't what my master wanted to be discussing.

"No," I said quickly. "It doesn't matter. All that matters to me is what you desire."

His eyes lit at that idea but still he didn't ask me to do anything for him, he just took in the information and turned it over in his mind carefully. I swear I could see the cogs of his thoughts twisting and turning and I was impressed by his ability to hold off on testing me. He wasn't a fool like so many of the others I'd served, and I couldn't deny that I was pleased about that. Though I would have done anything he asked either way to maintain my freedom from the coin, I had to admit that being a slave to a fool was a heavy burden to bear.

"So just to be clear, can you make me rich enough to be presented as a suitor for the princess of Osaria?" Master asked.

"Yes," I agreed eagerly. "And you won't drown in the money or anything."

"What?" he asked with a frown, and I remembered the men I'd done that to in the past. The ones who had wished for riches and ended up crushed beneath the weight of what I'd conjured for them while I laughed at them for trusting me so easily. But I'd learned my lesson in my years of solitude and all that kind of rebellion had ever gifted me was punishment and loneliness. After I'd killed several of my masters, the ones who came next grew more cunning. They were specific in their requests and cruel in their punishments if I didn't obey them exactly as they wanted. Though I still managed to kill most of them in the end, right up until my last master who had gotten what he wanted from me then hidden me away to languish in solitude and slowly fall into insanity. But he didn't know that the coin always returned here to this sacred place whenever it was left without a master, testing anyone who came to claim me with the temptation of the cursed treasure.

"Nothing. I just mean, your wishes will be fulfilled exactly as you intended them. I can do anything for you. Everything." I bit my lip, hoping I'd said the right thing. I couldn't go back in the coin.

"What are you exactly?" Master's friend asked, eyeing me like he was afraid of me. But I wasn't sure why. I was just me.

"I'm The Blessing," I said slowly, unsure if his mind didn't work very fast, because I had already explained this.

"But what is a Blessing? Are you a monster?" he pressed.

"No," I balked, looking down at myself. Did I look like a monster? Had I accidentally made myself big and spiky, with four heads and lots of teeth?

Phew, I was still a woman, unless I'd gotten that wrong. Maybe I needed more breasts, or less breasts, or more shapely knees-

Get naked, men like that.

I frowned, unsure if I was right about that or not. The desire I saw in my master's eyes wasn't aimed at me, it was aimed at the riches I'd promised him.

Topless then, everyone likes looking at breasts, and you have nice breasts.

"They weren't so impressed with my penis," I muttered in denial. Showing off parts of my body hadn't impressed them before, and I wasn't going to risk frightening them off again.

"Did you just say something about a penis?" Cassius asked, and I shook my head fiercely.

Stop talking to me; they'll think you're insane.

It might have been a bit late for that, but I forced myself not to reply to myself. You could only make one first impression after all. And I'd probably blown it. But my master was beginning to smile, and it was such a pretty smile. He really did have dimples. I hadn't seen dimples in...well, I wasn't certain I could even recall seeing them before.

"I think I like her," Master said, looking at his friend.

My heart swelled and swelled, growing into a sun of its own as pleasure skipped through every inch of my flesh at his words and my silver skin began to glow with it.

"She might be the answer to all of the kingdom's problems," Cassius agreed, his gaze still weighing me. "If she can truly do what she says."

"She might be the answer to all of *my* problems," Master murmured, reaching out towards me hesitantly.

I stared up at him hopefully. I hadn't felt the brush of anyone's skin against mine in so, so long and the idea of him touching me sent a tremor of anticipation running through me. Followed quickly by a flicker of fear. What if I just disappeared when his skin met with mine? What if I was only the memory of a person now, and the moment he couldn't touch me would be the moment I realised it and I just fizzled into nothing?

He pulled his hand back before it could make contact with my cheek and relief mixed with disappointment in my chest. But that was okay. I *was* very strange. I couldn't blame him for not wanting to complete that act. And freedom from the coin was more than I ever could have dreamed of so if he didn't want to touch me, he didn't have to. And it was probably better that he didn't, just in case.

"Can I..." I wasn't sure if I dared to ask but I *had* to. Because I couldn't shake the fear of not knowing for a moment longer. "Can I just stay out of the coin though?" I breathed, my voice cracking with desperation as my fingers trembled at the thought of him refusing me that taste of freedom.

Begging? That's super attractive. Besides, what master of ours has ever cared what we wanted?

"You want to stay out here?" Master asked, raising an eyebrow at me.

"It's just that I've been in there for such a long time," I hurried to explain, wincing in anticipation of a refusal, my heart pounding so fast that I could hear it whooshing in my ears.

"Sure, whatever. Stay out here if you like. So long as you're giving me whatever I want, that's fine by me," he agreed as if it was nothing. But it was *everything*. Absolutely everything. My heart cracked in two and splintered apart before reforming and beating stronger just for him, this saviour of my sanity, this keeper of my soul.

Wow, you did something right for once.

"Are you sure you think that's a good idea?" Master's friend asked anxiously, so rigid in posture it was like he expected me to pounce on him and start eating his face.

"Yes, I do," Master insisted.

I stared up at him and words failed me. Thank you wasn't enough. No words could express what that act of kindness meant to me. So instead, I swore with all my heart that I would serve him well. I would grant him anything and everything he desired to the best of my abilities. I'd fulfil his dreams and make sure that his life overflowed with everything he could ever desire.

He owned me, mind, body and soul. And I was his for as long as he wanted.

CHAPTER TWENTY TWO

The strange woman stayed on her knees before me, looking up at me like I was a damn deity or something, and I couldn't help the grin that pulled at my mouth. She was a stunning creature, though I wasn't entirely certain she really was a woman at all with the way she seemed to be able to shift her features - or grow a fucking penis if she wanted one - and the shifting metallic hue of her skin was more than a little unusual. Her purple hair swayed around her shoulders like she was underwater, and I found myself staring at it as it kept moving like that, despite the fact that there wasn't so much as a breeze blowing right now.

"So if I just tell you I want the wealth I need to present myself as a suitor for the princess of Osaria then you'll do the rest?" I asked her dubiously. I seriously wanted to believe in all the things she claimed to be, but I had more than a little mistrust of magic, and I was still waiting for some trick or curse to present itself.

Cassius seemed to be expecting an attack at any moment, barely blinking as he watched her unwaveringly.

"Yes," she breathed and the way she was looking at me made me feel like she might even love me, her eyes fixed on every move I made, and her lips parted to allow shallow breaths to pass between them as she stared. It was… well fuck, strange didn't even cover it. I didn't know what to make of it at all and I certainly knew I was deserving of no such emotion as love. No doubt she'd quickly figure that out for herself too.

I snorted a laugh at the turn of events, wondering if I really could be that fucking lucky.

"Why don't I just ask you to make me the emperor then?" I asked, wondering if Cassius had been right in thinking that wouldn't work based on the rules she'd laid out earlier. "Cut out the middle ground?"

"Well, I could make you the emperor of your own empire. But I couldn't give you anyone to rule over..." she said hesitantly, seeming almost afraid of giving me any answer other than a vehement yes.

"She told you she can't affect other people," Cassius muttered and I got the feeling this was pissing him off a bit. He'd come so close to claiming the coin for himself and now he had to watch me wielding its power instead. That had to sting like a salty little bitch, but it really wasn't my problem. Sucked to be him right now.

"Alright. Cassius here came up with an idea for me to enter the royal pageant."

The magical woman nodded like that made perfect sense, though I doubted it did with how little information I was giving her. "It's a series of fights and challenges where I would have to beat every other contestant in order to claim the hand of the princess and become emperor via our marriage," I explained and understanding sparkled in her eyes. "So can I wish to win this tournament thing?" I asked, testing the limitations of her power.

She bit her lip nervously then shook her head. "I can't make you beat someone else because-"

"That would affect them. Got it." I sighed. This power was starting to seem a little too restricted to me and I hadn't even made use of it yet.

Kyra's face dropped as she seemed to realise that I was disappointed and I frowned. She was seriously hung up on my opinion of her. I was all for people adoring me, but I wasn't sure I was so keen on my moods dictating someone else's like that. This blind adoration thing might actually get old fast if all she did was stare at me like I was her sun and moon combined.

"Do you wanna maybe stop grovelling at my feet?" I asked, beckoning for her to stand. "And maybe lose the creepy dog collar?"

She shot upright and smiled at me like she could only be happy if I allowed it. "I can make it so that the collar is not visible," she agreed, touching her fingers to the iron which was clasped tightly around her throat and making it shimmer out of existence.

I stared openly, feeling Cassius's attention riveted to her just as heavily as my own as we tried to adjust to this casual use of magic which should have been impossible.

The woman shifted a little uncertainly, her gaze never moving from me as she seemed to drink in the sight of me, and I wetted my lips as I tried not to let myself get distracted by the way her thin gown clung to her curves, leaving tantalising glimpses of flesh on show across her waist and chest.

"Are you ready to make your first command then, Master?" she breathed uncertainly.

I don't hate being called Master though.

I ran my gaze down her body, the way she said that word giving me ideas which probably weren't the best I'd ever had, but I couldn't help but notice how attractive she was. If she hadn't had silver skin and purple hair, I was certain she would have been a beauty worthy of the songs of heralds, but as I still didn't really have a grasp on precisely what she was, I was guessing it would be best not to try and make any moves on her.

I glanced at Cassius and he nodded his encouragement, urging me to attempt a command. I imagined he wasn't too concerned over the chance of it going horribly wrong for me though – if I died, he would be able to claim the coin and destroy it as he desired all the easier. But my gut was telling me that wouldn't happen and I was inclined to trust my instincts. They'd gotten me this far after all.

"Alright. Fuck it. I want you to make me into a suitor good enough for the princess of Osaria," I said, raising my chin and bracing myself for whatever the fulfilment of that command might cost me, though I was hoping I was right about trusting her word.

Kyra's bright eyes flared with magic and a warm breeze swept around us. I flinched at the graze of something against my flesh, shifting uncomfortably as invisible, grasping fingers caressed my skin and the clothes on my body were reformed. I gasped in shock as instead of practical cotton and linen, I found myself suddenly dressed in finest silk. My britches were a deep blue, inlaid with what looked a hell of a lot like sapphires around my waist and an ice white tunic fell over my chest, brushing softly against my skin like feather-light kisses.

I felt her magic removing every trace of dirt from my flesh and hair more thoroughly than any bath and I ran a hand through my dark locks, marvelling at the softness of them as I tried to get my head around the idea of something being capable of such incredible power. It wasn't natural, something long lost and terrifying, yet here I was bathed in it and didn't feel all bad. It felt like something I'd been missing my entire life.

"You look like a prince," Kyra breathed appreciatively as her magic fell from me like grains of sand spilling across my skin, making the hair on my arms stand on end and a shiver track down my spine before it retreated, leaving me in my finery looking just like one of the powerful, upper Fae bastards I hated so much, and she bit her silver sheened lip as she gazed at me with real warmth in her eyes.

"You look like a peasant in a nice tunic," Cassius contradicted, backing up a step from me like he could sense the magic hugging my body and I scoffed. I could tell he was putting on a brave front, not showing an inch of fear in the face of this wild power, but even a royal guard had to be shaken by this.

"Jealous much?" I taunted.

"Hardly. I'm simply stating a fact. You don't move like a noble. Or talk like one. You certainly don't act like one. They'll see you for what you are from a mile off. And just like the way an honourable fight gave me away to The Forty, the way *you* fight in the pageant will give you away too."

"So? I thought the rules said any man rich enough to pay the emperor a dowry could put themselves forward for her hand. Why does it matter if I'm low-born?" I asked.

"Technically, it doesn't. But they'll wonder where a peasant got all of that money, not to mention the fact that they won't fucking like it. And then rumours of some low born Fae entering the pageant will travel to the city, and Egos will hear tales of a handsome commoner who turned up out of nowhere with a fortune in tow just around the same time as you disappeared after heading out to find treasure buried in the desert."

"Point taken," I said with a sigh, having no desire to ever go anywhere near Egos again. I didn't need him now. Not if Kyra could do what she claimed she could do, so why would I return to him and risk him figuring out what I had claimed for myself?

If this coin and the woman linked to it was even half as powerful as she said, I would never have need of The Forty, The Den, or any of them ever again. My gut twisted a little at the thought of leaving Pip behind, but what other choice did I have? Besides, in my position he would have made the same choice in a heartbeat and I wouldn't expect any less.

"You'll have to teach me how to fake being a noble, Cass. I could do with a guard anyway if I'm supposed to be rich."

"The problem is, people know me in the palace," Cassius pointed out. "I can't just wander back in there-"

"Kyra, can you disguise him for me?" I asked, wondering if that would break her rules.

"If he agrees to it, I can," she said, the wind which billowed through her purple hair seeming to pick up in intensity as it was tossed about her even more forcefully. "That's the only way I can affect anyone with my power besides you directly."

"And maybe you could disguise yourself too? As Fae? You could be my maid or something? Instead of...well I don't think you actually got to the part where you told us what you were?"

"I'm a Blessing," Kyra repeated once more, smiling up at me from her tiny height like that actually meant anything at all.

"You're gonna have to clarify, little goddess, because that don't mean a damn thing to me," I told her.

"I'm not a goddess," she said, shaking her head like that idea was insane but she was the one breathing magic into the air all around us, so it didn't seem like that bad of a guess to me.

"What are you then?" I pushed but she just shrugged.

"I'm yours." She bit her lip and my gaze traced the movement, the sound of those words on her pretty mouth seeming all kinds of acceptable to me and I shrugged too, realising I wasn't going to be getting a clearer answer than that as she didn't seem to have one, so I let it go.

"Alright," I agreed, glancing at Cassius as he frowned like he didn't much like the idea of me claiming ownership over this creature who wouldn't tell us what she was, but she was the one who wanted to be owned, it wasn't like it had been my idea. "So, do you think you can manage the disguise thing?

Her eyes sparked with joy. "And then I could stay out of the coin?" she asked breathlessly. "The whole time?"

"Sure. Two disguises. No coin. What do you say?"

She nodded eagerly and I grinned at the bargain we'd struck.

"It'll take a hell of a lot to train you to pass for a noble," Cassius muttered, giving me an assessing look, which said he didn't think I could do it. But I could trick a whore into fucking me for free four nights in a row and outsmart all of the royal guards on a daily basis, so this sounded like a piece of cake to me.

"Can't I just ask for all the knowledge I need?" I asked, looking to Kyra who shifted uneasily.

"Well...knowledge isn't exactly a tangible thing," she said. "It's not like creating clothes or riches. The magic would have to affect your mind. The mind and the heart can't just be changed like that. They're too powerful on their own, to infect them with magic would destroy them. It can't be done."

"It looks like you have a whole lot of work to do if you expect to be able to enter the pageant then," Cassius said firmly, seeming all too pleased about that limitation to Kyra's power. "You don't even stand properly. Your legs are spread too wide."

"That's because my balls are so fucking big," I joked and Kyra laughed. The sound was almost musical, and I couldn't help but smile at her as she watched me with that burning kind of devotion again.

"Nobles don't tend to talk about their balls quite so much either," Cassius added, though I could tell he was amused too. His grumpy attitude barely lifted from his face. But real deep down, I reckoned he was laughing like a street cat at a fish market.

"Come now, if there's one thing about me that screams noble it's gotta be my arrogance," I contradicted. "No one's so full of themselves as a man with power. And money buys you power."

"You have a point there," he conceded.

"Speaking of money," I added. "Where is it?" It was all well and good having nice fancy clothes, but they wouldn't buy my way into the palace.

"I just thought it might be a little hard to carry," Kyra said. "Unless the palace is hiding inside one of the desert dunes? I assumed we had some travelling to do, but if it's digging-"

"We need to travel," Cassius cut her off, giving me a sideways look but I didn't care if she was a little odd, all the best people were in my opinion. It only served to make life more interesting.

"We could really do with a few camels then," Kyra murmured. "But I can't create a living thing. Maybe I could create enough money to buy some camels and then-"

"We've got camels already," Cassius interrupted. "It looks like we'll be using them to carry treasure out of here after all."

"Well let's just hope that Egos didn't have anyone following us. Because if he finds those bodies and ours aren't amongst them, he will hunt us for the rest of our days."

"I could make stones look like your bodies?" Kyra suggested brightly. "I could just flesh them up and make them all bloody and disgusting, and then anyone who saw them would take a single look and instantly think of you."

"They'd think of us because they'd look disgusting?" Cassius asked, his nose wrinkling and Kyra nodded excitedly.

I barked a laugh, smiling widely at her plan and nodding my agreement to it. "That sounds perfect. I could kiss you, little goddess."

"Okay," she replied breathily and I raised an eyebrow at her as she bit her full bottom lip and heat rose to her silver cheeks. "I mean, okay I'll do it. The stones thing. Not the kissing thing."

Cassius caught my eye and I shrugged innocently. It wasn't my fault that I tended to have this effect on women – if that was even what she was. She certainly looked mostly Fae but the unnatural colours of her skin and hair, and the constantly changing features of her face made it impossible for me to say whether or not she was attractive for certain. I tended to like my women a little more fixed in solid form and a lot less rainbow coloured.

Besides, she'd grown a penis not that long ago which wasn't really a plus for me personally, though I could think of a few guys in The Den who would have liked that feature. Especially if she managed to make it a little bigger next time. Either way, I had a princess waiting for me who was supposed to be the most beautiful woman ever born. And though I doubted she was anything quite as spectacular as that, I was going to fix my attentions on her for the foreseeable future. The princess was going to fall in love with me so fast and hard that she would barely be able to catch her breath between the kisses I laid on her untouched mouth.

"Let's get back to those camels then. I want to see my treasure," I announced, my attention catching on Kyra as she ran a finger along her bottom lip absentmindedly while her gaze rose to take in the trees surrounding us.

My pulse skipped as I watched her, something about the way she was drinking in the sight of everything like she'd never even seen it before entirely captivating to me. It made me look more closely at everything too, taking in the vibrant colours of the palm trees which towered over us and the way the dappled sunlight filtered down on us from above. The scent of the fresh flowers blooming in the grass seemed sweeter as she inhaled deeply, and I found myself following her lead. The sound of the waterfall permeated the air alongside birdsong, which I hadn't even noticed until I paused to pay attention to it.

Cassius cleared his throat loudly and I snapped around to look at him, giving his arched brow an innocent shrug as I turned away, moving back towards the falls. I ignored him as he continued to give me an irritated look, the feeling of his gaze upon the side of my face all too accusing. But he had nothing to worry about there. Kyra may have been stunning in appearance and alluring in all kinds of unknown and forbidden ways, but I wasn't utterly without restraint or common sense.

No. I definitely wasn't going to be attempting any kind of advances upon her. I'd take my women a little less silver, as usual, and keep my cock well away from creatures who wielded magic so unnaturally. I still had no idea what my so-called Blessing really was or what she might be capable of, and I wasn't going to be letting my guard down around her any time soon. For all I knew, if I got her near my cock, she'd accidentally turn it into an onion.

"I don't think he noticed," Kyra muttered to herself as she started following us. "It's *not* weird. It's normal...well if I don't reply then how can we have a conversation? No, they haven't noticed, I-"

I turned to look at her and a blush lined her silver cheeks as she fell silent, her golden eyes widening as they fell on me.

The moment stretched as we held eye contact and I just drank in the strangeness of her as I tried to get my mind around what was happening here. Magical entities didn't simply appear out of nowhere. Even magic-bearing creatures were rare these days, most of them reduced to nothing more than whispers and rumours which circled down to us from the past. The lost gods had taken the magic with them when they abandoned our kind, but it looked like they'd forgotten this piece of it when they went.

"You're very pretty," Kyra breathed as she looked into my dark eyes.

I nodded. "I know."

"I'm not sure it's a compliment coming from her," Cassius said with something of a taunt in his voice, and I smiled widely as I turned my attention on him instead.

"Jealousy doesn't suit you, mate."

"Oh wait," Kyra said slowly, shaking her head at herself irritably. "I meant ugly. I keep confusing the two."

I frowned at her as she passed me by because she hadn't fucking meant ugly. I was the opposite of ugly. There wasn't a single ugly thing about me aside from my arrogance and even that was charming most of the damn time.

"No, you were right the first time," I corrected her, but she laughed like I was the one who was wrong and waded out into the pool before the waterfall, heading back into the cavern so that she could create the decoy bodies for us. I caught Cassius sniggering at me too and narrowed my eyes.

"She's confused, she doesn't think I'm ugly. No one thinks I'm ugly," I insisted.

"*She* does," he said lightly and I cursed under my breath.

Cassius fished his sword out of the water on our way to the falls, strapping it to his hip tightly like that would be enough to stop me from lifting it again whenever I fancied.

We crossed through the waterfall once more and I felt the crash of power striking against me as it forced truth to cling to my lips again. We climbed back up onto the rock shelf on the other side of the water and I observed the bodies of the thieves I'd brought with us uneasily. Jadar was laying across the path just before the waterfall, his hands still clutching the jewels he'd taken from the trees moments before the curse on them had killed him.

"Why the hell were you hiding in a place like this anyway?" I asked Kyra as she paused to make two large stones look like the bodies of Cassius and myself. Not that they bore much resemblance to us with their skin turned inside out and blood staining the ground all around them, but the clothes looked right and there was the correct number of bodies here now.

"The Prophet who cursed me decided to put me here so that no one would ever find me again. He made it so that any time my coin was lost, it would return to this place to await discovery once again. Usually, the coin passed from master to master due to murder or theft, but on occasion it would simply be lost and would reappear here. A long time ago, Fae used to know of my coin and the power housed in it. They would seek out the cavern and claim the coin for their own. At least they did back then," she murmured, trailing off without explaining why the knowledge of her coin had been lost or how long it had been since she had been summoned from it last.

"Cursed you?" Cassius asked, latching on to that fact. "So, you weren't always like this?"

"No... I was Fae once," she sighed. "At least I think I was."

I arched a brow at that in surprise. I mean sure, she had a lot of Fae like features, but she was also a living embodiment of pure magic. I could feel it crackling in the air ever since the moment she had first appeared, could see it in the colour of her skin and hair and in the swirling darkness of her eyes, so it was hard to imagine she'd once been just a normal girl. I had to wonder if any part of the Fae she had once been even remained now.

"Why were you cursed?" I asked, eyeing the rock she'd glamoured to look like me with distaste. I wasn't nearly attractive enough in death.

"Because I killed an emperor," she said with a shrug before turning away from us and heading through the waterfall once more. It seemed to part around her body and her feet walked over the surface of the water as if it were solid.

Cassius's face dropped at her words and he caught my arm before we could follow.

"Maybe this is a bad idea," he breathed urgently. "What if she wants to make killing emperors a habit? We can't risk bringing her into the palace if she's holding some ancient grudge against the royal line."

I folded my arms as I thought about it. "You didn't even recognise the name of the emperor she asked you about before, so it seems like her grudge must be far outdated to me. Why would she harbour any ill will towards a man she's never met? Besides, she doesn't exactly strike me as the assassin type."

"She seems entirely unhinged to me," Cassius countered. "And we don't know her true nature. Everything she has said to us so far could be a lie."

"You can't lie in here, Cass," I said dismissively.

"*We* can't, but what if that creature can?" he hissed, and I frowned. "At the very least, we should keep our guard up. We don't know how volatile she could be. She seems confused and not entirely sane, how do we know we are safe in her presence?"

"Alright, you make a good point," I conceded because the girl was clearly at least a few kurus short of a gold bar. "But I don't think she has any power at all without my say so," I replied, tilting my arm and feeling for the chain which I could sense beneath my skin, though my fingers brushed against nothing but flesh as I hunted for it. "She can't even stay out of that coin unless I allow it. So if she does anything we don't like, I'll simply send her back in. Problem solved."

Cassius didn't seem totally convinced, deep lines forming on his brow, so I slapped him on the arm bracingly.

"Relaaaax. You look like I just unleashed a plague of death on the world," I laughed.

"What if you did?" he growled and I shook my head at him. Poor, sad little Cassius with his pointless valour and noble causes, trying to save the world while it crumbled around him.

"Then we'll deal with it. I've gotten myself out of plenty of tight situations, mate. It always works out. Don't worry about building yourself a shelter until the sky is actually falling, that's my motto."

"That's a terribly foolish way to live your life," he scoffed.

"And yet here I am, breathing air in and out of my lungs just the same as you are, but with a lot less stress about me. You're like one of those fancy, fizzy wines from Shamba that's been all shaken up in its bottle, the bubbles inside trying to explode their way past the cork, but me? I'm a crisp, smooth whiskey in a glass, chilling with a couple of ice cubes on a fine summer's day."

Cassius gave me a flat look at my colourful description, so I guessed he didn't appreciate it, but he did that restraint thing where he straightened his shoulders and held back the animal in him instead of snapping at me. Perhaps my guard companion wasn't as empty inside as I'd first thought, because the more I saw that beasty peeking out at me, the more I wanted to rattle the urn it was housed within to see if I could break it free.

It was probably too late for that though. He was too far gone, forged into a royal pawn who didn't even have wants for himself anymore. He'd seen my shiny new coin's power and the first thing he'd thought of was saving his precious kingdom from it. Sad that. He could have tried harder to get his hands on it, challenged me to a proper bloody fight and maybe he could have walked away with it too, then gone and wished for a nice new sun hat or something.

Cassius was still thinking, and he finally came to his long-drawn conclusion. Unlike me who made decisions on a whim, this man was cautious in fucking everything. It must have been so boring being him.

"Alright. I just hope we aren't making a terrible mistake," he said at last.

"Only one way to find out." I slapped him on the cheek then turned and strode away after my little goddess. This might have been one seriously strange turn of events, but I wasn't a fool. So if that girl wanted to be my Blessing, then I was gonna be all in with that, because the sound of all of my dreams coming true was pretty fucking beautiful, and I was starting to really like the idea of becoming a damn emperor.

CASSIUS

CHAPTER TWENTY THREE

We made camp a mile from the falls. The night was humid and the air stifling. I preferred the dry gusts of the desert to this thick heat beneath the trees any day. But after travelling through the Lyrian, neither Drake nor I were prepared to take on that journey again before a night's rest. We also had the pressing issue of the dragon we owed a debt to.

I pulled Drake aside as Kyra moved about the camp, creating a bright blue fire at the heart of a clearing in the trees. I watched it with unease as she tried out different colours on the flames, muttering curses as she worked. Her magic kept me on edge at all times, especially because Drake was now the master of it. It wasn't natural, only meant for the lost gods and not to be abused by reckless thieves for selfish gain.

"Perhaps you could ask the creature to create some treasure for Azurea," I suggested.

"Hmm, nah," he said dismissively, clearly not taking the threat to our lives seriously enough.

"The dragon will hunt us to the four corners of the world to ensure our debt is paid. And she will take it in blood," I hissed. "The answer is right here in front of us."

"Seems to me like the dragon specifically wanted that cursed treasure which we can't take out of that cave without ending up with our skin peeled from our bodies and turned inside out," he countered. "So giving her some imposter treasure in its place seems worse than just not giving her any at all."

"Then what do you suggest we do to appease the deal we made with her?" I asked darkly, seriously disturbed about going back on our word to that legendary creature.

Drake scored a thumb along his jaw for a moment before his eyes sparked with what I was certain would be a terrible idea. "Hey Kyra, can you make me unfindable to dragons?"

"Done!" she cried and Drake smirked at me, patting my arm with false sympathy.

"Seems like a you issue now, mate," he said and I glowered.

"Well good luck winning the pageant without my assistance. I'm sure Egos will make a nice coat out of your flesh when he's done torturing you." I turned my head away from him and he sighed wearily.

"Fine. Kyra, make Cassius unfindable to dragons too."

"Do you agree?" she asked me and I confirmed it, feeling like it would make far more sense to just conjure some treasure to appease her than this. I didn't want to scorn an ancient creature of the gods, but it seemed Drake wasn't feeling generous. As per usual.

A trickle of magic washed over me and I stiffened against it, the feeling unsettling, but it washed away just as quickly and Kyra went back to playing with the fire she'd built. I inspected my skin, expecting to find some mark of it, but there was nothing there, not even the lasting tingle of it in my flesh. But still, my heart rate wouldn't settle.

She started talking to herself again and anxiety warred through me about how unstable she was. "Not blue... Well, what is it then? Oh yes you're right, it's pink."

I frowned, observing her intently as I tried to assess how much of a threat she was. It truly did seem that she was under Drake's control through that coin, but she was still a weapon, and the fact that she was casually casting magic right in front of me now told me she *could* use it when she chose to. And as she didn't seem to be particularly familiar with how the world worked that made her potentially dangerous.

When she'd started setting up the camp and getting things wrong, she'd apologised profusely to Drake, her eyes flashing with fear as she told him she had forgotten a lot while she was stuck in the coin but he'd just laughed, seeming to find her amusing while accepting all of the things she created for him whether they were a bit off or not. Like the luxurious tent she had made for us to sleep in which smelled oddly like bananas, or the pool of heated water she had conjured for him to bathe in which had been filled with oil at first, before she remembered which liquid she should have created.

I'm going to walk a magical monster into the palace...and then what?

Had I made a poor choice here? Should I have been working harder to get my hands on that coin? Marching a common thief into the pageant still didn't sit entirely right with me. But the kingdom was at risk and I didn't see another way to take on Magdor. Even if I did destroy the coin, that wouldn't stop her from controlling my emperor for the rest of his reign.

So maybe this *was* the better option. And if I failed at gaining the evidence I needed to destroy her, I'd just take my chances at executing her myself. It might cost me my life but at least I would die knowing our kingdom was safe once more. That Austyn and her father would be free.

Drake was sitting cross-legged in front of a mountain of gold coins, counting every piece of the treasure Kyra had summoned onto the backs of our camels with a greedy glint in his eyes that made him look like some sort of demon. The beasts were currently settled down in the grass, their bellies full of the food Kyra had conjured for them and every now and then I heard their inner thoughts of contentment.

"I'm so rich...so fucking rich," Drake breathed for the millionth time, a laugh escaping him as he swigged on a bottle of wine which Kyra had created for him.

I chewed on the inside of my cheek, rising from the log I'd been perched on and approaching him. As my shadow blotted out the light of the fire and stopped him from counting, he glanced up at me with a scowl.

"Care to move out of the way, mate?"

"Rich people don't act like they've never seen a pile of gold before," I said evenly. How was I going to train this lout up to be fit to meet the emperor and his daughter? *Fuck it, he's never going to be fit for that, but I can make it seem like he is.*

"I'm not at the palace right now, so who cares?" Drake demanded.

I kicked his pile of carefully stacked coins and he scrambled around after them with a growl of anger.

I shook my head at the pathetic act. "Noblemen don't care if they lose a coin or two."

Drake ignored me, gathering each and every kuru up from the grass as fast as he could, muttering under his breath and I was pretty sure I caught the words 'turd-baked cunt' tossed in my direction.

Kyra was still having a conversation with herself about what colour a fire should be and my patience with my current company was starting to wear thin.

"Wow, look at all my money," Drake said under his breath as he finally got his coins back in order, but then his smile fell away. "I bet I could be richer. I should wish for more. Yeah, I'm gonna wish for more."

"Oh yes, now I remember, it's purple like our hair," Kyra said excitedly as she turned the fire blazingly purple then she scowled. "No, it's not purple, breasts are purple, see?" She yanked down her pale pink dress, exposing her pert breasts which were in fact a faint shade of lilac now and I cursed as Drake's head snapped up to look.

"Well maybe I am a whore, did you ever think of that?" Kyra growled at herself, pulling her dress back up. "We don't remember, so anything is possible – fuck it, it's blue." She changed the colour of the fire. "Like an arse," she said under breath with a decisive nod. "Wait...no, an arse isn't blue, is it?" she snapped at herself, taking hold of the hem of her dress and I rounded on her before this got out of hand.

"Red. Orange. Gold." I pointed at the fire.

Her eyes widened then a smile split across her face like a sunrise. "Oh thank you, sullen man," she gushed like I'd just made all of her dreams come true.

"I'm not sullen," I murmured, though I knew I should have just ignored the remark.

"Surly, then," she corrected, and my brow furrowed as Drake snorted a laugh at my expense.

"I am not surly," I said through my teeth, and she bit her lip, looking like she was thinking.

"Oh, I've got it this time! You're crabby. Like a crab, see?" she turned her hands into crab pincers with a flash of magic and snapped them at me.

"Yeah, that sounds right. Crabby old Cassius," Drake agreed and I ground my jaw, my hands curling into fists at my sides.

"I am not old, I am only thirty. And I am not cr-" I cut myself off, taking a breath and deciding to let it go.

Kyra giggled as she returned her hands to their usual form then made the fire a normal shade with perhaps a little too much gold in it. I nodded my approval and Kyra leapt to her feet as she began to dance around it in glee. It was hard not to stare at her with the way her skin began to continually cycle through every colour of the rainbow, as she started moving her body to a beat no one but she could hear with seductive movements I had never seen attempted in the royal court.

I was starting to wonder if there was any hope at all of her passing herself off as Fae once we returned to Osaria. Frankly, she may well have to go back inside the coin, or we'd give ourselves away the moment we arrived.

I did a slow circuit of the camp, eyeing the darkness between the unnatural palms which somehow existed all the way out here in the middle of the Lyrian. The air was moist and the chirrup of cicadas filled the air, alongside the grunt and croak of other small animals hiding away in the vegetation. The magic in this place made me uncomfortable, but as I turned my thoughts to Princess Austyn, I found an inch of calm to hold onto. I pictured her face, knowing it was a crime in itself that I hadn't tried to forget her features the moment I'd cast my eyes upon them, but I would no sooner let that vision go than allow an enemy army through the palace gates. It was mine, and a dark part of me was growing angrier and angrier about the fact that she would be Unveiled soon. That the men in the pageant would be able to feast their eyes on her, stash memories of her in their wicked minds to do whatever they pleased with. It made me want to cut out all of their eyes, so they never got the chance to behold her, and as my gaze slid to Drake across the camp, I felt a shudder of apprehension over him vying for her hand.

Would she be taken with him? Fall for his charm and let him touch her the way he'd touched a hundred women.

My grip tightened on the hilt of my sword and for a moment it was if the blade was humming in my grip, buzzing with power. But I was pretty sure it was just how hard I was holding onto it.

"Why's he walking in a big circle?" Kyra whispered to herself, as she bent over backwards and placed her hands on the ground while looking directly at me.

"I'm checking for signs of danger," I told her. "I'm a royal guard, it's a habit I guess."

"Ooh," Kyra cooed, kicking her legs up and somehow moving into a handstand which caused her dress to tumble down her thighs then whispered to herself. "Habits are so cuddly and fluffy."

I was pretty sure she'd gotten her habits mixed up with her rabbits, but as I opened my mouth to say it, Drake piped up.

"Was," he said, his eyes catching on the exposed skin of Kyra's legs before she thankfully dropped them to the ground once more and flipped herself upright again. "You *was* a royal guard."

"You *were* a royal guard," I corrected him with a tut. "If you speak like that in front of high-born Fae, they'll catch on to you in no time."

He shrugged, turning his attention to his coins again, making sure every single one was back in his pile before he acknowledged me, raising his chin and holding my eye as a decision shone in his dark gaze.

"Alright. Teach me to be a poncey twat," he commanded, and it was only for my love of my kingdom that I decided to try.

Kyra looked between us, biting her lip and I stiffened as she cast a fluffy pink cloud out of nothing to sit cross-legged on, floating closer to see better. Drake and I shared a nervous glance, the sight of this magic clearly setting him on edge too though he seemed to be adjusting to it far faster than I was. I swear my heart still leapt at every display of her power and despite her almost innocent seeming disposition, I half expected her to turn this power on us at any moment just for the hell of it.

"What are you waiting for? Make him into a poncey twat!" Kyra urged excitedly as she floated closer.

I cleared my throat, nodding and beckoning Drake to his feet. "Get up," I encouraged, and he did so, his cocky swagger already dripping from him.

"Shoulders back. You slouch." I moved behind him and straightened out his spine. "Like this." I strode away from him with my head held tall, showing him how the noblemen walked.

He watched me for a moment then strutted forward like a peacock, pushing his fingers into his hair, and smirking like he owned the whole world.

"Yeah...that'll pass," I snorted, and he gave me a slanted grin.

"That was too easy. What's next?" he asked.

"I can't teach you all the customs of the nobles in one night. And for you I'd need a decade."

He raised a brow. "Well, how long do we have 'til the pageant starts?"

I looked up to the moon. It seemed almost as if an entire lifetime had passed since I'd first been imprisoned and as I worked to count the days that had actually passed, shock jarred through me.

"It's in less than a week," I announced in concern and Drake suddenly looked half a fraction less confident than usual.

"Teach me then, mate," he urged.

I had more on the line than he did, so I had to give it my all, but as he casually rearranged his cock in his britches like it was nothing, I sighed.

"You can't touch yourself like that in front of the nobles. Ever."

"What? Not even if my balls are itching?" he gasped.

"I could scratch them for you if you command it. Would that be okay in front of the noble people, Cassius?" Kyra asked brightly.

"No," I balked as Drake barked a laugh.

"So what am I supposed to do? Just let my balls itch?" Drake asked seriously and I sighed. This was going to be a long fucking night.

"Yes, Drake," I growled. "You let them itch until they fall off for all I care, because I swear on the Fallen if you scratch them in front of the princess, I will cut them off."

"Hang on a second, so you're telling me that while you were on duty, you had to stand there with your balls itching up a storm, and you couldn't even do a little wall grind to alleviate them?

"What's a wall grind?" I demanded and Kyra flicked a finger, creating a small wall in front of Drake as she rolled onto her front on the cloud and cupped her head in her hands to watch.

"Thanks, little goddess," he said, giving her a smile, which was all too flirtatious in my opinion, before he started grinding his crotch on the wall, tossing me an overly sexualised look as I clenched my teeth and fought to hold back my irritation.

"Right, it was precisely as it sounded then," I deadpanned, swiping a hand down my face. "And no, we cannot do a fucking wall grind in the palace. No one should ever do that in the palace. Or anywhere for that matter. It's unseemly."

"Even if no one is around?" he asked in a mocking act of dismay, this entire thing clearly some joke to him, still grinding his junk on the wall like some sort of wild animal marking its scent.

"Of course not, we are taught perfect restraint," I said, lifting my chin and he finally stopped grinding, turning to me with a pitying frown.

"Fuck me, you had it even worse than I thought, mate. They cut the man right out of you, didn't they?"

My lips pressed hard together at those words, the truth of them cutting far deeper than I liked even as he sniggered at what had clearly been a joke. And though he might not have seriously gone around grinding against walls, I could tell his last words held a bite of truth to them when it came to his opinion of me. He might have been poor and hungry and fighting for his survival every day, but he had at least been himself during that time. I on the other hand, had become a creature of the crown and any semblance of the man I might have been outside of that was a hard thing to be certain of.

I didn't answer him, instead stowing my sword away and paying far too much attention to the act. Yes, there was an impenetrable box within me built of self-control and a thousand orders drummed into my being. The beast within it may have broken out on occasion, but it was always dragged back in again, collared and leashed. I was both the prisoner and the prison. This flesh was owned by the emperor, I'd handed it over the day I'd signed the contract given to me by Captain Marik. It had been my choice to make, so I wasn't going to pity myself of that choice. Especially not when it had saved my mother and sisters from losing their home. I wouldn't even regret that it had landed me here, preparing to take on the cuckoo in my kingdom's nest, because I had vowed I'd do anything for an opportunity to do just that for years. I couldn't go complaining about the way it had been presented to me.

"You'll need to learn to bow," I told Drake, changing the subject.

I curled my right hand into a fist, laid it over my heart then bowed at a forty-five-degree angle. He picked it up straight away and as we continued on with our training and Kyra circled us, clapping and laughing or sometimes just mumbling to herself, I had to admit Drake was a quick study.

I tried to improve his speech and the way he should address other nobles, but one evening wasn't enough for all of it, though he had made vast improvements by the time we sank down to the ground around the fire and called it a night.

At least the dog was teachable. He actually listened when I spoke, which was something I had only experienced in the company of my family. Royal guards weren't meant to voice their opinions or speak their minds.

Drake's comments about this not being the first con he'd ever run set me on edge more than they reassured me. He was a master of manipulation and a con man well practiced in getting what he wanted. Was I a fool for aiming this charlatan at the princess of our kingdom? Was I an even bigger fool to believe she wouldn't fall for his false charm?

My throat thickened and the tightness in my chest became almost unbearable as I pictured her laughing at his jokes, letting him draw her closer, seeking a kiss from his mouth.

"I need a drink," Drake muttered, looking to Kyra and I was jolted out of the darkness seeping over me as my attention was drawn to them.

I had tried to encourage him to be careful when asking for her gifts, to treat them with respect, and be wary before wishing for anything, thinking long and hard on each request. But he took advantage of her abilities as if he had owned them his entire life, no longer seeming the least bit concerned about the magic.

She dissolved her cloud, dropping to her knees in front of him obediently, staring at him like she was deeply in love with him.

"Oh, great Master of - er - the world. What can I do to serve your ugliness? Humbleness!" she corrected instantly, muttering curses to herself.

I breathed a surprised laugh, sometimes finding it hard to equate this creature with something to be feared. Although I could never be too careful.

Drake swiped a hand through his hair, dishevelling it in a way which somehow looked intentional.

"I think we will need a drink or six tonight. A bottle of..." He glanced over at me. "What's the most expensive drink in the kingdom – no, the empire?"

"Cartlanna honey wine," I said without hesitation.

"That." Drake pointed at me while staring at Kyra.

"Your wish is my remand," she said proudly.

"Command," I corrected quietly, and she blushed before a large bottle of the wine appeared in her grip. She placed it in front of Drake triumphantly and he nodded his approval.

"Thanks, little goddess," he said, throwing her a wide smile which made the currently copper coloured skin of her cheeks darken even further with her blush.

Drake plucked the cork out of the bottle with his damn teeth, and I darted forward, snatching it from his grip before he could drink it like a barbarian.

"That's worth a hundred kurus a drop," I gasped.

"It's free to me, mate, because my little goddess just conjured it up. Now give it back," he ordered, snatching a dagger from his hip, his eyes flashing murderously and all signs of the easy-going cad falling away to reveal the teeth of the monster which lay beneath that surface he presented.

By the Fallen, was he going to try and stab me over a bottle of wine?

"If you drink Cartlanna wine like that in the city, you're going to give yourself up in five seconds," I warned, refusing to so much as balk at his violent display.

He groaned, turning to Kyra again. "Cups?" he asked.

She nodded keenly and two golden chalices appeared in her hands, the most beautiful cups I'd ever seen. She handed us one each and I inspected mine with intrigue, trying to seek out some darkness in this power, but it was confoundingly beautiful.

"One for the lady perhaps?" I kicked Drake and he rolled his eyes. I was hellbent on treating Kyra well, for if she turned her wrath on us, we would pay dearly for it.

"Get yourself one," he said to her, and she smiled widely before conjuring another of the chalices for herself.

I poured out the wine then we dropped down to sit in a circle while Kyra watched me like I was about to perform a magic trick, and Drake looked like he was tempted to glug his wine before I gave him any instructions.

"Do as I do," I ordered, and Drake nodded, gesturing for me to go ahead with a lazy flick of his fingers. That mannerism was a pretty noble one at least – he hadn't been wrong about his arrogance being a bonus.

I clinked my chalice against Kyra's then lifted it to my lips. "To the Emperor Tarim Lunarelle," I said. "May his daughter bear glorious heirs." *But by Osaria, don't let them be Drake's or fucking Kahn's.*

Drake echoed the traditional words and Kyra joined in with a giddy grin.

I sipped the wine, the honeyed nectar rolling over my tongue and down my throat. I sighed contentedly as the alcohol fizzled in my gut. I'd always wondered what this tasted like. Even high-born Fae like me weren't privy to this level of wealth. A bottle of Cartlanna wine would have been the equivalent of two months' rent even for a royal guard.

Drake tossed back the contents of his cup and smiled widely. "That shit is delicious." He hurriedly poured out another glassful, his eyes flipping to me as he sensed my disapproval. "It's not like I'm gonna do this in the palace. But we're not in the palace right now, mate. So, let's drink like the heathens we are and just enjoy being away from all of that bullshit while we can." He clinked his chalice to mine with a roguish grin before sitting back and pouring himself another.

I nodded vaguely, but didn't down my drink like he was, recalling my captain's rules when it came to alcohol. I was permitted to have one glass of wine or tankard of ale on celebratory events like the emperor's birthday, summer's end, and the princess's upcoming Unveiling. To be drinking at all outside of those decreed holidays was something I should have been violently punished for. So, despite being out here in the middle of the Lyrian Desert with not a chance of being caught in the act, I supposed I really was still just a number, bound by the rules of my position.

Drake sank another glass of priceless wine and Kyra started copying him, not seeming remotely affected by the alcohol as she knocked back glass after glass and I continued to savour my single cup.

"Oh, *Cass*," Drake said dramatically, and I frowned at the nickname he was insisting on using for me. "Drink it, will you? There's an endless amount. And we earned it." He rested a hand on my shoulder, and I grappled with my inner restraints.

I'd never taken more than I'd needed of anything. Food, water, clothes. I was taught to live within my means, and the last time I had overindulged on alcohol, Captain Marik had severely punished me for it. I wasn't the only guard who had met that fate either. Once, one of my fellow guardsmen had turned up to training hungover and Marik had had him run laps of the palace without shoes on until he'd passed out, the ground so burningly hot from the sun that it had skinned his feet raw.

But no one was ordering me around now. In theory, I could do whatever I damn-well pleased, and yet it wasn't so simple.

My fingers twitched against my cup, but my muscles felt chained to my captain in that moment, holding me there, refusing to let me take even another sip.

"How did we earn this drink exactly?" I asked, the urge to devour the entire chalice of this delicious wine rising in me. Despite the tightness in my body and the years of self-control, a rebellious part of me was clamouring to be heard.

"We survived!" Drake announced. "Another day alive is always worth celebrating."

"So you're saying this is a special occasion?" I confirmed, a boyish grin pulling at my lips as I worked within the confines of my training to try and allow myself this indulgence. Fuck, why was this so difficult? Marik wasn't here, there was no whip in sight. Why couldn't I just break down the walls of my restrictions?

"Drink it," Kyra said excitedly. "Drink it, drink it, don't drink it, don't drink it." She slammed a palm to her forehead. "Wait, it was the first one. Do the first one."

Drake reached towards her as she went to hit herself again, his hand blocking the path of hers and making her look up at him in surprise. "Don't do that," he said with a confused frown and though she moved her arm aside so that he couldn't touch it, she did stop, blinking at him like he'd just saved her life instead of simply telling her not to hit herself.

"You're... sort of sweet for such an ugly man," she whispered, and shutters locked down in Drake's eyes at that. A chuckle of laughter left me as he sat back with a muscle in his jaw ticking, the dig clearly bothering him far more than it would have any other man.

I looked down at my wine once more as I considered my options. I could have one cup. Those were the rules on special occasions and finding an age-old magical creature who could bestow blessings upon the one who held her coin was surely something of an occasion.

Yes...that seemed logical. Arguably within the rules.

Convinced, I drained the glass in one long, delightful, thrilling gulp. Not a sip. Not a sup. A whole, fucking swallow.

Drake rounded on me with a laugh of satisfaction, his irritation falling away in favour of the wine.

"More," he said immediately as he refilled his own cup and Kyra's, but I held mine away, a shudder falling through me as I almost felt the slash of a whip against my back.

I gazed down at my empty chalice as the beatings of my past held me in chains. I was already a lawbreaker; another round of wine would hardly be a substantial crime to add to my list now. And yet somehow, I felt as bound to my captain's rule in this moment as I had during all those years at the palace. I'd already bent the bars of my inner cage, but now the bars were pushing back, and like a dog who'd been struck too many times by its master, I retreated.

"I can only have one cup. I...can't have more," I said in a strained voice, moving to place the chalice down and feeling their eyes boring into me. Fuck, I felt exposed, like they were seeing me for what I truly was. Just a hollow man built of steel. One of countless weapons forged to protect the empire, nothing more. Never more.

"But you haven't had your one cup yet," Kyra said, a twinkle in her eye like an actual star lived there as she pointed to it. I looked down, finding that the dregs at the bottom of my chalice had now swelled to refill it once more.

"Yeah, mate. Drink up." Drake breathed a laugh as I gazed at the wine, wetting my lips.

Technically, it wasn't a second cup of wine. And technically, that made drinking it within the rules.

I found I could easily lift the chalice to my mouth again, my heart thundering with defiance as I drank deeply once more, and every time I swallowed, I found that none of the wine had shifted from my cup at all. But I was within the rules, wasn't I? Certainly enough to feel as though I was, the nightmares beyond my cage not creeping in as I worked within the confines of the bars built around my soul.

"See? It's easy being bad, ain't it?" Drake said. "Much more enjoyable too. Unless you're a pious sort of man, Cass. Then I guess you'll be facing your sins at the door to the eternal garden." He laughed, proving he clearly believed in no such thing.

"The gods are lost. If there ever was a garden, it was lost with them," I said thoughtfully.

"So why all the struggle with sin?" he asked.

"Because of the pain in his eyes," Kyra answered for me, surprising us both as we looked to her, finding her hovering an inch off the ground. She promptly fell onto her arse, blinking innocently and looking between us, her eyes swivelling back and forth fast enough to make me dizzy.

"Pfft, what pain?" Drake scoffed. "Sleeping on too soft pillows at night? Being paid well and eating three meals a day. Oh, do stop breaking my heart," he deadpanned, drinking a deep gulp of his wine with a bitter expression.

Kyra continued to gaze at me intently like she expected me to correct him, but I wasn't going to share my past with the thief. Besides, he was right. I had chosen my suffering, walked willingly into the Royal Guard and offered up my life to do as they liked with. Perhaps I hadn't fully understood the extent to which they would carve out pieces of me, then mould, bend and break them into something new before they were returned. But I had known it wouldn't be easy, and the sacrifice had been worth it to free my mother from buying Marik's charity.

My stomach twisted at the thought of what she had done for us, and I worked to drain my chalice as it continued to fill.

Kyra continued to watch me without blinking, like she'd forgotten to do so, and I shook my head minutely at her to try and encourage her to stop. But what if this creature could see inside my head? Pick through my thoughts and rifle through my memories like pages of a book?

"What was it like living in the palace?" Drake asked me and Kyra's attention thankfully snapped onto him again.

"I didn't live in the palace, I-"

"Yeah, yeah, you know what I mean," he barrelled on over me. "You must have heard all kinds of gossip, seen all kinds of scandals too. Did you ever walk in on the emperor being ridden on the throne by a giant-titted servant girl?"

"Of course not," I said in outrage. "The emperor would never disrespect his marriage by taking a lover. And 'titted' is not a word."

"You're a liar on both counts," he accused. "Titted is the best word I know. And I bet you saw all kinds of things that would bring the empire to its knees if word ever got out. You don't have to protect them now, mate. Come on, tell me."

"If I ever saw anything of the sort – which I did not – I would hardly tell a street thief with a habit of running his mouth."

"My mouth doesn't run anywhere, Cass. Unless you count when it's running all over the pretty flesh of beautiful women." He gave me a cocky look and Kyra gasped.

"No, that can't be right," she muttered to herself. "He doesn't mean he eats women."

"I do eat women actually," Drake said, his arrogance spreading all over his face as Kyra gasped again, fear washing into her eyes.

"He means in a sexual sense," I clarified for her, giving Drake a dry look.

"Does cannibalism make you hard, Master?" she asked in shock and Drake cracked up laughing while I took pity on the creature.

"It's a turn of phrase, Kyra. He doesn't eat people," I said.

"Right, of course he doesn't." She started laughing as she realised her mistake and she and Drake shared a heated look that made my eyebrows lower. He had better not be thinking about making advances on her. She may not have been truly Fae at all anymore, even if she claimed she once was. But this magic wrapped around her was clearly some curse, and it could be a siren's lure too for all we knew. Drake could be under the spell of it, and once she had him in her trap, who knew what she would do with him?

I kicked him in the shin and he cursed, swallowing the last of his laughter as he spilled wine down his chest. "Hey," he barked at me, but then he got distracted as Kyra shifted closer to fill up his chalice and I frowned as the two of them spent all too long looking at each other.

I supposed it wasn't really my concern if he went and got himself drawn into her bed and ended up with his cock turned into a viper or some shit. But then again, I did need him for my plan, and I doubted he would be in the best of moods if he had to arrive at the palace with a snake for a cock.

As I continued to drink, an electrifying burn grew in my chest and all of my worries just faded the fuck away, leaving me half aware that Marik would have had me skinned alive for this, but also free from giving a damn. My mind was too fuzzy from how much wine I'd sunk, and technically I'd still only had one cup.

"Ha, fuck you, Marik," I chuckled to myself, then a little voice sounded in my head, drawing my attention.

"Wow, so bright, so glowy. Touch it. Taste it."

I spotted the large beetle which my animal Affinity had connected to, its body gleaming like oil in the light of the fire which it was walking purposefully towards, and I planted my foot in front of it before it could commit suicide.

"Tell me 'bout the princess again," Drake asked, a slight slur to his voice as he rose to his feet in a fit of excitement.

"What princess?" Kyra asked with equal fervour. "The one you're going to marry? Or another one?"

"No." I raised a hand in a warning, my teeth bared like a wolf about to strike. He couldn't have her even in his thoughts. He was conjuring up an image of her in that skull of his which could have been getting close to her reality, and I wanted to slice it out of his head and destroy it.

"*Yes,*" Drake begged, plucking a stick out of the fire and whipping it through the air so that the burning end of it left a trail of light in its wake.

Kyra watched him with glee, her hair raising up in an invisible wind and turning pink as it danced around her shoulders.

"Touch it, I will. So warm. So bright."

I realised the beetle had gotten over my boot and was two tiny steps away from casting itself into a fiery death. I pitched forward, knocking it away again with my finger and it went flying through the air, landing on its back with its legs wheeling wildly.

"Evil! Death coming! Run, run, run!" its thoughts flared inside my mind. I didn't think animals could actually speak my language, but my Affinity translated it as such.

"For the love of the Fallen," I growled in frustration, shoving to my feet as Kyra continued to watch the light show Drake was painting out for her with the glowing end of the stick he'd taken from the fire.

I stumbled on my feet, the world tipping as the wine sang a song in my veins and a high-pitched giggling started up in my head. I looked down to find a moth perched on my arm, seeming highly fucking amused about something.

"Big bald skin thing. Only hair on head. Ugly, ugly skin thing."

I shook my arm and the moth took off, its giggles carrying back to me and I swiped a palm down my face as I tried to block it out, the beetle still screaming in my mind too. I swear the alcohol in my blood was making my Affinity more potent.

"Tell me about the princess," Drake insisted as I moved to scoop the beetle into my hand, its screams only intensifying before I launched it away into the bushes and its cries of terror turned to a *weeeee* of joy.

"Tell me," Drake demanded and I gave in, too damn drunk to bother arguing with him as an idea struck me.

I beckoned Kyra to her feet. "You can alter the way you look, right?" I gestured to the ever-changing multitude of colours that were rippling across her skin, feeling less cautious of her magic now that the wine was numbing my inhibitions.

"Of course I can, sullen man," she said brightly. "Would you like me to turn into a horse? Drake told me about your fondness of them."

"When?" I snapped as Drake laughed obnoxiously then I cursed and backtracked. "I mean, I am *not* fond of horses. Not in a sexual way anyway."

"I didn't say anything about sexually," Kyra balked. "I don't think I want to be a horse now, Cassius," she said, biting her lip uncomfortably.

"I don't want you to be a horse either," I said in dismay.

"I can make you something which looks like a horse if you like? A willing one? Drake just has to command it and you agree and then-"

"I do not fuck horses!" I roared, and Drake lost his shit, laughing even harder as Kyra nodded quickly.

"Okay, sullen man." She winked and my jaw gritted.

"Can you do silver hair?" I asked, wanting to change the subject fast and she immediately tried, her hair flowing down to her waist and dancing in an enchanted breeze. But instead of silver it was white and shimmering.

"Sort of." My brow creased as the world began to spin a little. "Can you do longer eyelashes?"

Huge purple blotches appeared all over her body and Drake moved closer to watch with an amused look on his face.

"Is this right?" Kyra asked, looking down at herself hopefully. "Is this how she looks?"

I snorted a laugh, stumbling away from her and shaking my head as I drank more from my never-ending cup of wine.

My boot caught on Drake's leg and I collided with the ground before I even realised I was falling. Pain blossomed through my side and I realised I'd landed on a sharp rock. I tugged up my tunic as I rolled over, finding the blistering burn the torturer had given me splitting open.

Oh fuck.

Drake got to his knees, eyeing my wounds with a frown. The older bruises on my side had turned black and yellow and the slightly fresher ones lined my skin in purple from The Forty's fists.

"Kyra," Drake called and she appeared beside him in a flash. Like an actual fucking flash that damn near blinded me. "Can you fix his wounds?"

"Do you agree?" she asked me.

"No." I lurched away, shaking my head fiercely as the lick of blood spilled from the wound that had been cut open. This girl thought eyelashes were giant purple spots, what the hell would she do to me if she tried to fix my injuries?

"What's up, mate?" Drake asked, swaying above me.

"I could end up inside out like Jadar and the rest of them," I hissed and Drake tried to conceal a laugh.

He definitely thought it was funny and I had to assume that he wasn't grieving those men one bit.

"Don't you even care about your own men?" I growled as he looked like he was choking on a laugh he wouldn't let out, lost to some joke inside his own head.

"Why are you laughing?" Kyra asked. "Oh wait, are you crying? It's crying when the tears go up your nose right? Are they going up your nose or falling from your ears?" She moved to inspect him and he lost it, his laughter escaping him at last.

I snatched up the cup of Cartlanna wine as Drake's laughter rang louder through the trees.

"This stuff is strong." I staggered towards the fire. "Wait a second...*I'm* strong. I'm made of steel."

"What's that, mate?" Drake rose to his feet.

I tipped the bottle into my mouth like an absolute ruffian and stepped towards the fire.

"Look at me, Marik," I spoke to the sky. "I'm out here breaking your rules, and there's nothing you can do about it. I am made of steel."

"Are you gonna jump through the fire?" Drake asked excitedly.

"Oh no, he'll freeze," Kyra gasped.

"I'm jumping through it," I confirmed, rolling my shoulders. I was a royal guard. I'd been trained by the best fighters in the country. I'd been told I was invincible. And I damn well believed it tonight.

Yes...this is an astoundingly good idea. The best one I've ever had.

"Roasty toasty. The beastie will cook." A rogue spider said from a web in the trees to my right.

"Keep your words in your tiny spider mouth," I commanded and Drake and Kyra exchanged a look.

"Is he talking to me?" Kyra breathed and Drake shrugged.

"Burny, burny. Bye-bye, beast man," the spider continued to taunt me and I clapped my hands over my ears for all the good it would do me.

"Stop it," I slurred. "You don't know anything about anything. You're just a spider. You've got eight legs and no brain."

"No, I'm Kyra and I've got two legs and a nice brain, thank you very much," Kyra said firmly.

"He's not talking to you, little goddess," Drake murmured as I dropped my hands again, pointing to the web in the tree beyond me. "I think he might be talking to that spider."

I backed up a few steps, the golden flames roaring before me, seeming to arch up over my head as I watched, making this whole thing seem a lot more difficult than it had a moment ago.

"You're made of steel, Cass, you've got this!" Drake called as he sat down on the grass to watch, sprawling out lazily and swigging directly from the bottle of wine like a damn heathen. Though I had done the same not long ago, so I supposed I had to brush myself in the same tar as him now. I was just an outlaw, a vagabond, a rogue.

"Go on, sullen man! Jump to the moon!" Kyra cheered.

I jumped up and down a few times as I psyched myself up then ran flat out towards the fire, my heart pumping, freedom calling my name.

Cassius Lazar! Cassius Lazar!

I leapt upwards, the flames licking the bare soles of my feet as I soared through them, the scent of smoke and success rising up all around me as I flew like a damn phoenix straight through the heart of the flames. They were hot, my skin tightening and warming uncomfortably as I passed through them, but then I was bursting free of them, emerging on the other side like I was being reborn as a new man.

A thrill danced in my chest as my feet hit the ground on the other side, the scent of burning hair only dampening the feeling of utter success the smallest amount.

Triumph, victory, glory!

I skidded on the grass beyond the fire and crashed to the ground, rolling and rolling like a runaway bagel before slamming face first into a tree and darkness descended on me like the plague, the tiny laughs of a thousand bugs in the vicinity following me into the abyss.

AUSTYN

CHAPTER TWENTY FOUR

The night was deep and no sound called across the palace grounds except the soft coos of the caged night doves in the aviary, their soft trills so familiar that they helped slow the racing of my heart.

The day of the Unveiling was coming upon me too fast, and I couldn't stand it. It marked the beginning of the pageant, commencing the series of brawls and challenges which would provide one victor in the end. But first I would have the veil stripped away from me, my face gifted to the suitors who would finally decide whether my beauty was worth the price they'd paid to compete. Which was why I had to leave tonight. My final chance, my final hope.

Running made me feel like a coward, but I was down to my last option and the alternative didn't bear thinking about. I couldn't stay and see Kahn cut down the other suitors, claim me as his own, and force me to have his children.

Father was no longer present in his mind, and even though it pained me to leave him behind, what choice did I have? It was this or submit. And submission just wasn't in my blood.

I lay in bed, counting stars through the window which was cracked open as usual to let the cooler night air in. Though it was never truly cool in Osaria. The desert was a beast that seemed to breathe fire into the wind, baking the city until the streets cracked.

For the past two nights, I'd feigned a cough, and Zira had brought me some scarab nettles to rub against my skin to create a rash. The symptoms looked just like sand flu, an illness which was contagious and could spread easily from person to person. After the doctor had brought me medicine, she had commanded all my waiting staff to wear a cloth over their faces when tending to me, a fact I'd been banking on to pull off the rest of my plan.

Magdor had insisted I was faking my illness to postpone the pageant, but when the doctor assured her the medicine would heal me within a couple of nights, she'd gloated to my face that my little performance would achieve nothing and she'd left me alone in my quarters since.

I released a hacking cough, loud enough for the guards to hear beyond my doors, putting on a good show before calling out for my attendants. It was only a few minutes before Zira appeared with Jacinda in tow, their mouths and noses covered in cloth. Jacinda had her dark hair wrapped in satin and they exchanged a glance before hurrying forward and making a fuss as they pretended to tend to me.

"Ready?" I hissed to Zira and she nodded, a glimmer in her eye.

"Are you sure about this, Your Highness?" Jacinda asked anxiously, tugging on the sleeve of her uniform. I had been nervous to ask for her assistance with this plan, but Zira had assured me she would keep her silence and help me. I was placing my faith in her now, and I prayed I could trust her.

"Yes, but you must drink this. All of it, Jacinda," I urged, picking up the sleeping draft the doctor had left for me with my medicine and handing it to her. "As much as you can bear. It must seem like I drugged you, like I tricked you into drinking it."

She nodded quickly, taking the draft and pouring it out into a glass beside my bed before starting to gulp it down. My heart twisted at the risk she was taking for me and I hated her to do it, but Magdor had always thought of me as conniving, I was sure she'd believe me capable of this.

"Oh it...works quite quickly, doesn't it?" Jacinda slurred, drooping forward and slumping onto the bed.

"Come on, you have to get out of those clothes," Zira urged her, starting to tug at her uniform and together we helped Jacinda undress.

"Such soft skin you have, Your Highness. Like peacock feathers dipped in silk on a sweet, midsummer's day," she slurred, unable to resist a final compliment to me even as the draft stole her away.

I pulled off my nightdress, tugging it onto Jacinda's body before dressing in her clothes. She was asleep already as we pushed her into the bed and drew the covers up over her head.

Zira exchanged a loaded look with me, a thousand worries dancing in her gaze.

"Don't," I said firmly before she could voice any doubts, any words that might remind me of how foolish this plan could be. How perilous if it went wrong. "I must leave, Zira. I can't stay."

She swallowed, stepping closer and squeezing my arm. "I know. And I believe it will work," she whispered. "My cousin is waiting for us to the eastern border of the city. I just want you to know, I wish to stay with you."

"It's not safe," I said, shaking my head, knowing that if I was caught out there with her at my side, she'd be tortured and killed for this. At least if she stayed here, she could assure the guards I had threatened her. I was the princess after all, she was bound by law to do as I told her.

"No more crazy talk." I wrapped the cloth around my mouth and nose, and Zira bowed her head with a look of sadness before hurrying to tie my hair up in the satin Jacinda had been wearing, hiding every silver strand of it. There would only be torches alight in the palace and not everywhere, so the light would be low. I'd be concealed well enough, especially if I kept my head down.

I looked around my room for a moment, trying to hold onto the good memories I'd once had within it, not the bad. But it was hard when Magdor seemed to invade every corner, tainting the sweetness I'd once held here.

Zira took my hand, squeezing and giving me a reassuring look as she adjusted the cloth over the lower half of her face. "Ready?"

"Yes," I said, pressing my shoulders back. "Let's go."

She led the way to the door, pushing it wide and I stepped out after her without faltering, keeping in her shadow as the guards glanced our way. For two whole seconds, I failed to breathe, then they looked back at the wall opposite them, acting as though we weren't here.

We reached the end of the corridor and Zira pulled a tapestry aside, slipping into a secret stairway which was part of the servants' passages. I knew where to find every one of these. I'd played in them as a child, back when this palace had held nothing but secrets and adventure. A lick of that tantalising adrenaline ran up my spine again now as I followed Zira down the stairway, the cool walls hugging close on either side of us. I felt like a little girl, finding her way through the dark, and I realised how long it had been since I'd experienced any kind of excitement. My flesh was aching for it, my heart pounding in anticipation of more adrenaline, more danger.

The torches down here were few and far between, the flickering flames casting a deep orange glow in segments of the passages, only to leave us in darkness once more.

Zira moved easily through the passages, knowing every turn by heart just as I did.

I felt us reach the outer walls of the palace in the way the air chilled a little and the scent of flowers carried from the gardens. Our gardeners worked full time watering it daily, keeping the flowers blooming and the grass growing. It was wasteful, yet it was impossible to ignore how beautiful it was.

The river itself ran right through the heart of the grounds, weaving out into the city through a thick iron gate which ran deeper than the riverbed.

I turned my head and looked north towards the distant, lone mountain called Aguan, a place steeped in magical history. There was a fable about it which said a Prophet king had once lived atop it in a palace made of starlight.

The story went that he was in love with the goddess of the moon, Sirella. He used every kuru in the kingdom to build himself a beautiful observatory to watch the celestial body in the sky night after night, always pining for her, though the moon never looked his way.

But one day, there was a terrible drought, and the people of his kingdom began to suffer and die. The king hoarded the last of the water in his palace, locking the doors to keep them out and building a silver cage around the well in his courtyard which only he had the key to.

Day after day passed, but the rains never came. The king tried all he could, every spell he knew, every wish and curse and jinx. But nothing would bring the water back. So he turned to his true love and begged the moon for help, asking Sirella to send the rain and in return she could have his soul.

The moon was quiet for so long that the king believed the goddess had scorned him, that she was the one who had taken the rain away because she was tired of him watching her. So he promised never to look again, he vowed with all he was that he would never look her way if only she would send the rain to him. But the moon was quiet as always and still the rain didn't come.

The king demanded the last of his people were brought to his palace, his doors opened for the first time since the drought began. The city folk believed they were saved, that the king would share the water from his well and when he brought them to the courtyard, they praised him as he opened the door to the silver cage to let them in.

One by one, the people walked inside, hunting for the water they so desperately needed. But when they pulled up the bucket from the well, they found it dry. They turned to the Prophet king for answers, and it came in the form of death, a wicked spell cast from his lips which slit open their throats and let their blood flow into his well. And when the last of them lay dead, he took a chalice from his robes and filled it with their blood, quenching his thirst with the blood of his people.

Sirella turned to look then, seeing what the king had done and shuddering at what she found. So she sent the rain. A single cloud which poured down over the well, and the king gulped down the rain, praising the moon for her mercy. But she wasn't merciful, she was merciless, and she locked him within that cage as the water rose and rose, filling the palace until her bounty spilled over the mountainside while the king was drowned.

The kingdom was washed away and a river ran endlessly down the mountainside, carving its way through the land. And ever since that day, the river had remained there, feeding the earth and making it the perfect place for Osaria to be born, a gift from the moon.

I wasn't sure if I believed everything within the old stories, but I did believe in the lost gods. Though it seemed the power they wielded had bordered on cruel, and that particular fable about Sirella was one of the few stories where a god was kind – though why she hadn't saved the people before the king had murdered them made me question that too. It was probably exaggerated, changed over the years as the fable passed from mouth to mouth. Who knew what truth really lay in it, or if there was any left at all?

Zira pushed through a secret door, and I stepped onto the path outside the palace, breathing in the night air as we slipped into one of the gardens and walked side by side, our heads bowed in the usual way of the maids.

I kept stealing glances at the path ahead as we closed in on the gates, my heart drumming out a wild tune in my chest as I took in the row of guards there and the swords at their hips, the powerful men perfectly still, like extensions of the wall they stood before.

As we reached the gate, Zira lifted her chin and took the lead. "The two of us are showing symptoms of sand flu. The doctor ordered us to remove ourselves from the palace grounds if we ever suspected we were ill, so we can seek medical help before we infect anyone else."

One of the guards looked up at those positioned in a lookout on top of the wall, nodding to him and a beat later a clanking noise sounded and the gate started to open.

I took slow breaths, watching that gap in the gate widen and widen, giving me a glimpse to the path beyond. It was still the palace grounds there, and we'd have to pass one more gate to get out, but it was closer than I'd ever felt to freedom before.

Zira nodded to the men and I did the same before stepping forward to follow, all of them drawing away from us, the threat of sand flu clearly enough to make them cautious.

I was almost through when a voice rang out across the grounds behind me, making my bones turn solid and horror dagger through me.

"Stop them!" Magdor shrieked and I knew it was over before it had even begun.

The guards surrounded us in moments and I was corralled backwards by chest plates and strong arms, pain blossoming in my heart as I caught Zira's gaze and found her eyes full of apology. I wanted to banish that look from her face, but I didn't have a second to speak with her as Magdor arrived and plucked me from the middle of the armed men, her fingers knotting in the material of my sleeve.

"Foolish girl," she hissed then yanked me away as two guards fell into step behind us. I didn't fight, didn't run or scream or beg, because I knew the game was up and causing a scene would only make my punishment worse.

Magdor gripped my arm in a vice as she towed me back into the palace, her billowing navy nightgown whipping around her in the wind.

"How did you know?" I growled, my soul aching over my failure.

"The maid you drugged fell out of your bed and made such a thump that the guards ran in there to protect you. When they saw her face, they reported it straight to me," she hissed, her nails biting into my arm.

That was it? One fucking mishap and it was all over. I could have gotten out. I was so close to getting out.

I tried to turn back to see Zira, panic blooming in me over what they were going to do with her. But she wasn't there.

"You think the entire world revolves around you," Magdor spat as we made it inside and she led me down a deathly quiet corridor where moonlight poured through the arching windows. "You think that because you are a princess you can do whatever you wish? Well let me tell you your real worth, princess. It is this." She shoved me against a wall, taking a blade from who knew where as she placed the tip of it against my pelvis. I stilled, a tremor of fear rolling down my spine as I looked up into her cruel gaze. "It is the legacy your womb can provide, the heirs you can gift the winning suitor in the pageant. The rest of you will be enjoyed until your looks fade. And they *will* fade, Austyn. As leaves will surely fall in autumn, your face will droop, your skin will wrinkle and you will be cast aside for someone younger, fresher. So it is in your interest to ensure you remain valuable, and you can do that by being a good mother. By raising the sons and daughters you birth to Kahn."

"Kahn has not won the pageant," I snarled. "He has not won my hand."

"Not yet," she agreed, a conniving smile twisting her lips then she jabbed the knife into me a little harder, making me flinch. "But he will. And you will be much happier in life if you accept what must be done for the good of the kingdom, instead of being a selfish brat who only thinks of herself. Do you know what would become of you outside of this palace, Austyn?"

"I'd find freedom out there," I said passionately, knowing it to my core. "Any life would be better than this one."

She shook her head at me, a mocking laugh rolling from her lips as she lowered the knife at last. "You would not last a day outside these walls. There are men far more villainous than my son waiting out there to claim the warmth of pretty flesh like yours. And even if you somehow managed to avoid them, what then? You could not stay in the city, so where would you go? Would you do the impossible and try to cross the Lyrian Desert? Or head south to the kingdom of Berion to become some farmer's wife? And you think you would not be recognised? If the human traffickers didn't find you first on your travels, then it would be foreign soldiers or blood traders. You would either end up sold back to your father or sold to a far worse fate. There are many rich men in these lands who would pay to have you at their mercy, who would take from you until you were a shell of yourself. Is that what you want? To leave the safety of your home only to find yourself in a cage far worse than any fate you can imagine awaits you here? You're not thinking clearly, Austyn. You are and always will be an ignorant girl who knows nothing of the real world. But I would have thought you were smart enough to know that your fate here is the best you will ever be offered. And what a privilege it is to be gifted such a fate."

She gazed down her nose at me, seeming disappointed and perhaps even pitying of me. It made my bones rattle with rage. I wanted to rip that look right off of her face with nothing but my fingernails, but the ring of truth in her words had me standing there and doing nothing instead.

Perhaps I was ungrateful of my position in the world. I didn't know the taste of hunger or the struggle of poverty. Thousands of people in the city probably looked to this palace and dreamed of what it would be like not to have the burden of finding food before sundown, of not knowing when another coin would enter their pocket. And I was here taking it all for granted, wishing I could trade places with them just so that I could know freedom. But what if freedom was pain? What if it was starvation and suffering in a life I didn't know how to navigate?

Magdor stroked my cheek through the material over my face and my gaze sunk slowly to the floor. "There now, take a deep breath. We all must play our part. I have burdens too, my dear. But we must be grateful that our burdens are not as heavy as those of others, mustn't we?"

I twisted my head out of her touch and she clucked her tongue, backing up a step as she let out a long and weary sigh.

"Your maids will receive ten lashes for their involvement in tonight's plot and will be docked three weeks of pay," she said lightly and my head snapped up.

"No," I commanded. "I forced Zira to help me. I threatened her with a blade. And I tricked Jacinda into drinking that sleeping draft so I could take her clothes. They're not to blame. They've done nothing wrong."

"They should be thankful they are keeping their heads. If they were not bound to do your bidding, I would be less lenient. But rules are rules." She turned her back on me, sweeping away with her robe whipping out behind her as she turned a corner. "Take the princess back to her quarters!"

Two guards closed in on me a moment later and I was escorted back to my rooms. The second I stepped inside, the firm click of a lock snapped against my ears behind me and the deepest feeling of failure swept over me.

The lump in my throat wouldn't give way and I realised my hands were clenched so hard against my palms that my nails were nearly drawing blood.

I let out a scream that pitched through the entire palace, and I hoped every single person within its walls could feel the pain in it, I hoped they knew that their princess was a prisoner and I would be partaking in the pageant unwillingly at every stage of it.

My shackles were invisible, but I felt them growing tighter around my wrists as that scream ripped out of me and I wished the walls would crack and the whole palace would fall.

KYRA

CHAPTER TWENTY FIVE

Night might just have been prettier than day.
I sighed as I lay back on the sloping hill, enjoying the feeling of the lush grass beneath me as I ran my fingers through it and looked up at the stars.

"The sky is so far away," I murmured.

It was always that far away, there just used to be a coin's roof between us and it.

"I hope I never see that roof again."

"What roof?" The voice made me flinch in surprise.

I stilled as Master sat down beside me and I only turned my eyes to look at him. He was so much, this real Fae who existed so casually like he had always been there, just beyond my reach and waiting to rescue me from my eternal solitude. The moonlight was gleaming off of his inky black hair, a few wayward strands spilling across his forehead and falling into his eyes, and I couldn't help but wonder what it would feel like to brush them aside, run my fingers into those satin strands and just touch it.

It would probably feel a lot like being a crazy person who touches other people's hair.

He raised a dark eyebrow at me and I realised I hadn't answered his question, my heart beating faster as I got flustered by the feeling of having his attention fixed on me.

I forced myself to move, rolling upright and angling myself towards him while hugging my knees to my chest so that I could look at him properly. He was really nice to look at. He had the kind of face that could keep me captivated for hours on end and maybe that was just because it had been such an endless amount of time since I'd seen any faces at all, but it felt like it was more than that. Like his was the kind of face a girl could lose herself staring at, letting the depths of those onyx eyes swallow me up and devour me whole, while the devious curve of those lips forced my body to get the kinds of ideas I'd long since forgotten all about. He looked like a man who knew exactly how to use those lips for every kind of wicked deed from lying to kissing and so much more besides.

"The coin roof," I explained. "It's all I could ever see when I looked up for...a very long time."

"Looking up is always pretty good when you're out in the real world," he commented, his eyes reflecting the stars as he glanced up at them and an entire universe seeming to swirl in his gaze while I watched him. "It's what's closer to home that reeks of shit."

"Do I smell?" I asked in confusion. I wondered if washing in a pool of tears was really washing at all. Maybe I smelled like I hadn't washed in a millennia. *Maybe I smell of cheese.*

"No. I meant that the stars always look pretty because they're far away but the things closer to us tend to be a lot uglier."

"Like you," I pointed out.

"No, I'm pretty up close," he said, throwing me a smile which made something deep inside of me flip over.

He's flirting with us!

"I don't think so," I murmured as blood heated my cheeks and my heart skittered wildly at his attention.

Master frowned, obviously thinking my comment had been meant for him and I recoiled internally as I realised it sounded like I'd disagreed with him.

"You would be the first person I've ever met to think that," he said irritably.

"Would you like to be handsome?" I asked tentatively. "You could just ask for it and-"

"I *am* handsome," he snapped.

"Are you sure?" I asked.

Things like that were lost to me now. I hadn't seen any faces in so much time that it was like I'd forgotten where the features were supposed to sit, and I couldn't decide if his looked right or not. I was certainly captivated by him, but he was my master and I had been hungering for a master for so long that I was certain I would have been just as captivated by any other who had called me from my coin too. Maybe if I shifted his eyes so that they were both on the right side of his face it would help. Then I could look into both of them at once more easily.

"I'm sure," he growled and I chewed my lip instead of responding. I didn't want to contradict him again, but I was having trouble seeing it. I liked looking at his face, but I wasn't sure if it was because it was a nice-looking face or just an interesting one, and ugly was always more interesting than beauty anyway.

You would have killed for the attention of a man who looked like him once upon a time.

I wasn't sure if that was right, but I didn't want to speak to myself again with him here. I'd gotten myself into enough trouble as it was with one comment, so I wasn't going to risk a second.

Master looked out over the sweeping valley towards the desert beyond, seeming to be too irritated to talk to me again. I wondered if the fractured pieces of my personality would ever stitch back together into one person or if I'd always be this confused, divided thing. I was a broken girl, a forgotten legend, a shadow of whoever I'd once been, and I wasn't sure that I would ever find my way to being whole again, but maybe he could help me feel a little more like I was. Maybe this man with the coal black eyes and sin filled soul would be the one to pull me down into the dark and free me once and for all.

I knew I had no chance of aiming for the light anymore, but the darkness was my friend. It might have been where my monsters awaited me, but it was also the keeper of my secrets and where I felt most comfortable now. I could tell that we had that in common, he and I. So I was willing to be a slave to his desires, just as long as he used his power over me to offer me a taste of freedom once again.

"Cassius is still unconscious," Master said eventually, as if I'd asked. Which I hadn't. Cassius wasn't really my concern; my life was tied to my master's and nothing else really mattered to me aside from that. His wants were my sole purpose, and I could sense a need in him which still wasn't fulfilled, so I shuffled closer as I waited to hear more of what he required of me. "I was thinking we could talk without him for a bit."

"Okay," I breathed. He seemed to mean that. He wanted conversation from me. Nothing more. The idea was exciting and kind of terrifying too. The only person I'd had to talk to for a thousand years was myself and I didn't even like her.

"I'm not sure me and Cassius are totally on the same wavelength when it comes to me having my desires met," he said slowly.

I nodded understandingly but I had no idea what he meant. It seemed like the right thing to do though as he went on.

"And I think that he might just try to steal your coin from me," he added.

"No," I gasped, unable to believe that Cassius would do that to his friend. Ideas and bloodlust and death filled my mind as I thought of what it might take to stop that fate from playing out, but I knew it was no good unless that was what my master wanted. And if Cassius – or anyone else for that matter – claimed my coin from him then I would be bound as their slave in his place. It was my curse. The owner of my coin was the master of my power, and I was nothing but a pawn designed to fulfil those wishes.

You're so naive sometimes, it makes me sick.

"Yeah," Master said in a rough voice which he lowered as he glanced back over at Cassius who had one arm slung over his eyes while his other hand was wrapped around his sword's hilt. "And he's also been saying some things... about putting you back in the coin." He looked me in the eye as my heart pounded and I was struck by how concerned he seemed for me, the way he seemed to truly care, to truly want me to be safe from that fate.

I think he's more concerned for himself.

I didn't know if I agreed with that or not, but it was my duty to fulfil his desires and it was clear he needed something from me.

"What do you want me to do?" I asked softly.

"I think we need to do something about the coin so that there's no chance of him taking it. Or *anyone* taking it for that matter. So that I can protect you," he said.

Keep you for himself more like.

I nodded earnestly because even if I had a point. I didn't mind – I wanted him to keep me. I liked him. I wasn't sure why, but so far, he had given me no reason not to. He'd let me stay out of the coin when I'd asked to, and he'd given me the brightest smiles each time I'd used my magic for his pleasure. He even thanked me for it more often than not, and I wasn't sure I'd ever had a master do that before.

"I don't want anyone else to take it," I said. Someone else might make me stay in the coin, but my master was letting me be free. That was all I really wanted after such a long time in confinement, and I needed it to continue the way it was.

"So how could we hide it, do you think?" Master prompted, glancing at my mouth before dragging his gaze up and looking deep into my eyes.

He's definitely flirting with you.

I frowned, refusing to listen to myself and the ridiculous thoughts I was having as he drew a little closer to me, pinning me down with his dark gaze and the pure masculinity of his powerful body. The tattoos on his arms were still on show beneath the tunic I'd created for him to wear, and for a moment I could have sworn the one on his right bicep glinted in the starlight, making a knot tighten deep inside me as I looked between it and his face.

"Maybe, I could make the coin appear as an amulet? And place it on an unbreakable chain which you could wear around your neck?" I suggested, wondering if that was a terrible idea. Maybe I didn't have any good ideas left in my brain since it had been bottled up for hundreds of years. Or maybe the only ideas left *were* the good ones. The problem was, I couldn't tell anymore.

"Would you do that for me?" Master breathed, shifting a little closer so that I could smell the scent of him and taste it on my tongue. It was like smoke and sand and pure, brutal *man*. Why in the world had I thought he was a girl?

Because you're a damn idiot who lost your mind a thousand years ago.

"Ask for it," I whispered in return.

"I want you to make sure you stay mine," he said, lowering his voice in a way that made a shiver race down my spine. I liked the way he called me his. I liked him claiming me like that, like I was precious and important and real. It made me feel like we were sharing some secret beyond the bond of a slave and their master, and I smiled at him as I turned my magic to his desires.

The coin flew from his pocket, hanging in the space between us as I surrounded it with a band of platinum until it was contained within a ring of it.

Silver light appeared next, condensing into a chain which slid through a loop in the platinum which now held the coin before forming an unbreakable circle. I cloaked its appearance too, so that it looked like a golden amulet inlaid with rubies instead of a coin. The necklace dropped over his head and the last echoes of my magic flared in his eyes as it fell against his skin, hanging just above the open collar of his tunic.

My eyes tracked over the tattooed skin there, the hard planes of his muscular chest holding my attention as I looked to the buttons he'd left open below his throat, a swallow making my mouth dry out.

"You really are something special, you know that?" he murmured as he twisted the tiny coin between his fingers, inspecting my work.

"Special isn't always a good thing," I replied quietly.

I would have given anything to just be normal and to have never set foot in that coin. But that choice had been stolen from me by the man who had murdered my sister and this path had been the only one left for me to tread.

"Says the special one," he teased, leaning back on his elbows so that he could look up at the stars.

I couldn't help but stare at him as he laid there before me. He was so *real*. His hair was as black as midnight and his skin the richest bronze as if the sun kissed each inch of it every single day. His mouth hooked up naturally like he was happiness given flesh, and his dark eyes held more secrets than I could ever hope to untangle. It was a shame he was so ugly, but then I'd take a hundred ugly faces over another moment of solitude. A smile pulled at his lips as he noticed my attention on him, but I didn't look away.

He thinks you're staring because you like him.

I frowned. I *did* like him so why did it matter if he knew it?

Not the way you're thinking. He thinks you want to see him naked.

"I don't want to see him naked," I muttered beneath my breath.

Master's eyes swivelled to me, and he frowned.

"I wasn't talking to you," I said quickly, and he nodded, though he didn't seem very happy anymore.

Just about *you.*

I wrung my hands together, looking away from him awkwardly.

"I was wondering about what you said before, about how you used to be Fae," he said eventually, and I looked back to him with a surge of relief that he wasn't still mad at me.

"Yes?" I asked, as my pink hair swept forward around me, reaching down to my currently blue toes and tucking them in to keep them warm.

"It's just that you said that you were going to be able to disguise yourself so that you don't have to go back inside the coin, but from what I've seen you're not very...normal." He waved a hand at me and my heart tugged.

"I don't understand," I admitted, trying to ignore the fear I felt at the idea of going back into the coin.

Master pushed his hair back from his eyes and the muscles on his arm bulged as he did so. Somehow it seemed intentional, like he wanted me to

321

notice how strong he was, but I wasn't sure why.

"Fae don't tend to have multi-coloured skin and hair," he explained and a rainbow of colour skittered across my hands as he drew attention to it.

I've told you that a thousand times.

"Oh."

"So can you turn that shit off? Maybe make yourself look like you did before you were a Blessing?" he asked. "Otherwise, I think there won't be any other choice but to go back in the coin when we reach the city, and I would really rather keep my promise to you."

I recoiled, my eyes widening in alarm as panic loomed like a kraken before me.

"No, please," I whispered and for a moment I thought I could see pity in my master's eyes as he noted the desperation in my tone.

No man has ever had mercy on you before so don't go kidding yourself that this one is any different.

"You don't have to, providing you can look Fae," he said, his voice a little softer than before.

I nodded keenly. "I'll figure it out. I think my magic simply bled into every piece of me while I was trapped in there, but I can contain it again. I can remember what I was like...before."

Liar. You can't even remember your sister's name, let alone the colour of your own skin. We'll be back inside that coin the second we get close to civilisation, and he won't bother with you again until he wants more magic from you.

Tears welled in my eyes and I looked away from my master quickly, not wanting him to think he'd upset me, but the idea of that reality was like a punch to my gut which shattered my ribs and punctured my lungs. I couldn't breathe when I thought about returning to that prison and I knew I had to figure this out, make sure I could stay out here with him like he was offering.

"It's hard to imagine what you truly look like when your features keep changing," he said, his eyes roaming over me with interest like he was trying to see beyond the magic to who I was at my core. "Perhaps you're as attractive as me?"

"But you're not..." I chewed my lip again as irritation flickered in his eyes and forcefully reminded myself that he didn't like it when I pointed out how ugly he was.

"Are you trying to bait me or is that really what you think?" he asked in a growl. "I have never met a woman who didn't like my face before."

"You seem to care about your looks a lot," I murmured in response, not really wanting to answer. I did like his face, I just thought it could do with a bit of rearranging if he wanted to be more appealing.

He narrowed his eyes at me then waved a hand dismissively like he didn't even care. "If ninety-nine women fall at my feet and one turns up her nose at me, what difference does that make to me anyway?" he scoffed, but I wasn't sure if the question was really for me or just for the stars. Besides, it seemed like it did make a difference because his jaw was gritted with irritation and he wasn't looking at me anymore.

You could try lying.

"I'm not sure I remember how to lie," I hissed because my kind had never been meant to do that and though I knew all too well that it was possible now, it still wasn't something that came naturally to me. "I only seem to be able to tell the truth."

"And the truth is you find me ugly?" my master demanded as if I'd been talking to him.

I scrunched up my nose as I tried my hardest to do what I'd suggested and lie to him.

"I don't find you ugly," I said slowly and his eyes glimmered as if he'd expected me to admit that. "I find you…not…attractive."

"Not attractive?" he deadpanned and I could tell I'd angered him again. *Shit.*

"Umm…"

"I think it's time I got some sleep." Master got up and walked away from me and I bit my lip, wondering if I should tell him that he would probably look fine if I just switched his mouth and eyebrows about a bit.

Probably best to shut up at this point.

I nodded sadly. I might have been right for once.

When I was alone, I focused on drawing my magic away from my skin, my hair, my features. I needed to look Fae again if I wanted to remain free of the coin, and it was truly the only thing I desired anymore.

I laid flat on my back and stared up at the stars, asking them for strength as I tried to focus on what I needed to do, my fingers and toes pushing into the soft grass as I used the feeling of it to ground myself in reality.

As I started work, I realised how deeply I'd let the magic bleed throughout my flesh. My body wasn't even my own anymore, crackling and sparking with the power I fought to contain, and it hurt as I began to tear it from my skin inch by agonising inch.

My spine arched against the grass covered hill as I sucked in a harsh breath, the feeling of me forcing the magic from even the tips of my fingers akin to peeling the skin from my flesh and setting my bones alight for good measure.

I didn't know how long it had been since I'd allowed the magic to permeate my body like this, but it felt like my flesh had forgotten how to be without it, the skin mourning its loss with a flare of unthinkable pain as I gritted my teeth and dragged it back.

I stifled my screams as I worked to force it away without so much as pausing to question my dedication to this, each time the pain flared too hot I only had to remind myself of the alternative. If I couldn't do this, then I would have to return to the coin. And there was no fate worse than that which I could imagine, so any amount of torture was worth it.

So I bit down on my lip and buried my screams and tore the power from every inch of my body, forcing it back down into the well which existed inside me and making certain that it remained there out of sight and under my control.

It took me hours, during which time my other self constantly insulted me and made me doubt myself. My skin coated with a sheen of sweat and my heart raced to a beat so powerful that it sounded like the thrum of hummingbird wings in my ears.

The sun had risen by the time I was done, and when I finally collapsed where I lay, panting and trembling from the effort of what I'd done, a few errant tears slid from the corners of my eyes.

"I did it," I breathed to no one but the wind, certain that my body had returned to its original form. Whatever that looked like. I didn't remember or even care to in that moment. All I knew was that I had managed to force the colour from my limbs and hair, and that meant my master would allow me to remain outside of the coin.

A sob rattled my chest and my fingers twisted into the grass beside me as I breathed in the cooler morning air and stared up at the blue sky above me, welcoming each and every sight, sound, taste, scent, feeling and sensation which surrounded me in this beautiful, endless world.

I'd been alone and forgotten for so long that I'd given up all hope of ever leaving my prison again and yet here I was, soaking in the feeling of the sun warming my skin and breathing fresh air for the first time in an eternity that I couldn't even count the passage of time.

I gave myself a little longer with the tears of relief tracking down my cheeks before pushing myself upright and brushing them aside.

My fingers skimmed over my dress, shifting the colour to a simple white, the fabric held over one shoulder before encircling my chest and wrapping to one side, leaving an expanse of my midriff on show then curving around my hips and dropping down to brush my feet. The lower portion of the dress was thinner, the translucent fabric showing my legs through it as I walked and the breeze lifting the thin material so that the heat of the sun was less of a burden.

I felt…odd. I was myself again after oh so long and yet I still held no real memories of who that girl was supposed to be. It was unsettling and despite knowing that it didn't really matter anyway, I couldn't help the knot of tension which formed in my gut as I turned in the direction of the camp we'd made last night.

The sound of voices drew me back to the fire where Cassius had clearly woken at last, and Master had emerged from the tent I'd conjured for him to sleep in. Cassius didn't look in good shape, occasionally clutching his side where he'd cut himself on a rock last night, and darkness ringed his eyes. He rubbed the top of his head which had collided with the tree and I remembered how he'd gone crashing into it with a bang. Master had said to let him rest, but it didn't look like he'd gotten much of that even though he hadn't been awake for many, many hours.

They were discussing the best way for them to approach the palace and I crept closer a little nervously, plucking at the fabric of the white dress I had created for myself. The breeze tickled the skin of my stomach which I'd left bare, and I suddenly wondered if I should have covered myself up more. I didn't know what they were going to think of the girl I had been before I became the thing I was now and though I shouldn't have cared, I did. It mattered. And I wasn't even sure why.

I slipped between the trees at the edge of the fire, looking at their profiles where they sat deep in discussion, their gazes on the fire which burned endlessly before them, still powered by the bottomless abyss of my magic.

I waited several seconds, uncertain if I should interrupt or not then finally cleared my throat as they failed to notice me and I found I could no longer take the suspense.

Cassius leapt to his feet, drawing his sword as he pointed it at me, his brow lowering and his body tensing with the intention to use that weapon.

"What do you want?" he demanded, his gaze running over me like he was assessing whether or not I was a threat, and I blinked at him a few times as I tried to understand what was happening.

"Calm down, mate," Master said quickly. "Let the girl explain what she's doing here. Maybe she needs warming up." He gave me the kind of smile that made heat race to my cheeks and my heart do some kind of awkward somersault, and I bit my lip as I realised neither of them recognised me.

"It's me," I breathed. "I pulled the magic out of my skin overnight. It actually took a really long time and hurt like hell, but I think I got all of it in the end so here I am..." I shrugged, not really sure what else needed to be said.

"Holy shit." Master's gaze swept over me slowly, making me feel more exposed than I had even when I'd appeared naked before him the first time he'd summoned me, drinking in every piece of me from the top of my head to the tips of my toes.

My blush deepened at the intensity of his gaze on my features and I forced my eyes to Cassius instead, taking in the way he was looking at me and offering a nervous smile.

He slowly lowered his sword, taking in the changes in me with a faint frown. "When you said you were Fae before you ended up bound to that coin, how long ago were you talking about?"

"I lost count," I admitted, shrugging one shoulder as if the endless expanse of time I'd spent trapped in that hell was nothing at all, even though it was every fear I'd ever known embodied.

"Was it before or after the Fae fell from the grace of the gods?" he pushed and my master arched a brow at that suggestion.

"The fair folk," he muttered as he got to his feet too, his eyes roaming over me in a way that made me feel like he was truly seeing me. Not the magic or the power or the possibilities I presented him with. He was just looking at me. And the way his dark eyes were devouring me made me think he liked what he saw.

"I'm not sure," I said after a long pause where I tried to recall my life before I was this. But it was lost to me almost entirely. I could only remember the pain I'd felt over my sister's death and how the emperor's blood had felt as it coated my hands.

The way they were both staring was making me feel incredibly self-conscious, and I suddenly had the urge to know what the fuss was all about as I waited for them to stop.

"Your eyes are still the same," Master said eventually. "Still that endless shade of gold. But the rest of you is..."

He can't take his eyes off of you.

"I'm okay then?" I asked, ignoring myself. "I don't have to go back in the coin?"

"Yeah, you're okay, magic girl," Cassius said as he started kicking dirt over the last embers of the fire, wincing as he did so and clutching his side again. He looked kind of pale and I could tell he was trying to hide the pain he was in as he straightened his spine and continued his work.

"Okay doesn't cut it," Master muttered, his eyes still drinking me in before he swiped a hand down his face and turned away sharply. "Let's get moving then – I have a princess to marry after all."

A smile pulled at my lips as I realised I'd done enough to maintain my freedom and curiosity bit into me as I wondered what they'd seen as they looked at me, suddenly wanting to see me for myself.

The two of them began to load up the camels with the various things I'd created last night and I raised a hand before me to cast a tall, gilded mirror into existence right there on the grass.

I gasped as I found myself staring at my reflection, the distant echoes of recognition sounding deep within me despite how foreign my face looked to me as I stared at it.

I was a petite girl, with a fountain of ebony hair which tumbled down my spine in soft curls to caress the rounded curve of my rear. My skin was a sun kissed hue of brown which made the golden tones of my eyes almost seem to burn like sunlight beneath my thick, dark lashes.

I reached out a finger to paint the lines of my face, soaking in the sight of the girl who looked back at me. My lips were full and a dusky cherry colour which almost looked painted on, and my high cheekbones made the symmetry of my features seem somehow unreal, like I was looking at a painting of someone I once knew, not staring upon a true reflection of myself.

The longer I stared, the more I felt like I remembered this piece of myself, the smallest taste of the girl I'd been born as echoing in my heart until the beat of it seemed familiar too. There was a brightness to my golden eyes and a stubborn set to my jaw which suggested I'd once held my own desires and wants, known my own mind and been unafraid to voice it.

So much was lost to me, but in regaining this I felt like I was regaining something more, something I hadn't ever expected to find again. This was me. The house which held the fractured pieces of my soul, and I couldn't help but like what I saw.

I'd done it. I looked Fae again even if I felt anything but deep down inside.

And no matter what else happened now, at least I knew I wouldn't have to see the inside of that coin any time soon.

I watched as another relieved tear slipped down my cheek and I couldn't help but smile at my reflection as I pressed my hand to the glass and reclaimed ownership of the girl who was staring back at me from within it.

"Hi," I breathed, watching my own mouth form that word in reply. "Welcome back."

CASSIUS

CHAPTER TWENTY SIX

My head hurt. The soles of my feet hurt. *Shit*, my whole body hurt. Wine was not my friend. It was a temptress who danced with me all night long, then bent me over and fucked me in the arse with a pitchfork before leaving me there to recover alone. Her merry gifts had been stripped away to leave me with a foul mood the size of a mountain and no desire to ever play with her again.

I rode a camel at Drake's side, heading back towards the city and Kyra sat on her own camel, staring around at the desert in wonder. We'd left the oasis behind and now the dunes swept away ahead of us like a rolling sea frozen in time.

Once, we'd heard Azurea's bellowing roar in the distance and dread had slithered through my chest like a serpent. I'd been tempted to throw away the scale she'd given me for fear of it leading her to us, but Kyra had assured me she never would, and the scale was too valuable a prize to simply discard. When Magdor was dealt with, I would offer it to the emperor along with the Forken sword and hope it would help buy his pardon for my crimes. For now, they were mine to protect.

I clutched the wound on my side which was the keenest pain of all this morning after I'd split it open on that cursed rock last night. The blood that had leaked from it had plastered my tunic to my stomach and the ache was growing to a searing throb.

We travelled on under the baking sun and the horizon became so blurry and bright that I let my eyes fall shut, the steady movements of the camel beneath me the only thing grounding me as my limbs became heavier.

I am made of steel.

I forced my eyes open again, my grip tightening on the reins as I wetted my parched mouth. As the hours ticked by, shivers started to track down my spine and despite the raging heat, I was starting to feel cold down to my bones.

Drake and Kyra were ahead of me on their camels, talking idly as the world tipped and swayed. I reached for the water canteen strapped to my saddle, but my fingers wouldn't grasp the damn thing as the strength ebbed out of my body.

"I need to..." I couldn't get the words out. My mouth was too dry, and my thoughts were spinning like the wheel on a ship.

It's just a flesh wound, it shouldn't be this bad.

The world seemed to shift and suddenly I landed in a soft, fluffy bed of sand. The camel trod on my leg and I groaned further as another injury was added to my collection, but my limbs were leaden and I couldn't find a way to make them move.

The sky swum in a murky blue pool above me, close then far away.

I was on the verge of losing consciousness when someone struck me hard across the face.

"Say the words, Cass! Say yes!" Drake's voice sailed to me like a distant dream clinging to the edges of my sanity.

"Huh?" I managed to force out despite the heaviness of my tongue.

"Do you agree to me saving you, Cassius?" Kyra's voice. Her dark hair came into view and suddenly it was her I was looking at, not Drake. She was very pretty. Did she know she was pretty? Better tell her.

"You're very pretty, magic girl," I breathed and her golden eyes widened.

"Oh dear, I think it was the moss," she said, cocking her head.

"What moss?" Drake demanded.

"On the rock," she said.

"What rock?" Drake hissed, then reached for her, but she pulled away. "Kyra, help him. I *need* him."

"The rock that he fell on, Master. I saw all that lovely pink moss on it, and I thought oooh I remember when that man with the eyebrows died because he ate it that time. I think it's all kinds of toxic."

"What man? Kyra, for the love of the Fallen, he's going to die and I need him," Drake begged.

"You can touch it, but it can't get in you. Not your mouth, your nose, your ears, especially not in your blood, that would be very bad," Kyra said matter of factly then beamed, bouncing up and down and fading in and out of focus. "I remembered something, Master, isn't it wonderful?"

"Oh fuck, he's gonna die." Drake grabbed some sand, packing it against the wound on my side, and pain flashed through me, but I couldn't move anymore. Everything was fading and I turned my mind to the princess, wanting her face to be the last thing I held onto. My final crime in this world, but a sin I gladly committed.

I've failed you. Forgive me.

"I can do the saving. You just need to agree, Cassius," Kyra said.

"Say yes, arsehole. I need you," Drake insisted, slapping me again.

This fucking thief...

"Yes," I sighed on what felt like my final breath as the baking sun and sizzling in my veins made me want to fall into the comforting embrace of darkness.

Slowly, it receded. All of it. The pain, the blistering heat, the blinding ache in my side. The air glittered above me, my skin alight with power as a trickle of magic fluttered across my flesh, wiping away the wounds it found, digging deep to cut the infection out of my body.

I groaned, trying to protest to the magic surrounding me as I tensed in resistance of it, but I couldn't deny how soothing it was, how it was taking away all of my pain and leaving me whole again.

When Kyra sat back, I stared at her, bracing a little as magic continued to spark in her eyes and for a moment I wondered if her gift might turn to a curse. But she just smiled at me, a sweet relief in her expression before she looked to Drake for approval.

"Did I do well, Master?" she asked as he stared at me in astonishment, his eyes fixed on my stomach where my tunic was pulled up.

"You did fucking incredible, Kyra," he breathed in awe, leaning closer to me and whispering, "You good, mate? She hasn't turned your brain into a turnip or something, has she?"

"I don't think so," I said, propping myself up on my elbows and gazing down at my unmarred flesh. She hadn't just healed the wound on my side, she had healed away every last bruise and cut I'd still been left with.

I looked to Kyra again, this being who declared herself a Blessing, and I had to wonder if perhaps that word did fit her after all. She had just dragged me back from death's door. I would be taking the dark walk right now, hunting for the eternal garden, if it wasn't for her. Or perhaps my sinning soul would have been taking a turn onto the Bridge of Bones, crossing into Hellravia to be punished for my bad deeds. At least I only had a few of those that I could count, and legend said that once sinners had paid the price of their crimes, they would be free to leave hell and seek out the eternal garden instead.

Kyra leaned down to inspect me, her hair creating a curtain of darkness between us and Drake as she moved so close that her face was only a breath away from mine, her golden eyes swirling with the magic which lived inside her. She didn't touch me and that seemed intentional somehow, making me wonder what would happen if she did and whether I could survive it. She smelled like saltwater and fire smoke, and despite her Fae form returning to her, she seemed wholly *other* in that moment.

"Thank you," I murmured, and her eyes lit with pleasure at those words.

"You're welcome." She stood up, a wide grin lighting her face as Drake glanced between us with narrowed eyes.

"Right. On to the city then," he said, holding out a hand to help me up and I frowned at him, remembering it was he who had made the wish to save me. The choice hadn't come from Kyra.

I took his hand, gaining my feet and relishing the renewed flush of life in my body which I hadn't felt since before I'd been tortured in that wretched prison.

"Maybe it is you I should be thanking, thief." I kept his hand in my grip, drawing him closer as I tried to see the truth of why he'd done it.

"Oh, here we go," he drawled as he moved into my personal space, his face an inch from mine. "It's already happening, isn't it?"

I dropped his hand, frowning at him. "I just wish to thank you."

"No, you wanna kiss me, mate. It's written all over your face. Told you you'd fall in love with me. Everyone always does." He clapped me on the shoulder as I scowled, my gratitude falling away in an instant.

"Did you ever hear the story of Onix, the Fae who pretended to be a god and found himself at the end of Herdat's wrath?"

"Nah, my mommy didn't read me bedtime stories on account of her being dead and all." He shrugged and walked away while Kyra drifted after him.

My jaw tightened as I climbed onto my camel while Drake and Kyra returned to theirs. But I couldn't stay angry for long when I felt made anew after all these days suffering, and I stretched out my limbs and drank in the feeling of not hurting anymore. I'd be able to train harder during my morning workouts again, and find some solace to the anxiety plaguing me about the threat to the kingdom as well as the task that lay at my feet.

I hadn't always been an early riser, but Marik had ensured I was made one, and I had come to crave it too. Now, I needed to wake and fall into the routine of pushing my muscles to their limits. There was nothing like the trickle of sweat down my back at the crack of dawn, knowing I'd already out-worked ninety nine percent of the citizens of Osaria before they'd even woken up.

"We're travelling very far, aren't we?" Kyra said after a while. "On and on and on forever. You must like riding camels very much, Master."

"I'm pretty sure it's giving me ball blisters," Drake grumbled. "My beautiful cock is gonna get tarnished next."

"If he doesn't like it, why doesn't he command me to do something about it?" Kyra muttered to herself.

"Wait, you can transport us to the city?" I asked in disbelief.

"I can do anything Master commands," she said, smiling proudly and Drake turned to look at her with his jaw slack.

"You mean to tell me I'm out here baking in the sun like some common peasant-"

"You are a common peasant," I interjected.

"Not anymore, Cass." He ran his thumb over the medallion at his throat with a wry grin then looked to Kyra. "I command you to transport us to the city of Osaria with all of our camels and my gold."

"And Cassius?" she asked and Drake took his time making a show of deliberating that while I gave him a flat look.

"Yeah, I guess him too," Drake said, shooting Kyra a grin that made her blush.

"Do you agree?" she asked me and I nodded, though my muscles automatically tensed in preparation of the oncoming magic. I didn't know what to expect, and I didn't like to think on it too much as I waited for her to act, my hand going to the hilt of my sword as my instincts prickled.

She cocked her head to one side and suddenly there was a ripping sound that filled my entire head. There was a rush of movement in my periphery then I gasped as the Lyrian seemed to speed past us like I was watching it from the inside of a speeding train. My mind whirled as I stared at the landscape hurtling by while we all sat stationary on our camels and they honked in confusion.

"Holy shit," Drake whooped while I gripped my saddle, feeling as though I might be unseated somehow by all the movement, yet it clearly wasn't affecting us at all.

The world stopped rushing by just as suddenly as it had begun, and I found myself looking up at the white wall of the city from within a group of palm trees which lined the southern road, my lips parting and shock stealing all words from me.

"Fuck yes," Drake breathed, staring at Kyra in awe while I looked around us, making certain we hadn't been seen. "But hang on, I need to look like a count, Kyra." He gestured to his sandy clothes and wind-beaten hair. "I like the sound of Count Drake...Count Drake Nazari," he said dreamily. "And make *him* look like a guard. And not one that will be recognised at the palace."

He nodded to me and I agreed before Kyra weaved her magic again, the tingle of it becoming strangely familiar already. I certainly wasn't afraid of it as I had been initially, but the immensity of her power in the wrong hands was my new fear.

My bloodied tunic was replaced with fine, navy robes with a trim of gold around the lapels. The Forken scimitar was strapped around it, and Kyra altered the tanned red sheath to match the colour of my robes. Another curved dagger appeared at my waist tethered there by a deep crimson sash. A short beard grew on my chin and I frowned, reaching up to feel it. I'd never been allowed to grow any sort of facial hair as a guard, and it felt kind of good, the roughness against my fingers entirely new to me.

Drake was given robes of jade green and beige, and his hair smoothed out, the sand falling from it and floating away on the breeze. The stubble on his jaw became neater and as he lifted a hand to touch it, he eyed his palm in confusion.

"My hands are as soft as a swan's arse," he said, frowning deeply like he didn't like that.

I barked a laugh. "Counts don't have calluses."

Drake scowled but his irritation was forgotten as he met my eye. "You don't look any different. That stubble isn't enough."

"We can still see him as he is," Kyra said. "But he will look like a different man to the rest of the world." Her gaze travelled over me. "I might forget what you look like otherwise. Faces are easy to forget...then I'd never be able to make you *you* again."

I was relieved at that, not wanting to lose who I was even if it might just solve all of my problems considering the bounty that was no doubt on my head. But I didn't want to be someone else, I simply wanted to redeem the man I'd been.

Drake kicked his camel into a trot as we started along the brick road to the city and I kept pace with Kyra, sensing a sadness falling over her.

"Are you alright, magic girl?" I asked in a low voice.

She nodded, then shook her head, then nodded again. She kicked her camel to put some distance between us and I suspected she didn't want to talk about whatever was bothering her. What did a creature like her have to worry about?

Perhaps I shouldn't have cared to ask, but if her mood took a dive then we could pay for it dearly with that power she possessed.

We slowed as we reached the line of men and women who were waiting to enter the city gates, the gleaming white walls of Osaria stretching out endlessly in both directions as I caught a glimpse of the golden palace roof far off in the distance where it sat up on its hill above all else.

I opened my mouth to remind Drake that he didn't have to wait in line with the lower Fae, but he had already directed his steed past them, his cocky swagger firmly in place as he took to his new position like an arrogant duck to sparkling water.

Eyes turned towards us from every direction, and I caught more than few murmurs of interest from women as Drake peacocked the whole damn way into the city, a cocky grin lifting the corner of his lips which said he was enjoying the attention too damn much.

He tossed a wink at a couple of whores who called out to him from the back of a caravan headed out of the city and my jaw gritted in irritation. That man's libido would be the fucking death of this plan if he couldn't stop himself from flirting with every woman he laid his eyes on.

"Chin high. A man in your position wouldn't entertain the idea of mixing with lower Fae, let alone flirting with whores in public," I muttered to Drake and he obeyed, gazing down his nose at the civilians as it if was as easy as breathing.

"Where to? I normally take the backstreets when I head into the inner rings," he said.

"Next left," I directed as he took the lead. I had something I needed to do before we headed to the palace and I wasn't going to debate it with Drake. It was happening whether he approved or not.

I kicked the camel faster to overtake him, leading him down another few streets as we moved into the fourth ring; the first upper Fae section of the city.

We finally arrived at our destination and I dropped from the camel, tying it off on a tree outside a large white house with a small garden at the front. My heart warmed at the familiarity of this place and the thought of who lay inside.

"Where are we?" Drake asked.

Kyra jumped down from her camel, landing with the grace of a dancer and Drake reluctantly descended as well.

"This is my family's home," I told Drake. "I can't risk Egos finding them. I figured you could ask Kyra to protect them. And if you say no, I'll gut you."

Drake chewed on the inside of his cheek and I prepared myself for an argument which I was determined to win. I may have listened to his reasoning for only ever looking out for himself and I may even have been able to understand it in part, but I would not allow his selfish attitude to put my family at risk. But before I had to say so much as a word in defence of what I required from him, he nodded once.

"Fine," he agreed easily.

My brows raised at how little he fought this, wondering why before realising it didn't even matter.

"Thank you," I muttered.

I led the way inside and wondered how my mother was going to react. She must have heard I'd escaped from prison by now, and I'd no doubt given her several anxious nights of unrest since.

"Ma-mar?" I called and Drake sniggered. I shot him a glare, moving along the expansive white hallway.

Peach tea called to me from the kitchen, the scent so familiar it sent a wave of longing through me.

"Ma-mar?" I called again as I stepped into the room.

I spotted her at the table, her eyes puffy, her fingers knotted around a handkerchief. Her usually perfect make-up wasn't present and four of my seven sisters were crowded around her. Marla, Lyla, Fatima and Imani. Ma-mar looked up and fear crossed her features; her eyes were as dark as mine, but everything else about me was my father's and a fierce protectiveness crashed against my heart as I gazed at them all.

"Who are you?" she gasped, springing to her feet.

"Shit, remove the disguise," Drake hissed at Kyra and I nodded my agreement.

I felt a strange tug in my chest before my mother's face shifted into shock. "Cassius?" she whispered, her cheeks draining of colour as the others stared at me like I was a ghost stepping into the household.

"Y-You're dead," Lyla breathed.

"I'm not," I said, stepping closer. "I can explain."

"How is this possible?" Ma-mar seemed frozen, clutching the table like it was the only thing stopping her from collapsing.

"Cassius!" Marla cried, the first to break from the group as she flung herself at me. I caught her, crushing her to my chest as she sobbed against me. Lyla and Imani followed next, but Fatima held back, her sharp features pinched with anger.

"You're a criminal," she bit at me. "How could you bring such shame on our family? On Ma-mar?" She was one year my junior, the eldest of my sisters and the most imperious. If anyone was going to hold me accountable for the stress I'd clearly brought to my family's door, it was her.

"Come now, Fatima, give your brother a hug. Let him explain," Ma-mar pleaded as she gathered her wits, rising from her seat and pushing Fatima towards me.

My sister shook her head, folding her arms as she glared at me.

"I never meant for it to be this way, Fatima," I said with a sigh as Ma-mar stepped past her and pushed my sisters away too so that she could get nearer to me. She cupped my cheeks, tears spilling from her eyes as she gazed at me like she expected me to vanish at any second.

I pressed my hand to one of hers as guilt swam in my chest for all the pain she'd clearly been through because of me. "I'm sorry."

She shook her head, words failing her as she fell against me, hugging me tight and releasing a few sobs. My mother was a fiercely strong woman and I couldn't remember her breaking down like this since Father had died.

When she finally gathered herself together, she stepped back and wiped her cheeks as a smile broke free across her face.

"Tell us then. How are you here? And who are these fine people?" Ma-mar's gaze trailed over Kyra and Drake as she took in their presence, seeming to realise we had a guest above our rank.

"I know this seems strange," I said gently. I didn't want to lie to my family. But I needed to protect them, and I didn't want them fearing what I'd landed myself in. "This is Count Drake Nazari from the distant kingdom of Carubai, and this is his maid Kyra," I said, having chosen the most distant kingdom as the false home of this false count, in part because it was highly unlikely that there would be anyone else from his supposed kingdom in Osaria to spot the lie. But also because the Carubai people were said to be half savage and that would at least partially help excuse any of Drake's less than civilised behaviour if it was noticed. "The emperor pardoned me considering all the years of service I offered him, Ma-mar, but I can no longer work for the palace. He heard Count Nazari was looking for a new guard and offered me up as a candidate." I knew it was tenuous, but my mother wanted to believe that it was true so badly that I could see her buying it.

I'm a piece of shit.

"And why do you need him, Count Nazari?" Fatima asked suspiciously. "Don't you have your own guards?"

"Of course," Drake said, raising his chin and offering them half a smile to reveal his fucking dimples. "But I needed a man who knew the city and the royal family well. I actually deemed this man fit when I heard of his crime. After all, if I were to be given a death sentence every time I looked upon a beautiful face unexpectedly, I would have to be hanged five times over just for walking into this room."

"Oh," Marla breathed, raising a hand to fan herself at the compliment and throwing a wide-eyed look at my other sisters which suggested my sudden reappearance from the grave had just become the second most interesting thing to have walked into the room.

"That's very generous of you, Count, we're most grateful for you offering our brother work," Imani gushed, fluttering her long lashes at him flirtatiously and my muscles tightened.

Oh fuck no.

Drake grinned, his eyes raking over her then falling on my other sisters in the room in a predatory way which seriously wasn't going to fly with me.

I shot him a glare which I hoped made my feelings on his flirtatious smile very apparent, but he didn't seem to give a single shit about that. If anything, he seemed to take it as encouragement or maybe a challenge, I didn't know which but I wasn't going to stand for it whatever his motivations.

Keep your thieving hands away from my sisters.

"Cassius!?" Kaminah, Alia and Zaria ran into the room, throwing their arms around me and screaming their surprise at finding me here, and I was tangled up in another round of sobbing and explaining, feeling worse by the second about lying to them.

"Why didn't you come here sooner?" Zaria demanded, looking to Drake angrily. "Why didn't you let him send word?"

"Zaria, mind your tongue," Fatima hissed before bowing her head to Drake in apology on my sister's behalf.

"I had urgent business to attend to outside of the city. Cassius sent a letter to you with a courier while we were on the road, didn't you?" Drake answered Zaria's questions smoothly. "But the couriers are all being held up at the gates of Osaria on account of the new girding tax."

"Girding tax?" My mother frowned and I looked to Drake, wondering how he was going to finish this lie, having no choice but to go along with it. I couldn't very well tell my family the truth and get them caught up in the perils of what we were planning.

"Yeah, for the loins, you know," Drake said distractedly as he took in the sight of my newly arrived sisters. Kaminah was only in her undergarments and I thrust her sharply behind my back before he could get another eyeful.

"Go get dressed, Kaminah, we're in the company of a count," Ma-mar scolded her and Kaminah darted from the room, her laughter ringing back to us, and I guessed that my mother was distracted enough not to question Drake further on his fucking loin girding tax.

Drake's expression told me exactly how much he was enjoying this, and I managed to dig an elbow into his ribs as my sisters swarmed around us again. I gave him a look that was all threat and he blinked innocently at me.

Touch them and you're dead, thief.

"How lovely your hair is," Zaria cooed at Kyra, admiring her.

"Oh, thank you, it used to be purple but this is much better." She bit her lip and Drake's eyes narrowed.

"That's a joke," Drake said quickly and my sisters started laughing. Not just laughing. Giggling, staring at Drake with wide eyes and batting lashes.

I had to shut this down. Right fucking now.

"Ma-mar we're due at the palace. Drake is offering himself as a suitor for the princess," I announced, those words like acid on my tongue and my sisters' expressions dropped like stones. *What's worse: him fondling your sisters or your beloved princess?*

My heart beat harder and my hands curled into tight fists. *I'll bleed him out slowly if he lays a finger on any of them.*

"Oh, how exciting for you," Imani murmured, her disappointment clear.

Drake brushed a lock of hair behind her ear with a roguish grin. "I'm having second thoughts."

"Drake, we should really go," I said through my teeth and Imani turned scarlet as the rest of my sisters giggled wildly.

Ma-mar hurried towards me, taking my arm. "A word before you leave," she said firmly and I let her guide me out of the room, glancing over my shoulder as I watched my sisters fall all over Drake again.

I swear to the Fallen, if he gets handsy, I'll tear his damn head off and bury it in the garden.

He threw me a roguish grin and I ground my teeth, trying to curb my anger before I lost it and hauled him out of there by the scruff of his neck.

"My boy," Ma-mar said as we rounded into the hallway, her eyes glimmering. "Are you safe? Does this count treat you well?"

"Yes," I promised, cupping her cheek. "I'm fine, Ma-mar. Truly."

"Did the emperor really pardon you?" she asked, her gaze boring into me like she could sense the lie I was concealing and I hated myself for it. I had to sell it to her though, because the alternative put her in danger, and I simply wouldn't do that.

"Yes, but he has done so discreetly," I said. "It is best you don't speak about it with our neighbours. The emperor has offered me this gift because of how well I served him, and how close we are to the Unveiling. It was an accident that I saw the princess's face, that's all. He has forgiven me. But we mustn't spread word unnecessarily and let the emperor seem too lenient."

"Alright," she promised then smiled at me with the weight lifting from her eyes. "Is she very beautiful?"

A lump built in my throat, and I nodded stiffly. "Very."

"That's all you have to say?" She prodded me and heat burned along the back of my neck.

"Of course. What else?" I said a little abruptly and she gave me a knowing look that I needed her to stop aiming at me.

I pulled her into my arms, resting my chin on her head. She was so small and yet she was the strongest woman I knew. Most of my sisters had inherited the exact same quality. Anyone who thought women were the weaker of the species had yet to meet my siblings when one of them had been insulted. They were a vicious pack of dogs and would rip any man a new arsehole if they felt under threat. But they couldn't protect themselves from a man like Egos or the wickedness of Magdor, so I had to do it for them this time.

We headed back to the kitchen and I spotted Drake in a seat with Imani in his lap while the rest of them all leaned in close, listening to him telling some story which I had no interest in letting him finish.

I clenched my jaw at the sight, rage pulsing through my veins and making me want to fight him man to man.

Kyra was watching, seeming fascinated as Drake whispered something in Imani's ear.

"Kyra, ask them," I ordered, unable to keep the rage from my tone.

Drake spoke first as his sparkling gaze whipped onto my mother. "I want to offer you the protection of my household as a gesture for how grateful I am to have Cassius's assistance."

Ma-mar's eyes brightened. "That's very generous of you."

"So you all agree?" Kyra asked and my family all nodded.

Fatima didn't, folding her arms and frowning at me.

"You must agree," Kyra said uncertainly, biting her lip.

"Fatima," I growled. "You will agree to this. As your brother, I insist on it." *Great, I was playing the man card.*

She sighed dramatically. "*Fine.*"

Drake was still running his filthy hands all over Imani, one of them skimming up her spine while the other swept a lock of her hair behind her ear and I was damn close to ripping them off.

"Perfect. Now we need to go," I said through my teeth, trying to contain my fury as I glared at this thief who I had to fake respect for.

"Leave?" Ma-mar gasped. "But the Unveiling isn't until tomorrow. Where do you plan on spending the night?"

"I had thought to show the count to the Inn down on-"

"Nonsense!" she barked, shooting me a look which had me feeling like a small boy all over again, the power of my mother's stare never fading no matter how old I grew. "The girls will help me prepare the house for you. The count will of course take the finest room and we will arrange the guest space for – Kyra, was it?"

"It was," Kyra replied with a nod. "I think."

If Ma-mar noticed the oddness to that response she was far too polite to ever make mention of it and she smiled warmly as she nodded.

"Cassius, you will be in your old bed and we will prepare a meal fit for such wonderful guests." Ma-mar began barking orders at my sisters who for once did not complain or bicker over who did what, instead hurrying away, some of them to buy food from the market before it closed, others hurrying to get to work on preparing the rooms and the whirlwind of movement made my head spin and my heart swell with its familiarity.

There was no point in me trying to argue against Ma-mar's decision now that it had been made, so despite my very keen desire to get the thief far away from my sisters, I was left with no option but to agree.

"This is very kind of you, Madam Lazar," Drake said, flashing her a smile which made even her knees go weak as she laughed coyly, waving a hand dismissively.

"It is the very least we can do to show our appreciation for what you have done for our sweet Cassius." She turned to me, placing a doting hand on my cheek, making me squirm a little at being made to seem like a boy before him, but the look Drake was giving us was not one of amusement or mocking. It was more like…curiosity with perhaps the faintest hint of longing, though as I gave thought to that idea the look swiftly fled his expression.

"We will get out of your way while you make the preparations then," I said, giving in. "No doubt you have a lot to do, Imani," I added, shooting my sister a hard look as she lingered in Drake's lap.

Drake promptly lifted her to her feet, rising too, his palm trailing over her back and making fury burn in my flesh before he moved to join me.

"It is an absolute pleasure to accept your hospitality," he said to everyone, giving them a winning smile.

Even my mother seemed to buy it and she'd just witnessed him pawing one of her daughters without any shame. Gods, the man was infuriating. And now I was going to have to spend an entire night making certain he stayed well away from my sisters and kept to his own bed.

My shoulders trembled with fury as I smiled so hard that I was in danger of cracking a tooth, and I pointed the way towards the private courtyard to the back of my family home.

"The count and I have some preparations to make for tomorrow," I said. "We will do so in the courtyard to ensure we stay out of your way until dinner."

"I'll have Marla bring you refreshments shortly," Ma-mar said, nodding her agreement.

I led the way through the kitchen and dining chamber, opening the double doors there onto the wide courtyard which had long been one of my favourite places in the entire world. The huge lemon tree stood in the centre of the space, the wide spread of its leaves casting dappled shade across the cobbled ground below.

Wisteria grew up the white walls of the house, coating all four of them with the first blooms of the season in full force. Lilac sprays of flowers filled the air with a sweet and nostalgic scent, reminding me of long days spent playing out here with my sisters when I was a boy.

"It's beautiful," Kyra breathed, as she moved ahead of us, her head tipping back as she stared at the flowers which reached up past the windows of the house and climbed over the red tiles of the roof too. "Like something from a dream I wish I'd had."

But I had no time for her dreams and the second we stepped outside, I shoved Drake up against the lemon tree. "You touch my sisters again and I'll fulfil your prison sentence and castrate you."

Drake prised my hands away from his tunic, barking a laugh and not looking the least bit sorry. "They were all over me. Besides, I've got a sex Affinity so I can't exactly help it, women can just tell how incredibly good I could make them feel if only we had less clothes on as soon as they meet me. You can't blame me for that; if you have to blame someone then blame the gods." He shrugged, the look on his face setting my blood boiling, though I fought to hold my temper in, knowing my family would hear us if it got out of hand. It would be pretty hard to explain to them why I was arguing with the

Count I worked for, because he outranked me and I should know my place.

"I've protected them," Kyra sang, not seeming to notice the violent intentions in me, or maybe just not caring. "Their house cannot be found, and their bodies cannot be broken, cut, bruised or hurt in any way by malicious intent. And if by any chance anyone tries to steal them away, a swarm of angry bats will appear, helping them get free once more."

"Are you certain that will be enough to keep them safe?" I asked with a frown, concerned about the bats thing – it seemed like quite the choice.

"Of course it is," Drake said, moving further into the courtyard as he rolled his sleeves back, caring nothing for propriety and exposing his inked forearms before loosening a few buttons at his throat too. "You heard her: angry bats. No one is going to battle their way through a swarm of angry bats. Besides, Egos is going to think we're dead anyway so there would be no reason for him to ever even come here. I know him. He won't waste time and effort on punishing a dead man. His interests lay in gaining riches, not killing the families of people who have already paid the price of their failure." Drake shrugged and I could tell that he truly believed that, allowing my heart rate to settle a little.

It was the best I could do for the people I loved, and knowing that they would be safe went a long way towards helping me calm myself despite the knowledge that I was going to have to spend the rest of the day and night protecting my sisters' honour from the cad who had snuck into their home.

"Do you need to head somewhere to protect anyone?" I asked Drake as I tried to let my anger fall away.

Drake shook his head as he dropped onto one of the wooden chairs which surrounded a table in the centre of the courtyard at the base of the huge tree. "There isn't anyone."

"Oh," I breathed with a pang in my chest and he stiffened, seeming to feel the pity even in that single word.

"Not even a brother?" Kyra asked.

"No," Drake said stiffly.

"Or a sister?" she asked hopefully.

"No," Drake growled.

"A cousin?" she suggested. "Or a great, great aunt's cousin's friend?"

"Just assume the answer is no to all family members you're about to suggest," Drake said and I frowned slightly. He had no one but a bunch of thieves for family and they hadn't exactly been a decent bunch. The people who he had lived with, shared a life with and been surrounded by clearly meant as little to him as he did to them, and that fact in itself was enough to make my anger with him lessen. Even if he had held any affection for any of the thieves, he couldn't return to them now without Egos killing him. So he truly was alone in this world.

A giggle drew my attention to the dining chamber behind me and I whipped around, catching Lyla and Kaminah peering out to get a look at their guest with heated cheeks and wide eyes.

I growled beneath my breath, barking an order at them to go help Ma-mar with the preparations and closed the doors sharply to offer us some semblance of privacy.

But as I turned back to Drake and Kyra, moving to join them at the table, the sound of giggling reached me again, forcing my eyes to snap up to find Zaria peering out of her bedroom window trying to get a look at him too.

I exhaled slowly as I forced myself to remain calm and focus on all the things I needed to try and teach Drake before we entered the palace tomorrow.

I took in the way he sprawled in his chair, legs wide, arm hooked over the back of it and looking every part the cocky, ill-bred, lothario I knew him to be. This task was going to be close to impossible. But if I wanted any chance of getting into the palace and finding what I needed to remove the threat of Magdor from the throne, then I was going to have to make it work.

DRAKE

CHAPTER TWENTY SEVEN

I groaned loudly and obviously, swiping a hand down my face before clasping my hands before me and giving Cassius an imploring look.

"Please let that be it," I begged. An entire afternoon of practicing royal etiquette, greetings, the proper way to address people of different stations and a whole load of further mindless bullshit besides, and I felt like my skull might crack in two from the pressure of remembering it all.

Not least because I hated most of the pomp and pageantry that the nobility wasted time on. To me it all seemed like it was just put in place to force conformity and steal any semblance of freedom or fun from the Fae who abided by it. The nobility were so suppressed that I had to wonder how they hadn't all just died out, too afraid of saying the word cock to ever actually interact with one.

I really hoped my princess would relax her inhibitions quickly. I wasn't the type to spend five minutes fumbling beneath the sheets in a darkened room. So if she was coming to my bed then she was going to have to get used to all forms of worship and depravity at their finest because when I indulged, I took my damn time and wrung every inch of pleasure and more from the flesh of the women who joined me. Perhaps I would warn her of that when we met and watch the way her cheeks coloured with heat and desire as she saw the truth of my claims in my eyes.

"That will do," Cassius grunted, though I could tell he had further thoughts and corrections he wanted to make. "There are other things we need to get in order anyway."

"Such as?"

"When entering the pageant, your identity will need to be verified. There is an application which needs to be filled out too, and of course the matter of the payment to the crown."

"Kyra," I asked, turning my head to look at my little goddess who had made it up into the lemon tree during the mind numbingly boring lesson on the layout of the kingdom of Carubai where I was claiming to come from. Cassius had found some old books stored in his family office and had pointed out place after place on the map, correcting my pronunciation of most of them. But then we had gotten into an argument over the pronunciation of other places within the empire and in all honesty, he was just lucky I hadn't broken his nose.

"Yes, Master?" Kyra asked, flipping upside down and hanging from a branch of the tree by nothing more than the hooks of her knees.

I sucked in a breath, giving her a wide smile as she swung there, her dress bunching around her thighs and only keeping her undergarments concealed because it had gotten caught on the branch. Her raven hair tumbled down to brush the table before me, and I found myself forgetting what I'd been going to ask her as the desire to climb the tree and join her filled me instead.

"It will be rather hard to explain that behaviour to my ma-mar and sisters," Cassius muttered irritably as he looked at her and Kyra blinked.

"Is upside down not how things are done?" she questioned.

"Not usually. But there are at least six things which I can think of that are made far more enjoyable in that position," I replied.

Cassius banged his cup of water down on the table hard enough to force me to acknowledge his presence and I gave him a scathing look while he glowered at me.

"It would be preferable if you came down, Kyra," he gritted out.

"Okay." Kyra kicked her legs, forcing my heart to catapult up into my throat as she launched herself off of the branch, tumbling down so fast that I barely managed to lurch out of my chair towards her before she hit the table.

She rolled as she landed, the fabric of her dress flying up around her and concealing her from view for a moment before she tumbled from the table and into the chair she had been sitting in earlier.

Kyra swept her dress back down over her legs and a lock of ebony hair fell into her eyes for a moment before she blew it aside and settled back into her seat as if nothing had happened at all.

"By the gods," I said just as Cassius echoed the same sentiment, though I sounded more impressed in comparison to his somewhat horrified curse.

"Were you going to ask me for something?" she asked, cocking her head to one side as she looked at me, golden eyes glimmering, and I swear I felt the crackle of the magic contained within her lifting the hairs along my arms.

"Papers," I said somewhat dumbly as I had only half listened to what Cassius had been saying about the things we needed to get me accepted into the pageant. "Birth records, family tree, all the shit Cassius mentioned."

"Official invitations to the pageant were sent out several months ago," Cassius added. "They included the application paperwork for anyone eligible who wished to enter alongside the invitation itself marked with the royal seal which will need to be presented when we arrive at the palace to put your name forward. I caught a glimpse of them before they were sent out so I think I can help you create a convincing-"

"Like this?" Kyra held her hand out, a stack of thick parchment somehow clasped between her fingers, the ink on them glistening as if they had just been written out.

Cassius reached for them with a look of wonder on his face, leafing through them and reading each in turn before laying them before me to check them over too.

I gave them a quick look, the scribbles and symbols meaning nothing to me. Reading hadn't been something required for my survival on the streets, so I had never wasted any time trying to master it. Not that there had been anyone I could have asked to teach me if I'd wanted to. The only way for a kid from the slums to learn to read was by pledging their life to one of the many temples throughout the city and being taught to read the sacred texts about gods who had long since abandoned our kind.

It had never appealed to me, especially not after I had been forced to spend time with a holy man whose intentions were far less than pious, but even before that, a life of prayer and ritual in worship of gods who had stopped listening seemed pointless to me. It wasn't even like they could offer much in the way of food or shelter within the temples. They would buy meagre meals with some of the money that was donated from wealthy Fae but not with any kind of regularity which could be relied upon. Some saw it as better than fending for yourself on the streets, but I had heard enough rumours of the various kinds of sacrifice and worship required in the temples to know that I wanted none of it.

"Kyra," Cassius breathed, his finger skimming over the wax imprint of the royal seal. "These are utterly exquisite. The birth record even shows the appropriate signs of age, and the parchment is the twin of what they use in the palace."

"So they're good enough?" I asked, taking the way he was salivating over them to mean they were.

"These are more than good enough," he said.

"Perfect." I rose abruptly, allowing my chair to scrape over the cobbles. "Then I do believe we are owed a bit of respite from this endless training."

Cassius looked inclined to disagree but the sun was already waning, the shadows growing longer and the scent of something mouth-watering was drawing all of our attention back towards the kitchen.

"We will need to continue tonight, once my mother and sisters are sleeping," he said firmly. "There are many things which still give you away and we need to take every possible moment to prepare ourselves."

"Fine," I agreed, though I wasn't really looking forward to a night spent learning facts about the kingdom and enough about land management to be able to convince people that I was who I said I was. But Cassius insisted that a single slip up could cause the entire plan to fall apart, and I was still on board with the idea of becoming emperor, so I was willing to put in the work.

After dinner anyway.

I headed over to the double doors which led back into the dining chamber, pulling them wide and causing a series of gasps and giggles as three of Cassius's sisters all looked up at me from the table they had been in the middle of laying for our meal.

"I hope you enjoyed your time in the courtyard, My Lord?" Imani asked, fluttering her lashes at me as I drew closer.

"You have a beautiful home," I agreed, my eyes slipping over her and taking in the dress she'd changed in to. It was a stunning orange silk, the way it was tied revealing a long slit which ran up her thigh.

"Have you finished your business now?" Lyla asked, pulling my attention to her. "Perhaps you would like to join me on the balcony for a lemonade before-"

"The count is in need of a bath," Cassius snapped loudly from behind me. "He has spent a lot of time travelling over the past few weeks and I think it would be prudent to allow him to bathe before dinner."

"Would it?" I asked, knowing precisely why he wanted me occupied with a bath and making very little attempt to conceal my amusement over his horror at the thought of me spending too much time with his sisters.

"Yes. Forgive me for pointing it out, but you are smelling rather ripe from your travels," he added.

I barked a laugh. "Is that so?"

Kyra appeared so suddenly that I almost flinched as she leaned in close to sniff me. Not so close that she was in danger of actually touching me though, and I couldn't help but notice how carefully she avoided crossing that line.

"Hmm, I think I'd have to lick you to be certain," she murmured. "But that isn't really an option."

"Isn't it?" I teased, watching her eyes flash with what I had to assume was embarrassment, the colour in her cheeks only making me want to fluster her further.

"I can draw you a bath, My Lord," Imani said brightly, stealing my attention back to her.

"I already set water heating just in case," Lyla bit out, elbowing her sister as she hurried for the door.

"I can show you to the bathing chamber," Kaminah offered, but Cassius stepped between us firmly.

"That will not be necessary, I will show him the way." He took hold of my arm and practically dragged me from the room.

"What exactly do you think is going to happen if I am left with them for more than thirty seconds?" I asked him curiously as we began up a set of stairs which wound through the house, turning to follow the wall which lined the courtyard. "Do you think I will somehow start an orgy with all seven at once? I may be good, Cassius, but that would be an impressive fete even for me in such a short period of time. After a week then perhaps-"

Cassius whirled me around and slammed my back into the wall, his face in mine in an instant and his fist driving into my gut, winding me.

"Fuck," I laughed, pitching forward and clasping my stomach before he shoved me back again.

I probably should have been fighting back but the fury on his face just had me laughing louder, unable to stop myself.

"There are precious few things which are important enough for me to kill in cold blood for in this world," Cassius growled low, his brown gaze locking with mine. "But almost all of them reside beneath this roof. Do you understand me, arsehole?"

"I get it," I said, still laughing, but willing to give in on this point for the sake of keeping up appearances. I wondered if he would be interested in hearing how threats usually spurred me into taking the opposite kind of action, but I imagined that really would turn this into a fight, so I kept my lips sealed.

The sound of footsteps approaching the top of the stairs forced him to release me and we both turned in time to find Fatima arriving there, an empty pail swinging from her hand. She dipped into a soft curtsey as we approached, and I couldn't help but grin at how easily I was playing a count.

"I think I have this well in hand, don't you, Cass?" I questioned once we'd made it past her and his jaw ticked a little at the use of the nickname.

"I was named after a warrior of legend," he grunted. "A man who fought and won in over four hundred battles in the time before the Fallen."

"Yeah? Well, my name rhymes with snake. What's your point?"

Cassius stared at me for several seconds before finally cracking a laugh. "Sometimes I don't know whether I like you or despise you," he said, shaking his head as he led the way on.

"Both," I suggested. "Best to stick with both, mate. Don't forget, I'll turn on you in a heartbeat and stab you in the back if ever it suits my needs."

He blinked at me and I smiled broadly, giving his cheek a couple of little slaps and striding away before he could bat me aside, following the sounds of water pouring into a tub so that I could find my destination.

I took another set of stairs which turned yet another corner, following the edge of the courtyard once more and allowing the scent of the wisteria to float in through the open windows.

It must have been nice growing up in a place like this. Surrounded by siblings and parents who actually gave a shit if you lived or died. Cassius had had it all kinds of easy. If the size of the house and glimpses I caught into the various rooms I passed was anything to go by, none of them even had to share a room. Lucky, lucky.

I glanced around as I made it to the bathing chamber, finding Cassius hot on my heels but noticing that Kyra hadn't followed us up here.

I swallowed down the slight panic I felt at losing sight of my priceless treasure, but my fingers curled around the amulet at my neck and I relaxed a little. Unless she had been bullshitting me from the moment we met, she was bound to the coin which meant she couldn't have gone far. I had to imagine that being locked up in that thing for fuck knew how long had left her feet itching for movement, so she was likely just exploring while she had the opportunity to do so.

I forced myself not to worry about where she'd gotten to and stepped into the bathing chamber just as Cassius caught up to me.

Marla squeaked something unintelligible as she looked up from where she had been pouring a pail of steaming water into the copper tub which sat in the centre of the chamber before a set of double doors which were wide open and looked out towards the courtyard below. We were on the third floor here and the roof on the other side of the building was a little lower, offering a view over the top of the red tiles which showed the gold domed rooftops of the palace itself and I drew in a slow breath as I looked at it.

"I don't know why Ma-mar and Papa ever decided to place the bathing chamber at the top of the damn house," a girl complained from somewhere out in the corridor and the corner of my lips twitched as Marla gasped in alarm, slapping her hands over her mouth.

"I'd imagine hauling all of this water up here was a bit of a bitch," I commented in agreement just as Zaria stepped around the corner and the poor girl shrieked as she spotted me and her brother already inside, damn near sloshing the entire pail of water all down herself in her surprise.

"Do not curse in front of ladies," Cassius hissed while I fought a laugh and his sisters hurried to try and salvage the situation with murmured apologies and dipped heads.

They'd clearly been using another staircase, several of them hauling the pails of heated water up here so quickly that the tub was already near full.

I waved them off. "You don't have to apologise for speaking your mind," I said dismissively, turning back towards the open doors on the far side of the room which led to a tiny balcony and leaning my shoulder against the door jamb. "I can only imagine the inconvenience was thought worth it in light of that view."

The girls both agreed with me, hurrying around to finish up with the tub, telling me that they had brought goats milk, oats and fresh blooms for my bath to ease the ache of travel from my limbs.

I thanked them, unable to turn my eyes from the view and finding Cassius at my side as he came to look out at it too.

"The jewel of The Twelve Kingdoms," he murmured as we both watched the way the setting sun cast a blaze across the domed rooftops of the imposingly beautiful home to the royal family.

"The greatest prize in all the lands," I replied, my heart thumping faster and faster the longer I looked.

This plan of ours had seemed insane from the very first moment that Cassius had voiced it and yet somehow, tomorrow we would be walking through the gates which surrounded the palace, welcomed into the heart of the kingdom and I'd be given an opportunity to capture the hand of the princess. There was an entire empire right there, ready for the taking and I was standing here looking back at it, a street thug without a thing to my name besides grit and ambition.

Cassius seemed inclined to say something else, but he held his tongue, sighing as his own plots and concerns ate at him, his lack of trust in me clearly staying his words. He was clever to keep his secrets. I wasn't the one to be trusted with them.

"I'll leave you to bathe and ask Kyra to bring you something clean to wear for dinner," he said finally, stepping away from the view and heading to the door.

I looked down at the spotless silk garments I wore, a frown pinching my brow, but he had already gone, the door clicking shut and the sound of him chasing several of his sisters away from it calling to me.

I pulled my attention from the view too, turning and tugging my tunic over my head, draping it on a stool in the corner of the room before removing my boots and britches as well.

Once fully naked, I strode back across the room towards the tub, pausing for a moment as I felt the kiss of the sun shining in through the open balcony doors, a sigh escaping me as I took in the silence of this place. The tattoo on my upper right thigh warmed more than the rest at the feeling of the sunlight brushing against it as always and I scored my hand across the skin there absently as I focused on the lack of noise.

Yes, I could hear the distant hustle of the city which surrounded us, but above that I could hear the wind and birdsong. I couldn't make out individual voices much less the grunts and farts of a hundred violent men and women lingering close by.

I really hadn't ever known much peace like this.

"Oh my gods!" a shocked whisper reached me followed by a series of excitable giggles and violent hushing and the corner of my lips twisted as I realised I had an audience peeking out from the window on the far side of the courtyard. The slightly lower angle and the balcony between us meant they likely weren't getting a look at my manhood, probably just my bare, inked chest, but the desire to rile Cassius almost made me take a few steps forward to give them the full show.

Then again, Cassius would probably try to castrate me if he found out that his sisters had taken a look at my cock, no matter how innocently I might have claimed to have stepped out onto the balcony, so I decided against it.

I looked at the tub of milky white water with interest, noting the roses, carnations and cut blood orange slices which floated on the surface with a soft snort of surprise.

This certainly beat bathing in the river – especially a river full of dead kids with their hearts carved out. Even the bathhouses local to The Den had nothing like this, just pools of lukewarm water occupied by far too many bodies to ever truly be able to relax in.

I stepped into the water, letting myself sink all the way down beneath the surface before emerging once more, swiping the strands of ebony hair out of my eyes. I exhaled softly as I leaned my head back against the edge of the tub, my eyes finding that view of the palace once more and fixing on it.

My mind was buzzing with all of the commands and lessons which Cassius had been drilling into me, and though I was confident in my ability to pull off any con, I had to admit that there was a whole lot more to being noble than I had ever really thought about.

Customs, traditions, formalities and posturing were parts of their everyday lives and seemed so important to them that I had to question at what point they ever let loose and just enjoyed themselves. They had so much more than almost everyone else within the kingdom, and yet it seemed to me that all they did with it was covet it and relish in how very clever they thought themselves to have it.

I placed my arms on the edge of the tub, my eyes trailing over the ink there and my throat thickening a little. I had forced myself to look at the tattoos like this a lot in the years since they had been put upon my body. I made myself accept them and even grew to understand that it was yet another thing which people found attractive about me. I supposed I was lucky in that regard – the designs were intricate and beautiful, somehow powerful too. At least if I was going to be forced to bear scars, they had been ones considered desirable.

I no longer shuddered when I looked at them, nor was my head filled with the screams I could remember all too easily if I allowed myself to. Mostly, I just felt numb when I gave them my attention.

There was no point in me wasting energy lamenting things I couldn't change or wasting time on regrets. It was done. Over. Blood spilled and vengeance achieved. It was simply one thing in a list of shitty things which made up the entirety of the man I was. I was all sharp edges and broken pieces wrapped up in the sweetest kind of poison, which was perfectly designed to lure the unsuspecting close and encourage them to buy into the lie which I presented to them. I may have played the role of charm and banter, a thousand smiles always set waiting upon my lips from seductive to playful, knowing to friendly, but none of them held so much as a taste of the truth. Beneath the exterior, I was nothing but rot and ash, selfish desires which gave way to unthinkable acts without so much as a shred of regret left in their wake. That was what it took to survive the life I had been gifted. I would never apologise for it or even feel badly for it. Dog-eat-dog didn't come close to the reality of the slums. It was every monster for themselves where I came from, and no matter how well I hid my teeth, nothing would ever take away from the sharpness of the bite I could offer nor change how suddenly I might be tempted to do so.

My eyes moved to the palace once more and my fingers drummed against the edge of the copper tub as I looked at it, wondering if it might be the answer I'd always been seeking. The end of the life I'd been born into and the beginning of something so much sweeter.

Problem was, nothing ever tended to work out so simply as that. Especially for me.

My fingers moved to the amulet at my throat and I rubbed it between my fingers absentmindedly, wondering if Kyra truly held the power she claimed and would be able to offer me all she'd promised. It seemed more like the makings of a dream than a reality.

"Are you always this sad or do baths upset you?"

I jolted in alarm at the sound of the voice, twisting in the water so sharply that I sloshed a whole lot of it across the tiled floor.

"Shit, Kyra," I gasped, finding her sitting in a tall armchair there, her feet bare and legs kicking idly where she'd slung them over the arm of her seat, once again allowing her dress to bunch up and reveal her thighs to me. "How long have you been there?"

"I followed you here with Cassius," she replied with a shrug.

"No, you didn't," I said. "I looked for you and you were gone."

"Oh...well I went and helped Ma-mar in the kitchen for a while. She's ever so nice."

"She's Cassius's mother, not yours," I pointed out and she stared at me for several seconds like she didn't understand that then nodded.

"She told me to seek the light in all things," she said.

"That's an old saying from the Temple of Saresh."

"The god of the sun and all things living," she breathed, her eyes widening in realisation. "I remember now...only, that is all I can recall."

Her face fell and I sat up, water running down my bare chest as I turned to look at her properly.

"Your memories will return to you," I said, aiming to reassure her but she only shook her head.

"I think they're all too far gone for that," she murmured, her eyes brightening with tears for a moment, but she didn't let them fall.

"Then you can make new ones with me," I said firmly.

Kyra blinked at me, the tears clearing and her throat working as she twisted in her seat, folding her legs beneath her and leaning forward, the shift in her posture drawing my eyes to the curve of her breasts and my cock began to get all the wrong kinds of ideas within moments.

"Thank you," she whispered, and I nodded uncomfortably, not liking the idea of anyone feeling indebted to me. I wasn't a good man. Never would be. Anything I did served my own purpose first and foremost, and anyone who believed otherwise would only be rewarded with the sharp sting of shock when they realised the truth of that.

"Tell me how your magic works," I said, shifting the subject before she got any foolish ideas about me being something I wasn't, and I would end up forced to rectify her opinion.

"It is endless," she said with a shrug. "But not mine. All of the power in me belongs to my master."

"But where did you get that power?" I pushed.

Kyra's lips opened then closed, her teeth sinking into the bottom one as she thought, and I couldn't help but consider the fact that I was naked and the two of us were alone, despite being fairly certain that she wasn't anything even close to Fae anymore. She had shown me no signs of desire nor given me any real reason to believe that she was interested in the pleasures of the flesh herself.

I supposed being able to shift her body from one thing to another with magic meant that she didn't really have a body at all. So there was absolutely no point to the issue I was currently having beneath the milky white water, and I was going to have to concentrate on willing it away.

"I don't know," she admitted at last. "I think someone made me into this, but I... Everything I ever was is a blur now. An empty void. Or maybe I never was anything in the first place? Maybe I'm just nothing."

"You're not nothing," I growled, uncertain why those words had made my muscles lock or why I was filled with the desire to make her forget ever giving voice to them. "Nothing is what those above us want to believe we are. Nothing is what this twisted society claims we should be. But I have never accepted that to be my truth, Kyra, and neither should you. Anyone who thinks to make you into nothing should watch out for the day that they are forced to hear you roar."

"I find it hard to believe that anyone thinks of you as nothing," she said, her cheeks colouring as she took in my words, and I couldn't help the cocky shrug I gave her.

"Not anymore they won't," I agreed.

Silence fell between us as my gaze ran over her and she studied me just as diligently, making my skin prickle at the feeling of her eyes on me.

The air filled with a crackling, potent kind of energy which I swear sparked off of everything surrounding us, making my throat thicken and skin tingle. We just stared at one another, the link connecting us seeming to swell until I thought I saw the collar around her throat once more, the white gem blazing at its centre and the magical chain connecting us. I blinked and the vision disappeared again, leaving me unsettled.

"Show me what your magic can do," I said suddenly, needing to banish that image from my mind.

I dropped my hands back into the water, rubbing my wrists as if I wanted to scrub the feeling of the chain from my flesh before stopping, realising what that would mean. That link between us was the reason for her offering me this magic. Without it, I would be back on the streets, no princess for a bride and certainly no empire ripe for the taking. And despite the unappealing look of the magical chains which bound us to one another, I couldn't feel them and Kyra didn't seem to either, so I had to assume they were more symbolic than real.

Kyra smiled at the request and got to her feet, holding a hand out and igniting a flame upon it, the colour shifting to blue, purple, orange, green, pink, the flickering light seeming to swell and fill the entire room.

I stared at the power she wielded so casually, my mind unable to fully comprehend it. Even the Fallen hadn't claimed power over the elements, but it seemed that Kyra's powers held no such restrictions.

She clapped her hands together suddenly and all of the light in the room disappeared, making me suck in a breath as I found myself entirely lost in a void of darkness. Only the solid press of the copper tub and warmth of the water surrounding me reassured me that I was still where I had been, but my heart began to thrash in my chest as I failed to see a single thing, no matter how hard I strained my eyes.

My lips parted on her name, but before I could utter a word, a deep growl sounded from the far corner of the room, blood red eyes appearing out of nowhere and adrenaline pouring into my flesh.

I lurched back, water sloshing from the tub again as my hand reached towards the stool where I had left my clothes, hunting for the dagger I had left there with them as a curse escaped me.

The light flashed back into the room before I could even get close to reaching it. A blood red beast appeared in the corner of the room, its body something between that of a dragon and a wolf, sharpened fangs lining its snarling jaw.

It leapt towards us suddenly and my cry of alarm was swallowed by a roar which came from behind me, a flash of brilliant gold scoring across the room above my head as an enormous bird born of nothing but magical flames flew to meet the beast.

They collided with an explosion of multicoloured fire, and my mouth fell open as they disappeared, tiny sparks falling from the place where they had been, tumbling into the water and making it spark and fizz with power.

"By the Fallen," I muttered, my heart still thrashing and my knuckles blanched with how tightly I was gripping the edges of the tub.

"Do you want to see more?" Kyra asked curiously, not seeming the least bit flustered by that unbelievable display as she moved to stand beside me.

I could only stare up at her for a moment, my mind trying to marry the sight of this tiny, beautiful creature with the explosive force of power that I had just witnessed. She was so much more than I had even given her credit for. She was something beyond the realms of mortality, a true little goddess born of power and destruction.

"He *didn't* shit his britches," she muttered to herself. "He isn't even wearing britches."

I cleared my throat, pushing myself upright and releasing the edge of the tub as I regained myself, shaking my head to dispel the awe I had felt at seeing the extent of her power. And I had no doubt that she could do far more than that.

"You're incredible," I told her plainly. "I've never even heard rumours of power like yours. Are you certain you aren't a god?"

Kyra's lips parted then closed again, a crease forming between her brows before she finally shrugged. "No," she admitted. "I'm not certain. I'm not really certain of anything, but I don't think I am. I know things even if I don't remember them, and I know that I was bound to this life and given this power. I don't think that is how the gods were born, is it?"

I snorted a breath of amusement. "You're asking the wrong man for information on the gods," I told her. "I have no time or patience for forgotten deities who turned their faces from us."

"Oh," she said, seeming a little disappointed that I couldn't offer her any kind of certainty.

"But if I were to worship at the feet of a goddess, I could only hope that she would be half as breath-taking as you," I added, watching her disappointment turn to coyness as she flushed, her cheeks heating and lashes batting. "I'm going to get out of the water now," I warned her. "So you may wish to look away."

"Look away?" she questioned, but I was already heaving myself up and out of the tub, water sloshing around it and running down my skin as I stood with my back to her, taking the towel which had been left for me and using it to dry myself.

"Would I be able to get something fit to wear for dinner?" I asked her, looking back over my shoulder as I tied the towel around my waist. "Cassius seems to believe I need to change my clothes again already."

Kyra was staring at me, her teeth capturing her bottom lip as her fingers gripped the edges of the chair she sat on like she thought she might slip from it if she let go.

My pulse picked up a notch, my eyes roaming over her in a way that was wholly inappropriate as I questioned my assessment of her interest in pleasures of the flesh, before she burst that bubble with her words as simply as breathing.

"Are you sure you don't want me to do anything to fix your appearance?" she asked, her eyes widening with what I could have sworn was pity. "I know that you don't expect there to be a part of the pageant which focuses on looks, but what if there is and you lose points because of your face and-"

"No, Kyra," I barked, irritation prickling through me. "I would gain points for my face, not lose them."

"O…kay." She bit down on her tongue so hard that I was surprised she didn't make herself bleed with the effort she was making to hold in whatever thoughts remained in her head on this subject.

"We will be late to dinner at this rate," I said, my tone sharper than usual as I fought to contain my annoyance. I wasn't one to be riled easily but I also hadn't had anyone try to poke holes in my vanity before, and I couldn't say I enjoyed it.

"Oh, sorry, of course." Kyra didn't even move but her magic wrapped around me like a trail of soft fingers caressing my skin. Within moments the towel was falling to the floor and I found myself dressed in a pair of black britches and a white silk tunic, the edges of which were stitched with blood red embroidery, the quality of which I hadn't even seen worn by the nobility when I prowled among them lifting purses and liberating kurus from their too full pockets.

Kyra got to her feet before me, her own dress seeming to peel away from her body to reveal a set of bright pink harem pants and a matching top beneath it while her previous outfit just shimmered out of existence in the air around her. Technically, she was better dressed than a maid should have been, but I made no comment on it, seeing no reason for her to have to lessen the quality of her clothing. Surely it would only add to my appearance of wealth anyway.

"I suppose we'd best go fill our bellies then," I said, leading the way towards the door, my stomach rumbling at the delicious smells which were wafting up to us from the kitchen.

Kyra moved to walk with me as I headed out into the corridor, and though I kept my gaze ahead of me, I couldn't help but feel overtly aware of all the power she was able to wield oh so easily.

Sometimes it was easy for me to convince myself that she was nothing but a beautiful girl, but I would be a fool if I ever let myself fall for that. Kyra was a force of nature, a vat of power and an unpredictable creature beyond my comprehension.

She was just like me in that way. All kinds of dangerous hidden behind a pretty face.

I'd be certain not to let myself forget it again.

CASSIUS

CHAPTER TWENTY EIGHT

Between staying up late teaching Drake the ways of upper Fae, then waking throughout the night to do a circuit of the house and check he was still in his bed alone instead of joined by one of my sisters somewhere, I had gotten very little sleep. My ma-mar had had another feast waiting for us for breakfast and after our dinner last night, I truly couldn't remember the last time I'd eaten so well.

I was glad to be on the road to the palace because our presence was a danger to them – not to mention the danger presented by Drake's wandering cock - but I was sad too. I didn't get to spend nearly as much time with my family as I'd have liked since I'd joined the Royal Guard and it made me think of all I'd missed out on during our time apart. But sacrifices had to be made to free my mother from Marik's so-called charity. I shuddered, a violent hatred for that man rising me more keenly and making the scars along my back tingle with the echo of his whip.

I finally became distracted as we closed in on the palace walls, our camels laden with the gold that would buy Drake's way into the pageant, my mind hooking on the princess and her Unveiling today. I'd nearly lost my life for looking upon her face and now a lowly thief was going to see it for free. The entire kingdom would be permitted to see it, in fact. Yet still, the empire I'd devoted my life to had been willing to torture and execute me for the simple crime of having seen her early. I wasn't one to pout, but the injustice of that fact did sting.

My spine prickled as I tried to shake the strange emotion that had me in its clutches. It was so rare to me that it took me a moment to realise what it was. Jealousy. The acidic, burning kind that drove deep into my gut and stirred my demons from their slumber.

Drake's not going to win the pageant anyway. And it's not like I am any more worthy than him to see her face.

Marik's words carried to me from the past and I felt them root deep, never to be cut out. *"You are worth less than the dirt you walk on, Two-Eighty-Seven!"*

We approached the outer gates to the palace where a crowd had gathered. Drake lifted his chin and cheers went up from some of the civilians, but more still grumbled and glowered, the Royal Guard out in force to keep them back.

"Where was our invite?!" a woman hollered, her face twisting with disgust as she spat at the feet of Drake's camel before a guard roughly pushed her aside.

I frowned around at the crowd, surprised to find a lot of them in the well-worn and simple clothing favoured by those who lived in the outer rings of the city. I knew that this event had been heralded across the whole of Osaria, but I had assumed the majority of the crowd would be made up by the upper Fae.

"Why have they come if they aren't excited to see you arrive?" I muttered, drawing closer to Drake and shifting my hand to the pommel of my sword as I glanced around uneasily, my instincts telling me that I needed to be on edge here.

Drake scoffed softly, shaking his head at me without once letting the smile slip from his face. "Are you truly so ignorant as that?" he asked beneath his breath, and I noticed his own hand had moved closer to the dagger at his hip.

"As what?" I asked, my gaze scanning the crowd again. I had seen the odd gathering of unhappy civilians at the palace gates before, but they usually came to protest against tax rises or make their voices heard when begging for more funding for medical care or housing for the poor. I'd never seen them gather when nobles arrived at the palace for events like this. What would they hope to gain from this display?

"This pageant will see hundreds of nobles from all over The Twelve Kingdoms arrive in Osaria," Drake said, his tone patient, as if explaining something obvious to a small child. "There will be feasts, balls, galas, all kinds of events laid on with gluttony and wealth as the main guests. How do you think that makes the people who are watching their families slowly starve day after day feel?"

"But the arrival of so many people to the capital will surely result in more money being spread throughout the city," I protested, my gaze shifting over the crowd who looked almost on the edge of turning into a mob. "All kinds of purchases will be made, and many will benefit from-"

"Those merchants in the fifth and sixth rings likely believe that sentiment. They will gladly sell gowns and trinkets to the nobles and fill their purses with as many kurus as they can, but what good will it bring to those in the slums? You're a fool if you truly believe they should be grateful for the influx of wealth and greed which they will never see."

"Aside from the eventual wedding, the pageant is a celebration of the power and unity of The Twelve Kingdoms," I said. "It is an important reminder to all of the peace that reigns in our kingdom. No one wants to return to a time of war. The Battle of The Burning Men alone caused the deaths of-"

"Cassius," Drake interrupted, shooting me a hard look. "There isn't a man or woman alive who actually remembers a time of war. The Twelve Kingdoms have been united for a hundred years-"

"Two-hundred and sixteen," I corrected, and he just shook his head.

"Exactly. No one gives a shit. They care about living in squalor while the nobles have more than they could ever want. The rebels would gladly choose a bloody fight if it guaranteed food in their bellies when it was done."

I reached out to grasp his arm, my grip locking on my sword as dread filled me at his words. "Do you mean to tell me that you have connections to the rebels?" I hissed, eyeing the closest guards, glad that the noise of the crowd shielded our words.

Drake laughed loudly, shaking me off. "Do I look like a man who would dedicate his life to a hopeless cause? I may be able to understand what the rebels want, Cassius, but I have no affiliation to them. Why would I waste my time fighting to get food and better living conditions for all when I can just focus on guaranteeing such things for myself? Let the rebels spout their grand intentions until they grow hoarse from trying to make deaf ears listen to them. Let them throw their lives away in martyrdom by clashing with royal guards and those who support the upper Fae in all they do. Meanwhile, I will do what I always have – look out for myself and to hell with all the rest. That way of living has kept me alive so far and is about to see me walk through the gates of the palace itself too. The rebels will remain out here with nothing but their empty words of indignation to keep them warm at night."

I let him pull ahead of me while my brows stitched together at his words. He really was one selfish bastard. But was I any better? I believed in upholding the empire and the rule of the nobility. I just wished for them to bring about change which would benefit those who sought to revolt in the current circumstances. In reality, the rebels and I had the same enemy. Once Magdor was gone, it would be better for all of us.

We upped our speed, and I kept my gaze above the angry faces of the rebels in the crowd, focusing instead on those closer to the palace walls, the upper Fae who cheered and welcomed the late arrival, all of them clamouring to catch a glimpse of the suitor who may just end up as their next emperor.

We had timed this carefully, not wanting to arrive early and have him caught making conversation with the other suitors – time which could be used to discover his poor breeding before he so much as got his name listed for the pageant. Once he had been officially announced, I would relax a little, but until he made it through that first assessment, I was more than a little concerned about him being able to pull this off.

We were toeing the line of late, but that was preferable. The less time Drake had to reveal his lack of manners and propriety the better.

I cried out to the guards barring the gates, "Count Drake Nazari presents himself as a suitor to Princess Austyn!"

They beckoned me forward and I encouraged my camel towards them as I passed them the papers Kyra had forged for Drake. I didn't work often with the guards stationed at the outskirts of the palace walls, but I was anxious all the same as their eyes drifted over me. Thankfully, no recognition filled their eyes and I exhaled softly as their attention moved from me to Drake.

"You're travelling lightly, My Lord," one of them commented, taking note of the fact that there was only two of us in his entourage, but Drake only shrugged.

"I can't bare the slow pace of a full household," he said. "And it is a long way from Carubai to here – if we had come with more than just the three of us, I would not have made it in time at all."

The guard nodded in acceptance of his words, his attention slipping to Kyra next while she looked beyond the guards as if they held no interest at all to her, her focus on a butterfly which danced above their heads.

They took a moment thumbing through the papers before nodding and returning them to me, making a breath of relief tumble from my chest.

The gates were opened for us, and trepidation scored a path through my chest as I gazed at the path awaiting us beyond it.

I was going into the palace undercover. A vigilante with a single cause. Magdor had to be taken down. But before that, Drake had to convince the emperor that he was a nobleman worthy of his daughter's hand.

By the fucking Fallen, how are we going to pull this off?

Drake's smug-as-shit expression gave me cause for concern as the guards stared curiously up at him, clearly not recognising this nobleman.

"Don't overdo it," I murmured as I drew my camel up beside his.

He blinked, looking to me in confusion and I realised that expression had been wholly natural.

"Last chance for me to make you pretty," Kyra whispered, cupping her hand around her mouth as she rode her camel on my other side.

Drake scowled, drawing his shoulders back and I released a low chuckle, glad there was at least one woman in this world who was immune to his charm – well, if you could call her a woman. She certainly had female form, but the magic within her could have been responsible for her appearance. So I still didn't know what she really was, even if she had once been Fae, and I wasn't sure I wanted to know either. There were some things in this world that were best left alone, and magical creatures who lived in coins were certainly one of them. But here we were.

I was too deep in this plan now to second guess this creature's involvement, and if it led to saving Princess Austyn from Magdor's tyranny, then I knew I'd let all the devils of the world loose to ensure it. I felt the darkness of that quiet truth stirring within me, the part of me which had no limits, no bounds when it came to the princess. Thoughts of destruction and chaos in her name always had the monster in me purring, but lately it seemed it was rising too close to the surface, fighting too hard to get out.

The courtyard was full of white flower petals, and I sensed we were a little late to join the procession which must have already headed into the palace gardens. I'd wanted to be certain we weren't lingering among the other nobles who had come to offer themselves for the pageant, but I hadn't intended on us actually being late enough to cause a scene. I cursed, looking to Drake who didn't seem at all concerned about the time and urging him to hurry.

"Come on." I kicked my camel into a faster pace and Drake spurred his on as we darted out of the courtyard on the other side.

The inner wall came into view, and I spotted an entourage of wagons, horses and camels riding up to the arching wooden doors. The walls were starkly white, stretching out far to the east and west of the grounds while the highest points of the beautiful building were capped with golden domes, inlaid with sapphire detailing in intricate patterns. The grandest and largest dome of them all stood at the centre of the palace, the one that could be seen for miles around the city, standing atop the throne room of the emperor.

My gut twisted as I realised how sparse Drake's company was, but there wasn't much we could do about that. Kyra couldn't create living things and we couldn't have taken the risk of hiring people to fill the roles in case their tongues got loose, and they exposed our lie.

"Have courage, sullen man," Kyra whispered to me. "It's too late to back out. Unless you want to back out. Do you want to back out?"

"Shh," Drake hushed her. "Act normal. You're not a Blessing now, you're a maid."

"I'm a maid, I'm a maid, I'm a maid."

If we messed up and someone figured out who Drake and I were, our criminal bodies would hang from the palace walls as an example to the entire kingdom for months to come. Hopefully the disguise Kyra had laid on me was solid, but as I rode towards the inner palace wall, I felt like the truth was shining out at everyone.

I had to have faith in her power, no matter how unsettling it was.

Remember who you are. Remember what you stand for. What you were made for.

I am here for the kingdom. For the emperor. For the princess.

And I will not leave until my duty is done.

CHAPTER TWENTY NINE

O saria's palace walls spread out before us and for the first time in my life I was about to breach them as easily as slipping between the thighs of a well-paid whore. I'd dreamed of doing such a thing most nights for years, but I'd never really thought it would happen. No thief who'd set foot inside the palace had ever been seen again. It was about the only place in the kingdom that I was concerned I wouldn't have been able to rob. No matter how many times I'd dreamed of doing so, or how many times I'd tried to gain the information I would need to orchestrate it, I'd always come up against those same hurdles.

The palace was too well guarded, impenetrable, an impossible dream. But now the crown might just have been within reach, and I wouldn't even have to steal it – I could place it upon my pretty head and keep it sat there for good.

Perhaps I should have been thanking divine intervention or some long-forgotten god for this twist in my fate, but I wasn't. The only creature I was crediting for my current position was the girl currently riding to my left, and I wouldn't be letting her go no matter what.

Cassius exchanged a loaded look with me, and I gave him a confident smile. This was just a long game and I'd run enough hustles in my time not to be afraid of it. Confidence was key. If we believed that we were supposed to be here, then everyone else would believe it too.

Kyra was looking around at the outer gardens, her golden eyes sparkling with intrigue. She was holding it together and keeping whatever she felt off of her features, though she still muttered to herself from time to time.

Her black hair fell down her spine in a cascading wave and my gaze lingered on the motion of it as she swayed side to side on the camel's back. The camel slowed a little, falling into step beside mine and she gazed up at me with a smile gracing her lips. My attention lingered on her mouth for a few seconds before I forced myself to look away. She was utterly stunning in her true form, her lips just made for kissing and her curves created for worshipping. If she hadn't been a magical creature, I undoubtedly would have pursued her tirelessly, but I wasn't entirely sure there was enough humanity left in her for that.

She might have looked like a beautiful woman on the outside, but beneath her flesh there only seemed to be magic now. She was a shell for her power, and it seemed like what remained of the girl she'd once been had long since been tainted by it. Not to mention the fact that she kept insisting she found me ugly – which was a fucking joke if ever I heard one, but it also wasn't exactly an encouraging sign so far as her interest in me went.

Besides, I had a princess waiting for me. Supposedly the most beautiful woman in The Twelve Kingdoms, though I somehow doubted that. There was a hell of a lot of women in The Twelve Kingdoms and the chances of the most beautiful one of all just happening to be the princess seemed rather unlikely to me. But Cassius certainly seemed enraptured by what he'd seen of her, so I was sure she'd do just fine.

Cassius urged his beast forward and the camel honked in irritation as he drew ahead of us to announce my arrival at the final gate. I couldn't help but smile at the idea of it; one of The Forty being welcomed into the palace with open arms simply because I was wearing fancy clothes and carried bags of wealth with me. They had no idea who they were welcoming through their golden gates, and I was counting on them never figuring it out either.

"May I present Count Drake Nazari of Carubai, here to take place in the pageant," Cassius called, and the gates swung open before us.

I'd never had a family name before and the novelty of it almost made me laugh. Nazari had been the name of a man who had tried to cheat me in a game of cards once. I'd caught him out then beat him bloody before taking everything from him right down to the clothes on his back. I hadn't even wanted his fucking clothes and I'd tossed them in a pig pen on the outskirts of town, but I'd promised to take everything from him in payment for him trying to cheat me before leaving him bloody and naked in the street. And now I'd taken his name too.

They just let a wolf in with the sheep and they haven't even realised it.

We proceeded beyond the towering white walls and my heart thundered to a victorious rhythm as we stepped over that final threshold.

We'd done it. We were in. Fuck me, this was actually happening.

We headed into a wide courtyard with grey cobblestones lining it, white columns dividing the space with pink roses climbing up to adorn them. I looked up at the pale walls of the palace, my gaze rising to the gold, domed rooftops which crowned it, fighting hard against the grin which wanted to rule over my face.

"You're cutting it fine, Count Nazari," a guard said as he hurried forward to greet me. "The other suitors have already started presenting their pageant fees, I'm not sure if you'll make it in time to-"

"Nonsense," I replied dismissively, sliding from the camel's back and landing before him with my shoulders drawn back like I thought I ruled the damn world. Which I wasn't actually that far from doing if I managed to pull off this con. "Have your men help my guard carry it in."

I waved a hand in Cassius's direction as he started to order several guards to remove the chests which contained the treasure we were presenting to the emperor from the backs of the camels. It was somewhat gutting to have to let it all go, but Kyra had assured me that she would fill an entire room with gold for me in compensation once we'd pulled this off, and I had to maintain the illusion that this amount of money meant nothing to me.

"Of course, your grace," the guard murmured, easily cowed by my superior tone. I couldn't help but get a kick from that little show of power. It felt all too natural for me to be in charge like that – I swear I'd practically been born for this shit. "And I'll have some servants bring your things to your rooms. Will your companions need accommodation in the servants' quarters, or will they be housed with you?"

I was tempted to send Cassius to the servants' quarters just for the hell of it but as my gaze travelled over Kyra, I thought better of it. I wanted to keep her close in case I needed any more magic from her. Besides, I didn't like the way some of the guards were looking at her, and I wasn't sure she was equipped to be fighting off their advances in her current mental state.

With each day that passed she seemed a little more present, a little less stunned by the world and yet she was still so impossibly unpredictable that I would constantly worry about what she might say or do if I didn't keep her close.

"I'll house them with me," I said firmly.

Kyra slid from her camel and gazed up at the palace as she waited for us to move on. She looked more like a noble lady than a maid in her deep purple dress with her stunning looks and captivating aura, but I hadn't had the heart to ask her to scale it back a bit. She looked too fucking good, and she was clearly enjoying being free of that coin a whole hell of a lot too, so I figured it didn't really matter. Count Nazari clearly liked his maid to dress well. Who could argue with that if I said it was so?

I stepped closer to her, and she turned her golden eyes to me with a smile drawing up her full lips.

"Ready?" she breathed, low enough for only me to hear it.

"Let's go win me a princess," I agreed with a firm nod.

The guard led the way across the courtyard and through a huge, arched doorway.

Cassius and Kyra fell into step behind me, and I resisted the urge to glance back at them, knowing a noble wouldn't worry about the help keeping up. We proceeded through long hallways with pale walls and cream tiles lining the floor to keep the heat of the desert at bay. I enjoyed the feeling of the cool air on my flesh as we drew deeper into the building, and I silently memorised every turn we took. If this whole thing went to hell, then I was sure as shit going to rob the place before I had to run.

Our footsteps thumped over the tiles, and I worked to keep my face impassive while I took in the lavish décor of the palace from the priceless tapestries and paintings which clung to the walls, to the busks, vases and other sculptures which had each been set on its own pedestal within recessed archways lining the halls. The palace was designed to impress, and it did so with an effortless kind of beauty and impossible sort of wealth which had me wanting to hold my breath as I looked upon it all.

We finally reached a heavy wooden door inlaid with gold carvings of the old gods and the guard threw it open before us, making sure I didn't even have to face the inconvenience of pausing in my stride.

"Forgive the interruption, Your Majesty," he said, bowing low as he led us into the expansive throne room and my gaze swept over everyone in attendance so that I could assess them. It took a moment for me to focus as I gazed up at the domed roof far above and the paintings of the lost gods covering the entirety of it in such intricate detail that it stole my breath. Pillars lined either side of the huge hall and at the centre of it was a throne made of sapphire itself, gleaming like the most tempting thing I'd ever wanted to steal. Yes, that was a seat made for my arse, I could picture it now…me lording it over the entire empire while scantily dressed women fed me grapes and massaged my hands and feet. I was born for this; it was destiny humming through the walls and begging me to claim it. And dammit I would.

Aside from the guards stationed around the edges of the room and the servants who had gathered to the left of it, trying to remain unnoticed, there were seven other men standing to the right of the hall, each of them puffing their chests out and raising their chins pompously. The emperor was on his feet before the throne, seeming ready to leave, his almost bored looking gaze shifting in my direction as he took note of the guard's words. Here he was, the man who owned it all, and he didn't even have a smile on his face.

Well don't worry sad old man, I'll take all of this from you, and you can go live in some luxurious faraway villa on the edge of the world for the rest of your days. I'll be right here making the most of all your riches.

Everyone looked at us in surprise and pompous irritation. We really were late, but I had always enjoyed making an entrance.

"What is it? We are just heading to the Unveiling," a woman snapped as she strode forward to look at us, her navy dress sweeping out behind her as she moved.

She had long, dark hair which was twisted into a braid down her back and the sharp features of her face were oddly beautiful in a way which was unlike any other woman I could remember seeing before. There was something unnatural to her beauty, something lacking in warmth or heat, and her eyes were cruel and void of compassion.

I'd seen many a murderer in The Forty, but there were a few particularly mean bastards who killed for pleasure, and she had that same look in her eye as they had. I didn't need to look around at the tight set of Cassius's shoulders to know that this was Empress Magdor. The woman he blamed for the state of the kingdom and his poor, starving orphans.

Kyra gasped as she turned to look at the empress and Cassius hushed her aggressively while I fought an amused smile.

"We have a late addition to the suitors, Your Majesty. May I present Count Drake Nazari of Carubai." The guard gestured to me, and I stepped forward, pasting an apologetic look onto my face.

Magdor frowned at me. "It's a little late to-"

"Sorry about that. But I brought an extra chest of jewels to make up for it." I winked at her, and she scowled at me like I'd just slapped her. I guessed she wasn't impressed by me, but if that was the case then she was one of a very few people who'd ever felt that way. And no doubt I'd change her mind when I won this pageant.

Cassius moved forward with six guards in tow, and they all placed a heavy chest before the emperor, offering up my forged papers again to be checked. It seemed a little odd that the emperor hadn't acknowledged me yet and I moved away from Magdor to stand before him.

The emperor cast an imposing figure as he observed me from the comfort of his throne which he had dropped back into the moment his wife had stepped forward to speak. His hair was greying, and a neat salt and pepper beard covered his chin. He held his shoulders back and sat rigidly, but I could detect a little tension to his posture which made me wonder if he was in pain. I was damn good at reading people and as I looked a little closer, I detected a tinge of sickliness to his dark complexion and deep bags hung beneath his eyes. Emperor Tarim wasn't a well man.

"Your Highness," I said formally, dropping to one knee and bowing my head just like Cassius had shown me. I'd never willingly bowed to anyone before, but I figured my practice at being respectful to Egos over the years would set me in good stead here.

The emperor's eyes scraped over me momentarily and it almost seemed as if he didn't care whether I was here or not.

"Well at least the numbers are even now," he commented.

I wondered why he wasn't a little more curious about the stranger who had just offered himself as a suitor for his daughter. Didn't he want to know a bit more about me before he just accepted me into the competition? Was my money and gender all that he required of the man he intended to wed his daughter and one day rule his kingdom?

I held my tongue, taking Cassius's advice to only address him if I was asked a question directly, and the emperor's gaze slid over me slowly.

Eventually he nodded, gesturing for his men to accept the jewels and I released a breath of relief. I might have been one cocky arsehole with an unrivalled poker face, but even I had had my doubts about us pulling this off. But with that single nod, my fate shifted. I was in. I had the opportunity we'd come here for, and I was ready to dive into battle to claim this unobtainable prize with all I had.

"The Unveiling will begin shortly, your servants will await you outside," Magdor said brusquely, ushering me back to my feet so that I could join the other suitors.

I glanced over at Cassius and Kyra as they were led away, and my little goddess frowned slightly as she looked from Magdor to me, her lips parting on some thought, but Cassius hushed her once more and the doors were closed between us. I didn't much like being parted from her, but she had assured me that if I had need of her, I only had to rub the coin between my fingers or call her name, and she would be summoned to my side. Aside from that, I trusted Cassius to keep an eye on her in my absence. No doubt they were only being led to our rooms anyway, so there was no need for me to try and object to the separation.

I moved to join the other suitors and found seven sets of assessing eyes firmly placed on me. I was tall but not the tallest amongst them, one man had me beaten by a few inches and his steely gaze raked over me as if he was looking for a sign of weakness. Another man dwarfed me by a foot and was twice as wide. His face was not as repulsive as Cassius had described, but by the size of him I could only imagine that this was Kahn. I easily pegged him as the alpha of this group of puffed-up peacocks and made a beeline straight for him.

The other suitors eyed me with interest as I looked the giant right in the eye and gave him a wide smile, dimples and all.

"I hear you're the one to beat," I said to him, loudly enough to let the others know that they didn't threaten me in the least. No doubt it was earning me a whole host of enemies instantly, but I wasn't here to make friends. There could only be one winner and whatever way you cut it, they were standing between me and my goal which meant all they were to me was something I needed to knock aside by any means necessary.

"I will win the princess's hand and kill all of you who try to stand between us," Kahn replied confidently while I ran my assessing gaze over him. Being as big as a fucking ox was obviously an advantage for him, but I'd learned long ago how to find the weaknesses in my opponents so now all I had to do was figure out his. From what Cassius had told me he was as intelligent as a box of rocks, so I would be starting there and adding to the list as I went.

"Well, I won't be standing between you," I said, and his brow furrowed with confusion.

"What?" he demanded.

"I'll be standing above you. While you bleed out on the ground and cry to your mamma about the injustice of it all."

His frown deepened as he slowly realised what I was saying, and I slapped his cheek a couple of times in that patronising way which I knew drove men insane.

Kahn took a swing for me, and I danced aside with a laugh as his mother stepped forward angrily. Yeah, dumb as shit and not the fastest either – I'd beat him one way or another.

"That's enough!" Magdor snapped. "Save the fighting for the ring Kahn, this miscreant will soon be beaten and forgotten."

Kahn looked inclined to try and beat the fuck out of me here and now but as his mother's fingernails drove into his arm, he seemed to get hold of his rage enough to keep his hands off of me and leave it simmering in his eyes for now instead.

"We'll see," I taunted as I pushed between the suitors and took the lead as we followed the emperor.

I could feel all of their eyes on me as they were forced to walk behind me, and a grin pulled at my lips.

I've got bigger balls than all of you. And you ain't seen nothing yet.

Two guards opened a door at the end of a long corridor and the emperor led the way out onto a sweeping balcony which was filled with the heavy heat of midday.

The sun beat down on us, and I was wildly tempted to remove my tunic, but Cassius had assured me that that was unacceptable. Multiple times. Honestly, it was like he thought I was a total heathen incapable of so much as communicating with the so-called upper Fae without shaming myself. I mean, he wasn't totally wrong. It was more that what he saw as shameful, I tended to see as living my best life, and I wasn't inclined to change all that much about myself to appease his delicate sensibilities. But I could keep my lower Fae inclinations to myself for now in aid of claiming this prize.

The emperor took a seat beneath the shade of a palm tree which sat in a huge blue pot and Magdor dropped into a chair beside him, her cold eyes fixing on me and causing me to offer her a flirtatious smile. That went down about as well as me taking a shit at her feet might have, but she held her tongue, so I wasn't going to sweat it.

Two servant girls stepped forward to fan them as they made themselves comfortable, and I let myself get lost in daydreams of my own servants fanning me as I sat in the sun once I was emperor.

We were ushered into a line along the wall of the building by a couple of the guards and I gazed out at the view beyond the balcony which looked over sweeping ornamental gardens. Flowers grew in every colour, sectioned off with paths of white gravel which created a pattern only visible from above like this, the layout below appearing as a series of geometric shapes which created the image of a rosebush dotted with butterflies. It was pretty impressive if a little pointless and I let my gaze run over it while I waited for the main event.

"Her royal highness, Princess Austyn of Osaria," a guard announced as a door was thrown open to our left and my head snapped up as I turned to look at the woman I planned on marrying for the very first time.

The princess walked out, flanked by two plain-looking servant girls who kept their eyes lowered and their hands clasped before them. A veil of white fabric hung from a silver crown on the princess's head, covering her face and half of her body too so that it was impossible for me to get any idea of what she looked like.

Cassius had better not have been lying to me about what was hidden beneath that swathe of silk, because I was not going to risk my neck for her hand if she looked like a goose.

The princess moved to stand opposite us, and the guards left the balcony, closing the door behind them with a sharp snap. She wouldn't be wearing the veil again after today, but apparently this first sighting of her was for the suitors alone and I couldn't deny that I was damn curious to see her fabled face.

I folded my arms as the silence stretched, glancing at the other suitors who all stood with their hands behind their backs and their chests puffed out, their excitement evident.

I considered mimicking their posture but that really wasn't me and I could only bear to be so fake in the name of passing myself off as a nobleman. No doubt Cassius was self-combusting somewhere at this very moment in outrage, but if this girl was going to fall in love with me then she was going to need to see at least a little of the man I truly was, not just some show put on to impress people I gave no real fucks about.

"Gentlemen," Magdor purred, leading this ceremony despite the fact that her husband sat right there, and it should have been him. "Allow me to present the prize which you will all fight so desperately to possess."

She waved her hand towards the princess and the two serving girls stepped forward, one of them removing the crown and placing it on a low table behind them before grasping the edges of the princess's veil on her left while the other girl took hold of the right.

They glanced at the princess and though her body stiffened with tension, she nodded once before they slowly began to peel it back. They lifted the veil inch by inch, revealing the point where blue skirts met with a tight bodice around a slim waist then higher still, showing us the swell of her breasts as the corset pushed them up and my gaze caught on a lock of silver hair as it trailed over the dark bronze skin of her collarbone. It shone like metal in the light of the sun, and I arched my brow at the unusual colour while admiring the shape of her body. If we could just get a look at her face, then I'd soon know if this plan was going to work or not, because no matter how much I may have wanted the crown, I was no Balthazar, and I needed true lust to inspire me if I was going to be sharing this woman's bed.

The princess finally ducked her head, and the serving girls lifted the veil right off of her. A breeze caught in the thin material of the veil as it was removed, lifting it up and snatching it from their grasp, sending it flying away from them as they released it, twisting across the blue sky.

A smile tugged at my lips as I looked upon the face no man had been allowed to see before and drank in the sight which Cassius had been sentenced to death for gazing upon. She stared back at us, and her eyes glimmered with more than a little discomfort at being exposed before this line of men who had all come here to claim her.

I wondered what it would be like to be handed out as a prize to be won. Was she looking forward to her wedding day? To fulfilling the duty that had been laid out for her for her entire life? Had she been primed and groomed for this role so thoroughly that all she wanted to do was embody it? Or was she standing there gazing at all of us just as we were gazing at her? Judging, assessing, trying to get any small hint of a clue as to how her life might turn out with any one of us by her side and warming her bed?

It had to be a lot for her. Twenty-one years of life hidden away beneath a veil and now suddenly she was free of it and her duty had come to claim her. Was she excited, nervous, scared, angry? Right now, I would have to go with terrified, but that didn't mean to say she wasn't feeling all kinds of other things too. Perhaps I would enjoy uncovering her secrets and finding the woman who had been hidden behind that veil. Only time would be certain of that.

Her skin was a deep brown, several shades darker than her amber eyes which shone like two priceless jewels as she raked her gaze over all of us. Her unusually silver hair tumbled down her spine and caressed the soft curves of her waist, glinting like metal in the blazing sunlight and capturing my attention as I watched it move in the soft breeze, proving it was as smooth as silk despite looking as sharp as steel.

Her eyes fell on me, and I gave her my best smile, throwing in a flash of both dimples for good measure like we were sharing a private joke. And I guessed we were because with that one look, the two of us understood which suitor had captured her attention the fastest. She blinked at me in surprise and her lips pulled into a hesitant smile in response as a little colour flared in her cheeks, and I found myself oddly pleased to have alleviated a little of that fear in her eyes.

Yeah, Cassius had been right. She was pretty damn beautiful. She shone like a star fallen straight from the sky to land here before me in woman form. So now I just had to make her mine.

AUSTYN

CHAPTER THIRTY

I was still holding the breath I'd taken just moments before my veil had been stripped away. Twenty-one years I'd remained hidden. Now that time was abruptly over. And even after all the times I'd dreamed of this, I wasn't ready for it now that it was actually here.

Eight suitors lined up before me on the balcony, though I was sure I'd been told there were only seven. There would have been far more, but the price of entry had been set so high to keep the numbers manageable, making sure only the wealthiest of suitors could try for my hand – because what other criteria could possibly matter any more than wealth?

My heart pounded unevenly at the feeling of being so exposed before them. I'd been desperate to cast the veil aside for so long that I hadn't given myself any time to truly think about what it would feel like to stand here, stripped of my eternal hiding place. I was bared to the world now, my face, my feelings, my soul, all of it stripped back and laid out for the hungry wolves to devour, and it looked like they'd already arrived for the feeding frenzy.

I tried to decipher what they thought of my face, but with eight pairs of eyes slamming into my skin at once, I'd never felt so scrutinised. I was being ripped apart like a scrap of meat torn into by a bunch of dogs, and yet still they looked hungry.

Their muscles were tensing, their chests puffed out, chins tipped high and posture impeccably rigid. Apparently, it was a who-can-look-the-most-pompous competition. Was this supposed to impress me?

My gaze fell on the single man in the line-up who didn't look like someone had just pumped too much air into his lungs. In fact, he seemed utterly relaxed, his gaze trailing over me curiously but without that sense of proposed ownership somehow. He wasn't looking at me like he was here to buy me, more like he already owned the world and if that meant I came with it then he was game. He was undeniably handsome, his features seeming cut from stone with a rugged edge to them that made me wonder about him and where he'd come from. I even spotted the edges of tattoos peeking out from beneath his cuffs, the idea of a nobleman marking his flesh in such a way stirring my interest despite my determination to have no interest in any of my suitors.

His eyes were unlike any nobleman's I'd ever seen. They glittered with secrets and dark promises, a life filled with so much more than I'd experienced within my own life of rules and solitude. His handsome features were skewed in an indifferent kind of expression to the posturing nobles who stood alongside him. Not entirely without a hint of intrigue, but nothing of the raging excitement wafting from the other suitors. Their desperation tainted the air, the want in them like something feral hidden beneath their impeccable exteriors. He was somehow casually disinterested and yet completely engaged in looking at me. It left me feeling like he was absolutely in love with me and yet didn't want me at all. And I wasn't sure how that made me feel.

They all briefly bowed their heads. The bored looking one did so too a beat later, but with hardly any enthusiasm and a smirk which said this was a game to him. One he knew the rules to but didn't often play by. And that made my curiosity in him sour and blacken.

I wasn't even respected by these men. I was just a feather dangling above a bunch of cats.

My gaze scraped across the group from right to left, recalling their names from the descriptions I'd been given by Zira. Whoever the mystery man was, I didn't have a name for him. I tried not to let my eyes drift to him again as I gave each of the suitors my attention.

Kahn stood to the far left, towering above them all, his auburn locks still in place since the gifted potion from his mother had altered his looks. He was handsome but his face now seemed as though it were carved from the boulder he'd been born with the brain of, his nose the perfect sort of rectangle found on the statues in the walled gardens.

Next was Prince Amun Jah-Fal. Three times my age and son of the Ageishan King. Tall, thin and with grey hair that had been slicked with oil to try and make it appear black. His expression reminded me of a toad with a lily pad stuck up its arse. Maybe it had something to do with the weird shape of his eyebrows.

I grimaced as I turned away from him.

Shit, I have to stop wrinkling my nose. They can see me.

The veil was gone. I seriously had to remember that.

A low snort of amusement drew my attention to the mystery man again, but I stopped my eyes from trailing towards him. *What kind of nobleman snorts?*

Lord Tyron Kalaviv was next: a roguishly handsome man with the typical dark curls and ebony skin of the Forken Empire in the south. The only man not from our own empire and clearly here with the hopes of further bonding the two great powers in this world with our union. I wondered if he was hoping to turn the Osarians against the Quellioths in the war they were currently fighting against them. He was a renowned hero. A warrior.

I had to admit, I might have been slightly interested in him if he hadn't been paying my father to try and buy me and secure himself more power in the world. That single fact alone would have ruled out every one of these bastards if I'd had a choice in it.

To his right was Lord Theodore Darell, a fit-looking man wrapped in black robes, his bald head looking like it had been recently polished. He hailed from the kingdom of Tymera which lay to the far east where the Carlell river sprang up from the ground before starting its journey west where it passed through Osaria itself and gave life to all around us.

Tymera was said to be the one kingdom which still worshipped the old gods as reverently as they had back before the lie, a time when the Fallen still claimed immortality and full use of their Affinities. The city was said to be stunning, the buildings all built with the red stone mined from the foothills of the Greymorian Peaks at the edge of the world, their walls all adorned with silver effigies of the old gods. Priests chanted day and night, the sound supposedly heard from everywhere in the city at all times. Of course, I had never left Osaria and likely never would, but I loved hearing tales of the other kingdoms and the wonders they had to offer.

Next to him was Count Anis Cartoum from Falgesh in the far north where ice and snow were said to cling to the world at all times; he had the look of a demon about him with piercing eyes and overly long fingernails. Beyond that, was Prince Alexander Gurvine of the forest kingdom, Dunemare, a spotty teenager who looked like his head had been transplanted onto the body of an ox.

Beside him was Captain Jonty Hariot of the Cartlanna Fleet to the west. His face was weathered by years at sea, but he was young and primed with muscle. His hair was sun kissed and his eyes two pools of chocolate. Finally, there was the alluring enigma.

I beckoned Zira closer, whispering in her ear. "Who's that? You didn't mention his name before."

"Count Drake Nazari," the man answered for himself, evidently hearing me, his eyes sparking with amusement as he saw me flustered. "From Carubai."

I nodded, straightening my spine as I gazed upon his deeply attractive face, heat crawling up the back of my neck. His fine robes clung to his powerful frame, ink peeked out from the open collar of his tunic, and he was clean cut in a carefully put together and yet somehow entirely nonchalant way. He looked like all the others in some regards, presented as a package of prime nobility, but why did something about this one feel...off?

Carubai was the kingdom farthest from Osaria, set in the northeast of the empire and said to be a place inhabited by wild men and warriors alike. They were rumoured to settle feuds in blood – fights breaking out as easily as laughter and blood spilling on the streets daily. They were a savage people, and I could see some of that savagery in this late comer's eyes. The city itself was said to be set around a castle built of onyx stone, the Fae who resided there claiming their positions through brute force and strength. They had been the last kingdom to join the might of the Osarian empire, and my ancestors had tried to tame them as a part of the conditions of their allegiance to the crown, but it hadn't worked. Acquiring the brutal strength of their warriors had been more important at the time than any need to civilise them, the emperor choosing to ally with them rather than attempt to take them on.

Magdor moved before the men, and they bowed low to her. Lower than they had to me.

Count Nazari dipped his head a moment too late, the only one who didn't seem to be interested in simpering for her and Magdor eyed him with disdain while he gazed steadily back not seeming the least bit concerned with invoking her ire. A smile graced my lips and I battled to school my expression as Father raised a stern eyebrow at me.

"You may now approach the princess," Magdor announced and in seconds I was swarmed.

Lips on the backs of my hands, roses thrust between my fingers. This was it. The hounds were ripping in, trying to fight for their pound of flesh. Compliments flooded my ears and I shuddered, backing up, not liking this at all, instantly overwhelmed by their attention and their desperate work at trying to win me already.

My gaze landed on Count Nazari over their heads, wandering casually towards my father and joining him in the shade of the palm tree.

Apparently, the attractive question mark wasn't interested in speaking with me, and I didn't miss the insult in that. I was likely just another pretty trophy to mount on his wall, my opinions and personality all but meaningless to him.

"I'm quite warm," I snapped, wafting the men back. "One at a time perhaps?"

"Me first," Kahn muscled his way to the front of the group, and I retreated another few steps as I lost all sight of the other men beyond his huge form.

He was seeing me, but not really. And I decided I preferred the count's disinterest to the rabid attention from the others.

"You're very pretty," he said, his azure eyes twinkling. "Prettier than the moon. And I quite like the moon." He started rambling about moon craters and I zoned him out, starting a count in my head which would lead me to the moment when I could escape this show and run back to my rooms where I would no longer have to feign interest in these loathsome men.

"Your upper lip is curling," Zira said under her breath and I flattened the expression, letting my gaze trail beyond Kahn to where Count Nazari was speaking with my father.

What in Osaria was he saying to him?

My father nodded then laughed and I couldn't hide the bewilderment on my face. It was just too damn hard getting used to schooling my expressions when I hadn't had to for so many years. How the hell had he made the emperor laugh? A man who had been stone-cold to me since Magdor had claimed him as her husband was now *laughing* with a complete stranger right in front of me as if none of the distance between him and the man he'd once been even existed.

My blood heated and irrational anger tore through me over their interaction. I'd been unable to get more than a couple of sentences out of my father for years, and this man, this *stranger* was joking with him like they were old friends.

"You're snarling," Zira hissed but I didn't give a damn. To hell with how I was perceived. It didn't matter anyway. I was the princess and if these suitors wanted my father's throne, then they were going to have to go through me whether they liked me or not.

Count Nazari shot me a look then jerked his chin at me and I sensed it was an order. A summoning. Anger scored along my chest and set my pulse pounding furiously.

How dare he? *I* was supposed to be the one with the power here. And yet, I should have realised that I wasn't. I was their prize cow being prodded and poked, examined for good breeding. But fuck that.

I shook my head in a fierce refusal to his demand. He cocked his head, puppy dog like, though those dark eyes of his kept promising he was all but innocent.

I seethed as I drew my gaze away from him again and Kahn continued to try and come up with the words he needed to describe me.

Magdor stalked at the back of the men, eyeing them up as if assessing how strong they might be for the coming fights. Her gaze raked down the warrior Lord Kalaviv who was clearly one of the biggest threats. His biceps pressed against his tunic and several medals gleamed on his chest, speaking of the battles he'd fought in and won for his empire.

No one cared for the fact that I didn't want any of these men to win the brawls. I wished I could fight for my own hand and run away into the sunset with myself. My skill with a blade was likely superior to all of theirs, though I was curious about what their Affinities were. Probably peacocking and boasting about their status. And if there was an Affinity for shrivelled cocks, I truly hoped they were all fully gifted with it.

Women were not permitted to enter the pageant. Even if I had been attracted to the fairer sex, I wouldn't have had the luxury of being allowed to marry a woman like the rest of the empire could – heirs were more important than my happiness. And if that was all that was desired of me, maybe I could have married one of these pompous pricks, provided him with sons then taken a lover to fulfil my needs.

But of course, I would not be permitted to take a male lover for fear of bastards slipping onto the throne. My future husband would be held to no such standard though, and as my gaze fell over the men before me again, I couldn't help but wonder if any of them would be inclined to keep mistresses in the palace. My father had never done it openly, though I heard rumour once that he and Magdor brought a highly paid whore to their rooms on occasion, the act involving all of them, though I chose not to believe in such scandalous tales.

The idea of bringing a whore into the palace for my husband was somewhat abhorrent while also appealing in its own way – after all, if I didn't want him in my bed too often, what better way to keep him out of it than to have another woman satisfying the urges of his body?

But I'm the pretty little prize right now, and whoever wins will want me properly fucked before they get bored.

Bile pushed at the base of my throat, and I wondered if hurling myself off the edge of the balcony right now might be a preferable fate. But as I pictured my skull cracking on the flagstones below, my heartbeat quickened and I found myself deciding to live. I still had hope, though maybe it was a fool's hope. There simply had to be another option to all this, I just wished I could see it.

Lord Kalaviv pushed Kahn aside and Magdor's son cracked his knuckles as he backed away.

"Princess Austyn, how beautiful you are." Kalaviv lowered his tone as he bowed his head to me, his dark curls falling forward. "And how bored you must be." His eyes glittered with playfulness and I gave him a flat look.

"Yes, very," I said. "Men are often so dull."

He frowned like he was looking for the joke in my words, then roared a laugh, clearly deciding I was making one. But I was more than happy to assure him I wasn't.

"Something amusing, Lord Kalaviv?" I asked lightly.

"Forgive me, your highness, I did not expect you to have such…" He faltered on the end of that sentence, his gaze dipping to the swell of my breasts and lingering there before he looked back up at my face. "Personality," he decided and I, in turn, decided I no longer gave any care to schooling my expression. Perhaps if I was lucky, they'd dislike me so much that they'd return to their kingdoms and be done trying to claim me.

"Yes, an unfortunate side effect of the female form," I said dryly and I caught the sound of a snigger from Count Nazari's direction.

"Quite," Kalaviv agreed, clearly not picking up on my sarcasm, or preferring to ignore it.

"So you agree?" I pushed. "Women would be better off without thoughts and opinions of their own?"

Kalaviv opened and closed his mouth, stumped by me and I liked the zing of power that gave me. He stepped closer, painting on a charming smile as his eyes roamed over me again.

"Of course not," he said. "Women have many interests that I admire. Tell me, princess, what interests occupy your time? I hear the palace of Osaria is home to one of the finest sewing rooms in The Twelve Kingdoms. The spinning wheels are made from black dragonwood, is that correct?"

"I have no interest in sewing, my lord. But if you enjoy it so much, perhaps the empress will give you a tour?" I looked to Magdor who swept closer, her eyes as sharp as razors as she assessed the cut of Kalaviv.

"A tour? Good heavens, no," she tittered, waving a hand at me. "The princess can be very vivacious, can she not? My son has spent many years in her company, however, and knows how to handle her quirks. She has many of those, don't you my dear?" Magdor looked to me, playing her own game and not falling for mine. She only cared if Kahn won anyway, so if Kalaviv took a disliking to me, all the better for her.

"Well Princess Austyn comes from a long line of good blood," Kalaviv said haughtily, speaking to Magdor as if I was no longer there. "I am sure her quirks are most manageable. And I would be delighted to have the opportunity to manage them."

My teeth clenched together and I felt Zira's hand curl around my arm as if she expected me to strike him. I wasn't fool enough to start a war between our empires though, so I simply brushed past him and left him in my stepmother's company – a fate which was arguably worse than a punch to the face anyway.

I could feel Count Nazari's eyes on me like they were tunnelling into my flesh and it made my skin flush with unexpected heat. I suddenly very much had his attention. What was with men and competition? If I was as ugly as a dried-out trout would there be this much testosterone in the air?

"All of this is very formal." Captain Hariot stepped forward with an apologetic frown, his hands clasped behind his back. "I do hope I win my first brawl and have a chance to spend more time with you alone. Oh, and I'll try my best not to get too bruised. Unless you're into the wounded warrior type?"

He had a jovial kind of demeanour, and his eyes kept wandering around taking in the men he was in competition with. His attention lingered on Count Nazari and he bobbed his chin towards him.

"You must be drawn towards some of these suitors, a feeling in your lady waters perhaps?" he asked. "I am of quite the calibre, but there are some strapping young men here indeed. Which of them has caught your attention, princess?"

I followed his gaze to Drake who was still entertaining my father then ripped my eyes off of him and back onto the captain. "It hardly matters what I think. The man who wins the pageant shall steal my hand regardless."

"Yes, indeed." He slowly wetted his lips, his attention still on Nazari before he turned to look at me once more. "I am sure your eyes cannot help but wander in the meantime." He chortled.

"It is *your* eyes that seem to be wandering, Captain, not mine," I said and his gaze snapped onto me instead of the count, seeming taken aback by that.

"I am merely assessing the competition, your highness. It is my duty to take in the cut of these men, my opponents. There is nothing wrong with some healthy observation, be it here, or in the bathhouse. There are weaknesses to be found on a man's flesh that can only be noticed when he is bare, his

guard down as he washes his powerful body, his muscles lax and gleaming..."
He trailed off, looking over at the young Prince Gurvine, and I took the
opportunity to dart away.

I didn't get far before the demonic Count Cartoum descended on me like a
bat from the rafters, his dark cloak swinging out behind him and startling me.

"By the Fallen, where did you come from?" I held a hand to my heart and
Cartoum took in a rattly breath which seemed to involve a lot of his tongue,
like he was tasting me on the air.

"Forgive me for frightening you, your highness," he said in a raspy tone
that set the hairs rising along my arms. He reached out to caress a gold pendant
hanging on the necklace around my throat with the emblem of Osaria imprinted
on it. His long fingernails scraped over the metal and I winced away, but his
long arm kept extending unnaturally far so he could continue touching it.

"Pretty, pretty," he purred. "Such pretty things for a pretty princess. I shall
get you more pretty things when I am your husband, my lady. I shall drape you
in gold and it will make your blood taste all the sweeter-"

"Blood?" I balked.

"To the, er, mosquitoes, your highness. But do not worry, I have an Affinity
for scents. I brew perfumes made from the rarest substances across the land.
I can gift you a bottle of dandelion brew which will repel them from biting
you." He stepped into my personal space, shutting his eyes and sniffing long
and deep, wafting his hands towards his face as he breathed me in. "Your scent
could be bottled and sold for countless coin, my lady. It is best extracted from
the very heart of the source..." His fingers curled around my wrist, his palm
cold and clammy against my flesh as his long fingernails scraped against the
vein on my inner wrist.

I shuddered from his touch, snatching my arm away and Count Drake
Nazari was suddenly there, his hand pressing to my lower back as he steered
me away from the creep.

I was so relieved to escape his presence, that it took me a second to realise
how inappropriately the count was touching me, his hand so low on my back
that he was in danger of brushing his fingers against the curve of my arse.

I shifted away from him as we made it to the edge of the balcony and
Drake leaned against the stone railing, taking in the view with a lock of dark
hair falling forward into his eyes.

He'd pushed his tunic sleeves up in what I assumed was a reaction to the
heat of the day and I couldn't help but stare a little at his strong forearms and
the tattoos which caressed them, the patterns somehow captivating me more
than any design I'd ever seen before. It wasn't really proper of him to reveal
his flesh like that, but I got the feeling this man wasn't a fan of the rules he'd
been born into. Case in point – he was here and yet hadn't made a single
attempt to come speak with me until now. But he still didn't voice a single
word. If he wasn't interested in me then why had he come here?

Maybe it was about power for him...a man who looked like that probably
had a hundred mistresses.

A flush bit into my cheeks as I considered that, my gaze sweeping over these men as I wondered how many women they'd taken to their beds in their lifetimes. What would they expect from me on our wedding night? How roughly would they take my virginity from me?

With these huge men flocking around me, their large bodies pressing close and the lust in their eyes all too clear to see, it was hard not to think about that dreaded night. Would it hurt? Would they be gentle with me the way my maids promised they would be, or would they be rough the way that guard had been with the kitchen maid when I'd spied on them? The slap of flesh against flesh, heaving breaths and cries of pleasure echoed through my memory as my skin burned at the thought.

I'd lost Zira among the crowd and could see Magdor was now occupying her time by having her serve drinks to the men. So I was alone with Count Nazari, and the more the silence stretched, the more irritated I became.

"Well?" I demanded and he pulled his gaze from the view, arching a brow at me like he'd just noticed I was there.

"You seem flustered, princess. I do tend to have that affect." The corner of his lips tilted up in amusement and he looked back at the view, leaving me with a snarl forming on my lips.

"The last thing I would be flustered by is a man like you."

"A man like me?" he scoffed, looking to me again as I finally drew his full attention. "Do not judge me by the low standards of the men you have come to see all too much of while locked up in this pretty palace, princess. You know nothing of men like me."

"I know that your arrogance knows no bounds, that you believe the world is your orchard to pick the ripest fruits from whenever you like, and I know that you are here to claim my empire and add me to your conquests."

He released a breath through his nose as if dismissing my words, casually looking back at the view again. "The world has offered nothing to me. I have seized everything I have through brute force, hard work, cunning and determination."

"Then you are even worse than I thought, which is saying something," I said derisively, turning to leave but the count stuck his arm out to block my way on. He didn't touch me, but between his arm and the potted palm beside me I would have no choice but to press my body against him if I intended to leave, meaning I was effectively trapped in his company.

"Why would the gods have put all those shiny, priceless stars up in the sky if they didn't want us to try and claim them?" he mused and I scowled, giving up on trying to leave as I stepped closer to him instead, refusing to balk.

"And did you ever think to ask the stars what they want, Count Nazari?" I growled.

He frowned in confusion. "Call me Drake. And they're stars, princess. Things. Dust and beauty all tangled into something I really want to put in my pocket."

"Well, I am not a star," I hissed. "But I will remain as unreachable to you as they are. Count Nazari."

"Drake," he insisted. "I'm not fond of titles."

"I will call you a count without the O if you do not let me leave," I growled.

He chuckled as he dropped his hand, allowing me to pass without the indecency of having to tolerate his touch at least, and I marched away from him before he could say anymore.

I was soon forced to interact with the rest of the strangers who had come here to win me like a prize pig at a fair. The time rolled by, and the heat of the day intensified, until I was soon tired of stilted conversations with men who dismissed my snide comments as nothing more than jokes and hysteria from the summer sun. Or quite likely paid no attention to my words at all, neither caring what thoughts were in my brain, nor minding which of them spilled from my mouth. I was only a prize to be won after all.

I was relieved when my father finally called an end to the Unveiling and the suitors were ushered away by his guards. I waited to be dismissed too, noticing that Drake remained in place, folding his arms as he watched the other suitors depart the balcony and leaning back against the low wall with the clear intention of staying precisely where he was.

"Time to go," Magdor said to him, her tone sweet.

Even *she* was sucked in by that face. I wondered what it would have been like to be him. Your looks could be a blessing if you were a man in Osaria. Hell, just being an ugly man in Osaria was better than being a woman. They had endless options simply because of a lump of meat which hung between their thighs.

"I haven't finished speaking with Austyn," Drake said, shrugging one shoulder and I fell still in surprise at his audacity of addressing me by my first name while he just stared the empress down, looking like he didn't give a single fuck about who she was, or if he might have been in danger of offending her. And I had to admit, that was pretty damn attractive.

"Let the man have another moment with her," Father muttered from his seat, making my heart lurch in surprise as he involved himself in this and I looked to him curiously as he pushed himself upright.

Two guards moved to helped him out of his seat and I could tell he was feeling weak today as he allowed them to support him. My heart crushed in my chest as I watched them guide him away. How long was Magdor's cure going to take to find? He needed it sooner rather than later if his declining strength was anything to judge by.

As he passed me, I reached out to touch his hand, but his fingers didn't even twitch in response.

"Do you even notice I'm here?" I blurted and Father blinked as he looked down at me in surprise. "Do you care what's happening right now? Your daughter's being sold. Me. Austyn." I squeezed his hand and his eyebrows arched, clarity seeming to come to him for a moment.

"Austyn," he sighed, and I swear I could feel his presence at last, rising from the depths of his eyes to truly see me.

"Yes," I breathed, but Magdor got herself between us, knocking me back with a flap of her hand.

"Let your father rest, girl. You are acting like a child. It really is unbecoming. What is all this nonsense of being sold? You are a princess of Osaria taking part in a tradition that stretches back for generations. You are more fortunate than every girl in the empire combined. Have some dignity." She pushed me towards Drake, hurrying to guide my father away and clearly preferring to separate us than halt the count from having more time with me.

I shared a look with my attendant Zira who was waiting by the door which led back into the palace, but she was stolen away by Magdor as she urged my father back inside, leaving us alone with a couple of the guards.

I faced the final suitor and Drake prowled towards me like a predator stalking its prey, his broad shoulders pressed back and powerful frame dwarfing me.

I swallowed thickly as he approached. There was something about the way he moved, a confident swagger that graced his limbs and a fluidity to his movements which made him seem ready for a fight at all times. It was unnerving and even a little exhilarating. This man knew something of adventure which I yearned to understand too. He had lived during the years of his life while I had only ever been a songbird with clipped wings, cursed to stare out at the sky from the confines of my cage.

He moved so close to me that I almost backed up, stopping a mere hairsbreadth away from his chest brushing against mine. I should have moved, increased the distance, done something to deny the presumptuous behaviour he was displaying and yet a dangerous curiosity rooted my feet in place. I may not have been a match for the strength of his body, but I was more than a match for the strength of his soul, and I wouldn't be forced to back down.

I tipped my chin up to look him dead in the eye, the darkness of his gaze seeming even more feral up close, like he was nothing but a pit of secrets and sin, just waiting to swallow me whole.

He smelled like the richness of the desert and something fresh, crisp, like pure damned freedom wrapped around something so undeniably male that it made my mouth dry out.

"Hello again, wife," he said with a dark smile which showed off his dimples and made my pulse quicken.

"I'm not your wife yet," I growled, my brows raising at the balls on this prick as his gaze trailed over my face and caught on my mouth.

He dipped his head, my attention falling to his lips automatically as he drew so close he was inhaling my air, and for a single, insane moment I thought he was going to steal a kiss from me.

I should have drawn back, pushed him away, something, anything other than draw in a sharp breath which parted my lips and allowed me to taste his words as he hesitated there, just one insane decision away from kissing me.

"Yes, you are," he said in a dark and simple promise, the force of his claim so solid and undeniable that I just blinked at him in surprise, failing to so much as respond before he straightened and walked away. Not even staying for the whole minute he'd been gifted in my company, leaving me frozen, in his wake.

I was unsure if the heat in my blood and my hammering heart was due to rage or desire for that arrogant, brazen, cocksure arsehole, but either way, I was mad. Utterly, infuriatingly, irrevocably, *mad*.

Who the hell did that count think he was?

I turned after him, regaining my senses and refusing to let him get the last word over me like that. I wasn't going to let him rattle me. I had nothing to lose, so to hell with him.

"I shall choose to slit my throat before I marry you, Nazari," I called and he paused in the entranceway to the palace, but he didn't turn back. I felt the guards fighting not to look at me, keeping their gazes riveted somewhere over my head, but they could hear me alright. "The throne will never be yours."

Drake finally looked back at me, and I found him grinning like a cad, my words only seeming to spark his intrigue. "At least wait until after the wedding night to kill yourself, love," he said and my lips parted at the casual way he spoke to me, the high-born lilt to his voice seeming to fall away and leaving something rougher and all the more intriguing in its wake. "I assure you, you won't want to miss out on that. And once I have you panting my name in my arms and feeling more sated than in any other moment of your life, you can go ahead and follow through on that threat. At least then you'll die happy."

He strolled away with a laugh carrying back to me as I just stood there with my lips parted in shock and my cheeks heating with the words he'd dared speak to me. He disappeared inside, leaving me scorching beneath the midday sun as I fought the desire to chase after him and put him in his damn place.

How dare he speak to me like that? I was the princess of Osaria, and I would not be claimed by any man – especially not one who worked to fluster me and seemed to have no respect for rules or propriety.

The next time I saw him, I'd be ready for him though, and he might just find out that this delicate flower he sought to claim had thorns of her own.

DRAKE

CHAPTER THIRTY ONE

I followed a servant along corridors more opulent than any rooms I'd ever seen as he led me to my chambers. *Chambers. Plural.* I'd never had more than a single room to call my own and I was one of the wealthiest thieves in The Den.

This whole pageant idea was damn brilliant. Even if Cassius *had* come up with it. It didn't matter, I was going to win the tournament and marry the princess and be the emperor one day. And all because I'd found that coin.

I chuckled to myself as I thought back on that beautiful blush which had risen in the princess's cheeks as I'd forced her to give thought to the feeling of having my cock between her thighs, and I found myself a whole lot more interested in that part of this deal than I had expected to be. I'd been paying attention to her throughout that entire farce despite my gaze fixing on the gardens more often than her face. But it was how I worked. When I had a con to run, it always worked best when I gave myself time to study my mark before approaching them. And much to my delight, Princess Austyn had turned out to be far more than some pretty, delicate flower full of refined grace and empty of intelligent thoughts. She had a wicked tongue to her and a spark in her eyes which made me think that marrying her might not even be as tiresome as I had initially assumed. Better yet, she had looked genuinely angered by me possibly even offended even while trying to hide the glitter of intrigue in her eyes and disguise the leap in her heart whenever I pushed into her personal space. And I did enjoy the push and pull of attraction when it was tempered with rage.

I reached for the chain at my neck and grinned as I twisted the little coin disguised as an amulet between my fingers. Yeah, everything was looking up for me and I was chomping at the fucking bit to get started on the next part of our plans.

The servant pushed the door open, and his mouth fell slack as he looked inside and found Kyra jumping up and down on the large red cushions which sat in the centre of the wide space. It was intended to be sat upon, not jumped upon. Her raven hair spilled down her spine and a look of pure joy was on her face as she bounced on the plush cushions. She'd dragged her blue skirt into her fists so that she didn't step on it as she jumped and my attention caught on the curve of her thighs as she exposed them without a care, the wildness in her lighting a fuse inside me as I watched.

I raised an eyebrow at my Blessing as she finally noticed our arrival and looked over at us with a gasp of alarm.

"Is this not okay?" she breathed, her eyes widening in fear as she fell still, her hands still knotted in her dress.

The servant's mouth dropped open in shock. "What the-"

"No Kyra, it's not okay," I snapped as I pushed my way in past him. "Jump higher! I need to be sure there are no snakes in those cushions, or I won't sleep a wink tonight and you know it!"

"Sorry, Master," she gasped, and she started jumping more aggressively as I turned back to the servant who stood gaping in the doorway.

"The one time I trusted another man's assessment about there being no snakes present, I was bitten. Have you ever felt the venom of an emperian cobra sinking into your testicles? That is not a mistake I will ever make twice," I said aggressively.

"No, of course not," the servant muttered, glancing at my crotch in horror before lowering his head submissively.

Shit, I don't think I'll ever get over how good that feels.

I'd never given much thought to the way servants simpered and bowed to the upper Fae - in part because I'd always refused to bow myself and in part because I'd never once considered having anyone bow to me. But now that they were, I had to admit I was enjoying it. I didn't even care that it made me a hypocritical arsehole because I was riding a power high, and I had no intention of coming down from it any time soon.

"You can fuck off now," I added as the servant continued to linger.

He backed up quickly, muttering apologies and dragging the door closed behind him, and I turned to Kyra with a grin.

She was still holding her skirt up and I could practically see her arse, my gaze stalling there for several seconds. A pool of warmth built in my gut, and I took a few steps closer to her, unbuttoning the collar of my tunic and wondering whether she still thought I was ugly. I didn't want to admit how much that bothered me. Especially since she'd revealed her own captivating Fae form and the sight of her kept drawing my eye.

"Did I just hear you telling someone to fuck off?" Cassius growled as he appeared from a doorway on the far side of the room, and I tore my gaze away from Kyra's flesh somewhat reluctantly.

"It wasn't Master's fault," Kyra said quickly, and Cassius looked up at her where she still stood on the cushions.

I offered her my hand so that she could climb down, and she eyed it hesitantly before shaking her head and hopping down unassisted. I tried to ignore the flicker of disappointment that minor rejection stirred in me and gave my attention to Cassius instead. He looked all kinds of irritable, and I heaved an internal sigh at the lecture I could feel coming.

"It was just a servant," I said dismissively. In The Den I told people to fuck off at least eighteen times a day, so I really wasn't sure what the big deal was, but Cassius looked about ready to bust a gut over it.

"That is a royal servant who has most likely worked around nobles his entire life. As we speak, he is probably off telling everyone he bumps into about how the Count Nazari is completely lacking in common manners," Cassius hissed.

"And about his fear of snakes," Kyra added with wide eyes. "Maybe you should command me to make you snake-proof," she added as an afterthought.

"What are you talking about?" Cassius asked with a frown.

"The servant caught her jumping on the cushions like some wild creature let loose in the palace, so I pretended she was doing it on my orders because I'm afraid of snakes," I said with a slight shrug. The lie had come easily to my lips, I'd worked enough cons to know that thinking on your feet was part and parcel of the deal, and I doubted many people would mistrust a lie that made me look weak.

"Well now if any of the other suitors want to intimidate you, they'll know to hide a snake in your bed. Congratulations on giving them a piece of knowledge to use against you like that," Cassius muttered like he thought I was a damn idiot.

"Then the joke will be on them, because I'm not really afraid of snakes at all," I replied, with a scoff. The slums were full of snakes who liked to hide in the shadows of the buildings and prey on the many rats which lived about the place. I'd woken up to find a python in my bed more than once and I had no real fear of the creatures. Their bites hurt, but not as much as a stab to the gut and I'd sooner come face to face with a snake than a rat who might give me some disease. "I once bit the head off of a viper," I added for effect.

Cassius raised an eyebrow in disbelief, but Kyra's eyes widened with amazement, and I found myself wishing it were true. Though I imagined the act wouldn't be in any way enjoyable.

"Really?" she breathed, drawing closer to me.

"No, not really," I admitted, and her tinkling laughter rang out in response. It hadn't exactly been a joke, but if it made her laugh, then that was fine by me.

"Oh, well if you do turn out to be afraid of snakes then I could come to your bed with you and make sure that none appear in the night?" she offered, and I smiled at the idea of that. I wondered if she realised that what she'd just said could be interpreted as an offer of her flesh, but somehow, I doubted it. She seemed a little too innocent for that or at least uninterested in pursuing the idea with me. *Which is a damn travesty.*

"Maybe we should think about returning Kyra to the coin if she's going to draw attention with her peculiar behaviour?" Cassius suggested before I could reply.

Kyra recoiled like he'd struck her, scrambling away from him, and moving closer to me as her eyes widened in fear. I ground my teeth as I moved between them, tension lining my posture and my fingers flexing with the desire to ball into fists.

"*No,*" I growled.

I wasn't entirely sure why I cared so much about that point, but I could see that the idea of going back into the coin terrified my little goddess, and I refused to do that to her after everything she'd given me. I might have been a selfish bastard, but she'd only ever asked me for one thing, and I refused to go back on my word about it. Besides, I knew what it was to be trapped inside a place you wished you could escape, and I had no intention of forcing her back into her nightmare.

"She isn't ever going back inside the coin unless she chooses it herself," I said. "And I don't want you to mention it again."

Cassius's eyes moved to Kyra as she peeked out from behind me, and he sighed as he nodded.

"I'm sorry, Kyra," he breathed, swiping a hand down his face as he fought to regain his composure. "I'm just concerned about Magdor realising what you are. She wanted you for herself and I don't believe her motivations can be good. I fear what she planned on doing if she got her hands on you and I am just concerned about her figuring out who you are."

"I'll be more careful," she promised breathily. "I won't jump on the furniture again."

"That's all settled then," I said, ignoring the tension in the room and kicking my boots off as I headed for the cushions, feeling the weight of her adoring stare on me once more and not hating the feel of it.

I threw myself down onto the soft red cushions with a groan. I'd never sat on anything this comfortable in my entire life and I was pretty certain that I could get all kinds of used to it.

"Where is the coin anyway?" Cassius asked ever so casually like he had no plans at all to steal it from me, which I doubted. Sneaky motherfucker.

"It's safe, mate. Don't worry about it," I replied dismissively.

"It's just that, like I said, Magdor was desperate to possess it and if it fell into her hands then I can't begin to imagine the damage-"

"No chance of the empress getting her hands on it. Or anyone else for that matter," I added, fingering the necklace as I caught his eye with a challenge in mine.

"Is that it?" he asked, seeming impressed by the means I'd already gone to disguise it.

"Sure is, and this chain can't be broken. So unless someone rips it off of me or removes my head, it's not going anywhere." I grinned, pretty damn pleased with myself and Kyra for coming up with this.

Cassius seemed satisfied with that, and I leaned my head back, sighing as I soaked in the opulence of the rooms I'd been given.

The central space was wide, a long terrace with wooden shutters leading out to a balcony thick with potted plants coated in large, pink flowers situated ahead of my position on the cushions, the open grounds of the palace gardens beyond it should I wish to sit out there and take in the view.

There was a heavy wooden table behind me, a bowl of fruit left out on it alongside a pitcher of water which looked to have honest to the Fallen ice floating within it.

The space itself was painted a pale sand colour, four archways leading off of the central room, each with double doors set within them which all stood open, offering glimpses of bed chambers and a bathing chamber with a huge copper tub sat at the heart of it.

Luxurious didn't come close to describing it and somehow, it was all mine to use as I pleased. The common street thief a guest of the royal family themselves.

A breath of disbelieving laughter escaped my lips as I just sat there and took it all in, resisting the urge to pinch myself and check if this was all real and not some dream. But even my most ambitious dreams couldn't have conjured something this divine. This place wasn't meant for the likes of me. And yet here I was, my lower Fae arse resting upon cushions worth more than I could guess, and my eyes set on the throne which had sat above me and all those like me for generation upon generation. If I truly did manage to claim the thing for my own, I might just keel over and die of shock. But in the meantime, I intended to enjoy each and every decedent luxury which this opportunity presented me to its fullest.

Cassius moved to sit on the other end of the cushions, lifting the cushions there and moving them aside like he couldn't even allow himself that simple comfort and sitting just as rigidly as always once he got himself into position.

I could feel his eyes on me as I pushed my hair back out of my face, but I let the words he wanted hang in the silence between us, tipping my head back and looking up at the elaborate candelabra which hung from the ceiling instead, watching the way the metal frames around the candles cast ever moving shadows flickering across the curved ceiling above.

"So?" he asked stiffly, and I could tell he was practically bursting to know how the Unveiling had gone.

I kicked my feet up onto a dark coffee table which sat before us, and I could feel him trying to contain a cringe. Imagine the horror; a filthy street bastard placing his boots upon a table in the palace.

"Yeah, she's a sight to behold," I said, placing my head in my hands and spreading myself out to get more comfortable. "A bit forward for a virgin, I have to say. I was pretty surprised when she begged me to come to her chambers tonight and make a real woman of her. But I told her she'd have to wait 'til our wedding night for that." I smiled to myself, wondering how much he could take before he'd strike me, and I swear I could actually hear him grinding his teeth in fury as he fought to contain himself.

"And she didn't even mind about your face?" Kyra breathed, her eyes widening as she crept closer, taking a seat on the back of the cushions close enough for me to be able to see her even while I kept my eyes on the ceiling. "That's so romantic."

"The princess of Osaria would *never* invite you to her bed like that," Cassius snarled in outrage, ignoring my little goddess, which was a good thing because her words were enough to incite my own irritation.

I released a bark of laughter, my blood heating, and the desire to keep pushing at Cassius building in me beyond the point of fun as I considered goading him into a fight simply for the thrill of it. "Well at least not until I marry her after the pageant, eh?" I taunted.

"To do that, you would have to win the pageant and I highly doubt that a low born criminal like you would ever-"

"There's the truth then at last," I said, snapping my fingers as I pointed at him and pushed myself to sit up again. "At least now you're willing to admit that you think I'll lose."

"I never said I thought you'd win," he stated haughtily.

"But what if I do?" I asked and the question hung between us. He knew what I could do in a fight. He knew it wasn't impossible, and yet he'd brought me here all the same despite the fact that he clearly hated the idea of me winning this thing so much that it was eating him up inside.

"Then I suppose that will mean that you're worthy of her hand," he said in a tone of voice that made it clear he didn't believe any such thing. In fact, he looked inclined to rip my damn head off for the mere suggestion of it, and I had to wonder just how deep his infatuation with the sweet little princess ran.

"I'm not a fool, Cassius. I know you aren't just going along with this without a reason. And I know you manipulated me into participating in this pageant despite the fact that you don't seem at all enthusiastic about the prospect of me taking part, let alone winning. So that means you wanted to come back here for your own reasons. I only went along with you because your plan actually seems like a better one than any I could have come up with to take the power and authority of the emperor. In fact, the pageant will make it all too easy for me to gain everything I ever could have wanted with as little effort as possible. So come on, tell me why you were desperate enough to try and trick me into coming here. Tell me why you worked so hard to trick me into this position and make your own way back here. Tell me why you thought I was stupid enough to believe you wanted to come here and 'exonerate your name' when you're a criminal in the eyes of the crown and I know full well no pardon would ever be given to you."

"You're right," he said, dropping any pretence he'd been clinging to and just owning his actions. I respected him more for that much at least.

Kyra watched our exchange with wide eyes, but she didn't seem to want to voice an opinion. Or maybe she didn't have one. I guessed what we did or didn't do mattered little to her.

"So what is it then? What's so important to you that you wanted to come back here and be amongst the people who sentenced you to death for simply looking upon a pretty face?" I pressed, unwilling to let this go now that he was finally facing it.

Cassius didn't seem to want to answer but I was done with playing this game. We were here in the thick of the biggest con I'd ever attempted, and I refused to carry on without my eyes open to all components.

"Magdor," he growled, her name a curse on his lips. "Ever since she arrived in the kingdom, everything that the emperor had planned to do to improve our beautiful country has been tossed to the wayside. He's different since he married her, and I know it's more than infatuation with his empress. She is using sorcery or something even more sinister to manipulate him to her own purposes, and I fully intend to get the evidence I need to see her executed for her crimes so that Osaria can be free to prosper once again."

I raised an eyebrow at his impassioned speech and let out a low whistle. Sure, he'd made a lot of grand statements about the way he thought things should be and hadn't been at all shy about voicing his dislike of the empress before this, but I hadn't realised he was actually fool enough to try and stand against her.

"Magdor asked me to fetch the coin that housed Kyra, that alone is evidence of her witchery," Cassius said gravely.

"She wants me?" Kyra breathed and I nodded.

"And in the wrong hands, I believe you could be most dangerous," Cassius said. "Am I wrong in that?"

"No," she said, a tremor to her voice and horrors in her eyes which made my hackles raise. "The wrong hands have held me before. They have done such terrible, terrible things with my power."

I didn't like the sound of her being forced to turn her magic to the advantage of monsters, and I stared at her in discomfort for a long second before returning my attention to Cassius.

"Don't want much then, do you mate? Just the death of the damn empress," I muttered.

"Says the street thief who is trying to claim the hand of the princess and the crown to Osaria itself," he tossed back.

"Fair point," I conceded, the fight going out of me as fast as it had begun to rise.

His jaw tightened and I could tell there was no talking him out of this. I turned over his plans in my head and came to the conclusion that I didn't care. If he wanted to risk his life by going after some witch, then more fool him. And in the meantime, I'd continue to use his guidance to pass myself off as a count and win the princess's hand in marriage. It didn't matter if he thought I had what it took to win in the brawls or not – I knew for a fact that I did. Actually, it seemed to me like we could both get what we wanted from this arrangement simply enough, so I was quite happy to allow him to continue with his plans just so long as he continued to coach me in all I'd need to complete this con.

"Well, on your head be it, mate. If that's what floats your boat, I won't get in your way. You keep helping me and I'll keep on providing you with your cover story. Win-win. And when I'm emperor I'll give you your old job back as my royal bitch for good measure."

"A royal guard is a position of absolute prestige," he replied indignantly. "Only the best of the best are selected to join our ranks and-"

"And you're made of steel. Got it." I gave him an amused look and he gave up on trying to lecture me about the importance of his chosen profession.

Cassius sighed heavily and the arguments went out of him. "For now, we need to focus on getting you through the first brawl," he said. "A scroll arrived before you got back. You'll be facing Lord Kalaviv in the first round tomorrow. It will be a fight, man on man, no weapons will be permitted. Everyone has had their opponent chosen randomly by the judges. The scroll explained that each round will offer up a new challenge to the suitors, but it will not be announced until closer to the event. The suitors will gain points based on their performance, not just whether they win."

"Alright then. So I'm facing peacock with the flashy swords in round one? I can take him easy," I said confidently as I started unbuttoning my tunic. It was hot in the room, and I always preferred to give the breeze a chance at finding my skin if it appeared.

"Well, you need to do it like a nobleman to ensure you are awarded the highest points possible," Cassius said and I groaned at his serious expression.

"No dirty tactics then?" I guessed. Being noble certainly seemed to go hand in hand with being boring as fuck more often than not.

"It would help if I knew a little more about the way he fights," Cassius murmured to himself thoughtfully.

"He's from the Forken Empire and a war hero apparently, but anyone who has to announce themselves as a legend probably isn't one really." I shrugged out of my tunic, noticing Kyra's gaze trailing over my muscular chest and the ink that coated it, resisting the urge to smirk. *Ugly my arse.*

"You mean like the way *you* did when we met in the dungeons?" Cassius shot back.

I barked a laugh at that. "Fair point. But where I come from, everyone knows my name."

"And now those same people all know that you're dead too," he said, no doubt aiming to wound with that reminder, but I felt no loss over the end of that life, so his blow fell short of landing.

"I'll take that trade," I said, indicating our extravagant surroundings. Seemed like I was doing pretty damn nicely out of our new arrangement to me. Why would I grieve a life of poverty in the face of this?

"You really don't care about any of the people you've had to leave behind?" he pushed.

I considered the question for a moment. I'd joined The Forty at the same time as Balthazar when we were thirteen and I'd spent a hell of a lot of time with him over the last fifteen years. But we'd always been more like rivals than friends when it came down to it. And I liked Pip well enough, even looked out for him when I could, but he was just some street kid who made me laugh. There were other members of The Forty who I'd drunk and laughed with many times, but none of them mattered enough for me to grieve over losing them. I'd figured out a long fucking time ago that the only person I could afford to give a shit about in this miserable world was me, and I was planning on doing just that.

"No, not really," I admitted.

"You're as lonely as me," Kyra breathed and I frowned at her as her eyes glimmered with tears, making the gold in them seem to swirl with magic.

"I'm not lonely," I objected. "I'm just alone. There's a difference."

"Yes, there is a difference," she agreed. "I've been stuck alone for more time than I could count, wishing that the day would come when I might be surrounded by people again so that I wouldn't have to be alone anymore. You have been surrounded by more people than you could count for your entire life, but instead of taking joy in the relationships you could forge with them, you have chosen a miserable life of solitude. It's kind of sad when you think about it. You've turned your nose up at the one thing I yearned for more than anything."

I frowned at her for several long seconds, not liking the way that assessment made me not only seem like a total arsehole, but also like I was somehow missing something of my own.

"I never said I was miserable," I said eventually.

"You never said you were happy either," she replied and the look she gave me was like she was peering right into my soul, cutting me apart and seeing all of the damage which lay inside me.

I'd learned the hard way a long time ago what the cost of trusting someone was. And without trust, relationships never really had a chance to bloom, so I'd gone without them rather than allow myself to be vulnerable ever again. I only needed to look in a mirror to be reminded of what trust had cost me, and I fisted my hands as I fought the desire to score my fingers over the tattoos which had been forced onto my skin while I screamed for a mercy which never came.

I pushed myself to my feet, shaking my head irritably as I strode across the room in search of a bed. This conversation was starting to push my mind into a place I fought to avoid on a daily basis, and I just wanted to rest a while without having to hear their constant chatter.

"Where are you going?" Cassius called as I stepped into a wide bed chamber with a huge four poster bed at the centre of it. Silk sheets in shades of gold and silver lay across the thick mattress and a thin, gauze curtain surrounded it where it sat before a wide window which looked out on the gardens.

"I'm having a lie down," I replied tersely as I dropped my tunic to the floor followed by my britches and clambered onto the soft bed.

"Well enjoy it while you can - in an hour we need to start preparing you for the fight tomorrow," Cassius called firmly.

"Whatever," I mumbled as I closed my eyes, taking in the peaceful silence of the wide space which surrounded me and trying to focus on all that I had, instead of allowing any of their inaccurate assessments to permeate my skin.

They knew nothing of the life I'd lived or the choices I'd been forced to make for my own survival, and I didn't have to answer to a single one of them or their judgement on things they knew nothing about.

I'd always found it easy to shut my brain off and get to sleep when I needed to, but as I drifted off, one thought kept whispering through my mind.

If Kyra had spent all that time wishing she had people to care about, then was she right about me wasting time being alone?

The bang of a metal door sounded at the top of the stairs, and I flinched as I scrambled to the back of my cage, the iron bars which fronted it making me feel impossibly weak even though I wasn't touching them anymore. But in my restless sleep, my limbs had fallen slack, and I'd woken finding my leg pressed to them, the little strength I'd been holding onto sapped by the vile metal.

I pressed my back to the stone wall of my cage and drew my legs against my chest, wrapping my thin arms around my thinner body and trembling as the burn in my legs drew all of my attention. He'd finished with them yesterday, telling me the easy part was over as the pain of the marks he'd branded onto my flesh damn near blinded me and I dipped in and out of consciousness.

These weren't normal tattoos which he was branding onto my skin. I'd seen men having their bodies inked in the marketplaces on many occasions, and though they might have flinched and cursed beneath the tip of the needle as it was driven into their skin, they never howled with the agony I experienced as these patterns were forced upon me. And I was no weak child. I'd felt plenty of pain in my life through fists, the lash of a belt, even the crash of stones and rocks hurled at my skin for the crime of simply begging for food to fill my stomach. I didn't flinch easily, and I'd learned long ago never to show weakness or signs of pain. I could take a beating in silence, but I had screamed like a new-born babe while that ink had been forced beneath my skin.

"Bennit?" I breathed for the hundredth time since I'd woke a few hours ago.

There had been scraps of bread and a cup of water awaiting me in my small cage and I'd demolished them instantly, the hunger pangs barely sated by the meagre meal. But no matter how many times I'd hissed the name of the boy in the cage beside mine, he hadn't replied.

The brick wall which backed my cage ran around the left and right of it too, only the door was barred with iron so I couldn't see him in there, but the silence had had me trembling ever since I'd swallowed the last of my water.

Footsteps thumped down the stairs and I fought against the urge to close my eyes, staring out into the dark cellar as an orange light descended alongside the man who held the flaming torch.

My eyes burned from the onslaught of light after countless hours in the dark, but I welcomed it all the same. Better to see my fate coming, even if I couldn't run from it.

I watched as the hem of the ice white cloak descended the stairs on the far side of the dingy space, keeping my eyes from the table between here and there as I tried to pretend it didn't exist, the man who haunted my nightmares drawing closer.

He always arrived like that; his silence only ever broken once he began his work. I'd long since stopped begging or pleading with him, though Bennit still cried and begged. But he'd only been here a week, so he'd learn. Or not if his silence was as telling as I feared.

I watched as the priest drew closer, the height of my cage making it impossible for me to do more than stay seated here and keeping his face out of sight as he closed in on us.

He paused beside Bennit's cage, a heavy breath of irritation escaping him which proved my fears true. He was dead. Just like I'd be dead soon if I remained here much longer.

My throat thickened at the realisation that once again I was alone down here. Death come to claim the soul of yet another forgotten orphan who had been stolen from the streets and brought to this living hell. A shiver coursed through my weakened limbs and a foul taste coated my tongue. It was something between fear and grief, though I pushed both aside as forcefully as I could – neither would help me and they only made all of this worse.

The priest stepped away from Bennit's cage without a word and dropped down to peer into mine.

His dark skin was marred with endless scars which even extended over his bald head, and his eyes were white with blindness, but he still stared directly at me like he could see with something other than them.

He unlocked the cage and opened it, his hand lingering on the iron as if it didn't affect him at all, and I tensed in anticipation of what would come next.

I cried out as his hand snapped out like a viper and snared my ankle in the clutches of his filthy fingernails which bit into my flesh and drew blood as I kicked and struggled.

But it was no use, just like every other time he came for me, the full force of my blows and most desperate flailing of my limbs were never enough to fight him off. But I wouldn't give up. Not ever.

And as he strapped me to the table again, pinning my arm in place to one side of me and started up that chanting which haunted my every waking hour, I started screaming. Not from the agony of the foul ink that was being driven into my flesh even though it burned its way through me and tore me apart from the inside out as it merged with my body. No, I didn't scream from the pain, although that leant strength to my voice. I screamed in the hopes that someone might hear me, might come to my aid despite no one ever caring enough to help me before now.

So I screamed and I screamed and I ripped my throat raw as I stared into the lifeless eyes of Bennit, who lay dead in his cage, the ink which had been driven into his flesh now pooling on the ground around him as if his body could no longer contain it in death.

But no one came to rescue me. No one ever came for me.

CASSIUS

CHAPTER THIRTY TWO

While Drake was sleeping, I headed across the room to leave, knowing now was as good a time as any to start my hunt for evidence against Magdor.

I gripped the door handle, my sole purpose for living now seeming to thump inside my veins.

Protect Osaria. Stop the pageant. Save the princess.

"Where are you going?" Kyra called and I blinked out of my focused state, glancing back at her where she sat crossed legged on the coffee table, her skirt hiked up around her thighs and her feet bare.

My lips parted on any number of things that I might have been able to say about propriety or the way upper Fae tended to present themselves, but as she tilted her head at me with a naïve kind of innocence in her eyes, I found myself holding my tongue. I didn't get the feeling my advice would make much difference where she was concerned anyway, and Drake seemed content for her to behave as she liked. I had my hands full trying to form him into some semblance of a respectable man, and I couldn't take on the task of taming a mystical creature too.

"For a walk," I answered her question somewhat lamely.

"Ooh, can I come?" she asked, her eyes so bright they actually shone for a moment.

If anyone looked too closely at her, they might notice things like that. How there was something so captivatingly magical about her which meant she simply couldn't be a normal Fae. I knew Drake was against confining her to the coin, but I was starting to think it would be best if she at least remained in these rooms. There was no denying that she was a beautiful woman – or at least, she took the form of one - and I very much doubted she would be able to get far without drawing the eye of one man or another. It would only take one small slip for someone to notice something wasn't right with her.

"Sorry, Kyra, it's too risky. I need you to stay here."

Her expression fell and I glanced towards Drake's door, wondering how much longer he might sleep.

"But you have the very important task of protecting your master while I'm gone."

"I do?" she breathed, and I nodded.

"Yes, don't let anyone put snakes in his bed," I said with a small smile, and she nodded firmly, hurrying to sit in front of his door.

"No snakes," she said seriously.

In all fairness, if I'd been a servant on the receiving end of some nobleman's fury, I might have been tempted to shove a snake into his sheets. I'd often been tempted to do shit like that to my former captain. But that wasn't the way of guards. Those urges had been stifled, repressed, and beaten out of me.

Propriety, respect, and a ferocious protection of the Lunarelle royals was all I knew. Yet I was now a fugitive keeping the company of a thief. I had a hand in deceiving Princess Austyn into believing that Drake was an apt suitor, but it wasn't like he'd win the pageant. It was all in the interest of saving her father, getting the kingdom back in order and on its way to greatness again.

I ran my hand over the stolen scimitar at my hip.

Who are you kidding? You're as bad as Drake now.

No, I'll return it.

Later.

There was something running through my blood, keen and unknown. A thrill I couldn't shake.

Why does it feel so fucking good to forgo the rules sometimes?

I stepped into the immaculate corridor, laying my faith in Kyra's disguise to keep me safe from recognition.

I headed along the hallways I knew so well, passing by servants as they brought food to the suitors' chambers. They paid me little attention as I increased my pace, heading towards the east of the palace where the royal quarters were. Magdor had her own special quarters in the east tower, like a crow in a nest. The previous empress had never asked for such a thing so why was I the only one who thought that was suspicious?

I didn't know how I'd get dirt on her just yet, but I knew I had to. I had to catch her at her vile witchery. But then what?

Think, Cassius, think.

I reached the arching doorway which led to the eastern halls but found my way blocked by two guards that I knew. Rakus and Fikel. I'd trained with them, we'd stood beside each other for hours on end during our shifts and yet we'd barely shared any words beyond observations on the weather, current affairs, and comments on our training. How was it that I'd spent so many years in the company of these men, and I suddenly felt like I didn't know them at all?

My heart pounded as their gaze fell on me, but no recognition flashed through their eyes.

Thank you, magic girl.

I drew my shoulders back, marching towards them with every ounce of confidence that had been instilled in me during my years as one of them.

I'm still *one of them, dammit.*

"Good afternoon," I greeted them.

No response.

"I was getting to know the palace and thought I might take my liege on a tour this afternoon," I said, flashing them a smile I hoped might help them soften to me. It didn't.

"No one but the Osarian staff are allowed through these doors during the pageant," Rakus growled, his eyes darkening with a warning.

I wasn't getting past them. I'd been in their position before. If anyone tried to break the rules we were ordered to enforce, we were allowed to intervene with our blades.

"That's a shame. Good day to you." I turned right, heading out onto a large balcony which overlooked the gardens. It was quiet, sheltered by several potted palms and a red silk awning that offered some shade from the blazing sun.

I clutched the railing, staring across the grounds I knew so well. Every path, every shadow was my domain. I'd watched over it all for so many years and now I was outcast from that life.

"-no matter what he looks like," a female voice reached my ears.

"I'm not sure we can call him the gargoyle anymore. He's rather handsome," another woman replied.

I shifted to the edge of the balcony, glancing back towards the corridor I'd vacated, but the guards didn't have a view of me here.

"Magdor is despicable. How could she bring magic into the palace so freely?" the first spoke again.

My heart hammered as their voices drifted out of reach. What was I overhearing? Two maids discussing Magdor and magic? What if they knew something I didn't? Something about the emperor? What if they suspected what I did?

I threw caution to the wind, leaning over the side of the balcony and spotting a narrow ledge jutting from the wall beneath the line of windows. I tried to work out which rooms lay at this side of the castle and realised I was next to the princess's quarters.

I threw my leg over the railing and excitement pounded through my blood as I lowered myself onto the narrow ledge. I crept along it, pressing myself flush to the cool stone wall as I moved, knowing if I was caught the consequences would be dire. But why come here at all if I wasn't going to risk everything to prove Magdor's crimes?

A row of windowsills ran above me, and I reached up to grip onto one, taking in a slow breath.

I'm dead if someone spots me here.

Fuck it, keep going.

I carefully traversed the ledge, side-stepping until the voices reached me again.

"She thinks I don't know what she's up to," a female voice hissed. "But I know she's controlling my father. She has to be."

I nearly lost my grip on the window and my stomach swooped as I scrambled to keep myself in place.

By the Fallen, that wasn't just some servant girl speaking, it was the princess herself.

My eyes shot up to the cracked open window just above my head. If I straightened, I could peer in. But that made me all kinds of a lech. Then again...she had been Unveiled already. And I'd seen her before anyway...

The beast in me roused, a hungry devilish thing that crept into every part of my being and urged me on.

I straightened so I could look in, my pulse drumming solidly in my ears as I made that decision as if I had a right to.

Her back was to me and she wore a thin pink night gown, her silver hair woven into a long braid down her spine. Her attendant, Zira, was fussing about with her makeup but I could only focus on the woman in the room who owned every fibre in my flesh.

My heart rioted in my chest and adrenaline poured through my veins like liquid fire.

I needed to stop, but I simply couldn't look away.

"If she's got some Prophet offering her potions, what's to say she hasn't used one of them on my father?" Austyn growled.

"You think she's controlling him with magic?" Zira gasped.

"I don't know...maybe I shouldn't have said anything," Austyn said, a note of fear in her voice.

"You know you can trust me," Zira swore. "I'd never tell anyone anything you told me."

Austyn sighed. "Of course, I'm sorry. I know I can trust you. So...it's a possibility, isn't it? After what she did to Kahn, who knows what other kind of potions she's been feeding people," she said. "My father hasn't been the same since she arrived. You have to admit it makes sense."

My heart beat powerfully beneath my ribs as I felt like very wild thought I'd had about Magdor was finally validated. I'd questioned myself endless times, I'd driven myself mad thinking about this very thing, and now I was actually hearing my thoughts echoed by the princess herself.

Austyn held her suspicions about Magdor, and she was trying to work it out too. I supposed it could be possible that Magdor was outsourcing her powers, bringing elixirs or ingredients into the palace for her vile spells. If that was the case, perhaps she had people helping her. Perhaps my own guardsmen had been working to assist her, or the maids walking these halls were in her pocket.

"Austyn," Zira sighed. "That's a big accusation."

"But what if it's true?" Austyn pressed and I clenched my teeth, wishing I could storm in there and present all the suspicions I had too.

"How could you possibly prove it?" Zira whispered.

Austyn fell quiet and I frowned, sensing the toll this was taking on her. Magdor had stolen her father away from her, and it looked like she had stolen more than that too. There was something darker about her demeanour these days that made me want to go on a bloody rampage.

Austyn suddenly spun around and dropped her robe, revealing a set of lilac lingerie which was so sheer it was nearly transparent. My throat thickened and my cock swelled as I stared at her without blinking, my eyes scraping along the perfect sheen of her skin to the peaks of her nipples through the scraps of lace cupping her breasts. My hunger for her sharpened like a razor's edge and I found my throat raw with it. My fingers itched to claim her, the monster in me purred, urging me forward and in a moment of utter madness some part of me was tempted to go to her.

I forced my eyes up to her face and a whirlpool of amber stared back at me as I fell into the sea of her eyes. It was like the heart of the kingdom lived in there and I was hit with a longing to claim it for my own. All of it. I'd conquer the whole fucking world just to destroy anyone who told me I couldn't have her.

No.

I ducked my head, cursing myself as I clamped my eyes shut and conjured up a memory of being whipped by Captain Marik, every strike earned in this moment just as it had been back then. The scars on my back tingled and I felt the echo of them as if they were bleeding again now, the hot burn of each strike followed by the pain that bloomed like hell-born flowers along my flesh. They were my strength, a mark of my loyalty to the Lunarelles, and they helped push away my illicit thoughts.

"Pink or yellow?" Zira changed the subject.

"Pink," Austyn decided, and they fell into a conversation about dresses.

I clenched my jaw, hurrying back to the balcony and dragging myself over the railing.

I tried to remain in the punishment of my past, but I was lost to the clutches of those eyes again. My heart was beating harder than it ever had before and the imprint of her hourglass curves was making me harder than I'd ever been in my life.

I blinked firmly to try and force her body from my memory, but it remained there, her flawless skin branded in my head, my instincts so hungry for it that I had to squeeze the base of my cock through my britches to relieve some of the pressure building in it.

Great. Now I'm nothing but a pervert. Where's my fucking honour now?

Probably somewhere way down in the depths of hell waiting for my tainted soul to join it.

I pressed my back to the closest wall, swiping a palm down my face and

405

angling my thoughts to what I'd learned. If Austyn was right and Magdor was smuggling potions into the palace, that meant there was evidence no-doubt lying around in her quarters somewhere. Evidence of her breaking the law and using dark magic. Evidence that the emperor was under her control because of some atrocious elixir, and the punishment for that was unspeakable.

This was good, even though I'd committed a cardinal sin to attain this knowledge. What was another to add to my collection? I was already a damned man, though I'd still try to die as the most honourable one I could when the time came.

A shout caught my ear and I moved along the balcony, rounding a corner off to the west side of the palace and spotting a huge man with black curly hair training in a pit of sand. His dark skin glinted with sweat under the glaring sun, his tunic discarded at the edge of the square while he fought with a guard, tackling him to the ground and throwing fierce punches into his gut.

A maid stepped out from an awning erected beside it, clapping in praise. "Lord Kalaviv, your lunch will go stale in this heat."

My heart quickened as the lord rose from the bloody body of his guard and I took in the cut of him, from the confidence in his stride to the determination in his gaze. This was the man who was facing Drake tomorrow and it didn't look like he'd be easily beat.

He cracked his neck, dragging the fallen man upright by the hand. "Again," he snarled.

"But-" the maid called but he waved her off.

"I'll stop when I say I'll stop," he said, rolling his shoulders as another of his guards stepped forward to fight him.

I chewed the inside of my cheek as I watched him bring another man to his knees in a matter of minutes. When the sand was speckled with blood, I turned and headed back to our chambers at a fast pace, a knot tightening in my gut as I realised that I was sending Drake up against a lord who'd clearly had a lifetime's worth of training. Drake could make up some points with his technique, but he had little etiquette, so winning this fight was crucial to stop him from being put at an early disadvantage.

I needed more time, but the clock was already ticking.

When I made it back to our quarters, I marched towards Drake's bedroom and Kyra leapt to her feet in front of the doors.

"No snakes or enemies anywhere, sullen man," she said proudly. "Did you have a nice walk? You look a bit angrier than when you left. Do you enjoy being angry? Can someone be happy when they're angry? I hope they can, or else that means you're hardly ever happy."

"I'm not angry, I just need to speak with Drake," I said, trying to sidestep her but she darted into my way again.

"Oh, did I get the angry emotion mixed up with the happy one then? So you're always happy?" She frowned at me scrutinisingly then shook her head. "No, that can't be right otherwise your mouth would be in the upright position not the downward one. So you're definitely angry, sullen man. What happened?"

"Kyra, I don't have time for this," I insisted, but still she didn't move and as I didn't want to invoke the ire of a magical being, I didn't make any more forceful demands of her. "Please. I must speak with him."

"But Master is sleeping," she said. "And I really would like to hear about your walk. I heard one of the servants saying there's an orchard here where the apples grow as big as your head – is that true? I'm not sure I could eat that much apple, but I'd love to try. Will you take me there when Master wakes up?"

"I don't have time for this," I insisted, and her face fell as I crushed her hope in my fist and she nodded sadly, side stepping to let me by.

Guilt worked its way into my chest, and I hesitated as I took hold of the handle and looked to her, an apology forming on my lips and a promise to take her there when I had time. But then I remembered she was made of magic and perhaps this dejected look was just a ruse to lure me in so that I might be manipulated to her cause in future. Although, I had to accept I that hadn't seen anything cruel or monstrous about her yet.

I cleared my throat, pushing the doors open and finding Drake spread eagled on his bed, face up and butt fucking naked with absolutely no shame about him.

He cursed loudly, jerking awake and grabbing a blade so fast that I didn't even see where he'd gotten it from as he pointed it at me, baring his teeth in challenge as sweat gleamed on his tattooed chest. His eyes were wild beyond the point that I would have expected as merely a reaction to the interruption, and I frowned as I tried to figure out what had put that haunted, feral look upon his usually relaxed features.

Kyra padded into the chamber after me and I turned in an attempt to shield her from the sight of his naked body, but it was too late.

"Oh, it's very small. Or very big? It's bigger than mine was. Remember mine?" she gasped, staring unashamedly at Drake's body as he relaxed a little at recognising us, tossing the blade down on the sheets beside him and making no attempt whatsoever to cover his body.

"Yes, I remember." An amused smile twisted my lips, and I was surprised by who put it there.

Drake ran a hand over his face, seeming unsettled over something beyond seeing the two of us in his chambers before he dropped his hand again, glaring at us both and hiding whatever darkness had been haunting him as he grabbed some britches and tugged them on.

"It's big, Kyra. Get your sizes right," he muttered, but with less bite to his tone than I'd have expected, like the effort of engaging in such simple conversation was too much for him.

"Would you like it to be smaller? It must weigh you down," Kyra said brightly, and Drake's scowl quickly turned to smugness.

"Nah, little goddess, I'm good with how big it is – and so are the women I share it with," he replied, his voice taking on a flirtatious tone which had

Kyra running her eyes over his bare chest as she muttered something to herself which I didn't quite catch.

"You need to train," I said, wanting to move on from the subject of Drake's cock.

"What kind of training?" Drake questioned, raking his fingers through his inky hair, and pushing it out of his eyes.

"Fighting," I replied, earning myself a feral grin from him.

Drake followed me into the large central chamber bare-chested and looking more like his old self. He raised the dagger he'd aimed at me from the bed, and I had to stop myself from questioning when he'd grabbed it again. The man's sleight of hand was uncanny, and I had to acknowledge that his Affinities must have been something special to allow him to pull off such quick and subtle moves. Though he claimed to have so many of them that it was hard for me to tell which he truly possessed, and which were just bullshit pretences like that sex Affinity nonsense I refused to indulge in believing in for a single second.

"No weapons," I said, snatching the blade from him and tossing it onto the cushions.

"So you're looking for me to beat your arse with my bare fists then?" he questioned cockily and my blood heated at the challenge in his tone.

"I don't want you to do anything to my arse, thief. But if you can get past your fascination with it, I will teach you how to fight like a true lord."

Drake barked a laugh. "You're funny when you're not being a brainwashed bastard, Cass, you know that?"

"Well even brainwashed bastards have their moments, I suppose," I said, and Drake's eyes sparked with something wholly void of hostility for once.

I'd grown used to his easy smiles and laid-back way of presenting himself now, discerning the darkness with in him a little more easily than I initially had. If it was a mask, he wore it like a second skin. But something told me it wasn't; he was just both things. The cocky, arrogant arsehole who found it all too easy to charm his way through life and the cutthroat thug ready and waiting with a blade to drive into the back of anyone who crossed him. It may have been hard to marry the two sides of his opposing personality, but they were both as present and real as each other.

"Would you like me to make Cassius tell jokes every time he talks, Master?" Kyra asked. "I'm sure we can get him to agree if-"

"You will not get me to agree," I cut in.

"Sure you will," she countered. "Master can get you something nice to sweeten the deal. Like a horse girlfriend – or boyfriend?" She beamed.

"I don't fuck horses," I growled.

"Then why did Master tell me you did?" she asked in confusion, like the idea of Drake lying to her hadn't even occurred, and a growl built in my throat as Drake grinned widely.

"Yeah, Cass, why would I tell her that if it wasn't the truth?" he asked innocently, cocking his head to one side.

"Because you're a liar as well as a thief," I tossed back.

"I'd never lie about someone's sexual preferences, mate." He held a hand to his heart in mock offence. "You can fuck all the horses you like; I won't judge – just so long as the horse is willing. I ain't gonna see no pretty little mare forced to endure your advances against her will under my watch."

"This game is tiresome," I warned as Drake nearly choked on his own laugh. "You need to prepare for tomorrow."

"Go on then. Show me how to be a pompous prick. Though you're doing a stand-up job of it already right this second, I have to admit," Drake goaded me, but I didn't swallow the bait this time.

Kyra moved to sit on the cushions, crossing her legs and hooking her navy dress up around her thighs once more before picking up the blade and watching us keenly.

"Each fight will start with a bow." I pulled my tunic off, glad of the breeze flowing through the window as I dropped it to the floor. "Like this." I placed one hand behind my back and dipped forward.

Drake mimicked me, an irritating look on his face the whole time like this whole thing was one big joke to him. But he imitated me perfectly, so I had no reason to call him out just yet.

"Then take a fighting stance." I placed my feet, my right forward and my left behind before lifting my fists.

Drake copied me, though the look in his eyes said he thought this was ridiculous.

"Straight back, chin high. Look your opponent in the eye," I said. "It's a sign of respect."

"Right." He did as I commanded, and I was glad he picked up my instructions fast.

"No biting, no scratching and for the love of all Osaria, do not kick him in the balls. It will lose you valuable points."

Drake frowned in disappointment. "What's a brawl without a little ball kicking?"

"Because it is dishonourable. There'll be an audience judging you as the potential future of their empire. The princess will be watching and gauging your suitability too. This is a chance to show her your skill, your ability to protect her as her husband." My chest tightened at the mere idea of this thief claiming her, but he wouldn't win. Not against Kahn at least. And from what I'd seen of Kalaviv, it didn't look likely that he'd beat him either. "Most importantly, the judges will be watching your every move. You will be scored on skill, the kind of skill taught to high born Fae, so it is very important you get this right. Especially if you are to lose-"

"I won't lose," he scoffed.

"Well, I just saw Lord Kalaviv training out in the grounds," I revealed and Drake's brows lifted.

"And?"

"And he is a fierce opponent. Highly proficient with the strength of a soldier."

"Oh no," Kyra said in concern. "Shall I give you bigger muscles, Master?"

"My muscles are plenty big," Drake insisted, looking insulted by the suggestion that he might need help with this. "I've beaten far meaner bastards than some poncy lord."

Frustration flashed through me. "Not by fighting with honour, you haven't, thief."

"What do you even care if I win? You don't want me to win the princess and I'm here for the duration of the pageant regardless, aren't I?"

"No, Drake. You are not. Did you not even read the scroll explaining the rules of this tournament?" I pointed to the thing which had been left here for him on the oak writing desk by the farthest window.

"No," Drake grunted, and I sighed my everlasting aggravation with him.

"*Well*," I said through clenched teeth, working to keep my rage in check. "At varying stages of the pageant, the lowest scoring contestants will be removed permanently, but they are yet to reveal how long it will be before that happens. It could be after the first round for all we know. The traditions of the pageant vary throughout generations, and changes are made regularly so that suitors cannot prepare too well for the event and secure themselves undue advantage in the competition. Which means, Drake, we may have to leave the damn palace tomorrow if you do not gain enough points."

"Maybe you should do it, Master. It is quite nice here. I hope we can stay for a while." Kyra gazed around the room in wonder like she was seeing it for the first time all over again, and Drake's attention hooked on her for a few seconds.

His brow creased and I could see he was finally taking me seriously when he turned his attention my way again. "Alright then. Show me how to win with 'honour' -" he air-quoted the word "-instead of wasting air."

I blew out a huff of annoyance, knowing I had to keep my head right now. He may have been infuriating and all kinds of arrogant, but I supposed he *had* paid attention and executed everything I suggested skilfully so far. It was his smart mouth which was making this entire process so infuriating.

I ignored his presumptuous chatter and focused on what he needed to learn. All I could do was teach him as best as I could and hope it would be enough to buy us plenty of time in the palace. Every moment we remained here was valuable beyond words, buying me the time I needed to discover the truth of Magdor's sins, and I planned on making certain he did well enough to ensure our ongoing participation in this sham of a pageant for as long as I could.

From what I'd seen of his fighting skills back at The Den, I reckoned he had a chance at winning so long as he did exactly as I said. The problem was, Drake was a wild card. Unpredictable and a clear fucking menace when he wanted to be. He did have one quality that should keep his mind on track, however, and that was his desire for power and riches. He would play the part well if it meant it brought him closer to those things. Things that I would allow him to believe were within his grasp, but if I had to drive a sword into his chest myself to ensure that he didn't get his greedy hands on Princess Austyn in the end, then I wouldn't hesitate.

"Come on then." I beckoned him into a brawl, and he came at me like a rabid dog who'd been starved for a week.

He swung his fists wildly, landing two heavy punches before I rammed my own knuckles into his stomach. He wheezed, stumbling back before darting forward once more, his muscles firming, and teeth bared.

"Don't bruise my face," he snapped as I narrowly avoided his chin. "I want to look my best tomorrow."

"You could use Kyra to fix your face," I pointed out and his gaze darkened.

"I don't want you to hit my fucking face," he insisted, and I had to fight a scoff at his damn vanity. "The princess is going to fall in love with this face – it's our best weapon in this game we're playing."

"It makes no difference if she likes the way you look or not," I growled, throwing my shoulder into his and knocking him back a few steps which he followed up by aiming a fist straight at my fucking nose. Damn hypocrite.

I landed a punch to his side and a sweet satisfaction filled me at taking out a little of my frustration on him. Knowing that he wanted Austyn made me angry in a way I'd not known before. I refused to admit it was jealousy, but the searing discomfort in my chest told me otherwise.

We battled on, trying to knock each other to the ground with the ferocity of unchained heathens.

He curled a leg around the backs of mine and I struggled to stay on my feet, locking my arm around his neck before we crashed to the floor. Kyra released a whoop of excitement, enjoying every second of the show.

Drake started choking me and I shook my head. "This will lose you points," I rasped, and he released me.

I shoved him off of me and he rolled, slamming into the cushions and Kyra scooted backwards so that he didn't touch her.

"Wow, you're really bad at this," Kyra said to him. "Or are you good?"

"I'm better than good, little goddess, I'm the fucking best." He sprang upright, charging me down with a cry of rage.

"Don't let your anger get the better of you." I side-stepped and knocked him to the floor with a forceful shove. "Keep your head in the match. Think out your moves before you execute them."

He stood upright then leapt towards me, landing a hard kick to my chest. I hit the floor and coughed hard as he winded me. "Better," I wheezed.

I could feel the tingle of my Affinity racing through my blood like the memory of old magic lost to our kind which lit a fire in my soul at the thrill of the fight and I could see that same fire blazing in his eyes too. There was something so fucking energising about leaning into my Affinities like this, as if the powers the old gods had bestowed on our kind long ago were almost awakened by the use of them.

We continued on until we'd both beaten each other in several rounds, and we were panting from the exertion of our brawls. He was a force to be reckoned with. But even if he somehow beat Kalaviv, Kahn would still beat him on size alone. I had no doubts about that. But by the time that happened, I planned on having the evidence in place to take down his mother and him along with it.

You're not winning this pageant, thief.

Drake dropped onto a chair, panting as I poured us all a glass of chilled water left by the servants. He gulped it down and Kyra copied him like they were in a race, guzzling every last drop while watching him out the corner of her eye.

It was strange the way she seemed drawn to him like that, no doubt a side effect of his position as her master and yet it seemed like it was more than that too. Like she was…grateful? Perhaps even indebted to him in some way. She looked at him as though he had single-handedly saved her life, and she had pledged her soul to him in payment for the debt.

I personally saw plenty to be desired within the man she seemed to be unable to find fault in, but then again, I wasn't a magical entity bound to his will, so I had to assume her opinion was somewhat tainted by that.

I observed his tattoos curiously and finally asked the question that had been burning on the back of my tongue ever since the first time I'd seen them.

"How did a thief from the slums – albeit a damn good thief – afford tattoos as extensive and perfectly detailed as yours? There must be a small fortune of ink etched into your skin and I struggle to understand how you afforded it at all, let alone how you managed to convince an artist as gifted as the one who gave them to you to work countless hours decorating your flesh."

The mood in the room plummeted as fast as if I'd doused the entire place in ice cold water and Drake's inked hands fisted against his thighs as his entire posture stiffened.

"The dark never fades," Kyra breathed, shifting closer to Drake with pain in her eyes as if she already knew something I didn't, though she still held herself back from touching him.

For a moment I thought he was going to refuse to speak, but when he did, his voice broke the air like the crack of a whip.

"I neither paid for them nor wanted them," Drake gritted out, all amusement gone from his voice. "If I could cut them from my skin alongside the memory of how I came to have them then I would do it in a heartbeat."

"Someone did that to you?" I asked in surprise, the beauty of the designs which covered his body taking on a much darker aura as I ran my gaze over them again. The hours and hours of work which must have gone into placing them on his skin suddenly made my gut turn over instead of making my mind spin with the number of visits he must have had with the artist who created them. "How could they-"

"I neither wish to discuss it or remember it," Drake bit out. "But to sate your curiosity and dissuade any further discussion of this in the future, I'll tell you this much. I was held against my will for so long that I lost count of the

412

days and by the time I escaped, my flesh had been forever corrupted by the tainted ink you can see marking my body. I joined The Forty not long after that."

"You were just a boy?" I murmured in disgust, wondering what kind of monster would do such a thing to a child.

"I told you no one ever gave a fuck about me besides myself, Cassius," he replied irritably as if he wanted me to pay more attention. And I was starting to think he had a point because I hadn't once imagined he'd survived anything like that. Hunger and poverty? Yes. But this kind of abuse without a single person in the world who either knew or cared? That was a cruel fate indeed.

I looked at the man he presented to the world and saw what he wanted me to see, but there was more to him, darkness and horrors which haunted his past, layers of all kinds of memories which I doubted I would ever be able to fully comprehend because that kind of thing just didn't exist in the world I knew and had grown up in.

Drake shoved to his feet and crossed the open space in the centre of our suite, moving to the long table there and pouring himself another glass of water from the pitcher. I could tell he meant that as an end to this discussion, but I couldn't help but press him for further answers. I needed to know, to understand. I wasn't even certain why it bothered me so much, but I knew the lack of knowing what had happened to him would steal sleep from me unless I gained some level of comprehension here. What purpose did marking a child in that way serve?

"How did you escape?" I murmured, trying to figure out why someone would do such a thing to a child while holding my tongue on most of the questions I wanted to ask.

Drake downed his water without a word, but Kyra pushed to her feet, padding across the tiles towards him with her skin damn near glowing as she stared at him, looking like the mystical creature she was. Her lips parted in awe, and she seemed to see beyond the man standing before her to the truth of who he was in his soul, and I swear the air crackled with the power of all she was.

"Warrior born," she breathed, standing before him and looking up into his dark eyes as he towered over her, their gazes locking, something passing between them which was tangible and made my body tense with unease. "Through blood and bone and death."

Drake swallowed thickly, seeming caught in those haunting memories as he set his glass down on the table.

"Yeah," he agreed in a low voice. "It was something like that."

I sensed that he was done speaking about this and let the subject drop as Kyra continued to stare at him like he was the most fascinating thing she'd ever laid her eyes on.

Drake hesitated there, caught in her gaze for several long seconds before he broke the connection and looked down at the floor, clearly caught up thinking about things he'd rather forget.

I had so many more questions which wanted to burn a path right up and out of my throat, but I found myself unable to voice them, the ghosts which clearly haunted him in those memories warning me away. I knew he wouldn't speak any further on the subject and despite my curiosity, I respected that his secrets were his own to keep.

I cleared my throat, considering heading out to the bathhouse and giving him some space. "I might take a trip to the-"

"Where else did you go today?" Drake asked, interrupting me as his gaze snapped up to meet mine and I frowned at the accusation in his tone.

"I went looking for Magdor. Are you keeping tabs on me?" I growled.

"I like to be aware of everything going on around me, Cassius. Don't forget that."

I chewed on the inside of my cheek, shrugging as I turned away from him.

"Did you find anything?" he asked, and I sealed my lips. I still didn't trust him. And I certainly wasn't going to tell him exactly what I'd done today. I wasn't proud of what I'd seen despite the dark thrill that was quietly burning in my chest because of it.

"No," I said with a shrug.

I glanced at him, and his expression told me he didn't buy it, but I was saved from his questions as a knock sounded at the door.

I glanced at Kyra, making sure she appeared normal before calling out to tell the person outside to enter and a servant strolled in pushing a large dining cart.

Drake grinned, the shadows dropping from his gaze as if they'd never been there, and I was sure I'd never known a man who could don a mask as quickly and convincingly as he could. Among the guards we were trained to be stoic and supress all emotions, but Drake went beyond that, seeming to force his emotions to switch like the flip of a coin. Perhaps he was just a talented actor, but he was damn convincing either way. He strode forward and snatched a hunk of bread into his hand, lifting it to his lips before thinking better of biting into it like a savage in front of the royal servant.

The man eyed Drake curiously and the thief suddenly inspected the bread. "I want oat milk too." He whacked the bread over the servant's head, and I glared at Drake.

"Forgive me, sir, I'll have some brought immediately." The servant backed out of the room, bowing low and brushing crumbs from his hair as he went.

How the hell was this man supposed to pass as noble when he continually acted like an uncouth commoner?

Drake tore off a lump of bread and stuffed it into his mouth, chewing obnoxiously as crumbs flew everywhere, either trying to goad me or showing me just how spectacularly he was going to fail at passing for a noble.

"He looks like a hungry dog," Kyra said brightly.

"Yes," I agreed as Drake stuffed more bread into his mouth in defiance. "And this mutt has a lot to learn."

CHAPTER THIRTY THREE

We ate together in happy silence. Or at least I was happy. Master looked like the dark in him was working to swallow him up whole and Cassius was distracted, glancing towards the door and frowning so much that it made his face all scrunch and furrows appear in his brow.

I didn't need food to survive, but it had been such a long time since I'd had my pick of what to eat or experienced all the tastes each thing truly provided, so I just couldn't help myself as I moaned and sighed while we ate.

I grabbed a little ball of gooey chocolate deliciousness and moaned loudly as I placed it between my lips, closing my eyes and bathing in the pleasure of that taste. All the time I'd been stuck in the coin, I'd only eaten food I'd conjured from memory, and it had never tasted like this, or looked this good, or filled my stomach in such a real and satisfying way. I'd forgotten so much during my time in the coin that in recent years I'd only really eaten bland, grey, tasteless food and I hadn't even done that regularly. The taste of hunger had become so normal to me that I often didn't even notice it.

But here, in the real world where such delicacies existed to tempt me and an explosion of taste and satisfaction rolled over my tongue with every bite, I knew I'd never forget to eat again.

"Fuck yes," I moaned. "More."

Cassius cleared his throat and Master coughed around a mouthful of his drink, setting it down and giving me a look which made my toes curl as I met his gaze.

"Are you doing that on purpose, little goddess?" he asked, his voice gravelly as he pinned me in place with those dark eyes, and I slowly licked the chocolate from my lips as I looked right back.

"Doing what on purpose?" I asked.

"I suggest she doesn't eat in front of anyone else during our stay here," Cassius muttered, and I cut my gaze to him.

You're doing it again.

"Doing what?"

Acting like you lost your mind in that coin.

"I did lose my mind in there," I reminded myself and my master breathed a laugh before taking a final bite of his food and pushing his plate away from him.

"Did you always talk to yourself like that or has that changed since you became a Blessing?" he asked curiously, like he was interested, not like he thought less of me for it. He was clever and saw a lot, but he wasn't harsh or judgemental with his observations, only more curious for them and I liked that about him. He had an open mind even if he had closed his heart off entirely.

"I don't remember a lot about before," I admitted, trying for the thousandth time to recall even the simplest of details about who I had once been. All I had left were a few facts which I couldn't even corroborate with real memories. I knew I had loved my sister and that the emperor had caused her death. I knew that I had killed him and felt the heat of his blood on my flesh. I just struggled with everything in between like who I was and if I'd ever had dreams of my own or opinions that mattered.

You weren't like this back then. You were a force to be reckoned with before. Now you're just a broken fragment of the Fae you used to be. A memory caught on an ever-shifting breeze, impossible to capture and return to this body.

I bit my lip, not much liking that assessment but unable to deny the truth of it either because I didn't remember the truth.

"I'm going to take a trip to the bathhouse," Cassius said as he finished his meal too, carefully setting his knife and fork down, dabbing at his mouth with his napkin like a proper gentleman.

I looked to my master again as he sat back in his seat, legs spread wide as he sucked the last of his chocolate dessert from his fingertips and gave Cassius a taunting look.

"May the Fallen help us if you are required to dine in royal company," Cassius muttered, rising and nodding to me in farewell, like I was someone important.

I flushed at the attention, offering him a bright smile and he almost smiled back, making me wonder if he was still planning on getting my Master to put me back in the coin, or if he might just be starting to like me a little. I hoped he did. Then he wouldn't want me to go away anymore, and I'd have an even better chance of staying out here in the real world.

"You worry too much, mate," Drake replied dismissively. "Go relax in the bathhouse and make sure you have a good soak – with a bit of luck that stick up your arse will dissolve, and we can all have a lot more fun going forward."

"We aren't here to have fun," Cassius replied seriously.

"Well, you certainly aren't," Master agreed, and I giggled at Cassius's serious face before he turned and strode away.

As he tugged the door wide, a servant appeared beyond it, bowing her head to him before pushing an empty cart into the room and starting to gather the empty plates from our meal.

Master barely acknowledged her, looking towards the window as I felt that darkness in him pooling to the surface of his skin again and a shiver tracked down my spine.

I could almost hear the screams of his past, taste the blood from his memories and feel the pain in his heart. I wasn't sure if that was our bond speaking or if it was just that my past mirrored his. We had both been reborn in blood and ruin, and that wasn't a bond many people could feel for one another.

The servant retreated and the door closed behind her, leaving me alone with the man who owned me.

Stay quiet, you know they don't always like it when you speak too much.

I frowned because I did remember that; being punished for voicing my thoughts too often with other masters, but this one didn't seem like that. At least, I hoped he wasn't like that.

"Sometimes, when I was stuck sitting alone inside my coin for years and years in the dark, the only memory I could conjure was the feeling of sinking a blade into the flesh of the man who destroyed me," I breathed.

He turned those obsidian eyes on me in an instant, leaning forward and resting his elbows against his knees as he locked me in the intensity of his gaze.

"That's the only part of those memories I enjoy reliving," he said slowly. "The spill of blood against my flesh, the screams which weren't mine for once and the all-consuming feeling of finally making him pay for all he'd done."

His eyes brightened at that memory, and I licked my lips, almost tasting the blood on his hands which mirrored my own so beautifully. It probably wasn't something I should have wanted to have in common with him, but I did. I saw good in him alongside that brutality and seeing it gave me hope that there might still be some good in me too.

I pushed out of my chair and walked closer to him, my skin prickling with the desire to reach out and touch him while the fear in me held me back. If I tried to touch him and he turned out not to be real, I wasn't sure I could take it. But the longer I went without feeling the brush of his skin against mine, the more I thought about it, feared it, fantasised about it. I needed to know. Was I just a figment of my own imagination? Or did I exist just as he did? I didn't know and the need of that discovery was at once terrifying and intoxicating.

I hopped up onto the table in front of him, walking the length of it, his eyes trailing me like a wolf stalking prey as I crept closer, and heat blazed through my flesh. I sank down slowly, moving to sit right before him on the table, my legs falling into the gap between his thighs so that I could feel his powerful body surrounding mine as I drew close enough to taste his breath between us.

"Does it make us bad?" I whispered, wanting my words to be his alone as my fingers curled around the edge of the table and I leaned in, needing to be closer to him while still making sure I didn't touch him.

Master tilted his head to the side just a little, his eyes slipping over me as he considered the question while giving me his full attention, something in his dark gaze drawing me in and wrapping around me in a way I wasn't sure I'd ever felt before.

"I never held much faith in good or bad," he replied slowly. "But if this is what bad looks like then I'm not opposed to it. Tell me what it felt like when you killed the man who hurt you, little goddess."

I licked my lips, tasting the sin of that memory on my tongue and knowing full well I liked it. I could still hear his screams when I concentrated on the memory of them, still feel the heat of his blood on my flesh, the ache in my arm from the force of my blows.

I leaned in a little closer, tempting fate as the space between us dwindled and my heart took off galloping like a horse bolting for an open gate as a storm rose in the distance.

My tiptoes grazed his chair, landing on the edge of the wooden seat between his thighs as I pressed my weight down and leaned in to breathe my answer directly into his ear.

"It felt like freedom," I admitted in a low voice which scratched against my throat and left me feeling raw, exposed, shattered.

Master turned his head just enough to meet my eyes and I bit down on my bottom lip as I got lost in the galaxy which lived solely in his endless gaze. My fingernails bit into the wood of the table as I held myself there, suspended on the edge of a fall I couldn't come back from. The space between us was dwindling, fading, cracking apart and I was afraid of what might happen when it was gone. What it would be like if his flesh met with mine. Would the heat in his soul consume the fragile ash which made up the remains of mine?

His throat worked on a swallow, that truth just sitting in the space between us, asking to be devoured. I was captured by him and my need to know more of his secrets gnawed at me as I waited for him to make the decision which was building in his gaze.

"Take them from my flesh," he asked, a hint of pain and wounds unhealed to his tone that made my gut clench. I swear I could feel the agony of those tattoos being driven into his skin as if I'd been the one to suffer them myself.

"Yes, Master," I replied breathily, and his pupils dilated as his gaze remained fixed to mine.

I called on the magic in me to do as he asked, a rush of power cascading through my veins as it built in the air all around us and gusted through the room on an invisible wind. It tossed my hair around my shoulders and made the air seem to crackle as my nails bit into the table and I fought to hold myself there.

Master leaned back in his chair, looking down at his bare arms as if he could feel my power running into his flesh, but as I looked to the tattoos marking his skin, I frowned, finding them still there, the darkness of the ink seeming to thicken as I tried to force it from his body, impossibly fighting my power and refusing to do as I bid.

I began to glow as I drew on the well of magic inside me, trying to make it do as I commanded, and Master was forced to shield his eyes as I fought against whatever force was blocking my power from fulfilling his wish.

The light emanating from my skin burst from me in an explosion of power, and it felt like I combusted with the force of it as it ripped my hair around me in a maelstrom and set the windchimes hanging beyond the window rattling wildly. The glasses on the table shattered and cutlery was knocked to clatter against the tiles before the magic flared out and died down as quickly as it had arrived.

I was thrown flat on my back in the centre of the table among the shattered glass, feeling the slice of it piercing my skin as my chest rose and fell frantically, the impossible pressing down on me as I realised what I had done. I'd failed him. My one and only purpose was to make all of his commands come to pass, and yet something had blocked the magnitude of my power and refused to allow me to fulfil his wish.

"I'm sorry," I panted, pushing onto my elbows as I looked at him once more, backing up with fear stabbing into my heart, the enormity of my failure threatening to consume me.

I scrambled away across the table, not caring that it only made more glass cut into me and sent more of it crashing to the floor.

He's going to send us back into the coin.

I shook my head vehemently as the glow of my magic finally died down entirely and Drake was revealed beyond it, his gaze dropping to the tattoos still marking his body and a frown tugging at his strong brow.

"I can't remove it. There's old magic in them," I explained in a rush. "Something more powerful than me. I don't know what it is, but it goes beyond the depths of my power."

Drake pushed to his feet suddenly, the legs of his chair scraping across the tiles, and I almost fell from the table as I braced for his anger.

I winced as fury flashed across his features and I scrambled backwards, brushing against his wine glass which had been the only one remaining after my outpour of magic and knocking it over as I went, the spill of deep red liquid like blood across the wooden floor.

He's going to beat you or whip you or banish you forever.

Drake's hand clenched into a fist which slammed down on the table beside me with such force that the entire thing trembled beneath me. He bellowed in frustration, and I whimpered in panic, flinching away and cowering before him as I waited for the next blow to fall against my flesh.

This wasn't how I'd wanted to feel his touch for the first time, but I'd take it if it was what he needed. I'd accept any and every punishment he inflicted upon me for failing him just so long as he didn't banish me to the coin again.

"I can take it," I murmured, my eyes scrunched shut as I waited for that blow to fall, and I curled in on myself in anticipation. "All of it. Any of it. So long as I don't have to go back to the coin."

"You think I'm angry with you?" he bit out and his voice sounded so close to me that I couldn't help but crack my eyes open to look at him.

I found him leaning over me, his hands pressed flat to the table either side of me, the space between us infinitesimal.

"I'm sorry," I breathed again, wondering how many times I might need to apologise for this failure.

"It's not you, Kyra," he said, all gravel in his tone and savagery in his obsidian eyes. "It's that fucking priest, still haunting me from beyond the grave. I should have known better than to hope for the stain of his touch on my skin to be washed off so easily."

"I could try again?" I offered, still trembling beneath him as I tried to come to terms with the idea that he wasn't going to beat me.

"No," he grunted, a firm shake of his head dispelling that suggestion. "I might not like his mark remaining on me, but the ink on my skin has never been the real issue anyway."

"What's the real issue?" I whispered, my gaze roaming over his broad shoulders as he remained there, penning me in and holding me captive with the cage of his body over mine. Yet still he didn't touch me, and I didn't touch him.

"The mark he left in here," he replied bitterly, pressing two fingers to his temple before pushing off of the table and stalking away from me, leaving me lying there untouched and aching for his return.

"So you're not angry with me?" I called after him as he took a bottle of wine from the table and stalked towards his room.

"Not you, little goddess," he replied without looking back. "Never with you."

I bit down on my lip as the door to his chamber closed between us and I felt the rampant pace of my pulse slowly quieting.

"What now?" I breathed to the silence that fell in the wake of his departure.

Now you thank the gods that he didn't strike you, and work harder not to fail him again.

DRAKE

CHAPTER THIRTY FOUR

I woke in the middle of the night to the feeling of the mattress shifting beside me and I twisted around, grasping beneath my pillow for the dagger I'd stashed there.

Before I could locate it, my eyes fell on the figure in my bed, forcing me to still and Kyra bit her lip as she watched me. My heartbeat thundered in my ears and adrenaline trickled through my veins in response to being woken so abruptly. I couldn't force my thoughts into line quickly enough to tear my gaze from her mouth and the curve of her full lips which begged for far too much of my attention. What was she doing here?

She was barely a foot away from me, laying on top of the silk sheets while I remained beneath them, and her proximity was drawing a reaction from my flesh. She had changed into a pale yellow night gown, the silk trimmed in lace which brushed against the skin at her chest and thighs, making me all too aware of her body and how close she was to me.

"Are you awake?" she whispered, and I half wondered if she'd come here to offer her body to me, but the look in her eyes wasn't filled with desire, it was merely curious.

I cleared my throat, trying to banish the errant, lust filled thoughts which had pressed in on me all too easily at the sight of this beautiful creature creeping into my bed in the middle of the night and focus on her question.

"I am now," I murmured, my voice rough with lack of use as I gave up on hunting for my blade and shifted my hand to rearrange my overexcited cock instead. It had been too damn long since I'd had a woman and the unexpected torture of her company was only going to make that need in my flesh grow if she lingered here looking like that.

"You need to get up soon for the fight," she said.

"Really?" I glanced over my shoulder towards the open window which was letting in a cool breeze. It was still night, and the brawl wasn't until mid-morning, so I turned back to her with a frown.

"I'm not sure. Time doesn't really mean much to me anymore," she admitted, smiling shyly like she was embarrassed by that fact, but I found those kinds of details about the way she'd spent the last who knew how many years fascinating.

I probably should have been annoyed at her for waking me, but I couldn't quite summon any anger at her as she watched me with her wide, golden eyes, the weight of her stare making my body react in a way which was only really going to lead me to the kinds of thoughts I shouldn't be having.

I pushed my fingers through my hair and made an effort to scrub the alcohol fuzz from my brain, but I'd drunk three bottles of wine before passing out to keep the nightmares at bay, so I wasn't likely to manage that too easily.

Kyra watched me like I was the most interesting thing she'd ever laid her eyes upon, and I couldn't say I hated that. What man would object to a beautiful woman staring at him the way she did at me? The only problem was that in our current situation the only thing her proximity was doing was making my cock ache and my mind wander as I considered all the things I'd like to do to her body while we were alone here in the dark.

I shifted an inch closer to her then stopped myself with a grunt of effort. I'd never kept a promise to a woman I'd bedded before, and I wasn't sure if I should cross that line with someone who I had no intention of getting rid of. Besides, I wasn't sure if she even desired anything like that in her current form. She certainly didn't give me any indication that she found me attractive despite the way she watched me all the time.

Which doesn't piss me off at all.

I had to remember that this form was all magic anyway. She wasn't a woman, she was something…else. And I couldn't forget that. Especially when I was here to claim the most beautiful woman in the land. A princess. And yet as I stared at Kyra, it was hard to think of anyone but her. Hard to imagine any creature more desirable to me. But perhaps that was all a part of her gifts, ancient magic bound in tempting flesh.

"So did you have any other reason for waking me?" I asked, just to be sure, trying and failing not to think with my cock, but it was pretty fucking difficult when she'd climbed into my bed in the middle of the night dressed like that.

Kyra rolled onto her stomach and twisted towards me, resting her chin on her fist as she looked down at me. Her black hair fell around her face and coiled across the sheets between us, almost brushing against my bare skin. A strange feeling filled the space that separated me from it, almost like heat radiated from her and I wondered what it would be like to touch her. Would her skin feel as soft as it looked? Would I feel the spark of her power beneath her flesh? Or would my hand just pass through her the way Cassius's fist had when she'd first emerged from her coin?

"I was sitting in the dark, waiting for the monsters to come...but they didn't. It was so, so quiet," she whispered. "After a while I started to wonder if any of this was real or if maybe it was just this beautiful dream sent to tell me that I really *was* insane. Then I got this feeling, right here-" She tugged on the top of her nightdress, pulling the material down so that she could press her fingers against her heart.

My gaze lingered on her exposed flesh and the full curve of her breasts before trailing back up to her eyes which had suddenly filled with tears.

"-and I thought that maybe you weren't real at all. And I was still all alone inside the coin." A tear spilled down her cheek, glimmering silver in the faint moonlight which filtered in from outside.

I reached out to brush it away and she recoiled, a look of fear in her eyes which made me fall still.

"I won't hurt you," I breathed, dropping my hand to the space between us again, leaving it there on top of the silk sheets. "And I'm not going anywhere."

Kyra smiled hesitantly, blinking away the tears and the sight of it made warmth grow in my chest. I couldn't imagine what it would have been like to be stuck alone inside that small space for so long and now that she was free, I wanted her to know she could stay that way for as long as she was with me, that I'd never confine her to that hell again.

"You promise?" she asked, and I found myself nodding.

"You're safe with me," I swore, wondering at the words the moment they left my lips. It wasn't that I hadn't told those kinds of lies before, it was more the feeling that I wasn't lying at all. That I really meant that and intended to ensure it was the truth. I just didn't understand why I would care about her any more than I did about anyone else because I certainly had never made such an oath with the intention of keeping it before.

"I feel like I am," she agreed, twisting her fingers together like she wasn't certain she even wanted to admit that.

We fell into silence and I shifted against my pillows, placing a hand behind my head while leaving the other on the sheets between us. I wasn't sure if it was an offering or not, but I was starting to suspect that she was afraid to touch me for some reason and I wasn't sure what that would be.

"You said you don't remember who you were before you were bound to the coin," I said softly. "But what about after that? Do you have any memories of things you have done with the other masters you mentioned?"

Kyra started nodding then stopped abruptly, a frown pinching her brow. "Yes, but he doesn't know I killed them," she hissed to herself, and I arched a brow.

"You killed them?" I asked making her gasp and scramble backwards like she meant to run from me. "Wait," I called, and she fell instantly still, her fingers balling into fists as she knelt at the edge of my bed, the night gown she wore bunching up clinging to the curve of her hips and making me swallow thickly as I looked at her. "You don't have to run. You could just explain."

"Explain?" she breathed, her eyes darting to the door again nervously and

I waited, giving her a moment to consider that offer. "He can command me to stay anyway," she muttered, in argument with herself once again. "So it's not like I can run far. You remember what it was like with Master Ramish."

"What was it like with Master Ramish?" I asked curiously and she flinched again, like she never expected me to hear or react to any of the things she said to herself.

"He was...strict," she said with a shrug which was too casual for the dark look which passed across her eyes or the shiver which passed through her body.

"Strict?" I questioned, moving to sit up and patting the bed beside me, inviting her closer again.

"Yes," she breathed, a little more of that darkness passing through her expression before it was replaced with the hint of a wicked smile, the kind which teased at the bad in me, beckoning it forth. "Until he wasn't anymore."

I arched a brow, wanting to hear more but she remained quiet, muttering something to herself about saying too much, but I was pretty saw I caught the gist of what she was trying to keep to herself.

"He hurt you?" I asked, my voice low and my muscles tightening at the thought of it, the violence inside of me writhing with the desire to act. "Punished you when you didn't please him?"

Kyra nodded just a little and a low noise rumbled in my chest. I may not have been anyone's hero by any means, but I had seen and experienced enough of the way some Fae treated those they thought themselves above, to harbour a deep hatred of anyone abusing their position of power like that.

"I once saw a man kill his gally boy because he dropped a barrel of fish when he was unloading a ship down by the docks at the far west of the city where the ships hailing from distant Tymera docked. He hit him so fast and so brutally that his head was dashed against the edge of the ship's rail and his skull was shattered. The child couldn't have been more than ten. Dead just for making a mistake."

"What did you do?" she breathed, eyes wide and her posture falling unnaturally still.

I shrugged. "Nothing. It wasn't my business. But the royal guards did happen to see it too. I hung about, watching them while lifting coin from marks who crossed my path, expecting them to offer out punishment, a part of me hoping to see the bastard run through then and there for his crime. It was murder after all. The punishment for that is clear enough in the great empire of Osaria. A life for a life. Or so they claim. Turns out the only punishment the man faced was the price of a bag of gold kurus offered to the guards to look the other way as he tossed the boy's body into the Carlell River."

My jaw ticked at the memory of that day and the all too clear reminder of what value people like me held within this kingdom which claimed to be the crown jewel of the entire empire.

"You killed him," Kyra breathed the truth into the room and my lips turned up at the corner as I lifted one shoulder.

"I was on the lookout for a big mark anyway. It occurred to me that a man who could so casually part with a bag of kurus in payment for killing a child was in possession of far more wealth than he could possibly require. So I stalked him through the shadows once he finished his work overseeing the unloading of his ship, followed him all the way to the fifth ring where the wealthy merchants all live in their huge houses, working to lick the arses of the upper Fae and pretending they're just like them, hoping one day they might be accepted as such. I found a lot of coin stashed inside a safe beneath the floor of his office – but I needed his assistance in opening it for me. I will admit he was quite reluctant to part with his riches, but after I had relieved him of most of his teeth and several of his fingers, he found himself more willing to oblige me. I can't say that that kind of theft is my usual style, but I felt particularly motivated to carry it through. Unfortunately for the merchant, he happened to catch his throat on the point of my dagger as I was leaving, and I heard he bled out into his empty safe, left there to rot in the heat of the city until three days later, when a neighbour noticed the stench."

Kyra's breaths came a little shallower as I finished telling her my tale and I tilted my head at her, inviting her to share her truth with me in return if she so wished to.

Slowly, she shifted onto her hands and knees, crawling across the bed towards me and forcing my pulse to pick up as she drew closer, finally taking the position I'd indicated beside me and moving to sit there with her legs crossed as she turned to face me.

"Master Ramish was the nineteenth Fae to claim my coin," she murmured, her gaze lowering to her hands as she spoke, her brow tightening as she worked to recall the memory and I waited for her to go on. "He had heard of my gifts and what I was capable of but I... Well, I didn't always fulfil his commands the way he intended. If he asked me for a steak dinner, I would create a plate of grass because that is what a cow would eat for dinner. Or if he requested a hand sewn tunic of the finest design, I would make it to fit a small child instead of his large frame," she admitted, and I snorted a laugh.

"Why don't you ever play those games with me?" I questioned and her gaze swept up to look at me from beneath her lashes, the gold in her eyes glimmering faintly in the moonlight which made it in from outside.

"Games?" she questioned.

"I think I would quite enjoy them," I added, and surprise flickered across her face before she offered me a tentative smile.

"Even if I gave you a bed of straw instead of silk sheets?"

"There have been nights when I dreamed of the comfort of a straw bed, little goddess," I replied. "It would have been far preferable to cold stone and the stench of shit from the nearby streets. Every gift you offer me is far more than I could have ever dreamed of once. I may be enjoying the full benefits of your power, but I would be a fool to ever take it for granted."

"I..." Kyra trailed off, her eyes filling with tears once more and I cleared my throat, waving my hand at her to dispel the show of emotion. I hadn't said anything that wasn't true, but the way she was looking at me made me feel uncomfortable about it.

"Tell me what he did then, if he failed to find humour in the work you did for him."

"Ramish was not a tolerant man," Kyra said softly. "But he was clever. Cunning. He grew more careful with his commands, wording them in such a way that made it harder and harder for me to fulfil them in any way aside from how he desired. But I kept trying to sabotage him no matter what, feigning innocence whenever he lost his temper with me and shifting my body into smoke and magic if ever he raised his fist in anger at me. Until one day, I wasn't paying attention and he simply reached out and grasped my arm. I'll never forget the look on his face when he confirmed his suspicions that it was possible for him to touch me. And once he knew that was true, he started coming up with new commands. Ones where he would force me to stay in solid form and allow him to punish me for all the ways in which I infuriated him."

A coldness came over me which washed away all sense of amusement over the games she had once played with her power, and nothing but hatred for the man who had taken so much from her and rewarded her with pain and degradation filled me in its place.

"If that man still draws breath, then point me in his direction," I growled, seeing the scars of what he'd done to her plain enough on her face. "Call it payment for all you have offered me. I'll make him scream for you if you want to hear it, little goddess. I'll make him bleed so prettily."

Kyra drew in a ragged breath, her eyes meeting mine and the realisation that I meant that passing between us thickly. I didn't offer it lightly. It wasn't the kind of thing I did, solving other people's problems for them or inserting myself into business which had no impact on me. But Kyra's magic was offering me a life which I never could have even thought to steal for myself, and she had only ever asked for freedom from her coin in payment for it. I felt I owed her better than just the simple right to walk about beneath the sun and I would gladly offer her this if she wanted it from me.

"Ramish died many, many years ago," she replied, her lips lifting as she thought on that fact.

"How?" I demanded, the heat in my blood insisting upon an answer to that question.

"He believed he had me broken," she whispered. "After years of punishments and forcing my submission, he grew sloppy. He made a mistake. But that was all I had been waiting for. A single mistake which offered me an out."

"What was it?" I asked, the dark of the night seeming to wrap around her and showing me the truth, which was so easy to miss when first looking at her; that she had scars inside of her deep and terrible, just waiting for an outlet which she was more than capable of channelling when the opportunity arose.

"He made a command and forgot to tie it up in enough knots to stop me from sabotaging it," she said, a rough lilt to her voice which had me hanging on her words.

"What did he ask for?" I asked eagerly, a sick kind of thrill rising within me as I waited for her answer.

The smile she gave me wasn't a thing of innocence and wonder like those I'd seen on her before. This smile was one of a malignant goddess. One who had been scorned and abused and had finally reached her breaking point. One who had gotten her revenge. And I had to admit, I liked the look it gave her and the way her expression brightened at the memory.

"Water," she replied simply. "The fool asked me for water."

I didn't need to ask what she had done with that request. I could practically hear the rush of water crashing down upon the Fae who had thought to cage her and use her as if she were nothing but a possession. I could feel the explosion of power that must have spilled from her as his voice was lost to the water, his screams alongside any other commands he might have wished to make turning into bubbles without meaning until she was free of him at last.

"You really are a magnificent creature," I said to her, the awe in my tone clear enough that it brought a blush to her cheeks as we exchanged an intense look which acknowledged the similarities of our tainted souls.

The air between us seemed to grow thicker, harder to breathe and full of something I couldn't put a name to. The dark crept closer, the light abandoning us in the company of one another and making the words we had exchanged feel like secrets which bound us more honestly than the power of the coin.

"Are you worried about the brawl tomorrow?" she asked me eventually, breaking the spell the silence held me in, and causing me to release a breath.

"Not even a little," I replied. "No man can best me when I'm fighting for something I want. I didn't earn my reputation for nothing."

Kyra smiled at my accurate assessment of my skills, and she shifted to lay down beside me, just out of reach and still on top of the sheets, rolling onto her side as she looked at me.

"Can I stay here while you're sleeping?" she asked quietly.

"You want to watch me sleep?" I teased.

"Yes," she agreed eagerly. "Oh...apparently that's odd," she added as an afterthought, her expression tightening.

"Well, maybe I'm alright with odd." I gave her half a smile and indicated for her to stay beside me if she wanted to.

She beamed at me, throwing herself back onto the bed so violently that the whole thing bounced.

I released a laugh and put my hands behind my head as I closed my eyes again.

I tried to forget the fact that she was so close to me while my cock continued to make its ideas on the matter known, the silence somehow making me all the more aware of the needs of my flesh and the proximity of hers.

I bit my tongue to stave off the desire she was igniting in my flesh, reminding myself forcefully that even if she could touch me, she had told me to my face on multiple occasions that she thought I was ugly. Regardless of that, she probably wasn't even made of skin and bone like me, I doubted she even wasted time on emotions like lust. She was magic embodied. Of course she was beguiling, but she was also off limits.

I closed my eyes and worked to forget she was there, but it was damn difficult with the soft sound of her breathing just a few inches away and the sweet scent of honey blossom reaching me from her skin.

I ground my jaw, ignoring my cock and the urge to shift closer to her, forcing my mind from every sordid idea that came to it and blowing out a harsh breath as the torture of her proximity proved impossible to ignore.

Eventually I started to drift off and her voice reached me again just as I teetered on the edge of sleep.

"I know," she muttered to herself. "But I think I like him despite his face."

I bit my tongue in irritation against responding to that comment and forced myself to concentrate on getting to sleep as my cock practically wept in disappointment and I was forced to endure the bite of her fucking rejection yet again.

I really didn't give a shit that she wasn't attracted to me anyway. I had a princess and endless riches waiting to be mine, and I refused to let the less than flattering opinion of one crazy, alluring, magical being affect me.

"What the hell is this?" Cassius's furious voice roused me some time later and I pushed myself upright as I blinked the sleep from my eyes, my dagger in my fist and my muscles tensing at the note of threat in his tone.

"Shhh, he's sleeping!" Kyra objected as she sat up too, drawing my attention from the angry looking man in the doorway to her for a moment.

Her dark hair was a mess from laying in the bed beside me, but it suddenly restyled itself into perfect waves which fell down her back in a tumble of soft curls.

"You're supposed to be a suitor for the princess," Cassius growled, striding towards us with his jaw clenching so hard it looked like he might crack a tooth.

"I *am* a suitor for the-"

"What would people think if anyone saw the two of you sharing a bed?" he hissed.

I glanced at Kyra with a grin, fisting my solid cock and squeezing it firmly in an attempt to make the evidence of my arousal fuck off.

"Probably that she's just had a brilliant night," I taunted, and I swear his eyes actually flashed red with his rage.

"I did," Kyra agreed enthusiastically, bouncing up and down on the bed which in turn made her tits bounce within the thin material of her nightdress and Cassius flushed with rage.

"You are supposed to be a man of honour," Cassius barked. "The sort of man who the princess would be proud to call her husband. Not a lecherous fiend who beds his maid a month before their wedding!"

"Alright. Calm down there, mate, you're going to give yourself a haemorrhage or something if you aren't careful. I didn't lay a hand on you, did I Kyra?" I looked to her, then glanced away again quickly because my dick definitely wasn't going to get any less solid if my attention was fixed on her. I focused on the furious arsehole who had woken me up instead, aiming for that to do the trick.

"No. The only person to touch me was myself," Kyra agreed.

I released a laugh. "Well, that's understandable as you were sleeping beside me all night."

Cassius glowered at the insinuation.

"I don't understand..." Kyra frowned. "*Oh...*but why would I do that? ...I *know,* but Master doesn't exactly make me feel like-" Her eyes slipped to me and she promptly shut up as if someone had instructed her to. "I'm sorry about your face," she muttered, making irritation flare beneath my skin instantly.

"Right. And you're still alone in that opinion," I snapped as I stood and walked away from her, pulling on a pair of britches as I went, my cock finally seeming to get the hint that she wasn't interested and sinking like a ship full of holes.

Cassius gripped my arm as I tried to pass him and I paused, looking into his eyes as he held me in place.

"I'd take your hand off of me if you like your face in that arrangement, Cass," I said in a rough tone, a crocodile's smile on my face that warned him of the monster lying in wait beneath my skin.

"You should take better care of that Blessing," he growled, his voice low as he didn't back down. "She's too innocent and easily corrupted by your low morals."

He needed to take a closer look at her if he truly believed her innocent, but his claims were unfounded none the less.

"I never asked her to come to my bed in the middle of the night," I replied icily. "But letting her stay there *was* me taking care of her. She's been alone for fuck knows how long and she was afraid in the night for reasons I doubt either of us could ever fully understand. She wanted company, even it was just the company of a sleeping man. So why don't you mind your own business and take your damn hand back?"

Cassius held my eye for another long moment, clearly accepting the truth at last before releasing me.

I gave him a wide smile and patted his cheek. "Good boy."

I strode away from him before the fury that blazed in his eyes could come to anything more violent, and a knock sounded at the outer door just as I reached the central chamber.

"Enter," I called, liking the way the authoritative tone sounded in my voice. I'd never indulged in pointless dreams about becoming an upper Fae while I lived in The Den, but I sure as hell liked the feel of it now that I was indulging.

The door was thrown wide and four serving girls came in, pushing a large dining cart between them. They kept their heads low as they moved into the room, and I smiled to myself as I noticed them stealing glances at me from beneath their lashes. Kyra might not have thought I was attractive, but she was very much alone in that opinion.

"Your breakfast, Count Nazari," one of them murmured as the others began to lay plates of food on the table before the couch.

I eyed the meal with my stomach growling and Cassius and Kyra joined me, her nightdress replaced with a matching jade green pair of harem trousers and a short top with gold detailing on it that drew attention to the colour of her eyes. The guard looked like his anger with me had either lessened or had been quelled in the face of our company. Either way, I was glad to be done arguing with him. I was all for playing the part of a pompous count when I had to, but when the doors were closed, I was going to be myself again.

One of the servants approached me, bowing low. "Your outfit for the tournament, My Lord," she murmured, presenting me with a folded pile of white silk.

I held the tight britches and loose tunic out in front of me as I inspected them.

"Not the most practical colour for rolling about in the dirt and getting splattered with blood, is it?" I asked her, catching her eye despite the fact that she was trying not to look at me.

"Umm..." she hesitated, clearly not wanting to disagree with me while not wanting to insult the traditional garment either. "I'm sure it will look very fetching on you, My Lord," she said diplomatically.

"Most things do," I agreed, and a faint blush rose in her cheeks as she glanced at me then away again quickly.

"That will be all, thank you," Cassius said firmly, and the servants scampered from the room, bringing the cart with them before pulling the door closed behind them. "Stop flirting with every female you see," he hissed, pointing at me.

"I'll try, Cassius. But honestly that's like telling me to stop breathing. Besides, I have a sex Affinity so..." I dropped down before the feast which had been brought for us and filled a plate with a bit of everything on offer while Cassius scowled.

"If you eat too much you may get a cramp during the brawl and-"

"Where I come from, you don't ever turn your nose up at free food," I interrupted before he wasted any more energy trying to warn me off of filling my stomach. "You never know for sure when you'll get to eat again."

Cassius sighed and started on his own food too. "Fine, but don't come crying to me if it happens."

"I'm sure the princess will be more than happy to console me while she's wiping the blood of my opponent from my flesh."

"Don't get cocky, you haven't won yet," he reminded me.

"I was born cocky, mate. That's like telling the sky not to be blue."

"Would you like the sky to be orange instead?" Kyra asked, raising a hand like she was about to change it.

"No!" Cassius and I said at the same time, and I exchanged a look of amusement with him which seemed to be the end of our debate at least.

We finished our food quickly and I changed into the outfit required for the brawl. It fit me well and I couldn't help but run my hands over the expensive fabric appreciatively.

Kyra magically got herself changed into a deep red dress with silver gems glittering around the hem. She gave Cassius new clothes too and I tried to ignore the sight of all those whipping scars across his back as he changed his shirt. Wasn't my problem. He had signed up for that shit optionally. Seemed like he could have had a dandy old life being a milk maid or some shit instead, but he'd gone and handed his soul to the crown. Now the price of that foolish choice was laid right there in his flesh, and it spoke volumes about the royals he so willingly obeyed.

By the time we were ready to leave, the three of us looked like a group of high-born arseholes who I definitely would have taken pleasure in robbing blind.

"Can you make my head a bit clearer, Kyra?" I asked before we left. "A little of that wine is still swimming in my mind and I want to be at my sharpest today."

"Of course," she agreed with a bright smile which countered Cassius's unimpressed scowl perfectly as my hangover was washed away and I was left feeling as bright as a motherfucking button.

I wondered if I should have taken the warning she'd offered me about how she could twist the way she fulfilled my commands and try to be more precise when I gave them, but I decided against it. Doing so would have felt like declaring I didn't trust her, no doubt hurting her feelings in the process and reminding her of past masters like that prick she'd drowned who had been undeserving of her gift. So far as I could tell, all she wanted was to be set loose from the coin and she had told me more than once that she enjoyed using her gifts on me, so I wasn't going to spoil what we had going. All the time our arrangement remained mutually beneficial, I had no reason to fear she might try to harm me with her magic.

Cassius led the way from our chambers through the palace and out into the sweeping botanical gardens. The sun was beating down as usual and we took a twisting path between raised flower beds and arching pergolas covered in flowering vines. I had never seen anything like this in the city, though plenty of Fae living in the inner circles kept gardens or even grew flowers on balconies. But the beauty of this place was breathtaking, the blooms impeccable and not so much as a withered petal in sight. The work that must have gone into maintaining such perfection was astounding, and I couldn't help but stare at the varying plants and flowers that surrounded us at every turn.

Eventually we moved out of the formally arranged part of the gardens and onto a white stone path where the sound of a gathered crowd drew us on.

A fighting ring cordoned off with red and white silk sashes appeared at the foot of a long lawn and I smiled as the thrill of the fight began to rise in my blood.

A row of wooden stands were raised beyond the ring where several hundred high born men and women sat waiting for the pageant to begin.

To the right of the ring, a stage had been erected with a silk awning providing shade above three intricately carved wooden thrones, all of which currently sat empty in anticipation of the royal family's arrival.

Lord Kalaviv arrived ahead of me, surrounded by an entourage of twenty guards. He waved to the crowd, and they cheered him on as he pranced back and forth before them, hopping up and down like some strange bird, throwing his arms back and forth and kicking his legs up above his head.

"What's he doing?" Kyra asked in confusion.

"Warming up for the bout," Cassius murmured. "I suggest you do the same," he added to me.

"Not really my style, Cass. He looks like a fucking idiot. Besides, it's already plenty warm enough out here for me," I replied dismissively, the heat of the sun on my flesh already making me itch to remove the tunic.

"That's not the kind of warm I mean," Cassius muttered, but he didn't push the idea with me, clearly sensing how far he would get with that.

A huge cheer went up from the crowd and I looked around as Emperor Tarim, Empress Magdor and Princess Austyn approached from the rear of the stage. They climbed up and took their seats, smiling politely at their subjects as they acknowledged the praise.

The princess wore a light green silk dress which flowed around her, while Magdor looked harsher in a dark blue gown dotted with silver lilies, matching the emperor's fine tunic.

Austyn's eyes glimmered with unease as so many people looked upon the face that had been hidden for years, gasps and shrieks of excitement filling the air as everyone stared and I felt a surge of pity for her as I watched her fighting against the urge to squirm beneath their judgement. It had to be a lot of pressure to live up to, being dubbed the most beautiful woman in all The Twelve Kingdoms then having everyone look at you and decide whether or not it was true.

I wondered if she was even enjoying any of this because it sure as fuck looked like she wasn't from where I was standing. She may have been smiling, but the expression didn't touch her eyes and the rigid way she sat upon her throne made it look like she was ready to spring from it and sprint for privacy the moment she got the chance.

Cassius stilled beside me, staring at her face with his lips parted and a look in his eyes that said she was all he could ever want in a woman and more. My gaze raked over her again and I could definitely see the appeal, but I wasn't sure the drool was entirely called for.

"Kyra?" I asked, turning away from the princess to look at my little goddess. "What's that flower that only blooms once every ten years on that cactus that only grows in the heart of the Lyrian Desert?"

"An alorian bloom," Cassius responded before she could. "No one's seen one for the last few years as far as I understand. Though there are many pictures depicting the beauty of-"

"I'll have one of those please, Kyra. And make it subtle," I interrupted.

Kyra smiled at me conspiratorially as she cupped her hands together to create the flower before handing it to me. It was as big as my palm, smelling sinfully sweet in a way that made me think of old magic somehow, and I eyed the delicately beautiful layers of mauve and pink petals with interest as I gave her my thanks.

I slipped the flower beneath my sleeve as we headed down to the ring. A smattering of applause came as the crowd noticed our arrival, but I didn't care that Lord Kalaviv had gotten a bigger cheer than me. I only had to prove myself in the ring to win their fickle adoration. I didn't need the pomp and ceremony of bringing a whole host of guards and servants along with me any more than I planned on prancing about doing those insane stretches either. They'd be screaming my name once I had Kalaviv pinned in the dirt, which was all that actually counted anyway. And right now, there was only one person here who I was interested in impressing.

I moved beyond the fighting ring and headed straight for the stage, my gaze fixed firmly on the princess.

Her lips parted in surprise as I skirted the guards who stood before the stage, moving swiftly and quietly with the aid of my Affinities and hopping up onto it before any of them realised I'd gotten by.

The crowd hushed in surprise, and I was vaguely aware of Magdor frowning at me from her position to my left as I dropped to one knee before the princess, keeping my eyes fixed on her the whole time.

Austyn's amber eyes widened in surprise, the way her emotions were written so clearly across her features at all times meaning she had no hope of hiding what she was thinking, and I could tell she was a mixture of flustered, annoyed and pleased as she looked down at me.

"I got you a gift, dear wife," I said, giving her my best smile, dimples and all.

"A gift?" she asked curiously and I noticed a hint of shadow under her eyes which spoke of a restless night. What nightmare kept this girl awake, I didn't know. She certainly didn't want for anything in the world as far as I could tell.

"Yes, but you have to close your eyes first," I instructed.

She hesitated a moment, glancing to the crowd before back to me, twisting her fingers into the pale green skirt of her dress then finally submitting and letting her eyes fall shut.

I reached out and caught her hand, placing the flower into it and she gasped as the whole crowd fell completely silent. Touching the princess might have been a no go come to think of it, but there was no turning back now so I was going to have to just run with it.

I slowly brushed my fingers over her wrist, watching as goosebumps erupted along her flesh and smirking at the blush which found her cheeks before placing the flower in her hand.

"Is that an Alorian bloom?" Magdor asked in unveiled shock.

"Only the best for my love," I murmured, throwing Austyn a flirtatious smile as she opened her eyes.

Her gaze narrowed on me as I released her, and I could see her fighting the urge to dismiss the gift, but her eyes kept catching on it, appreciating the incredible rareness of such a thing and unable to bring herself to discard it.

"Its beauty is nothing next to yours," I added and she clucked her tongue, turning her cheek to me even as her attendants swooned close by. But apparently the princess wasn't so easily bought by sugared compliments, and I had to admit it appeared she had more depth than I'd expected to find in a girl no doubt raised to be Osaria's perfect little puppet. It was a welcome surprise though, and I was glad to find a woman of substance as my potential wife in place of some empty-headed vessel. It just made wooing her all the more challenging – which only made it more inviting too.

"Of course, beauty is boring without wit. It's what makes me such a catch," I added when she seemed disinclined to respond.

"How so?" she asked, disinterested in me now and I pushed my tongue into my cheek, determined to regain her attention now that she was withholding it. I wasn't a man used to being ignored, even the emperor and his wife were watching me closely. But not her. She was examining her damn nails like they had the secrets of the universe written into them.

No doubt she was aiming to put me off, but instead she was presenting me with a challenge which was only ever going to encourage me on.

I leaned in closer until she was forced to look at me again and I sensed the guards shifting around me as I overstepped her boundaries.

Austyn held up a hand to keep them at bay, curiosity bursting in her amber eyes as I played chicken with her. I could feel the crowd holding their breath, wondering if I really might be so bold as to lay my mouth on the princess. The game of it was all too fucking enjoyable and Austyn's eyes sparked like she liked playing it too.

I felt the rebel in her rising and for a second, we were just two people who wanted to say fuck you to the whole kingdom and I almost laughed at finding such a wild soul housed in this prim and proper creature before me. I wanted the kiss as much as I wanted to stick my middle finger up to the crown for all the meals it had robbed me of, and I wondered what Princess Austyn wanted to smite it for in kind.

"You're still wearing a veil," I whispered just for her. "This one's made of rules and expectations. Would you like me to tear it off for you, Princess?"

Her upper lip curled and she lifted her chin, her mouth so daringly close to mine, I wasn't sure which of us was challenging the other now.

"What you see is what you get if you win the pageant, Count Nazari. If there is more to be seen, you will never lay your eyes on it," she whispered in return and I drew back, standing at last while the crowd let out a collective exhale and broke into gossiping chatter.

"I'm damn good at peeling off layers, Your Highness," I said loudly and Magdor tutted as several women in the crowd giggled. "Metaphorically speaking of course." I gave the princess a filthy look that said the exact opposite of my words and she almost cracked a smile at Magdor's outraged expression. Perhaps that was the way to win her here – through enraging her stepmother at every turn. Couldn't say I had many objections to the idea of that.

I turned and took a running jump from the stage, soaring over the heads of the guards and rolling as I landed in the ring. I regained my feet quickly and held my arms wide like I was a performer on a stage – causing the crowd to applaud me as expected.

I drank in the attention and the murmured words of appreciation as they started to pay far more attention to me.

Lord Kalaviv stared at me in surprise from the opposite side of the ring as the crowd all broke into applause and I flashed my dimples at them. It looked like they'd changed their minds about who to cheer for already, and I wasn't going to complain about that.

My gaze hooked on a table set up beneath a low awning right at the edge of the ring where four men sat in fancy britches and shirts with sashes that marked them as the judges. They even wore little navy caps with the emblem of the royal family stitched onto them in gold, and their poncy faces said they were taking their roles very seriously. They didn't look nearly as impressed with me as the crowd were, in fact they were watching me with a scrutiny that said I was in trouble if I didn't find a way to make them favour me.

Dammit, Cassius had been right about this shit. But I wasn't deterred, because I was officially making it my mission to have the four of them eating out of my palm when they saw me destroy my opponents time and again.

A guard stepped into the centre of the ring, beckoning Kalaviv and I closer, and I forced myself to walk towards him in the stick-up-my-arse way that Cassius had shown me instead of using my normal swagger. It felt unnatural and wholly too restrained, but I was willing to play by his rules for now. Once I'd won the pageant and my bride, we would have to see how long I kept up the act.

My eyes slipped over the captain who had arrested me outside the countess's house and my heart leapt, but my smile didn't waver. His gaze slid down me then away before snapping back again as recognition hit him. But he couldn't work out why, couldn't figure out where he knew me from, I could see it in his eyes. It was almost too tempting to remind him, the thought of the shock he would get if he knew I was nothing but a street thief come to steal his kingdom right out from under him making a laugh bubble in my throat before I stamped it down again forcefully.

I turned my gaze to my opponent instead of the captain of the guard, dismissing him as if he was irrelevant and not a possible threat to my cover. Drake the thief was nowhere near as polished and well dressed as Drake the count and I'd never given my name when I was arrested, so I was confident that I could front him out. The mere suggestion of us being one and the same was too ludicrous anyway, so I felt assured in my own disguise.

"Count Nazari, Lord Kalaviv, are you ready to begin?" Captain Marik asked formally, seeming to dismiss the idea that he knew me and I could release the tension coiling in my gut.

I fought back the cocky response which sprang to my lips and nodded firmly instead.

"Then please bow to your opponent."

I held Kalaviv's eye as the two of us fell into a formal bow and the guard retreated, leaving us alone in the ring.

I stood upright again, waiting for the command to begin as my heart pounded with anticipation and excitement writhed in my blood. I was at home here. Fighting in the ring had been a daily occurrence in The Den, and I knew this peacock didn't stand a chance against me, no matter how many war accolades he'd claimed. Men like him didn't fight in the trenches nor on the front line. He was nothing but a trained dog, competent at party tricks but untested against a real wolf.

Kalaviv's bright eyes glimmered with confidence but that was okay. No one liked an easy opponent, and I was hoping he would help me put on a real show here.

"Commence!" Captain Marik shouted and Kalaviv leapt at me.

I ducked aside, avoiding the strike and resisting the urge to trip him as I aimed a punch for his face. He took the blow, following it with one of his own which collided with my shoulder as the crowd cried out in excitement.

We fell into a dance of violence, matching blow for blow as I fought against my instincts time and again, trying to play this part and missing more and more opportunities to land the kind of dirty hit it would take for me to get the upper hand. It was infuriating to say the least, forcing myself to allow those chances to pass me by while playing this pretty part.

I had to keep reminding myself about the goal here to keep my instincts in check.

It would be worth it for the throne.

Kalaviv lunged at me, his knuckles colliding with my jaw as he managed to trick me with a feint to his other side and I snarled angrily, grabbing his arm and twisting it sharply behind his back.

Cassius caught my eye from within the crowd, the set of his jaw and slight shake of his head warning me to stick to his damn rules. I cursed as I twisted my grip on Kalaviv's arm, planting a foot against his back and launching him away from me instead of trying to break it. Fighting honourably was no fucking fun at all.

Kalaviv shook his arm out as he maintained his distance from me, spitting a wad of blood to the sand which coated the floor of the ring and the crowd hummed with anticipation as we slowly began circling each other.

I wished I had a rock I could launch at his smarmy face to distract him long enough to place a knife in his gut. But as we weren't allowed to fight with weapons in this round, I guessed none of that counted as honourable either.

But this pretty bullshit was growing tiresome fast and I found myself unwilling to keep dancing to this beat.

I abruptly stopped circling, refusing to keep up this pretty game and forcing him to play by my rules instead.

Kalaviv eyed me as I remained entirely still for just long enough to unsettle him and the moment he shifted his weight away from me, my lip pulled back and I ran at him. It was far from subtle, but it would get the fucking job done and the way his eyes flashed in alarm was a pretty satisfying pay off to my plan as well.

He lurched aside before I could collide with him, his foot somehow catching mine and sending me tumbling to the sandy floor of the ring. Before I could right myself, the lord was upon me, throwing fists as I fought to buck him off and we grappled in the sand.

I threw my weight sideways before Captain Marik could start counting, and Kalaviv rolled away from me before I could follow him with my own attack, springing to his feet with a smug look which told me he seriously thought he would win this.

I closed the distance between us without bothering to assess his next move, swinging for his head with a furious combination of punches so that he was forced to retreat. My attacks grew wilder and I knew I was beginning to slip across the line Cassius had drawn for me, but this bastard was really starting to get on my nerves and I wanted to wipe the smile from his face.

He kept retreating, forced to block instead of attack, his forearms creating a cage around his face and allowing me to strike at his sides instead as I kept advancing, the crowd egging me on with their excited cheers.

Finally, I slammed a fist into Kalaviv's sternum hard enough to wind him and he stumbled back, losing his footing and allowing me to trip him.

He crashed to the ground and I dove on top of him, throwing my fist into his face. He was pinned beneath me as I hit him again, my lips peeling back in a brutal snarl as I kept pummelling him, not letting up in the slightest.

Captain Marik started counting and my heart sung with my oncoming victory. "One! Two! Three-"

Kalaviv swore like a common street thug, his teeth stained red with his own blood and he threw a punch straight at my throat, managing to slip past my guard and land it, causing me to rear away from the pain of it.

That's more like it.

I grinned at the dirty tactic as I lurched backwards, forced to put some distance between us once more but he grabbed the material of my tunic, yanking me back towards him with a violent jerk, allowing him to roll me beneath him.

My back hit the sand and he slammed a fist into my jaw, making my head ring as I tasted blood and I cursed at the injury to my face as the captain started counting again. This time drawing towards my end instead of my opponent's.

Kalaviv didn't release his grip on my tunic, twisting the fabric in his fist until the damn thing was choking me, my own attempts at escape causing the sound of tearing to fill the air alongside the roars of the crowd.

I snarled in anger as the ridiculous garment was used against me so dishonourably. I hoped the judges were striking out his points, marking him down for that shit.

"-three! Four-"

I was ruined if I stayed here. Losing the first round was too damaging to my trajectory in this tournament, so if I had to play dirty and lose points that way then so be it. But I'd be damned if I was going to lose this fight.

I threw my weight forward, slamming my forehead into the bridge of Kalaviv's nose, rewarded by the satisfying snap of breaking bone as blood flew, splattering my cheeks alongside his face and he was knocked off of me, crying out in pain. The crowd gasped, some booed, others cheered, but all were fucking shocked.

I leapt to my feet, ripping my ruined tunic off and tossing the material aside as Kalaviv clutched his face, his eyes simmering with rage for the damage to his nose. But I'd gained my advantage back, and I offered up a winning smile as I prepared to finish this once and for all.

Some of the nobles in the crowd cried out in a mixture of excitement and shock at the indecent display of my tattooed flesh and I spared a look for Cassius where he still stood at the edge of the ring, wanting to see his scandalised expression for myself so that I could laugh over it later.

But instead of finding him gasping like a virgin bride and clutching imaginary pearls like I'd been hoping, the moment my gaze connected with his he bellowed a command at me which only served to get the adrenaline pumping through my body even faster than before.

"End him!"

My heart pounded to a heady, beautiful rhythm as I turned my eyes back to my prey, intending to do just that. My opponent's blood coated my skin. My flesh was buzzing with the power of my Affinities. I felt focused, powerful and in touch with the gifts of the old gods which sang through my skin more powerfully than I could ever remember them doing before, like I had been born to do this and I was fulfilling my fate by standing upon the bloodstained sand preparing to secure myself an entire empire with nothing but the actions of my own flesh and blood. I was in my fucking element, and I was going to make this hurt.

Kalaviv wasn't making this easy for me, but I refused to back down and I absolutely refused to lose. Everything I'd come here for depended on me winning this fight and I wasn't going to leave this ring as anything less than victorious. But to do that, I was pretty certain I'd need to bend a few of Cassius's directions regarding my fighting techniques. And after Kalaviv's dirty trick with my tunic, I refused to play nice anymore. We were both clearly willing to lose points in this match going forward, because whoever stole this victory was going to come out on top regardless.

And if it was alright for the nobility to fight dirty, then it was definitely okay for me to do it. Unluckily for Kalaviv, down in the dirt was where I flourished.

It's time to show this princess exactly what her husband-to-be can really do.

AUSTYN

CHAPTER THIRTY FIVE

I watched the brawl with so much tension writhing through my body that I almost crushed Drake's gift in my hand. The flower was the rarest in The Twelve Kingdoms. We'd once had the cactus in the gardens but even that had failed to flower for several years despite the gardeners' best efforts, then the thing had up and died. *Where the hell had he gotten it?*

Drake was fast becoming the most mysterious person I'd ever encountered. Not that I'd met that many people in my life. Not up close anyway. And when he got up close, it was like the air crackled with energy. He gave off the sort of aura that said he owned everything and everyone in the vicinity. I didn't know how much I liked that. There were plenty of people in this world willing to own me, and he was definitely one of them. But still...there was something intriguing about him, something rebellious too. And after so many years of feeling trapped, and like every one of my breaths needed permission to be taken, Count Drake Nazari was feeding into that ache for freedom within me. When he'd drawn close and almost stolen a kiss, I'd thought of the scandal, of the horror Magdor would have felt over the defiant act.

It had been so damn tempting to see her eyes twist with shock, to hear the nobles gasp as the perfect illusion of their innocent princess shattered before their eyes. But then I'd remembered that Drake was a suitor here to win me, just like the rest of them. And I wasn't going to feed into his arrogance by offering myself up to him like every other countess and lady in this place clearly wanted to.

None of them were hiding their blushes or the way they fanned themselves every time he landed a blow against Kalaviv. It was clear he'd won their favour with his pretty smiles and theatrics, not to mention the removal of his fighting tunic which had left at least half of them with their damn tongues hanging loose of their mouths, but I would not be so easily persuaded. Though I couldn't help but look at the way his powerful body moved, the slick of sweat and speckles of blood decorating his deeply bronzed, tattooed flesh capturing more of my attention than I should have allowed.

Drake threw a bone-cracking punch to Kalaviv's jaw, and the crowd sucked in air while my heart rate picked up.

I'd never felt so alive. The scent of blood and sweat hung heavily in the air, and I wished I could walk out there myself and feel the thrill of the fight first hand. I watched Drake like a hawk, living vicariously through him and wondering what it must have been like to be able to pick your own destiny like he was able to. It was clear both men held an Affinity for fighting, but where Kalaviv favoured maintaining a powerful stance at all times, Drake shifted tactics like the wind. He was fast, almost impossibly so, his footwork as unpredictable as his attacks and unlike any formal style I had ever seen the guards of our kingdom use. Was that a style which was common in the distant kingdom of Carubai he called home?

There was one good thing I had found in this pageant, at least. I liked that it was feral, I liked the way the audience held their breath, and all eyes were locked on the fierce match instead of me for once. I relished the heat flooding my veins, the dryness of my mouth, the fear and excitement tangling into one illuminated being inside my chest.

This is what living is and I want more of it. More, more, more.

Drake started moving in a way that was anything but formal. I'd visited the guards' training grounds on occasion out of duty and seen them fight, but this was nothing like that. He was becoming more animal with every punch, every kick. Kalaviv couldn't keep up. Perhaps the lord's muscles were more for show than landing hits, maybe his heroic reputation had been bullshit after all. He certainly didn't look like an unbeaten war hero now.

I stole a glance at the judge's faces, trying to work out which contestant they were most impressed by, but they weren't letting their guards slip.

I knew each of them, the four of them chancellors of the emperor who had been a part of the royal court since before I could remember. I'd never liked them much, and I even recalled Father telling me they bored him to tears, but their knowledge of the laws and traditions of not just Osaria, but all of The Twelve Kingdoms was invaluable to the crown. During this pageant, they would be guarded by ten of Father's best men while they were housed in the northern town of the palace, and would only leave it when the rounds were in play to ensure they were never bribed or threatened into judging the pageant biasedly.

As Drake landed another ferocious punch to Kalaviv's temple, I found myself rising from my seat. My attendants hurried to mimic me and I shared a brief look with Zira, her eyes alight with anticipation.

Kalaviv managed to recover, feinting left before following with a harsh kick to Drake's chest as he fell for the distraction and he hit the ground.

The lord didn't slow as he lunged forward and stamped on Drake's calf, the dirty tactic proving how desperate he was getting in the face of his opponent. I grinned as the count rolled away from another kick, moving with that incredible speed once more and leaping upright, hissing through his teeth.

The pain only urged him on though, and suddenly he turned into nothing but a lion bringing down his prey. He faced Kalaviv across the ring, breaking into a sprint and diving into the fray without wasting any time on circling or baiting.

The crowd cooed and gasped as Drake dove at the lord with a feral cry leaving him which made every hair on my body stand on end.

My heart hammered wildly as he knocked Kalaviv to the ground, managing to maintain his position on top of him and I stepped forward once more as Drake's fists flew, breaking skin and sending droplets of blood flying while Kalaviv could do nothing but try to shield his face beneath him, the end of this suddenly in sight.

The scent of blood and sand and the roar of the crowd was nothing like I'd ever experienced. It was beautiful mayhem. We were animals stripped to our base desires, and there were no rules here, nothing but sweet carnage.

"One- two- three-!" Captain Marik called out and my heart started singing a tune I didn't know.

I didn't want to be bought. I didn't want this whole pageant to continue, but in that moment, I was so caught up in the fight that I simply needed to see the brutal end of it. And Drake was offering that end with every pound of his fists, showing no mercy to the man he held beneath him as every muscle in his body worked to seize his victory, and I found my eyes locked to him as if a cord had tethered them in place, allowing no alternative.

"Four – five!"

The audience bellowed so loudly it hurt my ears. A smile took over my features, so wide that I couldn't remember the last time I'd smiled like that.

Drake shoved himself upright, raising his arms into the air with a roar of triumph, drinking in his glory as the sun beat down on his tattooed, bloodstained flesh and for a moment he looked like a legend from the stories of the Fallen. A warrior born in blood and proven in battle time and again over the centuries, forever risking his immortal life and forever emerging victorious.

He stood there panting, looking to the judges as they exchanged words and the crowd continued to cry out and clap while we awaited their scores.

Finally, a folded piece of parchment was handed to Captain Marik and he looked down at it before lifting his head, everyone in the stands falling deathly silent to hear what he had to say. There were twenty points available to each contestant in a round, but a bonus of five points were awarded to the winner on top of their final score. For the dirty tactics he had engaged in, I wasn't sure how many Drake would have lost overall, though Kalaviv hadn't exactly fought cleanly.

"Lord Tyron Kalaviv secured himself eight points in the round and Count Drake Nazari was awarded twelve points for the round and five for winning the brawl, giving him a total of seventeen points."

The crowd cheered and I clapped along with them while Drake strode away from Kalaviv without offering him a hand to get up, ignoring the rules of honour and though there were mutters of disapproval, I only smiled wider. It made me think that Drake really wasn't playing a game, that this wildness in him was real to the bone. And realness was so very hard to come by in my world.

Drake strode up to the stage with a swagger that made my smile vanish like a ghost in the dark. He hid the limp in his leg damn well, but I could tell it was paining him and I took satisfaction in that pain as I remembered what that victory had bought him. Now, he was one step closer to owning me. To stealing my kingdom from my father and doing whatever he wished with it.

The closer he got, the more my lungs refused to let in air. Venomous rage was tangling with the adrenaline in my veins, and my jaw tightened as this tattooed beast strode towards me with a look that said I was his. That I was already won and bound.

I took the green rosette from Zira, my hands trembling with anger as I readied to pin it onto him. The first winner of the pageant. The enemy come to claim his prize.

I dragged in a slow breath, encouraging my heart to return to a normal pace as Drake approached, his footfalls heavy as he climbed the wooden steps onto the stage. He bowed to the emperor then knelt before me, his eyes sparking with the win and sweat gleaming on his body as his chest rose and fell heavily.

"You won," I said blandly, not letting on that I was at all impressed by his victory as I scrutinised him.

"Obviously," he said with a shrug like it was nothing. Like he wasn't battered and bruised and bleeding while speckled with his own blood alongside his opponent's. Like there hadn't been a single second where he'd doubted he'd be kneeling here before me at the end of the bout.

I plastered a false smile onto my face and he gave me a salacious look, running his tongue along his bottom lip in an utterly indecent way in front of the entire royal gathering who all tittered and applauded like he was some sort of hero.

Magdor released a noise of disapproval and I glanced at her, finding her giving Drake a calculating look that set my pulse racing. I'd been at the end of those looks before, the kind she gave just before she delivered her cruel punishments to me. There was no doubting who she wanted to win my hand in this pageant, and suddenly I was glad that at least Drake was giving her a moment of doubt over her son's domination in this game. Of course, I wasn't going to be jumping aboard Team Drake just because he'd angered Magdor, but I couldn't say I took no pleasure in seeing her usually unbreakable façade slip and her irritation at the crowd's clear enthusiasm for this new and unknown suitor slip through.

"Get on with it then, my dear," Magdor said encouragingly, though she said it partly through bared teeth as she pretended to smile and my amusement at her fury grew. "You may stand, Count Nazari."

I recalled the words I was expected to say to each winner, stepping closer to Drake as I gazed at his bare chest, wondering where the hell I was supposed to pin this rosette while taking in the unusual display of ink which caressed his skin.

Drake got to his feet so suddenly that my breath caught, his proximity practically indecent as he towered over me, his powerful, half-dressed frame so close to me that all I could see was him, the masculine scent pouring from his flesh making certain that every single one of my senses was assaulted by the undeniable aura of this man.

"Don't keep me in suspense, dear wife," he whispered, tilting his chin down to bring it closer to my ear and keep his words between us and that anger in me rose sharply again.

I dragged my eyes back up from his gleaming torso and found him goading me with a grin which seemed all too genuine and utterly infuriating all at once. Light shone from his eyes that spoke of a life well-lived, one where he was free and always would be. Where he got to throw money at anyone he liked, buy anything he wanted. And I was next on his list.

Well not if I can help it.

"Count Drake Nazari, I proudly present this rosette to you in honour of winning your first round. May the luck of the lost gods stay on your side and offer you more victories in the pageant," I drawled, not putting any heart into those words.

"I'm the luckiest man in The Twelve Kingdoms," Drake said, his confidence clearly knowing no bounds. "So no doubt it will."

I fought an eyeroll, closing the already too small gap between us and his scent rolled over me. All man. Perspiration, blood and freedom. A freedom I couldn't even dare to try and claim simply because I was born a woman. I wondered if he even appreciated the pure privilege he possessed simply because he'd been born noble with a cock between his thighs. How easy it must have been to be him.

"You didn't get away unscathed. If you're limping in tomorrow's fight, I doubt you'll do so well again." I relished the small ounce of power I took back from him, watching his expression flicker for half a second before his cockiness returned with a casual shrug.

"I'm not limping, Princess," he said, loud enough for everyone to hear. "If I staggered over here, it is only because I am crippled in the face of your beauty. It is a wonder I am not more wounded."

I scoffed as the crowd cooed, lapping up every drop of his bullshit, and I could see he was practically laughing with how easy it was to feed them it. But I would not be so easily fooled or won over.

I moved forward, painting on the sweetest smile I could manage and his eyebrows arched as he bought the lie I was presenting, pretending I had fallen for his sickly sweet words too.

I lifted the pin, pinching the skin beneath his collar bone and he frowned, a protest on his lips as he saw my intent, but then his lips locked tight, and his eyes dared me to do it instead. I could see he didn't believe I would, that we were just back to a game of daring and I'd be the first to back down. But he was wrong about me in more ways than one. And I had no problem proving it.

I stabbed the pin of the rosette into his flesh without care and he cursed under his breath as I slid it firmly into place, a trickle blood running down onto his pec as I released it and admired my work.

The crowd couldn't see what I'd done, but everyone around me sure as hell had and my attendants gasped between them as Drake stared at me with a snarl curving those ever-smirking lips.

"Thank you, Princess," he gritted out.

"You're most welcome, Count Nazari," I said, batting my lashes at him in mock admiration before returning to my seat, brushing the alorian bloom out of it with intent, causing it to fall to the floor and roll aside.

Drake was suddenly on one knee before me, scooping up the flower and placing it in my hand, stamping his lips to the back of it. The flower was crushed in my fist while his fingers locked even tighter around it, almost hard enough to hurt. He looked up at me with a dark and challenging look that told me this was a war he was willing to be a solider in.

He wasn't put off by my attack, in fact it was clear that it had only spurred him on to win me. I wasn't some tame animal to be collared and admired, I was a wild beast and he was going to learn that if he planned on capturing me, he was going to get bitten and mauled at every opportunity I could get.

He released my hand and the petals scattered down to the floor between us, the heat of his mouth remaining imprinted on my skin as he straightened.

"My apologies," he said in a way that said he wasn't sorry at all. He was destroying his gift before the crowd could see me discard it for good. "I'll get you another one, your highness."

"You won't find any in Osaria, Count Nazari," I said airily. "Pretty things tend to wither in this city."

Magdor scowled at the jibe I'd made at Osaria, but I didn't care. If she wanted me to pretend that I was happy about these proceedings then she was going to be sorely disappointed.

"Well pretty things tend to bloom in my company," Drake responded, his gaze burning with the intensity of a thousand suns.

My face dropped at the part he was playing once again. All for show. And I was so tired of being part of the performance. "Perhaps you should spend some time in the gardens this afternoon then, I've been dying for the fathom roses to bloom this season."

I gave him my cheek, dismissing him as I looked towards my maids, taking the class of chilled lemonade which Zira hurriedly fetched for me.

Magdor ushered him away, seeming pleased by my dismissal of the count, though it had nothing to do with her, or her vile son for that matter.

Drake glanced back at Magdor with no trace of warmth in his eyes then descended from the stage, walking on his injured leg and nearly concealing his pain as he strode away.

Zira and Jacinda took their seats on the cushions to my left and I stole a look at my father whose face had been unchanged throughout the entire brawl. He had clapped when appropriate, but he'd barely seemed to notice Drake or the interaction I'd had with him. My heart tugged as I tried to catch his eye, but he didn't look my way, always looking to Magdor instead.

"How handsome a couple you'd make. Two glowing stars joined eternally, burning forever and ever," Jacinda said with a sigh of longing.

"Oh, do calm down, Jacinda," I muttered, rubbing my eyes wearily and Zira smothered a laugh.

"He's not all bad," Zira whispered, glancing up at me. "Better than Kahn," she mouthed and I nodded, unable to deny that much.

But I didn't want this life. I didn't want a husband who'd claim my father's throne and never allow me to have a say in the kingdom's laws. I wanted to sit on that throne and seize the power which was rightfully mine. I wanted to make real change in our kingdom and the empire beyond, leaving my mark on this place I loved so dearly in a way that truly improved the lives of my people. Except it wasn't my right. Because of what I didn't have between my legs.

Fuck men. Especially men with midnight eyes and presumptuous smiles designed to steal women's hearts.

My heart is mine. And no one can have it. Especially not Count Drake Nazari.

CHAPTER THIRTY SIX

I wanted to race forward to help my master as he gritted his jaw and worked to keep walking on his bad leg, the pain of the wound practically my own as my bond with him begged me to help him, but Cassius reached out to stop me. His hand almost closed on my arm, and I gasped in panic as I willed my flesh to turn to smoke before he could touch me and risk ripping this pretty dream apart. If I found out that I wasn't real then everything I thought I had here would just melt away, and I feared I would find myself still trapped in the coin after all, alone, unwanted and forgotten all over again.

Cassius stared at me in surprise as his hand passed straight through my arm before looking around quickly to see if anyone else had noticed.

Super subtle. Sometimes I think you want to get us banished to the coin again.

"I'm afraid of being touched," I muttered.

"Sorry," Cassius said with a frown, though I hadn't actually meant to tell *him* that. I was only reminding myself. "But you can't go to your master now. He has to stand before the stage and accept his position in the rankings once the princess has finished offering Kalaviv her condolences on his loss."

"But he's hurt and I-"

"He's a big boy, he can manage for a little while and we can't risk anybody noticing anything strange about you or seeing what you can do. Look, he's speaking to the princess again now." Cassius jerked his chin to point him out and I bit my lip as I forced myself to remain where I was and tried to see him.

I stood on tiptoes to look beyond the crowd of Kalaviv's servants as their lord walked away from the princess looking a little like a kicked dog.

Master approached the stage once more, this time ushered to stand at the foot of it in the sand as the princess got to her feet, looking down on him with interest though her eyebrow arched like she wasn't totally impressed by him.

The guards who ringed the stage remained in place this time, forming a barrier between them but my master just called over their heads as if they weren't even there. His words were lost to the crowd, but my stomach knotted as a small smile tugged at the princess's lips in response to whatever he'd said.

The crowd on the other side of the ring were going wild, applauding and calling out my master's name as he threw them a rueful grin, still bathing in his victory. Master gave his full attention to the princess again as she called something else down to him. She was very beautiful. Her eyes glimmered and her long silver hair was so unusual, it drew my attention despite all the other people around us, making my blood hum with old and powerful magic. Memories tickled at the edges of my mind as I looked at it, but any time I tried to turn my attention their way, they flitted out of reach once more like little birds playing hide and seek with me.

I twisted a finger through a lock of my own hair thoughtfully, watching as the strand changed colour until it looked just like hers, the metallic silver sheen glinting in the sunlight.

Bad idea, idiot. You're supposed to be normal. Normal Fae don't just change their hair colour whenever they're feeling jealous.

"Jealous of what?" I breathed as I returned the lock of hair to my own midnight colour, allowing the curl to spring free of my finger.

Of the way your master's looking at her.

I frowned at Master as his eyes danced and he said something to the princess which made her eyes sparkle even though her face stayed resolutely impassive. Why should I care what way he looked at her?

Cassius released a huff of irritation so low that I almost missed it, and I glanced at him as he watched their interaction too. He had a smile on his face that spoke of his pleasure in our master's win, but his eyes were hard with disapproval and there was a set to his jaw which made that smile look painful.

Green doesn't look good on him either.

"Cassius isn't green," I mumbled and he looked at me as he heard his name.

"What was that?" he asked with a faint frown.

I didn't mean it literally, you dumb goose. I meant green with envy. He's jealous.

"Oh. Apparently, I think you're jealous," I explained to him and his lips pursed.

"What reason would I have to be jealous?" he asked, clearing his throat as his voice caught on the last word.

Because he thinks the princess is as pretty as your master, and he doesn't like how good they look together.

I gazed at Cassius with pity in my eyes. "I didn't realise how you felt about him... Well apparently, *I* did but not all of me. But it's okay, maybe it's not too late to tell him."

"Tell who what?" Cassius asked, his brow creasing.

"Master. You should tell him how pretty you think he is if it's upsetting you that he and the princess-"

Fail. Absolute fail. Sometimes I have no idea how we're the same person. I feel like you're doing this on purpose just to make me die of shame. Which would be an improvement because I have been desperate to die for about eight thousand years now.

"I... Kyra I think you're confused," Cassius said gently, his eyes shining with pity.

He's looking at you like you're a horse with a broken leg.

"Oh, I hope he doesn't like to have sex with wounded horses. Is it just the uninjured ones which arouse him?" I hissed, my wary eyes on Cassius but his attention was fixed on Master and the princess once more.

Gods, that's not what I meant. Focus on the broken leg part.

"What does that mean?" I muttered.

Too broken to fix. Ready for death. Which is true. I'm so ready for death it's unreal.

I frowned because that last remark hadn't held the certainty I'd grown used to from my other self. It was like I was repeating the same old lines I'd said a million times before, but now they didn't necessarily line up with the truth. I wondered if being out of the coin was changing things. Maybe I didn't want to die at all anymore. Maybe I was getting a taste for life again.

Maybe. But that's only because we're out here, and I'm not convinced that'll last. One mistake and we're back in the coin. Back in the dark. The cold. The isolation. All alone all over again.

A shiver of terror passed through me and I scrunched my eyes shut to try and push the monsters in my mind away. They couldn't come for me out here. They weren't allowed out of the coin. I was still here, I wasn't alone.

I blew out a harsh breath and opened my eyes again, forcing myself to focus on where I truly was and what was going on around me.

Cassius's tense smile remained fixed as he watched Master and the princess, and I followed his gaze on them too.

She pointed at the rosette which I was only just realising that she had pinned to his – oh by the gods – she'd pinned it to his naked chest and blood was trickling down his pec. She made some joke or quip about it if his reaction was anything to go by, not seeming upset by the fact that she'd poked a hole in him.

Magic burned through my fingertips as I looked at the blood, the taste of it rolling across my tongue as if I was the one bleeding and not a man who stood so far from me that I couldn't even hear his words. If he needed me I was here, though I was forced to fight my instincts and remain in place without getting any closer to him.

The crowd gasped and pointed it out, seeming to have taken whatever joke the princess had made about it as permission to comment on it, and Master did a spin and puffed out his chest like he was proud of where she'd placed it.

Cassius coughed a laugh, but it fell away as a faint blush lined the princess's cheeks while she looked over Master's exposed body, the firm lines of his powerful frame fully on show above the now bloodstained britches which hung low on his hips. The ink of his tattoos was like delicate artwork placed across his bronze skin by the most skilled of artists, and if the comments I could hear from the crowd were anything to go by, then many of the people watching agreed with me. There was just something about him that drew their gaze, from his appearance to the powerful aura which clung to him and the self-assured attitude which told them he had practically claimed the throne already. He was charismatic and captivating, and I watched in fascination as he drew the support of the crowd like moths to a flame.

You're staring at him too, if you hadn't noticed.

I frowned, wondering if that was true or not as my gaze followed the curves of his muscles where they stood out firmly through his skin, putting his undeniable strength on full display for all in attendance to see. His body gleamed with sweat after his bout in the ring which should have been off-putting, but somehow wasn't, making my mouth dry out as I continued to stare. My gaze drifted down to the muscles at the base of his stomach where they tapered into a deep V before they disappeared beneath his waistband, and I bit my lip.

Oh sorry, my mistake, you're just ogling him like a piece of meat because you like his personality.

"I *do* like his personality," I protested. Or at least I liked what I had seen of it so far.

Before I could respond to myself again, the empress rose from her seat and a chill ran down my spine. I could see the beautiful features which she presented to the world, but I could see the darkness beneath them too. Her true face was a wicked, rotting thing. A black skull with eyes of ice and a forked tongue, like a snake's. My heart beat faster as she approached the man my life was tethered to, and magic built in my skin just in case he needed me. She gazed down at my master with suspicion in her eyes and malice in her soul, and I shuddered at the thought of her getting any closer to him.

"She's evil given flesh," I murmured, and Cassius looked at me sharply.

"You mean Magdor?" he asked, almost reaching out for me again before stopping himself.

I nodded, fear trickling through me as I watched her call down to my master as if she was amused by his showboating, though I could tell she wasn't. She smiled but there was no warmth in it. The way she looked at him was assessing, calculating, like she was weighing him up and hunting for weaknesses.

A jewelled beetle crawled from the skeletal eye socket of her true form, rounding the back of her skull and disappearing once more, making my spine stiffen as I continued to watch her, expecting some foul act at any moment.

"What do you know about her?" Cassius asked, his voice filled with intensity.

"She hides her true face from the world," I breathed, rattled through to my core. "She cheats death and is death."

"Why haven't you spoken of this before?" he demanded, and I cocked my head at him.

"I tried to tell you when we arrived at the palace, but you kept hushing me. I assumed your hushing meant you didn't care to hear what I had to say on the matter."

Cassius's lips parted and I could tell he was thinking back to the day we had arrived as he swiped a hand down his face, seeming frustrated. "You could have told me about it after we were in our chambers."

"When we returned to our chambers you just did that pacing thing while looking all grumpy about life," I reminded him with a shrug. "And then I found that pond-"

"It was a bath that had been filled with milk and petals and-"

"It was delicious," I pointed out and he huffed a breath.

"Forget about that now. Just explain what you said about her hiding her face and being death. What does that mean?" he asked urgently like I had the answers he had been desperately hunting for. But all I could tell him was what I saw.

"She's evil," I replied, eyeing the creature who was wearing the face of an empress, wondering why he couldn't see what I could, while that coldness grew inside me again. "Evil given flesh and death given life. Any sane Fae should fear her."

Cassius seemed to want more from me, but I didn't know what else I could add to elaborate on it. There was a foul and twisted magic taking place in the body of the empress, but I knew only what my eyes were telling me and what my gut felt about her.

"What is she?" he asked, but I shook my head, having no more answers for him. "Kyra," he begged.

"I'm sorry, sullen man. That's all there is," I said apologetically, and he nodded, though creases formed on his brow as he fell into thought.

Lord Kalaviv's entourage moved away from us as he headed out of the ring. Anger and shame lined his features as he accepted his defeat and the fact that he was already at a clear disadvantage in the competition to claim the princess's hand in marriage.

A wild cheer went up as people cried out from the crowd that Master's current position meant he was first in line for the hand of the princess, though everyone here knew that could change before the day was out and the remaining brawls had taken place. Still, he would be rewarded for his win somehow, Cassius had said so while the fighting was going on and his seventeen points made it more likely he would remain in the competition once the eliminations began.

We headed towards the stage as my master finally turned away from it and strode towards us. I gave him a wide smile as I ran forward to meet him, excitement at his win buzzing through my veins like a vat of angry bees.

"You were amazing!" I said excitedly, almost launching myself at him before remembering I couldn't touch him and stopping myself at the last moment, my feet skidding on the grass and my arms wheeling in an attempt to prevent myself from falling.

Smooth.

I smiled widely, applauding him as he lifted his chin and gave Cassius a look that seemed to be waiting for his praise too.

"You won," Cassius said, his tone making it unclear whether that had been intended as praise or a simple statement of fact.

My skin prickled at the feeling of someone's eyes on me and I glanced up, noticing the princess's gaze travelling over me in an assessing way. I blinked at her in surprise, almost lifting my hand to wave before biting my lip, wondering if that was the right move or not. Her face was void of emotion like she had donned a careful mask and I couldn't tell if her intentions towards me were friendly or not from the simple act of her stare.

Scale it back, you're embarrassing yourself.

"Thank you, little goddess," Master said, his pet-name for me making me feel all hot and flushed as I blinked up at him, my attention instantly stolen by him once more. "We knew I was amazing before I beat that posturing bastard though," he added with a roguish smile.

"You're right, beating him wasn't that impressive really," I agreed, nodding seriously as I tried to ignore the feeling of the princess's eyes on me, wondering if she could see the truth of me or if she had some other reason to look.

"I didn't say that," he protested.

"Yes, anyone could have beaten him," I said quickly. "Even a new-born babe. Perhaps you'll go up against some real competition in the next round and have a chance to do something actually impressive."

Congratulations, you went from over-the-top adoration to just plain insulting him. Perhaps you should point out the fact that you think he'd look better with both of his eyes on the right side of his face and just seal in his disgust with you.

I decided not to reply to myself as both Cassius and Master were giving me the she's-lost-her-mind looks again, but I was beginning to think I was wrong about that idea anyway. No one else had two eyes on one side of their face, and Master's eyes were actually quite nice just the way they were. They were dark and deep, and his long lashes made me want to watch him blink and blink and blink…

You're a total lost cause. Watching people blink is not a hobby.

"It's better than *not* watching people blink," I pointed out, though thankfully Master and Cassius had started talking between themselves and they weren't listening to my ramblings anymore. They were discussing the finer points of the fight as Master moved towards a servant who held a pitcher of ice-cold water ready for him beneath a silk awning. I probably should have been the one to fetch him that glass come to think of it, but he didn't seem to mind the fact that I wasn't a very good maid. Actually, I didn't think I'd done a single maidly duty since becoming his maid. Perhaps I needed to work harder on my disguise. Then again, I wasn't entirely certain that I remembered what maids were supposed to do, and he hadn't exactly voiced any complaints, so perhaps I was concerning myself over nothing.

He drank the contents of one glass then took hold of the entire pitcher and poured the water remaining in it over his head, sighing happily as he flicked his wet hair back out of his eyes while water cascaded down his chest and soaked into the fabric of his white britches, making them cling to his body in a way that I was fairly certain was indecent.

Cassius looked like he was about to burst a blood vessel as more of the noble ladies pointed and swooned dramatically and I wondered if he was feeling jealous again. Poor Cassius.

The princess was looking over at Master once more as the water ran down his chest and I noticed a lot of the noble ladies in the crowd doing the same, pointing him out and fanning themselves as Master grinned at the attention, not seeming to mind it at all.

My gaze caught on the way the water dripped over the ink on his chest and I was struck with the desire to lick him. I'd bet he'd taste like all the best bad things, blood and sin and sand and man.

Do it then.

"I still can't touch him," I muttered, though I was still staring and wondering about the way he'd taste.

"I think the princess isn't your biggest fan." Cassius pointed out the rosette pinned to Master's chest with something of a smirk pulling at his lips.

Master raised his chin with a scoff. "She likes me just fine, mate. She knows I like it rough."

What did he like rough? The sea? Or was it the sky that got all whirly and angry when the wind blew?

Cassius didn't seem to like whatever it was that Master was implying though as he squared up to him, his hand going to the sword at his hip.

"I will not continue to warn you about your vulgarity regarding the princess," Cassius hissed in a low voice just for my Master and me. I wasn't entirely sure it even was for me too, but I was right there, leaning in to listen and shifting closer to the owner of my soul.

"Oh, what will you do? Behead me in front of all the nobles?" Master breathed, laughing at him and Cassius reluctantly dropped his hand, though his jaw kept ticking furiously.

"Phew," I sighed. "I thought I was going to have to kill you for a moment there, Cass," I said.

"Kill me?" he questioned, his eyes darting to me like he suddenly remembered I was an all-powerful being.

"Yes." I nodded seriously. "I saw it all in my mind, kind of like a premonition but more like a fantasy because it was really just my own thoughts. You were going to draw your sword then Master would have told me to save him, and I was going to reach right into your gut and pull your intestines out."

"What?" Cassius balked as Master laughed loudly.

"All of them," I confirmed with a sad nod. "And you have a lot of intestines so it would have taken me a long time just pulling and pulling and pulling while you cried at my feet. It was a terrible thing, sullen man. Truly horrific."

Cassius said nothing for several seconds, his lips parted on a reply which didn't seem to want to form on his tongue before he looked to Master instead of me.

"And you're still certain she's harmless?" he grunted.

Master laughed louder, drawing the eyes of the princess once more even though she had tried to stop looking this way twice already now. "Fuck no. I never said she was harmless. She's an utter savage, aren't you little goddess?"

His bright eyes drank me in, and I nodded in agreement. "Utterly," I parroted back to him, making him laugh more while Cassius took a subtle step away from me.

Magdor snapped something to draw Austyn's attention back to her though the princess's eyes briefly met mine, stilling my breath as she gave me a faint frown before she looked away once more.

The next two contenders moved into the ring, leaving me to look at her all I liked while she was distracted. She really was beautiful, regal, all the things any man might dream of finding in a woman.

I bit down on my bottom lip and felt my cheeks heating, a strange sensation building in my gut which writhed and twisted like a bucket of worms.

"Prince Gurvine's got this one in hand without even having to try," Cassius murmured as a beast of a boy bowed to a willowy man who seemed to be sniffing at the air.

"I want to use the bathhouse. This heat is exhausting," Master said, his gaze flicking to the brawl which was about to begin before he turned away from it, looking back towards the palace.

"We should watch the other bouts and see what we can pick up about the winners' fighting styles," Cassius objected. "Any advantage could be pivotal to you winning again in the next round and-"

"And that sounds like a great job for you," Master agreed dismissively, and I couldn't help but snort a laugh.

Cassius opened his mouth to object again, but Lord Kalaviv approached us suddenly and he was forced to hold his tongue.

"Good match, Count Nazari," he said, acting as though Cassius and I weren't even present as he moved to stand so close to my master that I was forced to take a step back.

He held his hand out and Master shook it with a hard smile, pulling him close and gripping his arm like they were great friends.

"It was for *me*, anyway," Master said, and I almost laughed again but Cassius caught my eye, warning me not to with a shake of his head.

As my master drew back, I noticed something glinting in his palm which he quickly concealed in his fist, and I cocked my head curiously as I wondered what it was.

"Indeed," Kalaviv replied curtly, not looking too happy about his loss though he was trying to front it out. "Would you care to join me to watch the remainder of the matches? I know many Nazaris back in my homeland, perhaps they're some distant cousins of yours?"

"Perhaps," Master agreed with a shrug. "But my father died when I was young and all I really inherited from him was my title and my estate. Mother remarried and I never had much to do with the Nazari side of my family after that, so I wouldn't really know. And thank you for the offer but I don't plan on watching the remaining matches, I'm in need of a bath."

"That's a shame about your father," Kalaviv said with a frown, not letting him escape so easily. "May I inquire as to how he died?"

"Trampled by a herd of elephants while voyaging in the south. Mother always did tell him that his exploits would end badly one day." Master shrugged.

I gasped. "Oh, that's so sad. I didn't know," I said, my heart twisting with pain for him as I thought of his poor father crushed beneath the feet of such enormous creatures. My memories of elephants didn't paint them as naturally violent, but then again maybe what I was thinking of wasn't a memory at all. Sometimes I felt like a vat of information with no source. I knew what an elephant was and had my own impression of the way they behaved, but actually trying to think of a time when I had laid my eyes upon one was impossible. Would I ever remember who I was, or would I always be this empty creature without any real sense of home?

Kalaviv's eyes turned to me in surprise. "Does your maid often voice her opinions while her betters are speaking?" he asked coolly, and I could see anger flashing in his eyes which reminded me of the masters I'd known before, the ones who favoured silence and punished failure harshly.

"Her *betters*?" Master asked roughly, all amusement slipping from his gaze as he took a step closer to Kalaviv, his eyes dark and full of threat which made my muscles tighten in a delicious kind of way. I held my breath as I watched him, uncertain if I should speak again or not. "I see no one here who is any better than her." His gaze stayed fixed on Kalaviv, and it was clear the comment had been aimed at him.

Tension stretched through the air, the feel of it brittle and just waiting to break, the memory of the recent fight between them stirring and the sour taste of testosterone rising once again as the challenge hung there unanswered.

Cassius cleared his throat, raising an eyebrow at my Master but he ignored him entirely, waiting for Kalaviv to respond. The lord narrowed his eyes in confusion, cutting a look at me which dragged down my body slowly before a knowing smile tugged at his mouth and he nodded.

"Ah, I see. She's that kind of maid, is she?" he asked, violence slipping from his gaze and something more improper taking its place, his eyes rolling over me in a way that made my skin feel sticky and filled me with the desire to bathe in boiling water.

"What kind?" Master asked, a low growl to his voice that should have been all the warning the lord needed, especially after the beating he'd just taken, but he didn't seem to pick up on it.

"The kind who services your cock as well as your home," Kalaviv replied, his gaze on me turning lascivious. "How is she? Perhaps you'd like to lend her to me as a consolation prize? I'm sure I could teach her better manners given a night in my-"

Kalaviv cut off with a strangled yelp as Master's hand snapped out and grasped his manhood tightly through the white britches he still wore from the bout, causing Kalviv to release a curse as he froze, his eyes bugging from his face and hand moving to his belt as if in search of a weapon. But he wasn't carrying one thanks to the rules of the brawl, meaning he had little option but to wait and see what would happen next.

I gasped audibly, my heart catapulting into my throat as the shock of the move struck me. Was he...defending my honour? Was that promise of violence in his dark and tempestuous eyes put there on my behalf?

It's a trap. He only wants to trick you into trusting him.

It didn't feel like any kind of trap though. It felt raw and brutal and an exhilarating kind of real.

"My liege," Cassius began but Master shot him a dark look, forcing him to bow his head and step back in deference, though the way his jaw ticked made it clear he wasn't happy about that.

Master stepped closer to the lord, his grip tightening and all amusement falling from his face as nothing, but cold, furious rage spilled from him.

"She is not a possession in my keeping to loan out on a whim," Master hissed, and a shiver ran down my spine which had no place being there on a day as hot as this one. "She is neither property nor for sale in any kind of way. She has a name. One which you are not worthy of hearing. She is worth far more than any price you could ever pay, and certainly far more than some kind of pity gift to allow you to feel like a big man again after being humiliated so publicly out there in the ring. And even if by some miracle she agreed to go to your bed out of choice, I would sooner cut your cock off than allow you to put it anywhere near her. Do you understand me?"

"Unhand me or I'll-" Kalaviv spluttered but Master pushed forward, squeezing harder and glaring right into his eyes, their noses brushing.

Kalaviv barely suppressed a wail of pain and Cassius subtly positioned himself to try and hide them from view of any prying eyes.

"You'll what? Cry out and tell everyone you tried to barter for a night with my maid as if she were some street whore for sale to you? Go ahead. I wonder what the princess would think of one of her supposed suitors looking to bed another woman within her own palace walls? Though after your performance in the ring today, it seems highly unlikely that she will ever have to worry about the burden of you becoming her husband."

Kalaviv tried to jerk free, but Master only followed, the thick muscle of his bicep bulging with how hard he was squeezing the lord's manhood.

Cassius moved strategically to continue blocking them from view, still trying to cover where my master's hand was placed in case anyone looked our way. I glanced around to see if anyone was paying attention, but they were all caught up watching the next suitors as they warmed up in anticipation of their brawl.

Kalaviv looked like he might pass out from the tightness of my master's grip and I strained my ears as I watched them, listening hard for the sound of a testicle popping, not wanting to miss it if it happened.

"Apologise," Master growled and Kalaviv looked even more horrified by that suggestion than he was by the threat being posed to his manhood.

"I'm sorry," he spluttered and Master's lip peeled back to reveal his teeth as he practically growled at him.

"To *her*." He gripped Kalaviv's chin, forcing his face around to me and I fell utterly still as I waited to see what he would do.

The lord's eyes flashed with disgust and hatred, the way he looked at me reminding me of all the worst Fae who had ever owned me. Something in me hardened as I looked right back at him, letting him see that he didn't scare me even though I knew it only made him hate me more. But I was sick of being made to feel lesser, being used without thought or consideration to who I was. Master had taken an interest in the truth of me and that had breathed life into a rebellious kind of defiance which I had forgotten I even possessed. I liked the taste of it and I planned on taking more.

Master squeezed tightly once again and Kalaviv gasped, giving in to what he knew he had to do and speaking to me through gritted teeth as he spluttered out an apology.

"I meant no offence," he ground out, though the fire in his eyes told me that his words were naught but lies. "I'm sorry if you thought I did."

"Hard not to be offended by the thought of spending a night in your bed," I said, the words spilling from me before I had so much as a chance to stop them.

Master barked a laugh, releasing Kalaviv suddenly, giving him a little shove so that he almost fell on his arse before managing to right himself while grasping at his cock with a curse.

"You're little more than savages," Kalaviv spat as he backed away, his eyes darting fearfully between the three of us as he attempted to retreat towards his own entourage once more.

"Savages?" Master scoffed. "Oh no. We're far worse than that."

"I have half a mind to inform the royal family," Kalaviv growled.

"Go ahead," Master replied. "I'll be sure to tell them the full truth of it. In the meantime, like I said, I'm headed to the bathhouse. I'd say I look forward to seeing you later, but I suppose that would be a lie." Master smiled tauntingly, a flash of teeth that was all warning and hunger for blood before he turned away dismissively and strode off without another word.

My heart thrashed wildly as I watched him leave, my emotions all stirred up and confused as I tried to make sense of what he'd just done. For me. He'd done that for me.

He only wishes to gain your full loyalty.

I had the sense to hold my tongue as I looked up at Kalaviv while he scowled at me, still cupping his groin protectively.

I took a step back, sensing the threat coming from him as he glared at me like that had been my fault, wondering if this truly would be the end of the matter or not.

"Your master will need fresh clothes prepared, Kyra," Cassius said, placing himself between me and the lord, his eyes encouraging me to escape while I had the opportunity. "You should hurry to catch him."

"Okay," I agreed eagerly, not wanting to linger in the current company and gladly taking the offer of escape.

I turned away from the angry noble, glancing once more towards the princess whose eyes briefly met mine from the stage, making something sharp twist in my chest as she did so. I dropped my gaze then, not sure what I was seeing in her face as she turned her attention my way and breaking into a run as I hurried up the lawn, chasing after my master.

He glanced down at me as I fell into step beside him, his gaze softening just a little in recognition. "Sorry about that," he muttered, his jaw hard as he still seemed to be fighting against his own temper.

"About what, Master?" I asked. "Shouldn't I be the one who's sorry for being a bad maid?"

He blew out a harsh breath, swiping a hand down his face and shaking his head.

"No. That arsehole should be sorry for thinking he's better than you just because he holds more money and power. My entire life I've been subject to the elitist bullshit of the upper Fae who like to think of themselves as so much more than the rest of us – but now look, I stand among them in some fancy clothes, calling myself a count instead of a thief and they're suddenly ready to call me one of their own."

"In all fairness you're shirtless, and I'm fairly certain your lack of clothing has caused something of a scandal," I pointed out and he cracked a smile at my words, flashing a single dimple at me as I tilted my head to look up at him while we continued to walk along the lawn towards the decorative gardens.

"No doubt Cassius has an entire speech planned out to chastise me with later," he said with a groan, though he didn't seem in the least bit apologetic for his actions.

"I imagine he will have prepared notes," I agreed.

"Just so long as he doesn't attempt to reprimand me for defending you to that entitled piece of shit," he muttered, his easy smile falling at the memory of what the lord had suggested about me.

"You don't strike me as the type to dislike whores," I pointed out and he shook his head dismissively.

"I take no issue with whores. They work hard for their coin and are among some of the best people I know. I take issue with men like him assuming Fae with less than them are either unfit for his company or for sale at his whim."

464

"I imagine he won't forget that message easily," I teased, twisting a finger through a dark curl of my hair, still getting used to the colour of it and finding I really liked the rediscovery of myself. I'd sat and stared into the mirror for over an hour last night, becoming reacquainted with the Fae I once was. It hadn't done anything to help stir any memories for me, but it had helped me to feel more like…myself? Or like I was real? I wasn't entirely sure which, but I was fairly confident it was a good thing either way.

"In all honesty, I feel like I didn't make it clearly enough," he muttered irritably. "Where I come from, I would have drawn blood for an insult like that."

"Do you often speak up in defence of those around you?" I questioned and he frowned at me, shaking his head.

"No. Of course I don't. That wasn't what I…" he trailed off, looking out into the gardens before shrugging and turning his attention to me again. "I am not a man to waste time fighting battles on behalf of anyone else. But… I would still feel inclined to kick his arse for insulting you. So make of that what you will. I have already given him a good kicking though, so I suppose I don't need to repeat the process."

I grinned at him. "You did," I said, taking pleasure in the memory of watching him beat Kalaviv in front of everyone, the feral hunger in his eyes and the way the lord had been forced beneath him. I wasn't sure I'd even remembered to breathe throughout the entire fight, my palms growing clammy and my mouth drying up as I'd watched it all play out through unblinking eyes, loving every single moment of it. "I thought he might cry at the end."

"That would have made my day." Master chuckled and I blinked at him in surprise, fighting the urge to flinch away as he leaned in closer to me, dropping his voice in a secretive way which made a flutter of excitement stir within me as I held myself there to listen.

"Would you like a gift?" he asked with a mischievous smile.

"A gift?" I asked in surprise.

He held out his hand and offered me a signet gold ring which I'd seen on Kalaviv's hand earlier. There was a ruby at the centre of it and I carefully plucked it from his palm, taking care not to touch him before I held it up to the light to look at the red colour better, my lips parting in surprise as I studied the offering.

"Thank you," I breathed. I'd never had a gift before, at least not in any memories I owned and certainly not from any master who had claimed me. The small token made a rush of emotions pour through me as I stared at it, my pulse hammering in my throat and clogging it up so that words stalled there, leaving me speechless as I just stared. This meant something powerful, the rush of it making me flustered as tears pricked the backs of my eyes and I blinked several times to try and hold them in.

He stole it, so it's not all that thoughtful.

"It's still the best gift I've ever had," I replied, pushing the ring onto my finger. It was far too big, but I didn't mind. People gave gifts to those they cared about. To those they *saw*. For him to have given this to me mattered because it meant I was more to him than just a means to an end. I was someone to him. Real. And maybe not quite so alone anymore.

My fingers shook at the thought of that reality, one where I wasn't just used but wanted. Where my company could be something desirable even when I wasn't fulfilling commands or making dreams come true.

It's too big because it's not meant for you. I'm not going to let you get all swoony over some stolen trinket.

I fought against the thoughts of the fractured part of me because she was just hurting really, afraid of this being true and caught in the trap of having been alone for altogether too long. But what if that was changing now? What if-

"Don't get too excited, Kyra," Master muttered, seeming surprised by how much I clearly appreciated the gesture, his hand pushing into his midnight hair as he brushed it out of his equally dark eyes. "And it might be a good idea not to wear that where anyone will see it."

"Why?" I breathed.

Because Lord Kalaviv will be looking for it and if he catches you with it, he'll have the guards cut off your head.

I wasn't sure if I wanted to have my head cut off, but I did like my gift all the same.

"Because it's a little bit stolen," Master admitted with a roguish grin and I didn't get the impression that he thought that made it worth any less at all. Thieving was how he had always survived, how he had always gotten what he wanted and when he'd stolen this ring, he'd done so for me. So surely that made it a gift just valuable as one he had bought?

Your standards have slipped a lot in the last thousand years.

"Okay." I dropped it into my pocket but the warmth of it slid into my heart. If I couldn't remember the last time anyone had gotten me a gift, so it was perfectly possible that no one ever had before. Which made this my first. Stolen from a man who had insulted me by one who had defended me. There was power in that. "Can I get you anything, do anything for you? Make you something or serve you in some way?" I offered, my attention dropping to his injured leg as the need to heal it itched at me.

"No, thank you little goddess, but I am quite content at the moment. The only thing I am in need of is a bath and my legs are quite capable of delivering me to the bathhouse without putting you out," he said. "Isn't there something you would like to do for yourself?"

"For myself?" I asked with a frown, uncertain what he meant.

"Yes. You know, don't you have any hobbies? Hopes? Dreams?"

"I dreamed of getting out of the coin. And you made that dream come true, Master. So now all I want to do is please you."

He stopped suddenly and turned to look at me. We had made it to the middle of the decorative gardens, completely alone for once amid swathes of stunning flowers and the gentle buzz of the insects pollinating them. A towering pergola arched over us, hiding us beneath a fountain of trailing yellow blooms and as I looked up at him, I couldn't help but wonder if I'd even mind if the rest of the world just faded away and all that was left behind was me and him.

My breath caught as I turned so that I was facing him, finding us too close together, the toes of his shoes bumping against mine, the almost touch enough to make my heart tumble into a race, though I made no move to back away.

"You don't want anything at all for yourself?" he asked, and the idea didn't seem to sit well with him, his brow furrowing and his stare intensifying until I felt captured by it.

He had looked at me plenty of times, studied me even and learned my face well, but this was different. This felt like he had peeled back the layers of what I was and what had been done to me an eternity ago so now he was looking right at the broken creature I had become while I was trapped inside that coin. He saw it and the longer he looked, the more he seemed to dislike what he found.

I bit my lip, sensing that if I said no to his question that he would be displeased, but not having any other answer to give him. It had been too long since I'd walked in the real world and been a real girl. Any wants, desires or dreams I may have once held had faded away and gotten lost to the abyss which now resided inside of me. He stared on, waiting for a response, a truth which I suddenly felt ashamed of, but when he refused to look away, it became clear that I had to admit it.

"I only want to make you happy, Master," I murmured, letting him see the honesty of those words as he searched my eyes for it with that frown still marking his brow, the words which every other master had loved to hear from me seeming too sour for him.

"Don't call me that," he muttered, his lips forming a hard line as he swallowed thickly, shaking his head a little as if he had just realised something he should have already known. "I don't think I like it anymore."

Panic bled into me at his words, the possibility of him no longer wanting me to belong to him rolling through me and the reality that presented filling me with an unending fear which made me want to turn and run as fast and as far as I could. If he was done with me, then he could discard the coin, banishing it and me, allowing the magic to return it to that hellish cave where no one ever came to look for me. My torture would begin anew, except this time, it would be worse because I had begun to regain myself. Just the smallest of pieces, but they were here, returning to me bit by bit and I liked them. I wanted them. Needed them. I couldn't bear for it to be over so soon when it had only just begun.

"But you *are* my master," I said in a rush, pushing forward as if I might touch him before jerking back, still too afraid to cross that line and risk the end of this pretty dream because I needed it far too much. "My purpose is to serve you and-"

"When that arsehole lord spoke about you like you were nothing but some object he could take possession of if I only allowed it, I fucking hated it, Kyra. I wanted to rip his cock off right there and then, and let him bleed out at your feet in front of all of those pretentious people who believe that being upper somehow allows for that kind of entitlement. I didn't fucking like it, little goddess, and I don't like the thought of you believing I have that kind of power or sway over you either. This magic between us may mean you're stuck with me, but I don't want you to think I want to own you like that motherfucker would have wanted to. So have your own thoughts and dreams and be your own person. Don't call me Master anymore. Just call me Drake, like everyone else," he said firmly and his onyx eyes burned with so much intensity that I was forced to nod.

"Okay... Drake." My heart raced at the taste of his name on my tongue, and I swallowed thickly as I stared up at him, wondering if he truly meant what he'd just said or if he'd change his mind now that I'd spoken his name. I hadn't had a single master who had ever looked at me like he was now. Like he saw *me* instead of only seeing what I could do for him. Like he cared about me being my own person outside of the magic which bound us. It was overwhelming and unexpected, and it made the broken fissures inside me ache with longing for all the things that I must have been once. Because I was afraid that after all this time, now that I had finally found someone who wanted to see who I was, it would turn out that I wasn't anyone anymore at all.

Drake smiled at the sound of his name on my lips, his dimples both showing, a bright kind of honesty lighting his dark eyes and something so undeniably genuine about the expression that I found myself forgetting to breathe all over again.

He shifted a little closer to me, eating up that too small space between us until I could feel the heavy weight of his presence pressing against me despite the fact that we were still a breath away from touching. His height forced me to tilt my head back so that I could keep looking at him as I hesitantly smiled in return, really feeling the emotions that went with that expression and trying not to tremble before him as he awoke things inside me which I had forgotten that I was even capable of.

"And do me another favour," he said, his voice low now, like what he spoke was a secret only meant for me.

"Anything," I agreed, sucking in a breath as a lock of my hair got caught in the breeze, whipping before my eyes and getting trapped in his fingers as he caught it on instinct.

He wasn't touching me, not really, but as I held his gaze and he carefully placed the lock of hair back over my shoulder without once touching my skin, I shivered. The near unnoticeable tug on the individual strands sent a burst of energy prickling across my scalp, and I had to bite down on my tongue to halt the soft moan which wanted to roll up my throat and escape me from the almost contact.

He was so close, so impossibly, tangibly close, and yet this distance seemed impenetrable at the same time. He wasn't done imploding my world yet though and as he asked his favour of me, I found myself stilling like a fresh spring freezing over at the first sign of winter frost, frozen in that moment and unable to continue while I tried to make sense of what he was suggesting.

"Try to think of something you'd like for yourself. You were Fae once, you had desires of your own. Maybe you should try to remember some of them. Or even just come up with new ones."

I found myself nodding, wanting to agree to whatever he asked purely for the fact that he had cared enough to ask it. Even though I had no idea how to even begin doing what he'd suggested. How could I remember what I'd wanted for myself before I was cursed when I couldn't even remember my sister's face? Dreams, wishes, wants, desires, all of that was long lost to me, even further removed than the memories of whoever I had once been, and yet there was something to his request, like a sweet taste on the back of my tongue which made me ache for something I could almost imagine. Like knowing I was hungry without having any idea of what I wanted to eat. His words made that want in me blossom and though it was more than a little terrifying I had to admit that I was curious so see if it could bloom.

"By tonight I want you to tell me something you want for yourself," he said firmly, seeing the uncertainty in my gaze. I found myself wanting to please him almost as much as I wanted to dive into the possibilities which could be gained by trying to discover my own desires.

"Okay," I breathed, like it was nothing. Simple. But the look in his eyes told me that he knew it wasn't.

I hardly knew where to begin with figuring it out, but I did know that I wanted him to keep looking at me like that, like he saw me and liked what he was looking at. It lit me up. *Woke* me up. and made me feel a little more like me every time he did it.

Drake nodded, seemingly satisfied by my response before turning away, breaking the spell of his nearness, and leading the way towards the bathhouse. My mind whirled with the knowledge of what he wanted from me, nothing at all coming to mind as I tried to consider what it was that I yearned for. It seemed an impossible task, yet I was determined to do as he'd requested.

I simply had to think of *one* thing I desired for myself. How hard could that be?

You can hardly even think of the right colour for the sky. And you might as well be reaching for it if you're foolish enough to try and reclaim the girl we once were.

The bite of my own doubts cast cold water over my ambitions, but even as they threatened to snuff out that little flame of hope which had begun to burn in me at the thought of reclaiming something of the girl I'd been, I threw myself over them, protecting them from the storm. That flame may have been small, but it was blazing brightly, and I refused to let it go out. I just needed one little desire to add to the fire, a single piece of kindling to help it grow. And if I managed that then maybe I could find another piece and another, more and more until eventually the blaze might burn right through me and return at least some of what I'd lost.

Likely it was a fool's hope, but that was still better than having no hope at all. So I clung to my tiny flame with all I had as my mind turned inwards, and I tried to come up with a single thing that I truly wanted for my own.

CASSIUS

CHAPTER THIRTY SEVEN

My hands curled into fists as I sat helplessly on the side-lines, watching the latest brawl from a seat a few rows back in the stands and imagining all the ways I might like to dismember the men in this competition.

The demonic-looking Count Cartoum fought with the pubescent teen Prince Gurvine, the count putting up a surprisingly good fight that spoke of his skill. He used some strange moves though, throwing sand randomly left and right and moving so fast, he had managed to disorientate the prince a few times. But Prince Gurvine had muscles of iron and was a frighteningly good fighter. He aimed for Cartoum's head repeatedly and with an agility that made him a fierce competitor.

Drake wouldn't take him easily if he was forced to fight him in another round, but then again, I was fairly sure I had underestimated his efforts before seeing him defeat Kalaviv. He may have used some less than proper tactics, but he had at least kept himself from going for the balls, so that was something. The points he had been awarded positioned him very well indeed, and I supposed I would have been over the moon about that had I not had the unsettling feeling in my stomach that this only brought him one step closer to claiming the princess.

I'd been unable to help my eyes from wandering to her throughout the brawl, and I'd witnessed the passion in her eyes as they watched Drake's movements. It had angered me to see her so beguiled by him. Was she pleased he was closer to winning her now? Was she being swayed towards the idea of a life with him?

It wasn't even that he was a thief that bothered me, it was that this pageant had been forced upon her and I had heard her express her disgust with this tradition many a time in the palace. Was she won over so easily already? Truly so accepting of her fate because of a pretty face and quick-witted tongue?

My hands fisted as I tried to equate this princess with the one I thought I'd known in ways. But perhaps I had been a fool, painting up a fake picture of her in my mind, pretending that I knew her, when really, I was just hoping I had. Maybe my lonely existence within the Royal Guard had made me a little delusional. Perhaps this was what she really wanted now that she had seen her options among the suitors. One option in particular.

A hard and unrelenting lump pushed at the base of my throat as I tried to let go of the jealousy searing the inside of my chest. I was teetering on the edge of my restraint, wanting to find something to destroy, burn and ruin in an effort to release some of this pent-up energy coursing through me. But instead, I simply sat there and reminded myself I was nothing and I had no right to feel this way. I was only a weapon branded with a number. Although, as I lifted a hand to brush my fingers along the scar that had now formed through the number behind my ear thanks to Drake, I realised I wasn't even that anymore. I was decommissioned, valueless, a creature bred for one purpose which it could no longer fulfil.

Count Cartoum finally went down, and he was awarded six points while the prince took fifteen. Gurvine approached the stage, still breathless from the fight and blushing as the crowd roared his name, applauding his victory while Count Cartoum was guided away by his entourage, a nasty bruise forming on his temple.

Austyn pinned Gurvine's rosette to his tunic and I watched her closely, my pulse thumping in my ears as I tried to work out what she was thinking. She looked dejected and her eyes kept skimming away from Gurvine to somewhere beyond the ring like she wished to be done with her duties.

The next set of suitors appeared for their brawl and my gaze shifted from the muscular bald man, Lord Darell, to Kahn. The more I saw of the empress's son, the more his altered appearance set me on edge. Apart from his size, everything about him had changed. His once shaved head was now overflowing with auburn locks, his face chiselled as if from stone and his muscles more defined.

I turned to the royals once more as the crowd reacted to the sight of him stepping into the ring, finding Austyn glaring at Kahn with undisguised distaste.

My mouth tugged up at the corner and my gaze lingered on her as I thought about how she'd pinned that rosette to Drake's chest and made him bleed. I was glad that she wasn't afraid to show him her spirit, at least. Though a twisted part of me was envious that she'd drawn blood on him, the idea of her hand spilling my own blood making my mind splinter with impure thoughts.

"My son has been gifted beauty from the Prophet of Jahalus," Magdor announced, rising from her seat. "He is now a fine suitor for a fine princess, wouldn't you agree, ladies and gentlemen of Osaria?"

The noblemen and women applauded, but some muttered under their breath, a ripple of concern passing through them over the use of magic, but there wasn't the shock and outrage I'd been hoping for. No doubt this news had already been leaked across the city, wagging tongues silenced and loyalties bought in the way only the nobles knew how. I sat up straighter as Magdor gazed around at them, her brows pinching together as she realised her words hadn't been received too well despite whatever work had gone into securing the support of the nobility.

I wasn't surprised. The people of this empire had long since learned the danger of accepting help from a Prophet. Endless tales of the cost of wielding magic could be heard in every tavern and around every campfire for miles. Nothing stolen from the lost gods came for free. And it usually wasn't what it seemed either. Only someone filled with despair and desperation would dare ask for the help of a Prophet, and even then, they'd expect the price of such magic to be steep indeed. For them to learn the empress had accepted a gift of beauty for her son left more than a few of them uneasy, no doubt wondering if the entire empire might suffer the cost of the magic thanks to her position.

A smug smile captured my mouth as she returned to her throne, feeling as pleased as if she'd just sat in camel shit.

The people of my kingdom don't much care for your ill-gotten potions, Magdor.

The fight started and I focused on every movement the men made, my training having taught me to see far beyond the outer layers people presented to the world. I was adept at assessing threats, to see danger coming far before it struck, and I was almost certain of Kahn's victory in this brawl already.

He wasn't just a powerhouse of strength; his movements were well practised and confident. Lord Darell danced around him for a minute or two, dodging the swings of Kahn's fists, but if there was one thing it seemed Kahn was adept at in life, it was this very thing. He was letting Darell do all the work, springing about, dodging blows while Kahn kept all of his energy ready for when Darell made a mistake.

One slip of the foot and Darell faced the first impact of Kahn's knuckles right to the chest. He was thrown from his feet to a round of gasps from the audience, slamming down onto his back almost theatrically, but the crunch that reached everyone's ears proved this was no play. Even the judges arched the odd eyebrow, and some of them noted things down on the parchments laid out before them.

Darell wheezed, brushing the sand from his bald head as he hurried to get up and waved a hand to the crowd like it was nothing. Kahn allowed him a moment to compose himself while guffawing at his opponent openly, and a smattering of applause sounded.

I watched Kahn closely as Darell moved into a fighting stance once more, picking apart his movements and dissecting his weaknesses. His gloating didn't last long as his gaze fell on the lord before him, and he raised his fists in preparation of an attack.

He hadn't once offered his back to Darell, keeping enough distance between them to prepare if the lord sprung at him. But Darell was too busy trying to pretend he wasn't hurt to dive into the fray once more. His movements were more cautious this time as Kahn allowed him to circle and close in, moving only his feet in a slow circle while Darell had to hop and bounce his way around the very fringes of Kahn's reach. As he was larger than any normal man, his reach was likely far more than Darell was used to in his opponents too.

Darell's brow was growing sweaty, his gaze set with determination, but every now and then, a wince crossed his features and his left hand moved to cup his chest where Kahn's fist had impacted. Between the heat and his injury, he was burning himself through the last of his reserves already while Kahn hadn't even broken a sweat. It was a pitiful display that had my own hands curling into fists, the desire to stand in his place flashing unexpectedly into my mind.

My gaze shifted to the princess and my foolish, hopeless self, indulged in a moment of madness as I imagined what it would be like to stand in that ring against Kahn, against any of these unworthy bastards. This pageant was outdated and the idea of anyone winning Princess Austyn like a trophy made me want to behead every contestant and cut down anyone else who demanded she take part in this barbarity.

To slay for her...to kill for her freedom, that would be a wish fulfilled indeed. I pictured myself bloody with Kahn's head swinging from my fist as I marched up onto that platform and knelt before her in an offering, the fantasy getting my heart pounding.

The crowd gasped, and I snapped out of the wild daydream, ripping my gaze away from the princess to look at the ring instead.

Kahn had knocked Darell onto his back again, but this time he was straddling his chest and throwing punches into his face which had already knocked two teeth out.

Marik started up the count as Darell failed to rise and I looked over at my old captain, my muscles tensing with the anticipation of the orders my body always expected from him. But I was unrecognisable thanks to Kyra, and it was a relief knowing this man who had haunted so much of my waking life no longer held me at his service.

Darell didn't rise again, and Kahn kept hitting him far longer than was necessary as he played with his food, a vicious kind of grin pulling at his mouth as the pain of the lord ignited some dark fire in him.

Kahn finally stood up, raising his bloody fists into the air as the crowd cheered for him and Darell was left unconscious on the sand, blood splattering the golden grains around him from his tenderised face. Kahn had stolen the round easily and he was awarded a staggering eighteen points while Darell took a mere three.

Marik whistled to some of the servants and a towering black horse was guided into the ring, pulling a stretcher along behind it. My heart lifted at the sight of Gallow, my horse wearing a fine golden bridle with his mane and tail braided neatly for show. I wasn't too far from where Darell's body lay and as Gallow sniffed the air, he lifted his head and looked right at me, stamping his front hoof. *"Yu-thar."*

The word sparked inside my head and my mouth lifted at his name for me. I supposed he had rarely heard my true name before, but I had often been addressed as 'you there' when I was wanted for some duty or another.

The little horsey accent he put on those words were endearing and I was glad he could recognise me. Of course, it was less endearing when he started trotting right towards me, yanking the bridle out of the servant's hands and dragging a half-conscious lord on the stretcher after him. He didn't stop at the front row of seats either, he knocked several people aside as he clambered clumsily up the stands towards me and Darell went tumbling out of the stretcher with a strangled cry.

"Gallow, you fool," I hissed, rising in alarm and moving to grab his bridle before he could trample someone.

He rubbed his nose against my face with a stubborn determination and I petted the star between his eyes.

"Apple," he demanded inside my head, and I cursed as the servants came to grab him.

"Get hold of that beast!" Marik barked as the crowd shifted away from Gallow in fright.

"I have him," I called, steering my horse back down over the stands and drawing him onto the sand where Darell had passed out again. "I possess a slight animal Affinity that sometimes causes beasts to act out of turn. Entirely my fault."

I inclined my head as I held the reins out for Marik to take, but he snatched them from my grip anyway and shoved them into the hands of one of the servants who was scrambling about trying to get Darell on the stretcher again.

We'd drawn a lot of attention away from Kahn who was now up on the platform receiving his rosette, and I could feel the princess's eyes pinned on us too.

Marik looked me up and down with distaste. "Aren't you Count Nazari's guard?"

"Yes, sir." I lowered my gaze in submission only to feel a roaring in my chest which told me I didn't have to submit to him anymore. So I raised my eyes again, though my back was ramrod straight under his scrutiny, too many years of training beating this perfect posture into me.

"Then I will be reporting your insolence to him," Marik said icily.

"Insolence, sir?" I questioned before he could turn his back on me. I never spoke back to my captain, but I had wanted to a thousand times, and now I was not his to command. The thrill of that truth sent a shiver of excitement through me. "I simply returned your horse to you."

"Yes, and the rogue animal shall receive punishment for its misgivings, and you shall likely receive the same for yours." He sneered, snapping his fingers at the servant holding the reins of my horse. "Tie the beast up outside its stable in full sunlight. No food or water for two days." He dismissed the servant with a wave of his hand and the man drew Gallow away as he pulled Darell along on the stretcher behind him.

My muscles tensed and my teeth locked together as that punishment fell on my animal, and I found myself stepping into the personal space of my old captain with a threat in my movements. His eyebrows arched as he took in my aggression and anger flared through his gaze, the kind which would have once seen me kneeling on hard stone while my back was torn open by the strike of his whip.

"Stand down," he spat, but I didn't move a muscle, feeling the audience's attention on us growing. "You dare to defy the Captain of the Osarian Guard?"

"Is there a problem, Captain Marik?" Princess Austyn called before I could respond and I turned, finding her striding across the sand while her maids hurried after her.

Magdor looked like she'd just swallowed a bee as she watched her go, leaving Kahn still kneeling on the platform, forgotten in favour of this unexpected drama.

"Not at all, Your Highness." Marik bowed, but I bowed lower, keeping my eyes on the ground as my heart pounded fiercely in my chest. "Please, return to the shade. There is no need for you to risk sunstroke for the sake of a rogue guardsman."

I felt Marik's eyes on me and heard every note of accusation in those words, certain he was wishing he could be the one to punish me himself.

"I am sure I can handle a moment in the sun, Captain," Austyn said dismissively. "You are Count Nazari's man, are you not?"

A lump pushed at the base of my throat as I hesitated, knowing it was respectful to raise my eyes now that I had been addressed directly. But I feared that the moment I looked at her, she would see the truth of me, her eyes able to cut through the magic hiding my face and beyond. Perhaps she would see right into the depths of my wicked soul where all my darkest fantasies of her were housed.

"The princess is speaking to you, guard," Marik said sharply.

Old habits died hard as I responded to the bite in his tone, standing straight and lifting my gaze. And there she was, so close to me, so familiar and so gods-damn captivating.

A small frown creased her brow as she looked at me, and I could have sworn my cover was blown from the way her eyes traced my face, her throat bobbing in some reaction I couldn't quite read.

"Forgive me," I started, but she spoke before I could go on, our eyes never breaking from each other's. There was an energy in the air that had my heart thrashing in the confines of my ribcage, and it was so potent that I had to wonder if she sensed it too.

"You are forgiven. Captain, you are the one causing a scene over a horse." Austyn's amber gaze snapped onto him accusingly.

"The horse knocked Lord Darell from his stretcher, Your Highness,"

Marik stammered and I relished the way he reddened before her.

"Yes, and the sky is blue, and the grass is green. Was there anything else?"

"The captain seemed to feel that the animal should be punished," I said, my tongue running away with me despite knowing I should have been keeping my silence, but my love of Gallow drove me to insanity it seemed, and I was unable to stop now that I had begun.

"Is that so?" Austyn asked, flicking a frown Marik's way and he stiffened.

"It is my duty to ensure that any horse within the royal cavalry is adequately trained," he spluttered. "A few days in the sun without sustenance will surely serve to remind the beast of its place and-"

"You intend to leave the animal standing beneath the blazing sun without food?" she gasped, and her maids echoed her horror, Jacinda placing a hand to her heart and looking in danger of fainting.

"Or water," I added, unable to hide the growl in my tone.

"Surely an animal is incapable of understanding such a punishment?" Austyn protested.

Marik's eyes had turned hard like two sharp stones and despite his deference to the princess, he did not back down.

"Apologies for any concern this has caused you, Your Highness." He shot a dark look at me like he was even more eager to see me punished now. "But I have been in control of the royal cavalry for many years, and I know the best ways to train a horse. A creature cannot behave like that and be allowed to remain within the ranks of our elite-"

"Count Nazari is in need of a horse," I blurted, seeing the threat of the knacker's yard flashing in Marik's cruel gaze. "I am certain he would be willing to purchase the beast and resolve the issue that way. He is not a man put off by free spirits or impulsive acts, so I am certain the steed would be a good fit."

"Your employer is a fan of free spirits?" Austyn enquired with a small scoff, though there was curiosity in her gaze too.

"Indeed, he is," I agreed, unable to take it back - though now I was regretting the words as she seemed to be more interested in them than I would have assumed.

"Well, that sounds like a perfect solution to me," she said abruptly. "Now can we get on with our day?" she demanded and Marik gaped at her, speechless while a smug smile fought to tilt my lips.

"Y-yes, of course. My apologies, Your Highness." He bowed low and I did the same, stealing a final glance at her as she swept away and returned to the stage, leaving my blood pumping hard and fast.

"Return to your seat," Marik snarled at me before turning and marching away.

I did as I was told and watched as Kahn finally received his rosette from the princess, his eyes wandering over her with all the hunger of a starving man. I didn't want Drake to win this, but Kahn claiming Austyn was an even more abhorrent idea.

I'll cut his hands off before I ever let him lay them on her bare flesh.

The final fight took place between the Cartlanna sea captain and Prince Jah-Fal of Ageisha. Captain Hariot fought with the strength of two men, battering the older man with more skill than I'd expected. My brows rose as I watched him play out the same tactic several times. Skirt around, aim for the backs of the knees. I tucked that nugget of information away for Drake if he had to face him in his next brawl.

Hariot finally succeeded in bringing his opponent to the ground and Jah-Fal was defeated, Hariot taking sixteen points while Jah-Fal was awarded eight.

Hariot made it onto my list of concerns, the strength and skill he possessed clearly something to take note of. I just had to pray luck was on my side and Drake would be able to win the next round. I knew of the old pageants and the tales of the rounds growing in barbarity. It had been many, many years since a princess had been the only heir to the throne, meaning it had been a long time since a pageant had been held in Osaria, so I didn't know what of the old legends were true. But the texts written about them spoke not just of savage brawls between the men, but fights with wild beasts, death-defying races, climbs, swims, all kinds of challenges to push the suitors to their limits and prove their worth as an emperor.

Drake may have been a damn good fighter, but what was to say he could win at the other brutal games he would face? At least for now, he was not in danger of elimination, but I needed to escalate my plan against Magdor before he was. He could even die in one of the rounds for all I knew, and then where would I be? Turfed out onto the street with no chance of ever finding my way back into the palace.

The royals were escorted away and white petals were scattered over them as they went. I waited for them to depart as was customary before taking my turn to head back to the palace. Although, I planned on stopping by the stables on my way there…

Someone knocked against my arm and I spotted Kahn beside me, stroking the emerald rosette on his breast. I was disgusted with what Magdor had done to him, turning him into a beautiful vision despite the fact he was nothing but an empty-headed cretin. Up close, the changes were all the more apparent, and I could almost sense the magic in his skin. Though it didn't feel the way Kyra's did, this felt like something dark and ominous, something that shouldn't ever have been let loose in our kingdom.

"Who trained your liege?" he asked bluntly, and I was more than happy for the opportunity to try and intimidate him.

"He was trained by a band of warriors in his youth in the treacherous foothills of the Greymorian Peaks to the north of Carubai," I said, naming the ruinous mountain range which bordered the entire eastern edge of the empire and marked the end of the world as we knew it. There was a single pass which led into those mountains, but none who had ever ventured into them had ever returned, and it was long rumoured that to cross them was to cross into death itself. Fae of old once took that pass when they grew tired of immortality, walking into the unknown to face their end among those mountains in ceremonies thrown to celebrate their passage from this world, sometimes after hundreds or even thousands of years inhabiting it. "Then he served in the royal battalion for four years before they had to remove him."

"Remove him?" Kahn's eyes narrowed, his overly long lashes shadowing them.

"He spilled enough blood in one battle to stain a hundred miles of sand red. Though his skills were greatly admired, they feared his bloodlust was growing too keen and it frightened the men he fought alongside."

Kahn ran a hand through his auburn locks, his face twisting with concern, though not nearly enough to sate the need to see this prick squirm.

"He always asks for a taste of his most fierce enemies too," I said, letting him see fear in my eyes as I lowered my voice and glanced around like I shouldn't be speaking of this.

"A taste?" he hissed, shifting closer with the need to know, but I shook my head and backed up.

"I've said too much." I turned to leave, but he caught my arm and drew me closer to him once more.

"Tell me," he demanded. "I am the empress's son, and I command you to tell me."

I took in a couple of breaths as though I were nervous of revealing this then leaned closer to him, speaking in a whisper. "He has me carve pieces off of them and serve them to him like bloody steak. He savours each bite, and when he is done, he adds another mark to his skin. He was told long ago by a wandering Prophet that it was the key to absorbing their power. It is why he is covered in so much ink. He wears their deaths like a cloak."

Kahn shuddered and my heart thumped harder with the game as I saw the terror crawling into his eyes over that.

"I must hurry to him now." I clapped him on the back then hurried away through the crowd with a smile growing on my lips.

The lies tasted sweet in my mouth, and I swear I had never known a freedom quite like the life I was living now. Though the price of it was another knife in the chest of the man I had been within these walls. The man who was crafted by gruelling training and correctional punishments. I still strived to be a good man, the kind the princess deserved to serve her. But it felt as though I were splitting apart, torn in two by the man I should have been and the man I was becoming.

I forced away my discomfort at how far down the road of sin I'd come and made my way to the stables, aware that my sins for the day were not over. I knew my old captain well enough and he would not allow my old friend to go entirely unpunished, especially not while he could still claim that Gallow was a part of the royal cavalry. Until Drake's purchase of the horse was official, he would use the time he still had to enact a punishment upon him, I just knew it. And Gallow was my one friend in this world, so I would gladly protect him with my life.

The stables created a perfect square and I strode through the archway that gave me access to the cobbled courtyard at the heart of it. Gallow stood there tied to a post beneath the baking sun, the white stones beneath his hooves reflecting the light and his black fur absorbing every drop of the heat it threw back at him.

I ground my teeth, both furious that Marik had continued on with this punishment despite the arrangement he had agreed to while not surprised in the least. He was a vindictive man, petty and cruel, and no doubt he planned on carrying out this punishment before arranging for the horse to be transferred into the ownership of my supposed employer.

All was quiet apart from one stable where a teenage boy was mucking out the shit and hay, shovelling it all into a barrow that stood to one side of the door. I whistled to catch his attention and his head snapped up, his eyes going wide at the sight of me.

"Can I help you, sir?" he asked quickly

I petted Gallow's flank and he snorted happily in welcome before I walked over to the boy, taking my time to reach him as his eyes darted everywhere around me like he could tell trouble was descending on him.

I slid a gold coin from my pocket, one of the many Kyra had created for Drake – which he would no doubt notice was missing later and make a fuss over. I twisted it through my fingers and the light caught the boy's eyes as he stared at it longingly.

"Here." I tossed it to him, and he caught it automatically, releasing the shovel so it went flying towards the ground. I caught the handle, flipping it up into my grip as the boy admired the coin.

"For me, sir?" he asked in astonishment.

That coin was more than he'd be paid in a month but seeing as Kyra could make the damn things out of nothing, it was no skin off my nose. Of course, there was a chance the coin could turn to dust in his pocket once the magic wore off, but perhaps not. I knew nothing of such things. And she certainly had never suggested that would happen.

"Yes, on condition." I moved forward, making him back up into the closest stable and the shade fell over us like a blanket.

The boy seemed to see the danger in me then, stumbling backwards a little too fast as he took in the size of me.

"Please," he gasped. "I know some boys in town who work the brothels. I – I have no experience in such things, and they would please you far better than I could-" he stammered, holding the coin out like even the prospect of being well fed for a month wasn't worth what he thought I was going to do to him.

"I'm not asking for that," I said with a frown, but the fear didn't slip from his gaze as if he expected me to grab him at any moment. "I am here to ask one thing of you, and one thing only." I used the shovel in my grip to point at my horse. "You will feed and water that animal whenever possible during the next two days."

"He is being scorched, sir," the boy gasped. "The captain commanded it."

That was Marik's fun little name for this punishment. I had faced it myself more than once, but Gallow would not suffer under my watch.

"Then you shall have to ensure you are not seen," I said, swinging the shovel towards him so the shit-stained end of it pointed in his face. "Do you understand me, kid?"

He opened and closed his mouth, but the argument died in his eyes as he slid the coin into his pocket and nodded firmly. "I understand. But...why, sir?"

I considered not answering, but I needed to quiet the boy's interest in me in case gossip spread among the servants. "Count Drake Nazari will be taking ownership of him, and I am to ensure he is in good health."

I tossed the shovel down and headed over to Gallow, the horse rubbing his face against me, a little whinny of content leaving him as the word *"Apple?"* flared hopefully in my mind.

"Not yet, boy," I murmured. "But soon."

I tickled his ears then reluctantly left him behind, making my way along paths and through courtyards I knew all too well, finding it strange to be doing so without orders to follow.

I headed into the palace, passing down the long, white corridors and taking the time to really appreciate the tapestries and oil paintings in a way that felt more meaningful than it had in the past, my time always focused on my duties. It really was a beautiful palace with tiny courtyards and balconies hidden sporadically around every other corner, hand-carved door frames and exquisite art everywhere I looked.

I took my time but eventually made my way back up to Drake's chambers. The sinking sun cast amber light through the windows which led out to the private balcony and Drake was bathing in it, sitting on the floor with his britches rolled up to the knee and his right leg outstretched. Kyra sat next to him, cooing over his injury. A red and blue bruise was shining across the bone and Drake was lapping up every one of The Blessing's soothing words and compliments over his fighting prowess. I noticed the rosette had been removed from his chest now and two dots of red showed where the princess had slid it through his skin, the sight of it making me brim with satisfaction.

As Kyra cooed and fussed even more, I kicked the door shut to grab their attention. Drake didn't so much as flinch at the noise, his instincts clearly as keen as my own, knowing full well that I was there.

"So?" he asked at last.

"So what?" I drawled.

"How did the final brawls go? I suppose I am comfortably in first place already and you're eating your words like a hungry little orphan with his mouldy bit of bread."

"That analogy leaves a lot to be desired," I said coolly, and Drake's head snapped towards me as Kyra continued to croon over him.

"Tell me, mate," he demanded, a bite to his tone and I cocked my head at him.

"You're interested now, are you? Makes a change."

"I'm always interested in things when they concern me," he said. "Come on, Cass, sound the winners trumpet and do a little celebratory dance for me. I'm first, aren't I?"

"Second," I delivered to him with a sweet satisfaction.

His face fell, like I'd slapped him, but he quickly schooled it into nonchalance. "Kahn?" he guessed, and I nodded. "Oh well, he's only first 'cause he got himself an easy target in his brawl. If he faced me, he'd be firmly in second place where he belongs right now, and the princess would be swooning over me even more than she already was – ow." He turned to Kyra who had just poked him hard in the bruise with the blunt end of a spoon, but she fluttered her lashes innocently. "Woopsie."

"Captain Hariot is positioned thir-" I started, but Drake spoke over me.

"Don't care, mate. Anyone below me is already out of the running in my eyes."

"That is a very foolish belief to hold," I said, but he was clearly done talking about this as he ignored me entirely, returning his attention to The Blessing.

Kyra continued to pout and fuss over the wound while Drake clearly enjoyed the attention, and I narrowed my eyes at him irritably.

"Just ask her to heal it," I said, shaking my head.

"I was just about to, mate," Drake said with a slanted grin. "Would you fix my leg, little goddess? Keep the colour of the bruise though. Just in case anyone sees it."

Kyra nodded quickly, shutting her eyes for a moment then Drake sighed, getting to his feet with a word of thanks. He strolled across the room, hooking a scroll from the dining table before approaching me.

"We were sent this." Drake thrust the thick parchment letter at me.

"What does it say?" I asked as I took it, eyeing the royal seal stamped onto the fine paper.

"I can't read," he grunted, gesturing for me to open it and I was stabbed a little too hard with that knowledge, especially as I'd been angry with him for not taking the time to read over the rules of the pageant. I was once again forced to acknowledge the privileges I had been afforded while he was fighting for survival on the streets, and I didn't like how that disturbed me.

I had been foolish not to think of it before. Of course he couldn't read. Orphans were not able to go to school in Osaria – another thing the emperor had been about to change before Magdor had arrived. Education was important for the advancement of our people as a whole, and he had once spoken passionately about the desire to offer it to all.

I ignored the tug of pity in my chest over this man's deprived upbringing and focused on the thousand issues this might present going forward as I tore open the seal upon the scroll and scanned the page. My heart sank as I read it and worries flickered through my mind.

"Fuck." I crushed the parchment in my palm.

"What is it?" Kyra asked keenly, her hair floating around her shoulders for a moment before she wrangled the magic and it fell naturally once more.

"You're invited to a formal dinner tonight alongside the other victors."

"Ohh, am I?" Kyra asked brightly.

"Er, no. Drake is," I clarified with a snort of amusement as her answer caught me off guard.

"Well, he was looking at me, so I had to assume he meant us," Kyra muttered to herself.

"And?" Drake questioned me with a shrug.

"*And* it's going to fit the traditions of The Twelve Kingdoms. Meaning every course will hold the customs of each land."

"So?" Drake shrugged again and I ground my teeth.

"Do you know the customs of every kingdom, *Count Nazari*? Do you even know the customs of your own alleged kingdom?"

"Obviously not," he said scathingly. "But you can teach me, right?"

I turned to the clock on the wall. There was only half an hour until the feast began. That wasn't nearly enough time to teach him everything he needed to know. And what if he messed it up and gave away the fact that he wasn't a real count? This could ruin *everything*.

"He can't," Kyra breathed ominously. "His expression says he can't. Look at his face, it's all scrunchy and worried and says, 'oh no the world is ending!'" She pointed at me and Drake frowned.

"Is that true?" he demanded. "There's really not enough time?"

"No, not even close to enough. I didn't realise this would be required or I would have been teaching you for days." Anxiety burrowed into my chest as I tossed the letter onto the nearest table and began to pace. There were so many layers to the customs around this meal, and even Fae who had been taking part in these kinds of things for years sometimes struggled to remember them all. But that would be no excuse. Anyone of high enough breeding would be expected to know the entire thing to perfection. Drake could not do it.

By the Fallen, what were we going to do? I couldn't risk Drake fucking this all up now. There would be a whole host of questions about the count once he proved he didn't even know the customs of his own land, let alone the rest of the kingdoms' traditions. Everything could fall apart thanks to this single damn thing.

"Shit...maybe I can say I'm too badly injured to attend?" Drake suggested but I shook my head.

"Tomorrow they will see how well you are and assume you lied. That would cause even more of a scandal," I growled, running a hand over my head.

"Tell them I have the shits then," he said with a shrug and I damn near choked on my own tongue.

"Nobles do not say things like 'I have the shits' and even if they did, they would surely send a healer for you, and though I cannot claim to understand healing Affinities in their entirety, I do know that a healer would instantly be able to tell that you were fit and well," I said, shaking my head and pacing faster.

Kyra started following me around the room, mimicking me as she clasped her hands behind her back and shook her head in frustration. I nearly bumped into her as I twisted sharply around and she vanished into a puff of smoke, making my heart lurch in surprise before she materialised beside me instead.

"I suppose *you'll* just have to go," Kyra gasped in realisation.

"That makes absolutely no sense, magic girl," I said as I took a measured step away from her, still disturbed by the power she had just wielded.

"I'll make you look like Drake," she said like it was obvious, and I wondered when she'd decided to start calling him by his name instead of master. Her smile suddenly fell away as she thought on her suggestion. "Oh, is that a bad idea? I suppose you wouldn't want to look that ugly, Cassius. It might make you very upset. Look how upset Drake is about it." She gestured to him, and his jaw ticked with rage at her words.

I released a low laugh and Drake turned to Kyra, taking in a deep breath. "Firstly, I'm *not* ugly. You've got things all mixed up and it's about time you got them straight. And secondly..." His eyes suddenly glimmered and a smile pulled at his mouth. "That's a fucking genius idea."

"Really?" she asked, her eyes wide with hope and he grinned as he nodded.

This idea was absolute insanity. "I'm not fit to attend such a thing," I said firmly, wanting to come up with a plan far less risky than this.

"Oh, but I am?" Drake blew out a breath of amusement. "You're high born, Cassius. That's good enough."

"It is not." My heart thrashed against my ribcage as I shook my head once more. "And I will not risk getting stuck looking like you forevermore."

"There are far worse fates, Cass," Drake said cockily, giving me that smouldering look of his which he always offered women.

I glowered back at him, proving I was unmoved by his peacocking.

"Of course, I'd probably have to kill you if you got stuck that way. There can't be two of me, mate. I'm one of a kind." He winked at Kyra and she laughed, batting a hand at him.

"Don't worry, Cassius, I'm more likely to turn you inside out than get the magic right anyway." She giggled at her own joke, and I stiffened as Drake approached me.

He slammed a hand down on my shoulder, meeting my gaze with a mixture of encouragement and threat in his dark gaze. "Don't worry about it. It'll be *fine*. Kyra will fix you up real nice, then you just need a few pointers from me. Simple."

I scowled. "I don't need any such thing."

"Oh yeah? Well, if you don't act like me they're going to figure out that something's up," Drake pressed. "I'm charismatic, charming, unforgettable. These are not talents you possess. But you're gonna have to figure it out sharpish."

I released a low growl, unsure of any other way around this despite my reservations.

I was going to the royal feast to lie to my own rulers. I would be spending the night fooling them all, fooling the princess. I would no doubt be given time with her, to speak with her, court her –

My mind hooked on that last thought and my throat thickened while the devil in me awakened. A night in the princess's company where I didn't have to stand guard, staring at a wall suddenly seemed like the most tantalising thing that had ever been offered to me in my life. And yet here I was refusing it.

Dressed in Drake's flesh, I would be free to speak with her to my heart's content, I would be able to get an inside look at the other competitor's demeanours too.

"Come on, mate," Drake begged.

"Yeah. Come on, mate," Kyra echoed as she jumped to his side. "Please, please, please with apple pie on the side."

"Fine," I agreed at last, sealing my fate and anticipation trickled into my chest.

"You'd better do me justice. I want the princess drooling over me tomorrow. Don't go ruining my reputation with your manners or any of that bullshit," Drake said, his eyes scraping down me accusingly. "For fuck's sake, you're too stiff. Loosen up, you arsehole. You're going to make me look bad." He shook my shoulders and I tried to relax my rigid limbs, but so many years of servitude made it difficult. He kept shaking me though until I'd changed my posture a little.

"Better," he said brightly, slapping my cheek in that way that made me want to rip his throat out. But as we were on a tight time limit, I thought better of it and managed to restrain myself.

"You'll get the seat beside the princess, no matter what." He shoved a finger in my face and I knocked it away.

"There will be a seating plan-"

"Fuck the seating plan up the arse with a cactus. You'll do this, Cassius. Because it's what I'd do," Drake insisted. "You'll sit beside her and you'll tuck your chair in so that you end up good and close to her. I mean it. If there isn't a thigh brush in your evening, then you will have failed. Do you understand me?"

I released a slow breath, realising it wasn't the worst thing in the world. I was taking on Drake's persona for a night, and the man had no care for rules or customs. That was the kind of freedom I had never indulged in, and it was all too tempting a gift to ignore.

"Fine," I said tightly, not letting him see my shift in mood over this.

"Good. Kyra, let's make Cassius look like me," he said.

Kyra smiled as she turned my way. "Do you agree?"

I nodded, trepidation flowing through my chest as her power hit me. My skin seemed to shiver and melt on my frame, my bones shifting and realigning into a new and unfamiliar posture as her magic ran over me, heating and cooling my skin simultaneously. I braced in the expectation of pain, but it never came, and as the odd sensation fell away, I knew without needing to see a mirror that it had worked.

A dark lock of hair fell into my eyes and I pushed it back before gazing at my hands, examining the slight shift in skin tone, the tattoos peeking out from beneath my cuffs and crawling up the backs of my hands.

Drake stared at me with his lips parting as he took a step closer, cocking his head and inspecting me, his eyes alight with intrigue. "Wow, I knew I was something to look at, but seeing it like this is really eye-opening. I'm fucking gorgeous."

I gave him a dry look. "Just get on with it." I froze as I found my voice wasn't mine anymore. It was his.

Kyra fashioned an elaborate cream tunic onto my body with golden buttons running up the middle and the kind of embroidery that would have taken days to perfect. The britches she created to match them were tighter than I'd normally wear, and I shifted uncertainly as I grew used to my new body within them.

"Right, so the rest of the bastards in the pageant think flashing their money and talking about how many horses they have will make the princess warm to them. But women don't give a fuck about any of that," Drake said. "Especially not one who's got a palace fit for the gods and already owns every trinket under the sun that she could ever wish for."

"Agreed. So perhaps she would be more enthralled by conversation about her interests and-" I started but Drake cut over me.

"Naaah, Cass." He waved a hand in my face. "She's a secret rebel. I've seen it for myself. She wants to play with fire and she might even wanna feel it burn, if you know what I'm saying."

"Shall I give Cassius a lit torch? Maybe he could set the princess's lovely silver hair on fire?" Kyra suggested.

"No, little goddess, it's a metaphor," Drake explained, and she scrunched up her nose as she tried to understand that.

"Like a flying lion?" she asked in confusion.

"That's a manticore," I said.

"Look, it ain't important what a metaphor is," Drake barrelled on. "Point is, you have to act like you don't want the princess. Like you couldn't give a fuck even though you do give a fuck, got it?"

"I'm not sure I understand," I said with a frown, though I couldn't help but want to try. Drake did seem to have a way with women that defied all logic and reason, and I certainly had never had any experience courting a woman for something meaningful.

Fuck, am I really taking advice from a thief?

"Look, I'll be the princess and you be me. Act aloof when I talk to you. Be a bit of a prick sometimes too. Give her a compliment then take it away again. Go on, try it." He fluttered his lashes at me, batting my chest. "Oh Drake, what big muscles you have. How handsome your smile is."

I gazed coolly back at him and he shoved my arm.

"Do it," he commanded and I huffed out a breath before trying to mimic his casual stance and his general air of owning the world. "Come on, be more aloof."

"Stop saying aloof," I hissed.

"Do it then, big man," he demanded, shoving me once again and Kyra nodded encouragingly.

I cleared my throat, trying to take onboard what he had said and nodding stiffly at Drake as I pictured the princess in his place.

"Good evening. You look very beautiful tonight."

Drake faked a girlish laugh and twirled a lock of imaginary hair around his finger. He was taking this too fucking far, but I didn't have the time to reprimand him for it.

"Now take it back, sullen man," Kyra whispered to me, her eyes wide as she watched.

"But I find most things beautiful. Including dirt. And....pig shit," I said abruptly and Drake stared at me before bursting out laughing.

"By the Fallen, you're fucked," he said as I scowled at him and his face fell as he realised that he was fucked too.

"How about I throttle you, bury you in the gardens and remain looking like you. Then I will act appropriately, and everyone will forget your previous behaviour while I win the pageant and leave Kahn bloody in my wake," I suggested and Drake gasped, pointing at me.

"There," he announced excitedly. "That's it, mate. You just gave me the tingles right down to my balls. That dark, forbidding shit is your angle. Go with that. That's more like me than your stick-up-the-arseness, so it's better than nothing."

"All this talk of sticks up things is making me hungry for some skewered potatoes. Is that still a thing people eat?" Kyra asked, then muttered under breath. "Wait...did people ever eat skewered potatoes?"

"I'll skewer whatever you want me to, little goddess," Drake said, giving her a look which was so far beyond inappropriate that I had half a mind to punish him for it. There was no chance I would be speaking to the princess like that.

"Oh," Kyra replied, biting on her bottom lip and forcing me to clear my throat.

"Focus on why we are here," I barked, and Drake snapped his head back to me again with a wry smile.

"Go with the menacing thing," Drake pressed, clapping me on the arm. "Just try not to talk too much and for the love of the Fallen, don't embarrass me when you *do* talk to her."

I pursed my lips. "I am a royal guard, I will not be an embarrassment."

"That's the problem," he huffed. "You're too...restrained. All of your personality has been stripped outa you and tossed away. It isn't coming back either, I can see that. It died a long time ago, mate. There was a wake with people mourning and everything before your personality was cremated and cast to ash on the wind. But at least try and pretend you have one."

I shifted my weight from one foot to the other, not liking that cutting assessment of me.

"I know that doesn't even bother you, Cass, because the part of you that would have been bothered by it is gone too," Drake said with a sigh that seemed like pity and it made me feel like the nothing I knew I was.

"Poof. Vanished," Kyra whispered mysteriously, emphasising his point and the way they looked at me made my chest shrink and compress. Maybe they were right, maybe I was just a shell with the memories of a man rattling around inside him. Maybe everyone could see it in my eyes, that I simply could never be whole if I tried.

The potential of who I could have been had been sacrificed to the crown. I had given it all up to protect my family from losing everything, and I had done so willingly. But now that meant I neither fit in with the nobles nor the commoners. I was made into something…other. Something no one could relate to anymore.

I gave in to Drake's demands of me, nodding my head like I had when Captain Marik had barked orders, quietly committing myself to the one thing I had left. The only purpose that made my life hold any value now. I would use this opportunity tonight to try and further my attempts at exposing Magdor, and keeping Drake in the pageant was crucial to that.

"You can't treat women like they're the apple of your eye or whatever other bullshit is circling through your repressed little brain right now. You've got to be aloof," Drake said.

"I swear to fuck, if you say aloof one more time-" I started but he cut over me.

"Just don't give her too much attention. If her maids are there, you need to give them at least twice as many compliments as you do the princess."

I clenched my jaw. "That is not at all appropriate."

"Women don't like appropriate, Cass. Have you ever even fucked a girl? Because I imagine you had to ask her to remove the stick from your arse first."

I glowered at him, my hands curling into fists. "That's none of your business and I do not have a stick up my arse."

"You do, it was surgically inserted by the kingdom," Drake chuckled.

I folded my arms, done with this conversation.

"It sounds painful," Kyra breathed. "Would you like me to magic it out for you?"

My jaw ticked and I refused to respond to her suggestion as Drake laughed harder.

"Go on, admit it. You're a virgin, aren't you mate? Fuck, actually, did that captain of yours have your balls removed? Are all the guards eunuchs?" Drake taunted.

Despite my efforts to remain impassive, my anger won out and I fisted his tunic, yanking him nose to nose with me as I bared my teeth. "I am not a damn virgin *or* a eunuch. And you may see the void in me, thief, but you would do well to remember why it is there. I am capable of unthinkable brutality, there is no torture method in this world that turns my stomach. I could pull out every one of your bones and keep you awake while I did it, and now that I have no collar or leash, I am free to aim that brutality at whomever I wish."

Drake shoved me off of him, looking keen for a fight. "You don't look free. You look as caged as all the guards in this place. You're still one of them, just a beast with its claws pulled out. One word from your old captain and you'd fall right back in line."

I lunged at him but Kyra dove between us, placing her hands out towards us and scrunching her eyes shut as we both came close to touching her. I stopped myself short of colliding with her, my respect for her greater than my desire to throttle the man on the other side of her.

"Well, you are just a thief pretending to be a god. The world will catch up on you, Drake. You think I am empty inside, then how about you? All you have is selfish desires and nothing of substance in this life to sate you," I spat.

"I will soon have all the treasure and all the power in the world, what could be more substantial than that?" Drake said, stretching his arms wide and laughing, either not caring about the truth of my words or seriously believing that all he needed were material assets to be content.

"Stop it," Kyra begged. "If you need new balls, Cassius, I'm sure Drake will wish some up for you."

"Yeah, I'll get you some shiny new balls, mate, how about that?" Drake mocked and a growl rolled up my throat.

"Stand aside, Kyra," I insisted, but she wouldn't move, shaking her head.

"I can't let you hurt my master." She shook her head more fiercely. "He may be ugly, but he's the best master I've ever had."

Drake flinched at that word. "Just get out of here, Cass," he commanded. "And forget your morals tonight. I don't have any and the princess has been lapping that up until now. If you ruin this for me, I will beat your arse."

Irritation flashed through me at the insinuation that Austyn was attracted to the cockiness of this common street thief. "I am not your puppet."

"No, but you are the kingdom's puppet," Drake said dismissively. "So go be a good boy and do what you need to do to save it."

"Tick-tock," Kyra said, waggling her index finger like a metronome. "Better get going."

I headed to the door as I swallowed back a stream of retorts, my heart pounding as I stepped into the corridor with Drake's voice calling after me, "Don't fuck this up, you neutered cunt!"

I shut the door as rage spilled into my chest, spotting a servant across the hall, his eyebrows nearly jumping into his hairline at what he'd heard. "Apologies, my guard is berating my maid."

He nodded, bowing his head low and I hurried away from him, cursing Drake under my breath. He was going to get us removed from the palace before

I could achieve anything with Magdor if I couldn't contain his outbursts.

I headed down a spiralling staircase and followed the sound of a string quartet towards the ballroom, mentally preparing myself for what was to come. Although, I wasn't sure there was any preparation I could have done to ready myself for seeing the princess up close, in a setting where I would be encouraged to speak with her.

My heart thumped with irrational desire over that, but I was a man wearing the face of a cad tonight. It would not be me she saw, and thank the Fallen for that. For the man truly keeping her company was nothing more than a disgraced guard who had indulged in one too many forbidden thoughts about her. And though I was quietly convincing myself that this was for the greater good, that this act was only in servitude to her in a roundabout way, I knew deep down that I was anticipating it for reasons that were entirely selfish.

The guards on duty bowed low to me and I arched my brows at being on the receiving end of the respect I'd dished out through all my years in their position. Little did they know, I wasn't in any way deserving of that respect. I was a criminal, and one wrong move could land me right back where I'd been when I had first met Drake, breathing out my final breaths before a grim execution.

I stepped into the grand dining hall where a white oak table stretched through the centre of the space, set with a golden runner along the heart of it. Arching windows lined one side of the room and a set of doors led out to a sweeping balcony washed in moonlight.

This place was more familiar to me than my own home. I had been stationed here countless times throughout countless royal meals, and I knew every thread in the enormous tapestry hanging on the far wall by heart. Sat on the ruby throne of Osaria was a white tiger with glinting silver claws and a proud sort of look on its face. Another was curled up at its feet, but its head was raised, and a fierce protectiveness seemed to fill its gaze. Trees arched over them, laden with oranges, apples, pears and a golden crown gleamed within the sun in the sky, held in the grip of a pale hand that was representative of the Fallen Fae, reaching down to place it upon the head of the beast. White tigers appeared in a lot of the art in the palace as they were featured within the Lunarelle family crest, their ferocity, beauty, and power all symbols of what the royals stood for.

I was the last to arrive despite the fact I was right on time, but the rest of the suitors who had won their rounds today were clearly eager to get as much out of their time with the princess as possible.

My eyes found Austyn instinctively, drawn to her as they had been even before I'd seen her face. It was her spirit which called to me, and the beauty of that could be rivalled by nothing, not the royal jewels housed within this palace, not all the treasure in the cave Drake and I had discovered, not even her beauty. She shone from within, and I wished to draw my sword and cut out the hearts of every man at this table so that they may never have a chance to dim that light in her.

Kahn, Captain Hariot, and Prince Gurvine all sat across from Austyn in fine robes, wearing trinkets, sashes and medals in representation of their kingdoms.

Behind the princess, standing either side of one of the high windows, were her two maids, Zira and Jacinda, both of whom were wearing matching yellow dresses, their heads bowed, and hands clasped neatly in front of them.

The princess made my heart stall as she rose abruptly to her feet and turned to me. It was only then that I truly took in her outfit and the way her silver hair was half pinned up into a delicate bun. She was dressed in a flowing golden gown that made her amber eyes stand out and her skin seem to shimmer. My throat thickened as her gaze floated down me approvingly and the victors rose from their chairs, obviously feeling compelled to do so too.

I fought the wave of bitter jealousy that accompanied her drinking me in, because it wasn't me at all. It was Drake she was admiring.

"Good evening," I said formally, bowing low and Austyn dipped her head in kind.

"Good evening, Count Nazari, I assume you have heard the news?" she asked, and I frowned.

"News, your highness?" I questioned.

"Lord Darell has withdrawn from the pageant," she announced, and Kahn sniggered, flexing his fingers which were lined with bruises.

The other men looked to him accusingly and I sensed the tension in the air. Darell had clearly been too badly injured to continue, and though nothing in the rulebook said Kahn's ruthless beating of him was prohibited, it certainly wasn't how anyone in this competition would want to be forced out of the running.

Everyone awaited my comment on that, but I was distracted by the beauty of the princess. I never simply had the opportunity to look at her eye to eye like this, my years of training demanding I bow my head to all royalty, but I wasn't a guard tonight. No, I was a man perfectly entitled to look, and the way she looked back made my flesh heat with desire.

"Are you going to stand there all night like a rabbit dazzled by the moon, or are we going to eat?" The princess dropped back into her seat and the rest of the men followed.

I rather enjoyed her sharp tone with me considering it was really Drake she believed she was speaking to.

"My apologies." I moved across the room, taking the remaining seat beside Kahn as a servant pulled it out for me.

Drake's instructions rang in my head, but I couldn't very well sit beside Austyn when there were no chairs laid out beside her. Though I had to wonder if he would still have found a way to do so.

The musicians played out of sight behind a curtain, offering the group of us some semblance of privacy – not from the guards who stood in every corner though.

I wondered what they would think of me now if they knew who was really sitting at this table with the princess. I supposed they would cheer when I was hung for it, no matter how many hours we had spent in each other's company previously.

Wine was poured for us in silver chalices, and I lifted mine under my nose as everyone did the same, swirling the cup as I breathed in the crisp scent of Cartlanna honey wine.

"Praise Cartlanna and its bountiful fields," Austyn said, starting the formal feast with the first custom.

The rest of us responded in unison with the scripted words which I knew from watching a thousand of these feasts from the shadows where my fellow guards stood now. "May the grass grow tall, the sun fall upon their crops, the rain moisten the earth, and may their bounty always be plentiful."

I sipped my wine in time with the others. This was a dance. Our movements synchronised and though I'd never done them before, my hands knew them as well as if I had. I'd committed it all to memory as I'd watched from the side lines, marvelling in the perfect rhythm of the feast of The Twelve Kingdoms.

The wine rolled over my tongue, and I took a larger gulp than necessary, figuring Drake probably would have done so anyway. Wearing his skin gave me a freedom I was starting to enjoy a little too much, and with no one around to tell me otherwise, I allowed my formalities to slip. I was hungering for a bite of life, and I was tempted to give in to my wants for once. Just for a night. What harm was there in that?

Kahn led the conversation, acting out his brawl with Darrel in a play-by-play of every punch he had landed. "And that was when I heard something snap." He slammed his fist down on the table, making the cutlery jump and I stared at him icily.

Prince Gurvine paled a little, but Hariot only straightened in his chair, eyeing Kahn's immense size.

"There was no snap," Hariot scoffed. "You may be big, Kahn, but your talk is bigger."

"Ha," Kahn scoffed, grabbing a glazed ear of corn from the latest platter to arrive and tearing into it with his teeth. "You'll find out soon enough."

Austyn's nose wrinkled as she watched the display. She had hardly eaten any of the food placed in front of her and she didn't look inclined to try any of the honeyed vegetables, seasoned rice and braised mushrooms laid out for us now. This course hailed from Ageisha; a kingdom famed for its mining industry and the jewels it bore. They were a fierce people born to a wild, mountainous land renowned for its ruthless beauty. The mountain range known as the Serpent's Spine was one of the most highly populated areas of wild beasts who liked to lurk in the dark of the many caves and passes there, but the Ageishan people had remained all the same, the riches of the mines too alluring even in the face of such dangers.

"My skill will see me through any brawl," Hariot said, puffing out his chest and stealing a glance at the princess as if he thought she might be falling for his peacocking. "I have sailed across the Iron Ocean and lived to tell the tale. My legs have withstood the roughest of seas, and I haven't taken a single tumble since my father placed me upon my first ship on my third birthday."

He slapped his own thigh as if to prove the strength in it and a frown inched into my brow. This man was a joke.

"I could defeat you in under a minute," I muttered, picking up my wine and taking a swig.

"What was that?" Hariot swung around, his surprisingly shapely eyebrows rising. "Don't you mutter under your breath at me, you cad. Speak for all the men to hear."

"And what of the woman you claim to be fighting for?" I demanded, my voice booming out louder than I'd intended.

Hariot glanced over at the princess, but I didn't shift my gaze from him, locking him in my sights and picturing the bloody mess I would so easily make of him in a fight.

"Yes, of course, she must hear too," Hariot simpered. "That goes without saying."

"Does it?" Austyn clipped and I couldn't help but look at her then, the power in her expression taking me off guard as she glared at Hariot. There was hatred there, but something deeper than that too. Injustice perhaps, that she had to sit here and entertain any of this.

How I wish you did not have to.

"Of course," Hariot gushed. "I meant no offence, princess."

Austyn looked away from him, flicking a hand in a gesture that was obviously dismissive.

Another course was served; a dainty dish of three asparagus sprigs dipped in the famed sauce of Berion. The southern city it hailed from was set among endless flat planes which made for some of the best farmland in all of the Osarian Empire, their crops sold far and wide throughout the kingdom as well as across the sea to trade with the Forkens, bringing much prosperity to our empire.

"May the wind fall at the backs of the mighty Berions," Austyn said, her tone flat.

We spoke the response in unison, and I cut into the tiny meal, picking up the knife and fork allocated for this course from the array of cutlery beside my plate.

I'd always wanted to try that sauce and as it hit my tongue, I released a groan that caused Austyn to look over at me.

I grabbed my wine, taking another long swig as I waited for her eyes to fall away from me. She was so beautiful it burned a mark into my heart. A mark that had been there ever since our eyes had first locked. Heat rose in my blood, the idea of her desiring me too exciting to ignore. Even though I knew it wasn't me she wanted at all. But tonight, I would know what it felt like to be someone she craved, and it tasted too damn good to deny it.

I made it through the rest of the courses without saying much at all and by the end of our Dunemare dessert, Prince Gurvine was filling the silence by describing the hall of fine wines he owned.

"You're awfully quiet tonight, Count Nazari," Austyn addressed me, and I sat up straighter in my seat. "Does wine not interest you?" She said it in a way that told me she was bored by this conversation as I was.

"Wine is good for drinking, not housing in dark cellars. Who cares how fine it is? I only appreciate that fact when it slides down my throat."

A smile tugged up the corner of Austyn's lips as she raised her chalice in my direction. "I will drink to that." She took a sip, and I watched the movement of her delicate throat as she swallowed.

Prince Gurvine got to his feet with a huff. "Well good night to you all, I am not going to remain here to be insulted." He looked to the princess as if hoping she might contradict him, but she did no such thing.

"Yes, run to bed little boy," Kahn boomed and Gurvine threw him a scowl before storming from the room.

"If he cannot take a simple jibe, he will be no good as an emperor," Hariot laughed, looking a little red in the face from how much wine he had consumed. "The throne needs a man of character, someone with charm, refinement, and above all else, clout."

"Clout?" Austyn tsked. "How about someone with a good heart who cares for the needs of their people?"

Kahn and Hariot guffawed at that, and Austyn shoved to her feet, tossing her napkin down on the table.

Kahn rose from his seat a beat later, his hulking form throwing a shadow over me. "Princess, Mother says it is okay to ask for some privacy this evening. We could go to the balcony so I can regard your pleasant form under the moonlight?"

Austyn's nose wrinkled and my teeth ground in my mouth, my hand curling tightly around the dinner knife in my grip. She quickly forced the look from her face, but I liked that I'd seen her true feelings. It was a glimpse into her thoughts. Beautiful or not, her mind somehow intrigued me more.

"Fine," she conceded. "But to make it fair, I'll have to spend time with each of you on the balcony."

Her eyes strayed to me, and heat rose in my blood as I sensed her desire to speak with me. The idea of her wanting time with me was too exciting to ignore, but the feeling dissolved as I remembered it wasn't me she wanted at all. It was Drake.

She headed away with Kahn and he laid an arm around her waist possessively as they disappeared through the balcony doors. The fact he had touched her so informally set my pulse racing and violence coursing along the inside of my flesh. I had half a mind to go out there after her and had I still been a guard, I would have been on her heels this very instant. I looked to the guards standing watch at the end of the room, their expressions vacant.

"Fucking useless," I growled.

Captain Hariot looked my way, his cheeks rosy from the wine he'd drunk. "What's that?"

I sighed, turning my attention to him to try and get my mind off the knowledge that Kahn now had Austyn in his grasp.

"Nothing," I said, slapping a Drake-worthy grin on my face and he smiled dreamily back at me.

"You really are something, aren't you?" He lowered his tone and his gaze rolled down onto my body then back to my face, leaving me feeling like his eyes were looking beneath my clothes somehow. "How do you rate your chances against Magdor's boy?" He slung an arm over Kahn's chair between us, leaning closer.

"I have more chance than you," I said with a taunting look.

"We'll see about that," Hariot said, wetting his lips as his gaze slipped to my mouth then back up again. "Perhaps we can talk more on this later? Kahn has invited me to the Frog Spawn Tavern after the formalities are done. He has some friends who are already getting the party started for us. Warming up the entertainment if you will." He waggled his eyebrows at me suggestively and I frowned.

"The entertainment?"

"Whores of course," he whispered low so the maids couldn't hear, leaning closer so his wine-tainted breath washed over me. "The finest in the land. They will do *anything* for a gold coin or two. You can be whoever you want to be in this tavern apparently. There is utmost confidentiality within its walls, it will all be very subtle." He tapped his nose then slicked his tongue over his lips again. "So any little fantasies you have can be explored safely there." His hand moved onto my shoulder, squeezing then starting to massage.

"Take your hand off of me," I warned through my smile.

He retracted it, chuckling softly as he retreated into his seat. "You seem far more uptight than you were earlier, Count Nazari. I would have thought a man like you would be familiar with the pleasures of such…entertainment."

I swallowed back the retort in my throat, knowing I had to play the part of Drake more convincingly, and right now I was giving the game away. I cleared my throat, settling back in my seat in a more relaxed pose as I forced my muscles to lose some of their tension. "Of course I am. But I doubt the entertainment Osaria provides at a price could even come close to what I am used to getting back in Carubai for free."

"Do tell me more," Hariot urged eagerly as I took a sip of wine. "I have travelled port to port, and I doubt there is much you have done that would surprise me. I am a well experienced man; I am sure I could teach you a thing or two about the pleasure that can be bought on faraway shores."

"I do not need to buy the company of women. If anything, they would pay good coin to have a night with me." I smirked like an arsehole.

"Mm, I believe that," he purred.

Austyn returned, her jaw ticking with annoyance as she marched back into the room and Kahn floated after her with a wide smile on his face. I twirled the knife in my grip, watching them and wondering exactly what had gotten him looking so pleased with himself.

Hariot leapt to his feet like a jack-in-the-box. "I'll accompany you next."

He shot to Austyn's side and bowed low, opening an arm in a gesture for her to turn around. She pursed her lips before twisting around and marching back outside again, leaving him galloping after her hastily.

I could feel the frustration flowing from her and wondered if I should pass up the opportunity to talk with her outside. What would I say anyway? I was going to fuck this whole thing up if I didn't act enough like Drake.

Kahn dropped into his seat with a smug grin, and I glowered, unable to stop my feelings towards him spilling into my expression.

"So, you got a new face, I hear," I said lightly, placing down the knife that was locked in my hand.

Kahn turned to me with a cocky smile. "Yes. Now Mother says I am more than a match for you on every level."

"Is that so? Well at least Austyn has no memory of *me* looking like a potato."

His face turned a nasty shade of purple. "How would you know what I looked like before?" he growled, and the air went out of my lungs.

Fuck.

I needed to recover fast. "It's all the servants talk about." I shrugged one shoulder, swirling my chalice as the crimson wine sloshed inside it.

Kahn's face went from purple to red and I wasn't sure what was worse. An angry vein bulged in his forehead, so I suspected red was the danger level.

The princess returned to the room before he could reach boiling point and I frowned as I noted the scowl on her face. It was clear she hated this whole thing, and I wasn't at all surprised.

Hariot bowed low, bidding the princess goodnight as he pressed a wet kiss to the back of her hand. I could practically hear the sucking sound as he tugged his lips off of her skin and my shoulders stiffened.

"Get your filthy, unwashed mouth away from her," I snarled, suddenly on my feet before I'd even realised I was moving.

Hariot bolted upright, looking to me in shock along with everyone else in the room.

I cleared my throat as Austyn wiped her hand down the side of her dress, looking to me with parted lips.

"I beg your pardon?" Hariot gasped, fucking flabbergasted by my rudeness.

I was consumed by a hot, thundering rage that had me stalking towards him and the princess at a fierce pace. I couldn't control it now that it was unleashed, and I didn't want to either.

"He has kept me waiting long enough for a moment with you, princess. Are you going to keep me in suspense any longer?" I asked, knocking Hariot aside and firmly placing myself between them, needing to increase that distance as soon as possible. And there was one clear way to do that. I was owed time with her on the balcony, and I was going to claim it now to get her away from that uncouth boar, even if it would put me at risk of her noticing the difference in the man she thought was accompanying her.

"You cannot speak to me so crudely," Hariot hissed, taking hold of my arm.

I yanked my arm free of his grip and slapped him on the cheek in that patronising way Drake always did. "I can do what I like, Captain. Now off to bed with you. Or to your whores. I don't care which so long as you are out of my sight."

"How dare you?" Hariot gasped. "I do not bed whores!" His eyes whipped beyond me in the direction of the princess. "Do you hear these lies he is trying to spread about me? How he tries to besmirch my name, My Lady?"

She didn't answer and I glanced back to find her walking out onto the balcony, completely dismissing us both. I followed her, ignoring Hariot as he called after me, cursing my name. But the name didn't belong to me anyway, so hell if I cared what he had to say about it.

I heard the maids whispering excitedly to each other before I stepped outside through a curtain of white silk and found Austyn standing there with her back to me, gazing out across the palace gardens.

My eyes travelled over the gold material hugging her curves and pooling around her feet on the tiled floor. Although I couldn't see her expression, I sensed she was weary of this interaction already, probably dreaming of returning to the privacy of her rooms far away from any of the men who were trying to win her in this twisted game.

"My apologies," I said in a low voice.

"For what?" she laughed humourlessly. "For outing Hariot's escapades? I may not have seen much of life beyond these walls, but I am not a fool. I know that every man in this pageant will have whichever woman he likes even if he is to marry me."

"Not every man," I vowed, though could I really do so on Drake's behalf? I would certainly castrate him myself if he planned on bedding other women whilst courting the princess, so I supposed I could guarantee it for now.

She clucked her tongue, glancing back at me and the way the moonlight lit her eyes made my heart stall in my chest. She looked like a magnificent goddess come to rain her fury down upon my flesh, and by the Fallen I would have welcomed it.

"Do not lie to me, Count Nazari," she warned. "Do not paint me as a fool in your mind, it will be the most dangerous thing you ever do."

"I am not lying," I swore.

She frowned at me then turned back to face the view, her head tilting as she gazed up at the glittering stars as if wishing upon every one of them that this night would end.

I could still hear Hariot ranting back in the hall, so as much as I didn't want to keep her here longer than she desired, I also wasn't going to allow her near that cunt again tonight.

The silence stretched and I forgot all about trying to be like Drake, falling into the stronger instinct I had which urged me to try and soothe that pain I saw in her.

"I know you hate this," I said quietly, and she glanced back at me, her brow creasing then quickly smoothing out. "You don't have to pretend."

Who would want to be bought and sold? My mother had lamented about the poor princess in her castle, forced to be a waiting womb to house a true heir. A boy. It enraged me that Austyn was so overlooked. This here was the true Lunarelle heir, the one who should be ruling the empire and bringing some good to this land.

"Excuse me?" she breathed, suspicion etched into her features.

"The pageant," I said. "You despise it."

Her eyes widened further then she schooled her expression once more, fixing on a mask that worked to shut me out entirely.

"Don't do that." I moved towards her, a tainted part of me taking over, and I couldn't fight it even if I'd wanted to. No, I was surrendering to this need in me, because right now the pull of it was a force strong enough to rival the gravity rooting us to the ground.

"Do what?" she whispered.

She was wrapped in chains so tightly, I could almost see them tethering her to this life she didn't choose. And I so wanted to break them.

I was moving too close. I could feel her breath on me. It tasted like wine and the deepest desire of my unworthy heart.

A small part of my brain was screaming at me to stop, but a bigger part of me was awakened, taking over. Just for a moment. What harm could one, single moment really do in the grand scheme of things?

"You try to hide your true feelings." I reached out as if to touch her face, then thought better of it and rested my hand on the railing next to hers. "You're a princess, so why should you have to hide?"

"And what are my true feelings?" She scowled, assuming I was trying to own her like the rest of them did. She definitely didn't want to be owned, and she didn't want her feelings to be guessed by some suitor who'd paid for the privilege of standing here either.

"You're angry. And so you should be," I growled, my own rage rising up to meet with hers. "I'd be angry too if I was placed on a pedestal and auctioned off to the highest bidder."

"What would you know?" she bit at me. "Men don't have to deal with such things."

"No. And women shouldn't have to either."

"Coming from a man who's trying to buy me? That's rich." She turned her back on me and my stomach knotted from the impact of her words.

Silence stretched on and I figured maybe I should have tried harder at being more like Drake. That was what she wanted. This honest bullshit wasn't getting me anywhere. I was just a dog with too many opinions and none of them really mattered. But just as I tried to form some cocky remark worthy of the man she actually desired, she turned back to me with her chin held high and defiance in her eyes.

"You're right, I don't want it. And I do hate it. All of it. Every moment is insufferable, and I despise every one of you for taking part in it." Her lower lip quivered with the fury in her words, the lash of them striking against me in accusation. I ached to tell her the truth, to bare who I was and show her I would never partake in the game she was trapped in, but I couldn't risk being exposed. Even if the princess hated Magdor, I was not going to wrap her up in this plot I was a part of and incriminate her if this all went to hell. She probably felt horribly alone in all this, and I wanted her to know she had at least one person on her side. Even if that person was just a guard, with no greater value in this world then the weapons in the royal armoury.

I nodded, a solid lump growing in my throat as she stepped towards me, looking hungry for blood.

"I'm the daughter of the emperor and I have no claim to my own throne. If you win, you'll seize it. You'll rule *my* country when my father dies and once you have your heirs from me, you may as well mount me on the wall like the trophy I am to you."

I clenched my teeth at such a possibility coming to fruition, words rushing to my lips which I had no right to say, but they were the truth, and fuck she deserved that if nothing else. "If I were fortunate enough to marry you, princess, it would not be for a throne."

"What then?" she scoffed.

For my entire career, I'd circled her like the moon circled our world. Just an empty lump of rock in the sky with only her to look at. I'd watched and admired, guarded and protected. It had taken me this long - *too* long – to realise I wasn't just a hard, cold thing with nothing but a single path to follow. I wasn't the moon; my core was molten and burning. I was a man of flesh and bone and heart. Every fibre of it wanted her. And she needed to hear the truth I had to give, even if it meant nothing because it was falling from the lips of a man who was not me.

"I've wondered for many years about what lay beneath your veil. The first time I saw you I knew there was something much deeper there which I'd never have predicted. There's a pain in your eyes that makes me want to carve out my heart and hand it to you in the hopes that it might ease your suffering. If I were your husband, I'd spend my whole life devoted to turning that pain into joy. Nothing would sate me more than that. Nothing would come close to fulfilling me outside of you. I am a dog without a master, but if I could, I would serve you and only you until my days were up."

Austyn stared at me as if she didn't know who she was looking at, and energy crackled between us that made it a task to breathe. It was a relief to have spoken those words after having held them within me, bottled up and desperate for an outlet, though it came at the price of knowing they were worthless. Sand cast to the wind.

Her hand slid along the railing and her fingers brushed mine. Electricity pounded through to my core, setting every nerve-ending in my body on fire. I'd devoted my life to protecting her. I'd already given her that, but now I was starting to crave something so much more. Something forbidden and tantalising at once.

I desperately wanted to close the distance between us, the space dividing us feeling as though it were full of fate-woven threads binding us together, drawing us nearer to one another. And the longer I stood there, the more of them there were, pressure mounting in my chest as I inched forward.

I was a ghost of a man hiding in the skin of her true desire, but all I wanted was to steal this moment from him and brand it as my own.

I stepped closer and her lips parted seductively, her eyelashes casting a fan around her big, amber eyes as she gazed up at me. Lust pooled in her gaze and ignited a fire in me that burned hotter than any furnace I had encountered. It was easy to forget I wore Drake's face as I leaned nearer, pretending that look was all for me, wishing for it even as I reprimanded myself for it too.

You're a sinner, a thief, a liar, and now you're a lech too. If you kiss her, it will be a filthy lie you can never undo.

"Drake," she whispered, and the spell was broken, cracking apart and sending sharp, jagged shards directly into my heart.

I moved back, but she closed the space between us the moment I did so, resting her hand on my pounding heart.

Her eyes widened as she felt that traitorous beat beneath her fingers. Drake's heart probably thumped to a casual tune no woman could ever affect. Even the princess. But mine was a racing, rioting lump of emotion that belonged to her even if she'd never once noticed me before now. She only saw me because I wore another man's face and was deceiving her with every breath that passed my lips. I had never committed a deeper sin than this.

"There is something so very different about you tonight," she said, her eyes narrowing with suspicion and my heart rate built to a crescendo beneath her palm, giving me away to her.

I captured her wrist, withdrawing her hand from my body, my throat thickening at the smoothness of her skin beneath my palm which was so unsullied by the taint of men. I did not want to be responsible for tarnishing it either.

She slid her hand backwards, my grip loosening to allow her to free herself, but instead she wound her fingers between mine.

A wild, tempestuous hunger grew in me, demanding more. More of her voice, her breath, her touch.

"What's the deepest desire of your heart?" I murmured, desperate to know. I longed to unravel her secrets one by one and devour each of them for myself. It was a selfish and urgent need I couldn't shake. I wanted every piece of this woman I'd admired my entire life, and I didn't want any other man to have a scrap of her.

"Promise not to tell?" she asked on a breath.

"I swear on all of Osaria," I growled.

She leaned in close, so close I couldn't think, my thoughts scattering so I lost my hold on reality completely.

Her mouth brushed my ear and lust drove a flood of heat through my body, making my muscles tighten and my cock stir to attention.

"To be free," she said against my skin.

I shut my eyes and my hands curled around her waist, drawing her flush against me as I fell prey to a dark fantasy of mine which I had dreamed of so often.

She moved into my body like it was designed to mould against hers, but this wasn't my body. And if she fit Drake so well, then it was clearer than ever that she wasn't meant for me.

I knew this would be the only night of my life I would ever hold her like this, perhaps ever touch her again at all. It was my sole chance, and it was already slipping from my grasp as the seconds ticked by and moved towards an inevitable close. So what was I going to do with it?

Break every oath I have ever taken.

"I would free you, princess. If I were the emperor, I would cast out all the old laws and give you the throne you're owed," I said, my tone fierce and full of honesty.

Her chin tilted up as her gaze roamed over my mouth and my fingers fisted in the golden material at the base of her spine, not letting her move another inch as I studied her.

Between the warm night air, the sweet scent of her skin, and the hungry look in her eyes, it was too much. I was only Fae. And apparently, I was the shitty kind because I was standing here with my greedy hands all over the princess herself with no mind to leave.

"Why don't I see the same man in your eyes I saw earlier today?" she questioned, though she remained solidly in my arms, every curve of her body pressed against the hard planes of mine and driving a desperate need in me that screamed to be acknowledged.

I needed to cover Drake's arse and there was only one way I could do that now. "I put on a front sometimes, that's all. If I'm an arsehole tomorrow, don't pay it too much attention."

She burst into laughter and the sound brought a devilish grin to my mouth.

"Oh, there he is," she said with a wild glint in her eyes.

She tip-toed up and fuck I was actually going to do this. There was no stopping me now. My demons were free and urging me on. Regrets were for tomorrows.

Her eyes fluttered closed, her lips so tempting I knew I would have to drive a sword into my chest to stop myself from crossing this line now. There was no way out of it. I was a slave to my urges, needing to feel the press of her mouth to mine and fulfil this maddening want for her, if only for tonight.

"Have you kissed a man before?" I asked, my lips almost brushing hers as I pressed my hand firmer to her back.

"Never," she answered, and a growl of possessiveness left me as I moved forward to claim it from her, to be her first kiss and make it worthy of remembering. At least it would come from someone who revered her down to her bones.

"Gracious Austyn!" Magdor's voice cut through the air, and I released the princess in alarm, turning to the empress with hatred coursing down my spine. "Whatever would the other suitors think if they saw you behaving so uncouthly?"

Of course it was her. Of all people to steal this from me, it had to be the vile woman who destroyed everything I loved in this city.

Austyn glared at her, drawing her shoulders back, a fire blazing in her eyes as she stepped out of my hold and moved to my side. "I'm not sure that's any of your business, Magdor. Leave us immediately." She pointed to direct her away, but Magdor didn't move an inch.

The empress's gaze flitted to me, her lip curling as she took in the cut of me. "It is best if you return to your chambers, Count Nazari, we wouldn't want any gossip circling, hm?" Her tone was light, but there was a warning there which I needed to heed. I couldn't put Drake in the firing line of this witch. I had no idea what she was truly capable of, and I did not want her eyes turning his way too often while I conducted my investigation.

"Yes, Your Highness," I bit out, brushing my fingers over Austyn's spine in one final farewell. Because that was it for me. I would never get this close to her again. And the knowledge of that drove a splinter of iron deep into my heart, never to be removed.

I pinned my eyes on Magdor as I walked towards her, bowing my head.

I'm going to take you down, you monstrous bitch.

I plastered one of Drake's cocky smiles onto my face and her cheeks grew red with anger in the same way that her son's had earlier. I sauntered back into the dining room, snatched a bottle of Cartlanna wine off the table and drank right out of the neck as I strode from the room. Kahn and Hariot were gone, no doubt having slipped off to join the secret sex party happening in the city. *Fucking rats.*

I heard Austyn following me, but I didn't look back as I left the dining hall, my mood descending into a dark pit.

I had been so close to tasting her lips, to kissing her the way she deserved to be kissed for the first time. But the ache I felt over that didn't come close to the guilt that was building up inside me like water against a dam.

What the fuck had I been thinking?

I drained a long swig of wine from the bottle, trying to drown out the weighted feeling inside me. I wasn't worthy of the princess, and I certainly wasn't worthy of claiming her first kiss. But the mere idea of someone else taking it made my blood run cold and an icy rage course along my limbs.

I headed down the corridor, walking back to Drake's chambers with heavy breaths falling from my lips, jealousy tearing into me at the images running through my head of her in another man's arms. As I rounded another corner, I snapped, hurling the bottle of wine at a wall, the glass exploding and wine splashing everywhere.

I came to a halt, taking in the destruction and running a hand down my face. I was trained in restraint, so why did I keep acting like some wild animal tonight? Why was it so hard to hold myself in check when it came to her?

Footsteps thundered behind me, and I frowned, turning back to see who was charging through the royal palace this late at night. But before I could tell who the shadow at my back was, a force collided with my skull like a tonne of bricks. My vision swam from the savage blow, and I hit the floor on my knees, trying to get up and fight, but the wine I'd consumed had dampened my wits.

The thwack of the same hard weapon struck me again and this time, the attacker took no prisoners, pain ricocheting through my skull before nothingness descended on me.

DRAKE

CHAPTER THIRTY EIGHT

I paced back and forth in the open living area of our chambers, chewing on my lip as I thought about what Cassius was trying to do tonight. Sure, he *looked* like me, but I wasn't convinced I'd ever met a man less *like* me in my entire life.

He wasn't going to pull it off. He would smile too much. Or not enough. And he definitely wouldn't make the right jokes. The princess was supposed to be falling for me, and instead she was going to be presented with a man who was just like every other pompous arsehole she'd ever met.

I groaned, swiping a hand down my face before dropping it as I let out a long breath. It didn't matter. I just had to hope that he took my advice and stayed fairly quiet. He had my face so he would at least look good enough, and I'd just have to tell her I'd been feeling unwell the next time I saw her to explain the lack of banter. It was the only option.

"Do you need something to help you relax?" Kyra asked from where she was perched on a windowsill across the room, drawing my attention her way.

The moonlight shining through the slatted shutters glimmered on her dark hair, and I felt like I was looking at the magic in her again as I let my eyes roam over her, this strange, ethereal being who had somehow become such an important piece of my life. I drank her in, my mouth drying out as I tried to arrange my thoughts again and I cursed myself as I fought against the desire she lit in me, the temptation she posed. I was here to marry a princess. I couldn't let myself be distracted by a creature who couldn't even be touched, no matter how often she drew my attention or how many times I found myself looking at her like this.

"I don't think I'll be able to relax until I can be sure he hasn't fucked this up," I muttered, turning from her as I paced away again, forcing my thoughts back onto the matter at hand.

"Cassius is a good friend and a good man. I'm sure he'll do a good job," she said earnestly. "Yes, I *know* I said 'good' a lot, but I thought great would have been overkill...well you don't actually know *everything*...he doesn't think I'm insane he just thinks I'm-"

I turned to look at her again and she abruptly stopped talking like she'd suddenly realised I could hear her.

An amused smile pulled at my lips as she squirmed with embarrassment, biting into the fullness of her bottom lip as her hands curled into fists at her sides.

"Sorry, Master," she muttered, dropping her eyes and heat flared across my skin at that word, irritation prickling at me.

"I told you not to call me that anymore," I replied, moving closer to her, my steps slow and unfaltering.

Kyra stilled as I stopped before her, the scent of her skin making me inhale slowly as I watched her, waiting while she fought against the instinct to show submission to me. She raised her eyes up to meet mine and my pulse skipped as I was captured in her gaze, her wide, golden eyes pulling me in. I placed my hand on the wall beside the window frame and leaned over her, wanting to be closer even though I knew there was no sense in that.

"Sorry," she breathed, drawing her legs up onto the windowsill and crossing them beneath her, making her skirt ride up to reveal the smooth skin of her thighs, my gaze lingering there a moment before shifting back to her face.

There was something intoxicating about her that went beyond the power that crackled beneath her flesh and had everything to do with the mysteries lying deep inside her eyes. There was darkness there and hurt too, but somehow her gaze still held a lightness and hope which I'd given up on for myself, but I was becoming addicted to seeking it out in her eyes. How did someone live through all she had and still maintain that outlook on life? How had she managed it when all I had lived through had only ever served to stain and harden my soul? I knew I was a selfish man, even a cruel one when I had to be, cunning, unforgiving, suspicious, murderous at times. All things I'd had to become to survive the life I'd been gifted by the gods who had abandoned us so long ago. And yet she wasn't like me.

The moonlight highlighted her high cheekbones, and I almost lifted my hand, wanting to run my fingers across her skin despite knowing she was untouchable, my fingers curling into a fist as I held them back.

"Don't be sorry," I replied, dropping my voice to a firm tone as I went on. "Just don't do it again."

A smile graced her full lips and my heart beat a little faster as my attention fixed on her mouth.

"I'll try not to," Kyra agreed, and I nodded in confirmation, but I didn't remove myself from her space.

"Have you thought of something you'd like to do for yourself?" I asked her, needing to distract myself from worrying about Cassius and the princess.

"Umm, kind of. But it's a bit strange," she admitted, a blush colouring her cheeks and making me want to know even more.

"Of course it is," I teased and she breathed a laugh.

The silence stretched as I waited for her to tell me what it was, but she didn't. She just sat looking at me, seeming to have an internal war with herself over whether or not to voice it while the air between us grew thick with the unspoken words.

"So?" I prompted gently, finding myself desperate to know what she desired, what someone who had the power to create everything for everyone around her, might crave for herself alone.

"I'm not sure if I should say it or not," she admitted. The height of the window put her closer to me than she would have been on her feet, and the distance parting us was less than it probably should have been, but I still didn't draw back. "I think I want it, and all of the pieces of me have agreed for once but..."

"But?" I questioned, curiosity burning a hole right through me as the war taking place in her eyes held me captive.

"I'm afraid," she breathed.

"What have you got to be afraid of, little goddess?" I asked, shifting my weight so that I was leaning into the arm I held pressed to the wall, the stone cool against my flesh. "You're the most powerful creature I've ever met. You can do anything, everything. Nothing should scare you."

"I'm afraid of the coin," Kyra admitted, eyeing it where it lay flush to my skin, hanging from the chain she'd given me. I hadn't put a tunic on again to combat the stifling heat, and I was almost certain her eyes trailed past the coin and over my body for a moment, but as her gaze snapped back up to meet mine, it was hard to be sure, and I was left uncertain over her once again.

"I promised I'd never put you back in there and I meant it," I said, letting her see the truth of that vow as she worried her bottom lip and fisted her fingers in the skirt of her dress.

Kyra's gaze warmed with some emotion I couldn't quite place as she accepted the truth of that promise, and I could tell just how much it meant to her. I wasn't a man who often did anything for anyone else, but I couldn't deny how much I enjoyed making her look at me like that. Like I was more than just a street thug or a pretty face, like she looked at me and saw something of worth despite all the reasons to see nothing beyond the selfish, hungry creature I was.

"And I'm afraid to be alone," she added softly.

"You'll never be alone while we're bound to each other either," I murmured, turning my hand over and looking at the skin where I knew the ethereal chain rested, despite being unable to see it.

She lifted her hand too, trailing a finger over her throat where a glimmer of white appeared, revealing the stone which lay there, marking her too. Some primal, un-awakened part of me liked that, seeing solid proof of our bond and our ties to one another.

"And I'm also afraid, that I..." She bit her lip, seeming frightened to even voice the thought which plagued her as I moved even closer, wanting to take away the fear in her eyes as I leaned down and breathed in the sweet scent of her skin. "That I'm not really real at all," she finished finally.

"You *are* real. You're right here in front of me," I said firmly, my fingers flexing where I pressed them to the wall, the desire to prove that to her somehow rising up in me fiercely.

Kyra looked up at me and it was like the stars were alight in her eyes. I could see the magic swirling in their depths, but I could see something that was entirely *her* too. She was still the girl she'd once been. Even if the magic and solitude made it hard for her to remember. She'd had dreams of her own once, a life of her own, and I could see a whole lot more than power in her.

Kyra's attention travelled over my face, and she frowned like she wasn't really sure what she was looking at. It shouldn't have mattered to me that she thought I was ugly. She was just one girl amongst hundreds who would disagree, but somehow it *did* matter to me. I wanted her to look at me differently. I wanted her to look at me the way the others did even if I shouldn't have been thinking about her like that at all. I was here to marry a princess. The most beautiful girl in all of Osaria. Or so everyone said. And though when I looked at Austyn, I could definitely see what all the fuss was about, I didn't quite see what I did when I looked upon Kyra's face.

"So, are you going to tell me what it is you want?" I asked her, wondering if there was anything I wouldn't grant her in that moment, feeling like our roles were reversed and I was the one dedicated to carrying out her wishes and desires, my sole purpose to bring them to life.

"It's not so much of a physical object," she began hesitantly. "It's more something I think I want to do."

"You think?" I teased. "So you're not sure?"

"Not yet," she said. "But I don't think I will be until I try it."

"The anticipation is killing me," I joked but I found that it really was. I ached to know what this strange girl yearned for. What it was that her magic couldn't provide and why she was looking at me like she thought I could.

She gazed at me, hesitating, and the silence filled with a thrilling kind of promise.

"Could you maybe...touch me?" she breathed like she was afraid to even voice the suggestion. "Just so that I *know* I'm real."

"That's what you want?" I asked, my heart leaping at the idea of it, the simplicity of it, and yet it felt anything but simple all the same.

Any time I'd come close to touching her before now, she'd recoiled or turned her body to smoke, and I'd begun to think that was just the way of her curse. She was more than just some mortal bound with magic; she was pure power itself. But the look in her golden eyes told a different story. She was afraid of this. And I wanted more than anything to banish that fear and replace it with something so much sweeter.

Kyra didn't look away from me as she slowly nodded, wetting her lips in a way that made me think she might just want this for more than one reason. But was I insane to believe that? Hadn't she made it clear she didn't desire me at all? And yet as I studied her intently, I could have sworn she was looking at me differently. Like she was seeing something she hadn't seen before.

I lifted my hand, and she drew in a deep breath as I reached for her, keeping my movements slow as I noted the fear in her eyes.

"You don't have to be afraid of me," I murmured. "I'd never hurt you."

"I know," she said, and I could feel the truth in those words as she held my eye.

I wasn't sure anyone had ever trusted me like that before. Implicitly, completely, like she had no reason at all to doubt my word. And it felt *good*. Perhaps Cassius's ideas about honour held some merit after all, though I would sooner eat my own foot than tell him that.

I moved a little closer, raising my hand towards her face and pausing just short of pressing my skin to hers as energy crackled between us, though I couldn't tell if it was magical or not.

My pulse was pounding as if this touch meant so much more than any kiss or caress I'd ever known. It was like I'd never touched a girl before, and we were both held captive in the moment before it happened, the two of us aching for it and fearing it at once.

I smiled at the ridiculousness of the idea as it presented itself, but it wouldn't go away.

There was a heat building in the space between us which held the promise of all her magic. I could feel it writhing in the air, dancing against my palm as I drew ever closer to the moment when our skin would meet, and our gazes connected as she held her breath in anticipation of it.

I pushed forward and my fingertips brushed along her cheek, sparks zipping through my flesh which had nothing to do with her magic and everything to do with her. Her skin was soft against the roughness of my fingertips, flawless and satin smooth as I traced my fingers over it, watching her power flare to life in her golden eyes.

Kyra exhaled slowly as my hand moved across her flesh until I was cupping her jaw in my palm, my fingertips pushing into her dark hair, drinking in this moment as I felt the significance of it writhing through the air.

"Real," I murmured, my voice rough, a ring of command to it like I was telling her it was so as well as proving it with this act.

She took a shaky breath as emotion twisted through her eyes, that fact sinking into her skin from the point of contact between us and stealing away her fear.

My heart was pounding too quickly, and I found I couldn't help myself as I took a step closer, wanting more of this. More of *her*.

Kyra's eyes widened as I closed the distance between us down to no more than a few inches. I could tell I was overwhelming her. She'd been alone for so long and this was too much. But it wasn't enough at the same time, and holding myself there was akin to driving blades through my feet to pin them to the ground beneath me.

I didn't move any closer despite every piece of me demanding I do just that. This had to be her choice. She had to choose it and want it, and her expression told me she wasn't sure if she did.

I didn't press forward but I didn't pull back either, and after another moment she lifted her own hand towards me.

She reached for my hair first, pushing her fingertips through it with a smile almost capturing her mouth and I fought the groan which was building in my throat at the feeling of her gentle touch against my flesh.

Her hand shifted lower, her touch gentle as her fingertips drew a line of pure energy all the way down the side of my face, tracing the shape of my jaw and feeling the bite of stubble against the pads of her fingers until she reached my lips.

My grip on her tightened as I ached to pull her closer, my hand shifting in her hair and causing her to shiver.

I wanted to feel her mouth on mine, but her gaze flickered with fear, and I stopped, the fingers of my other hand biting into the stone of the wall as I held myself back.

A curse nearly escaped my lips as I denied my body the pleasure it craved from her, but I held myself in check.

Kyra almost pulled away and I stilled, letting her take the lead as I knew she needed to. Her fingertips fell from my mouth, marking a trail over my chin and down my throat which bobbed beneath the pressure of her touch. She skimmed the necklace which held the coin, lingering as she felt my heart pounding beneath my skin, my muscles tensing as I forced myself not to move, to allow this without trying to take anything in return for it.

Her eyes lit with some deep emotion, and I wondered if I was making her heart race too, if she was feeling the things she might have felt before she became a Blessing, when she was just a Fae girl who must have felt desire and lust just like anybody else.

Kyra's fingers swept lower, tracing the lines of my tattoos, making them sing with her magic, heat radiating through each one she touched as if she was awakening something within them and calling it to her.

My muscles flexed beneath her touch, the effort it took to hold still increasing with every passing moment as she caressed the lines on my chest before trailing her fingers down my abs, travelling ever downwards, and making my cock harden in my britches.

She reached my waistband and I felt like I was about to combust with the desire she was building in me as her fingertips shifted along the line of the fabric while I forced myself not to react at all, though in the thin britches I wore it had to be damn easy for her to guess how much I was enjoying her attention.

My cock throbbed with the need for her, the tattoo on my right arm blazing with heat and my skin prickling with the feeling of my Affinities as my gift for pleasure and lust awoke with a fervour. I needed this like I needed air in my lungs, like I needed the thrill of the fight and the rush I got from pulling a job. The use of my gifts was as vital to me as breathing. I hadn't gone this long without the touch of a woman since I rid myself of my virginity, and I suddenly felt like I had reached my bursting point, my body aching with the desire to sate that need.

"Thank you," Kyra breathed, pulling her hand away but I didn't release my grip on her face. I couldn't. I wouldn't.

"Kyra," I began, unsure what I was even going to say. But I had to say something. I had to know if she felt this promise which was building between us, or if I was going to drown in desire for someone who could never want me in return.

"Yes?" she asked, and I took hope from the fact that she hadn't asked me to withdraw my hand from her face.

I tightened my grip, tilting her chin up as I eyed her full lips. Did I need to say the words? Or could I just close the distance which echoed between us and hope that she wanted this like I did?

We hung in that moment for several long seconds, and I knew if she'd been any other woman, I'd have taken this step by now. But she wasn't just some woman to me, some conquest to claim, or desire to sate. She was the girl who looked at me and saw more to me than any other had before and I wanted to be that man for her, the one who held true value, the one worthy of the look she was giving me. The problem was, I wasn't him.

She hadn't pulled back. She was waiting to see what I would do, and it turned out I was too. The tattoo on my right bicep was tingling, whispers seeming to collide in the air which I couldn't understand.

I leaned just a fraction closer, heart pounding, flesh demanding and my soul hungering for this creature who was a girl and something else entirely at the same time.

A flash of orange light lit the sky through the window at her back and my head snapped up to look as an echoing roar sounded across the entire city, making my pulse scatter as an enormous shadow moved through the clouds.

"Fuck," I swore as Kyra flinched back, my hand slipping from her face as she pulled away from me, breaking the spell which hung between us and casting me back into reality with a finality that made me curse.

"What was that?" Kyra asked, twisting to look over her shoulder at the dark sky as my attention fell back to her.

"Whatever it is isn't our problem. We could just ignore it," I said, leaning closer again, unwilling to relinquish the moment despite feeling it shatter around us.

"Why?" Kyra questioned like she really didn't know, and I felt that all too familiar slap of rejection from her which was only made worse by the fact that she seemed not to have even noticed she was rejecting me at all.

I straightened my spine, my eyes moving to the view beyond the window as fire flared to life in the distance again, though it disappeared as quickly as it had begun, making me frown in confusion. A house fire wouldn't just burn out like that.

I shook my head to clear it of the magical girl before me, stepping back as she watched me go without so much as a flicker of emotion on her face to tell me if she would rather I stayed.

"Of course I don't want him to *kiss* me," she hissed to herself. Her nose wrinkled at the thought and her gaze snapped up to meet mine as if she'd only just realised she'd been speaking aloud.

My jaw clenched as I drew back from her, raising my chin as her words dug into me and made me remember who she was, *what* she was. And that wasn't a girl who felt desire or lust or anything a hot-blooded mortal felt. And even if she was capable of such things, she'd made it clear on more than one occasion that she didn't feel that for me.

An echoing boom sounded somewhere in the distance, and I took another step back from Kyra, noting the way she relaxed as I drew away like she was relieved. I didn't know what the fuck that had all been about for her, but it clearly wasn't anything to do with wanting me.

"What the fuck is going on out there?" I muttered, peering out into the night once more while subtly rearranging my cock and forcefully thinking of things that would make it a whole lot less excited, though it was already sinking fast in the face of her clear rejection.

I focused on the memory of Balthazar fucking that ugly countess to finish the job of banishing the need from my flesh. Yeah, that would do it.

"Maybe it's a party?" she suggested as the sound of distant screams reached us on the breeze.

"Sounds more like the rebels causing shit again," I grunted, my memories flicking over the protests which had taken place in the city on and off over the last few years, more than one of them turning into rallies with brawls and looting breaking out, innocent civilians falling victim to the so-called champions of the people. The rebels may have claimed to be after a better life for the people of this city, but so far as I could tell, their actions only ever served to hurt those they claimed to fight for and had never once earned them anything from the upper Fae to help their cause.

I glanced at Kyra and found her eyes on me too, unspoken words hanging between us though I had no idea how to voice them or if I even should. She lifted a hand to the cheek I'd just been touching, and her expression filled with some deep emotion which I couldn't unfurl.

I wondered if she'd gotten what she wanted from me or if it had taken her by surprise the way it had me. Though it clearly hadn't ignited the same feelings in her as it had risen in me. Because I knew for a fact that I hadn't been expecting that.

The memory of her touch on my flesh seemed stained there as surely as the ink on my skin. And now I wanted more. Like a fucking idiot craving the moon when I was stuck on the ground, never able to grasp it for myself. I wasn't sure I'd be able to get her out of my head. Even for the sake of a princess.

An enormous boom sounded far closer to the palace and we both flinched as we snapped around to stare through the window again, a wave of crimson fire tearing across the sky and making my heart beat out of rhythm as a gigantic shadow swept over it.

"I seek the oath breakers. And I will tear apart this kingdom if that is what it takes to find them." The powerful voice seemed to echo right through my body and down to my bones, sounding solely inside my own skull and yet somehow, I knew that every man, woman and child within the kingdom had heard her too.

"Azurea," I breathed, recognising the deep and endless magic of the dragon's voice. My gut twisted with the realisation that she had come here for us, seeking the treasure we had promised and not delivered. "Fuck."

"Oh, she's pretty," Kyra breathed as Azurea blasted fire across the sky again.

I caught sight of more shadows moving before it, the smaller, thinner frames of fire drakes dancing across the sky as the city bells began to ring out an alarm and the royal guards ran to defend the people.

"Pretty terrifying," I growled, my eyes whipping back and forth across the view of the city as I took in the destruction the dragon had brought with her, summoning all kinds of monsters from the desert to help her in her hunt for the men who had betrayed her. "And she's after me. Or more accurately, she's after the treasure from that cavern where I found you – you know, the cursed gems which I couldn't lay a hand on without the risk of having my body peeled like a fucking banana and my insides plastered to my outsides."

"Oh."

"Yeah. Oh." I carved a hand through my dark hair as my mind wheeled with ideas on how I was going to fix this shit just as something collided with the palace walls with enough force to make the whole thing shudder around us.

The clamour of bells, screams of people and the roars of the monsters descending on the city filled the air and the scent of smoke poured in through the open window.

"Can you get rid of her?" I asked, looking to the magical girl at my side but she shook her head.

"Not unless she agreed, and even then, I'm not sure I could use my power on a creature as ancient and magical as a dragon."

"Right. Okay. Fuck." I started pacing, refusing to admit that I really should have just figured out a way to give the damn lizard her treasure back when we were in the desert instead of assuming she'd just forget about it in time. Cassius may have had a point with all of his 'never cross a dragon' bullshit, but I had no time for that now. I needed a plan.

"The scale," I said, snapping my fingers and turning to look back at the room. "Cassius has a dragon scale which can summon her. We just get the scale, use your magic to transport ourselves out into the desert and make her a mountain of gold to say sorry for the wait, and summon her away from the city to claim it, then this will all be fine."

"This will all be fine," Kyra echoed just as an agonised scream tore through the air far too close to us for my liking.

I looked outside just in time to see a pair of fire drakes fighting over a royal guard as they flew up past the window, their jaws locking around different parts of him before they ripped him in two and blood rained down from his corpse as the two pieces were devoured.

"Just fine," I muttered again, turning my back on the window, and heading for the door. "We need to find Cassius. Can you transport us to him?"

"Of course," Kyra agreed brightly as she moved closer to me, her clothes shifting around her until she was wearing a pair of black harem pants with a cropped top to match them. "Where is he?"

"I don't know – that's the point," I replied, and she frowned.

"Then how do I know where to take us?" she asked.

"You can't take us to him if you don't know where he is?" I confirmed and she shook her head as more screams sounded from the guards who were fighting outside. "Okay, we'll just find him the old-fashioned way then. I guess I'm gonna need a sword."

An enormous roar echoed through the sky just as the walls rattled again and my fist closed on the hilt of the sword Kyra had created for me as I threw the door to our chambers wide.

We headed out into the corridor where servants were screaming and running for their lives. I just had to hope I could find Cassius before that fucking dragon destroyed the entire city. Problem was, the feast should have ended ages ago and I had no fucking idea where he might be.

CASSIUS

CHAPTER THIRTY NINE

Consciousness returned to me in a slow ebb, like someone turning on a tap but only letting the water through drip by drip. Everything was dark and hazy, but I slowly regained my strength, and my eyes began to crack open. The memories came back in a wave, breaking through the pounding ache in my skull.

The feast. Austyn. *Some bastard attacked me.*

A dark stone ceiling glared down at me, and the rushing sound of moving water filled my ears.

Where the fuck am I?

I groaned as pain blossomed up the back of my head and made white spots pop in front of my eyes. I tried to sit up, but found my arms and legs tied down, the clinking of chains sending a sliver of anxiety through my chest. The drained feeling in my body told me they were made of iron.

I turned my head, spotting an underground river coursing along through the large, underground cavern I was in. Firelight flickered on the corner of my vision and as I twisted to face it, I found roaring flames beneath an iron cauldron. A hunched figure stood beyond it, bending over something I couldn't see.

The walls trembled suddenly, and the figure looked up at the ceiling before returning to whatever they were doing.

"Hello?" I rasped, but they ignored me, and I had the feeling I was not going to like it when their attention did fall on me.

A huge shadow loomed in my periphery and Kahn stepped into view, gazing down at me with a dark, bloodthirsty smile.

My upper lip peeled back, and my gut knotted with rage. "What the fuck do you think you are you doing? Let me go," I demanded, and I stilled as I heard my voice. I was still Drake. Which meant it was *him* this bastard saw lying here.

"You've upset Mother," Kahn growled, his eyes narrowing on me accusingly.

I grimaced, yanking at the chains which bound me, but it was pointless. The iron was thick and well secured, the power of the metal making me feel weak and nauseous at once.

"What do you want?" I snarled, my muscles tensing as I bucked against my restraints once more.

A distant boom sounded above us, and Kahn glanced up at the ceiling with a frown lining his brow.

The hunched form beyond Kahn stood upright and as she turned, her face was revealed to me.

Magdor.

"*You,*" I hissed. "Release me this instant. I am a Count of Carubai."

She let out a low laugh, pushing her hood back and unveiling her black hair which fell about her like a sheet. My eyes landed on the large chest with bottles and jars within it that she'd been bent over. She held a jar in her hand filled with a glimmering purple liquid which she promptly poured into the cauldron, a hissing, spitting sound reaching me from within it. Whatever potion lay in there bubbled angrily and black smoke coiled above it, filling the air with a putrid scent.

Magdor tipped her head back and began to chant something in a language I couldn't understand, taking an iron blade from the table beside her. She waved the blade around as her chant grew more frantic and I yanked against my restraints, my muscles flexing as I put as much power into fighting the iron as I could.

Kahn watched me with an amused gleam in his gaze, leaning closer to me with a smirk. "Not so cocky all wrapped up in iron, are you Nazari?" he taunted.

Magdor's chanting pressed into my ears, and I felt something twisting around me in the air, like a presence I couldn't see. But I could feel it, some horrid, intangible thing hanging there like a shadow.

"What is this?" I demanded as Kahn moved back again and my eyes fell on his mother once more.

She cut into her own arm with a groan and the darkness seemed to press deeper into the room, seemingly urged on by the blood that spilled from the wound.

"Witch!" I accused. This woman was just as foul as I'd suspected, but that knowledge didn't give me any comfort now that I was chained down before her on a stone table like a fucking sacrifice.

"Drake Nazari," she spat the name like it was dirt. "I am afraid you have gained too much favour with the princess."

The walls trembled once again and Magdor paused, frowning as she turned to her son. "Kahn, go and find out what all of that noise is," she commanded.

"But I want to watch, Mother," he complained.

"Do as I say," she snarled, and he pouted like a child, giving me one, last, wistful look before turning away and following Magdor's order.

His footsteps retreated and I was left alone with Magdor, which somehow made me more fearful for my life than when her beast of a son had been present.

My shoulders tensed as she approached, her face contorting as she gazed down at my body.

"You will die for this when you are discovered," I growled, holding on to the small hope that that might happen. But I might not live long enough to see her meet the wrath of Osaria.

She ignored my words, reaching out and hooking her slim fingers into my tunic, ripping it open. My stomach tensed under her roaming gaze, and I roared my fury at her, pulling at the chains once more, but I was stuck in this hellhole, and I didn't even know where exactly that was.

Magdor turned towards me with the bloody knife, and I stiffened, my abs taut as she hovered the blade over my stomach like she was deciding where to cut.

"If you kill me, you'll start a war with my kingdom," I snarled, praying she'd buy it.

She pressed the ice-cold blade to my chest, the iron making bile rise in my throat at that simple touch and I knew she'd barely even begun yet.

"I'm not going to kill you, Nazari." Her mouth pulled up into a cruel smile then she slid the knife across my skin, slitting it open.

I sucked air in through my teeth as blood poured from the cut and pain rippled through the shallow wound.

"What do you want then?" I demanded, my training making me draw my attention from the pain onto survival instead. I could weather torture, I had done so before, but I sensed that wasn't her aim.

She didn't answer, moving away and dangling the dagger over the cauldron instead. My blood rolled off of the blade, dripping into the potion and a flash of red preceded a tendril of crimson smoke. I shuddered as I watched her stir the contents, the dark presence in the room growing closer once more, the air thickening around me and the taste of blood coating my tongue as she chanted in that strange language again.

My hands curled into fists as I glared up at the dark ceiling, desperate to think of a way out of this.

A splashing noise caught my ear and I turned to look at the underground river, watching the deep water surge by and disappear further into the dark cave system. A hulking shape came into view and I squinted as a rowing boat emerged, heading downstream. Two figures sat in it, one small and one large. But it wasn't until the boat hit the shore that I got a good look at them. A muscular man in ebony robes jumped from the vessel, dragging a young boy in rags after him who looked pale and shellshocked. The man had a swathe of black silk pulled up over his face so all I could see of him was two murky grey eyes.

Magdor hurried forward, snatching the boy from his arms, and shoving a bag of coins into the man's hands. "You are late," she hissed.

"Do you know what I had to get through to fuckin' make it 'ere?" the man hissed.

"No and I do not care," Magdor said. "Get out of here this instant. I have work to do."

"What is this?" I questioned, trying to work out what I was witnessing.

The man's eyes slid to me, his brows raising for a moment in recognition and my heart stuttered as I realised he knew me – no, he knew *Drake*.

"Hey – help me!" I barked at him, but he didn't turn back as he jumped into his boat and started rowing upstream into the darkness, fighting the current so the river couldn't sweep him beneath the low, rocky cave roof on the far side of the cavern.

Magdor dragged the boy along by the scruff of his neck. He could have been a teenager, but the scrawny size of him made it hard to tell. His eyes were wide with terror as Magdor walked him towards the cauldron and anxiety warred beneath my flesh.

"Please, Your Highness, I was told you needed a new servant. I promise I'll serve you well," he said, and she shoved him to his knees.

He gazed up at her with fear in his expression and my heart jerked in response.

"Magdor," I snarled. "Enough of this."

"Yes, you will serve me," Magdor spoke to the boy, ignoring me, her voice suddenly lower, more gravelly.

The air around us thickened with that cloying presence, accompanied by a pungent scent that made me thrash harder against my restraints.

"Stop!" I roared, and the boy looked back at me with terror sparking in his eyes.

Magdor lifted the knife and began to chant in words that made no sense to me, but filled the cavern with the stench of that foul power. Panic clawed at my insides as I was forced to watch whatever twisted magic she was wielding here.

"Get away from him," I commanded for all the good it would do.

She caught the boy by the throat in a surge of motion and rammed the blade into his chest so fast that I could only stare on in shock, silenced by the unspeakable act she'd committed. He was just a boy.

My gaze met with his as panic and agony filled his expression for one endless second before his eyes rolled back into his head and he sagged in her grasp. Magdor tossed his limp body to the ground and dropped onto him, her hood falling forward to cover her head as she lowered her face to his chest.

"What are you doing?" I shouted. "Let me go!"

A vile crunching noise reached my ears and nausea gripped me as the darkness in the room deepened further, and I found myself choking on the taste of death in the air. I couldn't deny what was happening, couldn't turn from it or make it stop. Because I knew in the pit of my soul that she was *eating* him, devouring his flesh like a starved animal, ripping through bone and muscle with nothing but her teeth.

"Get off of him!" I cried in vain, knowing he was long beyond help as blood oozed around his lifeless form and the sound of her feasting on him drove into my skull.

Magdor's head snapped up and she turned to glare at me, her mouth smeared with blood, a lump of something equally bloody gripped in her hand.

My throat closed up as I realised what it was. His fucking heart.

"What's the matter, Nazari?" she asked, her voice a deep, demonic thing. Her features changed, the skin peeling back and shifting until her face was nothing but a skull of shining black bone. Fear cut into me as I eyed her snarling mouth full of serrated teeth and the fiery eyes of this witch's true form, and my stomach twisted in revulsion as a golden beetle scrambled across her face into a hollow eye socket.

"Who are you?" I hissed, drawing on the courage my training had instilled in me.

Magdor rose to her feet, biting into the heart in her grip like it was nothing but an apple. Her features smoothed out once more and she returned to her Fae form, her raven hair floating down to her waist. Her face was more beautiful than before, her skin smooth and gleaming, as if something in this demonic ritual had offered her a slice of youth.

"I am the creature who will control you for the rest of your days, Drake Nazari." A contorted smile gripped her mouth as she reached down, grabbing the mutilated boy by the arm. She hauled his body to the river's edge and tossed him into the water, his lifeless form sailing away on the rapid current.

Horror bled through me as I realised she was responsible for the dead children that had been turning up in the eastern river for years. How long had this monster been brutally murdering kids for her twisted magic?

I gritted my jaw, glaring at the beast who'd brought such terrible misfortune on my beautiful city, who had caused the deaths of so many innocents.

If I was going to die here, then I wanted her to know I had always suspected her. That I'd been so close to figuring out how she was doing it, and now I was right at the heart of her lair with the evidence shining back at me.

"How unfortunate for you then, Magdor," I said coldly. My training had taught me never to show weakness in front of an enemy and hell if she was going to see me so much as flinch in her company. "Because I am not Drake Nazari."

Magdor regarded me with her head cocking to one side, her face a picture of beauty but all I could see was the monster she'd revealed herself to be.

"What is that supposed to mean?" she asked in suspicion. "I see the man before me with my own two eyes."

"I am not him," I said firmly. "This is a disguise."

Her brow creased as she stepped closer to me, her gaze travelling down me like she was hunting for the truth. "A disguise? That would require magic and what purpose would it serve you?"

"It means I can fight his brawls for him in the pageant," I lied quickly.

Her eyes flashed with doubt as she saw the logic in that. A nobleman might go to such measures if they weren't capable of fighting themselves. She strode towards the open chest beyond the cauldron and snatched a small bottle out of it.

"I will indulge you then. But if this is just a ploy to delay the inevitable, Nazari, then you really are wasting your breath. Better we finish this sooner rather than later." She strode towards me, uncorking the bottle and the scent of ammonia hit my nostrils.

She pinched my nose, and I kept my lips clamped together, fighting against the inevitable. I thrashed and fought as hard as I could, but the iron was making me woozy, and my lungs soon burned for air. Still, I was not going to make this easy on her. I'd been trained to hold my breath underwater for several minutes, and this hag was going to have to wait if she wanted me to drink that acrid-smelling substance.

She waited as long as it took and I glared at her the entire time, my lips pursed, and my face turning blue. Eventually I was forced to take a breath and she poured the liquid straight into my mouth.

I jerked violently against the iron chains as the horrid mixture hit the back of my throat, coughing and spluttering to try and keep it out, but some of it went down. My eyes seared as the disgusting taste engulfed my senses, and I feared what poison she had dosed me with.

Magdor stepped back, tilting her head as she watched me and I could feel the change in my appearance beginning already. A wave of magic crept along my skin, my bones reformed, my skin shivering and the dark strands of hair which had been falling into my eyes retreating, revealing my true face to her.

Her eyes narrowed and recognition filled her eyes followed by shocked disbelief.

"You?" she blurted, her brow furrowing in confusion.

"So you remember me?" I asked, regaining an inch of power from her.

"Cassius Lazar," she hissed like I was a plague on this world.

She clutched my throat, her upper lip rolling back as she dug her sharp nails into my skin. I didn't wince as she increased her grip, her rage lighting a dark fire in her eyes. "There is only one way you could look like this. So where is my coin?!" she roared, her hand crushing my oesophagus so I couldn't tell her even if I'd wanted to. Which I absolutely didn't.

She retracted her hand, glaring at me with such fury it spilled from her in waves. "Where is it?" she snarled. "You stole it from me!"

I bit down on my tongue, refusing to answer and she stormed away from me towards the cauldron.

"I will seize your mind and your tongue, and you will tell me everything." Anticipation rushed through her voice, and fear writhed through my stomach as I watched her. I was immobilised; even with all my strength I couldn't break through iron chains and as the foul metal sapped my energy with every moment it was pressed to my skin, I knew my chances of escape were even slimmer.

"Is that potion how you control the emperor?" I demanded, needing to hear an answer from her lips before I was forced under her control.

Her eyes narrowed, suspicion crawling across her expression. "And what would you know about that? You are just a guard. Less than a dog. A mindless lump of muscles set to protect the palace walls."

"I am not blind," I hissed. "Since you arrived in the palace the emperor hasn't been himself. The city has fallen to disrepair. The laws he was on the cusp of passing were pushed to the wayside. I know it was you because I've watched you like a hawk. The way you saunter around the palace as if you own it. The way the emperor has faded since he married you, the way his words do not sound like his own anymore."

She released a breath through her nose. "And what would you have done with this grand knowledge? You are just a vessel, Lazar. They cut out your essence and replaced it with nothing but rules and Osarian law. No one would have believed your word over mine."

"I am more than some vessel," I snarled, but even *I* heard the doubt in my own words.

Magdor sneered at me dismissively, and my heart squirmed and writhed in my chest as if it didn't want to be in there anymore.

"Is that what this is really about?" she simpered, her mocking clear. "You seized my precious coin and wasted your breath wishing for a new face, a new life? A nobody trying to be somebody? Is that what your pathetic little mind dreams about?"

Anger flared inside me. Though I battled hard not to react to her words, my heart twisted and came apart. That wasn't what this was, but she had one thing right. I *was* a nobody rising above my station, and the truth of that fact undid me.

"So does Nazari truly exist, or have you always been him?" she demanded, and I didn't see the point in lying now.

"He exists," I grunted.

"How does he play into this then?" she went on. "Are you trying to win the princess so you can share her?"

"I am not here for the princess, I only seek to protect the palace. I've been watching you for a long time. And I almost had you the night I saw Austyn's face. Do you really think I would break Osarian law for the sake of seeing her? I was following *you*, Magdor."

"How noble," she scoffed, scooping the ladle out of the cauldron and my shoulders tensed. "So this is some ploy to bring about my downfall? You are more of a fool than I could have imagined. A guard playing hero." She laughed coldly. "You are just a worthless creature hiding in the flesh of a Fae."

"I could say the same to you."

She glared at me before facing the cauldron, and instead of forcing the elixir on me as I expected, she drank several deep gulps herself. My arms tensed as I watched, tugging against my restraints despite knowing it was pointless.

She convulsed for a moment, holding a hand against her stomach and I prayed she had accidentally poisoned herself. But that hope was quickly crushed.

The thickness in the air seemed to deepen as she began to chant again, and I shifted against the hold of my chains, feeling a heavy gaze settling on me, though I couldn't discover the source of it.

From the depths of my being, I knew she had summoned something else to join us here in the dark of this hidden cavern, something even more vile than herself, something which hungered for pain and death above all else.

When Magdor turned to me, her eyes glowed with some terrible power and fear strummed a chord in my heart. Because if she stole my will from me like she had the emperor, she would get her hands on Kyra. She wouldn't hesitate in killing Drake and taking the coin from him. And I would be helpless to stop it.

DRAKE

CHAPTER FORTY

A boom sounded throughout the palace, the walls trembling as we sprinted down a stone corridor just along from the dining hall where Cassius should have been.

"Where the fuck is he?" I growled, throwing open a door at random.

A man sitting on a latrine in the room shrieked in fear and I scowled at him. Apparently, he had literally decided to shit himself in response to the terror he felt over a dragon laying siege to the castle, and I yanked the door shut in his face before he'd even stopped shrieking to cut off the stench of him.

"It will be okay," Kyra offered, looking up at me as I hesitated, trying to figure out where to hunt next. "I know you're worried about your friend, Master, but-"

"My friend?" I asked with a frown, not taking the time to point out that she'd done the Master thing again, though I wanted to. Whenever she called me that, it just left me feeling cold, wrong, twisted up inside.

"Yes," she said with such obvious belief in the fact that I didn't have the heart to correct her. I didn't have friends, only people I hadn't fucked over yet. "I think I have an idea to help you find him."

"What is it?" I demanded, turning my attention from the allure of her face. I needed to harden myself to this girl and aim my focus where it was desired instead of indulging in fantasies of something that wasn't going to ever happen.

A smile gripped Kyra's beautiful features and I hated how much it pleased her that I was listening to her idea. What kind of arseholes had she been forced to serve before me? "If you command me to find him, then I could create a magical compass that points to him and you can track him down and keep your dragon deal and save the kingdom and-"

"Yeah, okay I want that," I agreed instantly.

Kyra's eyes lit up and I almost laughed at the pride shining in her gaze. She seriously thought I was acting like a good person right now, and if she wanted to believe I was a better man than I was then that was okay by me. I'd play along, but no doubt she'd be disappointed in the end. I was doing this to save my own arse before anyone else's. If a few street urchins and washer women survived the day as a side effect of that then so be it, but it wasn't my aim.

Kyra took the lead, racing away along the corridors beyond the dining hall, and I broke into a run as she used a glimmering golden arrow on her palm to guide us towards Cassius.

She set a quick pace and I was forced to hurry to keep up with her as we moved through the darkened palace, tightening my grip on my sword whenever a crash thundered through the stone around us, or the roar of one of the monsters beyond the walls reached us.

Pounding footfalls made me skid to a halt, years of running through the streets from the guards making me recognise their boots without question. I caught Kyra's arm, propelling her to the side of the corridor just as they appeared.

"Return to your chambers, My Lord," Captain Marik barked as he spotted us. "This is no time for a nobleman and his maid to be out and about. We will see the monsters off."

"I'm sure you will," I agreed, the slightly scathing tone to my voice not missed by the captain, and he narrowed his eyes on me as he thundered past with his men, heading for the exit.

A bellowing roar sounded overhead, and I threw myself towards Kyra as the sound of shattering stone ripped through the air, the wall crumbling as something struck it from outside. My palms hit the wall and I pressed her to it, using my body to shield us as the masonry began to fall apart.

"Ask me to save you," she gasped, her eyes wide as I met her stare, and I realised my own stupidity a moment before the words escaped my lips.

"Save us," I said just as the roof gave out and a dome of solid power blasted from Kyra, surrounding us in a cocoon of silver energy, the bricks cascading over it like rain rolling down a windowpane.

My lips parted in awe as I looked around at the insane display of her strength, the entire side of the castle ripping away from us as a huge grey fire drake used its claws to try and break inside.

"Did you just try to shield me with your body?" Kyra asked, a depth to that question which made something writhe uncomfortably in my gut.

I was saved from the truth of that accusation by the fire drake lunging at us hungrily.

I swung around with a bellow, my sword carving through the air and slicing into the scales of its front leg, spilling blue blood across the floor as it lurched after me and I danced aside.

My skin hummed with my gifts as my Affinities all came into play and I fell into the rhythm of the fight, my sword striking the creature again and again as I scrambled over broken stone and half buried floor, leading it away from Kyra.

The fire drake roared loudly, rearing back and opening its tooth-filled jaws, a whooshing sound building as it summoned the fire in its gut and prepared to blast me with it.

I roared right back at it, hurling my sword with all my strength, and watching as it flew end over end before flying straight into the fire drake's open mouth, burying itself in the back of its throat.

The fire drake reared away, a bellow of pain escaping it as it toppled back out of the hole it had torn into the palace wall, tumbling down to the courtyard far below. The fire it had been summoning exploded in its chest as it hit the ground and I gripped the edge of the broken wall, watching as the beast died, a victim of my sword and its own flames.

I raised my eyes to the sky, spotting more of the creatures as they flew across the city beyond us, hurling fire and chaos down upon anyone unlucky enough to end up in their paths.

"Bring me the oath breakers!" the dragon's voice echoed in our minds once more, and I shifted back out of sight again despite knowing Kyra's magic still kept the beast from locating me.

"I'm going to need another sword," I muttered, one appearing in my hand before I'd even finished the request and I thanked Kyra before turning my mind to what we needed to do. "Let's go," I barked, and she nodded, summoning the golden compass needle again and pointing to the far end of the corridor.

"I'm worried about Cassius," Kyra breathed as we made it beyond the rubble of the broken wall and started running down another corridor. "I have a bad feeling."

"Why are you so convinced something is wrong with him?" I asked her as she began muttering to herself about time running short.

"I can just *feel* it," she murmured. "He's my friend. I'm connected to him, almost as I am to you, though nowhere near as strongly. But ever since I realised I cared about him, my link to him grew into something tangible, you know."

"No, I don't know, Kyra," I replied with a frown. "That's obviously a Blessing thing."

"Is it?" she asked in surprise, stopping so suddenly that I collided with her.

She almost fell to the floor, and I grabbed her hand to catch her. Her power slammed into me so hard that I was nearly knocked from my feet too until somehow, she was the one holding *me* up and not the other way around.

"Sorry," she said, releasing me as my veins crackled from the force of her power. "I'm still not used to the touching thing."

I shook my head as the cloud of her energy withdrew and I was able to think clearly again.

"It's alright," I said, trying to make sense of the scrambled thoughts I'd been left with.

"Come on, we need to find him," she insisted and the concern in her gaze made my eyes narrow as I tried to figure out why she cared so fucking much. Not that long ago, Cassius had been all about destroying her and the coin which held her, so why was I just now learning about them being secret little friends? What had I missed?

"To be honest, I didn't get the impression the two of you were all that close," I said, cutting my eyes down the dimly lit corridor as I took in the tapestries lining the white walls and wondered where the fuck she was even leading me. I certainly hadn't been this deep into the palace before, and I was pretty sure we were coming up on areas we weren't supposed to trespass into. Though with the palace currently under attack, I wasn't sure how much resistance we might find waiting for us anyway.

"I was alone for a long, long time, Drake," she whispered, making me look to her again as her golden eyes seemed to glimmer in the dark. "The two of you were there when I was finally released. You're all I have."

I bit my tongue on the rest of the questions I had about her and Cassius as I took in the truth of her words, swallowing down my irritation and making a mental note to question him on it further when we found his wandering arse.

"Alright," I grunted. "Let's find the arsehole then."

Kyra beamed at me, then held her hand out between us and the golden arrow on her palm pointed down a corridor to our right.

We quickly headed in that direction but came up short as we found our way on barred by six royal guards in full armour, weapons raised and ready to fight.

"The royal family is sequestered inside until the threat is alleviated," one of them said. "I'm sorry, My Lord, but I cannot let anyone pass this way."

"Understood," I said, turning around and giving Kyra a firm look even as she gave me an imploring one.

We rounded a corner so we were out of sight and Kyra instantly shifted closer to me.

"He's that way," she insisted, holding the compass up as proof.

"That's the royal quarters," I said firmly, knowing that those rooms were going to be heavily guarded in every direction, and there was no way we'd be able to get into them without causing one hell of a stir. At least not directly.

"So, what do we do?" she asked desperately which seemed kind of crazy for an all-powerful entity, but I had a plan. I always had a fucking plan.

"We need to find another way. Lucky for you, this is my thing. Breaking and entering comes a lot easier to me than prancing about like a count."

"Oh, I'd love to see you work," she cooed, and I scoffed.

I'd hardly call thieving work, but then again maybe she was right; it was how I'd earned a living for most of my life, and though I didn't pay taxes on my income for it, that had only made it all the more profitable for me. That said…Egos's cut had always been far greater than any tax ever would have been, so maybe it wasn't that amazing for me after all.

"Come on then." I turned and hurried back the way we'd come, ignoring the sounds of screams which swept in from the closest windows. I knocked on the walls as I went, hunting for something I was almost certain would be here.

I cursed as I failed to locate anything other than solid stone for several minutes, seeking out any sign of a hidden passage. But surely all palaces this big had them. More than a few of the estates I'd robbed did, so this wouldn't be any different.

"Knock a penny, hop a penny, dance a penny tune," Kyra murmured as she followed me, rapping her own fist against the wall too. "Mock a penny, drop a penny, party like a loon."

"You have a beautiful singing voice," I teased.

"Thank you," she breathed, and I almost felt bad for teasing her, but the girl honestly couldn't hold a tune any better than a brawling alley cat. "Well, even if he *is* lying, he was being nice by doing so. So why don't you keep your big nose out of it or just stop existing like you keep threatening to do?"

I glanced at her, wondering if the conversations she had with herself were meant to be overheard, or if she believed she was conducting them in her head most of the time, because she certainly acted as though none of what had just passed her lips had been heard by anyone other than herself.

Kyra fell silent, tilting her head as if she was trying to listen to something, and I knocked my fist against the wall again, eliciting a hollow sound in response.

"I think I found it," I hissed.

Kyra sighed and moved closer to me. "I'll never leave me," she muttered, eyeing me sadly.

"That's really confusing. But I'm guessing if she's you and you're you too, then maybe you shouldn't really want her to leave?" I replied as I slid my hand along the wall, trying to locate a way into the passage.

Kyra remained quiet as she drew closer, biting her bottom lip as she considered my words. I reached up to pull on an unlit torch bracket. The sound of sliding stone filled the air, but no entrance appeared.

I frowned at the wall, looking along it until I spotted a tapestry. The bottom corner of it lifted slightly like it was caught in a breeze and I pointed at it as I hurried closer.

Kyra jogged after me and I pulled the tapestry back to reveal a hidden stairwell which ascended into darkness.

"A little light?" I asked.

She stepped ahead of me, and a glowing purple orb appeared above her head, illuminating the way on. I followed her inside and dropped the tapestry behind us just as another shuddering boom rattled the castle walls.

"Well, we always had purple lights in the coin," Kyra muttered. "He doesn't mind, or he'd say he minds-"

"I love the purple light, Kyra," I said loudly, interrupting the argument she was having with herself over it.

"Really?" she asked, turning to look back at me from a few steps above.

"Really," I confirmed. "Everything you do is unbelievable. You couldn't get it wrong if you tried."

Her lips parted but she didn't say anything, and I wondered if she was having an internal discussion over it with herself again. I probably should have found that unsettling but somehow, I didn't, I was just fascinated by her and the way her mind worked, unable to imagine how I would have coped if I'd been cursed with her fate. I guessed she was doing pretty well all things considered.

I passed her on the stairs, and she began to follow me as we climbed higher. I kept going, up and up until we must have climbed four floors, then entered a dark corridor where we could finally take the direction of the compass once more.

"Where the fuck are you, Cassius?" I snarled, mostly to myself but partly to him because what a fucking time for him to choose to go AWOL. No doubt he was on some one-man mission to catch Magdor in the act of whatever witchcraft he was so certain she performed, but I wasn't the least bit interested in that shit given the current circumstances.

My fancy new boots weren't as suited to moving as silently as my old ones, but I managed well enough despite the stone floor, not that I really expected anyone to hear a soft footfall while the walls were rattling, and monsters roamed the night.

We came to the end of the hidden passage and there were two doorways awaiting us: one to the left and one on the right.

Kyra summoned her golden arrow and it pointed firmly to the right.

I raised an eyebrow at her and moved to push on the wooden door, easing it open silently. Another stone passage lay beyond it, and we hurried on. My heart started to beat a little faster, my thieving habits kicking in as we moved deeper into forbidden territory, my Affinities for stealth and cunning growing sharper as I drew on those skills. Awareness pricked at me. I had no doubt we were well within the royal family's private quarters now, and the idea of it sent a thrill of longing through me.

How close might I be to the crown jewels?

We also could have been just moments away from getting caught, and I wasn't sure what would happen then. Perhaps I could say that Austyn had told me about the secret passages and asked me to come see her, which would probably be less of a crime than breaking and entering, but how would I explain Kyra's presence? Maybe I could say I'd brought her as a chaperone, but would anyone buy it? So, I was sneaking to the princess's quarters and my intentions weren't to get her alone in her bedroom... Unlikely, but if anyone could sell it then I was willing to bet I could. I'd just have to convince the princess to go along with it – but I could probably use my general charm or even my sex Affinity to help with that.

The passage came to an end, and I stilled before a door with a small hole located in the centre of it. I pressed my eye to it and found myself looking at a large room with a fireplace on the far side of it and a thick red rug lining the floor beneath a dark, wooden table. There didn't appear to be anyone inside it, so I eased the door open.

Kyra stayed close enough to me that I could feel the echoes of her power brushing against my skin, making the hairs raise along the back of my neck as I was taunted by her nearness.

I stepped into the circular room with a frown. The fire had burned low which suggested someone had been here earlier, but the place seemed deserted now.

It looked like some kind of office or private study, sadly void of anything of value aside from reams of books and papers. And though I knew there was value in knowledge, I was a street thug who couldn't read, so I had no way of figuring out if any of the scriptures here were worth stealing.

I turned to push the door closed behind me and found myself looking at a huge painting of the emperor, seeming younger than he was now with a beautiful woman by his side who must have been Austyn's mother.

The hole I'd looked through had been cleverly disguised within the pommel of his sword.

Kyra eyed the compass on her hand, but the thing kept spinning around and around, flailing left and right like it didn't know which way to direct us at all. I frowned at it and Kyra sighed.

"He must be invisible," she murmured. "But I don't know why he's not talking to us."

"I don't think Cassius is invisible," I replied, but I was beginning to feel a lot more uneasy about this whole thing than I had been.

I'd been quick to dismiss Kyra's concern for Cassius initially, but now that we were in the furthest reaches of the palace, I couldn't help but wonder what the hell he was doing here. There was no way he could have gained access to this part of the castle legitimately, and I was beginning to think that maybe Kyra had been right to be concerned for his well-being.

"If the compass thinks we've found him, then I'm guessing we must be either right below him or right on top," I said. There were no windows in the round room we'd entered but after the stairs we'd climbed, I was willing to bet we were pretty high up in one of the towers. With that in mind, I guessed that Cassius was below us somewhere.

"So, we need to go down. Maybe you should command me to create a hole in the floor?" Kyra suggested excitedly.

"Maybe. Or we could just take the stairs," I pointed out. "It might be a bit more subtle."

"Right," Kyra agreed with a look in her eye which hinted that she was disappointed with my choice.

I resisted the urge to laugh and crossed the room to the only door instead.

I tried the handle, but it was locked, and I released a breath of frustration.

"Have you got a hair pin?" I asked and Kyra produced one magically, holding it out to me.

I dropped to my knees, manipulating the lock with well-practiced skill and after several achingly long minutes, the door clicked open.

"Wow," Kyra breathed.

"I'm a man of many talents," I replied with a smirk.

"No, I just meant; wow, I can't believe you wasted so much time doing that when you could have just asked me to unlock it."

I stared at her for a few seconds, feeling like an idiot for not realising that while also wondering if any of my hard-earned skills would be worth remembering anymore. With her by my side, most of my tricks and talents were seeming more and more irrelevant and all the things that had made me impressive were now unnecessary. Hell, she was making it possible for me to be the next emperor and if that came to pass, I would never want for anything again in my life. And yet the idea of my skills being debunked sent a trace of loss through me which I never would have expected. I'd been looking after myself for a long fucking time and I was proud of the things I'd learned in my bid for survival. My skills were the things that defined me and made me the man I was. If I didn't need those anymore, then what was even left to me?

I decided it was better not to think about that too much right now and turned my mind back to the task at hand instead.

"Whatever Cassius has gotten himself mixed up in, it can't be good," I said as I prepared to open the door I'd unlocked. "So just be careful, okay? Stick behind me."

Kyra's eyes widened and she nodded before following me through the door. We stepped into a tightly circling staircase and started heading down. The further we went, the colder it got and the more distant the sounds of battle came from above.

We passed several doors which led back into the palace but didn't stop to check any of them. Kyra shook her head at each of them, her connection to Cassius telling her that wasn't where he was.

We clearly weren't about to walk into a royal parlour or the princess's bed chamber. No, we were headed far too deep for that. If I were to hazard a guess, then I would say that we were closing in on a dungeon or something of the sort. The kind of place where no one could hear you scream. And the only place in the palace which was fit for that would be all the way at the bottom. In the murky depths of the building, far below the glamorous facade they wanted the world to see.

Down here would be the darkness they hid from their subjects. Down here would be the truth.

AUSTYN

CHAPTER FORTY ONE

"Open up!" I yelled, hammering my fist on the door to my chamber. The guards had locked me inside the moment the attack had begun, and my heart was still beating furiously at what I'd seen through the crack in my window. A monster breathing fire down upon the city, my people.

"They'll never let you go," Zira said, catching my hand to try and draw me away but I yanked it free again, continuing to bang on the door.

"I am your princess and I command you to open this door!" I shouted, but no reply came.

Heated rage washed through my veins as I gave up, wheeling around to look at my maids as they stared at me in wide-eyed concern.

"What do we do?" Jacinda breathed in fear, then clapped her hands over her ears as a thunderous roar shook the walls, far closer than it had been before.

"It's coming this way," I breathed.

"What is it?" Zira questioned, moving closer to Jacinda to comfort her.

"I don't know," I said, knotting my fingers in my hair as I tried to decide on what to do.

"A large fire drake?" Jacinda squeaked.

"It was far too big for that. And did you hear that voice?" Zira ran a hand over her throat, looking to me with the colour draining from her face.

Another booming roar sounded out and the frosted glass of the window reflected the light of crimson flames.

I ran to the only window that opened, peering through the crack again and trying to see more. We'd crammed in close together to see out the moment that voice had carried through our heads, and in the distant had been a huge beast wheeling through the clouds. I didn't know what vengeful thing had come here to destroy my city, but I could not stay here and watch Osaria fall.

I couldn't see any sign of the creature now, but it was hard to see much at all.

The royal guards were shouting something at the gates, and a bellowing voice carried from one of them. "It's headed for the palace!"

A roar sounded somewhere right above me then a force hit the wall to my right like a cannon blast, throwing me onto my back as the masonry exploded and I hit the floor hard, skidding into my maids.

Jacinda screamed, hurrying to pull me to my feet and checking me over for injuries as Zira placed herself in front of me protectively as if she expected death to appear at any moment. A scaly, spined tail whipped through the air before disappearing out of sight up into the sky, and my throat tightened at the thought of whatever monster had been large enough to knock down that wall.

"Get to safety," I commanded, running past Zira before she could try and grab me. I was a little bruised but had no further injuries and the adrenaline in my blood kept me from really feeling them anyway.

"Austyn!" Zira cried in panic, but I was already climbing out of the hole in the wall, lowering myself down the crumbling roof tiles.

My heart leapt as the roof shuddered beneath me, but I managed to swing myself over the edge of it before it gave way, dropping onto a balcony below. I landed in a crouch, shoving quickly to my feet, and pushing through the wooden doors that led into a maiden's lounge.

I ran through one room to the next, my mind fixed on the armoury where I could fetch weapons. I wasn't going to hide away like some mouse down a drain. My city was under attack, and I was damn well going to be out there fighting for it.

I shoved through a heavy door into a corridor and came face to face with Lord Kalaviv buckling up armour as he walked. He swung a huge broadsword in his grip, a twisted look on his face that was full of bloodlust.

I moved to step back before he saw me, but Kalaviv's eyes locked on me, and his eyebrows lifted in surprise.

"Princess," he gasped, running forward, and grasping my arm before I could escape. "What are you doing down here?"

I was unarmed and as I glanced down the corridor beyond him, I realised I was all alone. No guards, no one watching as they always were.

"I'm going to fetch my sword of course," I said, yanking my arm free of Kalaviv's grip

He chuckled at my expense, apparently thinking I'd made a joke.

"My sweet lady, you do have such wit about you," he purred, moving closer again and tucking a lock of silver hair behind my ear.

I flinched away from his touch, shifting sideways to try and make a run for it, not wanting to waste any more time than I already had. But Kalaviv stepped sideways to block my path, his huge body forming a wall I couldn't get past.

"Come, I shall escort you back to your rooms, Your Highness. You must be protected," he said, offering me his arm.

"No, I am going to fight," I growled, and the walls shuddered as something impacted with the palace somewhere above us.

A tremor ran through my flesh, and I surged forward, trying to get around him, but Kalaviv caught my waist, tugging me against him, his hands grasping my side in a way that was horribly overfamiliar.

"The men will handle the monsters, my sweet one."

"I am not your sweet anything," I hissed. "Take your hands off of me."

"I don't mean to frighten you," he said, softening his tone. "I am protecting you." He puffed out his chest like I might swoon and thank him, but I scowled and tried to shove away from him again.

"Hush now, you are growing hysterical with fear," he said soothingly, holding onto me even tighter.

"I am not afraid." I threw my fist out and it slammed into Kalaviv's gut, making him wheeze even through his chainmail. He released me and I ducked past him, running as fast as my feet would carry me to get away from him.

"Wait - get back here!" he boomed as he took chase. "You must stay inside. You are too precious to go out there."

"You mean my throne is too precious," I spat back at him, pushing myself faster as I raced down corridors left and right to try and lose him.

My breaths fell heavily from my lungs as I turned another corner and relief filled me as I spotted a painting that held a secret passage behind it.

The heavy stomp of Kalaviv's boots were drawing closer and I didn't slow my pace at all as I ran to the painting, seeking out the catch on the left edge of it and pulling. The painting swung forward, and I stumbled into the dark space beyond it before yanking the hidden door shut behind me with a click.

I held my breath, listening as Kalaviv drew closer, his footsteps slowing as he neared the painting and I feared he'd seen me go this way.

"Princess Austyn!" he cried, so close, it made my heart flinch.

I didn't let out a single noise as I remained there, pressing a hand to my mouth to stifle even the sounds of my breaths.

The entire palace trembled once more and Kalaviv cursed, his footsteps carrying away from me and making my shoulders sag with relief.

I squinted through the gloom, pressing one hand to the wall beside me and feeling my way forward. The well-walked servants' passages would be lit with sconces, but this part of the tunnels clearly wasn't used often enough. At least I knew every one of these paths intimately, and it was easy for me to find the top of the stairs and start hurrying down them.

The gloom swallowed me up as I ran deeper into the belly of the palace, entering a lit area of the tunnels and racing down the familiar winding pathways towards the royal armoury.

I finally slipped through a tapestry that let out into a grand corridor with suits of armour standing in the recesses of the walls on every side.

I made it to the armoury door, heading into the long training room where my father's armour and weapons glinted proudly on the walls. I came here to train whenever I could, my Affinity with metal making every sweep of a blade feel as natural as breathing. But I hadn't had any formal training since my youth, since the Maggot had taken up residence in my home. I was skilled enough to know I would be useful to the city tonight though, and the idea of having a real chance to be of use to Osaria set my soul alight.

I stripped out of my dress and pulled on the close-fitting black britches and shirt I wore for training along with my boots before grabbing my chest plate and strapping it on. Next, I wound up my hair tightly in a knot before pushing on my helmet to hide my face. I placed my father's sword in a scabbard on my hip and sheathed a sharp little beast of a knife in my boot.

Finally, I took the silver bow and arrows my father had gifted me for my sixth birthday, the Lunarelle family crest engraved on the head of every arrow. The metal sang in my palm, each arrow hand crafted and made of purest silver, the tips as sharp as diamonds.

My Affinity for the metal was making my blood hum in anticipation of wielding it as I hooked the quiver over my back which fit both bow and arrows inside it. Then I hurried back out of the armoury and took the stairs up flight after flight, following the sounds of roars and the crashes that were coming somewhere to the east of the palace.

My stomach lurched as I rounded a corner, nearly running straight into a battalion of guards.

"Get in line," the one at the front barked at me, mistaking me for one of them.

I nodded quickly, slipping to the back of the ranks and mimicking their movements as they ran in sync with one another. The royal guards were like one entity in battle, a hive mind created by the crown and possessing all of their souls. I wondered if there was much left of the men within them. The only one I had seen any life to had been my father's personal guard, Cassius Lazar. A lump rose in my throat as my mind turned to him and I quickly focused on the task at hand.

"It's attacking the eastern tower!" a maid screamed as she appeared through a door, slamming it shut behind her and pressing her back to it. "There are monsters everywhere. They're going to get in. By the Fallen!"

The guards continued past her, saying nothing and I slowed my pace in confusion.

"We should head to the eastern tower," I called in the best man voice I could muster, stepping towards the door the woman had burst through.

"Get back in line!" the head guard barked at me. "Captain Marik's orders were to protect the nobles in their quarters."

"Move," I snapped at the woman, and she staggered away from me.

"Hey!" the guard yelled at me, but I was already gone, rushing down the corridor beyond the door and heading towards the bellows of the beast.

I made it into the spiral stairway that circled up the eastern tower and the monsters' roars echoed through the space, reverberating through my skull. My pulse ticked out of rhythm, but I didn't slow, knowing this might just be the definition of insanity, but I wasn't going to back down now. I had my arrows, and one well-aimed shot to the heart of the gigantic beast leading this madness could end this for good.

I couldn't see anything through the stained-glass windows that ran along the edges of the stairwell, but shifting shadows out there made my skin prickle.

A scuttling noise carried from above me on the stairs and I slowed my pace, drawing my sword and taking a slow breath as I waited for whatever was moving this way, the metal kissing my palm and promising me its loyalty in this fight.

The scuttling grew louder, and I pressed my back to the wall, ready to launch an attack and trying to prepare myself for what I was about to face. I had never been in a true fight before, and I had no idea if I was capable of this, only that I would try to be with everything I had.

A screech sounded before a monstrous creature leapt before me on the stairs. It was twelve feet tall with eight hairy legs as thick as saplings and a scorpion tail which arched over its back, its stinger red and primed to sink into my flesh. It was a scorpious spider, a monster which dwelled deep in the desert, and one that I had never seen outside of horror stories and books that warned of the beasts which roamed beyond the city limits.

I acted on instinct instead of the terror which told me to flee, leaping forward with a battle cry and swinging my sword at its ugly head where fifty white eyes stared back at me.

It shifted aside before I could strike true, and my sword slashed through one of its legs instead. The beast shrieked horribly, throwing its weight at me as it caught me in its pincers and we crashed into the window.

The glass shattered under the impact and the monster lost its grip on me, a cry leaving my throat as I fell through the air before my back hit a slanted roof beyond the tower. I started rolling and scrambled onto my knees, clinging to the tiles to slow my fall before gaining my feet.

I'd lost my grip on my sword, but I spotted it as it caught the light of the moon, laying further up the roof right in front of the scorpious spider.

Miraculously, I had survived the attack with only a few scratches, my chest plate and helmet having taken the brunt of the shattered glass and the impact of my fall.

My heart beat to a wild rhythm and a flood of excitement rushed through me instead of the terror I should have felt at all this. I had never felt so alive in all my years in this palace, and my instinct was to be right here in the heart of the fray.

I took the bow from my back, nocking an arrow and drawing back the string as I lined up the shot with the creature's head. But before I could release the arrow, an enormous, terrifying beast rose up beyond it in the sky, giant, red-tipped wings catching the light of the moon as it wheeled overhead.

It was impossible. The last of them had left this world centuries ago. There was no way this creature could be in existence now. But as the monster swooped overhead and released a plume of hellfire from its jaws that ignited the sky in a haze of blood red flames, there was no denying what it was.

A dragon of the lost gods.

CASSIUS

CHAPTER FORTY TWO

Magdor convulsed more and more, and I stopped fighting against my restraints as she jerked and groaned, shock making me fall still as I stared at the gruesome display. The cloying feeling of that dark magic she had called to us only grew stronger, a sense of dread burrowing deep into my bones.

She released a guttural noise that sounded as if it had come somewhere from the pit of her stomach, and the ritualistic chanting pouring from her lips turned into a rasp as she fought to go on with it.

I was helpless in the face of this tainted magic, the iron holding me down making my muscles weak and useless.

Magdor buckled over, grasping her stomach and crying out, the chanting finally ending as she groaned in pain and panted hard. I didn't dare to hope she'd somehow done herself harm though, instead watching her with trepidation as I waited to see what would happen next.

She snapped upright, her eyes two hollow pits of black bone as blood trickled down her cheeks in a pair of agonising tears. A grimace pulled at my features as she moved towards me, her back straightening and those empty eyes flashing with a wild hunger. My heart broke into a gallop as though it were looking to burst free of my chest and escape the horrors which closed in on us in this chamber.

"Stay back," I commanded.

I bucked against my iron chains, a renewed terror filling me as the witch drew nearer.

If she takes control of me, I'll never save Osaria. Austyn will be forced to marry her son. The emperor will never be free of her.

"You want the coin?" I snapped, desperately trying to think of a way to hold her off. "I don't have it anymore. A thief took it after I made this command."

Her lips curved into a knowing smile. "Liar." She moved to the end of the stone table, climbing onto it between my legs and crouching there like some kind of demon spider.

I recoiled into the stone, trying to bring a knee up to hold her off, but I couldn't do anything except jerk against my restraints and watch this unfold. She crawled over me, resting her knees either side of my hips and leaning down so her hair created a curtain around us.

Her cold, empty eyes bored into mine and I ground my jaw as I glared back at her, refusing to show fear even in the face of this monster.

"Get off of me," I snarled, but her response was an empty laugh.

She lowered her mouth to my chest, and a wave of nausea gripped me as her wet lips moved down my body. Her tongue slicked out against my skin and repulsion filled me as she groaned in delight, but there was nothing sexual about this. No, her hunger was for my flesh, just as it had been for that innocent boy's.

I bucked my hips violently, but I couldn't get her away, the thundering pulse of my heart racing so fast that I feared it would burst at any moment. Was she going to fucking eat me?

She dug her teeth into my stomach, encasing my navel with her lips and I roared in agony as the razor-sharp points of her teeth drove deeper.

"Bitch!" I fought as hard as I could against the strength-sapping iron, but she continued to bite down and pain raced through my skin as she sliced her teeth through my flesh.

The thought of being devoured bite by bite was a horror beyond anything I had known before. Any torture was preferable to that.

When she lifted her head, a circular ring of bloody teeth marks was imprinted on my skin, and I scowled at her, fighting the fear which threatened to undo me.

I am made of steel.

Her empty eye sockets flickered with an unholy flame, and she threw her head back, her dark hair tumbling around her shoulders as she released a low growl.

I bellowed a roar for all the good it did me, wondering if my voice might travel far enough to the ears of someone willing to come seek me out. But even if they did, I was in the grip of a monster, and her power clearly ran far deeper than anything I could have predicted.

She hunched forward and coughed heavily, raising a hand to her mouth.

A disgusted look had taken up permanent residence on my face, but she didn't pay me any attention. Blood wet my ankles and wrists from the strength of my fight against my restraints, coating the iron manacles as I struggled in their hold.

"What the fuck do you want from me?" I demanded, but she didn't bother to acknowledge me.

She coughed once more then lowered her hand from her mouth, revealing a large, shining golden beetle in her palm, a doting smile on her face as she looked at it like it was a new-born babe.

"Take his mind," she whispered to it as I gazed on in horror.

She let the bug crawl from her hand onto my stomach and I jerked wildly to try and get it off. Its little legs brushed across my skin as it moved, darting towards the bloody marks around my navel with intent.

"What is that?" I barked as Magdor sat back on her heels to watch, excitement lighting her eyes.

When the beetle reached the wound, it starting burrowing into my body and I cried out at the horrible feeling of the vile little creature driving itself under my skin.

"No!" I roared as it made its way beneath my flesh and a bump raised on my stomach, starting to scuttle upwards.

The pain of it was nothing in the face of the panic that was rising in me, the beetle tearing its way up my body from the inside.

I couldn't do anything but thrash and beg that this thing would stop its ascent as I cursed Magdor's name under the name of every lost god, begging for them to wake from their slumber and come save me from this hell of a fate.

A shadow rushed through the room and my gaze whipped sideways just in time to see Drake slamming into Magdor, throwing her from the table. She hit the ground, rolling into a crouch, and baring her sharpened teeth at him with a growl.

"*You*," she spat.

"Drake," I gasped as he raised a sword in his grip, pointing it at Magdor as she rose to her feet, her back straightening and making a cracking noise that was wholly unnatural.

Drake lunged forward again, swinging the sword with a furious blow, but Magdor moved with inhuman speed, darting out of reach and appearing behind him. She grabbed a fistful of his hair, yanking him backwards and throwing him across the cave with impossible strength.

He hit the wall with a yell and Kyra screamed as she ran to his aid, falling to her knees beside him.

"Master, tell me what you need," she gasped, but he was already back on his feet, running to intercept Magdor again.

"Kyra!" I cried, looking down at the beetle beneath my flesh as it scrabbled its way over my ribcage, fighting to get higher. The magic girl ran to my aid as Drake swung violent blows at Magdor, keeping her running as she shot out of the way of his strikes.

Kyra looked down at me with wide eyes as she took in the bug moving up my chest, the bump in my skin climbing ever higher.

"Get it out," I spoke through my teeth as I fought to bear the foul sensation of its sharp pincers cutting into me.

"Hang on, Cassius. I'll rescue you." Kyra fetched a silver cup from Magdor's potion stores and slammed it down over the beetle to halt its movements, looking around for something to help her remove it.

Drake cried out as he was thrown into the stone table I was chained to, his sword clattering onto the ground.

Kyra whirled away from me and the cup went flying as she rushed to help him, kicking the sword back in his direction before Magdor could descend on him. Drake's hand curled around the hilt the moment Magdor collided with him, the monstrous woman driving her teeth into his arm and tearing a lump out of his flesh. He roared in anger, swinging the sword up, but she sped away again before the blade's edge could cut into her.

"*Kyra*," I begged, and she swung back to me as the beetle made it to my collar bone.

She grabbed the cup and slammed it over the bug once more, a deep frown furrowing her brow.

"I'll bash it dead," she decided, and I nodded, anything but letting it get further than it already had. But as she lifted the cup and smashed the bottom end of the cup down on the bug, the beetle bit deep into bone, trying to burrow away from her hand.

"Stop!" I cried and Kyra dropped the cup in dismay.

"Sorry, sullen man," she said, looking around for another answer. "Maybe Drake can wish it free."

My eyes wheeled onto Drake as he slammed into Magdor, finally catching her, and cracking her head back against the cave wall. She slumped to the ground at his feet, and he raised his sword as if unsure whether to strike at her again.

"I need help," Kyra called, and Drake turned, racing over to us in an instant and looking down at the bug as she pointed it out on my body.

"Cut it out!" I commanded; my voice hoarse as the creature made it to my throat.

"What the fuck is that?" Drake gasped.

"Get. It. Out," I snarled as the beetle crawled up the side of my neck, the sickening feeling of its legs scraping a path beneath my flesh making my entire body tense and my heart thunder in my chest.

"You can wish it free," Kyra suggested.

"No time." Drake snatched a dagger from his hip and slammed his palm onto my throat to stop the thing advancing. The tip of his blade scored into my skin and pain burst through the wound as he twisted the dagger.

"Motherfucker," I snarled.

He squeezed the cut and I ground my teeth hard as he forced the vile insect from my skin. It tumbled to the floor, and Kyra leapt onto it, smashing her heel down on it again and again until the thing was crushed and unmoving.

"You could have wished it free," I hissed and Drake shrugged innocently.

"Did you see that?" Kyra breathed to herself. "Well, that's not a nice thing to say. I'm sure Cassius cares that his brain hasn't been eaten."

"We need to apprehend Magdor and bring her before the royal court," I said urgently, looking over to where she lay still on the ground.

"Are you insane? That's the fucking empress, mate. If we drag her into the palace tied up at our mercy, they ain't gonna believe we're the good guys," Drake said.

"We must. Didn't you see what she was?" I hissed.

"A monster," Kyra whispered.

"Yeah, but she's still the empress. I ain't looking to get hung for treason, I've got a throne to win," Drake said, pushing a hand into his dark hair.

"Untie me and I'll do it then," I said, and he shrugged, heading over to Magdor and aiming his sword at her as he kicked her leg, checking she was still out cold. Then he knelt down, rummaging in her robes and producing an iron key.

He returned to me, sliding it into the shackles binding me, freeing my legs and my right arm.

"Kyra, can you heal me?" Drake murmured to her, nodding to the bloody bite mark on his arm.

"Of course," she said brightly and the magic fluttered out from her and into his wounds, healing them up as if they had never been there.

"Hurry up," I pressed.

Magdor sprang to her feet with a shriek of fury and my heart jolted as her eyes locked onto Kyra, the witch rushing towards her with greed and desire filling her expression.

"*Fuck.*" Drake abandoned me, launching into an attack and swinging his sword out to intercept her.

I tried to get up, but I was yanked backwards as my left wrist remained tethered to the table and I cursed in frustration.

Magdor moved with unnatural speed, darting past the length of Drake's sword and lunging for Kyra, but her hands slid through The Blessing's skin as if she was made of smoke.

Drake collided with the witch, locking an arm around her throat and holding his other wrist with his hand, jerking tight enough to cut off her air supply. In the act, he dropped the key and it tinkled across the ground, anxiety pouring through me as it bounced away from me.

"I've got it, sullen man." Kyra ran for it, snatching up the key and racing towards me again with determination in her golden eyes.

That dark presence seemed to throb and pound around us again, and as Drake fought to hold the bitch in his grasp, I could have sworn I caught sight of a red glow seeming to burn through the back of his tunic.

"Drake – watch out!" I yelled, though I didn't know exactly what I was warning him of.

Magdor reared back suddenly, forcing Drake off of her and slashing her nails towards his face. He planted a kick to her chest before her strike made contact and spat air through his teeth.

"Not the fucking face!"

Kyra jammed the key in the lock of my manacle, twisting it. I yanked my arm free at last, running forward to help Drake as I fought to shake off the effects of the iron. As Magdor rushed at him once more, I caught a handful of her hair and dragged her backwards.

"We have to subdue her!" I called to Drake as a howling roar seemed to fill the space around us, and that dark presence intensified like it was trying to come to the aid of its twisted mistress. "We must expose what she is."

Drake began to say something, but she slammed her hands into his chest and sent him crashing backwards, his head cracking against the rough wall as a curse fell from his lips.

Magdor shrieked like a wraith, seeming to find some new well of strength as that heavy power built in the room, turning in my arms and throwing me away from her.

I stumbled, catching hold of her arm and taking her with me. My legs hit the cauldron with a resounding dong and I forgot my morals, forgot fighting with honour and punched her straight in her warped face, making her head snap back violently before I grabbed a handful of her raven hair and rammed her whole head into the liquid.

Drake cursed as he pushed away from the wall, blood staining his neck from a wound hidden in his hair as I fought to keep Magdor submerged in the concoction, and he scrambled forward to help.

Kyra screamed from somewhere behind me, my attention snapping to her as she clutched her ears and sank to her knees, power spilling from her in a flood of golden glitter as the dark presence which Magdor had summoned seemed to writhe and pulse around her.

"Kyra!" Drake bellowed, turning as if he was going to go to her.

Magdor reared backwards like a demon, coated in the purple potion which stained her hair and her contorted face.

She threw a punch to my stomach which knocked the wind out of me, and I hit the ground hard on my arse.

Drake seized Magdor's arms, trying to hold her in place as she fought like a banshee and the darkness in the cavern thickened, making my ears hum with a potent power.

Kyra screamed louder as I scrambled to my hands and knees, and her eyes suddenly snapped open, the gold which was normally contained to her pupils filling them entirely as a defiant cry spilled from her lips, and she threw her head back.

Power crashed from her so violently that I was knocked to the ground again, my fingers biting into the rough rocks as I fought to pull myself upright, the entire cavern filling with glittering golden light.

I squinted at her as the oppressive presence of whatever Magdor had been summoning retreated, and for the briefest of moments I could have sworn I saw the outline of golden wings glowing against Kyra's back as she spread her arms wide and continued to scream.

The force of her power slammed into me, sending me rolling away and knocking Magdor and Drake from their feet too. The dark presence howled violently as it was forced away from the cavern, the heaviness in the air dissipating as the golden glow faded too.

Kyra fell forward, the visage of ethereal wings disappearing as she collapsed onto her hands and knees, panting heavily.

"Herdat, return to me!" Magdor cried desperately, scrambling across the rocky ground like she meant to follow the thing wherever it had gone.

Drake shoved himself upright, yanking Magdor up too with a fistful of her hair as she wailed wildly, still crying out the name of a lost god. But surely that couldn't be what it was? Herdat was the god of death and ruin; she was the most feared of all gods, and she had left this world a long time ago, along with all the rest. There was no way she could be back, summoned by the will of one Fae.

Drake swore as he fought to tug Magdor along with him and they staggered backwards, moving closer and closer to the raging river while his face set in a brutal, determined mask.

Magdor forgot her grief and whirled on him, screaming as she collided with him. She moved like a wild animal, slashing at his skin with the sharpened points of her fingernails and finally striking his face, carving four long scratches into his skin which split and spilled blood instantly.

"Bitch!" he roared in anger. "Kyra, I wish for a metal fist!"

"Done," Kyra replied, raising her head to watch the fight through a spill of inky hair as she remained panting on the cavern floor.

I gained my feet, running towards Drake and Magdor on the edge of the water. Drake's right fist shone silver as he slammed it into Magdor's face, and the crunch of breaking bone filled the cave.

"No!" I bellowed as I tried to grab the witch's arm, but she fell back with a shriek of fury.

She hit the water with a scream, blood pooling around her before she was dragged beneath the turbulent water.

I moved to leap into the river to fish her out, desperate for the world to see what she was, but Drake caught my arm, yanking me back.

"Are you crazy? You'll be swept downstream with her." He pointed and I spotted swathes of her robes floating on the surface, careering along the current at a fierce pace before being sucked into the tunnels which delved further beneath the ground and out of sight.

My lips parted, panic threatened to set in, but my training got in the way of it. I had to keep my fucking head and figure out what to do from here.

Drake clapped his metal hand to my shoulder, his eyes dark. "She's gone, mate. Nothing we can do to change that now."

"She floated away, should we have stopped her floating away?" Kyra asked as she appeared beside us, still panting, and looking exhausted.

I realised too late that Drake probably could have commanded something into existence to stop this from happening.

I sighed, rubbing my fingers into my eyes. The heat of blood washed down my neck and I lifted a hand to the neat cut Drake had made against my flesh to carve the beetle out of me.

"Thank you," I said earnestly as I gazed at Drake. "You saved my damn life."

He smirked and his eyes filled with warmth for a second, despite the bleeding wounds that coated his skin and the adrenaline and fear which was only just starting to fade from the air surrounding us. "Well don't expect me to make a habit of it, Cass."

"I wouldn't dream of it." We stared at each other, assessing, weighing, acknowledging. And I wondered how this lowborn thief had somehow wormed his way under my skin – kind of like that beetle.

I wasn't sure I'd ever had a real friend outside of my horse before, but it was starting to seem like he was one. Despite all the evidence he'd tried to present me with to prove he was a heartless cutthroat who would only ever use the people around him for his own gain, he had come when I needed him. And there was no selfish reason I could think of for that, which meant it had to be as simple as it seemed. He actually gave a shit about it me.

My attention shifted to Kyra, and she smiled up at me so brightly that she practically glowed again.

"I'm glad you aren't dead, sullen man," she breathed, and I could see real relief in her eyes at those words, making my gut twist with the realisation that she had cared about my fate too.

"For a moment there, I could have sworn I saw…" I trailed off as I ran my gaze down her, the memory of those ethereal wings pushing at me as I tried to wrap my head around the idea of it.

"What?" she asked, and Drake cocked his head at me in question too.

"Wings," I said, my mind spinning with the idea of that as I wondered if I could have truly seen it or not.

Kyra's brow furrowed in confusion, and she looked over her shoulder as if searching for any evidence of that.

"Did you hit your head in that brawl, Cass?" Drake taunted, his gaze roaming over Kyra too.

"What did you say you'd seen again, Cassius?" she asked me curiously, pinning her focus on me once more and I frowned at her, wondering how she could have forgotten that so quickly.

"Wings," I pushed, but this time instead of frowning she just laughed, shaking her head at me as if I'd lost my mind and Drake arched a disbelieving brow at me too. "Never mind," I muttered, turning my attention to the more pressing issue of what we'd just done.

I gazed around at the lair I was in, the spilled potion, the chest of jars and bottles which were surely enough to incriminate Magdor. Though how I was going to prove this place belonged to her, I wasn't sure.

"We had better alert the guards." I made a move towards the exit, but Drake snatched my arm, yanking me around to face him.

"How the fuck are we supposed to explain this?"

"With the truth," I said frankly. "We'll tell them she brought me here."

"And why would they believe that? How are you going to tell them what happened without bringing the coin into it? I won't let you expose Kyra like that." His expression darkened in warning, and I bristled at the challenge he presented.

"We'll say we don't know why she was after us," I growled. "We cannot let her get away with this."

"Cassius," Drake hissed. "Magdor's gone. Drowned, dead, who knows? Who really cares? Doesn't look like she's coming back, mate. So let's just return to our rooms and pretend it never happened. All you really wanted was to get rid of the bitch anyway, so it seems to me like we've accomplished that. We don't need to draw any attention to our involvement in it."

I shook my head, ready to walk away again when he went on.

"Without Magdor, we don't have an admission of guilt or any real evidence aside from a room of dubious shit – there isn't even anything to prove this place was hers," he pressed. "Without her, the Royal Guard can twist this any way they want. And right now, it looks like we just killed the empress of Osaria and are standing in a den full of shit *we* could have brought here for all they know."

I clenched my jaw, stubbornly wanting to have faith in the system, even though doubts were crawling in. "They will believe us. We only need to explain-"

"Not everyone is as honest as you, Cass. I've been on the receiving end of the Royal Guard's mercy more times than I can count. And *you* may not have kicked the shit out of street boys for amusement, but I've met plenty of them who did. So I'm not going to risk ruining what I have here for the sake of your morals."

"The evidence is right here," I snarled. "The kingdom must know what Magdor has done."

"They'll want to question us," Drake growled. "*All* of us." He glanced over at Kyra who was now sitting on the stone table, swinging her legs. He lowered his voice to a whisper. "Do you think she'll get through a line of questioning without them figuring out what she is?"

My gaze trailed over the innocent, magical girl with my gut tying in knots. No matter what vendetta I had against Magdor, I couldn't risk Kyra being exposed. The coin would be seized. She'd be forced back into it, and who knew what would be done with her then? They could kill her or abuse her power. And after she had come here to help save me, how could I repay her with that fate?

I shut my eyes, fury making my blood hot as reality descended on me. "Magdor will get away with everything."

"She's dead," Drake whispered. "That surely means the emperor will be free now? Everything will be okay again just like you wanted. You just won't get a medal for it."

"I don't want a-"

"Sure, sure." He slapped my fucking cheek a couple of times in that patronising way which made me want to break his pretty face before turning to face Kyra and raising his metal fist. "Can you undo this now? As much as I like it, I'm not sure it'll count as honourable in tomorrow's brawl."

Kyra slipped off the table, her eyes falling on his hand until the metallic sheen of it fell away and he was left flexing his fingers as his flesh returned to normal.

"And if you could heal me too that would be amazing," he added, pointing to the scratches on his face as if that was the most worrying thing to him right now. But it was the large gash in the back of his head which continued to bleed down his neck that I would have been most concerned about.

"You're so fucking vain," I grumbled at him as Kyra granted his request and healed him, cleaning away the blood and grime until he looked like a gentleman once more. Or at least as like one as he was capable of appearing, with that street-born swagger and casual posture.

"I'm failing to hear an insult there, Cass," he said. "Now stop the jealous bullshit and agree to let Kyra heal you too."

"Are you sure you have the energy?" I asked Kyra with a frown, remembering the way she'd looked after fighting off that thing which had been present here with Magdor.

"It hurts me to see you hurting," she replied, the honesty in her response surprising me and as I felt her magic humming in the air between us, waiting on my consent, I could tell that was the truth.

I nodded once in acceptance and she smiled as her power washed through my body, healing and cleaning me the way she had for Drake.

"You'd better get the disguise back over your face again too. Then we can get the fuck out of here," Drake added, and I agreed to that, allowing Kyra to disguise me as Drake Nazari's guard once more.

My heart clenched as I gazed between the two of them, knowing I had to accept this fate. We would return to our rooms, and pretend we knew nothing about this when it was announced that Magdor was dead. And if her death released the emperor, then maybe everything I'd hoped for would come to fruition anyway. Maybe there would be no pageant at all by tomorrow. Maybe it would be outlawed. Maybe Austyn would be given the freedom of choice at long last.

"Come on," Drake urged as he led the way through the cave towards a door hidden in the shadows. "We have a dragon to appease."

"What?" I gasped.

"Oh right, yeah that dragon we pissed off is attacking the palace," Drake said, tossing me a grim look and a distant boom far above us proved that he was telling the truth. "So I had the clever idea to use that dragon scale she gave you to summon her to us, give her a heap of gold and tell her to fuck back off to the desert. Sound good?"

"Alright," I said heavily, scraping a hand over my short hair, feeling ready for anything now that Kyra had healed the weakness from my body. "The scale is in your quarters."

"Oh. So I didn't even have to bother coming to find you after all," he said, giving me a sweeping look, and the stupid little thought I'd had about him coming here to help me popped before my eyes. "Lucky for you I didn't know you didn't have it on you, eh?"

"Yes, Drake, lucky is exactly how I feel about this turn of events," I deadpanned, not liking the way a knife was twisting in my chest over learning the truth.

Fool. Did you really think he gave a damn about you?

Kyra shifted closer to me, a knowing look in her eyes. "He was always going to come look for you, Cassius. He was worried about you. You're his only friend after all," she whispered loud enough for Drake to hear too, and he scoffed.

"You really need to stop trying to convince yourselves that I'm a good man," he warned, his eyes skimming between the two of us with his usual helping of far too much bravado. "It will only make it hurt more when I prove the truth to you and break your little hearts."

"Liar," Kyra muttered, but he ignored her, and I was saddened that she had so much faith in him.

"Kyra, I wish we were back at our rooms," Drake said.

"As you wish," she replied. "Let's go turn that dragon's frown upside down."

DRAKE

CHAPTER FORTY THREE

I stumbled a step as we arrived back in my chambers at the far end of the palace, my gaze moving around the space as I got my bearings and I tried to get my head around that insane use of magic. It felt like the contents of my stomach had been left behind down in that dank room where Magdor had been up to fuck knew what, but as I drew in a deep breath, I managed to realign my thoughts to this new reality.

An almighty bellow sounded in the sky outside the open window, and I turned my head to look over the city, my stomach lurching at the sight of fires burning across it now, the drone of the city bells ringing on and on. The clamour of men fighting filled the air too, the clang of swords and roar of battle cries adding to the cacophony of noise and making it sound like the city was at war. Which I guessed it was.

Monsters had attacked before this, stealing victims away into the night or finding their deaths on the blades of the royal guards, but never like this, in such numbers and with such fury. Azurea had done this, brought this down upon the people of Osaria. All because she was greedy. And maybe a little because I shouldn't have tried to get out of a deal with a dragon. But mostly because she was a cunt.

"Where's the fucking scale?" I demanded, looking to Cassius who had been staring through the window too, his mouth falling slack at the destruction taking place out there, but the bark of my voice broke him out of it.

"It's here," he growled, taking off into his room, his boots pounding across the tiles.

Kyra slipped closer to the window, the flash of flames beyond it brightening her eyes.

"I remember…" she murmured, almost to herself and I moved towards her too, my gaze drawn up onto the parapet where a lone soldier was fighting against an enormous scorpious spider, the eight-legged beast lunging at him with its stinger tail snapping out repeatedly. I'd heard that being stung by that thing was one of the worst fates a Fae could suffer. The poison slowly melted your insides, keeping you conscious throughout the entire thing as it worked from the least vital organs to the most. Then the creature would begin to devour your extremities while you still lived, the process taking several days to complete if it took you back to its lair. Fuck that for a fate.

"What do you remember?" I asked as I watched the soldier who continued to fight valiantly against the huge beast, though I had to wonder if he was just staring his death in the eye because that thing was fucking huge, and it looked damn hungry too.

"Fire, lies, anger," she breathed, turning to me with the flames from outside reflected in her eyes. "The dragons belong with the gods."

"The gods clearly forgot this one," I muttered bitterly, and Kyra blinked, a veil seeming to lift in her gaze as she nodded.

"We should fix this," she said.

"We will," I agreed. "Just as soon as Cassius finds that-"

"I have it," Cassius barked as he strode back towards us, showing us the jet-black scale in his hand before pushing it into his pocket. The Forken scimitar he had decided to keep for himself was now strapped to his waist, and he'd changed into a fresh shirt after Magdor had destroyed the one he'd worn to dinner. "But if you had simply heeded my warning when you first decided to ignore the promise you made to that creature then none of this-"

His words were cut off by a scream of terror which made the hairs stand up along the back of my neck. I turned to look at the parapet where the scorpious spider had managed to back the soldier up against the tower wall, its stinger striking against the bricks repeatedly while the soldier – who I now realised was actually a woman – fought to parry the blows with a short sword. It was definitely a losing battle. She was one wrong move away from being stung and there was no remedy in this world for that.

"The princess!" Cassius gasped, breaking into a sprint and I lunged for him, grasping his arm, and yanking him to halt before he could take another step towards the window.

"What princess?" I demanded, my brow furrowing in confusion.

"That is her fighting up there," he snarled, wrenching his arm from my hold. "I would recognise her even in the darkest of nights by the simple beauty of her aura alone."

He didn't give me another moment to object before he was running again, heading towards the window I wasn't blocking and leaping straight at it despite the shutter being closed.

Wood shattered and broke apart as he collided with it, and I scrambled after him with Kyra right beside me as we looked out to see him hit the balcony of the rooms below ours and roll before leaping to his feet and racing away towards the far wall. He instantly began to climb a trellis covered in roses to get up to the parapet above, and as Austyn yelled another battle cry, I had to admit he had been right about the identity of the soldier fighting that beast.

"There was an open window right there," I pointed out, bobbing my chin at the one beside the broken shutter which Cassius had just leapt through like a possessed maniac.

"Are we going after him?" she asked, and I grunted an agreement as I took a running jump out of the open window. I could hardly become emperor without a princess to marry, and Cassius had taken the fucking dragon scale with him too.

I rolled as I hit the balcony below, leaping to my feet and yelling out for Cassius to wait as I craned my neck to see him scaling the wall high above us.

"I could fly us up there?" Kyra suggested as she landed at my side, falling into a crouch instead of rolling. She looked like one of the legendary Ageishan assassins in her dark clothing and that deadly look in her eyes. I had no doubt that she could kill better and more ruthlessly than any of the cutthroats I'd known in The Den if the notion took her, and for some reason that only made me like her more.

I glanced around before shaking my head at her offer. "We can't use magic like that out here – too many witnesses about to see. But if you want to make me immune to the sting of a scorpious spider then I'm up for that."

"You've got it," she agreed, and I felt the brush of her magic coating my skin as I broke into a sprint and tore away across the balcony.

I leapt up onto the trellis and began to climb after Cassius who was shouting something about smiting all beasts in his path while a fire drake swooped towards him, and he was forced to stop his ascent in favour of swinging his sword at it.

I continued to climb as the fire drake swooped around him, slashing its talons and catching his shoulder, causing blood to splatter down onto my cheek as he cursed at the wound, the sound of the beast's pain following a moment later as Cassius struck it with his sword.

The fire drake launched itself away from him and he instantly continued to climb, crying out for the princess even though I had to doubt she could hear him over all the noise the scorpious spider was making. But the fire drake wasn't done with him yet, and as I climbed after him, I yelled out a warning as the flying lizard came for him again.

Cassius turned his head, swinging his sword just as the drake belched fire at him and I swore as the brightness of the flames forced my eyes from them. My heart raced with panic as I saw his end in that fire and I found myself hating the idea of that far more than I should have.

"Not today, you scaly bastard!" Cassius roared and an ungodly shriek followed just before the fire drake plummeted from the sky, blue blood spilling from the stab wound to its heart and its huge body damn near knocking me free of the wall as it passed.

I looked back up to find Cassius climbing again, despite the fact the back of his shirt was on fire and the flames were licking their way up his spine.

I pushed myself harder, the fire drake's attack having let me close the distance between us, and I made it to his side as we got nearer to the roof of the building.

"Does he know he's on fire?" Kyra asked from beside me and I wasn't certain if her words were for me or herself.

"A glass of water, please, Kyra," I asked, holding my hand out just in time for one to appear and I tossed the contents over Cassius's back, dousing the flames while he just ignored me and kept climbing.

The back of his shirt was almost entirely destroyed, and a patch of charred and blistered skin showed through the ruined fabric, marring his flesh. *By the Fallen.*

Cassius didn't so much as glance at me in thanks for me stopping him from burning to death, and he heaved himself up over the balustrade with a battle cry while I tossed the empty glass away from me to shatter on the cobbles far below.

I hauled myself up next, drawing my sword as I made it onto the roof with Kyra right beside me, and we chased after him as he raced towards the scorpious spider who still had Austyn trapped against the tower wall.

The princess was parrying blows from the creature's enormous stinger as it struck at her repeatedly, the force of the strikes knocking chunks of masonry from the tower walls every time it missed.

"For Osaria!" Cassius roared as he sprinted for them, swinging his scimitar with all his strength and severing one of the creature's eight legs before it even reacted to our presence on the roof.

Blue blood sprayed from the severed limb, coating him from head to toe as the monster shrieked in agony and twisted around to seek out its new prey, two of its legs slamming into Cassius and sending him tumbling away across the roof where his head cracked against the brickwork so hard, I swear I almost felt it myself.

"Oh, that looks like fun, can I fight too?" Kyra asked, drawing a pair of stunning daggers out of thin air and giving the creature a look so monstrous that I wasn't even certain which of them was more beastly.

"Sure," I agreed. "Just remember to keep your magic hidden."

Kyra's smile turned manic, and she darted forward as Cassius rolled to his hands and knees while the scorpious spider ran for him.

I cursed myself for getting involved in this madness then gave in to the call of the fight as I ran forward too, raising my sword and crying out to draw the beast's attention my way as I took a running jump and severed another of its legs.

"Drake?" Austyn's surprised voice found me as I spun away with my agility, managing to avoid the blood shower which followed my strike as I sped beneath the belly of the beast.

A roar announced another fire drake swooping down onto the roof and I lost sight of the princess as a cloud of fire separated us, instead focusing on the fight as I aimed a savage blow at the belly of the monster above me.

My sword crashed against the armoured plating which covered the scorpious spider's belly and I twisted aside as I failed to pierce it, my arm yanking painfully as I fought to keep hold of my weapon.

The monster moved with unexpected speed, leaping aside and making room for its stinger to crash down, aimed right for me.

I threw myself aside, rolling across the roof and keeping up the movement as its stinger slammed down again and again, the monster chasing after me with a furious screech.

Cassius leapt over me suddenly, a roar of fury leaving him as he swung his sword over his head like a battle axe, bringing it down on the tail of the beast just as the stinger struck the roof once more.

Blue blood burst from the wound as he hacked into its flesh, the stinger left dangling from the half-severed appendage as the scorpious spider yanked it away with a howl of pain.

I leapt to my feet and ran for another of its legs, carving through it like I was felling a sapling, laughing wildly as the monster pitched sideways, almost crushing me beneath it.

The tattoo on the left of my back felt as if it was on fire, burning against my skin, while energy coursed through me. The thrill of the fight gave me a high unlike any other as I leaned into my Affinities and bathed in the power of wielding them.

Kyra whooped excitedly from somewhere behind me and I twisted around, finding her locked in a battle with a scarrion beast. The millipede-like monster reared back on its hind legs, bearing sets of razor-sharp teeth at her before it lunged with unnatural speed, blocking my view of her and making my heart catapult into my throat.

I ran towards the creature, its long, red and brown body twisting around and around, coiling over something which just had to be my little goddess.

"I'm coming!" I yelled as my heart beat a war rhythm in my chest. But before I could get any closer to the thing, I was forced to jump aside as its severed head was thrown my way, the lump of flesh thumping wetly against the roof and rolling past me, leaving a trail of blood behind it.

Kyra grinned as she scrambled up onto the headless corpse of the monster she'd just killed, the knives she held now wet with blood and a feral look in her golden eyes which made me bark a laugh.

"Nice work," I commented, and she flushed with pride before turning and running off to find her next victim.

Cassius's yells of battle made me turn his way again and I found him fighting to finish the scorpious spider, slashing at the creature's face while it tried to snatch him into its pincers and eat him whole.

Austyn was fighting beyond him, her movements fluid as she fought against the fire drake which snapped and lunged at her, backing her up towards the edge of the roof as it herded her there with blasts of fire from its powerful jaws.

I spun my sword in my hand as I broke into a sprint, heading for the drake as it blasted fire at Austyn. She was forced to leap aside, her boots smacking against the edge of the parapet and the fall below calling her name as her arms wheeled to keep her balanced. A shriek of fright escaped her as she teetered on the edge.

I yelled out at the fire drake, trying to draw its attention away from her as I ran for it, seeing her death hanging in the balance as she ran out of room, and it lunged at her again.

Cassius slashed at the scorpious spider's bulging eyes, catching it in the face and breaking away from it as it jerked back, hurling his sword towardss the fire drake just as it raised up onto its back legs, heading straight for the princess.

The sword caught the drake in the side of the neck, and it toppled forward with a dying howl, making me lose sight of the princess beyond it and all knowledge of her fate was stolen from us.

Her screams were lost to a tremendous roar tearing from the scorpious spider as it pounced at its now unarmed prey.

I spun my sword in my hand as I broke into a sprint, hacking through yet another of the scorpious spider's legs just as the thing managed to slice its pincers into Cassius's gut, carving into his flesh and spilling his blood like wine from a chalice.

Cassius bellowed in agony as the monster carved into his body and my gaze met with his as his death hung in the space between us.

"Kyra!" I roared as I ran on, cutting through another of the scorpious spider's legs, felling the beast like an overgrown tree and springing aside as it slammed down onto the roof just where I'd been standing a moment before.

I leapt up onto the creature's spiny back and ran for its head as it kicked and squirmed pathetically, trying to get up on its few remaining legs.

Cassius was punching the thing in the face as it still slashed at him with razor sharp pincers, cutting into him over and over again and spilling so much blood that I knew he didn't have long for this world. The thought of that sent my gut twisting with fear as I upped my pace and ran for him.

I raised my sword above my head and leapt forward, throwing all of my weight down into the blow and sinking the blade deep through the many eyes of the monster that was trying to send Cassius into death, spilling blood and gore as it heaved a final cry of pain and finally died.

Kyra appeared beside me so suddenly that I was almost certain she had materialised from thin air, but I had no energy to waste on worrying about witnesses as I jumped down from the beast's back and made it to Cassius where he was half pinned beneath its dead body.

"You must get to the princess," he coughed out around a mouthful of blood, and I cursed his unending loyalty even in his dying moments.

"Do you agree to Kyra healing you?" I barked, slapping him as his eyes rolled back and the end threatened to come for him before he could even agree.

His eyes lit with surprise, moving to Kyra as she dropped to her knees beside us, and he nodded.

"Yes. But you must get to Austyn. You have to-"

"You heard him, Kyra," I growled, and she nodded.

"The princess," Cassius gritted out, but I was already on my feet, doing what he wanted regardless of his fucking orders.

I ran from the two of them, trusting in Kyra's magic as she worked to save the most infuriating man I'd ever known. I made it to the twitching body of the fire drake which had been trying to kill the princess before Cassius had thrown his fucking sword at it like he had a death wish.

I climbed over the body of the beast and dropped down beyond it, fear capturing me for a moment as I failed to spot her anywhere. But as I took a step towards the edge of the roof to look for her on the ground far below, a muffled curse spun me back to face the fire drake once more.

The glint of silver armour caught my eye beneath the corpse, and I threw my weight against the monster's scaley body, knocking it aside and finding a thoroughly crushed, thoroughly alive princess trapped beneath. Her helmet had fallen off, lying beside her on the roof tiles, and her silver hair pooled around her like liquid moonlight.

"Well look at that," I said, giving her my best cocky grin while she panted beneath me, all bloody from battle and looking nothing like the primped little princess she was supposed to be. "I knew I liked you for a reason."

AUSTYN

CHAPTER FORTY FOUR

Drake offered me his hand to help me up and I took it, still stunned to find that he had come to my aid. My palm slid into his and his fingers wrapped around me as he pulled me to my feet so fast that I had to steady myself against his chest.

I was half aware that his guard and maid were watching us, but I couldn't draw my eyes from his face. Between the time we had shared on the balcony earlier tonight, and finding him here now, wet with blood for me, I was starting to feel something I had never felt before. Could this man really be someone I could trust? Someone who didn't flinch at seeing a woman fight in battle, who actually encouraged it.

I acted on instinct alone, knowing now was not the time, but I was high on the wildness of battle and the freedom I had claimed out here in this fight. I fisted his shirt, drawing him down to me so our lips met, fire coursing along my spine at the reckless act. But I was tasting freedom for the first time in my life and there was no one here to stop me from being rash now.

He stilled in surprise and for a moment I thought he was going to pull away, but then he yanked me closer by one hand on my back and cupped my jaw in his grip, dominating the kiss as he pressed his tongue into my mouth. It was the first time I had ever allowed a man to touch me like this and it set my pulse skittering across my body as I met his tongue with tentative strokes of my own. I didn't know what I was doing but Drake's mouth moved against mine like he had done this a thousand times, and that didn't bother me somehow. I just wanted to learn this, to know how to express this passion in me and offer it to the man who had fought at my side up here against the monsters that had come to destroy my city.

His kiss was filthy, savage, ruinous and I let it devour me from the inside out, burning up in the heat of it. This was already the wildest night of my life and I wanted to squeeze every drop of adventure out of it before I was forced back into my cage.

Drake was the embodiment of the freedom I had never been able to possess myself, and I tasted that on him now, drinking it into myself and taking a piece of it for my own. His life was what I wanted mine to look like. Him with his carefree smiles and easy choices. He could do anything he wanted, *be* anything he wanted, and I hated him for that almost as much as I liked him for it.

Our kiss was a battle of its own, our wills colliding and neither of us bowing to each other's wants. We took from each other as much as we gave, our fingers biting into one another's flesh as we stole this moment of bliss among the chaos that was awaiting us beyond it.

And though I knew Drake Nazari was a suitor, that he had come here to claim me and my throne just as all the other suitors had, I was starting to wonder if there was a chance for freedom in a life with him. That maybe if he could kiss me in the face of a battle and not sneer at the sight of a princess dressed in the blood of her kills, then perhaps there was a match to be made here that could benefit us both.

CASSIUS

CHAPTER FORTY FIVE

I watched as Drake and Austyn kissed with the passion of two lovers driven together by fate, their want for each other a tangible thing that set off a painful tearing feeling down the centre of my heart.

Drake claimed the princess's first ever kiss with hungry movements of his mouth, lost to her and all the desire she clearly had for him. My hand shook around the hilt of my sword, the pain of seeing her possessed by another man turning to a violent envy that made me lift my blade, my teeth baring as a hateful anger burned along the core of my being.

Kyra moved closer to me and the gentle presence of her drew clarity to the edges of my thoughts before I could act on that primal instinct and attack the man who held Austyn in his arms.

"Ow," she breathed to herself. "Do kisses always hurt the people close enough to watch them?"

I didn't have an answer to that, embroiled in my own tempestuous thoughts as I tried to hold onto the single sliver of restraint she had returned to me. I could not attack Drake for this and give away my own feelings on the matter. She wanted him, that I could not deny. And I had no right to be jealous of him, even if I didn't believe him worthy of her affection. He was a street rat deceiving her, but I was playing my part in that deception, so if I were to resent him for that, then I had to resent myself in kind.

After what felt like an eternity, their lips broke apart and perhaps that was worse, because the lust-filled look Austyn gave him hollowed out my chest and left it barren. His thumb skimmed down her neck and his eyes moved to Kyra, his throat bobbing for a second before he looked back at the princess. I couldn't quite decipher what he was thinking, but as a smirk lifted his lips, I had no doubt it was something depraved.

"How did you know it was me up here?" Austyn asked as Drake scooped down to pick up her helmet and hand it back to her.

"I would recognise you even in the darkest of nights by the simple beauty of your aura alone," Drake purred, and my spine straightened as I recognised those words as my own. So his thievery extended to speech now too? Would he steal the very essence of my soul if it was of use to him?

Whatever bond I had thought was forming between us was a filthy lie I'd fallen for. Drake had only come to rescue me from Magdor because of the dragon scale now sitting in my pocket. I was just a tool for him to use to gain as much power, wealth and beauty he could lay his hands on.

Austyn looked flushed from what Drake had said, biting her lip as she backed up and yanked her short sword out of the side of the dead fire drake. She took a moment to tuck her hair up and placed her helmet back on just as a deafening roar echoed across the city followed by the words of a dragon seeping through the inside of my head.

"Bring the oath breakers to me and the slaughter will cease."

"What is she talking about?" Austyn gasped. "Who are the oath breakers? Who would be fool enough to break a promise to a dragon?"

"Someone with really big balls, I'd bet," Drake said with a knowing nod.

I shot him a cold, accusing glare and he shrugged innocently at me.

I spotted Azurea descending from the clouds above the city, fire pouring from her open jaws and screams echoing up from those unlucky enough to be caught in her blast.

"No," Austyn gasped, running to the edge of the roof closest to the destruction. "How can we get to them to help?" She gazed over the palace grounds to the two walls ringing it, keeping us contained within it.

Drake moved closer, checking on Kyra who was holding a hand to her heart and frowning like she was confused about something. I took a moment to extract my sword from the dead fire drake, wiping the blood off on its flank as I prepared to continue in this fight. I had danced with death only minutes ago, yet now I was whole again, not a single wound on my flesh. Kyra's magic truly was powerful, and I had to be grateful she was on our side in this battle tonight.

I turned to thank Kyra, but found her staring intently at Drake.

"Did you enjoy your kiss?" she asked him, her tone a little too bright and I wondered if I was a fool to believe I heard a note of jealousy to it.

"Yeah, sure," he murmured, eyeing her face closely.

"She must like you very much to kiss such an ugly man," Kyra said, and Drake scowled.

"Not everyone finds me as unappealing as you do, it seems," he bit back, ever touchy about any disparaging comments on his appearance.

I left them to bicker as I ran to Austyn's side, looking out to the city as I buried the feeling of my shattered heart and focused on what needed to be done.

"If you remain concealed, perhaps the guards will let us out to fight, Your

Highness," I suggested and I felt her eyes on me through her helmet, but I refused to meet her gaze. If I did so, I would crack, and I had to become what I was born to be now. A warrior with no other purpose than to serve her and the empire.

"Do the women of Carubai fight alongside men?" she asked.

"Some do, My Lady," I said, though I wasn't sure if the words were a lie. I certainly needed a reason to cover for the fact that I was not protesting to her fighting in this battle, and that Kyra was fighting alongside us.

I had seen Austyn's proficiency with her blades, her metal Affinities were well spoken of in the palace. I knew that she'd been trained in her youth, but her talent had been left to stagnate since the emperor's mind had been addled by his new wife. It was clear from what I had seen of her skills that she would make one of the finest soldiers this land had seen if she were only given proper training.

"So will you follow my orders if I give them?" she asked.

"I would follow you to the moon if you commanded it," I said quietly and I felt her surprise at that comment, but a fire drake swept overhead and stole all of our attention before she could respond.

The drake opened its jaws, its eyes pinned on the princess as she raised her sword, ready to meet it, but I could see the blaze of fire building in the back of its throat. I lifted my own sword, my animal Affinities suddenly tingling as I set the beast in my sights, and its gaze shifted onto me. I felt my mind link to its own in that way I had only felt with docile creatures before, and its furious, hungry thoughts burst into my head.

"Kill, devour, burn!"

I forced my will against it with a roar of effort, trying to twist its mind elsewhere and I staggered forward as I felt its desires shift beneath the power of mine.

"Turn, fly, retreat," the fire drake's voice filled my head once more.

The drake tucked its wings, sweeping past us on the roof and someone fisted their hand in the back of my shirt, yanking me backwards as my foot met nothing but air and I realised I'd nearly fallen off the roof.

I found Austyn there, looking out at me through the slit in her helmet with shock and confusion pooling in her amber eyes as she released my shirt.

"What just happened?" she asked.

"I have a slight animal Affinity," I said.

"Slight?" Drake boomed as he joined my other side. "You just stopped that fire drake from burning Austyn alive, mate."

The drake shrieked as it flapped its wings, rushing back up towards us, my grip on its mind now gone and its own wants returning. And its wants were clearly aimed at devouring us.

"Do it again," Austyn urged. "Make it fly us out beyond the palace walls."

"That is insanity," I said, shaking my head, but Drake's hand slammed down on my shoulder, turning me to him.

"You can do it, Cass. Or are you gonna show the princess how small your balls are? Oh wait, they cut them off entirely, right?"

"Fuck you," I gritted out, the challenge in his eyes making me determined to prove him wrong as I sheathed my sword.

I jerked his hand off of my shoulder, still furious at him over kissing Austyn, knowing he was just out for his own damn skin tonight as usual. But we had to call the dragon to us and doing so here on top of the palace would be damn foolish while the grounds were teaming with guards. Anyone could see us, and expose us as the oath breakers who had brought this plague down upon the city.

The fire drake snarled and I focused on how I had made the connection with it before, trying to find a way into its head before it could attack.

"Burn – burn – burn," its thoughts burst into my mind before I took them into my grasp.

It wasn't entirely effective and the effort of forcing my will upon it took all of my focus as I made it turn in the air, just close enough for us to climb onto its back.

Austyn dove onto it without a flicker of hesitation and the beast shrieked angrily while I worked to keep its hunger for us subdued.

Drake leapt on next, and I threw caution to the wind as I dove after them, grabbing onto the scaly back of the animal as it flexed its black wings and took off. I had to keep my mind entirely locked with it as I fought to stop it from bucking us off every time its will battled with mine. But somehow, impossibly, I got it to fly forward, sweeping over the palace grounds and beyond the walls which ringed it, closer and closer to the raging dragon who was flying low, burning the streets with huge plumes of flames. I could feel the heat of them as we closed in on her and my throat thickened as I glanced back to check on Kyra. But she wasn't there.

"Fuck – Drake, we left her behind," I gasped, losing my mental grip on the fire drake and it bucked sharply, launching us off its back.

I cried out as we fell, smashing into a slanted roof and skidding down it rapidly. Drake stopped his own fall, slamming a dagger into the tiles and holding on while I went tumbling towards the edge with Austyn crashing after me.

I skidded off of the roof with a curse, grabbing onto the edge of it and hanging there by one hand. Austyn went flying over the edge beside me and I grabbed her wrist, her whole weight dangling from my left arm as I gritted my teeth and held on. I used her momentum to swing her back up with a roar of effort leaving me, using every scrap of power in my muscles to toss her onto the roof.

She scrambled forward, grabbing my shoulders and heaving as she helped to pull me up.

Drake skidded down the roof towards us, probably by accident considering he had no good motives in his bones, and grabbed hold of me, helping to drag me back up.

I moved onto my knees between them, and my heart lurched at the sight of the giant ant-like creature that scuttled over the rooftop ahead of us. It clicked its pincers and charged forward, the three of us breaking apart and one hard kick of my boot sending it flying over the edge of the roof as it got close.

"Fuck you, you fucking ant thing!" Drake called after it.

Austyn got to her feet, raising her sword as she gazed up at Azurea who loomed over us in the sky, her eyes sharpening on the princess. *No.*

"I am Austyn Lunarelle and you will leave my city in peace and return to the dark you came from!" Austyn screamed before sprinting up the roof to meet the dragon head on, her sword discarded as she pulled her silver bow over her shoulder, nocking an arrow and loosing it into the air. *By the fucking Fallen.*

Azurea roared as the arrow sliced through her hind leg and fire plumed in her mouth in a twisting inferno of hell that would incinerate anyone and anything it touched.

"Austyn!" I cried in panic, knowing I couldn't get to her in time, and even if I could, it would only equal both our deaths.

"Azurea!" I bellowed to get her attention, but the beast could not see me. There was only one thing I could think of to protect Austyn as I snatched the dragon scale from my pocket, placed it in my palm and thought her name. *Azurea.*

The flames stuttered out in the dragon's throat, her head lifting and her eyes snapping directly onto me. Yes, she saw me now. Kyra's magic was peeling back and allowing the beast to perceive me once again, and I raised the scale in my palm as it began to glow blue with some ancient magic.

"Oath breaker," she snarled.

I turned as Drake stared at me in shock at what I'd done, but I didn't waste a moment to explain that I would gladly die to save the woman who had been so close to meeting her end.

Austyn released another arrow, but Azurea knocked it from the sky with her wing, her gaze not moving from me as she bore down from above, and I had no choice but to fucking run, leading her away across the rooftop.

CHAPTER FORTY SIX

I n the blink of an eye, I shifted through space and appeared between Drake and Austyn, running across the roof tiles, chasing after Cassius as if I had fallen from the fire drake's back too and hadn't been left behind at all.

"Thank fuck," Drake muttered as he spotted me, throwing me a dazzling grin before powering on after Cassius with the Dragon chasing after all of us as we ran. The monster's gaze was only fixed on the ex-guard as he waved that glowing scale above his head, drawing all of her attention onto him.

Austyn glanced at me then drew in a sharp breath as she did a double take, her eyes sweeping over me from within the helmet which covered her face.

"Where did you-" she began but the dragon bellowed a roar and fire blasted from her mouth, setting the roof of the building that Cassius was charging across on fire and sending lumps of it crashing down onto the streets below.

"We can follow that way, right Kyra?" Drake called, pointing to the roof of a building adjacent to the one we were sprinting over, and I nodded.

"Yep. That way," I agreed, magic flowing from my body and subtly creating a path ahead which hadn't been there before, wooden planks appearing between gaps parting rooftops and making a route towards Cassius as he continued to lure the dragon after him.

Drake leapt from the roof onto the closest plank, running across it with practiced agility which spoke of the number of rooftops he had traversed like this when he was nothing but a street thief.

"Come on," he called, looking back to us as Austyn hesitated, glancing down at the drop below.

"It's easy," I urged her. "Like chewing on nails."

"What?" she asked with a frown, and I shrugged because my inner me was telling me that wasn't easy at all, and I wasn't certain what was.

"Like riding a fire drake?" I suggested and her frown deepened.

"You weren't on that fire drake so how did you even catch up to us?" she asked suspiciously.

"Sure I was – I was just on the arse end, by the tail...underneath." I cleared my throat as an internal groan sounded from within me and I blew out a breath, swiping at my brow with the back of my hand as if I'd also just survived that madness.

Wow, your acting skills are truly awful.

"Shut up," I hissed at myself, pretending I couldn't sense Austyn's confusion.

"What did you just say?" she asked, and I balked, realising she thought I'd told her to shut up which probably wasn't ideal.

"Look up," I said, pointing and by luck, Azurea wheeled around above us with a tremendous roar as Austyn looked skyward.

"Run!" Drake bellowed and Austyn forgot all about her hesitation as she took off across the plank at a furious pace and I ran right on her heels, magic brimming within me and hunting for an outlet.

The dragon chased after Austyn instead of Cassius, roaring her fury as she blew out fire at our backs, the heat of the flames licking up my spine as she barely missed us.

"This way!" Cassius yelled from a rooftop to our left and Drake stopped to wait for us, ushering Austyn on ahead and meeting my gaze with concern in his dark eyes.

"Spear?" he asked, and I nodded, making one appear in his hands and pausing at his side as he raised the thing, aiming it at the dragon as she came for us once more, her eyes set beyond him while my magic still kept us invisible from her.

Drake threw the weapon as she swept overhead, the spear tearing through the dragon's wing just as I caught sight of something sparkling from within a large fleshy pouch on her belly. Azurea howled in agony and wheeled aside as red blood sprayed the street below from the wound.

"Nice," I commented, and he grinned.

"Damn right." Drake jerked his chin in a command for me to chase after the others.

I did as I was told, running towards them and leaping onto the roof where Cassius and Austyn were taking cover behind a huge chimney stack, the two of us joining them behind it.

"You struck the beast?" Austyn asked Drake in shock. "With what?"

"I used a piece of broken wood as a spear," Drake replied, lying so beautifully that she didn't question it any further. "But it won't stop her for long. We need to lead her out of the city." He gave Cassius a pointed look and I realised the princess was stopping us from doing just that. They didn't want her to witness my power, so we couldn't leave to summon the dragon away from here. The look in Cassius's eyes said there was no way he would abandon her here either.

"If only the oath breaker hadn't been such a fucking fool," Cassius ground out.

"Maybe they had a good reason to break their promise to her," Drake said. "Maybe the dragon was a rude cunt."

Cassius glared at him while Austyn snarled. "There can be no good reason for bringing this hell to my city. I'll see the perpetrators hang for bringing this danger here," she hissed, and I raised my chin, moving to place myself between her and Drake as I sensed the truth to that threat.

"Well, I guess it could all just be some misunderstanding," Drake said. "Either way, I say we all focus on just leading her the hell out of here."

"Agreed," Cassius ground out and I relaxed as Drake gave me a reassuring look. "The north wall is the closest. Let's try and get her out into the desert."

"Or kill her before she causes any more carnage," Austyn growled, nocking an arrow in her bow.

"Bloodthirsty suits you, princess," Drake commented, and Cassius's growl only deepened but he was already on his feet and leading the way on.

I broke into a sprint to catch up to him, the wind whipping through my hair and the thrill of this game bringing a wild smile to my lips. The sound of Azurea's roar made the entire world tremble around us, and I knew she was hunting for us again.

The others chased us as we leapt from rooftop to rooftop, the dragon coming after us at speed, the wound in her wing magically healed already and her fury only seeming to have increased.

Eyes peered out at us from the houses below, fearful expressions watching our passage and cowering from the beast that hunted us while we aimed for the distant sands of the Lyrian Desert ahead.

"We aren't going to make it," Drake cursed, throwing a look back over his shoulder as the dragon gained on us.

"That's the spirit," I encouraged, and he shot me a frown.

I hate you.

"Mutual," I muttered to myself.

A huge gap opened up ahead of us and I cursed as I realised the gap was far bigger than any that had come before now. The roof of The Temple of Saresh, the keeper of the sun and giver of life, shone in the moonlight as it beckoned us closer, the only option as Azurea closed in on us once more.

"We can make it!" Drake bellowed. "Don't slow down."

"Oh fuck," Cassius cursed, spotting the huge gap between the roof we were on and the temple ahead of us, but as the dragon blasted fire at our backs, we were left with no choice but to jump.

I whooped excitedly as I leapt from the rooftop, spreading my arms wide and feeling the exhilarating sensation of the wind streaming through my hair as gravity relinquished its hold on me for several unending seconds before I began to descend. It felt so freeing, so right, and I wanted to hold onto that feeling with all I was.

Drake's fingers locked around mine as we free-fell towards the temple roof, and I sucked in a breath at the shocking sensation of him touching me. My skin buzzed with a power I just managed to contain within my own flesh, stopping myself from hurting him with it as I focused on the way his skin felt against mine.

I *was* real.

He'd said the words and I'd felt them right down to the core of my being. I was broken, fractured, twisted beyond repair and less than a shadow of the girl I couldn't quite remember even being, but I was real. And I felt it even more so as I soared through the sky, holding the hand of the man who had set me free from my eternal prison.

Drake released me as the roof of the temple loomed and he threw himself into a roll as he hit it. I mimicked his movements, laughing as the golden painted tiles slammed into my flesh with punishing brutality, feeling every bit of the pain of my landing as it only served to prove my existence in this harsh world further.

I ended up flat on my back, grinning up at the stars as Cassius and Austyn rolled to a stop to my right and I watched as the enormous shadow of Azurea shifted across the moon above us, her head tilted down as fire glowed in her jaws.

"I will take all from this city until the oath breakers meet with my vengeance!" Her voice echoed through our skulls, and I breathed in deeply, tasting the smoke of her fire as it built and built.

"Osaria will never fall while I still draw breath!" Austyn cried in reply, pushing up onto one knee and raising her bow as she nocked a silver arrow and took aim.

A whisper of power shivered through the air as I looked at the princess of Osaria on her knees before a beast of the old gods, and I felt an unseen energy dancing all around us as if the gods themselves were stirring in recognition of this act.

Azurea roared, fire blossoming from her throat and I sucked in a sharp breath as Austyn roared right back at her, releasing her arrow with a deadly precision which made the energy surrounding us shift and grow, though no one but me seemed to take note of it.

My eyes remained glued to the passage of the arrow as it carved a path through the air, puncturing the crimson flames which billowed towards us and shooting straight through the centre of them towards the heart of the beast.

The world seemed to come to an utter standstill as the arrow pierced the dragon's flesh, the cheers of an unseen crowd cracking through the air as Azurea's flames guttered out and a cry of purest agony escaped the dragon's lips.

"By the Fallen," Drake breathed, his voice a soft touch upon my senses as we watched the dragon begin to fall from the sky, a cry of celebration going up as all those looking on from the relative safety of their homes watched the beast fall.

A sense of victory was thrumming through the air but at the same time, a pang of sadness tugged at my heart as I watched what was likely the very last of the immortal servants of the gods begin to topple from the sky, her great journey coming to an end in this place after a life that must have been so full of knowledge and adventure.

My eyes widened as I realised the monstrous creature was going to land right on top of us and Cassius yelled a warning as he took hold of Austyn's arm and propelled her to her feet.

All four of us broke into a run, sprinting away across the golden roof of the enormous temple even as fate sent the dragon crashing down towards us at an unstoppable pace.

"Kyra!" Drake called, and I looked to him, expecting some command to save his life but finding nothing there aside from his concern, our gazes colliding barely a moment before Azurea crashed into the roof of the temple with the force of a comet falling from the sky.

Austyn screamed as she was knocked from the edge of the tiles, Cassius leaping right after her without a moment's hesitation while Drake and I continued to try and outpace the crumbling rooftop as it fell apart beneath our feet.

"Tell me to save you!" I cried as I reached for Drake, desperation clawing at me as I felt the wings of fate thundering closer. He was mortal. So incredibly, fragilely, fleetingly, mortal. And I wasn't sure if I was anything at all without him.

But before any words could pass his lips, the tiles beneath our feet fell away. The only thing I heard amid the crashing of the building as half of the roof was torn apart, was the screaming of my own heart. Everything I had just begun to believe in was falling away from me so fast that I was powerless to stop it.

It was real. I was real. If only it hadn't been so brief.

CASSIUS

CHAPTER FORTY SEVEN

Austyn fell beneath me, her arms reaching out wildly in an effort to grab hold of anything to stop her fall. My heart beat chaotically in my chest as terror consumed me and awoke every instinct of my training. If only I could wield gravity and fall faster to catch her.

By some miracle she landed in a red cotton awning over someone's balcony, and I collided with it a second later, the two of us rolling into each other in the middle as the material tore beneath us. I grabbed hold of her, surrounding her with my body as we fell, slamming into the hard stone of the balcony below and taking the brunt of the fall to my back.

Austyn's body shook from the adrenaline as I held her, giving her enough room to breathe, ignoring the pain splintering up my spine.

"Are you alright?" I rasped.

"Yes, I think so. Thank you – er, remind me of your name again?"

"Cass," I said, figuring it was half true.

"Thank you, Cass. Are you hurt?"

My heart lurched as Azurea fell from the roof above, colliding with the side of the balcony, her huge talons ripping through the stone like it was paper and shattering the structure beneath us, the world flipping on its axis once more.

I crushed Austyn to my chest as we fell, but it seemed like half the building was coming down with us, the pounding of bricks and shattered stone slamming into my body over and over. Azurea roared as she was struck by the blast too, a huge lump of rock colliding with her head as she clasped at the silver arrow buried deep in her chest. Her enormous tail swiped the building, sending another spray of shrapnel everywhere before she hit the ground below us with an echoing thud that sounded her demise.

We landed on the dragon's scaly back just as the street buckled beneath her weight and we fell into the dark of the sewers far below, Azurea's body slamming into the water and sending a wave out into the gloom.

I lifted Austyn into my arms without a second thought, traversing across Azurea's outstretched wing onto the brick path that ran along one side of the tunnel of water, the darkness in the sewer pressing in.

The building we had fallen from groaned and more masonry crashed over us from above, casting a plume of dust into the air which I squinted against to try and see. I dropped to the ground with Austyn beneath me, bracing myself against the bricks as I tried to shield her from the falling stones, but as I looked down at the princess, I found her frighteningly still. Through the gloom, I could just make out a dent in the metal of her helmet, her eyes shut and her features still.

"Princess," I gasped in terror, tugging her helmet off and cupping her cheek in my palm as panic cut my heart to ribbons. I leaned closer, my ear to her mouth and the softness of her breaths fanned against my skin, filling me with relief. She was alive, but for how much longer?

I slid her helmet back into place to protect her from any further tumbling stones, though the falling brickwork slowed until it finally stopped altogether. By some hand of god, I hadn't sustained any life-threatening injuries. I could still run, and I would. As far as I could until the princess was safe within the hands of a healer.

"Stay with me. I'll get you out of here," I swore, looking up at the hole far above us in the roof of the sewer. It would be a difficult climb, especially while I was holding her, but I would find a way.

I scooped her against my chest just as a strange red glow fell over us and I lifted my head, finding an enormous ruby dragon egg laying on its side among the rubble on the path in front of us, the ethereal light emitting from deep within it. I knew that egg. I'd seen it before, deep in a canyon in the Lyrian Desert where we had first encountered the dragon of old.

Azurea stirred and every bone in my body froze as I looked to her, praying I had imagined it, because surely she could not still live on with an arrow piercing her heart?

But as she tried to regain consciousness, my muscles bunched in preparation of a fight, because it was clear she was not cast from this world yet. I cursed the lost gods as I held Austyn tighter, not wanting to let go of her in a bid to engage the beast.

Azurea shifted, rolling onto her side and revealing a fleshy pouch on her stomach where that egg must have been contained. Her most precious of possessions.

She clawed at the arrow wedged within her chest, trying to tear it from her body, but it wouldn't shift. The dragon shuddered and fire rippled deep within her body, her ribs lighting up from the inside and the glow of heat rippling out to spread through her wound and along the length of the arrow. The silver melted under the intensity of Azurea's fire, and I watched in horror as the molten silver flooded out of the wound, spilling down her flesh as she began to heal.

I moved to place Austyn down, planning to smite the dragon fast and finish her once and for all. But before I could make another move in the direction of that plan, a lightning bolt of a crack shot up the side of the egg and the deep glow burst out from within it, so bright I had to squint against it. With the crack, came an echoing boom that carried across the city, seeming to sound from the very earth itself.

A blast of energy exploded out of the egg and slammed into us, throwing me onto my back on the ground while I held onto Austyn with all my might, snared by the fear of what further misfortune was coming for us.

The ground shook violently beneath us, starting as a low rumble before growing to a furious crescendo that threatened to cave in this whole place. I acted with urgency, pushing upright with Austyn in my arms, running into an alcove with a stone arch above it, tucking the princess tighter against me as the earthquake tore through Osaria, bringing another bane upon its people.

The windchimes hanging from windows and doorways all around the city started chiming in a wind I couldn't feel, but I could feel something far more powerful than a storm brewing. There was magic in the air, the kind of power I had sensed from Kyra, only this was far greater, far more menacing and omnipotent. It spoke of ancient deities and monstrous beings more frightening than even Azurea who lay before me in all her divinity.

Screams carried across the city as people ran for their lives, but I stood firm, knowing I was safest in the arching structure of the alcove while the tremors ripped through the ground and sent buildings quaking above us, threatening to topple and crush anyone beneath them. Although, if this place caved in, we were done for.

The dragon egg glowed brighter and brighter, and the crack within it deepened until I was almost certain it was going to split apart entirely.

Azurea growled deep in her chest, lifting her head and licking the air as if she could taste the old magic closing in on us.

I knew I was witnessing something unimaginably almighty unfolding, but I had no idea what it was, only that I was sure it was something to be feared.

"When the shell gleams, the lost will be found."

DRAKE

CHAPTER FORTY EIGHT

The press of soft hands to the side of my face was the first thing I noticed, several seconds passing as I focused on that sensation and the sound of my name on lips which called to me from somewhere beyond my oblivion.

The pain came next. Agony crashing through me in a torrent that stole my breath as I sucked it in, the press of an endless weight crushing down on top of me almost making me pass out again.

"Just say yes," she begged, those hands tightening, and my entire world dominated by that feeling as I forced my eyes open and found her there, her golden eyes swimming with moisture as she pleaded for me to speak that word. "Agree to me healing you, Drake, please."

A groan crossed my lips which was filled with all the pain in my body, and the call of the darkness was almost enough to make me turn to it for some relief from this torture, but I was unable to turn away from her.

"Just one word," she urged. "Only one."

"Yes," I forced out, an agonised cough following the word before light spilled through every piece of my being and I was consumed, devoured, and remade in her magic.

Bricks and masonry were swept aside as if they were nothing more than leaves in a breeze, lifting from my body and allowing her to use her incredible power to heal me until I was brand new once more.

"What the fuck happened?" I asked, though even as the words escaped me, I remembered the roof, the arrow, the falling dragon. "Is it over?"

"No," Kyra breathed, a note of prophecy to her tone that made my heart thump out of rhythm before she threw herself at me, her arms winding tight around my neck and her body crushing me to the ground.

The scent of her engulfed me like a summer breeze, sea salt and fresh blossom all rolled into one, this explosion of life given flesh. Kyra's magic hummed and buzzed throughout her body, my skin tingling from the contact with her as I slowly closed my arms around her in return, the feeling of accepting such an embrace utterly alien to me. I had never had a parent hold me this way. I had never lingered in the company of a lover long enough to experience it either, and I didn't know how to react to the pure relief she clearly felt in restoring my life to me from the cusp of death.

The ground rumbled beneath us, the sound of countless windchimes sounding from beyond the temple walls, and I cursed as a new pain suddenly exploded through my flesh.

A cry broke free of my lips as I released my hold on Kyra, my spine arching against the stone floor of the temple and my muscles bulging as my fingers dug into the floor while I fought to hold myself still through the burning sensation tearing through my body.

"Drake?" Kyra gasped as she scrambled to her feet and nothing but a bellow of pain fled from my lips in reply, my flesh beginning to heat and burn in deliberate lines all over my body.

My eyes rolled back into my head and suddenly I was in that room again, strapped to that table while foul ink was forced into my skin, the man who had tortured me for so long chanting in that way which had haunted my nightmares ever since my escape from that hell.

I could feel the bite of the needle as it drove into me, but instead of focusing on one place like it had when he'd placed the tattoos upon me, I could feel it everywhere at once, each piece of ink on my skin doused in acid as it ate into me, until I could have sworn they were etching themselves right into my bones.

A warrior born of sin shall rise.

A cacophony of voices all spoke inside my skull, the tattoos coating my skin burning impossibly hotter as my bones cracked beneath the weight of them, forcing their way deeper inside me.

"Make it stop," I begged of Kyra, forcing my mind away from memories of that place and back to her, back to the stone floor of The Temple of Saresh, where I knew she was with me.

A golden glow pressed through the closed lids of my eyes, tranquillity calling out to me from within in it and I managed to turn my head that way, forcing my lids to part so I could look to my little goddess and see the raw power she was wielding for me. The glow around her grew brighter and brighter, the light blinding me until my eyes watered, but I didn't look away.

"It's not working," she gasped, her features lost to me in the brightness of the light that surrounded her. "I can't stop it, Drake. Tell me what to do."

The power rumbling through the ground only drove into me harder, and I cried out again as I felt the marks of my tattoos sinking deeper and deeper inside me until I was certain they were branding my fucking soul.

The golden light of Kyra's power died out as if it had been snuffed by the breath of a god, and I was released from my torture in the same moment, panting heavily on the stone floor as my body shook from what I had somehow survived.

"Drake?" Kyra breathed as I groaned, rolling onto my hands and knees, raising my head to look at a doorway carved into the rear wall of the temple.

Nothing but darkness lay beyond the white stone entrance, skulls lining the edge of it with candles lit inside their empty eye sockets. There were marks carved into the bones, marks which I recognised as I forced myself to my feet.

My clothes hung from my frame in tatters, my limbs shaking from the torrent of power that had washed through me, my body feeling almost as if it wasn't my own as I took a step forward. There was a tightness to my skin that hadn't been there before and a fluidity to my movements which surpassed even my usual level of control over my body.

The windchimes continued to rattle out in the city streets, but with every step I took towards that doorway, the sound seemed more muffled, my focus moving to an ancient hum radiating from within the darkness ahead of me.

I made it to the doorway and paused, turning to look at the Fae skulls surrounding it, reaching out to run my hand over one of them and feel the lines of the design which was carved into it. I knew that pattern. The same mark adorned my right thigh, the lines of the tattoo glowing as I looked down to see it through the scraps of fabric which had been my trousers.

"I don't like this," Kyra breathed, moving close to my back, the caress of her power brushing up against my skin.

"Then don't follow me," I replied in a dark tone which didn't sound like my own at all, but it didn't matter. My destiny awaited me within this place. I could feel it calling for me from beyond here, demanding I come to claim it.

Kyra sucked in a breath at my dismissal, but I couldn't so much as turn to look at her, my gaze focused entirely on the darkness before me.

Warm air spilled from within the chamber, like the breath of some long slumbering monster washing over my skin, but still, I didn't turn back.

My fingers fell from the skull, and I raised my chin, meaning to answer the call of my fate.

Kyra's hand snapped out to encircle my wrist, holding me in place and forcing me to turn to look at her. Her ebony hair was tangled and the black clothes she wore torn and dusty, more smudges of it staining her skin and the less than perfect appearance made her seem so much more Fae for once. Like I might have just been looking at a girl instead of the most powerful entity I had ever known.

"I can feel a change coming for us," Kyra whispered, her golden eyes wide with fear. "If you step foot in there, you won't be able to turn back. They'll have you in their thrall."

"Who?" I demanded, the call of that place only deepening with every moment I lingered here.

"The gods," she breathed, fear lacing her words. "I feel them stirring."

My heart leapt at the possibility of that, every fearful, cautionary tale I'd ever heard about the deities who could be as cruel as they could be generous flashing through my memory in warning.

"What else do you feel?" I asked of her, though I knew my mind was already decided on this.

Kyra hesitated for several moments, an unseen wind stirring her hair and making her skin glimmer as she tightened her hold on my wrist. "Afraid."

I studied the truth written into her features before releasing a breath and turning back to the doorway that continued to beckon me closer with every passing second.

"I've had one enemy for my entire life, little goddess," I said slowly, the ink on my skin tingling with energy. "And I've never let fear beat me yet."

I tugged my hand free of her hold and took a step into the dark, ignoring the sharp inhale of her breath, and walking willingly towards my fate, because I already knew there was no alternative to it now.

I was a man of sin, a street thief, a liar, and a savage. But I would never be a coward.

CASSIUS

CHAPTER FORTY NINE

"**M**an of steel. Oath breaker. I know you are here," Azurea's deep, feminine voice filled my head and struck a chord of fear in my heart.

I turned fast, tucking Austyn away into the shadows of the alcove, knowing there was only one thing I could do to save the princess now, and that was to face the monster and draw its eyes away from her.

I stepped out of the shadows as that ruby egg continued to shine, though not so brightly that I couldn't look at it anymore. There was a humming, living energy spilling from that thing and it set my heart pounding to an unfamiliar tune, one that seemed to lure me in.

I drew my sword as Azurea lifted her head, pushing herself up in the water, her eyes settling on me and seeming to see right through to my bones.

I side stepped towards her egg and she bared her teeth as a vicious snarl left her.

"Do not dare move any closer. She is the most precious creature in all the land." Azurea sniffed the air and shivered as the quakes in the ground finally eased, though the windchimes and bells continued to call out all across the kingdom. *"Do you know what you have done?"* she spat venomously within my mind.

"What *I* have done?" I asked, fighting to keep my voice even, knowing that showing anger with a dragon was only a death wish in itself. "You have attacked my city and murdered innocent people."

"Place down your weapon," she commanded, ignoring my accusation. *"Kneel, and pray for your end to be swift, man of steel."*

Fire flickered within her jaws and my heart stuttered as I refused her words, raising my sword higher. "If I am to die, I will do so on my feet as a true warrior of the crown."

"Then you shall burn for me slowly," she hissed, and that red fire licked her lips as she bore down on me.

I lifted my sword, preparing to leap forward and strike true in one final act that I hoped would finish her for good. But the flames were already pouring from her jaws, and as I saw my death coming for me, I moved forward to embrace it with a roar. The sound was full of every true emotion I had ever felt, my love for my family, for my kingdom, and my love for a princess who lay in the shadows behind me, a woman I would protect with my dying breath.

The flames were all I could see as they circled down from Azurea's jaws and the heat of them were so intense, I knew I would be consumed by them within moments and cast to ash. There was a cracking sound behind me accompanied by a wave of energy that blasted through the air and made my ears ring, but I was too focused on my enemy to pay it any heed.

As the first of Azurea's flames nearly licked my arm, a creature not much larger than I swept in front of me with a shriek, leathery white wings with ice blue tips outstretching as the fire surrounded it.

The flames guttered out against the white beast's flesh and Azurea screamed a high-pitched scream that made me clamp my hands over my ears, the sound echoing through my skull.

My eyes were dancing with white spots from the intensity of the firelight, but as I blinked them away, I realised my saviour was a small dragon. One glance sideways showed me the ruby egg was now in pieces and as I turned back to the beast in utter confusion, my gaze locked with the most incredible blue eyes of the new born dragon.

A gentle power washed into my chest, taking me captive as it surrounded my heart and urged me towards this breath-taking beast. In the back of my mind, I feared this was a trick to lure me to my death, but I still couldn't stop myself from approaching her.

She cocked her head to one side, and I noticed two icy blue horns just poking through the top of her slim head. Every scale on her body looked almost luminescent, the white glinting blue as she moved, and my lips parted in awe at her beauty.

The beast moved forward to meet me and the sword fell from my fingertips, clattering as it hit the ground.

I raised my hand, hearing a heavy pulse within my ears that was beating faster than my own, and I realised it was coming from this mystic creature. Slowly, her heartbeat fell into the same rhythm as mine and as I reached out, utterly captivated by the magic of her, she rested her nose to my palm. Her scales were so much smoother than I had expected and as she opened her mouth, a single blue flame kissed my palm.

I knew I should have flinched away from it, expecting pain, but somehow, I knew to stay there as the flame spread over my wrist before disappearing into my flesh.

"No!" Azurea bellowed, lunging forward behind her baby, but the young

dragon spread her wings to warn her back.

Her mother held off as if some magic was keeping her at bay, releasing a noise of anguish as she thrashed in the sewer water.

The single blue flame slid deep into my veins, and I watched as it travelled up my arm, a lump forming in my throat over what was happening, sure I should have been terrified, but feeling nothing but delight as it ran deeper into my body.

I felt the moment it met my heart and I gasped as warmth spread through the middle of my chest, that living flame dancing there and burning brightly.

"Do not speak her name," Azurea boomed inside my head. *"You are unworthy. She is not for you!"*

I frowned, unsure what she meant, but it became clear as I met the gaze of the small dragon again, her gleaming blue eyes like two sun-drenched oceans. I knew her name as if I had always known it, as if the world had been waiting for me to speak it for a thousand lifetimes. And there was simply no way I could stop it from leaving my lips.

"Emberliss," I said, and the word set a shockwave ringing through the air that made Azurea roar in anguish.

The young dragon released a cry of happiness, rushing towards me and nuzzling my face, as I was released from the magic keeping my instincts at bay.

I backed away from her in fright, looking to her mother as she paced in the water of the sewer, throwing her head back and bellowing furiously.

"Go to her," I urged, sure this would see my end as Emberliss kept moving towards me like a duckling who had imprinted on a wayward goose.

Emberliss released another soft cry, pressing closer to me and my back hit the wall as her tongue ran up the side of my face.

Azurea's bellows grew more frantic, and she turned to us, the magic barrier keeping her back fizzling out of existence. She swept Emberliss away from me with her wing and opened her powerful jaws, flames circling in the back of her throat in a promise of death.

I swore, lunging for my sword, but Azurea knocked it into the water with one of her talons, her lips peeled back in a ferocious snarl.

"What have you done?!" she screeched, and I winced away from the voice as it tore through my skull. *"She is* mine. *A gift from the lost gods. How dare you imprint upon her!"*

I didn't know what that meant, and I shook my head as I raised my hands in innocence. "I don't understand."

"Well you will understand this," she hissed. *"Now that I cannot kill you, I will curse you instead. Your arrogance will cost you everything, man of steel."*

"Wait, undo it," I commanded. "I did not mean to."

"It is already done," she snarled fiercely. *"I can no easier pull the sun from the sky, you fool. The magic is binding, it cannot be reversed. You have corrupted the only dragon born in this world for a thousand years!"*

Emberliss growled, trying to get past her mother's wing to reach me, and

I didn't just see her panic, I felt it in the centre of my heart, and it made me panic too.

"Stay back," I told her, raising a hand, fearing what Azurea might do to her.

I didn't know why I cared, but I did. I loved that creature as if it were my own child, and that knowledge set my mind whirling with terror.

Emberliss was kept back by her mother as the might of Azurea's next words sent me falling to my knees before her. *"Hyesha ola norenti savan. Man of steel, I curse you from your bones to your soul."*

The scale in my pocket started to burn, searing through my trousers and I grabbed it out, meaning to throw it away from me, but instead, it grew against my palm, wrapping over the flesh and encasing it in more scales which were the colour of blood. They rushed up my right arm and I yelled, trying to tear them off of me, but they were stronger than iron. And worse than that, they burned like living hellfire was binding itself to my flesh.

I yelled out in agony as they spread rapidly onto my chest and up my neck before climbing the side of my face.

"Stop!" I shouted, but Azurea continued on, a savagery in her eyes that made me certain no words I spoke would ever convince her to free me from this.

"I have longed for a child for a thousand years, and you have stolen her just as she has come to me at last. So I shall return the favour, man of steel."

"No, please," I rasped, buckling forward, and pressing my hands to the ground as the sharpened scales on my body spread over my back, tearing through my shirt so it fell in tatters around me. The scales gripped my shoulder blades, binding to flesh and bone, the fiery touch of them more painful than anything I had ever experienced.

Emberliss released a screech of rage, and I felt her panic ripping a hole through the centre of me as she tried to come to my aid.

"Stay back," I gritted out through my teeth, not wanting Azurea's ire to turn on her. "Get out of here!"

"Do not speak to her as if she is yours to command!" Azurea shrieked and the scales spread quicker across my skin, encasing my other arm as the dark, cloying power of them gripped me tighter.

Nausea filled me from the impossible heights of pain, and I was sure no man could survive this, not even one forged into a steel warrior of Osaria.

The ground was shaking beneath me, and debris started to fall from the street above. It felt like the world was ending and I was at the very heart of it, waiting to see the apocalypse come tearing through the doors of the afterlife.

"Gaven herash notin ova. Your soul is mine," Azurea hissed. *"And it will remain so until the curse is done. Verin ashar guren lidash."*

The ancient language sent a flood of magic over me, and I shuddered from its cruel touch, the scales urged on by its power and running down the length of my legs. I was burning from the inside out, and I was near blinded by the flames coursing through my veins.

Through it all, I felt that single blue flame within my chest gifted to me by Emberliss, spreading out as if trying to hold back the potent power of her mother's curse. But it was no good. The curse sank in and the moment it connected with my heart, I collapsed forward onto the ground, writhing as my voice was ripped raw by my roars of torment.

"Corrupt one," she branded me. *"You are tainted now, as you have tainted my daughter. This power will not unleash you until it is done."*

The fire in my limbs faded enough for me to catch my breath and I panted as I gazed up at the monster above me. "What is done?"

"Evran ilis ukan," she said icily in that wicked tongue which bound me in old magic. *"You have stolen my heart's desire, so you will hunger for the death of yours in kind. You will ache for their end until the need drives you to the brink of insanity. You cannot run or hide, you will be pulled towards them with the force of gravity, and they will suffer in your company. You will only be released from the curse by their death at your hands, or else you will succumb to the curse of the Dragonia Verake, and become my monster, a plague on this world that will spill the blood of innocents until the streets of Osaria run red."*

"No, wait. I can bring you as much gold as you want, I can pay the debt," I rasped as I thought of what those words forewarned. My heart's desire?

My mind turned to Austyn, and I fought the urge to look over at her where she was hidden within the shadows, terror consuming me at what this curse could mean for her. Because there was no desire deeper in my heart than my want for her.

"No treasure can save you now."

The scales started to recede across my body, sinking away into my flesh as if they hadn't existed at all. But I could feel them there, waiting to return and twist me into the monster she spoke of. There was no worse fate for me than that, to be turned into a weapon against Austyn.

"I will take any other punishment. Kill me if you must!" I demanded as terror flooded me. There was some deeply wicked thing taking root in me now, forcing down the morality in me and latching onto every damning thought I'd ever had. It was gripping the most villainous parts of my being and drawing them to the surface, making me ache for the blood of the princess.

"Please," I gasped, trying to hold onto the man I was, but he was already slipping from my grasp.

"No. This is the price of what you have done. Ambris elus vertatis," she hissed, and I felt my tongue weigh down with those final damning words. *"You cannot speak of the curse. It is your secret to bear alone. And bear it you will, man of steel."*

CHAPTER FIFTY

My pulse thundered as Drake stepped further into the darkness of that chamber, every piece of me demanding I turn and run from this place aside from my foolish heart which refused to abandon him to the fate he had so adamantly accepted for himself.

Let him die. Maybe the next master won't be so pig headed.

"If he dies, I may as well die too," I hissed, knowing it was the truth because the end of him would mean returning to the coin, returning to the dark and the emptiness, returning to the broken thing I had become. And I knew I was still broken in many ways, but I was also becoming something again. I wasn't healing exactly, but maybe I was growing, learning to be something new. And that would all end if he died here now.

Drake kept walking away from me, moving further into the darkness of the chamber while the hum of power beyond anything I could claim made the air vibrate all around us. He could feel it now too. I could tell by the rigid set of his shoulders, though he didn't turn back.

Well, if you don't want him to die then you had better follow him.

I swallowed thickly, magic rising up within me as I accepted the truth of that statement and steeled myself to step over the threshold.

I could hear the skulls surrounding the door screaming, the echoes of their deaths lingering on eternally and pushing images of torment, agony and bloodshed into my mind which weren't my memories at all.

I could see men and women fighting in endless places, from battlefields to darkened streets, jungles to castles, beaches to mountainsides. Each of them fought with a strength unlike anything I had ever seen, their movements perfect, their strikes powerful. Yet still each of them fell as I was forced to live through their deaths within the confines of my mind, the truth reaching out to scrape at me with bony fingers and accusing glares.

One by one the warriors found death in bloodshed, each of them falling into the dark, several of them overwhelmed by countless enemies while others were tricked or betrayed. These Fae had been almost impossible to kill, and yet they'd all died in the most violent of ways in the end.

"All who walk beneath the sun fear us," the whispers of a thousand dead voices filled my mind and a flicker of a memory stirred within me.

My breath stalled in my lungs as I remembered a chair beneath the trees, a warm breeze and blood on my hands.

My eyes were fixed on Drake's back as he strode further into the gloom and through a tear in his shirt I could see his tattoos, a faint light seeming to outline them, making my hands tighten to fists. Recognition which I hadn't been able to fathom before pressed into me, forgotten memories stirring in my head.

I suddenly knew those markings. They were the names of the gods, written in a language beyond Fae comprehension, the beautiful images representing each and every deity. That language held unimaginable power. None aside from the gods could even speak it and most couldn't so much as recognise it when they laid their eyes upon it, save for those few names. Many, many moons ago, before I had been given to the curse of the coin, those symbols had adorned the most holy of all places. And they had adorned the skin of the Tirbeshi too.

"Wait," I gasped, my voice like a drop of water falling into an ocean as it hit the silence of that room and dissipated as if it had never even been at all.

My memories were fast and fleeting, skipping away from me whenever I focused on them too closely, but suddenly, I did remember this. The Tirbeshi Warriors were selected to become vessels of the gods' power, warriors to serve their will, granted strength and ability far beyond what they had been born to hold.

But that power came at a price. Most died under the needle, the ink used to mark them made with the blood of the gods themselves, the weight of it far too powerful for almost anyone to handle. It had been called the first test and of all who attempted it, less than one in a hundred had survived the marking. But after that, they had to face the hands of the gods.

Every terrifying tale I'd ever heard about the true birth of a Tirbeshi Warrior pressed in on me at once as if my mind had only been waiting for me to think of them and my memories hadn't been closed off to me for longer than I could possibly recall. The horror of those tales engulfed me, stealing all fear I had over crossing the threshold to that chamber, leaving me with the desperate need to rescue Drake from that fate before it was too late.

I broke into a run, the magic in me flaring to life and whipping my hair out behind me as I raced into the dark after him. The screams of the fallen warriors were cut off so abruptly that the silence was almost painful in contrast and the temperature plummeted as I chased him down, making my skin erupt in gooseflesh.

"Master, you need to listen to me," I begged. "This place is tainted with old magic. I can feel the gods stirring. They're turning their focus this way, and you can't be here when they do. I remembered something about your tattoos, something from my past and-"

A huge boom resounded through the darkened chamber and a tsunami of magic exploded from the centre of the room as cold and acrid air washed over us, knocking me from my feet and sending me sprawling to the ground.

Drake swore as he kept on his feet before me, a golden light spilling through the room from his flesh. My heart raced in terror as the tattoos which stained his skin all began to glow and burn with ancient power.

The shredded remains of his clothes were burned off of him, leaving him naked before me, his back to me and the names of the long-lost deities brightening all over his flesh with every passing moment.

A huge sarcophagus lay in the centre of the chamber and more bones decorated the walls around us, the watchful eyes of the skulls making my skin prickle with the sensation of being observed by countless dead.

Everything in the room was that same pale, bone colour, the scent of rot clinging to each part of it and the echoes of a thousand warriors' deaths brimming in the air. This was a tomb, but not one that had been in existence during my Fae lifetime. Someone had done this, scoured the world for each of these long-dead warriors and stolen their remains from their proper burial sites. Someone had brought them here, used the power lingering in their bones for their own designs and created this chamber within the heart of The Temple of Saresh.

It wasn't right. These warriors had given their lives for their gods, had served their purpose, and been lain to rest. They shouldn't have been forced back into the world of the living, used against their will like this, their peace disturbed and their joy in the after stolen from them. I knew that was what had happened. I could feel their souls tethered to this place now, ripped back from death and their rest within the eternal garden, forced to take part in whatever hell this chamber had been designed for.

"You eluded me for a long time, child," a voice rasped from beyond the sarcophagus, and the chill that passed through my flesh was all consuming.

Pure terror bled through my veins and made my head snap around to take in the robed figure lingering in the shadows.

"No," I gasped, scrambling backwards as the horror of my past stepped closer to us, potent fear enveloping me even while my memories danced just out of reach, but I knew that voice. I knew that man.

"You," Drake snarled, and my gaze snapped to him, finding his entire body rigid with tension, his hands tightening into fists and his lip curling back on a snarl as somehow, he recognised him too. "I killed you."

"It is hard to kill that which does not draw breath," the robed man replied, taking another step closer to us, and pushing back the hood of his robe to reveal his face.

My lips parted in a silent scream as I took him in. His bald head and imposing stature were the same as I remembered, the spotless white robe he wore remained unchanged, his features unmistakeable even with my memories little more than scattered dandelion seeds on a breeze.

Inside my head all I could hear were the screams of my own torture, the agony of my fate when he had cast it upon me and stolen all I was and all I ever would be while binding me with the very symbols which covered Drake's body now, so many, many years later.

Kalir.

The architect of my ruin took another step closer to us and I remained frozen there on the ground as I stared up at him, taking in the scars which now marked his dark flesh in countless places across his hands, throat and face where I could see it beyond the confines of the white robe. His eyes were opaque with blindness, though they remained riveted on the target of his attention and through my utter panic, it took me several moments to realise that wasn't me.

He was staring at Drake. His entire focus locked on the man who owned me, not seeming to have noticed I was here too.

"I left you bleeding out on your own filthy floor," Drake hissed adamantly. "No man could survive those wounds."

"I am no mere man."

Kalir moved closer and something snapped inside me, the fear immobilising me turning into something far more powerful as I realised that he wasn't here for me. He was after the man who had pulled me from the dark and helped me find some small semblance of the scattered pieces of myself.

My own fear didn't matter in the face of that, my own reasons for needing to run from here falling away as I realised I had something so much greater to achieve here. It wasn't my miserable existence I needed to fear for. It was that of the man who had become my whole world since the moment he took charge of my destiny by claiming my coin for himself.

I was on my feet in a flash of movement, breaking into a run and drawing my daggers as I placed myself between Drake and the servant of ill tidings who stared his way with a greed I knew could only equal something terrible.

"No, Kyra!" Drake barked. "He's mine. Give me a sword."

My postured tightened but the magic which bound me to Drake's will forced my compliance and I forged him a sword while cladding his body in golden armour for good measure, not once moving my focus from Kalir even though he seemed to have forgotten us entirely.

The man who had once been the royal Prophet to an emperor whose name I couldn't recall stepped up to the sarcophagus with a rolling chant building in his throat.

Kalir placed his palm down on the lid of the stone sarcophagus just as a furious roar escaped Drake's lips, and I gasped as he broke into a sprint with his sword raised and murder flickering in his dark eyes.

"*Wait*," I begged as a thunderclap of power echoed off of the stone walls, but Drake was beyond listening to my pleas, his own fury taking control of him as he leapt up onto the sarcophagus and swung the sword straight for Kalir's neck.

The sharp blade cut through flesh and bone in a blow powerful enough to sever the chanting man's head from his neck. But instead of cleaving him apart, a blast of power exploded from him, and Drake was hurled away while the wound to Kalir's neck healed as if it had never even existed at all.

I cried out as I flickered in and out of my corporeal form, appearing at Drake's side in a swirl of purple smoke as he slammed into the wall and the bones of the fallen Tirbeshi Warriors clattered down on top of him.

The moment the bones fell from their place against the wall, they began to move, skeletal hands grasping at Drake's limbs and skulls gnashing their teeth as they rolled towards him.

"Fire, Kyra," Drake demanded as he kicked out at a skull which was rolling closer to him.

A blast of raging blue flames exploded all around us, incinerating the bones and freeing him from their attention.

"We need to run," I urged as Drake made a move towards Kalir again, my hand snapping out to grasp his arm.

"No. That thing dies for what he did me. He locked me up and scarred my flesh while I watched countless others die beneath his needle. I won't let that nightmare draw breath a moment longer." Drake yanked his arm free of my hold and I cried out a warning as he ran for Kalir again.

The chanting grew in pace, the walls starting to vibrate with the sound of the words I couldn't understand, and an unimaginable power began to swell within the chamber of death surrounding us.

Drake bellowed a challenge as he leapt for Kalir again, this time aiming for an arm and bracing against the clap of power which blasted from the Prophet's flesh as his blade carved into it.

He swung his sword again and again, aiming for Kalir's limbs and hacking at them until both an arm and a leg lay severed on the floor, the Prophet's blood washing over the white stone of the tomb and even through those injuries, he didn't stop chanting.

As Drake swung his sword again, an echoing boom sounded and he was thrown back once more, colliding with me as I shot forward to help him, the two of us tumbling away across the floor.

"What is he?" Drake hissed as he shoved to his knees again, the light glowing from his tattoos brightening while Kalir's body reformed itself once more.

"Death," I replied, a ring of truth to the word which no one could deny. "We need to get out of here."

Drake looked like he would rather pull his own teeth from his mouth than turn tail and flee from this place of blood and ruin, but as the sound of the chanting grew louder and the thing in that tomb made the walls tremble with its power, I knew it was the only choice.

"No. I need a sword which can destroy whatever the fuck he is," he snarled, and I swore as my magic followed his command, imbuing his blade with some deep power I didn't fully understand.

Drake shoved to his feet once more, hefting the sword in his grip and racing back into the fight. He leapt around the sarcophagus and swung his sword at Kalir again, his tattoos glowing so brightly they were almost blinding. As another wave of power crashed through the room, it slammed straight into the Prophet, and he absorbed every bit of it.

Drake's movements took on a stunning fluidity which was utterly breathtaking, almost seeming to dance through the air while rushing at Kalir.

His sword arm moved so fast that it was hard to follow its passage as he hacked into the Prophet, staining the white of his robes with blood as an ungodly shriek escaped his lips.

I ground my teeth as I was forced to watch, my power seeming useless to me in that moment while I was trapped, awaiting the will of my master. I wanted to fight too. I wanted to give myself to the movements of battle and feel the spill of blood on my skin.

Kalir whipped a blade of his own from within his robe and blocked the next blow, a hiss escaping his scarred lips as he was forced to turn and fight.

"You wield the power of the Esworn," he snarled, parrying another blow before Drake whirled around and cut a bloody line into his back before he could block it again.

I flinched at that name, hating all it implied; that I was less than Fae, unworthy of my own name, unworthy of anything other than servitude.

"No. I wield the power of vengeance," Drake said in reply, ducking beneath a strike of Kalir's blade and thrusting his sword up and into his chest with a furious cry.

Kalir's mouth parted, blood spilling from his lips as he gasped like a fish out of water and I sucked in a sharp breath as I stared at him, watching his death play out right before me while my magic buzzed and tingled like crazy within my flesh and my heart thrashed with the desire to join this fight.

Drake shoved the sword in harder, coming nose to nose with the man who had scarred his body with the marks of the lost gods, grinning at him wickedly with carnage flaring in his dark eyes.

Kalir continued to gasp and tremble as his life spilled out of him, but a creeping coldness began to work its way up my spine, and I shivered as I looked around for the source of it.

A heavy pulse began to throb through the air and a wild shriek sounded within my own skull a second before the dying Prophet slammed his hand against Drake's chest and dug his fingers into his skin.

"I claim you, vessel," Kalir hissed, blood spraying from his lips and I screamed as I saw this for what it was. A withered soul clinging to a false illusion of life while seeking out a body to house itself in for its true resurrection.

"Let me help!" I screamed. "Just say yes."

Drake's eyes moved to mine just as Kalir's body fell slack at his feet like a puppet with its strings cut, and the dark essence of his spirit burst free of the bloodstained corpse.

The darkness which remained of Kalir swept up into the air above Drake's head and fear slammed into me endlessly as I saw that wicked fate coming for him, the fate which Kalir had been planning when he'd marked Drake's skin all those years ago. A Tirbeshi Warrior whose body he could steal for his own, strong enough to withstand the presence of a twisted thing such as him.

"Yes," Drake called, his wide eyes fixed on the shadow as it shot towards him, and he threw his sword up even as he blindly put his trust in me to save him and my heart swelled at his belief in me.

My body fell apart and I shifted in the blink of an eye, becoming a cloud of purple smoke which billowed across the chamber and got between Drake and Kalir's spirit as the dark presence shot towards him.

A scream vibrated through my being as I felt the impact of his twisted soul crashing into mine, but the magic in me swelled, forcing him back and refusing to allow him to pass through me to get to my master.

Kalir roared as he flung the full force of whatever stolen power he had at me, trying to break through and steal my master's body to use for himself, and my entire being vibrated with the energy required to fight him off.

But Kalir wasn't like me. He might have been powerful and knotted up with magic he had stolen from the gods over the countless years he'd spent clinging to this semblance of life, but the immortality they had once granted all of us wasn't a gift they offered out anymore, and he wasn't bound to their power the way I was.

I had been shackled and chained, branded and remade. The magic of the gods had been driven into me so forcefully that I'd had to give up my Fae body and feel every agonising moment of them remaking it around the cracked remnants of my soul to claim the power I now owned. I wasn't some scrap of a soul clinging to a façade of immortality. I *was* immortality. Which meant that he was no match for me.

Drake yelled a battle cry as he swung his sword, decapitating the body which Kalir had now abandoned before hacking into it again and again, turning the flesh into little more than a bloody lump of meat while I fought to overpower his spirit, making sure Kalir had nothing else to return to within this place.

"I banish you to Hellravia!" My voice echoed off of the bone-lined walls as my power flared. The purple smoke making up my being engulfed Kalir's soul, absorbing his attacks and taking the pain of every strike without so much as flinching.

It didn't matter how much he hurt me. It didn't matter if ending him would mean my end too. All that mattered was Drake's life. He had to be okay. He had to live on beyond this hellish place.

A blast of raw power slammed through me as Kalir's screams filled the chamber, and I knew that I was screaming too beneath the force of his attack, but I wouldn't back down, instead focusing on the one thing now tethering me to this world and refusing to allow myself to be ripped away from him.

With a surge of power, I threw my magic out of myself in a wave, all of it slamming into Kalir's spirit in a demand for it to pass on into Hellravia where he'd find unending torment at the hands of Herdat and her army of untold monstrous creations.

The blast echoed off of the walls, bones falling from them to hit the ground and the entire temple trembling around us.

Kalir screamed one final time before he was blasted away from me, his spirit shattering and power ripping from him.

The purple smoke reformed into my flesh at the tremendous swell of my power, and I fell from the air, crashing down onto the lid of the stone sarcophagus with such force that the breath crashed from my lungs, and I was left panting and in pain atop it.

Drake leapt up onto the sarcophagus with me, his hand moving to my cheek as he stared down at me with a wild look in his eyes, the tattoos on his skin still glowing with power.

"What did you do?" he demanded, a bite to his tone making me flinch as the agony of my fight with Kalir still drove into every piece of my body.

"We need to go," I breathed, swallowing against the pain. I fought to push myself upright despite the way my power kept flickering weakly within me and my body felt lined with razor blades every time I moved. "There's something else here."

As if my words had called on it, the heavy presence I'd felt earlier began to grow within the room, the temperature dropping all around us as Drake's tattoos blazed brighter and fear pressed in on me more deeply than any pain I felt.

Drake straightened, looking towards the head of the sarcophagus almost as if someone had called his name, and I hissed through my teeth as I forced myself to sit up, reaching for him as he retreated.

"Don't listen to it," I urged, glancing towards the door as the power continued to build around us and I began to fear that we were already too late. "Whatever it's offering will come at a cost. You have to-"

"Warrior born in sin," a voice shook the air which was neither masculine or feminine, somehow seeming like a combination of all things and making a whimper pass my lips as memories of my rebirth danced through my mind. *"Born in the age of lies, filled with greed and lust for all things."*

"Drake," I hissed.

He stepped away from me, his fingers brushing across the stone lid of the sarcophagus as the ink on his skin pulsed with the power of the lost gods, tempting him closer with promises untold, but I knew how the gods liked to play with the lives of Fae. And I knew of their wrath in the years which had passed since a lie had broken their faith in all of us. Nothing they offered him now would be a gift, only a curse set to ruin him and all he touched.

"Look at me, Drake," I begged, and he turned his head, lifting his eyes to meet mine, though what I found looking back at me wasn't the man I had begun to think I knew. There was greed and hunger and a want for power I hadn't seen in him before that moment. Or perhaps I'd just been denying that it was there, ignoring him when he told me plainly that he was a selfish man with a heart full of sins. "You can't trust them. You can't believe what they say. The gods are angry, vengeful, please don't take this gift from them. You can't-"

"Can't?" Drake asked me, his tone hard while his palm moved to press down on the white stone lid before him and the tattoos on his skin flared with power. "I've never let anyone tell me what I can or can't take in this life, little goddess."

I swallowed a lump in my throat as those words struck at me, but I refused to give in.

"Listen to me," I urged. "You don't need this. You have me. I can do anything you want, anything you need. You don't have to-"

"So I'm to become your creature as you are mine?" he asked. "A slave to your power just as you are a slave to my will?"

"I'm not," I began, shaking my head, but I couldn't go on with that sentence because I knew as well as he did that that was the truth of me. "Please, Drake," I begged, the power in the chamber pulsing so heavily that I almost cried out at the weight of it.

"Your destiny holds great power," the voice spoke again, and I could see a decision forming in Drake's eyes which he wouldn't be able to turn back from.

"No," I begged, lunging forward in desperation, reaching for him even as the power in this place grew so thick that I could scarcely breathe. "Drake, you can't! You have to-"

"Return to the coin, Kyra," Drake commanded just as my fingers brushed against his arm.

The darkness in his eyes captivated me entirely and horror radiated through me at the command. My head shook in disbelief as my body began to fall apart, purple smoke swirling up around me as I shifted out of existence, fear and betrayal colliding within my flesh so potently that I was choking on them.

Drake's dark eyes met mine, and I found a hardness there which was as unavoidable as the command he'd just given me, his coldness stilling my heart in my chest and tearing away the sense of security which I'd so foolishly begun to rely on while I was with him.

He had sworn never to do this to me. He'd given me his word that I would never have to return to that hell again and yet my body was still falling apart, the seconds between here and there dragging as I tried to cling to this reality with all I had, desperate not to find myself in that prison again.

"You promised," I gasped.

Pain of a wholly different kind tore through me, cutting into the fabric of the girl who I'd just been starting to remember, forcing me back into the trap of my own addled mind as I was ripped away from reality and banished to my own personal hell.

The screams inside my head blotted out all sounds except Drake's voice as he spoke one final thing to me. Words that broke his promise and my heart in a single, soul-crushing blow.

"I was a boy born to nothing and I grew into a man dressed in sin, little goddess. There's only one thing you can ever rely on from me when words pass my lips. And that's lies."

I crashed into the middle of the coin as the sound of his voice and the taste of free air were stolen from me entirely, my spine colliding with the pool of tears which marked so many years of my endless solitude that I'd long since lost count of them.

I made no move to stop myself as I began to sink within the evidence of my own sorrow, the saltwater lapping up around me and swallowing me whole while the feeling of my heart shattering into a thousand pieces consumed me and nothing but my own poisonous self-hatred filled my soul.

I had been so very foolish to believe in the sweet promises of a man who owned my power. I had been so fucking stupid. So insane to think any master would see me as more than a tool to grant their wishes.

As I sank to the bottom of the pool of tears, I didn't do anything to stop myself from drowning because I was drowning already, the nightmares of this place rising up to devour me one by one until there was nothing left of me at all. But even then, I'd linger. After the monsters of my mind had picked every piece of flesh from my bones with agonising slowness, I'd still be here.

In the dark.

Alone.

Told you so.

Enjoyed A Game of Malice and Greed?
Come to the discussion group to chat about it with other readers!

And if you don't want to leave Osaria just yet, you can read the prequel novella about Kyra's mysterious past A KINGDOM OF GODS AND RUIN.

AUTHOR NOTE

So…how did you enjoy delving into the latest dark corner of our twisted creation? The world of AGOMAG was one which grew roots all of its own and sprouted flowers and thorns we didn't always expect and yet somehow seemed to fit in place all too perfectly.

When it comes to fantasy stories, one of the most exciting tasks for us is not only creating characters whose struggles translate from the magical to the relatable, but also developing worlds without the boundaries we are stuck with in the real world. And I can say that we have barely touched the surface with these corrupt idols and angry gods.

And of course, we couldn't resist a curse or two, a touch of heartbreak and a dash of betrayal, because the hardest fought stories always have the most worthy conclusions…right?

In true fairy tale fashion we've started off with once upon a time, so now I guess you'll have to wait and see what's to come before the happily never after…

Love, Susanne & Caroline xoxo

ALSO BY
CAROLINE PECKHAM
&
SUSANNE VALENTI

A Game of Malice and Greed
(M/F, Fantasy Romance Series)
A Kingdom of Gods and Ruin
A Game of Malice and Greed

Brutal Boys of Everlake Prep
(Complete Reverse Harem Bully Romance Contemporary Series)
Kings of Quarantine
Kings of Lockdown
Kings of Anarchy
Queen of Quarantine
**

Dead Men Walking
(Reverse Harem Dark Romance Contemporary Series)
The Death Club
Society of Psychos
**

The Harlequin Crew
(Reverse Harem Mafia Romance Contemporary Series)
Sinners Playground
Dead Man's Isle
Carnival Hill

Paradise Lagoon

Harlequinn Crew Novellas

Devil's Pass

**

Dark Empire

(Dark Mafia Contemporary Standalones)

Beautiful Carnage

Beautiful Savage

**

The Ruthless Boys of the Zodiac

(Reverse Harem Paranormal Romance Series - Set in the world of Solaria)

Dark Fae

Savage Fae

Vicious Fae

Broken Fae

Warrior Fae

Zodiac Academy

(M/F Bully Romance Series- Set in the world of Solaria, five years after Dark Fae)

The Awakening

Ruthless Fae

The Reckoning

Shadow Princess

Cursed Fates

Fated Thrones

Heartless Sky

Sorrow and Starlight

The Awakening - As told by the Boys

Zodiac Academy Novellas

Origins of an Academy Bully

The Big A.S.S. Party

Darkmore Penitentiary

(Reverse Harem Paranormal Romance Series - Set in the world of Solaria,
ten years after Dark Fae)

Caged Wolf

Alpha Wolf

Feral Wolf

**

The Age of Vampires

(Complete M/F Paranormal Romance/Dystopian Series)

Eternal Reign

Eternal Shade

Eternal Curse

Eternal Vow

Eternal Night

Eternal Love

**

Cage of Lies

(M/F Dystopian Series)

Rebel Rising

**

Tainted Earth

(M/F Dystopian Series)

Afflicted

Altered

Adapted

Advanced

**

The Vampire Games

(Complete M/F Paranormal Romance Trilogy)

V Games

V Games: Fresh From The Grave

V Games: Dead Before Dawn

*

The Vampire Games: Season Two

(Complete M/F Paranormal Romance Trilogy)

Wolf Games

Wolf Games: Island of Shade

Wolf Games: Severed Fates

*

The Vampire Games: Season Three

Hunter Trials

*

The Vampire Games Novellas

A Game of Vampires

**

The Rise of Issac

(Complete YA Fantasy Series)

Creeping Shadow

Bleeding Snow

Turning Tide

Weeping Sky

Failing Light

Printed in Great Britain
by Amazon

19053959R00349